FATE BREAKER

VICTORIA AVEYARD

HARPER TEEN

An Imprint of HarperCollinsPublishers

HarperTeen is an imprint of HarperCollins Publishers.

Fate Breaker
Copyright © 2024 by Victoria Aveyard
Map art by Francesca Baraldi
Map © & ™ 2024 Victoria Aveyard
All rights reserved. Printed in the United States of America. No part of this
book may be used or reproduced in any manner whatsoever without written
permission except in the case of brief quotations embodied in critical articles
and reviews. For information address HarperCollins Children's Books, a
division of HarperCollins Publishers, 195 Broadway, New York, NY 10007.
www.epicreads.com

Library of Congress Control Number: 2023940809
ISBN 978-0-06-311606-1 — ISBN 978-0-06-337608-3 (intl ed)
ISBN 978-0-06-339113-0 (special ed)

Typography by Jenna Stempel-Lobell
23 24 25 26 27 LBC 5 4 3 2 1
First Edition

to those who walk in darkness, but never lose hope

and to me as I was at fourteen, looking for this story

I finally found it

FATE BREAKER

1

THOSE LEFT BEHIND
Charlon

A fallen priest named his gods and prayed to each.

Syrek. Lasreen. Meira. Pryan. Immor. Tiber.

No sound came from his lips, but that didn't matter much. The gods would hear him either way. *But will they choose to listen?*

During his days in the church, Charlie used to wonder if the gods were real. If the realms beyond Allward still existed, waiting on the other side of a closed door.

By now, he knew the answer. He was near sick with it.

The gods are real, and the distant realms are here.

Meer in the desert, its Spindle flooding the oasis. The Ashlands at the temple, a corpse army marching from its depths.

And now, Infyrna, burning up the city before his eyes.

Cursed flame leapt against a black sky, even as a blizzard roared against the smoke. The Burning Realm consumed the city of Gidastern, and threatened to consume their army too.

Charlie watched with the rest of their bedraggled host, every warrior horrified and staring. Elder and mortal, Jydi raider and Treckish soldier.

And the Companions too. They all wore the same fear on their faces.

But it did not stop them from charging forward, their battle cry echoing through the smoke and falling snow.

All rode toward the city, the Spindle, and the flames of hell itself.

All but Charlie.

He shifted in the saddle, more comfortable on his horse than he once was. Still, his body ached, and his head pounded. He wished for the relief of tears. *Would they freeze or boil,* he wondered, watching as all the world seemed to break apart.

The blizzard, the burning. The battle cry of Elder and Jydi alike. Immortal arrows twanged and Treckish steel rattled. Two hundred horses pounded across the barren field, charging for the flaming gates of Gidastern.

Charlie wanted to shut his eyes but could not.

I owe them this much. If I cannot fight, I can watch them go.

His breath caught.

I can watch them die.

"Gods forgive me," he murmured.

His saddlebag of quills and ink felt heavy at his side. They were his weapons more than anything else. And in this moment, they were utterly useless.

So he returned to the only weapon left to him.

This prayer came slowly, from the forgotten corners of another life.

Before that hole in Adira. Before I defied every kingdom of the Ward, and made a ruin of my future.

As he recited the words, memories flashed, sharp as knives. His workshop beneath the Priest's Hand. The smell of parchment in the dank stone room. The feel of a gallows rope around his neck. The warmth of a hand laid against his face, Garion's calluses as familiar as anything in the realm. Charlie's mind lingered on Garion, and their last meeting. It still stung, a wound never fully healed.

"Fyriad the Redeemer," he continued, naming the god of Infyrna. "May your fires cleanse us and burn evil from this world."

The prayer tasted wrong in his mouth. But it was something, at the very least. Something he could do for his friends. For the realm.

The only thing, he thought bitterly, watching as the army charged.

"I am a dedicant priest of Tiber, a servant to all the pantheon, and may all the gods hear me as they hear their own—"

Then a barking howl split the air like a thunderbolt, and the horse flinched beneath him.

Across the field, the city gates buckled, rattled by something within. Something big and powerful, many somethings, all screaming like a pack of ghostly wolves.

With a swoop of terror, Charlie realized he was not far from the truth.

"By the gods," he cursed.

The Companions and their army never faltered, the wall of bodies charging straight ahead. For the flames—and the monsters within them. The city gates crumbled, revealing hellish demons the likes of which he had only seen in godly manuscripts.

Flaming spines, ashen shadows.

"Hellhounds," Charlie breathed.

The monsters leapt into the army without fear. Their bodies burned, the flames born of their fur, their too-long legs black as charcoal. Snow sizzled against their burning coats, sending up clouds of steam. Their eyes glowed like hot coals, their open jaws spitting waves of heat.

The manuscripts were nowhere near so fearsome as the real thing, Char-lie thought dimly.

In the pages of the old church books, the hellhounds were sharp and small, burned and twisted. Not these lethal, loping wolves bigger than horses, with black fangs and ripping claws.

The manuscripts were wrong about something else too.

The hellhounds can die, Charlie realized, watching one crumble to ashes after a sweep of Domacridhan's sword.

Something like hope, small and ugly as it was, reared up inside the fallen priest. Charlie held his breath, watching the Companions fight their way through the hounds into the burning city.

Leaving Charlie alone with the echoes.

It was torture to watch the empty gates, straining to see anything inside.

Have they found the Spindle? he wondered. *Have the hounds gone to defend it? Is Taristan still here, or have we missed him again?*

Is everyone going to die and leave the saving the realm business to me?

He shuddered at the last thought. Both for his own sake, and the world's.

"Certainly not," he said aloud.

His horse whickered in reply.

Charlie patted her neck. "Thank you for your confidence."

Again, he eyed the city of Gidastern, a city of thousands reduced to a flaming graveyard. And perhaps a trap as well.

He bit his lip, worrying the skin between his teeth. If Taristan was there, as they suspected, what would become of the Companions? Of Corayne?

She is barely more than a child, with the world on her shoulders, Charlie cursed to himself. *And here I am, a grown man, waiting to see if she makes it out alive.*

His cheeks flared with heat, and not from the flames. With all his heart, he wished he could have pulled her back from the battle. He winced, a knife of regret in his chest.

You never could have saved her from this.

Another noise rose from the city, a single guttural call. But it came from many mouths, both human and otherwordly. It sounded like a death bell. Charlie knew it too well. He heard the same thing at the temple in the foothills, rising from countless undead corpses.

The rest of the Spindle army is here, he realized with a jolt. *The Ashlanders, Taristan's own.*

Suddenly his nimble fingers wound around the reins, his grip like iron.

"Flames and hounds and corpses be damned," Charlie muttered, throwing back his cloak to free his arms. One hand went for his short-sword. "And damn me too."

With a snap of the reins, he urged the horse forward, and she broke into a run. His heart rammed in his chest, matching the beat of her hooves against the ashen ground. The blizzard swirled, the clouds red with flame, all the world turned to hell. And Charlie rode right into it.

The gate loomed, with burning streets beyond. A path unfurled, beckoning the fugitive priest.

At least it can't get worse, he thought.

Then something pulsed in the sky, behind the clouds, a thump like a tremendous heart.

Charlie's spine turned to ice.

"*Shit.*"

The dragon's roar shook the air with all the fury of an earthquake.

His horse screamed and reared up on her hind legs, her front hooves pawing helplessly. It took all Charlie's will to keep his saddle. His sword fell to the ground, lost to the ash and snow. He watched with wide eyes, unable to tear his gaze away.

The great monster burst through the dark clouds over the city, its jeweled body red and black, dancing with the light of flame. The dragon twisted, born of the god Tiber and the glittering realm of Irridas. *The Dazzling Realm*, Charlie knew, remembering it from scripture. A cruel place of gold and jewels, and terrible things corrupted by greed.

Fire curled from the dragon's jaws and its claws gleamed like black steel. Hot wind blasted over the walls, carrying snow and ash and the bloody, rotten smell of dragon. Charlie could only watch as the Spindle monster crashed down into the city, toppling towers and steeples.

His quill had traced many dragons over the years, drawing patterns of flame and scale, claw and fang. Batwings, serpent tails. Like the Infyrna hounds, the reality was far more horrible.

There was no sword he could raise against a demon such as this. Nothing a mortal could do against a dragon of a distant realm.

Not even the heroes could survive such a thing.

The villains might not either.

And certainly not me.

Shame rose up in his throat, threatening to choke the life out of Charlon Armont.

But for all the Ward, for all the realms, he could not go any further.

The tears he wished for finally came, burning and freezing in equal measure. The reins twitched in his hand, tugging the horse away from the city, from the Spindle, from the Companions. From the beginning of the end of the world.

Only one question remained now.

How far can I go before the end comes for me too?

In all his twenty-three years, Charlie had never felt so alone. Not even the gallows had seemed so bleak.

It was past nightfall by the time he was finally out from under the blizzard and the ash clouds. But the smell of smoke clung to his skin like a brand.

"I deserve it," Charlie muttered to himself. He swiped at his face again, wiping away long-dried tears. His eyes felt red and raw, just like his broken heart. "I deserve every awful thing that comes my way now."

The horse blew hard, her flanks steaming against the winter air. Exhausted, she slowed and Charlie obliged, easing her to a halt. He slid gracelessly from the saddle, bowlegged and sore.

He did not know the map of the Ward so well as Sorasa or Corayne, but Charlie was a fugitive, not a fool. He could navigate better than most. Grimacing, he drew a parchment map from his saddlebags, and unfolded it with a squint. He was still some miles from entering the Castlewood. Ahead of him, the mighty forest ate up the distant horizon, a black wall beneath the silver moon.

He could keep heading east into the Wood, using the thick trees as cover against any pursuit. Adira lay in the opposite direction, far to the west through enemy territory. He thought of his little shop beneath the broken church. Among the quills and ink, the stamps and wax seals.

I will be safe there, Charlie knew. *Until the end. Conquerors eat the rot last.*

Unfortunately, the path back to Adira wound too close to Ascal. But he did not know where else to go. There were too many roads to walk.

"I don't know," he grumbled to his horse.

She did not reply, already asleep.

Charlie made a face at her and rolled up the parchment. He set to his saddlebags, still intact, with his gear and food. *Enough*, he noted, checking the stores. *Enough to reach the next town and then some.*

He did not risk a fire. Charlie doubted he could even get a fire going if he tried. He'd spent his fugitive days in cities mostly, not the wilderness. He was usually never far from a seedy tavern or cellar to sleep in, his own forged papers and false coin in hand.

"I am not Sorasa, or Andry, or Dom," he muttered, wishing for any of the Companions.

Even Sigil, who would drag him to the gallows herself for a sack of gold.

Even Corayne, who would be just as useless as he was, alone in the winter woods.

Angry, he pulled his cloak tighter. Beneath the smoke, it still smelled of Volaska. Good wool, spilled gorzka, and the warmth of a crackling fire at the Treckish castle now far behind.

"I cannot do anything useful out here."

It felt good to speak, even if he spoke to no one.

"Perhaps they can hear me," he said, mournfully looking to the stars.

They seemed to taunt him. If he could somehow punch every single one from the heavens, he would. Instead, he kicked at the dirt, sending stones and fallen leaves skittering.

His eyes stung again. This time, he thought of the Companions, and not the stars. Corayne, Sorasa, Dom, Sigil, Andry. Even Valtik. All left behind. All burned to ashes.

"Ghosts, all of them," he hissed, scrubbing at his watery eyes.

"Better a coward than a ghost."

Lightning jumped up Charlie's spine and he nearly toppled over in shock—and disbelief.

The voice was familiar as Charlie's own quills, his own seals painstakingly cut by hand. It trilled, melodic, the lightest touch of a Madrentine accent curling around the Paramount language. Once Charlie likened that voice to the silk that hides a dagger. Soft and dangerous, beautiful until the moment it decides not to be.

Charlie blinked, grateful for the moonlight. It turned the world to silver, and Garion's pale cheeks to porcelain. His dark mahogany hair curled over his forehead.

The assassin stood some yards away, a safe distance between them, a thin rapier at his side. Charlie knew the weapon too, a light thing made for speed and swift parrying. It was the bronze dagger tucked inside Garion's tunic that was the true danger. The same one all the Amhara bore, to mark them as assassin, the finest and most deadly upon the Ward.

Charlie could barely breathe, let alone speak.

Garion took a step forward, his loping gait easy, and lethal.

"Not to say I think you are a coward," Garion continued, one gloved hand raising in the air. "You have your brave moments, when you put your mind to it. And you've been to the gallows how many times now? Thrice?" He counted on his fingers. "And never once pissed yourself."

Charlie dared not move.

"You are a dream," he whispered, praying the vision would not disappear.

Even if he isn't real, I hope he lingers.

Garion only smiled, showing white teeth. His dark eyes gleamed as he prowled closer.

"You certainly have a way with words, Priest."

Exhaling slowly, Charlie felt some sense return to his frozen hands. "I didn't run away. I went into the city, and burned with all the rest of them, didn't I? I'm dead and you are—"

The assassin tipped his head. "Does that make me your heaven?"

Charlie's face crumpled. His cheeks flamed against the cold air, and his eyes stung, his vision swimming.

"I am loath to say it, but you are truly ugly when you cry, my darling," Garion said, his form blurring.

He isn't real, he's already fading, a dream within a dream.

It only made the tears come faster, until even the moon drowned.

But Garion remained. Charlie felt the warmth of him, and the rough swipe of a gloved hand upon his cheeks. Without thought, Charlie caught one of the hands in his own. It felt familiar even beneath layers of fine leather and fur.

Blinking slowly, Charlie looked on Garion again. Pale in the moon-light, his eyes dark but brilliantly alive. And *real*. For a moment, the realm was still. Even the wind in the trees stopped and the ghosts in their minds lay quiet.

It did not last long.

"Where have you been?" Charlie said roughly, dropping Garion's hand. He stepped back and stifled a very undignified sniffle.

"Today?" Garion shrugged. "Well, first I waited to see if you were going to run into a burning city. I'm very grateful you did not." He grinned. "At least becoming a hero hasn't knocked the sense out of you."

"Hero," Charlie spat. He felt like crying again. "A hero would have gone into Gidastern."

Garion's smile disappeared like a slate wiped clean. "A hero would be dead."

Dead like all the rest. Charlie winced, his shame like a knife in his gut.

"And where were you before today?" Charlie demanded. "Where were you for *two years*?"

Garion flushed but did not move. "Maybe I grew tired of saving you from the gallows?"

"As if it was ever difficult."

Charlie remembered the last time all too well. The feel of coarse rope against his neck, his toes scraping the wood of the gallows platform. The trapdoor beneath him, ready to be sprung. And Garion in the crowd, waiting to rescue him.

"The last one was just a shitwater outpost with a garrison dumber than donkeys," Charlie muttered. "You didn't even break a sweat."

The assassin shrugged, looking proud of himself.

It only incensed Charlie.

"*Where were you?*"

His plea hung in the freezing air.

Garion finally dropped his gaze, looking down at his polished boots.

"I watched Adira whenever I could," he said in a low, sullen voice. "Between contracts, when the winds and weather allowed. Made it as far as the causeway so many times. And I *always* listened for news. I was not . . . I was not gone."

Charlie sucked down a cold gasp of air. "You were gone *to me.*"

Garion met his eyes again, his face suddenly tight. "Mercury warned me. He only does that once."

Mention of the lord of the Amhara, one of the deadliest men in the realm, sobered them both. It was Charlie's turn to look at his shoes, and he toed the dirt awkwardly. Even he knew better than to cross Lord Mercury, or tempt his anger. Garion had told him enough stories about Amhara fallen. And Sorasa was proof of them. Her fate was merciful, by all accounts. Only cast out, shamed and exiled. Not tortured and killed.

"I'm here now," Garion murmured, taking a halting step forward.

The distance between them suddenly felt too far, and also too close.

"So I won't wake tomorrow to find you gone?" Charlie said, near to breathless. "To find this all—"

"A dream?" Garion offered, amused. "I'll say it again. This is not a dream."

The wretched hope flared again, dogged and stubborn.

"I suppose it's closer to a nightmare," Charlie mumbled. "What with the end of the world and all that."

Garion's smile only widened. "The end of the world can wait, my church mouse."

The old nickname lit some fire within Charlie, until the air went hot on his skin.

"My fox," the priest answered without thinking.

The assassin closed the distance with his easy grace, neither slow nor fast. Still, he caught Charlie off guard, even as his gloved hands took his face. And Garion's lips met his own, far warmer than the air, firm and familiar.

He tasted like summer, like another life. Like the still moment between sleep and waking, when all went quiet. For a split second, Charlie forgot the Spindles. The broken realm. And the Companions dead behind him.

But it could not last. The moment ended, as all things do.

Charlie pulled back slowly, his hands on Garion's own. They stared at each other, both searching for the proper thing to say.

"Will Mercury hunt you?" Charlie finally asked, his voice shaking.

"Do you want the truth, my love?"

Charlie did not hesitate, even as he wound his fingers with Garion's. "I am willing to trade a broken heart for a living body."

"You always were one for pretty words." Garion smiled him off, though his eyes went cold.

"What do we do now?" Charlie murmured, shaking his head.

To his surprise, Garion laughed.

"You fool," he chuckled. "We *live*."

"For how long?" Charlie scoffed, dropping his hands. He glanced into the darkness, to the city on fire and the Spindle still torn.

Garion followed his gaze, looking over his shoulder. There was only the blackness of the night, and the bitter cold of the moon.

"You truly believe it, don't you?" he said softly. "The end of the realm?"

"Of course I do. I've seen it. I know it," Charlie snapped.

Despite his frustration, somehow it felt good to quarrel with Garion. It meant he was real, and imperfect, flawed as Charlie remembered. Not some shining hallucination.

"The city behind us burns, you saw it too."

"Cities burn all the time," Garion replied, swishing his rapier through the air.

Charlie put out a hand and the assassin stilled, the light sword hanging at his side.

"Not like this," Charlie breathed, forceful as he could be. He willed his lover to listen, to hear his own terror. "Garion, the world is ending. And we *will* end with it."

With a long sigh, Garion sheathed his blade.

"You really know how to destroy a moment, don't you, darling?" He shook a finger at him. "Is this that religious guilt all you priests carry, or just your personality?"

Charlie shrugged. "Probably both. Can't allow myself a single moment of happiness, can I?"

"Oh, perhaps a single moment."

This time, Charlie did not flinch when Garion kissed him, and time did not stop. The wind blew cold, rattling the branches overhead. It stirred Charlie's collar, kicking up the smell of smoke.

Wincing, Charlie stepped back. He furrowed his brow.

"I'll need another sword," he said, glaring at the empty sheath at his hip.

Garion shook his head and sighed, frustrated. "You're not a hero, Charlie. Neither am I."

The priest ignored the assassin. He drew out his map again, laying it flat on the ground.

"But there's still something we can do."

Garion crouched down next to him, a look of amusement on his face. "And that is what exactly?"

Charlie eyed the parchment, tracing a line through the forest. Past rivers and villages, deep into the woods.

"I'll figure it out," he muttered. His finger drew a line over the forest on the map. "Eventually."

"You know how I feel about the Castlewood," Garion said, sounding annoyed. His lips twisted with distaste, and a little fear too.

Charlie almost rolled his eyes. There were too many stories about witches in the forest, born among the echoes the Spindles left behind. But Spindlerotten witches were the least of his worries now. He smiled slowly, the air cold on his teeth.

"Trust me, I did not run from a dragon only to die in a cackling old woman's cauldron," he said. "Now help me figure out a path that won't get me killed."

Garion chuckled. "I'll do my best."

2

DEATH, OR SOMETHING WORSE
Andry

Blessed are the burned.

The old prayer echoed in Andry's head. He remembered how his mother used to say it, over the hearth in their apartments, brown hands outstretched to the redeeming god.

I certainly do not feel blessed now, he thought, coughing up another gasp of smoke as he ran. Valtik's hand was cold in his own, her bony fingers surprisingly strong as she led them through the city.

Taristan's undead army lurched through the streets behind them. Most were Ashlanders, born of a broken realm, little more than skeletons, rotted to the bone. But some were *fresh*. The dead of Gidastern fought for Taristan now, the citizens of his own kingdom turned to corpse soldiers. Their fate was almost too horrific to comprehend.

And more will join them, Andry knew, thinking of the soldiers who rode into Gidastern. All the bodies left behind. The Jydi raiders. The Elders. The Treckish war band.

And the Companions too.

Sigil.

Dom.

The two giants stayed behind to defend the retreat, and buy whatever time they could for Corayne. Andry only prayed their sacrifice was enough.

And that Sorasa was enough to protect Corayne alone.

Andry winced at the thought.

They sprinted through what felt like hell itself, a maze filled with monstrous hounds, the corpse army, Taristan, his red wizard, and a damned dragon of all things. Not to mention the dangers of the city itself, the buildings burning and collapsing around him.

Somehow, Valtik kept them ahead of it all, leading Andry out to the city docks.

Only a few small boats remained in the harbor, with most already heading out to sea. Soldiers piled onto anything floating, wading out into the shallows or leaping from the docks. Ashes coated their armor and faces in heavy soot, obscuring any insignia or kingdom colors. Treckish, Elder, Jydi—Andry could hardly tell them apart.

Everyone looks the same against the ending of the world.

Only Valtik somehow escaped the ash falling all around them. Her shift dress was still white, her bare feet and hands clean. She stopped to stare at the burning city, every street echoing with death. Shadows moved through the smoke, lurching into the harbor.

"With me, Valtik," Andry said gruffly, looping his arm through her own.

With me. The old battle cry of the Gallish knights returned some strength to his legs. Andry felt hope and fear in equal measure. *We might yet survive this or we may be left behind.*

"Without the stars, without the sun, the way is red, the path undone," the witch chanted under her breath.

They ran together, toward a fishing vessel already moving, its sail unfurled. The old woman didn't hesitate, stepping into seemingly open air. Only to land safely on the deck of the boat, not a hair out of place.

Andry boarded with less grace, leaping after her.

He landed hard on the deck, but his body felt oddly light. Relief surged through his veins as the little boat cut through the burning harbor, leaving behind the corpse army crawling on the shore.

The ship was barely larger than a river barge, big enough for perhaps twenty men. But the vessel was seaworthy, and that was more than enough. A mismatched band of soldiers, raiders, and immortals crewed the deck, urging the boat out to sea.

Smoke stretched far out over the waves, black fingers reaching for the horizon. But a single band of sunlight remained, gleaming low across the sea. A reminder that all the realm was not this hell.

Yet.

Grimly, Andry looked back to the city in ruins.

Gidastern burned and burned, columns of smoke reaching up into the hellish sky. Red light and black shadows warred for control, with ashes falling over everything like snow. And beneath it all were the screams, the howling, the sounds of splintering wood and cracking stone. The distant, shuddering beat of gigantic wings somewhere in the clouds. It sounded like death, or something worse.

"Corayne," he murmured, her name a prayer. He hoped the gods could hear him. He hoped she was already far from this place, safe with Sorasa and the last Spindleblade.

"Is she safe?" He turned to Valtik. "Tell me, is she safe, is she alive?"

The witch only turned, hiding her face.

"VALTIK!" His own voice sounded distant.

Through his spotting vision, Andry saw her move to the prow of the little boat. Her hands gnarled at her sides, fingers curled into pale claws. Her lips moved, forming words he could not make out.

Overhead, the sail filled with a cold blast of wind, pushing them faster and faster out into the frozen embrace of the Watchful Sea.

Purple fish swam through the little pond in the courtyard, their fins creating ripples on the surface. Andry watched and breathed deeply. Everything smelled of jasmine and cool shade. Andry had never been here before, but he knew the courtyard anyway. This was the house of Kin Kiane, his mother's family in Nkonabo. Across the Long Sea, as far away from danger as anyone could be.

On the other side of the pond, his mother smiled, her familiar brown face more vibrant than he remembered. She sat in a chair without wheels, wrapped in a simple green robe. Valeri Trelland's homeland suited her better than the north ever did.

Andry's heart leapt at the sight of her. He wanted to go to his mother, but his feet would not move, rooted to the stones. He opened his mouth to speak. No sound came.

I miss you, he tried to shout. *I hope you are alive.*

She only smiled back, wrinkles crinkling at the corners of her green eyes.

He smiled too, for her sake, even as his body went cold. The jasmine faded, replaced by the sharp tang of saltwater.

This is a dream.

Andry jolted awake like a man struck by lightning. For a moment, he hung suspended in his own mind, trying to make sense of his surroundings. The rocking of the waves, the hard deck of the boat. A threadbare blanket tossed over his body. The freezing air on his cheeks.

The smell of saltwater, not smoke.

We are alive.

A short, broad figure stood over the squire, illuminated by moonlight and lanterns slung in the rigging. *The Prince of Trec*, Andry realized with another jolt.

"I did not know Galland allowed their squires to sleep on duty," Prince Oscovko said, darkly amused.

"I'm no squire of Galland, Your Highness," Andry replied, forcing himself to sit up.

The prince grinned and shifted, the lanterns illuminating more of his face. He sported a black eye and a good deal of gore all down his leathers. Not that Andry minded. They all looked worse for the wear.

Slowly, Oscovko held out a hand. Andry took it without question, hoisting himself to unsteady feet.

"They don't allow you to make jokes either, do they?" Oscovko said, thumping Andry on the shoulder. "Good to see you made it out."

Andry's jaw tightened. Despite his easy manner, he saw anger in Oscovko's eyes, and fear too.

"Many did not," the prince added, glancing to shore.

But there was only blackness behind them. Not even a glimmer of the burning city remained.

It is no use looking back, Andry knew.

"How many men do you have?" he asked sharply.

His tone caught Oscovko off guard. The prince blanched and gestured along the small fishing boat. Quickly, Andry counted twelve on the deck, including Valtik and himself. The other survivors were just as battered as Oscovko. Mortal and immortal alike. Raider, Elder, and soldier. Some wounded, some sleeping. All terrified.

Off the bow and stern, in either direction, tiny lights bobbed along at their pace. Squinting, Andry made out black shapes in the moonlight, their own lanterns like low stars.

Other boats.

"How many, my lord?" Andry said again, sterner than before.

Down the deck, the other survivors turned to watch their exchange. Valtik remained at the prow, her face turned to the moon.

Oscovko scoffed and shook his head. "Does it matter to you?"

"It matters to all of us." Andry flushed, his cheeks growing hot against the chill. "We need every soldier who can fight—"

"I gave you that already." Oscovko cut him off with a wave of one bruised hand, slicing it through the air like a knife. His face fell, torn between sorrow and desperation. "Look where it brought us. *Both of us.*"

Andry held his ground, unyielding, even in the face of a prince. His days at a royal court were long behind him, and he was not a squire anymore. Courtesy didn't matter. There was only Corayne, the blade, and the realm now. Surrender was not an option.

"Eat, drink. Tend your wounds, Trelland," Oscovko finally said, sighing out his rage. His anger turned to pity, his eyes going soft in a way Andry hated. Slowly, Oscovko took his shoulder. "You are young. You have not seen battle like this before, you do not know the toll it takes."

"I've seen more of this than you have, my lord," Andry muttered back.

The prince only shook his head, mournful. Whatever anger he carried was eclipsed by pain.

"It is a longer journey home for you than it is for me," Oscovko replied, giving his shoulder a squeeze.

Something caught fire in Andry Trelland. He shrugged off the prince's hand and stepped into his path, blocking the deck.

"I have no home to return to, and neither will you, Oscovko," he growled. "Not if we abandon the realm now."

"*Abandon?*" Oscovko's anger returned tenfold. "You're right, Andry Trelland. You are no squire. And you're not a knight either. You have no idea how much these men have given. Not if you're asking them to give more."

"You saw the city," Andry countered. "You saw what Taristan will do to your kingdom, to the *rest of the world.*"

Oscovko was a warrior as much as a prince, and he seized Andry's collar with blinding speed. He glared up at him, his teeth gritted, and dropped his voice to a harsh whisper.

"Let these men go home to their families and die with glory," he snarled, his voice low and dangerous. "War is coming, and we will fight it from our own borders, with the full might of Trec behind us. Let them have this much, Trelland."

Andry did not waver, staring back at the prince. He matched his furious whisper.

"You can't die with glory if there's no one left to remember your name."

A shadow passed over Oscovko's face. Then he growled like an animal denied a kill.

"A cracked glass holds no water."

The voice rang out over the boat, cold as the icy wind. Both Andry and Oscovko whirled to find another figure standing close at the rail. She was taller than Andry, taller even than Dom was, with dark red hair plaited into braids. Her skin glowed whiter than the moon, pale as milk. And like Dom, she had the look of the Elders. Immortal and distant, ancient, set apart from the rest of them.

Quickly, Andry dipped his brow.

"Lady Eyda," he murmured.

He remembered her arriving with the Jydi and the other immortals, their boats gliding out of the blizzard. She was fearsome as any warrior, and mother to the Elder monarch of Kovalinn. All but a queen.

Oscovko let go of Andry's collar, turning his frustration on the immortal.

"You'll have better luck speaking riddles to the bone witch," he barked, waving a hand to Valtik at the prow. "The Wolves of Trec have no more patience for immortal nonsense."

Eyda took a lethally quiet step forward. The silence of her movement was unsettling.

"The enclaves thought as you did, Prince of Mortals." She said Oscovko's title like an insult. "Isibel in Iona. Valnir in Sirandel. Karias in Tirakrion. Ramia. Shan. Asaro. And all the rest."

Andry remembered Iona, and Isibel. Domacridhan's aunt, the Monarch, with her silver eyes, golden hair, and stony countenance. She called the Companions to her castle, and sent so many of them off again to die. There were other Elders just like her, holed up in their enclaves, ignoring the ending of the world.

The high, cold halls of the immortals felt so far away now. Andry supposed they always were.

Eyda kept on, her eyes on the stars. Venom dripped from her words.

"All my kin, content to sit behind their walls and their warriors, like islands in a rising sea. But the waters will drown us all," she spat, turning to Oscovko and Andry. "The waves are already at the gates."

"Easy for an Elder to sneer at mortal dead," the prince bit back.

Squire or not, Andry winced.

The immortal did not quail. She towered over them both, her eyes flashing like struck flint.

"Count our number, Wolf," she sneered. "We gave as you gave."

Like Oscovko, she wore signs of the battle all over her armor.

Once-fine steel was battered and scratched, her dark red cloak torn to ribbons. If she had a sword, it was long gone. The prince looked her over then glanced out to sea, to the other boats fighting along through the night.

Despite Oscovko's opposition, Andry felt bolstered by Eyda's support. He locked eyes with the immortal lady, her unblinking gaze filling him with fierce determination.

"I must ask you all to give more."

Andry barely recognized his own voice as it carried over the boat. He sounded older than he felt, and bolder than he knew himself to be.

Sighing, Oscovko wrenched his eyes back to Andry, meeting his glare.

"I cannot do that," he said desperately.

This time, Andry took the prince's shoulder. He felt the immortal lady's attention boring into his back, her gaze like iron. It only strengthened his resolve. *One ally is better than none.*

"There is one Spindleblade now," he said.

Andry willed Oscovko to feel the desperation he carried in his own heart. And the hope too, small as it was.

"One key to cracking the realm. And Taristan of Old Cor *does not have it.*"

The words landed slowly. Each like a knife in Oscovko's armor.

"The girl does," Oscovko muttered. He passed a hand over his head, disbelief in his eyes.

Andry leaned closer, his grip tight.

"Her name is Corayne," Andry said, close to a growl. "She is still our last hope. And *we* are hers."

To that, Oscovko said nothing. No agreement. But no argument either. And that was enough for Andry Trelland. For now.

He took a step back, releasing his grip on the prince's shoulder. With a start, he realized all the boat was watching. The Jydi raiders, the Elders, and Oscovko's men too. Even Valtik turned from the prow, her blue eyes like two stars in the night sky.

Once, Andry would have crumbled under so much attention. Not anymore. Not after all he had seen and survived.

"You don't even know if she's alive," Oscovko murmured, low enough for only Andry to hear.

Andry fought back a wave of revulsion.

"If she's dead, so are we," he shot back, not bothering to whisper.

Let them all hear me now.

"You saw what a broken realm looks like." Andry pointed back through the darkness, to the part of the sky with no stars. "You saw the city burning, the undead walking, the hounds of hell and a dragon bearing down on us. You know what fate awaits Allward, and every single thing in it. Your homes, your families."

A ripple moved down the deck as the soldiers exchanged heavy looks and whispers. Even the immortals shifted.

"None of us can escape what comes, not if we give up now." Desperation rolled through Andry's body like a wave. He needed every sword and spear before him, broken and defeated as they were. "It may not seem like much, but we still have hope. If we keep fighting."

Lady Eyda was already with him, but she offered Andry a single, grim nod. Her Elders reacted in kind and bowed their heads to Andry. The lanterns gleamed off their armor and furs, dancing among faces pale-skinned and dark, heads golden and jet. But their eyes were all the same. Deep as memory, strong as steel. And resolute.

The Jydi followed suit without hesitation, rattling their weapons.

Leaving only the Treckish warriors, battle-hardened and weary. And loyal. They looked to their prince for guidance, but Oscovko did not move. He surveyed Andry against the lanterns, tight-lipped and grim.

"I will return to Vodin with my men," he said, his voice booming.

Down the deck, the Treckish soldiers seemed to deflate. A few sighed out in relief. Andry gritted his teeth, wanting to scream with frustration. He felt the last of his patience ebb away.

But Oscovko wasn't finished.

"I must return—and raise the rest of Trec's armies, to fight this war properly," he said. "To defend my people—and the realm entire."

Heat flushed across Andry's cheeks, and he was glad for the shadows.

"Galland spilled *our* blood in Gidastern," Oscovko roared, slamming a fist against his chest. His men nodded in reply, a few fists clenching. "We will return the favor."

Andry startled when Oscovko threw back his head and howled, baying at the sky like a wolf. His men responded in kind. In the darkness, Treckish soldiers on the other boats matched the call, their howls echoing like ghosts on the water.

When the cold air hit his cheeks, Andry realized he was smiling.

Oscovko smiled back, and it was the smile of a wolf.

"What of you, Trelland?" he said, pointing. "Where will you go?"

Andry swallowed hard.

The others looked on, waiting for an answer. At the prow, Valtik stood firm, unblinking and silent. Andry hesitated for a moment, waiting for her infuriating guidance. It did not come.

Oscovko pressed in, eyes flashing. "Where will *your girl* go?"

With a will, Andry wrenched his gaze away from Valtik. He found Lady Eyda instead. But in his mind, Andry saw another Elder monarch.

He thought of Corayne too, and all he knew of her. With the last Spindleblade in her possession, she was even more of a target than ever before. She would seek out somewhere protected, strong enough to keep her safe from Taristan. Strong enough to fight back against him.

And somewhere we all know, he thought, remembering the ragged hope Corayne kept alive. *She will only go where she thinks we can follow.*

"Iona," Andry said, all conviction. The great city of immortal Elders rose up in his memories, walled by mist and stone. "She will make for the Elder enclave, in the Kingdom of Calidon."

And I will follow.

3

SO I MIGHT LIVE
Corayne

The gray horse ran through a gray world.

Ash and snow spiraled together, hot and cold.

Corayne felt none of it. Not the horse cantering beneath her. Not the tears on her cheeks, carving tracks down her dirty face. Nothing broke through her shield. The emptiness was the only defense she had against all behind her.

Against the death. The loss. And the failure too.

She held on to the invisible shield as long as she could, holding it tight against her heart. She dared not look back again. She could not bear the sight of Gidastern, swallowed up by smoke and flame. A graveyard to so many, including her friends.

Somehow the empty field was worse than the city's corpse.

No one followed. No one waited.

No one survived.

So Corayne did as she knew best, as her mother would have. She put the horizon ahead of her, and followed the smell of saltwater.

The Watchful Sea was her only companion, its iron waves battering the shore. Then night fell, leaving nothing but the sound of the sea. Even the blizzard faded away, the sky clearing. Corayne glared up at the stars, reading them as she would a map. The old constellations she knew were still there. They had not burned with the rest of the world. Out over the sea, the Great Dragon clutched the North Star in its jaws. She tried to take comfort in something familiar, but found even the stars were dull, their light cold and distant.

The horse kept on, never slowing. Corayne knew it was some magic of Valtik's, one last gift.

If only she gave the same strength to me, she thought bitterly.

She could not say how many hours passed in the burning city. It felt like years, her body aged a century, haggard and exhausted. Her throat burned, still scratchy from smoke. And her eyes stung from too many tears shed.

Reluctantly, she tried the reins. Part of her doubted the horse would listen, bound instead to a dead witch in a burned city.

But the mare responded without hesitation, slowing her pace. It blinked at her mournfully.

"I'm sorry," Corayne forced out, her voice raw as her throat.

Her nose wrinkled. *All my friends are dead and now I'm apologizing to a horse.*

Slowly, she slid down from the saddle, her body aching after hours on the road. It hurt to walk but still felt better than riding. Reins in hand, she forced onward, the mare keeping pace at her side.

In her head, she heard the voices of the undead army, little more than beasts, moaning and gurgling as one. United behind Taristan and Erida, and What Waits above them all.

Corayne leaned against the horse's flank, chasing the mare's warmth. Reminding herself she was not alone, not truly. The horse smelled of smoke, blood, and something colder, half-familiar. Pine and lavender. Ice.

Valtik.

Corayne's heart clenched and her tears gathered again, threatening to fall.

"No," she forced out. "No."

Jewels gleamed in the corner of her eye. She turned her head to see the Spindleblade in its sheath, the sword lashed to the horse's saddle. The gemstones in the hilt winked with every step of the horse, weakly reflecting the stars overhead. Corayne knew the stones and steel all too well. It was a perfect match to her father's Spindleblade, the one left shattered in a burning garden.

"A twin," Corayne said aloud, her voice low.

Twin blades, twin brothers. Two fates. And one terrible future.

Though she never knew him, Corayne wished for her father, Cortael of Old Cor. If only so she could pass the burden back to him, and give up all hopes of saving the world herself.

Why me, Corayne thought, as she had so many times. *Why must I be the one to save the realm?*

Corayne dared not touch the sword, not even to check the steel. Andry Trelland taught her how to tend a blade, but she could barely look at it, let alone clean it. The Spindleblade took her father's life. Took too many lives to count.

As they walked, her fingers trailed over her leather jerkin and beaten ring mail, then her pair of fine vambraces on her forearms. Despite the grime of battle, the pattern of scales, outlined in gold, still gleamed.

Dirynsima. Dragonclaws, Sibrez had called them. A gift of Ibal, from Isadere and their Blessed Dragons. *Another lifetime ago.*

She tipped her arm, examining one vambrace in the starlight. Steel spikes lined the edge of her forearm, sharp as a blade. A few were dark red, crusted with blood.

Taristan's blood.

"You're indestructible to most things," Corayne said aloud, repeating what she told her uncle hours ago. "But not all."

The Dragonclaws were twice blessed, both by Isadere—and Valtik. Perhaps whatever they did, Jydi bone magic or Ibalet faith, was enough to harm Taristan. The thought gave her some comfort, small as it was. But not enough to sleep. No matter how tired she was, Corayne could not make herself stop walking.

I'm too close to the open Spindle, she knew. *Too close to What Waits. And He waits for me in my dreams.*

Even awake, she could almost feel His presence, like a red fog at the corners of her eyes. She remembered when she fell through the Spindle at the old temple. Barren, cursed, a dead world corrupted and conquered. The Ashlands were a broken realm, cracked with Asunder, the hellish realm of What Waits. He found her there, His presence a shadow without a man to cast it.

The King of Asunder waited for her now at the edge of her mind, a hand extended. Ready to pull her down.

She remembered every word He told her.

How I despise that flame inside you, that restless heart of yours, He whispered then.

She felt her heart now, still stubbornly beating.

You cannot fathom the realms I've seen, He said, his shadow rippling with power. *The endless ages, the limitless bounds of greed and fear. Put down the Spindleblade. And I will make you queen of any kingdom you wish.*

She bit her lip, the sharp pain enough to bring her back. The voice faded in her memory.

Despite her hatred, Corayne found herself staring at the blade again, watching it as she would a dangerous creature. Like the sword itself might spring from its sheath and stab her too.

Quickly, before she could think herself out of it, she drew the blade in a single, singing motion.

The naked steel reflected her own face.

Shadows pooled beneath her eyes. Her black braid was a tangle, her sun-bronzed skin gone pale in the northern winter. Her lips were cracked by the cold, her eyes rimmed red by smoke and sorrow. But she was still herself, beneath the weight of the realm's fate. Still Corayne an-Amarat, with her father's grim look and her mother's dogged resolve.

"Is that enough?" she asked the silence. "Am I enough?"

To this, she received no answer. No direction. No heading or path to follow.

For once in her life, Corayne had no idea which way to go.

Then the horse startled, raising its head and pricking its ears in a way that made Corayne tremble.

"What is it?"

The horse, being a horse, did not answer.

But Corayne did not need one. Its fear was answer enough.

She whirled to face the horizon, looking back toward Gidastern. Something like a candle burned in the darkness. At least, it looked like a candle. Until the cold wind blew, carrying with it the smell of blood and smoke.

Corayne wasted no time leaping into the saddle. Behind her, the light grew and loosed a haunting roar.

Infyrna hound.

Corayne gritted her teeth, watching the candle split into many, the vicious barks echoing across the miles. Beneath her, the horse lunged into a gallop. The mare remembered Taristan's burning hounds as well as Corayne did.

His army will not be far behind, Corayne knew. Her stomach dropped to her feet. *If not Taristan himself.*

She kicked her heels, willing the horse to move even faster. Corayne could barely think as they galloped along the dark coast. Her body ached with exhaustion, but she could not fall.

For the realm falls with me.

Valtik's magic lasted and the horse rode on.

Light grew slowly in the east, turning the black sky to deep blue. The stars battled valiantly against the sunrise, but one by one, they blinked out of existence.

Darkness still clung to the land behind her, pooling in the shadow of the hills and trees. A black column of smoke rose in the west, the last remnants of Gidastern. Smaller trails of smoke pocked the sky, like flags to mark the hounds as they careened across the wilderness.

A few were close, less than a mile off.

Corayne tried to think around the fog of exhaustion. To figure out some way through the path ahead, whatever it might be. If they were here, Sorasa and Charlie would tell her to head for the closest village, to throw some unsuspecting garrison at the hounds. Dom would turn and fight, Sigil laughing at his heels. Andry would make some valiant, stupid sacrifice to give the rest of them time. And Valtik, impossible and inscrutable, certainly had some incantation to turn the hounds to dust. Or she would simply disappear again, only to turn up when the danger had passed.

But what about me?

Part of Corayne despaired. The rest of her knew she could not. The realm would not survive her sorrow, or her failure.

She thought of the map, of the landscape around her, the northern reaches of Galland.

Erida's kingdom. Enemy territory.

But the Castlewood was near, the great forest of the northern continent. It stretched for endless miles in almost every direction. To the south lay the Corteth Mountains, then Siscaria and the Long Sea. *Home.* Corayne's heart ached at the prospect. So much of her wanted to point the horse southward, and ride until they crashed into the waves of familiar waters.

To the east were more mountains. Calidon. *And*, she knew, *Iona*. Domacridhan's enclave, an Elder stronghold. And perhaps the last place upon the Ward where she might find help.

It seemed impossible. Miles away, at the edge of a fading dream.

But the enclave burned a hole in her mind, its name a whisper in her ears.

Iona.

The enclave was still hundreds of miles away, beyond the Castlewood and across the mountains, hidden in Calidon. Corayne could hardly fathom what the enclave looked like, shrouded in mist and glen. She tried to remember how Andry and Dom had described Iona, without remembering Andry and Dom themselves. It was an impossible endeavor.

She saw Andry's face, his warm, kind eyes, his lips pulled into a gentle smile. His laughter never had any bite to it. Only kindness and joy. Corayne doubted the squire ever carried an ill thought for anyone. He was too good for all of them.

Too good for me.

Above all, she remembered his blazing kiss against her palm, his lips pressed to her skin in the only goodbye they would ever have.

Her palm itched on the reins, threatening to burn like everything else.

Then the smell of smoke filled the air, somehow heavier than her bottomless grief.

The scent was overpowering, but not so terrible as the keening scream of a hellhound as it thundered over the hill behind her. Its overlong black legs ate up the landscape, leaving a burning trail with each footfall. Flames leapt along the beast's spine, and its open mouth glowed like hot coals.

Corayne felt a scream of her own rise in her throat, but only dug in her heels. Beneath her, the horse obeyed, somehow gaining speed.

The hound drove on, snapping and barking. Its brethren answered, their howls echoing beyond the dawn.

"Gods help me," she murmured, tucking low against the horse's neck.

Despite her galloping horse, the hound closed the distance between them. Over one maddening hour, the hound gained, inch by inch. Every heartbeat felt a life age. Every faltering step a lightning bolt in Corayne's chest.

The sun climbed in the sky, melting frost along the road. Corayne felt only the warmth of the hound's flames.

It snapped at her horse's hooves, jaws black and burning.

This time, Corayne did not call on the gods.

She saw the Companions in her mind, all dead behind her.

Dead so I might live.

It will not be in vain.

In a single motion, she reined the horse and drew the Spindleblade, the steel flashing in the morning sun. It flamed brighter than the hound itself, snarling as it leapt for her horse. Already moving through the air, its body like an arrow from the string.

With all her strength, Corayne swung the blade, a lumberjack with an ax.

The Spindleblade cut through flame and flesh. There was no blood as the hound's head fell from its shoulders. Its corpse fell to embers and ashes, leaving nothing but a burned path in its wake.

The world went achingly silent, but for Corayne's heartbeat and a trailing wind. The ashes blew slowly, until even the embers winked out.

Sweat dripped down Corayne's face, and she heaved a single, shuddering breath.

Her heart pounded, most of her in shock. The rest surged with triumph. But there was little time to celebrate, or even breathe a sigh of relief. The silence loomed up again, as much a reminder as anything else.

You are alone, Corayne an-Amarat, she thought, her heart welling up with sorrow. *More alone than you ever thought you could be.*

She wheeled the horse again, back onto the path toward the distant forest. Ashes fell from the Spindleblade. She wiped it clean with her sleeve, thinking of Andry and how he tended their blades with sure hands. The memory made her breath catch, only for a moment. With a snap, she slid the sword back into its leather sheath.

Corayne did her best not to think about the last thing Taristan's sword killed.

Her best was not enough.

The sun wheeled across the sky and hours passed. The Castlewood did not seem to move any closer, but neither did the remaining Infyrna hounds. Perhaps the loss of their brother kept them at a distance.

Can monsters feel fear? Corayne wondered as she rode on.

Taristan is a monster. And I saw fear in him, she thought, remembering his face in their final moments together. When she took his Spindleblade for her own, and a dragon crashed down onto the city. He was afraid then, his bloodshot eyes wide with terror, as much as he tried to hide it. Neither

Taristan nor Ronin controlled the great beast. It roamed freely, destroying whatever it wanted to destroy.

Where the dragon might be now, Corayne had no idea. And she did not want to spend precious energy thinking about it. There was nothing to be done about a dragon loose upon the Ward, obedient to nothing and no one.

Just when Corayne thought Valtik's mare might ride forever, her inexorable pace began to slow. Only a little, barely enough to notice. But sweat foamed on her flanks and her breathing grew hard. Whatever magic Valtik imbued the horse with came to an end.

"Well done," Corayne muttered, patting the mare's gray neck. "I don't have much else to give you but my thanks."

The horse whickered in response and changed direction.

Corayne didn't have the heart to rein her back, and let the horse angle off the old road and down a wooded bank. There was a stream at the bottom, half choked with ice. But the water ran clear, and Corayne was thirsty too.

When the mare bent to drink, Corayne slid from the saddle, landing on bowed and aching legs. She winced, bone-tired and saddle-sore. All she wanted to do was lie down and sleep, no matter the danger. Instead, Corayne tried to think as Sorasa would.

First, she loosed the Spindleblade from the horse's saddle, and slung it over her shoulder. She only trusted Valtik's magic so far, and a spooked horse could mean disaster. Then she assessed her surroundings with a sharp eye, noting the dip of the bank and the tangled tree branches hanging over the stream. Good cover from the sky, should a dragon be lurking. The ground formed a little valley with the stream down the center, barely deeper than she was tall, but it offered some cover too. Not enough to sleep, but enough for a moment's peace. Enough for Corayne to exhale, if only a little.

"Iona."

Corayne tested the name on her tongue as she mulled over the possibilities. She knew little of Dom's home, but enough. It was a fortress city, well hidden in the valleys of Calidon. And filled with immortal Elders. If even half of them were fearsome as Dom was, it would be a safe place indeed.

If they even open the gates to me, she thought ruefully. *Iona refused to help us once. They might do so again.*

Even so, it was her best option.

Perhaps the only one.

As her horse drank, Corayne refilled her own waterskins upstream, then tried to clean her face. The icy water was a shock, waking her up a little.

Again, she glanced at the sky, peering between the branches. The sun angled cold and golden among the clouds. Too beautiful to stand on such an awful day.

She turned back to find the mare with her head raised and ears twitching, over-alert.

Immediately Corayne went for the Spindleblade on her back, hands closing around the hilt in seconds. But before she could draw, a low voice echoed over the stream.

"We wish you no harm, Corayne of Old Cor."

4

THE LIONESS

Erida

They will kneel or they will fall.

Siscaria and Tyriot kneeled.

So became the Queen of Four Kingdoms.

Erida of Galland, Madrence, Tyriot, and Siscaria. Her domain now stretched from the shores of the Auroran Ocean to the bitter cold of the Watchful Sea. From sprawling Ascal to the jeweled islands of the Tyri Straits. Forests, farmland, mountains, rivers, ancient cities, and bustling ports. All of it fell beneath Erida's command, and her shadow grew long indeed.

My empire, with no boundaries but the edges of the realm itself. All the realm in my own two hands.

She'd had more than enough time to think of her destiny on the road home, as their journey was longer than planned. Parts of the Long Sea were too dangerous for the Queen to sail, even with a fleet around her. Pirates thrived in times of war, and they stalked the waters like hungry wolves. Erida and her company were forced to travel overland from Partepalas to Byllskos, where she received Tyriot's surrender. Or rather,

Tyriot's abandonment. The Sea Prince and his royal cousins fled their palaces, rather than surrender to her conquest. Erida laughed at their empty halls and empty docks. She left behind a few lords to manage the coastal cities and carried on, rolling over the continent in an inexorable wave.

Siscaria surrendered easily. Erida placed her uncle, Duke Reccio, in control of the Siscarian capital. Their bond of blood made him more loyal than most of her own nobles.

She had rejoined her armada soon after and a hundred Gallish ships, galleys, and cogs turned north to Ascal. The nobles were eager for home, but none so much as Erida herself. Her own flagship led the way, an immense war galley done up as a pleasure barge, with all the comforts of a royal palace.

After two months of travel, Erida despised it.

She suffered through countless meetings, feasts, and oath takings, all her time wrapped up with loathsome courtiers scratching for favor. Everything seemed both endless and immediate. Some days disappeared in the blink of an eye. Some seconds dragged, clawing over her skin. She felt so now, through the last agonizing miles of the long way home.

Patience, Erida told herself. *This torture is nearly at an end.*

She knew what waited in Ascal. And who.

Taristan was already there, returned from Gidastern. His letters had been vague, scrawled in Ronin's spiky handwriting, but she gleaned enough. Taristan was victorious too.

She expected nothing less. He was her match in every single way.

Erida squinted north, where the shores of Mirror Bay narrowed into the mouth of the Great Lion. Ascal sprawled, the city of islands and bridges strung across the river. Her heart skipped a beat, her body tightening with anticipation.

She would be home before nightfall. Even the tide rose to her favor, pushing on the fleet, a favorable wind filling their sails.

"We've made up time," Lord Thornwall said, holding the rail at her side. His red beard had finally gone all to gray. The conquest had been hard on her greatest commander.

Lady Harrsing held her other flank, leaning heavily against the ship. She bent like a crone, huddled in her furs against the damp cold. Erida would have commanded her down below, but she knew Harrsing would only wave off her concern. The old woman had faced worse than winter in her many years upon the Ward.

"What of the final counts?" Erida asked her commander, eyeing him sternly.

Thornwall heaved a great sigh. He did his best to condense two months of conquest.

"One thousand of Lord Vermer's men lost to the Tyri rebels before the surrender," he said. "And we received word from Lord Holg that the Tyri princes still attack from their islands."

Erida fought the urge to roll her eyes.

"I trust Holg's ability to defend Byllskos in my absence. Especially against coward princes who flee at the first sign of danger."

"We lost nine ships to the pirates on the Empress Coast." Thornwall's face darkened.

Erida shrugged. "Pirates scatter at the first sign of danger. They are scavengers at best."

"Scavengers," he agreed, nodding. "But smart, organized somehow. They're infiltrating harbors under true flags and good papers of passage. Sweeping past patrols only to rob treasuries and set fire to ports. I see no end to it, not unless we shut down passage entirely."

He drew a deep breath. "I believe they have allied with the Tyri princes."

Erida all but laughed outright.

"I've never heard of such a preposterous thing," she said. "The princes hunt pirates for sport. Theirs is a long history of bloodshed."

Next to her, Lady Harrsing sighed. "A common enemy makes strange allies."

"I care little for the errant princes, and even less for ramshackle pirates," Erida snapped, feeling her patience run thin.

"You gained three crowns of the Ward in as many months, Your Majesty," Thornwall said, swiftly changing the subject. He eyed her brow, where Erida would soon wear a crown fit for an empress. "It is no small thing, what you have done."

Since her coronation, Erida knew Thornwall's great value. He was intelligent, strategic, brave, loyal, and, strangest of all, honest. Erida saw it in him now, tentative as he was.

"Thank you," she said, and genuinely meant it.

Lord Thornwall was not Erida's father, but she valued his praise just the same. And as commander of Galland's armies, Lord Thornwall knew more of war than almost anyone else. A corner of his mouth twitched, betraying a frown.

"Kneel or fall," he murmured, echoing the words now rippling across the realm. "The threat worked on Siscaria and half of Tyriot."

Thornwall looked down at his hands. They were callused by the hilt of a sword, his fingers ink-stained by maps and paperwork.

"Larsia will follow, still weary of war." He ticked off a finger, counting. "Perhaps the border kingdoms will as well. Trec, Uscora, Dahland, Ledor. Gods know they hate the Temur more than they hate you, and would rather be your ally than be caught between a Temurijon cavalry and a Gallish legion."

Erida watched his face intently, as she would any courtier. She saw weariness in him, and conflict. *Torn between his loyalty to me, and his own weakness*, Erida thought, clenching her teeth.

"But Ibal, Kasa, the Emperor of the Temurijon." Thornwall met her gaze sharply.

Erida kept her face still, even as frustration rose up inside her. *There is fear in him too.*

"Those are wars, the likes of which this realm has never seen," Thornwall said, his words like a plea. "Even with the continent beneath you. Even with Taristan beside you."

She heard what he would not say.

You will not win.

His faithlessness was like a slap across the face.

"We are Old Cor reborn, Taristan and I." Her voice went hard and unyielding as steel. "The empire is ours to reclaim and rebuild. It is the will of the gods as much as my own. Or have you lost your faith in the gods, in holy Syrek, who drives us to victory?"

Her usual tactic worked almost too well.

Her commander flushed and blustered, set off balance by an invocation of his god.

"Of course I have faith," he sputtered, collecting himself.

Lady Harrsing gave a cluck of her tongue. "It is the will of the gods, Lord Thornwall."

The will of a god, at least, Erida mused to herself. At the thought of Taristan's master, Erida's stomach twisted, and warmth bloomed in her chest. She dropped her furs entirely to keep from sweating.

Next to her, Thornwall bowed low, eyes flitting between the Queen and the old woman.

"I know you have the . . ." He paused, struggling for the right word. "*Godly* army."

Erida nearly laughed aloud. She had many words for Taristan's corpse army, away in the north. None of them came close to *godly*.

"But we are only men," he answered softly. "Legions of thousands, but men still. Tired of war. Eager to go home and bask in victory. Let them sing songs of you, your glory, your greatness. Let them renew their strength, so they might rise to fight for you again. And again. And again."

That was enough to give Erida pause. She pursed her lips, thinking on her commander's advice. As in younger days, she found herself looking to Lady Harrsing for guidance. The older woman stared back at her now, brow furrowed into a thousand lines of care. After many years, her face was easy to read.

Listen.

"It is not in you to falter, Your Majesty. I know that. You do not tire, fail, or flag," Thornwall pushed on, imploring. "But the men are not you."

Erida barely nodded. Her commander was no simpering courtier. His flattery was poorly done, albeit true.

"I see your point, Lord Thornwall," she said through clenched teeth. "We shall discuss this further when we are safely back in the capital. I give you leave."

He knew better than to argue, dipping into a low bow.

"Yes, Your Majesty."

She did not watch him stalk off, content to watch Ascal on the horizon.

Bella Harrsing remained, eyeing her beneath the folds of her fur cap, her look shrewd.

"Your victories are the greatest blow you could ever deal to Lord Konegin," she said. "And anyone who might support his treasonous attempts to usurp your throne."

Erida flinched at the mention of her cousin. His name was like a knife through her heart. She scowled and showed her teeth.

"I can think of something worse," she growled.

His head on a spike.

Bella Harrsing chuckled low in her throat, the sound a wet rattle. "I'm sure you can, my dear. The Empress Rising, the court calls you," she added, dropping her voice. "I hear their whispers even here."

"As do I." Erida relished the thought, her sapphire eyes glittering. "Even the lords who used to sneer in my face. Now they kiss my hand and beg for favor, hanging on my every command."

Her body buzzed, excited and frightened and gloriously proud, all in one. As always, Erida wanted a sword of her own, some weapon to wear as all the men did. Even her useless courtiers who could barely hold a fork carried blades to feel dangerous. She had nothing but her skirts and her crowns.

"Queen of Four Kingdoms," she whispered. Slowly, she pulled off a glove, revealing the emerald ring of state. It winked on her finger, a flashing green eye.

Lady Harrsing stared at the jewel too, as if entranced. "Old Cor reborn," she muttered, repeating Erida's own words. "It was your father's dream once. And his father's before him."

"I know," Erida answered without thought. Such hopes were hammered into her since birth.

"And you have come closer than any king before you," Harrsing said.

Slowly, tentatively, she put out a gloved hand, letting it hover over Erida's arm.

On instinct, Erida leaned into the old woman's familiar touch. Childish as it felt.

"He would be proud of you."

The whisper hung in the air, nearly torn apart by the wind. Erida clutched to it all the same, holding it tightly in her chest.

"Thank you, Bella," she murmured, her voice shaking.

Ahead, Ascal bloomed like a bruise. Golden walls and cathedral spires rose, banners of gold and green glinting against the bloodred clouds. Ascal was the greatest city in the realm, home to half a million souls. Her own palace sat at its heart, walled onto its own island, a city unto itself.

Erida traced the familiar skyline, noting every tower, every flag, every bridge, canal, and temple dome. In her mind, she walked the path laid ahead of her, a grand parade route from the deck of her ship all the way to the New Palace. There would be cheering from the commoners, flowers strewn in front of her horse, shouts of triumph and adoration. She was a conqueror returned, an empress rising. The greatest ruler their kingdom had ever known.

And her reign had only just begun.

Her grip tightened on the rail, keeping herself still. It took all her restraint not to jump into the water and swim all the way back to her palace, her throne, and Taristan most of all.

Slowly, she pulled away from Harrsing's hand. The old woman let her go, unable to stop a ruling queen from doing anything. She narrowed her eyes to Erida, but the Queen did not explain, her mind elsewhere. Without a word, she turned, putting her back to Lady Harrsing and the city.

Let me stay, darling.

She was used to the voice by now. When it came, she did not flinch or startle. Only her eyes flickered, jumping up to the red sky overhead. It was barely noon, though it looked like sunset in every direction.

Let me in.

As always, she answered in the same way, almost teasing him.

Who are you?

What Waits spoke with His usual velvet, His voice coiling around her mind.

You already know. Let me stay. Let me in.

His touch lingered, ebbing slowly, until only echoes remained.

5

LAY DOWN THE BRANCH
Corayne

Corayne fell into a warrior's stance with the sword pointed in the direction of the voice. Sorasa Sarn had taught her well.

Many silhouettes gathered on the bank above her. The sun blazed at their backs, fading their edges, and Corayne had to squint against the light to see them clearly.

"We wish you no harm," one of them said again, taking a slow step forward. He did not fear the sword in her hand, lethal as it was.

Corayne doubted any Elder would.

Immortals, all of them. She knew it instantly. They had the same look as Domacridhan, their eyes deep and distant, their faces grave. The one closest moved with unearthly grace, his motions fluid as the stream beneath her boots.

He shared Dom's milk-white skin too, but nothing more. The Elder had deep red hair and golden eyes, yellow as a hawk's. Where Dom was broad and imposing, a scowling mountain, this one had the look of a willow tree, with long, lean limbs. The Elders behind him shared the same coloring, all six of them.

They wore mail and leathers beneath their cloaks, in varying shades of purple and gold, like fallen leaves. They were forest people, their garb used for camouflage in the trees. But they stuck out oddly in the empty hills.

"You are of the Castlewood," she said, her voice high and cold.

The immortal dipped his brow and swept back a graceful arm. "Of Sirandel, Lady Corayne."

Corayne racked her memory for any scrap she knew about his enclave. She came back with little, only that Elders of Sirandel died with her father. They fought Taristan once, and lost.

Will they fight again?

She raised her chin. "How do you know my name?"

The Elder's hawk eyes softened as he looked her over. His pity made Corayne's skin crawl.

"By now, your name is known in every enclave of the Ward," he murmured.

Corayne took it in stride. "And *you* are?"

The Elder bowed his head again, then sank to a knee. In another life, another Elder kneeled before Corayne. In the shadow of her old cottage, not a ditch at the end of the world.

Corayne bit her lip to keep from screaming.

"I am Castrin of Sirandel. Glorian-born son of Bryven and Liranda."

She waved him off with a shake of her head. "That isn't necessary."

Castrin leapt to his feet in a blink, wringing his hands. "My apologies, my lady."

This time, memories of Dom and his incessant apologies, his useless titles, almost knocked Corayne to the ground. She turned her head and lowered the sword, hiding her face from Elder scrutiny. Her eyes burned and her throat went tight, every breath a hard-won gasp. She wished for Dom with all her heart, for any of them. Some part of her wondered, if she reached far enough, with all the will she had in her body—would they appear?

"My lady, are you injured?"

It took all her restraint not to snap at the Elder, bewildered as he was. She remembered Dom long ago, before he gained some insight into mortal ways. Castrin was somehow worse.

"No," she bit out, turning back around. Slowly, she returned the Spindleblade to its sheath.

The other Elders looked down with unsettling eyes, tracking her, like wolves at the edge of a forest clearing. Strangely, she felt some relief. She was safe in their company, as much as anyone could be in a realm breaking apart.

"I suppose I should ask why you sought me out," she said, shifting her weight to lean up against her mare. The horse's warm body felt good beneath her shoulder. "But I think I know. Has your monarch seen reason, now that a Spindle burns at the gates of your forest?"

Castrin's lips thinned. He glanced past her, in the direction of Gidastern. *Does he see the smoke of a city burned, or the charred paths of Infyrna hounds loose upon the Ward? Does he know what lies behind me?*

Judging by the revulsion on his face, Corayne guessed he did.

Shaking his head, Castrin looked back to Corayne. "We bid you come with us, to the safety of Sirandel, and our monarch's protection. Valnir is keen to meet you."

Her back against the horse, Corayne crossed her arms.

"I'm going to Iona," she said quickly, her mouth moving faster than her brain. The plan formed as she spoke. It felt right somehow, almost destined. *For there is no other plan to make.* "You are welcome to guard me as far as your enclave, and offer me respite for a night. Your Valnir and I will talk, but I must be on my way."

Behind Castrin, his Elder warriors exchanged slow, shocked glances. Castrin blinked, sharing their confusion. They clearly did not expect her opposition. These Elders had little experience with mortals.

Finally he bowed again. "Very well, my lady."

Corayne grimaced, the title like sand in her mouth. "My name will suffice, Castrin."

He bobbed in acquiescence. "Very well, Corayne."

Her eyes stung again, albeit less than before. The more pain she felt, the more she numbed to it. Like spending too long in the cold, until there was no cold anymore.

"I heard tell of your companions, Corayne. Mighty and cunning. Noble heroes all," Castrin added, searching her face. Corayne did her best to remain calm. "Where are they?"

Her voice stuck in her throat, lips barely parted. She could not bring herself to say it, but the Elder did not relent.

"Domacridhan of Iona?" Castrin pressed. "He is a friend."

Corayne's breath caught and she spun on her heel, putting her back to the Elders. She all but leapt into the saddle, her blood pounding in her ears.

"He was my friend too," she whispered.

Every mile behind her, every day passed, was another stone in the wall around Corayne's heart. She focused on the rhythm of the horse beneath her. It was easier to count hoofbeats than it was to remember her Companions, and their fate. Even so, they haunted her, their faces swimming in her dreams.

The Castlewood was ancient and twisted, a maze of roots, brush, and branches. At first, every direction looked the same. Gray with winter, green with pine, brown with the needles and dead leaves underfoot. But the Elders knew paths no mortal could find and their horses charged through the tunneled branches. Corayne could only follow, feeling lost, swallowed up by the labyrinth of trees. She even lost track of the days, trailing their number like a grief-stricken ghost.

"Corayne an-Amarat," Castrin called out, his voice filtering through the haze of memory.

She reined to a halt and turned to find the immortal riders already dismounted.

They looked back at her expectantly, their yellow eyes like darts of sunlight through the trees. Castrin bent at the waist and swept out a graceful arm, the picture of a courtly gentleman.

"We have arrived," he said.

Her brow furrowed in confusion. The forest around them seemed no different, filled with rocks and roots and ice-choked streams. Pine trees towered over naked oaks. The aspens shimmered, a few still clinging to their golden leaves. The birds were louder here, the sound of water against stone more musical, but little else changed.

"I don't—" she began, her eyes wavering.

Then her vision shifted, and Sirandel bloomed.

The two trees behind Castrin were not wood, but hewn stone, the bark carved by master hands. They even had roots, pouring right into the dirt. The few leaves still clinging to the smooth branches were not leaves at all, but colored glass, intricate and impossible. Red, gold, and purple, they cast shimmering shadows on the forest floor. The trees arched together, forming a simple kind of doorway.

Or a gate.

"We will walk the horses from here," Castrin explained, taking his mount in hand. "Even you will know the way."

Corayne started to bristle, but he was right. Never in a thousand years would she have found her way to Sirandel alone.

She slid from the saddle and her boots hit rock instead of dirt. There was stone beneath the underbrush, camouflaged like the rest, leading through the gate on a secret road. Carved foxes watched from the roots of the trees, one perched on either side like a pair of gate wardens. Corayne felt their unseeing eyes. She suspected there were real guardians in the trees, hidden Elders of Sirandel, who watched the gate.

"Is an enclave like a city?" she said, squinting through the forest. She couldn't see any guards, but the stone trees grew more numerous with every step. Their glass leaves glittered like Castrin's eyes.

Castrin shrugged. His horse followed him without being led, so used to his master and the Sirandel road.

"It depends," he answered. "Some enclaves are little more than outposts, others villages or castles. Ghishan is a mighty cliff fortress, a jewel in the Crown of Snow. Tirakrion an island. Then Iona is a proper city, the oldest of our enclaves. It is there many of our people first entered this realm, from a Spindle long shifted."

"Shifted?"

"Spindles do not just open and close, my lady. They move," Castrin replied. "Over centuries, of course. It will be long years before the burning Spindle of Gidastern appears somewhere else."

Corayne's eyes widened. She pictured the golden needle that was the Spindle, spitting flame as it sliced across the Ward.

"I did not know that," she said, worrying her lip. "Is the Ionian Spindle how you came here, Glorian-born?"

A shadow crossed Castrin's face as they walked. This time it was Corayne asking the painful questions, and the immortal trying to avoid them.

"I crossed as a child, many hundreds of years ago," he said stiffly. "We were exiled from a kingdom I do not remember. First through the Crossroads, and then, yes, to the land that became Iona."

Exiled. Corayne tucked Castrin's words away like jewels to be turned over later.

"The Crossroads?" she murmured, a picture of innocent curiosity.

"The door to all doorways, we called it once." Castrin's eyes went faraway and Corayne wished she could see into his memories. "A realm behind all the realms. With a Spindle to each land in existence. Its gates always moving, always shifting."

Corayne's throat tightened with the implication. "But the Crossroads is lost, like Glorian."

"It is," Castrin replied stiffly. "For now."

She did not miss the way his yellow gaze lingered, first on her face. And then on the Spindleblade. A chill ran down Corayne's spine but she hid it well. She wore her old self as a mask, letting her wide-eyed and curious nature rise up like a shield.

There was a Spindle in Iona once, a door to all doorways. A way for the Elders to return home. But there isn't anymore.

A whistle snapped her thoughts in half and she looked back to Castrin. He whistled again, low and haunting. With a start, Corayne realized he perfectly mimicked an owl. Another whistle answered, hooting out of the trees.

In a blink, the immortals around her doubled, more guards appearing from the woods. They wore soft, purple leathers, embossed with the sigil of the fox. Half were red-haired and yellow-eyed like Castrin. The others varied in their coloring as any crowd in a port city. Bronze-skinned or moon-pale, black-haired or blond, even one silver-gray.

Castrin raised a hand to the guards, palm open in friendship. "I bring Corayne an-Amarat to Sirandel, under the Monarch's own command."

One of the guards narrowed his eyes and sniffed the air. "You bring hounds of Infyrna as well, Castrin."

Corayne's heart dropped into her boots.

"They're still following us?" she hissed out, looking back the way they came. She half expected to see fiery bodies flitting through the trees.

Castrin scoffed out something akin to a laugh. "They are still following *you*," he said. "But they will be dealt with. The forest slowed them as I hoped it would, and you are safe within Sirandel. Even from beasts of the Burning Realm."

Corayne swallowed down a little of her fear. "What of the Castlewood?"

The immortal blinked. "I don't follow."

"Your forest. Your lands." Corayne waved at the woods around them, ancient and stretching for miles in every direction. "Are the hounds burning their way through, destroying as they hunt me?"

Castrin exchanged confused looks with his immortals, all of them blank-faced.

"That is no concern of ours," he finally said.

With a hand, he motioned for her to continue down the path.

Corayne tipped her head, feeling as confused as Castrin looked, albeit for very different reasons.

"This realm is not our own, Corayne. It is not ours to keep," the Elder explained. He began walking again, forcing her to follow. "It is not yours either, Daughter of Old Cor."

A sour taste filled Corayne's mouth. Her terror did not disappear, it only changed. Again, she eyed the immortals around her, distant and detached from Allward, like the stars themselves. Anchored in a lonely sky, doomed to watch and never interfere. *But these immortals are not doomed. They have chosen to stand back.* She bit the inside of her lip to keep herself from saying something rude, or hateful. Ruefully, she thought of Dom again. Once, she thought him foolish and idealistic. Now she longed for his noble idiocy.

At least he cared about the rest of the world.

She fell silent, watching Castrin and the rest carefully, step after step.

The path turned into a proper road, and the stone trees around her grew tall. So perfect was their placement and artistry that Corayne hardly noticed she had walked into a structure, the arches above her formed by live growth and sculpted stone, woven together by immortal hands. The glass leaves became windows and skylights, filtering the sun in chips of color. Birds fluttered among the branches, and Corayne caught the red flash of a living fox among the roots, darting past its stone cousins.

"Sirandel," she murmured.

City or palace, she could not say. More Elders wove between the columns and Corayne suspected this was a great hall. They flashed in and out of sight like the fox, moving both too fast and too slow, blending into their enclave with little effort. Their clothing—steel, leather, or silk—was patterned in purple and gold, all in the image of fallen leaves.

Archways tunneled through the trees, as did winding staircases. Some spiraled up into the high canopy, to watchtowers above the branches. Others dove into the tree roots, underground to chambers unseen. There were no walls to guard the enclave, only the Castlewood itself. Sirandel felt more like a cathedral than a fortress, alone in the wilds.

"Your home is beautiful," Corayne said softly, and she meant it.

Castrin replied with a true smile.

Eventually they reached a terrace, raised up among the roots, wide and flat enough to serve as a banquet hall. *Or a throne room*, Corayne realized, drawing a sharp breath.

At the far end, the stone trees wove to form a curved wall, with more colored glass between the branches. Carved roots curled, forming a great seat. Overhead, the living trees gave over to stone entirely. They were fully indoors without Corayne even realizing it. And they were surrounded, purple-armored guards lining the perimeter around them. They were fearsome, but not so fearsome as the Elder who sat the Sirandel throne.

"Your Majesty," she said, her voice echoing through the great, high chamber.

Without hesitation, Corayne bent to a knee before the Monarch of Sirandel.

Lord Valnir eyed her from his seat, his lips pursed together. Only his yellow eyes moved, tracking Corayne as she lowered herself.

Like Castrin, he was tall and lean as a willow tree, with porcelain-pale skin and long hair streaked red and silver. He had the bearing of a king but wore no crown, only jeweled rings on every finger. A purple cloak hung half off his shoulder, clasped with gold and amethyst. He blinked yellow eyes behind dark lashes, looking her over from head to toe. The dim light of the forest, filtered by the stained glass, cut strangely across him. He seemed a predator, keen as the fox sigil of his enclave.

Slowly, he leaned forward into brighter light. Corayne did not miss the scar around his neck, barely visible over the collar of his cloak. White and pink stood out against his pale skin, ringing his throat like a chain.

He bore no weapons she could see, only the branch of an aspen tree.

It lay across his lap, silver-barked and golden-leaved, trembling in a phantom wind.

"Rise, Corayne an-Amarat," he said. His voice was soft, ragged even. She wondered if the scar had anything to do with it. "And be welcome here."

She did as commanded, willing herself not to shake. Even after Erida and Taristan, it was hard not to feel intimidated by an Elder ruler.

"Thank you for your welcome," Corayne forced out. She wished for Andry so badly. He would know how to act in the hall of a great lord. "I'm afraid I cannot stay long."

Valnir's brow twitched in confusion. "I suppose you mortals are always pressed for time."

For a moment, Corayne said nothing. Then she pressed a hand to her mouth, stifling a laugh as best she could.

From his throne, Valnir glanced at Castrin, bewildered.

Corayne only laughed harder. It was the only respite she had, a brief escape from the doom awaiting them all.

"I apologize, Your Majesty," she said, trying to steady herself. "It isn't often I hear jokes about my inevitable death."

Valnir furrowed his brow. "I did not intend that."

"I'm aware," she answered. Her tone hardened. "Domacridhan of Iona was the same, for a time."

Silence fell over the chamber, heavy as a cloud.

On his throne, Valnir shook his head. Whatever color there was in his pale face drained away.

"So he is dead."

"I cannot say for certain." Corayne strangled the hope still fighting in her heart. "But only death or chains would keep him from me."

A low snarl escaped the Monarch's lips. His teeth gleamed and Corayne half expected fangs.

"Like Rowanna, like Marigon, like Arberin," he hissed, clenching a fist. Fury churned behind his mask of immortal stoicism. "Vederan blood spilled for this wretched realm. Dead for nothing."

"His death will not be in vain so long as I live, Your Majesty." Corayne squared her body to the throne and put a hand to the sheath on her back. "And so long as I bear the last Spindleblade upon the Ward."

All around the chamber, Valnir's guards put arrows to the string, moving too fast for Corayne's mortal eyes. They watched, poised to strike, as she drew the Spindleblade, letting the sword reflect the many lights of the hall.

Valnir glared at the sword, his red brow etched in an unforgiving line. With a shrug, he waved down his guards.

Corayne laid the blade on the flagstones, its jewels glowing like coals in a hearth.

"I see you know it," she said. "And what this sword means."

Fast as Elders could be, they were more terrifying when they chose to move slowly. Valnir did now, pushing off his throne. He clutched the aspen branch in one hand, the golden leaves shuddering with each step. He sneered at the Spindleblade as he stalked across the floor, long-legged and prowling. Another hiss escaped his mouth.

Corayne fought the urge to run, every instinct in her warning that she was little more than prey before the immortal king.

"I know this sword better than you can possibly imagine," he said, his eyes wide and glaring. Not at Corayne, but at the Spindleblade. "The Princess of Iona came to us some months ago, weaving tales of woe. She brought word of my kinsmen dead, and this realm on the brink of ruin. She asked for warriors, for my entire enclave to rise in battle."

Corayne scowled. "And you turned your back on her."

"Better to turn my back on one instead of many," he snapped.

Again, she wanted to run, but held her ground.

"She is dead, too, you know," Corayne said softly. Valnir recoiled, as if struck. His face tightened with anguish. "Princess Ridha burned with the rest of Gidastern."

The Monarch rounded on his kinsman, moving so quickly his limbs blurred. He pointed the golden branch like a spear. "Is that true?"

Without hesitation, Castrin dropped to a knee and bowed his head, mournful.

"We never reached the city. Our orders were to retrieve Corayne and come back." He glanced sideways at Corayne, stricken. "But Gidastern burns on the horizon, and Infyrna hounds roam the Ward."

Corayne let his words wash over Valnir. He stared at the blade again, his grief shimmering with tremendous anger.

"Another Spindle torn, my lord," she said.

Valnir didn't look up from the sword.

"But no more, if you speak truly," he breathed. "If that is the last Spindleblade in the realm, and you its wielder, then we have nothing else to fear from Taristan of Old Cor."

"I wish with all my heart that were true." Corayne sighed and took a step toward the Monarch, dangerous as it felt. "But my uncle does not act alone. He is a servant of What Waits, who seeks to break this realm apart, and claim the pieces for His own."

Valnir waved a hand at her. "Through the Spindles, yes. Ridha said as much, and Isibel before her, when all this nonsense began. But Taristan can't tear any more Spindles without the sword in your hand. So long as we keep the blade from your uncle, the realm is safe."

Then something glittered in his eyes.

"Better yet, we destroy it," he growled. "And ensure no Corblood conqueror can ever threaten the realms again."

Corayne lurched forward, planting herself between the Elder and the Spindleblade. She put out a hand, as if she alone could stop Valnir should he choose to act.

Thankfully, the immortal pulled up short. He narrowed his eyes, confused and enraged. "You wish to keep it? For *what*? Yourself?"

Corayne all but scoffed in frustration. "Taristan's damage has already been done. I've closed two Spindles, but there are two more open still. One in Gidastern, beyond anyone's reach. And one—I don't know where. If I did, I would be there already. But the open Spindles will eat at the world, like cracks spreading through glass. Until everything shatters. And What Waits—"

"Waits no more." Valnir whirled, his long cloak sweeping over the floor. Leaves circled in his wake as he prowled back to the throne. With a sigh, he sank back into his seat, the branch across his knees again. "The Torn King of Asunder conquers this realm like so many others."

Corayne's jaw tightened.

"So many *others*?" she echoed, her brow furrowed.

Valnir gave her a leveling look. "Do you think this is the first realm What Waits seeks to conquer and consume?"

A hot flush washed over Corayne's face and down her neck.

"No. I have seen the Ashlands with my own eyes, sir," she forced out, trying to sound as stern as Valnir looked.

In her head, she saw the broken realm beyond the temple Spindle, a land of dust and heat and death. Nothing grew. Nothing lived. There were only corpses crawling over each other, and a weak sun in a blood-soaked sky. *How many other realms fell to such a fate? How many more will fall after we do?*

Valnir's gaze changed, if only a little, more thoughtful than before. And perhaps, a little impressed. One long-fingered hand rose to his neck, and rubbed at his scar, tracing the old line of uneven flesh. With a jolt, Corayne realized what the scar was from.

Not a blade.

A noose.

Her mind spun. *Who in all the realms would try to hang an Elder king?*

"Tell me of your journey, Corayne an-Amarat," Valnir said finally, his eyes still faraway. "Tell us all."

Exhaustion loomed over Corayne, threatening to crush her. But she could not falter. Princess Ridha had failed to sway Valnir and his people. Corayne knew she did not have the luxury of failure anymore.

She spoke as quickly as she could, as if she could outrun her own sorrow. By now, she knew the story well enough.

"My mother is Meliz an-Amarat, Captain of the *Tempestborn*, known as Hell Mel in the waters of the Long Sea." The Elders looked on blankly. Her mother's fearsome reputation held little sway with immortals of the forest. "And my father was Cortael of Old Cor, a prince born, heir to the empire long dead."

She winced as recognition flickered through Valnir and his guards, and even Castrin.

Corayne bit her lip. "I know members of this enclave, your own kin, died with my father, at the first Spindle torn."

Elders were strangers to grief, and they wore it poorly. Valnir went sullen at the mention of the dead.

"You know Domacridhan survived, and set out to find me, just as Princess Ridha set out to find allies among the enclaves."

The Monarch was even less accustomed to shame. It curdled on his face and Corayne half expected him to huff like a child.

She kept on.

"I did not believe him then, when he told me what my father was. Corblood. Spindleborn. A child of crossing, as you are all. Nor did I believe that made me Corblood too, an heir to the old empire. And another wielder of the Spindleblade. I thought—" Her voice wavered, overcome with memory. "I saw it as a chance to leave my mother's cage. To see the world."

Valnir raised a single scarlet eyebrow. "And?"

She swallowed a scoff. "I've seen too much of the world since then."

And worlds beyond this one too.

Corayne kept on, keeping her momentum as best she could. When she finished, her mouth felt dry and her heart rammed in her chest, living the pain of her journey all over again.

A look of pity flashed in Valnir's eyes, his brow furrowed in concern.

"You have accomplished many great deeds, Corayne an-Amarat. Too many, most would say." He ran a white hand over his face before touching the scar again. "We will say prayers for Domacridhan and Ridha tonight, and the rest of your fallen. The men of Trec? Your Companions?"

"The Jydi too," she answered hoarsely. Her voice began to fail her. "And the Elders of Kovalinn."

Valnir did not rise, but his body recoiled against the throne. His face went tight and both hands gripped the tree branch in his lap, fingers wrapping around the fragile aspen.

"*Kovalinn?*" he hissed.

"They met us on the shore outside Gidastern, sailing to our aid," she explained. "Just in time."

Just in time to be massacred with the rest of us.

"And who led them?" Valnir demanded, his voice rising to shake the stones. "Certainly not Dyrian. He is barely more than a child."

Corayne shook her head. "The Monarch's mother led his people. Eyda, they called her."

Valnir stood too quickly, his yellow eyes filling with hot, angry tears. His fists still clutched the branch, holding it out like a shield.

Sunlight gleamed in his red and silver hair, the streaks like blood. Corayne realized she had seen hair like that before, on the shores of the Watchful Sea. Lady Eyda had similar coloring. Different eyes, but the same red hair and milk-pale skin. *She looks just like him, actually*, Corayne realized, the pieces of the puzzle slotting together in her mind.

"Eyda of Kovalinn. Eyda of the Exiled, banished from Glorian with the rest of us." The Monarch heaved ragged breaths, his chest rising and falling beneath the brocade. He half snarled again. "Did she live?"

"I do not know, Your Majesty—"

Her words caught as the aspen branch snapped in two, the sound like the crack of thunder. Its golden leaves scattered across the stone floor and a harsh wind blew through the enclave, stirring the world.

Corayne flinched as Castrin leapt forward, hands outstretched.

"My lord—" he shouted, but Valnir cut him off with a slice of one hand.

"I lay down the branch," the Monarch of Sirandel said, the force of his voice shaking the air.

Corayne felt some simmering magic ripple with his words, like the beat of a bird's wing. It reverberated through the room and the Elders kneeled, as if leveled by their lord's power.

Then Valnir stretched out a now empty hand, long fingers crooked.

"I take up the bow," he said.

It sounded like the end of a spell, or a prayer.

From the shadows, another guard appeared, clad in more armor and mail than the rest. She bore a great yew bow across her hands, the curve of the wood perfect and smooth. Corayne expected more jewels and artistry, but the black wood was unadorned. Only the bowstring gleamed, oiled to deadly perfection.

Without a word, the Elder guard knelt at Valnir's side, extending the bow toward him.

The Monarch eyed the weapon for a long, shuddering moment. Corayne's throat tightened, her heart thudding so loudly she knew the immortals could all hear it.

"I wish the road ahead of you was easier. I regret the path you must walk," Valnir said, meeting her eyes. His fingers closed on the grip of the bow and lifted it high.

"But I will walk it with you. To death or victory."

6

A WOLF AT THE DOOR
Erida

Erida knew how important the love of the common people was to her own survival. As well as the respect of her nobles. It was a difficult thing to balance, the line between love and fear. She played the same game at her first coronation. Then, Erida was barely fourteen, still a child, ascending the throne of the realm's greatest kingdom. She wore green silk and gold jewelry, a flag all her own. It was the best she could do, hoping to look older, unafraid, fit to rule as Galland's first queen.

Now she was godlike, worthy of an empress's throne.

Gone was the green silk, replaced with a golden gown and golden armor, an equal balance of queen and conqueror. The armored breastplate was more like jewelry, with metal molded to her torso, set with fiery gems that flashed every time she took a breath. A belt of gemstones ringed her waist, a rainbow of color to match the kingdoms now beneath her rule. Emerald for Galland, rubies for Madrence, dark purple garnets for Siscaria, then Tyriot's sea-blue aquamarine. Her cape was cloth-of-gold edged in velvet, the fabric flashing like the sun itself.

On her finger, the emerald of Galland burned in the red sunlight. It glowed brightest of all.

Erida took even breaths, steadying herself as her ship sailed forward, and the roars of the city around them grew. It sounded like a distant waterfall, a crashing hum, constant and unending. She raised her chin and shut her eyes, letting it wash over her.

Devotion, reverence, worship.

Is this what gods feel like? she wondered.

Her eyes opened and the world blurred, a riot of color and sound. She thought nothing of the other courtiers joining up behind her, great lords and military commanders among them. Erida could only focus on the steps in front of her, careful never to falter, move too quickly or too slow. She barely even noticed the horrific smell of Ascal.

Her galley was too big for Wayfarer's Port and docked in Fleethaven, alongside other ships of the Gallish navy. The circular docks were deep and wide enough to dock twenty great warships like horses in a stable. Sailors looked on from every deck, craning for a glimpse of their great queen.

Erida made her way down from the deck with care, her attendants holding up the edges of her skirts and long cape. She kept her head up and her eyes forward, her face a perfect mask.

There had been much debate over how she would traverse the city. A carriage would be safest, but hide her from view. A litter would be too slow. A single horse might spook among the crowds, throwing the Queen to the cobblestones.

A chariot waited instead. Gold as her gown, a lion-faced shield roaring at the front of the basket. One of her Lionguard waited patiently, holding the reins of six white chargers harnessed to the yoke.

She climbed up beside him, letting her attendants manage her skirts, as she raised a single hand to the people crowding the streets, alleys, windows, and canal edges. The rest of her full Lionguard took formation around the chariot, astride their own horses. Then reins snapped and the chariot moved. Erida lost her balance, only for a second, as they lurched forward.

She felt like a bride again, come to wed her destiny.

They took the Godswalk, the widest avenue in the city, paved with smooth limestone. Soldiers of the city garrison lined the way, holding back commoners and nobles alike. It was too deep in winter for most to throw flowers, but the wealthy tossed roses into her path, sending up petals like bursts of fresh blood. Erida's own retinue tossed coins back, whipping the crowd into a frenzy. They chanted Erida's name until her head spun.

The Lioness, some called her. *Empress* shouted others. And Erida felt drunk on their love, drunk on her power.

Statues of her forefathers watched as she drove past, staring from various squares and pedestals. She knew each one by name, her own father among them.

Konrad III's statue was a perfect likeness, sculpted from white marble. Erida herself had commissioned it upon his death, employing the most skilled sculptors in all the realm. It felt like the least she could do then, as he lay cold and dead.

As her chariot drove past, Erida could only stare, tracing her father's unmoving face and unseeing eyes. Even victorious, it made her heart ache.

I am what you wished for, Erida wanted to tell him. *A conqueror.*

Empty marble eyes stared back, his stern mouth closed forever.

No matter how hard she yearned, how fervently she reached, how powerful she had become, her father was beyond her grasp. Death separated all things, from empress to insect. All the same, she wished and reached, hoping to feel some brush of his love and pride.

There was only emptiness.

They continued onto the Bridge of Faith before circling around the magnificent cathedral tower of the Konrada. Built by Erida's great-grandfather, the Konrada honored every god in the Ward, all twenty.

In her heart, Erida knew the falseness of such gods.

And the truth of one, his face carved from shadow, and not stone.

Let me in.

The whispers still echoed, always at the edge of her mind. Always waiting.

Let me in, and I will make you the grandest queen this realm will ever know.

They drove on, leaving the Konrada behind. Erida would return for her triple coronation, but now her thoughts narrowed to the New Palace. It loomed ahead of them, a stone beast. The palace was its own island in the middle of Ascal, a city unto itself.

Her heart swooped as they drove onto the Bridge of Valor, with the Grand Canal rushing below. She'd crossed it a thousand times in her life, but never like this. A hundred soldiers of the palace garrison lined the bridge, their swords raised to form a tunnel of steel.

Cheering echoed along the canals, from every corner of the city. All the world seemed to be screaming for her.

Erida tried to bask in it without being overwhelmed. She faced forward, to the gates of the palace, a mouth of iron jaws. Her grip tightened on the bar, both to hold on and to hide her trembling fingers.

They were through the gates in the blink of an eye, the thick palace wall passing over her head. The horses slowed as they entered the great gateyard of the New Palace, kicking up dust and gravel. The walls of the palace gleamed, cleaned to perfection. Lord Cuthberg, her seneschal, had prepared the palace well for her return.

The red sun tinged the realm with pink, and everything took on a rosy edge. It felt like looking through stained glass.

Distantly, Erida wondered if this all was a dream.

Her aching feet said otherwise.

The knight pulled the horses to a gentle stop while the rest of her Lionguard fell into rows. They formed up behind her chariot, allowing Erida to step down into their midst. In her golden armor, Erida was almost one of them.

Something buzzed in her ears, a whine to drown out all else. Her eyes landed on the steps of the palace, and the great oaken doors beyond. Home to the throne, the great hall, and her royal residence.

She almost saw through her seneschal and the other assembled courtiers, their faces blurring. All of them bowed, like flowers in a field bending toward the sun.

Only one set of eyes remained, locked on her own face. His body did not move, his head lowering only an inch. It was enough.

Taristan was a vision in blood red, as she was a vision in gold.

Erida pitied whatever attendant had forced her husband into a velvet surcoat, a ruby chain, and polished black boots. He wore no cloak despite the chill of winter. It made him stand out against the other peacocks huddling in their glossy furs. Even Ronin, who bent oddly, burrowed into a dark red cloak.

The Prince of Old Cor was as Erida remembered, more than three months ago. Before he rode north to Gidastern with the sniveling wizard and a corpse army.

She'd had word since then. Too-short letters, half written in code, alluding to another Spindle torn, another gift given. Another victory. But little else.

Erida kept her mask up, but her fingers quivered, hidden by the folds of her long cape. She tried to think of the crown, of the throne, of What Waits and the little whisper at the back of her mind. Of anything but her own husband.

Does that make you mine?

Taristan asked her as much three months ago, alone in their rooms. She did not give him an answer then, and found she still had no answer now.

He stared at her, unblinking, while the rest of the world looked at the ground.

Upon closer inspection, there was something strange across his face. A swipe of red, the skin torn. A barely healed wound. Impossible as that was for someone like Taristan, invincible to all things, stronger than any who walked the Ward.

A cord snapped into place between the two of them, and Erida could hardly stand it. She wanted to close the distance more than anything. She wanted to know what had happened in Gidastern, she wanted to hold him in her arms. It took all her will to wait.

"Hail, Erida the Lioness, Queen of Galland, Queen of Madrence, Queen of Tyriot, and Queen of Siscaria," her seneschal shouted, his voice echoing off the walls of the bailey.

Erida barely heard a word of it.

Across the long yards, Taristan held her gaze. His eyes gleamed with a familiar red sheen. From What Waits or the bloody sky, Erida did not know.

"The glory of Old Cor reborn," Thornwall called out from his own place in the line. He stood up from bended knee.

Next to him, Lady Harrsing matched his shout.

"Empress Rising," she said firmly.

"Empress Rising," the crowd echoed.

Taristan's lips moved with them, his voice drowned out.

When silence fell again, cut only by the distant thrums of the city, Erida offered the smallest nod to her court.

"It's good to be home," she said slowly, her voice regal and deliberate.

Lord Cuthberg scurried to her side, moving like a jeweled insect. He chattered incessantly, the words washing over Erida in a numbing tide.

"—the Temur ambassador arrived yesterday with his retinue. I put them in the Lady's Tower for now. Ambassador Salbhai requests an audience—"

Erida's jaw clenched, her teeth grinding together. *I'd rather burn the tower down with all the Temur in it*, she thought. Instead, she forced a painful smile.

"Very well, see to it," she spat out.

Only then did Taristan move, taking long strides to reach her. His polished boots crunched on the gravel.

Erida felt as if the air had been sucked out of the gateyard. She kept still, her chin high, unflinching before the eyes of the entire court. In her mind, she cursed her thundering heart. Taristan was a prince of Old Cor, blessed by What Waits, the most dangerous mortal to walk the earth. There were many good reasons to fear him.

Erida only feared his indifference, his distance, and another second beyond his grasp.

She remembered all too well the white scars on his chest, the black void of his eyes when the red sheen ebbed away. The feel of his heart beating beneath her palm.

She hoped they would not remain memories.

When he sank to a knee before her, her fear evaporated into thin air.

Her fingers were suddenly hot, held in his familiar, burning hand. She stared as he pressed her knuckles to his fevered brow, though his skin was dry. He was not ill. This was usual for Taristan, his flesh blazing with the power of What Waits. Reverent, he pressed his lips to her hand and stood again, moving with warrior speed.

"My queen," he said roughly, her hand still in his own.

She could not smile. Even now, she would not give the court the satisfaction of her happiness. That was for Erida and Taristan to share alone.

Her eyes roved over his face, tracing the strange cut on his cheek.

She wanted so badly to touch it.

"My prince."

Erida loathed the idea of marriage for most of her life.

She had no desire to enter a bridal cage, and trade her throne for an overstuffed lord. Most of her days were spent outfoxing betrothals, playing foreign princes against each other as she moved armies into place. Her survival depended on the support of her nobles, and their support rested on what she could give them. Instead of marriage, she promised glory, gold, and conquest. The empire reborn.

Even so, her advisors pushed for marriage. Harrsing, Thornwall, they wanted their queen wed for her own safety. Her loathsome cousin Konegin wanted her wed for his own benefit. She dodged them all. *Find me a champion*, she told them once, knowing the target too small to hit.

Taristan found her instead, offering his hand—and all the realm.

The Crown Council balked at such a match. Taristan was no one. No land, no titles, no gold. He claimed Corblood but little else, naming himself the successor of Old Cor, a prince of the fallen empire. That wasn't enough for Erida either.

But it was enough to keep her curious. She watched, wide eyed, as the handsome rogue drew a dagger and cut a line across his palm. She remembered his blood being too dark, darker than she imagined blood could be. Even so, she leaned closer, only to watch him heal before her eyes. Only to see the gleaming scarlet of someone else in his gaze.

Erida once wondered if she would ever regret her decision to marry Taristan of Old Cor.

Now she laughed at the thought, her face pressed up against Taristan's chest. Only silk separated her from hard muscle and hot skin. He burned through his clothes and she leaned into the feeling, even as a bead of sweat rolled down her back beneath her gown.

They were alone, finally, back in the solar of the royal chambers. The long gallery looked over the palace lagoon, where her own pleasure barge moored. In the windows, the sky glowed red with sunset, and the first stars winked to life. A small part of Erida wanted time to slow, and leave them suspended here, locked together, with nothing but their two beating hearts.

The lion inside her won out, roaring for more. Hungry to devour the rest of the realm.

She pushed back, allowing herself to look at Taristan fully. His face was clean-shaven, his dark red hair combed back. But for the gash across his cheekbone, he could pass for a pampered, handsome prince.

Taristan stared back, studying her with the same intense scrutiny. Grinning, he slipped a hand into the jeweled belt around her waist, using it to drag her closer again.

"I feared the worst," Erida said, raising her chin to stare up at him.

Taristan quirked his brow. "Death?"

The Queen shrugged, a smile tugging at her lips. "Oh, I don't worry about that. Not with you."

Her consort was a man of few words, even alone with his wife. He fell into his usual silence, stone-faced. Once, she thought it a wall between them. Now Erida saw it for what it was.

An invitation.

She pressed closer. The heat of him radiated, even through her armor and silk.

"I thought you may have," she said, her breath catching. To her annoyance, she felt herself flush. "Forgotten me."

Above her, Taristan made a harsh sound deep in his throat. He leaned until their foreheads nearly touched, his black eyes voids to swallow her whole. Erida wondered what she would find if she tipped forward into such an abyss.

Is there only darkness? Or is What Waits somewhere in the deep, a red presence hidden in shadow, waiting to rise to the surface?

Let me in. Let me in, she remembered. *Does he hear it too?*

"You are Queen of Four Kingdoms," Taristan muttered. Court life had not changed his blunt manner. "The lowest beggar in the street knows your name."

Erida pursed her mouth and held her ground, unmoving. Taristan towered over her but she felt just as tall, the might of four crowns like steel up her spine.

"That's not what I meant."

"I know," he answered, so softly she almost missed it.

Then he closed the final distance between them, his lips pressing firmly to her own. Where his eyes were an abyss, empty and impossible to read, his lips were an inferno, impossible to misunderstand. They burned over her, trailing from her mouth to the corner of her jaw and back again. She welcomed them gladly, her own mouth parting, her fingers suddenly in his hair, her nails scraping along his scalp. He gasped into her and she grinned, a lip in her teeth.

Then the red sheen flared deep in the black, a bolt of lightning in an otherwise empty sky. She saw What Waits swim to the surface of Taristan's mind. It was only a small reminder and Erida took it in stride. She had not opened her own mind to the Torn King, but He stayed all the same. She knew He waited, pawing at the door, a wolf howling to be welcomed in.

What Waits could wait a little longer, as could all else.

Her fingers trailed across Taristan's cheek, running down to cup his jaw. Again, she eyed the gash across his face, marring otherwise handsome skin.

Erida touched the cut gently, tracing it with her finger. His skin flamed beneath her own. He didn't flinch but his eyes hardened, all black again. What Waits disappeared, diving back into the depths. For now.

She remembered the cuts Corayne left on Taristan's face last time. Three ragged lines, little more than a scratch. They healed, but not so quickly as they should have for someone like Taristan. *Some kind of magic,* he told her then.

This wound was worse, scabbing over in a dark line.

"Was this Corayne?" she asked, searching his eyes.

Gently, he pulled her hand away. He shifted, putting some inches between them. Erida shivered at the loss of his warmth.

"Corayne and her witch," he answered. A rare flush spotted high on his cheeks.

Erida furrowed her brow. She saw shame in Taristan, as much as he tried to hide it.

"And what else?"

His white throat bobbed over his collar, pale veins webbing beneath the surface. She noticed a patch of red skin, raw and shining. Like a *burn*.

Without hesitation, Erida seized the soft velvet at his throat and pulled it away to reveal a swath of burned flesh. Her eyes widened, raking over the skin. It was healing, but slowly. *Normally.* Like any other mortal man.

Erida felt her mouth open in shock. Then she grabbed his sword hand and raised his knuckles. The white skin turned pink over the bones, showing common scrapes and scratches. It looked like the hand of any swordsman in her army, any knight in the training yard.

Battered, battle-worn.

And mortal.

She felt his gaze like a weight across her shoulders. Grimly, she met his eyes.

"Taristan, what is this?" Erida bit out.

It sounded like an accusation.

Taristan heaved a long, slow breath. The flush crept down his face, making the white veins in his neck stand out even sharper.

"Corayne and her Companions closed the first Spindle," he said, fighting to keep his voice level. Even so, she heard the rage trembling in him. "The first one I opened."

Her stomach dropped. Puzzle pieces fitted together in her mind, and she hated the picture.

"The first gift given," Erida hissed. "So if a Spindle closes, you lose—"

"What He gave me." Red edged slowly back into his eyes. Taristan twitched and Erida wondered what he felt, what he heard in his head. "That is the nature of failure, I suppose."

"Then go back!" Erida put her palm to his chest, pressing against him. "Right now. Take an entire legion if you must."

As much as she wanted to pull Taristan into their bedchamber, Erida wanted this more. She took his shoulders and shoved with such force even Taristan staggered, surprised by her ferocity.

She gave no quarter, shoving him again. This time he braced, firm as a brick wall. Her vision went hazy at the edges, the room wavy around her.

"Take the sword and *rip* the Spindle back open," Erida snarled. Suddenly her collar felt too tight, her armor heavy and constricting. The entire chamber seemed to close in. "You're too vulnerable this way."

Taristan caught her wrists when she pushed him again, his fingers locking in a gentle but unyielding grip.

"I've been vulnerable most of my life," he said evenly, glaring into her.

Erida's head throbbed in rhythm with her heartbeat. She dropped her gaze to his hip, to the sword belt that was always there. Until now.

Her knees almost buckled beneath her.

"Where is your sword, Taristan?" she breathed, desperate.

Stoic as he was, Erida saw her own rage mirrored in him. In his clenched jaw, the narrowing of his eyes. The shame was still there too, ugly and unfamiliar.

"I suppose you can lend me another," he answered dryly, his voice hollow. He was never one for jokes, even in victory. In defeat, it was like watching a fish try to walk.

Erida ripped herself from his grasp. "There are no Spindleblades in the vaults of Galland."

With shaking hands, she undid the jeweled belt and threw it to the floor. The ceremonial armor soon followed. The gold-dipped iron clanged dully. Trembling, Erida found her way to a chair by the window. She sank into it, combing her fingers through her hair until her braids fell undone, her maids' work turned into a mess. She took a steadying gasp of air, schooling her breathing. She willed herself to calm down, to think logically, even as the chamber spun around them. One by one, she dropped her many rings, gemstones the size of grapes rolling over the fine carpets. Only the Gallish emerald remained, green fire on her finger. It ate up the red light of sunset, the heart of the jewel dark and endless.

She stared into it. For a second, she thought she glimpsed a sheen of bloodred.

Her eyes snapped back to Taristan.

"Where is Corayne an-Amarat?" she growled.

Silence was his only answer.

Erida wanted to strike him again.

"So she got away from you. Fine." She waved a hand, the emerald winking. "Did you send scouts after her?"

He put a hand to his hip, leaning to compensate for the magnificent sword he no longer carried.

"My army isn't the kind to . . . scout," he said thickly.

Erida could only sneer. She remembered the Ashlander horde, half rotten and lurching. Deadly, but brainless. Sometimes literally.

"I'll have Thornwall dispatch riders to every corner of the Ward. And I'll triple her bounty," she said, leaping up from her chair. "She will be found, and her Spindleblade too."

Taristan's low sigh stopped her.

"*My* Spindleblade. I shattered hers."

Gnashing her teeth, Erida whirled on him.

"How did that girl manage to steal a sword out of your own two hands?!"

She tried to imagine it, tried to balance the mercenary lord before her with the ugly mouse his niece was.

"Taristan, what happened in Gidastern?" Her voice quivered.

"The Burning Realm lives up to its reputation."

Outside the windows, the red sun slipped beneath the horizon, its blaze disappearing. The salon went dark and cold too quickly, the candles unlit, the hearth weak and low.

"How many died?" Erida murmured. She ran a hand over her arm, shivering through the thin silk.

Taristan shrugged. "How many live in Gidastern?"

He would not meet her gaze. Erida realized she did not know what regret looked like on his face, or whether he could feel it at all.

Her own remorse was smaller than she expected. There was only severe, necessary logic to think of.

"Did any escape?" she demanded. "Does anyone know you did this to my city?"

Taristan's red silk went black as the shadows grew, spilling over him.

"The horde followed me in soon after. I doubt any survived to tell of what happened."

"Good."

The word came out almost too quickly, an arrow loosed before the archer could take aim. It was easier than sitting with the knowledge of a city in ashes, its people slaughtered. Her own banner trampled and bloody. Erida let the thought well within her, only for a second. She remembered the corpse army, ragged and clawing, a nightmare in daylight.

And a weapon too.

She felt Taristan's reluctant gaze, watching as the scales balanced in her head.

The equation was easy, in the end.

With her chin high, Erida drew up her spine and folded her hands together, standing as she had every day of her royal life. She was marble and gold, unfeeling, a queen.

An empress. And empires are born in blood.

"Gidastern burned in a terrible fire. These things happen," she said, waving a hand. Then her fingers curled, clenching into a fist. "What is one city for an empire?"

Deep in her mind, something smiled. She could feel it, unfamiliar lips pulling over too-sharp teeth.

Taristan watched her with something like fascination. She recognized that look too. She saw it on her own courtiers all the time.

"What of the dragon?" Erida murmured, her eyes flitting to the window. As if she might glimpse the beast itself.

Born from another Spindle. Erida knew that better than most. She was at Castle Lotha with Taristan when he opened it. She remembered the burning thread of gold suspended in the air, the portal to Irridas, the Dazzling Realm. *But the dragon came through later, after we were long gone from that place.*

The red flashed in his eyes, so bright it ringed yellow and rotten.

"The dragon," he growled, shaking his head.

She wrinkled her nose, brow furrowing. "I thought Spindle creatures answered to you. I thought they were under your control."

"A dragon is not a walking corpse or even a kraken," he shot back, viperous. "They are greater minds than that, more difficult to overthrow. Even for Ronin."

Perhaps he's useless now, and we can be rid of him, Erida thought joyfully.

"And where is the little rat?"

Taristan shattered her hopes with a quick gesture of his hand. "In his hole."

The Archives.

Erida wanted to lock the doors to the archival vaults and leave the sniveling red wizard to starve. Instead, she forced a polite nod better suited for the high table of a boring feast.

"The Spindle in Gidastern remains, we have that still. It is dangerous enough not to need a guard. No one will be able to close it now, not even Corayne an-Amarat," Taristan offered. The leering red in his eyes faded a little. But he kept pacing. Erida half expected the carpet beneath him to catch fire. "It burns even now, consuming everything within the walls."

"Victory, but at such cost," Erida mused.

She felt like tearing something in two. Instead, she counted her legions, and wondered how many riders she could send north before the moon rose.

"You lost the sword." She bit her lip. "And you lost Corayne too. She still lives."

He snarled low in his throat. "She does. Somehow."

Erida felt his anger tenfold. "What of her friends? Are they alive?"

To her infinite surprise, Taristan cut a rare, wolfish smile. His eyes glimmered, black and red, jet and ruby.

Mortal and demon.

"See for yourself," he said.

7

A SECOND HEART
Domacridhan

The world ached.

Or it certainly felt that way to Domacridhan of Iona, immortal prince, a warrior of many centuries, strong and swift, deadly with blade, bow, and bare hand. Fearsome as the breaking dawn.

And currently chained to the wall of a dungeon.

His ankles and wrists were bound with tight links, his neck collared. Something that was hopefully water dripped onto his face. He kept his head tilted just right, so as not to find out for certain. And to better see through his bars. A torch burned somewhere, its light weak and flickering. He could just make out the cells on the other side, thanks to his Vederan eyesight.

Sigil was blind in the dark.

Across the corridor, she slept sprawled across the ground. The chain attached to her ankle jingled in the silence, shifting whenever she moved. The wreckage of her dinner sat at the low gap in her cell bars, cup empty and bowl licked clean. Judging by smell, the food was foul, to say the least.

The Queen's prisons left much to be desired.

Somewhere among the cells and passages, a door creaked open.

Dom swallowed hard, throat bobbing roughly against the iron collar around his neck.

Morning already, he thought.

Across from him, Sigil woke to the sound of stomping feet, the only noise their guards would make. She roused quickly, blinking against the growing light as their torch approached.

The jail guards rounded the corner at the far end of the long row of cells, one of them carrying a tray. Both were pale and greasy, low soldiers, the kind who cared little what they did, so long as there was payment.

Neither guard acknowledged his existence, as usual. They stopped only to pull out Sigil's empty tray, and then shove another one with her breakfast through the gap in her bars, using a long stick. Both were careful not to get within reach of the bounty hunter.

Their single torch turned her dark eyes to lit coals. She grinned at them, a tiger in its cage.

But after so many days underground, even Sigil had taken on a strange pallor, her bronze skin going sickly. Her leather armor was gone, leaving only a bloodstained shift and torn breeches. She leaned to one side, compensating for her wounded leg. Broken or simply bruised, Dom still didn't know. But their weeks of imprisonment were good for healing, if little else.

"I'm injured, chained, and weak, gentlemen," she laughed, grabbing eagerly for the bowl of gray sludge. "The stick seems excessive."

The guards ignored her. Both wore swords, as well as a brace of daggers, and chain mail beneath their tunics. None of it would be much use against the likes of Domacridhan and Sigil, should the chance present itself.

The chance never did.

Sigil and Dom kept time by the guards. The food didn't change, but the guards did, a morning and evening shift going back and forth. Dom couldn't move even to scratch out the days on the wall, so Sigil did as best she could.

"Fourteen," she whispered as the guards scampered away with their torch. She used the fading light and her ankle chain to scrape a line down the stone wall.

Fourteen days in the dungeons of Ascal, entombed beneath the New Palace. Dom stifled a snarl of frustration.

"Two weeks here," he hissed. "Two weeks lost."

"Three weeks, if you count the journey from Gidastern," Sigil said from across the corridor. "But you were unconscious for most of the way."

"Don't remind me," Dom hissed, his head thumping again. What little he remembered was painful enough.

Ridha. Dead. His skin crawled. *And then . . . not.*

His last memories of the outside world were hazy. The city burning. The stink of a corpse army. A river, a boat, and his usual seasickness. Ronin had kept him from fully waking, the weight of his magic pressing Domacridhan into a deathly twilight.

Until they chained him to a wretched wall in a wretched cell, and let him return to his wretched senses.

He was grateful for Sigil's company, though even she seemed to have lost her reckless joy. She grieved as he did.

For all of them.

As he did every "morning," Dom prayed to his gods, even if they could not hear them. He begged Ecthaid, god of the road, to guide Corayne on her path.

She is safe with the others, he told himself for the thousandth time. *She has the only Spindleblade. And Sorasa will keep her alive, no matter the cost.*

He had to trust in the Amhara assassin more than anything else. The world depended on her now, and on Corayne's ferocious heart.

Sigil's overzealous slurping shattered his thoughts. Somehow, Dom was grateful for the disgusting distraction.

"Better today?" he said.

"There's meat in it now," she answered, shrugging her broad shoulders. Even without her leather, she was still mountainous, a hulk in her cell. "I think it's rat."

Dom was quietly glad for his Vederan nature. Their jailers had not fed him yet, but the slow pangs of hunger were easy for the immortal to ignore.

Unlike his position. His spine flared with discomfort, every muscle protesting his stance against the wall. The mysterious liquid dripped too close to his eye and he hissed, turning his head again.

"What shall we talk about today?" Sigil said as she walked the bars of her cell. Unlike Dom, she wore only a single shackle around her ankle, its long chain connected to a ring on the far wall.

He tipped his head back, careful to avoid the drip.

"Three weeks," he growled. "They could be back in Vodin by now. Or Sirandel, in the Castlewood, if they can find it. Or they took to the sea, with the raiders. Or—"

"Or Corayne and the others could be in another cell, locked up in this maze with the two of us," Sigil snapped. She scowled in his direction, eyes fighting against the dark. "Or—"

Dom curled a fist, one of the only things he could do.

"Do not say it."

Sigil braced her head between the bars, fitting her face into the gap.

"I won't if we talk about *something* else," she shot back at him. "We've gone over every inch of what-if's and maybe's. You Elders may have centuries to dwell but we mortals have to *move on*."

He glared at her across the corridor, his face hot with anger. Not that Sigil could see it.

"Even I know you're lying," he muttered.

Her bowl clonked off the bars of her cell, splitting in two. Unsatisfied, Sigil kicked blindly at the pieces.

"Well, it's one of the only things I can do down here!" she shouted, throwing up her hands.

After another furious pace across the cell, she fell into her usual routine. Hands braced against the packed dirt and cut stone floor, she started her exercises. With every sit-up, she hissed a long breath.

"They aren't questioning us," she muttered as her body bobbed up and down. "They aren't torturing us. They aren't even going to just let us die. What does that Corblood bastard want?"

Dom watched her exercises with envy. What he would give for a single free limb, let alone run of the entire cell.

"Taristan wants us to suffer," he spat, glaring up. He imagined the New Palace above him, with all its stained glass and gilding, its great halls crawling with silk rats and steel vipers.

On the ground, Sigil scoffed. Then she turned her head, yelling up at the stone ceiling.

"We're suffering!"

Dom barely heard her over the thrum in his ears, his own blood pounding. It roared like a crashing river, like the lion on Erida's cursed flag.

"Taristan will keep us alive until his victory is complete." Dom bared his teeth to no one. In the shadows, he saw Allward fall, consumed by What Waits and His realm of Asunder. Borne into flame, fallen into the abyss. "When he sits a throne of ashes, king of a broken realm, he will make us kneel. And watch."

Sigil slowed and blew a lock of black hair out of her eyes.

"He's going to have a hard time tearing apart any more Spindles without a sword," she said thoughtfully. "He doesn't have it. Not if we're still rotting down here. He doesn't have the sword —and he doesn't have *her*."

Dom remembered it all too sharply. Sorasa's whip on Taristan's wrist, the Spindleblade falling from his hands to land at Corayne's feet. And then their fading silhouettes, reduced to shadows in the smoke.

"I certainly hope so," he murmured.

Sigil looked in his direction, her eyes narrowed to slits as she tried to see. "Save some of that hope for yourself, Dom."

"You've got enough for us both, Sigil." He chuckled darkly. "The iron bones of the Countless?"

The bounty hunter leapt to her feet in a flash. She curled both arms over her head and slammed her hands to her chest with a resounding slap.

"Will never be broken," she answered, a true smile on her face. It was the only thing that seemed to cheer her in the darkness.

Even in the dungeons of a conqueror queen, the battle cry of the Temur shuddered them both.

Until the scrape of a key in a lock splintered through the air. Dom turned his head so quickly his skin caught on the collar, scratching painfully. He barely noticed, his Vederan eyes narrowed on the end of the corridor.

"Sigil," he hissed. "Someone's coming."

She went wide-eyed in the darkness. "It isn't the right time."

Down the corridors, a door hinge creaked, the sound of it like thunder. The jingle of keys and clank of armor followed, the many noises a haunting song in the darkness.

Dom strained against his bindings again, twisting his wrists against old iron and good steel.

Sigil pressed her face out of her cell as far as she could, straining to see anything beyond the blackness. Her massive hands curled around the bars, knuckles going white.

The torchlight returned, growing steadily as it traveled along the corridor. Dom strained his ears, listening as carefully as he could. Footsteps came with the light.

Not two pairs of boots but—

Dom's eyes widened.

He held up seven fingers, hoping Sigil would see them in the growing torchlight. Across the cell, she nodded grimly and slunk back from the bars, careful not to clink her chain. When she reached the far wall, she gathered the slack she could, looping the iron chain around her arm. It was the best weapon she had besides her own two fists.

Dom could do nothing but wait. He swallowed again, raising his chin, his jaw clenched. Ready to bite if he must.

Then the light rounded the far corner of the corridor, and Dom realized there were two torches coming toward them. Their usual jail guards led the way, followed by four soldiers. These men were not jailers, but knights of the castle garrison. One carried a dark shape over one shoulder, slung like a pack of dirty laundry.

Dom barely noticed it, his eyes flying to the rear of the formation.

Ronin smirked back at him, his white face glowing in the darkness, his robes the color of scarlet rage. Dom's vision tipped sideways, his blood roaring again.

"Good morning," he said as they approached. "It is morning, did you know?"

Angry as he was, Dom felt a burst of grim satisfaction. Ronin limped along at a ragged pace, leaning heavily on a cane. Any magic the wizard possessed was not enough to heal what Valtik did three weeks ago. Dom could still hear the deep crack of snapping bone.

Dom drew a ragged breath. "Bring me Taristan."

The wizard's laughter echoed cruelly off the stone walls.

"Domacridhan, I know this is a new situation for you," the red wizard sneered, passing his cell. "But you're a prisoner of the Prince of Old Cor. You don't get to demand anything ever again."

"Cowards, all of you," Dom barked, his neck flexing against his collar.

In her cell, Sigil scowled, still pressed against the wall with the chain in hand. Ronin was careful to keep to the middle of the corridor, out of her reach.

Dom grimaced. "What's it like to be outsmarted by a teenager? *Again?*"

The wizard stopped in his tracks, a milk-pale hand twitching at his side. He turned himself around with some effort, relying on his cane. Dom glimpsed the outline of some kind of brace beneath his robes.

"I would hardly call dumb luck being outsmarted—" he started, all but huffing. Then he stopped short, allowing himself another small laugh. He shook his head and slicked back his thin blond hair, plastering the greasy strands to his scalp. "No, I won't gloat. It is unbecoming of a wizard, and the left hand of the Torn King."

With Taristan at His right, Dom thought, his skin crawling.

The Elder's unease pleased the wizard. Ronin's grin widened, stretching across his face until Dom thought his head might split. He took a menacing step toward Dom, while the jailers made for an empty cell, and shoved a key into its lock.

"Besides," Ronin purred, still smiling, "we all know who the true brains of your Companions is." He tipped a finger, a signal to the knight. "And *she* isn't much use anymore."

Ice shot through his veins, and Dom's body went numb.

Distantly, he heard Sigil snarl and slam against her own bars. She shouted something in Temur, a curse or a threat. Her cries rattled uselessly against stone walls and iron bars.

The knight with the sack over his shoulder stepped into the open cell, while the others looked on in silence. Ronin kept his eyes on the immortal. Dom felt his gaze like a needle.

Time slowed and the knight slung off his burden. The sack wasn't tied shut and it opened easily, emptying its contents.

Sorasa Sarn rolled out onto the cold floor and Dom's vision slanted, his head spinning.

Ronin laughed, the sound like shattering glass.

"Honestly, I expected more from an Amhara."

Something snapped in Domacridhan, bone-deep. Like an earthquake breaking a mountain. He knew only fury, only rage. He felt nothing, not even the snapping of the chains around his wrist, the steel links shearing apart beneath his own force. Whatever immortal soul he carried disappeared, reducing him to little more than beast. Six harried, terrified heartbeats thrummed alongside his own. The knights and guards looked on him as they would a monster, the whites of their eyes flaring. Sigil's heart raged, mirroring her anger.

But Ronin's heartbeat remained even.

The wizard was not afraid.

Weakly, beneath the rest, another heart drummed. Steady but slow. And stubbornly alive.

"Sorasa, *SORASA!*" Sigil's cry rebounded off the walls, her voice coming from seemingly everywhere.

Dom's free hand went to his collar, his fingers working to grip the metal edge.

"She's alive," he bit out.

It calmed Sigil, but only a little.

"Tsk, tsk, Domacridhan," the wizard said, ticking his head back and forth. With another twitch of his fingers, he gestured to the knights again.

Wide-eyed as they were, they locked Sorasa in her cell and made for Dom.

Metal groaned as Dom pulled away the collar, its screws tearing out of the stone behind him. With both shoulders and one arm free, he went for his other wrist next.

The jailer's key jingled closer, the lock on his cell door clicking open, and three of the knights surged in. Dom caught the first knight by the gauntlet, his open palm wrapping around an armored wrist.

In the corridor, the fourth knight yelped, coming too close to Sigil's cell. She moved lightning fast, thrusting an arm through the bars to grab him around his throat.

The other knights surrounded Dom, leaving their compatriot to fend for himself as they overwhelmed the immortal. To his surprise, they left their swords sheathed, using all their weight to pin his arm back against the wall.

Dom cursed them in his own language, loosing five hundred years of immortal rage. His teeth snapped, inches from their armor, fighting to find any gap of skin. Desperation set in slowly, his window of opportunity disappearing with every passing second.

One of the knights put his forearm to Dom's neck, throwing all his weight into it. Steel slammed against his throat.

"You accomplished nothing but a few new bruises," Ronin said above the din. He stood at the bars of Dom's cell, leering with his red stare. One hand still clenched the cane.

The other hung at his side, his fingers gnarled like white roots.

Dom tried to choke out a retort but failed. He hissed, giving one last lurch to throw off the three knights. It was no use. They held firm, their armor crushing him against the stone wall.

Ronin's voice went slow, syrupy, as if traveling through dark water. Dom fought to keep his eyes open while his lungs screamed for air.

"I'd wish you sweet dreams," the wizard said. His face wavered, until there was only his eyes, two pinpricks of bright red in a white moon. "But there are only nightmares ahead of you, Domacridhan."

The white fingers twitched, and Dom felt like he was falling, drowning. Dying.

The blackness swallowed him up.

When he woke, there was a new collar and a new chain around his wrist. The steel gleamed into the semidark, catching the smallest ebbs of light from the distant, flickering torch. He tested both, neck straining, arm tight. Neither gave.

Across the passage, Sigil sat against the wall of her cell. Like the steel, her open eyes caught the scarce light. With a sigh, she raised her bound wrists, showing off a tightly wound leather cord.

Dom frowned. "I'm sorry."

"Well I'm *insulted*," she said, her voice thick and groggy. "You're nailed to a wall and Sorasa is drugged into oblivion. But Sigil of the Temurijon is just another prisoner."

"We'll use that to our advantage. As soon as we can," he answered, for himself as much as her.

His gaze trailed, shifting through the bars to the next occupied cell, two over from Sigil, leaving an empty space between them. Ten feet of open floor at least.

Sorasa still lay where she fell, thrown to the ground in a discarded pile. She faced away from them, toward the wall, one arm hanging oddly, the other beneath her body. Her short, ragged hair fanned out around her head in a black halo. They took her weapons, Dom knew, as they took his own. She looked strange without half a dozen daggers and poisons belted to her. The jailers left her in her leathers at least, and her old, well-worn boots.

Dom still smelled dried blood and his heartbeat rammed, drumming against his ribs. She was wounded at some point. In Gidastern, or afterward. It was too difficult to think about, knowing she was here. Knowing she had been in Ronin's hands, and Taristan's, for however long.

He sniffed again. *No fresh blood, at least.*

"If she's here with us—" Sigil's voice broke off.

"Then she isn't with Corayne," Dom finished for her. He squeezed his eyes shut. It was scarcely darker than the dungeons. "She didn't make it out of the city."

Corayne is in grave danger, worse than I ever let myself imagine.

"There's still Valtik. Trelland. And what a surprise, Charlie escapes the noose again." Sigil leaned heavily against the bars, bound hands behind her head. "Wily little priest."

Any words of assurance died in his throat. As much as he wanted to, Dom wouldn't lie. There was no point in it.

Without Sorasa, they are doomed.

Sigil's sigh sounded ragged in the darkness.

"Her heart still beats?"

"It does," he said.

"Fine," Sigil muttered.

Then she cupped her hands, opened her mouth, and shouted anything and everything in Sorasa's direction. The cells rattled with the sound of her voice, until it was almost deafening.

But nothing Sigil did could rouse the Amhara assassin. Even Dom did his best, calling her every curse and foul name he knew, every insult he'd ever dreamed up for the hateful Sorasa Sarn. It was a welcome distraction from the sinking feeling in his chest. He felt chained to an anchor, dropping through an endless sea.

Two days passed.

Plates piled at the gap in Sorasa's bars, cups of water left untouched. And the Amhara was just a shadow, left to rot like her food.

"Her heart still beats?"

Sigil yawned like a lion and sat up, her chain clinking.

Dom didn't bother to listen for the low, steady beat. It was already in his head, second nature, keeping rhythm with his own pulse.

"It does," he answered, teeth gritted.

Using the bars, Sigil heaved herself up against the cell wall.

"Her heart won't be beating much longer if she doesn't get some water," she muttered. For once, Sigil of the Temurijon sounded subdued. Even worried.

Dom craned his neck. "What?"

Her scoff echoed across the cells. "Mortals can die of thirst, Elder."

Immortal as he was, Dom could ignore such things if he chose. He licked his dry lips, trying to imagine what it was to waste away in a mortal body. He eyed Sorasa again. She was always small and lean. But against the shadows, she seemed skeletal.

He narrowed his eyes, squinting for a better look. "How long does she have?"

"Who knows what the Amhara trained into her, but—" Sigil hesitated, weighing her response. "A few days. Three or four, maybe."

Again, Dom tested the collar, and the chains. Again, he felt like he was drowning.

The chain clinked against Sigil's shackle as she walked, pacing the cramped space. "Certainly they would not save her from Gidastern just to let her die down here in the dark?"

To let her die in front of me, Dom thought. It was torture, plain and simple. And not for Sorasa. *This is what Taristan wants, to take every Companion from me, as he took Cortael.*

"Who knows what the red wizard did to her," Sigil muttered, spitting in the dirt.

Dom tried not to think of it, but he heard it anyway. The creak of a wooden rack, the hiss of hot iron. Knives on whetstones. And worse magic than even he could fathom, born of blood and broken realms.

"She would hold up to questioning better than most. Even the iron bones," she offered. She thumped her chest with her bound hands, albeit half-heartedly. "What could she tell the beasts that they don't already know?"

He eyed Sorasa again, refusing to blink, trying to catch any quiver of movement. Her chest rose and fell so slowly, barely visible even to his eye. That had not changed in two days. Nothing more, nothing less.

"We'll find out what they want when they come for us next," he growled.

"Good luck to them." Sigil tested her chain again, kicking at the ring on the wall. "They'll have to kill me first, and spark war with the Temurijon. The iron bones of the Countless will never be broken."

"You have a high opinion of yourself, Sigil."

"Bounty hunters can be princesses too, Elder," she shot back. "The Emperor is my cousin, and to spill my blood is to spill his own."

Dom could barely shrug, his body too restrained. "What if that blood spills in darkness, with none to see?"

In her cell, Sigil paused, thoughtful.

"You're a prince," she finally said. "Won't your people rise to avenge you?"

Growling, Dom shook his head.

If Ridha's death cannot bring Isibel to fight, nothing can, he knew.

"They rise for little. Least of all me."

"Can Elders die of starvation?" Sigil asked suddenly, returning to her exercises.

Dom thought of his stomach again, and his last meal. It was too many days ago to count, his memory hazy.

"We might find out," he sighed.

Sigil bent into a sit-up, bound hands crossed over her chest.

"And you still can't move at all?"

Despite the circumstances, Dom wanted to laugh, his lips twitching. "No, I choose to remain like this."

"Strange time to finally grow a sense of humor, Dom," she replied.

He tipped back to look at the ceiling, tracing the cracks between the stones and wooden beams. Looking anywhere but the unmoving body a few cells away, her face still obscured. Her heart still beating.

"It was bound to happen eventually," he sighed.

They lapsed into easy silence, a common pastime in the dungeons. Dom's vision hazed, his aches fading a little as he dozed, suspended between full awareness and sleep.

"What can we do, Dom?" Sigil whispered at last.

He blew out a long breath. He wished for his sword, for an inch of slack in the chain. For Taristan and a plunging dagger to end all this. Anything felt better than this purgatory, hanging over a cliff edge.

"We can hope, Sigil," he said. "That is all."

8

FOX AND CHURCH MOUSE
Charlie

They fell into their old rhythm easily. It felt like turning onto a familiar path, his own footsteps already worn in the dirt. Sometimes, when Charlie's brain buzzed with the heat of the campfire and the closeness of Garion's body, he could pretend it was the old days.

Charlie was still a priest when he first met Garion. It was summer in Partepalas, and Prince Orleon had just come of age. The King of Madrence ordered barrels of wine opened at every square throughout the city and Madrentines raised their cups to the heir to the throne. Various knights and country lords entered the city for the celebrations, many stopping at the city churches to pay respects to their god. Most went to Montascelain, the great cathedral dedicated to Pryan. The god of art and music was Madrence's patron, and its priests sang in the streets as forms of worship.

One of the many reasons Charlie chose to worship Tiber instead.

The god of commerce, coin, and trade was not so popular in a city like Partepalas, where they valued beauty above all things. Charlie's dedicant order maintained a smaller church near the port, in the shadow of the city's iconic lighthouse. Workmen crewed the lighthouse in great shifts to keep the flames high, and the light turning on oiled gears. The great beam passed over the stained-glass windows at night, flashing through the pews and altars like a beam of sunlight.

After squinting at scripture all day, illuminating the tales of Tiber with painstaking care, Charlie had trouble seeing at night. He was glad for the lighthouse as he walked the length of the church, extinguishing candles as he went. Smoke trailed to the lofty ceiling, painted with Tiber's face and his usual mouth of jewels and gold coins.

If not for the sweep of the lighthouse's beam Charlie never would have seen Garion beneath a pew, huddled in the shadows. His was bone-white, drained of blood. If Charlie believed in ghosts, he would have run screaming from the church hall, all the way back to the priest dormitories.

And Garion would have died of his wounds on the cold stone of Tiber's sanctuary.

Instead, Charlie dragged him out into the dim light of the last few candles. He was a priest of Tiber, not Lasreen or even Syrek, whose orders knew some medicine. But Charlie was the orphaned son of farmers. He could dress a wound at the very least.

It was enough to stabilize Garion and set him upright. Charlie figured he was another country knight come to the city for the prince's birthday, who got more than he bargained for in a back alley.

The priest soon realized how wrong he was.

The wounded man was not a country fool but a blooded Amhara, cunning and vicious as an assassin upon the Ward. Vulnerable only for an instant.

But the instant was enough.

They talked through the night, Garion on the edge of death, and Charlie on the edge of panic. With every passing second, the priest wanted to run and fetch his superior, or simply leave the Amhara to his healing. The man was a deadly assassin, who might kill him as soon as his strength returned.

Instead, something kept Charlie rooted, an instinct that he did not understand then. He watched the color slowly return to the assassin's face, his white cheeks gaining a little more warmth with every passing hour. In the meantime, Garion spoke to stay awake, and Charlie listened with a priest's inviting ear.

The assassin regaled him with stories of the greater world, beyond Madrence, beyond even the Long Sea. To lands barely dreamed, of deeds both astounding and awful.

"You are quiet, even for a church mouse," Garion mumbled sometime before dawn, his eyes dancing with the light of one last candle. One of his hands brushed Charlie's own, only for a moment.

"You are gentle, even for a fox," Charlie answered back, surprising them both.

Over the following years, the names stuck.

Fox. Church mouse. Called out in the street, laughed in gardens, whispered in bedchambers. Wept in a basement in Adira, with no one to listen but the quills and ink.

Now the names echoed through the cold air of the Castlewood.

The trees protected them from the harsh winter wind, but also from the sun. Charlie found himself drawn to pockets of light every few hours. Sometimes he wished they'd kept the horse. But in his heart, he knew she would only slow them down as they headed east.

Garion shook his head at him for not the first time that week, or even that day. He watched Charlie from the edge of the clearing and cut a crooked smile.

"How in Lasreen's name did you survive up in Vodin?" he muttered, laughing. "The Castlewood is high summer compared to the Treckish wilderness."

"In Trec, I slept in a king's castle and feasted in front of roaring hearths," Charlie answered. He watched his feet as they walked, careful not to trip on an errant root. "Your hospitality leaves much to be desired."

"I'd be offended if I didn't know your sense of humor." Garion wove through the tree trunks with Amhara grace, swinging himself over a little stream. Charlie followed with a grumble, icy water splashing against his boots. "Besides, that's a fine jacket I stole for you yesterday."

Indeed, Charlie was glad for the rabbit-lined jacket. Together with his fur cloak from Trec, it kept him from freezing over entirely.

"The woodcutter will certainly be missing it," Charlie muttered. It was as good as a thank-you. "But you didn't have to rob his cabin. I have a few coins left."

Garion made a tutting noise and wagged a finger. "The last thing we need is a woodcutter to bite into one of your coins and discover it's a forgery."

A branch shook as Garion grasped it, easing himself over a tangle of thornbushes.

"Besides, we'd do better in Badentern," he said without so much as a puff of exertion.

They had been a week in the woods at least, and Charlie was sore all over. His feet throbbed in his boots, but he kept on, scrabbling through the thorns.

"We're not going to Badentern," he grumbled for what felt like the thousandth time. "We're not going to Badentern because that's not where Corayne will go."

Garion's smile disappeared. "Charlie."

It sounded like pity.

"If there's a chance she's alive, I must believe it," he said in a low, stern voice.

Garion followed along, like a panther at the corner of Charlie's eye.

"And if she isn't?" he prodded.

Charlie winced and slipped on a patch of ice, but caught himself just in time, waving off Garion's attempts to help.

"If she is dead, then the Ward must be warned."

Garion blinked in reply, then spun in a slow circle. He eyed the gnarled trees and overgrown ground, before turning back to gape at Charlie.

"Who is going to warn the realm from here?"

Charlie's lips twisted in annoyance. Both with Garion, and with their circumstances at large. He thought of the map in his saddlebags, now slung over one shoulder. And the fox inked into the Castlewood, drawn among the oaks and pines.

He thought of something else too. An army of soldiers like Doma-cridhan, immortal and mighty. And willing to fight.

"Elders," he said. His voice echoed through the quiet woods. "There are Elders in this forest. Somewhere. Dom spoke of them once."

Garion shook his head again. While he was raised in the famed guild of assassins and knew much of the world, his teachings were limited indeed. He carried little beyond the knowledge needed to kill, and escape.

"Elders and other realms, it's all Spindlerotten nonsense," the assassin said. He kicked at a stone on the ground, sending it skittering into the undergrowth. "If the world is ending, I don't want to spend it wandering these infernal woods, looking for Elders we're never going to find. You don't even know where they *are*, church mouse."

For once, the nickname rankled, and Charlie scowled.

"I can find them," he said hotly. "Alone if I must."

With maddening speed, Garion loped to his side. Charlie gritted his teeth, trying not to be annoyed by his partner's ease in the woods. Meanwhile, his every step felt like a battle with the mud.

"Now you're truly being foolish," he said, eyeing the trees.

His manner grew more suspicious, his assassin's instincts falling about his shoulders like a coat.

"Once, Amhara trained to kill Elders. Generations ago." Garion's lips went white as he pursed them together. Such was the way of his memories. "Not for gold, or contracts. But for glory. It was considered the greatest feat an Amhara could ever accomplish. Even then, few succeeded."

In his mind, Charlie saw another Amhara assassin, her blade smiling in her hand. And a brooding immortal following her like a shadow, annoying her to no end.

"Sorasa nearly killed an Elder a few times," he muttered to himself.

Garion's voice dropped. "I've never seen an immortal before."

"I've only met the one." Charlie's throat tightened with emotion. "Hardly impressive."

He swore as he lost his footing again, this time sliding against a broken tree stump. Though every part of him wanted to stop and rest, he pushed off the rotted wood and marched on.

Garion followed. Charlie felt his gaze and quirked an eyebrow.

"You've changed, Charlie," the assassin said.

Charlie snorted. "What gave you that impression?"

He looked down at himself, his belly still round beneath his coat. But he was leaner than ever before, thinned out by hard days of travel. He knew his face was probably gaunt and pale, his stubble patchy, his skin grimy with dirt and sweat. And his lovely chestnut hair, once oiled and braided, looked worse than old straw. A far cry from a robed priest in a god's church, or even a forgery master in his workshop.

Garion read his thoughts easily, shaking his head.

"You've never believed in anything like this before. Even your gods," Garion said softly.

Gratitude swelled in Charlie's chest. "Will you believe me, then?"

"I'll try" was all he managed to say.

Then, without warning, Garion burst into motion. Like a cat, he scrambled up the closest pine tree with startling speed. Charlie blinked, startled, before following as best he could. He tried the lowest branch and immediately gave up.

"Well, what do you see?" he called into the branches.

Garion was already in the canopy, balanced precariously on a tree limb that looked too small to hold his weight.

"There's some villages to the southwest, perhaps five miles off," he said, shading his eyes against the bright sunlight above the trees. "I can see the smoke trails. And there's the river due east, working through the forest."

Charlie winced as Garion shifted in the branches, climbing to an even higher spot.

"What are you looking for exactly?" he shouted.

Garion waved a hand. "A castle? A tower? You'd know better than me."

"And I know next to nothing," Charlie muttered to himself. He had no idea what an Elder enclave looked like, let alone where it might be. Again he kicked a stone into the trees.

"That cloud does look a bit like a dragon," the assassin said with the edge of a laugh.

"Don't start," Charlie growled.

Garion tsked, shimmying back down the trunk of the pine. He jumped the last six feet, landing gingerly on his toes.

Show-off, Charlie thought again.

Then he cupped his hands around his mouth and spun, facing north. Charlie heaved a breath and yelled, his voice loud enough to shake a few birds from the branches.

"VEDERA OF THE CASTLEWOOD," he boomed. Overhead, an owl hooted in annoyance, awakened from her sleep. Charlie paid her no mind, his focus on the woods. "I AM LOOKING FOR CORAYNE AN-AMARAT."

Next to him, Garion clapped his hands to his ears. "Lasreen's eyes, warn a man next time," he muttered, watching Charlie with something between fascination and confusion.

Charlie ignored him and took another breath. "VEDERA OF THE CASTLEWOOD. I HAVE NEWS OF SPINDLES TORN."

Garion tipped his head. "What's a Vedera?"

"It's what the Elders call themselves," Charlie said out of the corner of his mouth. "VEDERA OF THE CASTLEWOOD."

Next to him, Garion curled a lip with annoyance. "This isn't going to work."

Charlie shrugged. "I'm used to it."

"Fine," Garion snapped back. With a scowl, he raised his hands to his mouth anyway.

Together, they screamed into the dark reaches of the forest, their voices reverberating off branch, earth, and stone.

"VEDERA OF THE CASTLEWOOD. I AM LOOKING FOR CORAYNE AN-AMARAT."

Garion kept at it even after Charlie's voice died, his throat raw from shouting. They had not reached the river yet but stopped at a quiet stream for the evening. The landscape changed little. Trees, trees, and more trees, but it was a good place to sleep. Charlie ignored the freezing temperature to plunge a hand into the stream and drink greedily. The snowmelt water was a balm on his burning throat.

"To the tomb with this," Garion finally said, his voice low and rasping. He sounded like a ghoul raised from the grave.

"Fine," Charlie rasped back, glad to be finished with such foolishness.

To his relief, Garion began the work of building a fire, so Charlie set to making a small camp as much as he could. He laid out their cloaks and furs, creating a nest in the hollow of a tree. Neither spoke for a long while, grateful for the silence.

Garion roasted a pair of rabbits for their dinner, meager as they were, starved by winter. As he gnawed on a greasy bone, Charlie dreamed of better days. A little table in the sun outside a Siscarian taverna, a glass of pale red wine in hand. Or warm bread, fresh from a bakery on the banks of the Riverosse in Partepalas. Even venison, roasted and seasoned by Andry Trelland's careful hand. Eaten hot in the foothills of the Wolf's Way, with nothing but stars above him. His Companions alive and arguing in their usual way.

"Do you have any other less . . . noisy ideas?" Garion whispered, tossing his bones into the undergrowth. He took a greedy pull from his waterskin.

Charlie chose his words carefully, trying not to speak too much. He gestured to his saddlebags, his papers and pots of ink inside.

"I can't exactly forge my way out of this one," he said softly.

Garion's face tightened, the firelight glowing in his eyes. "I can't fight it either."

A corner of Charlie's mouth lifted. "For once we're equally useless."

They shared an easy smile over the fire. Despite the circumstances,

Charlie wondered if this wasn't a dream too. He stared at Garion a while longer, looking for a shadow, a flaw, an impossibility. Any indication all this was just a delusion, or the wanderings of a dead man.

Garion read his thoughts easily. "I'm real, church mouse," he said, his voice almost lost entirely. "I'm here."

Heat spread across Charlie's cheeks and he looked away, spitting a piece of gristle on the ground.

"I take it back. I'm not useless. I can cook, at least," he said sharply, dispelling the tension. "Under proper circumstances."

Leaning back on his elbows, Garion rolled his flashing eyes. He sprawled against his cloak and furs, leaving ample room beside him. A lock of dark hair fell over his brow in a disturbingly lovely way.

"We didn't exactly have cooking lessons back at the citadel."

He grinned when Charlie stood, closing the short distance between them.

"Another strike against Lord Mercury," Charlie said, laying down next to him. Together, their warmth made the freezing air almost comfortable.

Garion took another sip of water, wetting his throat. "He sent me forth with the same contract as the others. To kill Corayne an-Amarat and any who stand in the way."

Corayne. Her name tore through Charlie's mind, still a searing wound.

"I suppose Mercury owes me some gold. I all but killed her too," Charlie hissed. "Leaving her to die. *To burn.*"

He turned Garion's words over in his mind. *Sent forth with the same contract as the others. Meant to kill Corayne. And her Companions too.*

"How long have you been tracking us?" he finally said.

Again, Garion's lips twitched, twisting into a pained frown. Charlie saw shame in him still, and something else beneath.

"Since you arrived in Vodin weeks ago," Garion said. "Her death was bought many times over, a glorious contract for any Amhara."

"Well, now there are twelve Amhara less than there used to be," Charlie said flatly.

Garion's eyes went wide, his beautiful face torn, weighing the implication. "Luc and the others found you first?"

For Charlie, Garion was far easier to read than Sorasa. His skill lay with the sword, not subterfuge or scheming. Garion was a weapon in Mercury's hand, while Sorasa was his snake. Venomous and willful.

Charlie tried not to think of her, burned with the rest.

Instead, he thought of that day in the mountains, high upon the Wolf's Way. Dom and Sorasa went to hunt for dinner, and Sorasa returned covered in blood, silent as the bodies she left behind.

"They found Sorasa and the Elder," Charlie said.

Garion paled. "She killed them all?"

"Dom helped," he replied, shrugging.

The cold wind rustled in the trees, shuddering the branches. Garion looked sick, his eyes unfocused as he took in the news. Charlie saw the same pain in Garion, the one Sorasa bore too. The guilt. The rage. More than anyone, Garion knew what a cost Sorasa had paid.

As Charlie knew what a cost Garion paid now, to be here, his blades unbloodied.

"We are both betrayers. In blood and bone," Garion said finally, heaving a deep breath. Charlie felt the heat of him radiating through the winter air.

The priest forced a grim smile. "Betrayers for the good of the realm isn't so bad."

Garion did not match his grin. "If only I could pay in flesh as Sorasa did once," he cursed. This time, he reached for his own ribs.

Charlie knew why. He remembered the tattoo inked along Garion's side, a symbol on each rib, every mark a testament to his days serving the Amhara. He didn't have so many as Sorasa, but enough to mark him as a dangerous killer. Charlie had traced them many times, with fingers on flesh, then quill on parchment. He traced them even now, fingers twitching at his own side.

"Lord Mercury will be on the hunt soon enough. If he isn't already," Garion hissed. Charlie felt his body tighten up beside him. "With the twelve dead, and me . . . off the path. He might finally leave the citadel to finish the job himself."

Charlie propped an arm behind his head and looked up through the tree branches. They could barely see the stars.

"As if dragons and torn Spindles weren't danger enough."

Garion could only snort in reply.

"Do you think the Elders heard us?" he breathed, watching the branches overhead.

Fear curled in Charlie's belly. "If they're anywhere nearby, yes."

A rather large if, Charlie mused. He knew Garion thought the same thing. The Castlewood was hundreds of miles wide, impenetrable even to the armies of Galland. There was a reason it was still wilderness, as good as a green wall across the kingdom.

"They say there used to be Spindles all through the Castlewood," Garion said, half-asleep. His eyelids drooped. "The trees fed on them, turning into doorways themselves. Before I went to the Amhara, my mother used to tell me stories of unicorns springing out of hollows just like this one."

Grimacing, Charlie shifted against a knotted root poking him in the spine. He eyed the tree hollow around them, the trunk of the great oak parted like a pair of curtains. It looked unremarkable, empty but for dirt, dead leaves, and two weary travelers.

"Well, I don't fancy being stabbed by a unicorn," Charlie retorted, putting a hand to Garion's hair. He brushed it idly, the familiar dark waves a river in his fingers.

Garion made a low, satisfied noise, his eyes falling shut. Another might think him asleep, but Charlie knew better. Amhara assassins rarely dropped their guard, and Garion was a light sleeper in the best of times.

"Not anymore, of course," Garion added dreamily. "Those Spindles disappeared a long time ago. But they left echoes behind. There are still witches in this forest. Spindlerotten."

"I believe the preferred term is Spindleblessed," Charlie murmured back. He looked to the stars again, then the trees. A small part of him expected lightning-blue eyes and the smell of lavender. "You've never met a witch before. Best not to speak ill of them."

On his chest, Garion raised his head and opened his eyes, almost nose to nose with Charlie. He studied the fallen priest with intensity, his gaze passing slowly over his face.

"You're certainly not the church mouse I remember," Garion rasped.

Charlie swallowed equal parts sorrow and pride. "But you are still my fox."

9

EAGLE AND CROW
Andry

There was no cold like the cold of the sea.

Andry did his best to keep warm after a week of sailing, when all his clothes felt somehow both wet and frozen. He envied Oscovko, who'd returned to shore days ago. His men were probably halfway back to Vodin by now, traveling overland back through the Gates of Trec. It would take weeks to rally the Treckish army, and Andry all but salivated at the thought of a warm castle.

Especially now, as he rowed hard with the rest of the crew. He glanced down the deck of Lady Eyda's chosen vessel, the largest of their mismatched armada. It was a Jydi longship, crewed by immortals and a few raiders who'd managed to escape.

Luckily their journey would soon be at an end. Ghald was near, the raider city fading out of the gray clouds.

The city sat at the tip of a peninsula, a knife jutting out between the Watchful and the Glorysea. The city sat across the only habitable land, the rest of the coast jagged with cliffs, fjords, and pine forest. Such were the lands of the Jyd; green, white, and gray, a frozen world of hardy folk.

Horrible winds roared from the north as their boats fought slowly into the port. Andry strained along with the raiders and immortals, his palms blistering on the worn wooden grip. But every stroke brought them closer to shore, until they passed the protective stone wall in the harbor. The wind died, letting them glide the rest of the way.

When the ship finally anchored, the crew wasted no time. The Jydi all but leapt from the benches, vaulting over the ship's rail to land on the dock below.

Andry's body ached after the hours rowing and he stood up gingerly, careful with his few belongings to survive Gidastern. His teakettle was not one of them. He mourned its loss for the thousandth time, wishing for nothing more than a warm cup of tea.

As he belted his sword back around his waist, he circled slowly, taking in the raider city of Ghald.

Longships jammed the port. Sails of every color flapped in the wind, striped or painted with symbols to mark the clans. Andry spotted bears, horned fish, wolves, eagles, and even a few dragons, their jaws breathing faded red flame. He had no idea what emblem belonged to which clan but tried to memorize them anyway.

Corayne will want to hear about this, he thought, his mouth filling with a bitter taste.

Beyond the docks were the markets and storehouses, meant to hold grain, steel, coin, treasure. Whatever came back from the summer raids. There were longhouses roofed with thatch, shingle, and turf, some with tiered spires. They reminded Andry of the cathedrals of Ascal, carved from wood instead of stone.

Almost all of Ghald was made of wood. Even the palisade wall was cut gray timber, sharpened to cruel points. Andry gulped and thought of a single candle bringing the entire place down around them. Let alone a dragon.

Gidastern was half stone and she still burned, he thought, glancing at the heavy gray sky. *Ghald will suffer the same fate in half the time.*

Then Andry's eyes narrowed, tracing the cramped streets of the raider capital.

But not without a fight.

Upon closer inspection, he realized Ghald was more a military encampment than city. Armories and stables dotted the streets, and forges sparked from every corner. Hammers rang on anvils while traders shouted in the markets, haggling over the price of good steel. He saw axes flashing in a training yard, and almost everyone wore some kind of armor beneath their furs. Men and women alike, hailing from all the clans. Hide tents lined the interior walls, done up in rows like an army camp. Ghald overflowed with raiders, far more than she could hold.

The sight filled Andry with some confidence, small as it was. Like the Treckish warbands, the raiders fought for glory as much as gold.

And there was no greater glory than saving the realm itself.

The Elders rallied together, following Lady Eyda off the ship. Andry hesitated to join them, hanging back. He was no immortal soldier. Instead, he offered an arm to Valtik, planting himself next to the witch.

"Ah, it is good to see you," she crowed, her smile growing even wider.

Andry sighed and pulled his cloak, hiding his sword beneath its folds. "I've been here the whole time, Valtik."

The old woman clucked her tongue, tsking at him as she worked at a new braid, weaving bits of fresh lavender into her gray hair.

"Avoided me the whole voyage through," she said. "You're lucky I am forgiving."

In spite of himself, Andry barked a dry laugh. "You're lucky I don't chain you to my arm. You're not disappearing on me again, and especially not here."

"My Jydi will fight, with shield thick and steel bright." She raised her gaze to survey the city around them. "And the rest—they will give up the branch living."

Andry could only shake his head. "I don't know what that means, Valtik."

She grinned in reply, and tightened her grip on his arm.

Forever the dutiful squire, Andry let her lean on him.

"Come, Andry," she said, patting his hand. "With me."

The familiar cry was an arrow through Andry's heart. His throat tightened.

"With me," he whispered back.

Valtik led them all through the city without breaking stride, her bare feet passing over wood, dirt, stone, and snow. Eyda and her immortals followed silently behind. The Lady of Kovalinn still wore her torn cloak and battered armor, the loss of Gidastern written all over the steel. Andry knew they made for a strange, if not threatening sight.

Many faces turned to watch their passing, pink-skinned or black, pale or bronzed. But all with the same cold flush. Though the native peoples of the Jyd were fair, the clans offered protection to any who took up the raider ax. Mortals from all over the Ward lived among the fjords and pines.

Andry did his best to put his faith in Valtik.

She knew Ghald well, navigating the streets into the heart of the city. The buildings grew more intricate in their adornment. More and more Jydi came to watch, and Andry's skin crawled under the eyes of so many. He breathed a sigh of relief when they reached the top of the hill, leveled off into a square. The crowd of onlookers held back and they walked on alone.

Massive longhouses lined three sides of the square while a grand wooden cathedral loomed over the fourth. Andry marveled at the many-gabled church crowned in carved dragons, their jaws holding the sun and moon. Black tar gleamed on the plank walls. The church seemed a dragon too, its shingles glittering like scales.

Andry shivered, remembering what a true dragon looked like. He eyed the clouds overhead and prayed it had not followed them into the north.

"The eyes of Lasreen see all above, and all below," Valtik murmured. "Sun and moon, eagle and crow."

As she muttered, a flock of birds took flight from the church, their wings black against the sky. Andry shivered beneath their flickering shadows.

Without hesitation, Valtik led them through the doors of the church, the interior black beyond. It felt like being devoured.

Andry blinked fiercely, willing his eyes to adjust before he tripped over something.

The church was warm, at least. A fire burned in the center of the square chamber, open to the many angled roofs stacked above. The smoke smelled sweet, perfumed by an herb even Andry couldn't name. The interior was just as intricate as the gables outside, every column carved with imagery. Andry knew more of Galland's god Syrek and his mother's chosen, Fyriad, than Lasreen. But even he recognized the carvings. Most told stories of Lasreen and her loyal ice-dragon Amavar, journeying through the land of the dead or wandering the Ward to collect wayward ghosts. After the dragon in Gidastern, Andry could hardly look Amavar in the face.

Bone witches stood in the shadows, most of them in gray shifts. One of the witches wore black, standing behind an ancient stone altar at the rear of the church. He watched them with blind, white eyes.

A few Jydi warriors stood among the witches, easy to pick out in their furs and armor. Many wore clan colors and collars of precious metal. All had some kind of weapon, be it an ax, sword, or spear. *Chiefs*, Andry knew, his heart leaping in his chest.

Valtik drew them around the hearth fire to stand before the altar. She dropped Andry's arm and he expected her to kneel, or at least bow to the blind witch. Instead, she shrugged.

"This is all," she said, sounding apologetic. "Those left in the fires are doomed, trapped under His thrall."

A murmur went through the church, rippling between the witches and warrior chiefs.

"Doomed," Eyda rasped behind them, her low voice cutting through the whispers like a knife. "So there is no saving the ones lost to Taristan's necromancy?"

Behind the altar, the blind witch lowered his brow to the stone beneath his fingers. His lips moved without sound, speaking some prayer no one could hear. The chiefs did the same, offering prayers for the Jydi dead in Gidastern.

"A soul taken by What Waits is a soul taken forever," the blind witch said when he straightened. Somehow, he knew where Eyda stood, and turned his face to her. "They are part of Him, with no tie to sever."

"I thought the Elders knew all," one of the chiefs grumbled. He pulled at his braided red beard, his bare wrist tattooed with the jagged ring of a mountain range.

Eyda eyed the chief as she would an insect. "It is not for us to know the depths of evil, in the hand of What Waits, or in Taristan's *mortal* heart."

The redbeard all but growled. "Instead you led the Yrla to die."

Andry stepped between the two of them, lest the Lady of Kovalinn cut the Jydi chief in half.

"The Yrla answered the call first, and bravely so," Andry said sharply, with a grateful bow. He thought of the dozen or so survivors now roaming Ghald, the last remnants of their clan.

Another chief bowed her gray head. She wore a white wolf pelt around her shoulders.

"Indeed," she said, cutting a glare at the redbeard. "We will remember their sacrifice."

The redbeard ignored her and took a step down from the altar, his eyes on Andry. His lips pulled back from yellow teeth, halfway between a smirk and sneer.

"You are far from home," he said, eyeing Andry up and down. "You look like our southern brothers, but you speak like the conquerors, like the dogs of the Green Queen."

The Green Queen. Andry scowled and cursed Erida's existence.

"I was a squire of Galland, born in the palace of Ascal," he replied, his voice level. It echoed high into the rafters. "Trained to be a knight."

Around the church, a few of the chiefs hissed, including the redbeard.

Andry did not react, waiting out their anger.

"*Was*, my lords," he finally said, deliberate. "As a boy, I learned about the summer raids. You were a plague on Galland's northern shore, even to the city of Gidastern herself. The Jydi would glide out of the night to loot shrines and villages, stealing away with anything they could carry. Leaving burned towns and dead bodies behind."

In front of him, the redbeard puffed out his chest with pride. The raids were not just their livelihood, but tradition.

"I feared you first," Andry admitted. "Then I dreamed of turning back your raids with my own sword. Protecting the north, bringing peace to the Watchful Sea. Serving my queen, and her kingdom."

Andry had no skill for speechcraft, but he knew honesty. It was easy to tell the Jydi the truth of his past, so they might better understand the dire circumstances of the present.

"Now I walk among you, and I pray for your help." He held the red-beard's stern gaze, expecting the chief to hiss again. "We all do, no matter our differences and long histories. That's how desperate we are."

To Andry's relief, the redbeard did not argue.

"Gidastern is gone," he continued bluntly. "There's nothing we can do about it. But we can move forward—"

The chief with the white pelt held up a pale hand. Her fingers were crooked, broken and healed a dozen times.

"Save your breath, Blue Star," she said, cutting him off.

Blue Star.

Andry glanced down at his own chest, at the tunic over his ring mail. His father's sigil remained there, across his heart. Somehow, the thread-bare blue star still held on, a deep cobalt like a twilight sky. *Like my father's eyes*, Andry thought, trying to hold on to a face he could barely remember.

He looked back up to the chief, his breath caught in his throat.

Like Valtik, she only shrugged.

"The Jydi do not need convincing," she said. "We foresaw the breaking of the realm long before any of your kings or immortals cared to notice. It's why we have gathered in Ghald. To prepare. And to fight."

Andry blinked, startled. All attempts at a rousing speech died on his lips. He all but deflated, his shoulders drooping.

"Oh," he sputtered. "Well. Good."

From the altar, the blind priest raised his head. Like Valtik, he wore lavender in his braids.

"The Rose of Old Cor lives, does she not?" he asked. "Is there a war left to be fought?"

His weary voice carried through the church. *The Rose of Old Cor.* Andry heard her name even though no one said it. *Corayne* echoed off every column and carving, haunting as a ghost.

Is she alive? Andry had asked Valtik only once, and she refused to answer. He was too afraid to ask it again.

When Valtik giggled, Andry turned on her, wide-eyed, only to watch the witch throw up her hands.

"She carries on," she said lightly, as if talking about the weather. "Her path is drawn."

Andry's knees buckled and the earth tilted beneath him. He wanted to laugh and cry in equal measure. The witch only giggled again as he seized her by the shoulders. Andry's vision narrowed to the old woman in front of him, her lightning-blue eyes threatening to drown him.

Someone grabbed his arm but he shrugged them off easily.

"Valtik, you knew all this time?" he demanded, glaring down on her. "You didn't say anything, you didn't tell me?"

"Timing is all things," she answered, patting his face. "From the saving of the realm to the ruin of kings."

Again, someone took Andry by the shoulder. Again, he went to shrug them off, only to meet the iron grip of an Elder.

Eyda loomed at his shoulder, a warning in her eyes.

Quickly, the church came back into focus. The bone witches gathered at the altar, ready to defend their own. And the redbeard chief ran a finger down the blade of his ax, a naked threat.

With a steadying breath, Andry relented. Valtik giggled again and stepped out of his grasp, leaving him to recover. Too many emotions warred across his mind, all of them swirling around one thought.

Corayne is alive.

"You say her path is drawn," Eyda said evenly, addressing Valtik. "Can you tell us where that path leads?"

The witch spun slowly, examining the gabled ceiling. "You are on it. The lanterns are lit."

Andry fought back another wave of frustration.

"If her path is our own, then Iona is correct," he said sharply. "We'll find her there. And maybe then I can be rid of you once and for all."

"Be careful what you say before the eyes of Lasreen," Valtik chided. She gestured to the carvings on the towering columns and spiraled her wrist. The smoke of the hearth fire twisted oddly through her fingers. "In her temple, all things are seen."

"Good," Andry hissed. "She can see how *annoying* you are."

While the bone witches recoiled at the insult, Valtik giggled.

"Annoying indeed," she said airily. "But only in need."

Andry felt his eyes roll into the back of his head.

The chief with the wolf pelt mirrored his impatience. Huffing, she took a step down to the hearth, facing Eyda head on. Her pale green eyes flashed over them in turn.

"The clans of the Jyd are in agreement," she said. "The Corblood girl is the last hope of the realm. She must be defended, and our own dead avenged."

Then the chief put a fist to her chest, thumping her armor once. "Yrla came first, but Sornlonda, the Snowlands, will follow."

The redbeard thumped his chest eagerly. "Hjorn will follow."

Another chief did the same. "Gryma will follow."

So it went through the church, fists beating against leather, with every chief pledging their clans. Andry did his best to commit them all to memory. The eagle of Asgyrl. Sornlonda's wolf. The redbeard's great mountains of Hjorn. Blodin. Gryma. Lyda. Jyrodagr. Mundo. He repeated them over and over, but the Jydi words blended together in his head.

Corayne would already know them all, he thought. He braced himself for the usual sting of her memory. Instead, he felt only joy. It took all his will not to sprint out of the church and down to the harbor, where he might hail a ship all the way to Iona.

"We are the clans of the Jyd," the Sornlonda chief said. She struck her chest again. "We are many."

Her fellow chiefs gave a short, low hoot, like a battle cry.

"We are strong."

They did it again, deeper than before. It shook the air of the church.

Sornlonda's face darkened. "But not enough to face a great army alone."

Andry knew enough of the Gallish legions, let alone Taristan's undead horde, to agree. He nodded grimly.

"Your strength is on the water, in raiding," he said. "Quick attacks and quick retreats. If Corayne makes it to Iona, the Queen of Galland will pursue her with every soldier she has in her legions, every siege engine. Every ship in her fleet."

The chief offered a wolfish, bloodthirsty smile. "You have a taste for war, Blue Star."

Heat flooded Andry's cheeks, but he kept on.

"Prepare your longships for winter seas. Make sure no one can move an army through the Watchful, or along the coast. The warbands of Trec will do the same along their border," he added, thinking of Oscovko and his army. "We may not be able to stop Erida and Taristan, but we can slow them down."

When the chiefs hooted out their war cry again, Andry almost shouted with them. Instead, he put a hand to the sword at his hip, his fingers following old instinct as they wrapped around the hilt. It felt like the only thing he knew how to do anymore.

"Together," he said softly, his voice lost to the echoes.

With me.

10

THE CROWN FIRST
Erida

Outside the window, night fell across Ascal. Erida watched the bloody remnants of the sun fade while lights sprang up across her city. She inhaled slowly, as if she could breathe in the many thousands who lived within her walls. It steadied her enough.

"I should see them," she said, turning back from the window. Her mind flew down to the dungeons beneath the palace, and the prisoners jailed there. "All three of them."

"Only the assassin might be of some use," Taristan said. "But Ronin was not . . . gentle with her."

Erida flinched. She knew the work of torture well enough. Her own dungeons held many chambers for such things, her interrogators and executioners well trained in the art. It was more than necessary for any ruler, especially someone with a kingdom as vast as her own, and a court so untrustworthy.

Something told Erida that Red Ronin was even worse than her own agents. The bitter, Spindlerotten wizard had far more tools at his disposal.

"Is she dead?"

Erida finally looked back to Taristan, too much distance between them. Her cloak still lay discarded, golden as her armor. So much of her wanted to do away with the rest of their clothing, to lay herself bare, but there was work to do still.

He only shrugged at her, his detached manner returning. Taristan cared little for the captured Amhara.

"Not yet. The guards report she has not awoken from her last interrogation, since they brought her back to the cells."

Erida narrowed her eyes. "And when was that?"

"Near three days ago," he answered.

Again, she flinched and thought of Ronin, his red-rimmed eyes and too-wide smile glowing in the shadows of a dungeon.

Erida shook her head to chase away the vision. "What of the immortal?"

She remembered Domacridhan too well. The monstrous, menacing Elder loomed tall in her mind, with a barely concealed rage simmering below the surface. He reminded her of a storm out at sea, threatening to break on shore.

Taristan's rare smile returned. If Domacridhan was a storm, Taristan was the cruel wind keeping him at bay.

"He lives, rotting in the cells. It's a harsher punishment than even Ronin could concoct," he said. Erida detected the smallest thread of pride. "When the end comes, when our victory is absolute, only then will he see the sun again. One last time."

There was no flare of red in Taristan's eye. The dark satisfaction was his and his alone. It shivered and delighted Erida in equal measure.

"Will he know where Corayne is?" she asked.

He shook his head.

"Doubtful. Domacridhan is only a few things. Brave, idealistic. And stupid." Taristan scoffed low in his throat. "He was a shield to Corayne, little more."

"He is an Elder prince."

"Do you wish to ransom him?" Taristan raised an eyebrow and barked out a laugh. "Wring some gold out of his queen?"

She waved off the thought with a swing of her hand, her emerald blazing.

"No. Let him lie in darkness," she answered. "We'll take the gold ourselves when we wipe his enclave from the face of the realm."

Across the room, Taristan grinned, lips parted, like he held the world in his teeth. To Erida, he almost did.

"Indeed we shall," he breathed.

The yards between them stretched and Erida felt cold despite the close air of the room. It was his warmth she craved, almost too hot to bear, enough to blaze without burning.

He held her gaze and Erida wondered if he could read the desire on her face. The want. It felt all-consuming, even as she pushed it away, until her own heart was just a distant echo, beating in the back of her mind.

The crown came first. The work was still at hand.

She drew a breath and broke the silence between them.

"I can't believe I'm saying this, but I must speak with Ronin."

Taristan's black eyes narrowed, confused for an instant. Then he relented with a shrug.

"He is in the archives," he said, indicating the doorway.

A jolt went up Erida's spine. She closed a fist, raising her knuckles to show the emerald of Galland.

"Am I not Queen of Four Kingdoms, an Empress Rising?" she said, all but laughing. "Can I not summon a single Spindlerotten wizard?"

Taristan shrugged again.

"Not unless you send someone to carry him up the tower stairs," he said, sounding almost apologetic. "The witch snapped his leg."

If only she snapped his neck.

"I must admit, I'm jealous," she said aloud, flushing. "Very well, I will go to him."

With a will, she took measured strides toward the door. Every step was deliberate, too fast. She feared she might take any chance to linger.

Then his fingers grazed her wrist as she passed, and all her restraint fell to ashes.

Again, her lips burned with his own, until nothing remained.

Both snarled at the knock on the door.

"Your Majesty?" said a faltering voice from the hall.

Again, she growled behind her teeth. Taristan's head dropped, his forehead braced against her bare collarbone. Dimly, Erida wondered when he'd drawn aside the top of her dress, but it didn't matter anymore.

She pulled it back into place with a huff and went to the door, wrenching it open with a glare to freeze blood.

Lord Cuthberg, her seneschal, cowered on the other side. Her ladies-in-waiting flanked him, along with Lady Harrsing, bent over her cane. Only for Harrsing did Erida's fury abate a little.

"Your Majesty, my deepest apologies," the stout old seneschal sputtered, bowing low. As the highest administrator in her palace, he wore a golden chain of office and fine clothing to rival her wealthy lords.

Erida didn't miss the way Cuthberg's gaze fluttered past her, finding Taristan still standing in the salon. The seneschal whimpered again, all but covering his eyes. Cuthberg had a head for numbers and organization, but no spine.

The Queen ignored him, turning her focus on Lady Harrsing.

"Bella, you should be resting after our long journey home," Erida said with a small, true smile. "Shall we dine together tomorrow?"

To Erida's dismay, Lady Harrsing looked apologetic. She bowed as low as she could despite her cane, and the ladies followed suit.

"My dearest queen," Harrsing said. Her silver hair caught the candlelight. "The Temur ambassador awaits. We dine together tonight. All of us."

At her side, Lord Cuthberg twitched, bowing again.

With a burst of annoyance, Erida remembered his nattering in the courtyard, upon her arrival. *The ambassador requests an audience*, he'd told her, and she had agreed.

"Of course." Erida did her best to don her court mask: lifeless eyes and a demure smile. "Lord Cuthberg, escort my husband to his attendants and see he is ready for the ambassador."

Erida half expected her seneschal to drop dead.

"I would prefer to dine in my chambers," Taristan ground out, looking just as uncomfortable as Cuthberg.

"Your preference is noted," Erida shot back, gesturing to the door.

To her relief, he didn't argue. He didn't linger either, pushing past her without so much as a backward glance or a trailing hand. It felt like a bucket of cold water over hot coals.

Cuthberg scurried after Taristan, who swept down the long passage and out of sight with a few quick strides. Erida pitied whatever attendants awaited him.

The crown comes first, she told herself again, shaking off the buzzing sensation of Taristan's lips on her own. Without him, it was easier to be Queen of Galland instead of Erida.

She stepped back from the door and allowed her ladies to sweep in, a flock of pretty birds in silk and lace. Lady Harrsing followed after them.

Erida fell back into the old rhythm without thinking. Maids appeared alongside her noble ladies, and together they went through the usual motions. So did Erida. She tipped her head back, letting nameless hands wind through her hair, combing out the old braids to set them anew.

Only Lady Harrsing sat, the others too afraid to look idle in Erida's presence.

"Bella, we've had quite the day," Erida said, letting someone unlace her gown. Another pulled it over her head, revealing her undergarments. "I cannot say how long I will be able to treat with the ambassador this evening."

"Little more than an hour will be good enough," Lady Harrsing replied, leaning heavy on her cane. "Ambassador Salbhai had a long journey too, and he will not be riding off again so soon."

Erida caught the meaning easily.

"Ah," she said, already frustrated with the presence of an ambassador she did not know. Let alone one from the Temurijon, the only empire in existence to rival her own.

"I do not have the patience for this, nor the time," she muttered, tipping her head to allow a maid to remove her necklaces. Another polished the emerald on her finger.

"Your Majesty does as she wills," Harrsing allowed. Her pale green eyes were still sharp as ever. Erida felt them like two icy daggers. "But it serves us well to keep the Temur behind their mountains for as long as possible. I have no desire to see the Countless in my lifetime."

I cannot say the same, Erida thought, careful to keep her face still. She had desired such a thing for too many years: to test her legions against the horseback army of Emperor Bhur. To win, and stand above all others in the realm.

She eyed Harrsing again, reading the lines of age on her face. She was seventy years old at least, a mother and grandmother many times over, to children all over the realm, in every kingdom.

Lady Harrsing stared back, letting the Queen look.

"I do desire to see one thing, though," the old woman added, flicking her gaze down to Erida's stomach.

The Queen huffed out a dry, withering laugh. She wanted to tease Bella for her prying but refrained. The eyes of her ladies were many, their gossip swift.

"Lady Harrsing," Erida clipped in a scandalized tone. She hoped the gentle chiding would be enough to turn her curiosity.

Behind her, the ladies arranging her clothing for the evening slowed in their work, looking on. Erida felt like a lion behind bars, caged and observed by weaker beasts.

To Erida's relief, Harrsing relented. She put up a hand in surrender.

"It's an old woman's privilege to wonder, and speak out of turn from time to time," she said, smiling idly. Like the Queen, she wore a mask too.

Erida saw through it easily. She knew better than to mistake Bella Harrsing for anything less than a cunning politician, who survived for decades in the Gallish court. Lord Thornwall commanded armies across the kingdom, but Bella navigated equally dangerous ground in the palace.

"I am mother to a kingdom, and birthing an empire," Erida said, over loud. "Certainly that is enough for now."

"For now," Harrsing answered, nodding agreement. But her sharp eyes flashed. "For now."

Slowly, Erida nodded back. She knew what Harrsing meant, what she wanted to say but could not in mixed company. Even now, with all the power in the world in her hands, Lady Harrsing still tried to protect Erida of Galland. It made the Queen's heart twist.

Powerful as I am, I still need stability in the eyes of my lords, Erida thought. *I need an heir to sit the throne I build.*

"It has been a strange winter," Harrsing muttered, turning her gaze to the windows. Darkness pressed against them, broken only by the lights of the city. "There's word of snow in the south, and fire in the north."

Fire. Gidastern. Erida kept still, swallowing down her discomfort.

"And the sky," one of the ladies breathed, forgetting herself.

"What of the sky?" Erida asked sharply.

"Surely you've seen it, Your Majesty," the girl answered, not daring to meet the Queen's stare. "Some days it looks red as blood."

"Red as victory," Erida corrected, her tone sharp. "Red is the color of mighty Syrek, the god of Galland. Perhaps he smiles on us."

Her undergarments came off next and Erida went to the vast copper tub by the fire, the water steaming. With a low purr, she sank into the water, feeling the long journey home slough off her skin.

Lady Harrsing remained perched in her seat, an imperious bird watching over the Queen.

"One hour at most," Erida reminded her, tipping her head back to let the maids wash her hair. "I've only just returned to the city. Certainly Ambassador Salbhai will not think me rude? Besides, he can treat with the other diplomats. Lord Malek and Lord Emrali would certainly leap at the opportunity to entertain a Temur ambassador."

Something strange flashed in Harrsing's eyes. Erida thought it might be shame.

"Malek and Emrali have been recalled to their courts in Kasa and Sardos," Lady Harrsing finally said, reluctant.

With a splash, Erida shifted in the water. She weighed her options quickly, keenly aware of the many observing eyes around her. If the kingdoms of Sardos and Kasa had called back diplomats from Erida's court, there was certainly trouble afoot. If not danger.

But Erida of Galland feared no kingdom or army upon the realm. The water splashed again as she shrugged her shoulders, making a show of her disinterest.

"Very well," she said, gesturing for Harrsing to continue.

The lady nodded.

"A great number of other nobles have arrived in the city already, ahead of the coronation."

Indeed, Ascal seemed more crowded than usual, and not just with lords and ladies of Galland. Commonfolk would be flocking in from the countryside to celebrate their queen, toasting her victory with free ale and wine. Not to mention delegations from Madrence, Tyriot, and Siscaria were on their way, to witness the making of their new monarch.

"What news of Konegin?"

Her treasonous cousin's name tasted sour in Erida's mouth.

Around the chamber, her ladies slowed. Only the maids kept at their work, scrubbing Erida's arms down to her fingernails.

Harrsing heaved a breath and banged her cane once on the ground, frustrated. "There has been little word since his failure in Madrence."

Erida did not miss the careful wording. His *failure*. It was a gentle way to describe an attempted usurpation.

"I've made my own inquiries but received little in the way of news. I suspect he is on the other side of the Long Sea by now, seeking a hole to hide in," Bella muttered.

"My cousin gambled his life and future on seizing the throne. He will not give up so easily," Erida replied.

Around the room, her ladies lowered their eyes, hands trembling.

Erida almost scoffed at them. She had little desire to coddle terrified children. But her ladies were of noble blood, descended from kings and high lords. It was in no one's interest to make them afraid.

Animals are most dangerous when they are afraid, Erida thought.

She looked on her ladies in turn, daughters and wives of powerful men. Seeking greater power in their proximity to the Queen. Spies, all of them.

Erida felt like an actor on a stage, pantomiming for a crowd in the street. She summoned all her court training, all her days spent schooling her face and voice.

"We seek to build a great empire, with Galland at her heart," Erida said, sincerity welling up. She realized the maids were listening too, slowing in their work to let her speak. "I want peace across the realm, and prosperity for its peoples."

The histories will remember me well. Victorious, generous, magnificent, holy. And beloved, she thought. Even as she spoke, she traced the paths the gossip would take, through the palace, the city, the noble families, and the commonfolk across the Ward.

"I want to build greatness and glory. A land worthy of our gods." It wasn't a lie. Erida tasted the truth of them, seductive as it was. At the edge of her mind, a warm red presence glowed with pride. "And I will do what I must to make it a reality. For us all."

"Of course, Your Majesty," Harrsing said from her seat, her voice cracking the quiet in half. "Lord Konegin's treason will not be tolerated."

Erida allowed a maid to help her from the bath. Another wrapped her in a robe warmed by the fire.

"He will be dealt with," she said. Combs slid through her ash-brown hair, pulling her back and forth. "I must cut off the head of the snake before his venom sets in."

If it hasn't already, she thought. *Certainly he has allies still at court, people who would put him on the throne if they could. I must root them out.*

Death had shadowed her first coronation. Erida suspected it would haunt the next one too.

11

THEIR SOULS TOGETHER
Corayne

One night in Sirandel turned into two, then three, then a week. Corayne did her best not to let the days melt together. But time felt different in the Castlewood, beneath the trees in the shifting pockets of sunlight. She told herself the spent days were useful. The Elders needed time to gather their warriors from the far-flung corners of the forest. And Corayne needed time to heal what wounds she could. Her bruises disappeared, her scrapes and burns fading away.

But the memories remained. They cut too deep to ever close.

At least sleep was peaceful here. Either she was far enough away from a Spindle, or What Waits could not penetrate the Elder enclave. She dreamed only of the little cottage by the sea, and the smell of lemon groves.

By the seventh morning, she knew Sirandel enclave well enough to find her way to a training yard alone. Corayne braided back her hair as she walked, sorting out a few tangles with her fingers.

The yard was always empty when she arrived, left open for her use. The Elders heard her coming long before she was close enough to see them. She eyed the stone circle, big enough to hold many sparring pairs.

Moss filled the old markings carved in the stone, while sculpted trees wove together overhead. Colored glass spit a rainbow across the flat circle.

Corayne danced in and out of the shards of light, going through the motions Sigil and Sorasa drilled into her. It was harder without them, but her muscles remembered, and she relied on instinct.

The Elders outfitted her well, replacing her burned clothes with a selection of fine velvet tunics, leggings, and plain leathers. All in rich browns, golds, and purples, to blend with the winter forest. There was also a cloak of Sirandel, embroidered with foxes, the hood lined in impossibly soft fur. It reminded her so strongly of Dom's Ionian cloak that she could never wear it.

The immortals left her to her own training, approaching only to leave water, food, and an array of weaponry she might find better suited to her form. She brought the Spindleblade with her each day but hesitated to use it. The sword was Taristan's, not hers.

Corayne preferred a shorter, lighter saber, its blade slightly curved.

With every arc of her sword, she pushed herself a little bit faster, a little bit harder, until her breath came in short gasps.

It will not be in vain, Corayne told herself for the thousandth time.

"Forgive the intrusion."

Huffing, Corayne let the momentum of the sword turn her around to face Valnir himself. Grand as he was, the Elder hesitated at the edge of the stone circle.

"How long have you been watching?" Corayne grumbled, wiping her brow with her vambraces. She was careful to avoid the spikes of the Dragonclaws.

Valnir blinked at her, stone-faced. "Perhaps an hour."

Not for the first time, Corayne wanted to scream at the social norms of the Elders.

"What can I do for you, my lord?" she said, trying not to sound annoyed. *Is it finally time to move? Have your warriors assembled?*

To her dismay, the Elder monarch took a step forward into the training ring, his purple cloak trailing behind him. The bow was on his back now, like another limb.

"You have been well trained," he mused, circling around Corayne with a keen eye.

She itched under his attention, his yellow gaze excruciating.

"Thank you," she said begrudgingly. "I am eager to be on the road, sir."

"I know this," he answered, his eyes dropping to the Spindleblade. With a jolt, Corayne realized there was nothing she could do if Valnir decided to seize the blade or smash it to pieces.

Her heartbeat rammed against her ribs.

Valnir went still for a long moment, as if weighing his words. Then he drew aside his purple cloak, shifting to show more of his neck. A mighty vein thrummed under the white skin. With a single finger, he traced the line of gnarled flesh across his throat. The scar looked wrong on an immortal body.

"They only need rope to hang you mortals," he muttered, half his mouth curling into a scowl. "For us, the executioner must use weights and steel chain."

As much as she tried, Corayne could not stop herself from picturing such a sight. Cords of steel wound around Valnir's neck, heavy iron hooked to his feet.

"Why?" she said, eyes going round.

His voice was gentle. "I was not the only one."

Her mind spun, recalling another Elder. *The same eyes, the same hair. The same face, nearly.* Slowly, Corayne understood. *And the same scar on her neck.*

"Eyda. The Lady of Kovalinn."

Valnir dipped his head and backed into the training circle, giving her some space.

"My sister," he said. "So it was, the two scions of our great family became its ruin."

Corayne remembered Eyda on the shores of the Watchful Sea, leading an Elder army and a Jydi clan. *To their doom*, she thought bitterly. Part of her wanted to twist the knife, to make Valnir admit his own mistake. His refusal to fight doomed Princess Ridha, and his sister too.

But Corayne saw the sorrow behind his eyes, and the terrible shame. *He knows it already, and he is doing everything he can to make it right.*

"As there were Spindles in Allward then, there were Spindles in Glorian too." Valnir folded his hands while he paced. "Doorways to many realms. Irridas, Meer, the Crossroads, the Ward. It was our belief that these Spindles posed a threat to our own realm and needed to be closed at all costs."

Corayne heard the controlled anger roiling in his voice. "Your people did not agree."

"Glorian is the light of the realms, and light must always spread," he replied. "Our king said so himself. It was our duty to cross the infinite lands, bringing Glorian's greatness wherever we roamed."

"My own blood is of the Spindles," Corayne offered, wincing as Taristan's face rose in her mind. "I understand the call to wander, as much as someone like me can."

Valnir barely seemed to hear her, his eyes sliding out of focus.

"I am comforted in knowing I was right about the Spindles," he murmured. "In the end."

Swallowing hard, Corayne looked down at the sword on the bench, tracing the familiar blade. Some days it was a burden, others a crutch.

Today it felt like a compass, its needle pointing in no direction she knew.

The Elder watched with yellow eyes.

"Forged in the heart of a Spindle," he breathed, reaching out to touch the sword.

"May I?" he asked, indicating the hilt.

Somehow Corayne knew he would accept whatever choice she made. Slowly, she nodded her head.

His long fingers wrapped around the hilt, and with a flash of steel the sword pulled free, the bare blade held up to the forest.

"A thread of gold against hammer and anvil, and steel between all three. A crossing made, in blood and blade, and both become the key."

The edge turned in Valnir's grip, catching the sun, every strange letter flashing against the patterned light.

"That's what it says on the sword," Corayne breathed. As she had so many times, she tried to read the language of the blade, woven in beautiful, inscrutable script. "You speak Old Cor?"

Grimly, Valnir returned the Spindleblade to its sheath, and placed it gingerly down on the bench. He treated it with gentle reverence, as a parent would a child.

"A little," he murmured. "Once."

Again, she took in the way he handled the sword, his eyes filled with sudden softness. As if looking upon a friend. Or a child.

"You made them," Corayne blurted out.

His smile was the thin curve of a crescent moon. It did not reach his eyes.

"You made my father's sword. You made Taristan's." Corayne's voice shook. "You made the Spindleblades."

"Among many others. Only two survived to enter this realm." Valnir shook his head. "I have not looked at a forge since."

She eyed his neck again, the scar gleaming at his throat. "They put you in a noose for it."

Valnir shrugged. "The noose was only a threat."

Some threat, Corayne thought, swallowing hard.

"Death or exile. It is clear what we chose, my sister and I," he continued, putting a finger to the steel's edge. A single drop of blood welled up. "We entered the Ward as outcasts, with only a like-minded few. We were not welcome in Iona, so we built Sirandel. And after the Spindles shifted—"

He drew back his hand, a flash of pain crossing his beautiful face.

"Glorian Lost made exiles of us all."

Corayne felt the same pain lingering in her own heart, at the edge of everything always. She knew, in some small way, what it was to be lost, without hope of returning home.

Then Valnir gave an exasperated sigh, looking to the trees. He clucked his tongue.

"Come, there is commotion in the great hall," he said, still staring away into the maze of the hewn forest. At what, Corayne did not know, her mortal eyes and ears pitifully useless.

"Fine," she said, throwing the Spindleblade over her shoulder.

It lay heavy against her back, a constant anchor as she followed Valnir dutifully through the enclave. Her boots crunched over stonework and dead leaves, but he made no noise at all.

All the while, her thoughts swirled, a storm in her head. *Valnir marches now not because it was the right thing to do, but for revenge*, she knew. *And perhaps some redemption too.*

* * *

Valnir's great hall stuck out so vividly now, Corayne hardly believed she had ever missed it in the first place. She passed between two arching trees, their petals worked in golden glass, to find the chamber roving with Elder warriors. They gathered in small groups, speaking in their own language, their whispers both melodic and otherworldly. Corayne marveled at their weaponry, knives, bows, and spears, all gleaming and ready for war.

The crowd cleared the way for them, opening a path to the throne. Valnir made for it while Corayne hung back, hoping to be lost in the crowd. Until something strange caught her eye and her racing heart stopped short. Her chest tightened and the air felt crushed from her lungs.

Two figures waited before the throne, one of them kneeling, his form familiar.

Corayne tried to say his name. It came out in an embarrassing squeak. He still heard her.

On the ground, Charlon Armont whirled as quickly as he could. He moved gingerly and Corayne feared the worst. Then she realized there was an even more horrible possibility.

"Are you real?" she forced out, her voice shaking. "Am I dreaming?"

She half expected to jolt awake in her bed, tangled up in soft linen sheets. Her eyes stung, already fearing the prospect.

But Charlie let out a low, raspy laugh.

"Am *I* real?" he croaked.

Then he gestured to the great hall of stone trees, the Elder warriors, and Valnir standing over him. Charlie stood out horribly in comparison, a young mortal, travel-worn and pale, his brown hair a tangle, his robes dirtier than his boots.

A smile crooked on his lips. "I'm the most real thing in this place."

Corayne shrugged off the Spindleblade, letting it fall to the ground. She lunged forward, all but tackling Charlie around the middle. He toppled sideways, held up only by the man standing next to him. Corayne hardly cared, too busy wrapping her arms around his shoulders.

"You're all sweaty," Charlie grumbled. He made a show of trying to swat her off.

Corayne pulled back, taking him in again. *Stubble on his cheeks, shadows beneath his eyes. Muck everywhere. And real.*

She wrinkled her nose. "Well, you *stink*."

His mud-brown eyes creased as he smiled back. "Quite a pair, then, the two of us."

Just *the two of us* echoed in her head. It was almost too much to bear.

"How did you find me?" she forced out, still clutching his forearms.

Over his shoulder, one of the Sirandel guard shifted into her eyeline.

"We found him," the guard said. "It was not difficult. They filled half the Castlewood with their noise."

Suddenly his rasping voice made sense. Corayne's eyes widened.

"Did you *shout* your way into Elder custody?" she scoffed.

Charlie shrugged. "It worked," he said, sounding just as surprised as she felt. "What about you?"

Her grin faded. "A search party found me the morning after—" She stumbled, the words too difficult to say. "After."

Slowly, Charlie pulled his arms from her grip.

"I'm sorry for running away," he said, his face turning pink with shame. Something glimmered in his eye and he scrubbed it away before a single tear could fall.

Corayne wanted to punch him.

"I'm not," she said quickly, taking him by the shoulders again. This time, she held on too tightly, forcing Charlie to hug her back. "It's the only reason you're here now. With me."

Even as she said it, she heard another voice in her head echoing the call. *With me.* Andry used to say it so many times, Corayne couldn't believe she would never hear him say it again.

Charlie looked her dead in the eye, the same pain shining in him.

"With me," he replied.

"I take it these are your Companions."

Valnir's low voice, breaking them apart. The Elder monarch looked them both over, before his gaze strayed to the stranger still standing next to Charlie.

"One of them is," Corayne said, eyeing the unfamiliar man.

She read him as she would a map, eyeing his leathers and rapier. Her focus snagged on the familiar bronze blade poking out of his jacket.

"I am Garion," the stranger said. "Of the Amhara."

"*Oh*" popped out of Corayne's mouth before she could stop herself.

Charlie flushed pink again.

Corayne looked between priest and assassin, delighted. Mismatched as the pair were, one a lithe killer with the bearing of a dancer, the other a fugitive priest with inky fingers, they seemed to fit together.

"A pleasure to finally meet you," she said, taking Garion by the hand. "Charlie's told me next to nothing."

Garion eyed Charlie sidelong. "We'll soon remedy that."

"Lord Valnir, my friends need to be seen to," Corayne said, turning to the immortal. "If they are to join us for the journey east."

Charlie's relief disappeared. "And when might that be?" he said through gritted teeth.

It was not Corayne's place to answer. She looked to Valnir. A week ago, his yellow stare frightened her. Now she saw it as just another obstacle in the path forward.

He gripped his bow and studied the intricate carvings of the wood, tracing a fox with one finger.

"Dawn," Valnir breathed.

Murmurs rippled through his assembled immortals.

Next to her, Charlie scowled.

"Dawn. Fantastic," he muttered.

Charlie and Garion were given chambers near Corayne's own, branching off within the same underground structure. It wasn't stuffy like a cellar, the ceiling punctuated by marble roots and skylights to flood the rooms with shards of light. Candles burned in branch holders, chasing off any shadows or dampness. Food crowded one of the many tables. Rabbit, pheasant, vegetables, and wine, all rich in variety despite the winter. Soft carpets cushioned the stone floor, patterned with leaves of every shade. There was even a copper tub positioned in front of the crackling fireplace. When Corayne joined them, both Charlie and Garion had already scrubbed clean.

Corayne positioned herself on a cushion, twitchy and excited, her body unaccustomed to joy after so much sorrow. Her cheeks ached from smiling but she couldn't help herself.

By the sumptuous bed, Charlie pulled on a new linen shirt with a sigh. He raised a sleeve and inhaled deeply, savoring the smell of clean clothing. He already wore tan suede breeches and new boots, his long hair combed through.

At the fireplace, Garion was back in his Amhara leathers, as Corayne expected. If he was anything like Sorasa, Garion wouldn't trade his good leathers for the finest clothing in Allward. But he did lay out his weapons for cleaning, his rapier and six daggers varying in size.

"Do you have any injuries? You can send for a healer, but I warn you, they aren't much good," Corayne chattered, all but bouncing on her cushion. "Not much call for healers among immortals, I guess."

Charlie pursed his lips at her. "You look crazed."

"Perhaps I am," she shot back. Then she eyed Garion. "I promise, I'm not usually so—"

"She is," Charlie finished, cutting her off. His voice was still raspy and he gulped at a glass of wine, draining it down. Then he flopped onto the bed, tucking his hands behind his head and crossing his ankles. "Oh thank the gods," he sighed, relaxing against the blankets and pillows.

A corner of Garion's mouth lifted into a beautiful smirk. He looked at Charlie through dark lashes, in a way that made Corayne understand exactly why Charlie loved him.

"Garion of the Amhara." She scooted on her cushion to face him fully.

The assassin turned his focus to her. His smile came easy, widening. Unlike Sorasa, there was no snap of danger behind his dark gray eyes. He seemed more inviting, friendly even. But perhaps that was a weapon too.

"Were you sent to kill me like the others?" she asked, watching his face closely.

From the pillows, Charlie guffawed. "If this has all been a trick to assassinate Corayne, I will never forgive you."

"Darling, do you know me at all?" Garion answered, clicking his tongue as if to scold him.

"Too well, in fact," Charlie sneered.

"Hmmm," Garion hummed low in his throat. He leaned against the wall, half in shadow, coiled like a dangerous, beautiful cat. "Sorasa Sarn is not the only Amhara to turn her back on the Guild."

Corayne winced. "*Was*," she blurted out, regretting it instantly.

She heard Charlie shift among the pillows and swing his legs to the floor, his boots hitting the ground with a thump.

"You saw—you saw them go?" he stuttered.

"I saw enough. That's—I can't say it all again." Her throat tightened and she swallowed hard. "I don't know how anyone could survive Gidastern. Even Sorasa and Sigil. Even Dom." She felt sick even skirting around it. "Certainly not Andry. He'd give his life before leaving anyone else behind."

Out of the corner of her eye, something flashed. She turned just in time to watch a single tear fall off Charlie's face.

"And Valtik?" he murmured.

Corayne swiped at her own stinging eyes. "Honestly, Valtik is probably playing bone dice somewhere and laughing at the end of the world." She was only half joking. "I think it's just us. We will have to be enough."

"We aren't dead yet," he said.

The words were too familiar to Corayne by now. She echoed them anyway.

"We aren't dead yet."

Before an uneasy silence could truly settle, Garion huffed. "So where are we supposed to be going tomorrow?"

"And so abysmally early," Charlie grumbled.

Corayne set her jaw. "We set out for Iona enclave. In Calidon."

Charlie leaned heavily against the table, as if already exhausted by the long journey. "Why Iona?"

"It's the largest Elder city. Dom's home. And it's where all this began. The Spindleblades, my father. I feel like some cord is pulling me there. It's the right path, it has to be," she said, putting a hand to her heart. "Not to mention the fact that Taristan has Erida's army and a horde of the undead. He will come after me to get the sword back, and I don't intend to just stand on the side of the road until he shows up."

"And—" Her voice caught. "I think it's where the rest would go. If they could. If there's a chance they're not—"

Then words failed her entirely, her throat threatening to close.

Across the room, Charlie dropped his eyes, giving her a little privacy in her grief.

"Well, I don't know what a good plan sounds like anymore, but I suppose this has to be good enough," he finally said. "Perhaps the letters will help a little. If they ever make it where they need to go."

Again, Corayne ached with memory. She wanted to go back to Vodin, to the morning before they rode out of Trec. When she and Charlie sat at a feasting table, a stack of parchment between them, the air smelling of ink. As she wrote, Charlie forged a dozen seals of the highest crowns across the realm, from Rhashir to Madrence. Each one calling for help, each one laying bare Erida's conquest, and corruption.

"If we're lucky, they just might." But even Corayne did not dare to hope. The letters would take weeks or months to reach their destinations, if they made it at all. And then, they had to be believed on top of everything else. "Will Isadere sway their father? Will the King of Ibal fight?"

Charlie cared little for the Heir of Ibal, and he scoffed. "If they look away from their holy mirror long enough."

It was hardly what Corayne wanted to hear. She bit her lip sharply, nearly breaking the skin. "I can't believe it's just us."

By the table, Charlie's face softened. He was clean-shaven again. It made him look younger, closer to Corayne's age.

"I should say something wise and comforting. But even as a priest, I was never good at that sort of thing." He eyed the many candles on the tabletop, the light of their flames dancing on his cheeks. "I don't know what lies beyond this realm, Corayne. I don't know where our souls go. But I want to think they go together, and we will see them again, one day. At the end of it."

In one swift motion, he licked his thumb and pointer finger. He pinched five candles in turn, snuffing out the flames with the smallest hiss of smoke. Corayne winced as each candle went out.

Then he grasped another candle, still burning, and set the five back to light again.

"Pray with me, Charlie," Corayne murmured.

She expected him to refuse.

Instead, he took a knee beside her, one hand clasped in her own.

To whatever god would listen, she prayed for guidance. For courage. And for the realm beyond to be as Charlie said. Their souls together, waiting for the rest.

12

THE BULL, THE SNAKE, AND THE HURRICANE
Domacridhan

The next day, the jailers returned. This time, they came with a Lionguard knight, his armor golden in the torchlight. He walked proudly, chest thrust forward, but Dom caught the way his gaze shifted, flickering over the prisoners on either side of the corridor. Even the Queen's guard knew to fear them.

The Elder bristled against his many restraints. Part of him wanted to rip the guards apart. The rest wanted them to force a cup of water down Sorasa's throat. On the other side of the corridor, Sigil slammed against the bars with bound hands.

"She's going to die on *your* watch," she snarled at the jailers. "Is that what the prince wants?"

Neither the jailers nor the knight answered.

"You're going to end up in one of these cells with us if she dies," she taunted, wagging a finger at him.

"I'm not sure which is more frightening," Dom said from his wall. "The cells—or the cellmate?"

Smirking, Sigil threw back her head and barked a guttural laugh.

One of the jailers glanced back at them, his face drawn with concern.

"You need to help her," Dom called.

To his relief, the guards stopped at Sorasa's cell, keys jingling.

The knight hung back, allowing the jailers to enter the cell first. He kept one hand on his sword, his gauntleted fingers wrapped around the hilt of the blade.

"You're sure she hasn't moved?" the knight muttered.

The jailers stepped over the abandoned bowls of rotting food. "Yes, sir. She hasn't eaten, hasn't drank for almost three days now. Since the wizard brought her down."

Dom felt his heart in his teeth.

"Very well," the Lionguard said, nodding, his lip curled with disgust. "Then this is the wizard's doing, and the wizard's problem."

"Yes, sir," the jailers said in unison, ducking their heads.

The knight waved a hand, already impatient. "Get her up."

Both jailers exchanged darting looks, reluctant to touch an Amhara assassin. Even an unconscious one.

"I said, move her," the knight snapped. "Go on."

"Go on," Dom heard Sigil mutter to herself. She watched Sorasa with wide eyes, looking as nervous as he felt.

The jailers were careful in their movements, keenly aware of both Sorasa and the prisoners watching. She was small enough for one to carry, and a jailer slung her easily over his shoulder. Her head lolled in a way that made Dom feel sick, and her shoulder was clearly dislocated. Her arm swung as the jailer made his way out of the cell, his partner close at his side.

For the first time since Gidastern, Dom saw Sorasa's face. Like Sigil, she was paler than he remembered, her skin losing its bronze glow in the dark. She had bruises too, half-healing, and a gash over one eye. Even so, she looked peaceful, as if only sleeping. Nothing compared to the last time he saw her face, when they were trapped in a burning city, with hellhounds and the undead around every corner. But her eyes were open then, alight like two copper flames.

What he would give to see those eyes open again.

The jailers moved quickly, and the knight followed on their heels, his long green cloak billowing out behind him.

"Don't die on me, Sarn," Sigil muttered as they passed her cell.

Dom said nothing. He only listened to the steady, unyielding beat of her heart. And then the fading steps of the jailers, their boots scuffing the floor, as the knight's armor clattered with every stride.

Then the heartbeat quickened and Dom thought his own heart would stop. Something flickered in the corner of his eye, half seen, like the beat of an insect's wing. He turned his head sharply, neck scraping against the metal collar.

Just in time to watch Sorasa Sarn open her eyes and kick out a leg. She hooked a bar of the closest cell with her knee, her good arm going around the jailer's shoulders. He gave a short cry of shock, only for Sorasa to throw his whole body, slamming him into the iron bars, his teeth shattering in a spray of bone.

Again, the powerful wave rose up in the immortal.

"DUCK, SORASA!" he roared, but she was already moving.

The knight's longsword cut through empty air, clanging off the iron bars. Sorasa rolled under the blow, going not for the knight, but the other jailer.

He yelped and dropped his torch, the flames smacking against the stone floor. The shadows shifted rapidly.

Sorasa had him in a second, seizing him by the neck of his tunic to throw him backward. He landed flat on his spine, choking out a breath. With a swift kick to the throat, Sorasa made sure he never tasted air again.

Sigil whooped in triumph and rattled her own bars, her chain singing.

The keys sang above it all, rattling on their ring. But now, they spun on Sorasa's finger. She leered as she walked, her focus on the knight. Torchlight wavered on her face, the flames painting her in rippling shadows. For a moment, she seemed more beast than mortal, a giant spider moving through the darkness. Her lips parted, showing her teeth in a terrible smile.

"Snake," the knight snarled, charging at her with all his strength.

But Sorasa sidestepped him neatly, her back to the cells. With a quick sweep of her good arm, she tossed the keys behind her.

They slid across the floor, hissing through the dust and straw to land in front of Sigil's cell.

"Keep him busy," Sigil crowed, scrabbling through the bars for the ring.

"Take your time," Sorasa hissed back.

One-handed and unarmed, the assassin twisted in circles around the knight of the Lionguard. He was too big to fight in the narrow corridor, the sweeps of his sword catching cell bars instead of Sorasa Sarn.

Dom struggled against his bindings to no avail. His ankles and wrists ached, his neck rubbed raw, but none of it mattered. He followed Sorasa's arcing path with wide, unblinking eyes. His breath came in short gasps, and he willed the knight to stumble, to leave some opening in his guard.

It's all she needs, he knew. *One wrong step. One second lost.*

A lock clicked, a cell door whined on ancient hinges, and Sigil of the Temurijon stepped out into the passage. All six menacing feet of her. Her unbridled laughter echoed off the stone.

Only then did the knight falter, stepping backward, his sword pointed out in defense. Not attack.

"THE PRISONERS HAVE ESCAPED!" he boomed, shouting for anyone that would listen.

Anyone that might save him.

With a few lunging steps, Sigil took Sorasa's side, pressing the keys into her good hand.

"Knew you were fine," the bounty hunter grunted, her wrists still bound. It didn't seem to bother her as she squared off to the surviving knight.

"Of course, Sigil," Sorasa said over her shoulder, turning away to let them duel.

Her eyes shifted in the torchlight, finding Dom. The copper flames burned again, beacons through the darkness.

He half expected her to take her time, to bother him in her usual way. To his relief, she made quick work of the lock in his cell door.

In the passage, Sigil stalked toward the knight. "Are you going to run, Brave Champion of the Lionguard?"

He snarled beneath his helmet. "Never."

"Then I'm sorry to kill you," she answered, laughing again. "Although, I suppose I have to kill you either way. Maintain the element of surprise and all that. You understand, I'm sure."

Still grinning, she charged into the knight with all the force of a raging bull.

In the cell, Sorasa studied Dom's chains as he studied her face. The last three weeks were written all over her body. Dark shadows circled her eyes, her cheekbones sharp, her face more hollow than he remembered. Her fingers were bruised and burned, a few nails missing. Old blood and ash striped her leathers, black and dark reds. Her clothes tore at the seams, tattooed skin poking out beneath. But underneath the blood and bruises, she was still Sorasa Sarn. Ruthless, fearless. And stubborn as a kicking mule.

In spite of himself, Dom could not help but smile, a grin spreading over his face.

She raised her chin to him, her heartbeat a drum in his ears. Again, she spun the ring of keys.

"Elder," she said.

"Amhara," he answered.

Her eyes flicked over his many chains and bindings, an eyebrow raised. "Can't say I'm sure where to start."

The usual frustration overtook his relief. "Sarn," he cursed, his smile dropping.

"Fine, fine," she answered, smirking.

As Sigil danced with the knight, Sorasa set to his chains. She started at the wrists, fitting different keys to different locks. His first arm came loose with a snap, his joints aching. When she freed the other wrist, he bit back a moan low in his throat.

"Easy, Dom, almost there," she murmured, her tone oddly gentle. "Can you handle the neck?"

He answered by prying the collar off himself, the steel bending in his grasp.

Beneath him, Sorasa grinned.

The last chains fell from his body, and Dom lunged from the cursed wall. He was an aching hurricane, all pain and rage. His foot struck iron and the cell door exploded off its hinges, falling backward with a dull clang. Everything came into sharp, impossible focus, even as time seemed to slow.

Dom felt like a giant released, a dragon rising. A beast unbound.

As a priest bows before a god, Sigil bowed out of Dom's way.

Beneath his helmet, the knight's face went white, his mouth gaping open. The sword dropped from his hand, landing hard on the floor. He turned and ran, fleeing before a tidal wave of immortal fury.

Dom held no love for violence. He made quick, quiet work of the knight.

And silence fell again.

Sorasa finally slumped, leaning back against the bars. Heaving a ragged breath, she braced her bad arm beneath her knees, her other hand against her dislocated shoulder. With a sick, echoing pop, it slid back into the socket. Dom could not help but wince, seeing the rare flash of pain across her face.

A half second later, Sigil wrapped her in a bruising embrace. Sorasa winced over her shoulder, fighting her off.

"I don't need broken ribs on top of everything else," she ground out, straightening up again. But she still listed, keeping one hand on the bars for support. With the other, she grabbed the cup of water off the floor of her cell and drank greedily.

Sorasa wore her mask even now, but Dom saw right through it. He picked up the knight's sword, gripping it firmly, before striding back to her.

Gingerly, he put out a hand.

"I'll carry you if I must," Dom said.

Her eyes snapped to his, full of venom.

"I'd rather die," she spat, shoving off the bars. With a snap of her wrist, she threw the cup down the corridor and set off at a trot.

"That might happen," he grumbled after her, matching stride.

Sigil fell in line, stopping only to pull a pair of daggers off the knight. She gave one to Sorasa and used the other to cut her bindings. With a hiss, she clasped her wrists, soothing the rings of raw skin.

"What now?" the bounty hunter said.

Behind them, the torch on the ground flickered, dying.

"Follow me," Dom said, his vision adjusting to the darkness. Luckily the other torch still burned around the far corner, its rippling fire growing stronger with every step.

Sorasa scoffed at his side.

"Follow *me*," she cut in. "I'm the only one who knows where we're going. And what we're going to do when we get there."

"The first thing we're going to do is feed you," Dom snapped back.

In the shadows, Sorasa hissed. "You sound like the squire."

Then she kicked at the Lionguard knight's body, shifting his corpse on the floor. His golden armor gleamed up at them, catching the distant torchlight.

"This should just fit you, Dom," she said, eyeing the body.

The immortal wanted to argue. Instead, he found himself shoved into steel plate and a green cloak, a helmet crammed over his skull. Between Sorasa and Sigil, they made quick work of lacing him into the armor. He watched, helpless, as Sorasa belted the sword around his waist, her fingers quick and sure.

"It's a bit tight," he grumbled. After weeks chained to a wall, the armor felt like a new kind of prison.

Sorasa only rolled her eyes. "You'll live," she bit out.

They rounded the corner of the corridor, just to face down another long line of empty cells. The passage angled steadily upward, to gods knew what. Dom strained his hearing, but there was nothing but the sound of their own hearts.

Sorasa quickened her pace, stupid as it was to push herself.

"Erida is in the palace, triumphant in her return from Madrence," she said. "We should pay her a visit."

For once, Sigil looked reluctant in the face of a fight. She put out a hand, grasping for Sorasa's shoulder.

"We have to get out of here," she said, her dark eyes flashing.

The assassin shrugged her off neatly.

"Do I look like I want to stay?" Sorasa scoffed. "We're leaving, we're just going to make the most of it."

Though Sigil looked skeptical, Dom felt a strange sense of calm. He didn't need to ask to know Sorasa already had a plan, and another plan beneath that one. After all, she'd had two long days to puzzle it out. He found himself falling silent, where once he would want to argue. To needle the assassin, poke at her intentions. Search for the lie in her words, for any evidence of deceit or betrayal.

I am not Amhara anymore. He could still hear her words spoken weeks ago, as if they still hung in the air.

By now, Domacridhan of Iona certainly believed them. His heart tightened and swelled, overcome for an instant.

Then he shut his feelings away, as Sorasa once told him to do.

You don't need it.

He saw only the path in front of them, and the sword in his hand. The way forward was easy. They just needed to stay alive to walk it.

13

THE DYING SWAN

Erida

The great hall had long recovered from the wreckage left in Corayne an-Amarat's wake. New chandeliers hung from the vaulted ceiling, each one individually bolted to the stone. Every surface shone, each slab of marble polished, the wood-paneled passages oiled and gleaming. Rugs were freshly washed, statues dusted. New banners of Gallish green and Corrish red hung heavy at every arch. Lions snarled and roses bloomed, wound together for queen and prince consort.

And guards lined the walls, done up in armor with good swords at their sides. More guards than Erida ever remembered there to be in her palace.

She entered her great hall with the usual fanfare, a simple green gown trailing out behind her. After her parade through the city that morning, she couldn't stomach the thought of putting on another complicated, overwrought dress weighed down by jewels. Her hair was unbound too, waving gently down her back beneath a plain circlet of hammered gold.

The message was clear. Queen Erida was tired from a long journey, exhausted by pageantry, and would not linger.

Her ladies and Lionguard kept pace, a few measured steps behind their queen. Three knights followed along this evening. Three others flanked Taristan, already seated at the high table.

"All hail Erida, Queen of Galland, of Madrence, of Tyriot, and Siscaria. The Empress Rising," boomed Lord Cuthberg from the dais, shouting out her titles.

Her lips twitched, wanting to smile. But she maintained her still, demure mask as she climbed the steps to the high table.

Throughout the great hall, the other tables were already crowded. Erida glimpsed a rainbow of silk and fur, all dappled with candlelight. High nobles of the court stared back at her, murmuring and watching. Most were well-known courtiers—lords and ladies, military commanders, and a few nobles already come in from the countryside for the coronation.

Among them, the delegation of the Temurijon was easy to spot.

They occupied their own long table, just a few steps below her own. The Temur men and women were black-haired and bronzed, dressed in rich but functional clothing. Better suited for travel than the feasting hall.

Erida knew the realm as well as any, the maps in her council chamber hard-drilled into her since childhood. She measured the path from Ascal to Korbij, the Emperor's great seat among the steppes. It lay thousands of miles away, on the banks of the Golba, the River Without End. She suspected the ambassador and his company set sail downriver many months ago, perhaps even half a year, to reach her.

The ambassador himself sat at the high table, to the left of her own chair. A place of great honor and respect.

Salbhai was an older man, with a high-boned face and a keen, ebony-eyed stare. He wore an overcoat of black silk, patterned with rose-gold feathers, bound at the waist with a belt. His own hair had gone to gray, as had his beard. Both were plaited into a braid, held in place by a circle of copper wire.

As a diplomat and politician in his own right, he was skilled enough to serve Emperor Bhur and treat with rulers of the realm. Meticulous in his manners, Salbhai stood to bow as the Queen approached.

She inclined her own head, polite to a fault.

"Ambassador Salbhai," she said, taking her seat. On her right, Taristan sank into his own chair, glowering in his usual way.

Erida caught a flash of scarlet robes at the corner of her eye and fought back a wince. *Too injured to be summoned but not so injured as to miss dinner*, she thought, cursing Ronin. The wizard sat on Taristan's far side, curled in his chair like a goblin.

"Your Majesty," Salbhai said, sliding back into his seat.

He had a kind look about him, his eyes cheerful and merry. Erida distrusted him immediately.

"Would your companion like a seat?" she said, eyeing the Temur guard behind Salbhai's chair.

Unlike his compatriots, the Temur soldier was baldheaded and young, his crossed arms bulging beneath his black surcoat.

"The Born Shields do not sit, Your Majesty," Salbhai said plainly. "I believe your Lionguard are the same."

Erida blanched. The Born Shields were raised to defend the Emperor himself, born to the saddle, the sword, and the bow. She eyed the guard again, then Salbhai, sizing them up as best she could.

"My Lionguard protects the crown and the prince consort," Erida said evenly, forcing herself to take a sip of wine.

Salbhai did the same, matching the Queen. He was polite to a fault.

"I am the blood of Emperor Bhur, down the line," he said, nonchalant. "A Born Shield guards me as he would the Emperor. To spill my blood is to spill his own."

Erida took another sip to hide her grimace. Her stomach twisted.

I have mistaken merriment for amusement, she thought. *The ambassador knows he is untouchable in my court. He can do whatever he likes, unless I wish to declare war on the Temurijon.*

Again, Salbhai mirrored her, his black eyes bright.

"I am honored by your presence, truly." Erida forced a graceful, winning smile. "To know that the Emperor holds me in high enough esteem to send someone of your caliber—it is flattering indeed."

"You are Queen of Four Kingdoms," he answered. As with all diplomats, Erida listened to more than his words.

"The Empress Rising," Salbhai continued, his eyes glittering. "You are perhaps more like Emperor Bhur than you know."

Erida sorely doubted it. Bhur was an old man, gray and fading, with little taste for glory anymore. When he eventually died, his sons would war for his empire, and carve up the once mighty Temurijon.

I will not make the same mistake.

"I should like to meet him one day," Erida replied, smiling.

On the battlefield, beneath a white flag.

Salbhai grinned too, showing even teeth. The smile did not reach his eyes. "I believe you shall."

The servants moved the length of the high table, laying down elegant platters of food, each one richer than the last. The kitchens were eager to impress their victorious queen and her guests. Erida indicated a roast swan, skinned for cooking and redressed with its feathers, wings raised as if to take flight.

With a neat slash of her knife, Erida cut the swan meat.

"And to what exactly do I owe the honor of your arrival, Ambassador?" she said. "It cannot be my coronation. You would have to be Spindletouched to foresee such a thing, and journey here in time."

Salbhai shook his head. "I was only in Trazivy when I received orders."

The map in Erida's head narrowed, the scale of the realm shrinking. She forced a bite, giving herself time to think without speaking. *Only a month's ride between Trazivy and Ascal. Even less by boat*, she knew, recalculating.

"And those orders were?" Erida muttered, dropping her voice.

The ambassador twitched a smirk. "I see no use in burying my purpose here."

Erida's grip tightened on her knife. "I will dig it up if you do."

"Of that, I am certain, Your Majesty," Salbhai laughed, grinning openly at her, as if she were some amusing child instead of a ruling queen. "You have undertaken wars of conquest across the east, rapidly bringing three kingdoms into your domain. And you are hardly finished in your work."

Before Erida could form a reply, Salbhai continued, cutting off any retort.

"Emperor Bhur is a conqueror too." He leaned closer, until Erida could see the dark freckles spread across his nose. Born of days in the sun, not the shadows of an imperial court. "He holds all the northern territories under his thumb. But for the little kingdoms, and even they know the truth of their freedom."

Trec, Uscora, Dahland, Ledor. Erida rattled off the border kingdoms in her mind. Buffers between the Temurijon empire and the rest of the realm.

"What is your aim, Queen Erida, Empress Rising?" Salbhai murmured, staring into her as if he could read her mind. "Will your eyes ever turn north? Will your hunger reach across mountains? Will you threaten my people, and test the Countless upon the open plain?"

A year ago, Erida would have relied upon her small smile and downcast eyes. A young, unwed queen was easy to underestimate, and an easier character to play.

It did not suit Erida anymore.

Her courtly mask dropped. Her smirk was a snarl, her sapphire-blue eyes flashing with all the might of the oceans.

I am Erida of Galland, Queen of Four Kingdoms.

I am subject to nothing and no one.

"Do you threaten me, Lord Ambassador, Blood of the Emperor?" she hissed back at him.

Her smirk widened as the ambassador recoiled.

"We hold no desire for your kingdom, Galland or otherwise," he said quickly, scrambling to regain some ground. "Stay on your side of the mountains, Your Majesty, and we will remain on our own."

As quickly as it disappeared, Erida's court mask returned. Her smirk softened, a gentle laugh on her lips. The lies slid through her teeth like breath.

"That is all we ever desire, Ambassador," she said, returning to her dinner.

At her side, Taristan glowered at his own empty plate, clearly listening. She caught the flare of red in his eye and felt the heat of him rise, flickering like the candles.

Salbhai scowled. "We will need a show of goodwill, to cement this truce."

Again, Erida laughed. "I'm sorry to say I have no children, and no betrothals to make. Yet. That can be negotiated when the time comes."

Internally, her stomach twisted. Erida knew too well what it was to be a prize mare, sold off to the highest bidder. She already regretted the need to do the same with her own child, whoever they might be.

14

FATES WRITTEN
Sorasa

Dom and Sigil followed close on her heels. *Too close,* Sorasa thought. She could feel them hovering like nursemaids. Both thought her half-dead, weakened by hunger and torture. Their naked concern made her skin crawl.

Put the pain away, she told herself, repeating the old Amhara saying. *You don't need it.*

She did what she could, ignoring the howl of her empty stomach and the dull ache of her shoulder. Not to mention the dozen other little bruises, cuts, burns, and fractures. She faced far worse in the citadel, during the first years of her training. A dark, cool cell in the bowels of the New Palace was easy compared to weeks of abandonment in the Ibalet deserts, dying of thirst beneath an inescapable sun.

If anything, the days of silence, withdrawn into her own head, had given her all the time she needed to think.

And plan.

She navigated the dungeons quietly, turning each corner, steadily moving up the spiraling levels. Sorasa had never been imprisoned here before, but other Amhara had. Their experiences were detailed in the citadel, carefully recorded and stored among their archives. She pieced together what she remembered over the long, silent days. Until the dungeon map laid out in her mind, perfectly drawn from memory.

"How did you escape Gidastern?" Sigil blurted out as she bounded along beside the assassin.

Sorasa bit back an exasperated scoff. The last thing she wanted was another interrogation, especially under the circumstances.

"How did *you?*" Sorasa replied.

"We didn't escape, we were captured. After—" Sigil faltered, her dark eyes wavering to Dom.

Behind them, Dom loomed in his usual way, a storm cloud of contempt. His expression darkened beneath his stolen helmet. Rage and sorrow warred across his face, made even more severe by the shadows. Sorasa remembered the last she saw of him in the city, turning to fight alongside his immortal kin.

"I don't remember getting out of the city," the assassin forced out, filling the silence for Dom's sake. "But I remember Corayne, riding alone through the city gate, out onto the road."

"Why did you leave her?" The deep, familiar timbre of Dom's voice rumbled in her chest.

Sorasa's face went warm, her cheeks flaming with shame.

"To buy her a chance."

I expected to pay with my life.

Their silence was answer enough. Even Dom knew what she meant, his eyes flickering in the torchlight.

"And then I was on a boat," she sighed, walking on. "Tethered somewhere between sleep and waking. Everything smelled of death, and the sky looked like blood. I thought I was in Lasreen's realm, wandering the lands of the dead."

The days on the river were hazy at best. Sorasa had used what will she had to pray to Lasreen, her deity above all others. She even searched the heavens, looking for the shape of a faceless woman or Amavar, the dragon companion of the goddess.

Neither came, and the days wore on, wavering in and out.

"I reached Ascal in darkness, leaving the smell of death at the edge of the city. I know now it was the corpse army, Taristan's horde." Sorasa tried not to picture it, the rotting soldiers of the Ashlands, the brutalized people of Gidastern. All bound to the red wizard, ensnared forever. "They wait in the countryside, ready to obey their master."

Sigil pulled a face. "How many?"

"I do not know," Sorasa answered.

Her hand twitched in annoyance, wishing for her familiar bronze dagger. Like her other weapons, it had been taken away weeks ago. Instead, she gripped the hilt of the knight's long knife.

"Unfortunately Taristan and his wizard think highly of the Amhara, and knew to keep me bound throughout the journey." She shook her head. "It took some time for me to resurface and return to a useful state of mind."

Both bounty hunter and immortal chewed her words, wounded by them. Sorasa knew enough of their tempers to see the twitching distaste on their faces. They went quiet, their boots the only sound as they rounded another corner.

Among the echoes, Sorasa remembered.

Ronin brought her back fully for his interrogations. By then, it felt like a reprieve. Sorasa preferred pain to oblivion. The red wizard asked stupid questions of her, most of them useless. She resisted them anyway, drawing out the process of his so-called torture. As with the cells, she'd faced worse among the Amhara. Sorasa Sarn did not fear a pulled tooth or splinters shoved under her fingernails. Ronin resorted to neither, hesitant to pursue anything that would leave real damage. He relied upon forced drowning mostly, putting a bag over Sorasa's head and dumping buckets of water over her. She knew well enough how to suffer such things. With every punishment, she set the bar for pain as low as she could, reacting to the slightest discomfort. She made a show of it for Ronin's sake, her eyes rolling, her body jumping against the restraints.

It was only his magic that truly concerned her. Against that, she had no training.

Her only respite came from the interrogators and the changing guards. They did not intervene on her behalf. But they were useful, whispering to each other, carrying news from the palace above them. Even as she screamed, spitting out water, choking against a garrote, locked in an iron maiden, or dancing on her toes with her wrists bound up, she listened.

Sigil finally spoke up, shattering the tense quiet.

"If the Queen is returned, she moved quickly, to make it all the way back from Madrence," she muttered. "I wonder why?"

"Calidon is too mountainous to attack in winter, but Siscaria and Tyriot kneeled without bloodshed," Sorasa replied neatly, grateful for the change of subject. "She had no cause to linger in the east, exhausting her army. Her soldiers will be grateful to go home, victorious and drunk on glory. Besides, there's a coronation to be had. She's Queen of Four King-doms now, and she's going to show Galland exactly what that means."

Sorasa felt the incredulous looks of both Dom and Sigil.

"All this you learned in the dungeons?" the Elder growled.

Sorasa braced for his usual suspicions. She was long used to them by now.

You are ruthless and selfish, Sorasa Sarn. I know little of mortals, but of you, I know enough. Dom's words echoed in her head, too sharp a memory. His distrust stung then. It burned now.

She turned to face him, expecting fury or doubt. But there was only concern, his white face almost soft in the torchlight. It stopped her cold.

Their eyes met, emerald on copper.

"I didn't know you could get any paler, but here you stand," Sorasa spat, whirling around again. Her heartbeat rammed. "We need to get you both out into the sun again, you look terrible."

"You look worse," Sigil sighed. "What's your plan, then?"

"I heard pieces of things, here and there," Sorasa said, quickening her pace. "Pirates stalk the Long Sea, threatening port cities. Every ship into the harbor could be a hunter. Sea travel is slow and dangerous now."

"Corayne's mother is making herself useful," Sigil said, half smirking. "I knew I liked her."

"If the Queen is here, Taristan is too," Dom said, sneering up to the ceiling. As if he could see right through the floors of the palace. "We can still kill him."

"Are you going to prance off and let him knock you around again?" Sorasa wanted to grab him by the collar, lest the Elder run off to his death. "Or are you going to listen to me?"

"Tell us your plan then," he snapped back, crossing his arms over his armored chest. The lion molded to the breastplate roared at her from eye level. To anyone else, he seemed a knight of the Lionguard, deadly and imposing.

Sorasa turned to Sigil instead, meeting her gaze with a hard look.

"There is a Temur ambassador here," Sorasa said slowly, letting the ramifications sink in.

Sigil's keen dark eyes narrowed. Torchlight danced, reflecting in her gaze. Sorasa watched as the gears turned in the bounty hunter's mind and a grin split her broad face.

"I assume you've already thought what I'm thinking now," Sigil chuckled, taking Sorasa by her good shoulder.

Her grip was almost bruising but Sorasa leaned into it, her own smile small and sharp.

"Among many other things," she said.

A jailer lay dead at his post, his throat opened. Blood pooled beneath him, spreading slowly across the dirty floor of the guardroom.

Sorasa blinked slowly against the blinding glare of too many torches, willing her vision to adjust after days in the dark. Across from her, Sigil did the same. Dom required no such time, his own body braced against the iron-banded oak door. He listened, all his focus on the next chamber, and the beating hearts within.

He held up five white fingers, closed his fist, then five again.

Ten.

Sorasa wiped the Lionguard dagger on the dead guard's tunic, cleaning the blade. The other dagger twisted in Sigil's fingers, the hilt clutched in her fist. Dom still held the longsword, the torches flashing the length of the steel. Grimly, he leaned back from the door, moving without sound to stand in front of it. Even in full armor, he moved silently, with little effort.

All three knew their survival rested on speed, silence, and secrecy. All three knew the edge they stood upon. All three felt the fate of the realm in their hands.

The Elder moved first, swifter than any mortal, kicking the door down. It splintered under his force, the lock blasting inward as the oak swung on screaming hinges, flying open to reveal a small room of shocked guards.

There was hardly time enough for the men to grab their weapons, let alone call for help. Dom's sword cut through the closest two, separating heads from shoulders.

Sorasa's dagger buried in another neck, striking the guard at the far end of the room, his hand already on the next door. She slid below another guard's outstretched arm, stealing his sword and cutting him down in the same motion.

Sigil struck behind her, punching with one fist and stabbing with the other. Teeth skittered across the stone floor and bodies crashed through battered wooden furniture, sprawling over chairs and the single table. Sorasa stayed low, agile enough to wheel under any strike. She collected blades as she went, throwing one just to pick up another.

Silence fell as the bodies piled up, until there was only one guard left alive. He shuddered under the table, one hand on his throat, trying to stem the flow of blood.

Sorasa showed him the only mercy he knew.

When his heart stopped, she surveyed the guardroom with a cold eye.

There were no windows. The guardrooms were still underground, but coals crackled in a small fireplace, warming the chamber. She checked the chimney and cursed. The shaft was too small to climb, even for the Amhara.

A deck of bloodstained cards splayed over the table, alongside a few piles of coins, upended cups, and half-empty plates. Sorasa grabbed the leftover food like an animal, tearing at a piece of stale bread and dried meat. It tasted better than anything she'd ever eaten before.

Sigil busied herself with the wooden chests next to the fireplace, kicking open one after another. She pawed through bottles of bad wine, a few books, and stacks of old tunics. Then she checked the bodies themselves.

After a few seconds, she donned a leather belt and sheath, sliding a sword into place.

Sorasa followed, grabbing a sword before retrieving the Lionguard dagger. The rest of the gear was useless to them. Sorasa preferred her leathers to chain mail, and none of the jailers were anywhere close to Sigil's size.

The Elder waited at the next door, his pauldron braced against the wood, his ear pressed up to listen.

As before, Sigil and Sorasa flanked him, watching for his count.

This time, he held up three fingers.

So it went through the palace dungeons.

Blood ran beneath doors and over stone. Green tunics fell in their wake, jailers and castle guards alike. Dom listened, Sigil looted, and Sorasa led, taking them past bunk quarters and storerooms, tracing paths remembered from a scrap of parchment. They gathered supplies with every step. Sorasa shouldered a bow, a quiver of arrows at her hip, while Sigil squeezed herself into a coat of chain mail and jacket.

All this they did in relative silence, the only sounds the hiss of steel or the wet rattle of a dying breath. Until Sigil threw open one last chest, half hidden behind a tapestry.

She bit her lip, subduing a whoop. Sorasa leapt to her side, heart rising in her throat.

Sigil's broken ax smiled up at them, the edge catching the candlelight. Even snapped in two, the Temur weapon had never looked so beautiful, the long wooden handle wrapped in black leather and copper. Grinning, Sigil picked up the two pieces, and fixed them to her sword belt.

Beneath the ax was a greatsword, still in its sheath, attached to a fine belt. Sorasa recognized the intricate Elder craftsmanship, a pattern of galloping stags worked into the oiled leather. She passed the blade over to Dom wordlessly.

He exhaled a long breath, turning the sword over in his hands. With a flick, he drew it an inch, exposing the Elder steel within. His ancient language stared up at him, etched into the sword.

Sorasa's own hands found the Amhara dagger at the bottom of the chest, beneath a tattered old cloak the color of moss. She pushed it aside with shaking fingers, drawing out the bronze blade as she would a baby from the cradle. Her belt was there too, dangling with her pouches of powders and poisons. She snatched it up greedily, buckling it into place around her hips. The weight felt like a warm embrace.

Their old gear, battered by too many battles, was a strange comfort. Sigil donned her padded armor, the black leather plates linking together neatly despite a good many rips. Dom drew out his Ionian cloak, half-destroyed, the green-gray fabric near to ruins. Stags ran the length of the hem, embroidered in fraying silver thread. Sigil opened her mouth to scoff but Sorasa cut her off with a sharp look. It surprised them both.

Dom didn't notice. Stone-faced, he tore off the cleanest square he could, tucking the little piece of his enclave away.

The rest he left, abandoning it forever.

Sorasa felt a little like the old wool: bloody and frayed, worn through. But still alive.

"This way," she murmured, indicating the next door.

The dirty floors were gone, swept clean to reveal flagstones and mortar. They trekked down the last passage, to the final stairway dividing the dungeons from the barracks above. Fresh air seared down Sorasa's throat. She breathed greedily, sucking it down, filling her lungs with cold, damp hope.

The palace lay ahead.

And only death behind.

"The guards change one hour after sunset," Sorasa said, eyeing the landing. Dark red light spilled down from the top of the stairs. The last rays of a dying sun.

One hour until someone discovers the bodies.

Sigil ran a thumb down the edge of her broken ax. "I hope it's enough."

Dom took the first step, and then the next, never looking back. With his armor, helmet, and green cloak of the Lionguard, no soldier ahead would dare stop him.

"It will be," he rumbled, breaking into a silent run.

Low as it was, Sorasa heard his whisper, nearly lost to the spiraling stone.

"With me," he said.

She bit her own lip, nearly drawing blood. The response welled up in her throat anyway.

With me.

The last time Sorasa Sarn crept through the winding halls of the New Palace, she had no fear. Back then, Sorasa cared little for the state of the realm, or the ramblings of a preening Elder prince. Her task was finished, Corayne an-Amarat delivered safely to the Queen of Galland. The Amhara played her part and moved on, lingering only to serve her own curiosity.

She knew how well that ended.

Now, she rolled through the passages in a rushing tide, the realm's fate chasing behind her. The New Palace flared in Sorasa's mind, big as a city, its many passages like veins beneath skin. She thought of tunnels, servant hallways, crawlspaces and attics. Cellars, crumbling towers, vaults, little chapels abandoned for the night. The Amhara Guild collected it all through countless years and contracts, creating a map for its assassins to learn.

There were certainly more guards than before, a fact Sorasa took great pride in. The watch patrols had at least doubled since her last visit.

But they were still no match for Amhara knowledge or Dom's senses. Together, they moved quickly, avoiding or punching through all obstacles. There was no time to fear, no time to think about anything other than the next inch forward.

Sorasa's plan spiraled, every step built hastily on the next. It felt like laying the stones of a road before an oncoming horse. Quickly, she navigated the barracks, then the gardens, cutting through the hedge maze toward the old keep.

Neither Sigil nor Dom spoke. They trusted Sorasa to get them where they needed to go. Even Dom didn't argue, to Sorasa's surprise. His doubt was familiar, if annoying. His faith was more difficult to navigate.

The black towers of the old keep blazed with torches, green banners streaming from every window. Guards prowled high above them, but none below. There was no cause for alarm in the palace.

Yet.

Sorasa wasted no time explaining and grabbed for the closest banner. She crawled up its length as easily as climbing a ladder, despite the dull ache in her shoulder. Sigil and Dom trailed along, following her up the steps to the lowest window of the keep. At Dom's signal, she slammed her elbow through a pane of glass, shattering it inward to spray across the floor of an empty spiraling stair.

She landed inside with the grace of a spider, the other two close behind. There were no bedchambers or personal quarters in the old keep, but offices for the Queen and her council. Meaning it was mostly empty.

They tracked the few guards, moving behind their watch pattern. Sorasa killed only one when he stopped short, examining an old tapestry. She shoved him headfirst into a closet, folding his legs over his body. Her work was quick. Not even a drop of blood stained the floor.

She felt Dom's glare the whole time.

"I won't remind you how many corpses you left in the dungeons," she hissed, latching the closet door shut.

From the passage they entered a dim library, dusty with disuse. Papers covered one of the many tables, while rugs patterned the wooden floor. Sorasa kept moving as she checked the adjoining room. With a grin, she returned with a bottle in her free hand, a brown liquid sloshing in the glass.

Dom and Sigil watched, wordless, as she doused the chamber, pouring out the bottle. The torch went next.

Flame puddled across the library. The dust, the papers, the carpets and old heavy drapes went up like candles, an inferno sparking to life.

Sigil smiled through the flames, striking a fist to her chest.

The burst of triumph didn't last. Sorasa's throat tightened as the heat hit her face, the smell of smoke strangling. For a split second, she was back in Gidastern, the city burning around her, the screams of the dead filling her ears. The flames danced, taking the shapes of Infyrna hounds and corpse soldiers, all jumping and leaping.

An armored hand touched her shoulder and she flinched. The vision broke and she whirled away from Dom, putting her back to the library.

"Keep moving," she bit out, though she was the one frozen.

They went from room to room, fire trailing through the honeycombed chambers of the castle.

Dom loosed a low growl, stopping them short. "Half a dozen guards coming this way, they're running."

Smirking, Sorasa turned to the wood-paneled wall of the corridor. "Good."

With a well-placed fist, she knocked at a corner of the paneling. It swung backward on greased hinges, revealing a small, dark hallway, the kind used by servants. They ducked in without question.

The low ceiling forced Dom and Sigil to stoop and angle sideways, their broad shoulders scraping against the old walls. Sorasa had no such trouble, all but skipping through the passages.

"If we're lucky, the fire will cover our tracks," she said. As they ran, she watched the walls, studying the stonework. "The guards will be too busy saving the old keep to check the dungeons."

"Oh, I just thought you hated libraries," Sigil muttered.

Sorasa's true laugh echoed off the stone.

"And if we're very lucky . . ."

The assassin trailed off, stopping at the top of a curving stair. She ran a hand over the wall to her left, the exterior of the keep. The square black stones were rough beneath her hand, their age obvious. She took a step down the stair, her fingers passing from the pitted black rock to pale yellow stone.

"If we're very lucky?" Dom prodded.

Her palm went flat against the wall. It felt cool, smooth. New. She took another step down the spiraling stair, then another. At the bottom, a door curved into view, the wood gleaming. Polished oak.

"I'll let you know if it happens," Sorasa answered, to his annoyance. Even as she smiled, she tried not to think of the flames consuming everything around her again. "Shall we?"

Dom nodded stiffly and she wrenched open the door below, leaving behind the old keep.

Sorasa kept a sharp eye for servants, though they would hardly question a Lionguard knight. Part of her was surprised by the ease of their journey through the palace. The doubled guard should have been more of an obstacle. But most of the palace soldiers were halfwits and Erida thought herself safe in the heart of her kingdom. She had no cause to look for danger. Her war was far beyond the walls of Ascal, not inside her own palace.

The Queen's pride made her shortsighted, and Sorasa intended to use it to full advantage.

The servants' stair led down to another narrow passage. It ran long and straight, dimly lit by torches, with squat columns arching overhead. Storerooms marched along the right, cave-like and tunneled together. Most were piled high with stores of food, meant to feed the palace through the winter.

"We must be close to the kitchens," Sigil said, grabbing a whole onion from the closest sack. She bit into it like an apple.

Sorasa jabbed a thumb over her shoulder. She barely noticed the dried meat in her hand, half of it already in her mouth.

"Behind us," she said. "Ahead is the royal residence. There's a stairwell all the way up to Erida's own chambers."

"And what is above us?" Dom eyed the ceiling. It was not stone, but thick wooden beams, holding up the floor above them.

"You already know," she answered, reading the sharpness of his features.

Beneath his helmet, Dom furrowed his brow. His gauntleted fist closed on the hilt of his sword.

"The great hall," he growled.

His cape wound around Sorasa's fist, as if her grip would truly stop Domacridhan should he choose to bolt. Still, she pulled it taut.

"Don't even think about it, Dom," she said through gritted teeth.

He glared down on her. "I thought you wanted to be useful," he hissed back.

"Useful, not *dead*. Taristan will kill us if we're found, or worse." Sorasa loosed an exasperated sigh. She fought back the familiar urge to beat some sense into the immortal. "You agreed to this. Sigil will get the Temur out of here. We burn what we can, head for the lagoon, and swim out."

Dom wrinkled his nose and grimaced. He opened his mouth to argue, only to stop short, tipping his head.

With the wave of a hand, Dom ushered the three of them into the closest storeroom. They pressed in, only to face endless rows of ale and wine, stored in giant barrels. There was also a wall of mismatched bottles, liquors imported from every corner of the Ward. It looked enough to drown a Treckish war band.

Sigil slipped behind one, the barrel taller than she was. Dom kept his eyes on Sorasa, his glare like green fire. He backed her into a corner, hiding them both from the doorway.

Sorasa ignored his infernal closeness and listened for the gentle pattern of footsteps. Out in the passage, a pair of servants idled by, chattering in low voices.

Only when Dom sighed did Sorasa uncoil. The servants were gone.

Scowling, she put both hands to Dom's chest and shoved with all the strength she could muster. It felt like pushing against a brick wall.

"Do you think you're going to take Taristan on in front of Erida's entire court? Save the realm in a blaze of glory?" she laughed, throwing back her head. "I thought your time in the cells would give you a little more perspective, Dom."

"I find it difficult to manage perspective when facing the end of the world," he said tightly, throwing off his helmet. It clanged against the wall.

Without the helm, he was too easy to read. Sorasa had seen it all before, the frustration and rage of Prince Domacridhan. He mourned without knowing how, and now he faced another failure. Not just losing Corayne, but walking away from Taristan. To leave him alive was to admit defeat, something Dom still had not learned how to do.

"You can't beat him, Dom," she said softly, keeping her distance. The tight air of the storeroom heated with their presence, warmed by their bodies and breath. "None of us can, not now. Not even together."

To that, the Elder had no answer, his face like stone.

Sigil looked on, stern for once. She took a step toward the Elder, as if handling a spooked horse.

"I have to warn the Temur." Her voice took on a softer edge than Sorasa knew Sigil possessed. "The ambassador is here to negotiate, but there's no negotiating with Erida anymore. Not with Taristan by her side."

Sigil kept her eyes on Dom, imploring.

"If we can get the Temur out of the city, they can go to Emperor Bhur." Her jaw clenched, a muscle twitching in her cheek.

Dom did not answer, his gaze fixed on the wall.

"That is the most useful thing we can do, Dom," Sorasa said, trailing the path of Sigil's logic. "If the Emperor can be convinced to fight, the Ward might have a chance against Erida's armies."

"Neither of you need me for that," Dom spat out, whirling around. In the armor, he looked the picture of a brave knight, bound by duty and honor.

Or caged by it, Sorasa thought.

"You're right, we don't," she snapped back at him. "But *Corayne* does need you."

By now, Sorasa lost count of how many times Dom had been injured in front of her. Stabbed, burned, bruised. Strangled by a kraken's tentacle.

Nearly trampled by stampeding horses. Laid low by the tolling of a bell, high in the tower of a temple lost.

Somehow, her words cut deeper than all the rest.

His face fell, the grim scowl sliding away.

Any Amhara knew how to spot an opportunity, and Sorasa took hers. She twisted the knife in his heart.

"Corayne is still out there, alive," she pleaded, her own desperation coloring her voice. "Don't abandon her for Taristan's sake."

The Elder met the assassin's eyes, a storm in him. She weathered it, refusing to break his stare.

"For Corayne," he finally growled.

Some tightness released in Sorasa's chest and she exhaled slowly, grateful.

A dull pop sounded and she spun, only to find Sigil holding a glass bottle in one hand, a cork in the other. Smirking, she raised the bottle of clear liquid, letting it slosh. Sorasa caught the sharp, acrid smell of gorzka.

"For Corayne," Sigil echoed, taking a gulp. She winced as the Treck-ish liquor burned down her throat.

Dom rolled his eyes at her and shook his head. "Sigil—"

The bounty hunter waved him off. "I'm about to play the part of a drunk foreigner, stumbling around a palace I don't know. I should smell the part at least."

He pulled a face but didn't stop her. "Fair enough."

Sigil raised the bottle again. Her eyes met Sorasa's over the glass, her gaze darkening. The Temur woman toasted once more, this time to Sorasa herself.

The assassin did not raise a bottle in return, but dipped her brow all the same. They spoke easily, without words, seeing what Dom could not. Again, Sorasa's throat tightened. All these months, Sigil was a wall behind her, someone to lean on, as close to a trustworthy friend as Sorasa had. After almost losing her in Gidastern, farewell felt like salt in a still-bleeding wound.

But Sorasa respected Sigil too much to embarrass her with goodbyes.

Our paths have already been laid, our fates written by godly hands.

She only hoped the ink of their lives wove together for a little while still.

15

THE RIGHT TO DIE
Domacridhan

Sorasa had her uses, this Domacridhan knew too well. They would have never escaped the dungeons without her knowledge, her wiles, or her simple endurance. To suffer long days without food or water, let alone after torture, and still fight. It was more than admirable. Immortal as he was, Dom could not fathom the pain she faced then, or the pain she ignored now.

But still he hated her.

For Corayne.

Sorasa's plea was worse than a knife in the gut, worse than any betrayal he once believed her capable of. Because there was no fighting it. Her logic was sound, her reasoning inarguable. Stoic as he looked, Dom raged inside. He felt chained again, back in that infernal cell. Only now his bars were Sorasa Sarn. She alone kept him from leaving the storeroom and climbing up the servant stair, to wait in the Queen's chambers for one last chance at redemption. Taristan was invincible still, but without his Spindleblade. Perhaps the loss of it was enough, a single chink in his otherwise demonic armor.

Even Dom knew it was a foolish hope.

Sorasa is right, he knew, cursing her for it.

Raging against Sarn was familiar, at least. An easy crutch to lean on, an easy fuel to burn.

But it didn't make waiting any less torturous. Dom listened intently to the feast above, trying to pick familiar voices out from the scrape of plates and chairs. It was no use. Too many heartbeats, too many bodies. He suspected hundreds of courtiers sat above them, eager to welcome their ruinous queen home. He hated Erida too, little that he knew of her. Her marriage to Taristan was enough. She willingly tied herself to a beast in mortal skin, all for a few jewels in a crown.

He focused on footsteps instead, tracking the courtiers as they finished dinner and the servants in the halls nearby. The guards were easiest to pick out, their footsteps heavy with the weight of weapons and chain mail. A contingent of knights clanked overhead, marching out of the hall and up a grand stair. Dom bit his lip, listening hard. Lighter footsteps followed the knights up the tower, to the royal residence and a distant bedchamber high above.

Erida and Taristan, he knew. His stomach turned, skin crawling with every step they climbed. Until the sound of them faded away, even the clatter of the knights lost to his immortal ears.

It took all his will to stay put, to listen.

And to wait.

Sorasa and Sigil were right about the Temur. Even Dom could admit that. The Emperor was still the greatest obstacle in Erida and Taristan's path.

Besides Corayne.

Dom's heart clenched. He thought of Corayne, wherever she might be, alone and wandering through the wilderness. He knew little of sending magic but reached for a whisper of it anyway, letting the ache in his chest guide. He found only darkness in the corners of his mind, only fear and doubt. Corayne was beyond his protection.

For now, he told himself, growling low in his throat. *For now.*

Shouts echoed distantly, booted feet rushing overhead, and Dom grimaced.

"Fire!" one of them shouted.

"It's time," he said reluctantly, donning his helmet.

Across the storeroom, Sorasa squinted over the cache of liquor, each bottle a little glass jewel. She paused in her examination to survey Dom, her copper glare spearing him through his armor.

"Keep to the plan," she warned. "I'll be right behind you."

Sigil nodded without hesitation.

After a long, excruciating moment, Dom did too. He did not doubt Sorasa Sarn, not anymore.

His faith flagged anyway. Not in the bounty hunter. Not in the assassin.

But in his own immortal heart.

The New Palace was mostly as he remembered it. Gilded and polished, fit for the wealthiest mortal kingdom in the Ward. But there were far more roses than before. Woven into tapestries, blooming from vases. Beneath his helmet, Dom sneered at them, the thorns winding around the paws of the Gallish lion, a rose in its roaring mouth. He wanted it all to burn, and Taristan with it.

Sigil ran alongside him, her steps swaying and off balance. She played the part of a drunk well, as Dom played the part of the knight.

Up ahead, the guards around the great hall were already in chaos, rushing back and forth.

"Fire in the old keep," one of them shouted, pointing back along the passageways.

Another spotted Dom on the approach. His eyes swept past Sigil entirely and he dipped into a low bow. The other guards mirrored him quickly, deferential to a knight of the Lionguard.

"My lord, fire—"

"Attend to your duties," Dom barked out, doing his best to seem like a knight. That is, stiff and over-proud.

Beyond the guards, the great hall looked half-empty, with only a few courtiers still within. They peered out, drunk and curious, half-interested in the commotion.

The Temur remained, their heads bent together around a gray-haired man who looked to be their leader.

Sigil wasted no time, grinning toward her countrymen.

"The iron bones of the Countless," she called out, thumping her chest, "will never be broken!"

At their table, the Temur whirled, turning in Sigil's direction. A few answered the call instinctively, speaking the words of the Temurijon. All looked confused, their bronze faces furrowed with suspicion.

Dom did not speak Temur, but he knew what Sigil told them next. *Move. Now.*

Watching her, Dom felt some tension release in his chest. The Temur welcomed Sigil as they would an old friend, chattering happily in their own language. Whatever her game, they played along without hesitation, and even the ambassador took her under his arm. Quickly, they made for the doorway, abandoning their table at Sigil's behest. To anyone else watching, they simply looked like courtiers done in for the night. One even tipped his head to the guards as they passed, leaving the great hall behind.

Dom let them go, sparing only a single glance at Sigil. She winked back at him, until the Temur closed around her.

"Prince Taristan and Her Majesty have safely retired for the evening, my lord. Should we abandon our posts to aid in the keep?" the closest guard said, but Dom ignored him.

Go! he screamed at himself, willing his feet to move. His task was done, Sigil safely delivered to her kinfolk. Despite his immortal nature, the Lionguard armor felt heavy on his limbs.

It was no mystery as to why. Every step was another inch away from the Queen's chambers. From Taristan and Erida. Guarded only by mortal knights. The temptation of it was nearly blinding.

Keep to the plan.

Sorasa's voice echoed in his head. Dom listened for her heartbeat in vain, but it was lost to the sounds of the hall. And beneath it, the steady crackle of flame as it consumed the old keep.

Reluctantly, Dom turned to leave. It felt like the closing of a door, like surrender. In his chest, something tore. He barely heard the guards calling after him. Their voices warbled in Dom's ears, faded and faraway. He could only keep walking, one foot in front of the other.

This was the plan, this was the chance. He need only keep moving. Sorasa would do the rest.

Dom alone heard the snap of wood, the splintering of barrels, the cracking of many, many glass bottles beneath their feet. He braced, fists clenching, squaring his shoulders.

The explosion rippled, the force of it breaking against Dom's back. He turned into the concussive wall of sound, just in time to watch the floor of the great hall crumble inward, collapsing into the storerooms below. As in the old keep, great columns of flame jumped up, fed by the liquor stores below. The barrels of ale and wine became a lake of fire, the bottles of spirits spitting glass. A swell of heat pulsed out in a wave, breaking against Dom's face, heating the steel of his armor so quickly he ripped off his helmet.

He watched, wide-eyed, as tables and benches fell to the storerooms below, courtiers toppling with them. At the far end of the hall, the dais remained, hanging out over the open wound that was the floor.

The Temur were already out of harm's way, safely ushered along by Sigil. But the lords and ladies of Erida's court screamed, fighting their way out of the great hall any way they could.

"Evacuate!" a guard yelled somewhere, his shout barely audible over the roar of flame.

"Get outside!" "Get over the bridge!" "Save the Queen!"

Many voices called back and forth, the servants, nobles, and guards spilling out into the corridors in all directions. A few loyal soldiers fled deeper into the hall, fighting against the blaze to reach the Queen's tower on the far side. But most fled.

It was better to run and risk treason than stay and be burned alive.

Sigil and the Temur broke for the nearest way out, and Dom followed, catching up in an instant. Many of the courtiers ran after him, desperate sheep in need of a shepherd.

Despite his hatred for Galland, Dom threw the exterior doors wide and stood back, waving for the courtiers to escape into the courtyard.

"This way!" he boomed, putting out an arm to hold the door wide.

Outside, he glimpsed the main gate, the Bridge of Valor arching beyond it. Back into the streets of Ascal. Only the canal separated the palace from the great city, its alleys and gutters a sanctuary just out of reach.

The grateful courtiers ran for him, seeing a knight of the Lionguard, a protector. They surged out of the palace, coughing violently against the smoke. Great black plumes rose out of the collapsed floor and Dom was reminded of the dragon for a second, its jaws pouring ashes. With a sniff he realized it was not just the hall on fire.

The old keep still burned too.

The Temur vaulted into the open air of the courtyard, never breaking stride. Dom watched, stone-faced, as Sigil shoved the last of them out the door.

Without thinking, she grabbed Dom's neck and pulled, trying to drag him along.

The immortal did not budge. It was as good as trying to rip up a tree stump.

Sigil hissed, the flames gleaming in her eyes. "Keep to the plan," she snarled, throwing Sorasa's words back in his face. "*This* is the plan."

"I don't see her," Dom snarled back, breaking Sigil's hold. He looked back to the hall again, expectant. But there was no Amhara shadow among the nobles and servants. No copper eyes finding him in the smoke.

The bounty hunter gnashed her teeth, hovering in the doorway. Behind her, one of the keep towers went up in a plume of flame. The Temur ambassador called out in his language, beckoning back to Sigil.

She winced, true pain written across her face.

"Sorasa will be right behind us," she bit out. "She knows what she's doing."

Dom did not doubt it.

He put a gauntleted hand to Sigil's shoulder and pushed, sending her falling back on her heels. She wheeled her arms to keep her balance, a shocked look on her face.

Dom was already gone from the door, retreating back into a palace gone to ashes.

"So do I."

He shoved against the tide of the panicked crowd, wading through the courtiers as he would water.

Sorasa is going to bring the entire palace down, burn this island, and every person on it.

What was an opulent hall only moments ago looked Spindletorn, burning as Gidastern did. Tapestries flamed along the walls and stained glass cracked in the windows, shattering across what remained of the floor. Every piece of the hall seemed primed to feed a fire, the lacquered wood melting, the wine-soaked linens turned to flame. Dom tried not to breathe too deeply. The smoke stung his nose and eyes anyway. He felt the steel of his armor heat against his clothing, growing hotter with every step. He soldiered through it all. It was too easy to turn from the discomfort, his focus narrowing to the path laid out in front of him.

The edge of the ruined floor charred, the wood burning and rushes flaking away as the hole before him grew. A few guards pressed against the walls, inching their way forward in an attempt to reach the Queen's tower. Their terrified faces glowed white against the red tongues of flame.

Dom didn't hesitate, leaping down into the crater.

Puddles flamed across the stone floor. Fire ate through the barrels, their hoops like empty rib cages. A few glass bottles popped, shattering as the alcohol inside ignited. He stalked past them all, ignoring the heat rising all around him, inside his armor and out.

Ahead is the royal residence. There's a stairwell all the way up to Erida's own chambers.

Sorasa said as much not an hour ago. He followed her voice as he would a signpost. The passages were stone, giving no quarter to the fire still raging behind him. He ran, dreamlike, ashes spiraling in his wake. Embers landed in his cloak and he ripped it aside, abandoning the mantle of a dead knight, leaving it behind to burn.

The stair was as Sorasa said, at the end of the long corridor.

He climbed eagerly. He did not tire nor falter. He did not fear anything but failure, or worse, disgrace. When he reached the top, hundreds of steps spiraling out below, Dom drew his greatsword. The blade drew quietly from its sheath, gleaming dimly in the weak light of the servants' passage.

A heartbeat thumped behind the only door on the landing. The rhythm was strong and steady.

Dom threw open the door without warning, kicking it wide to reveal the Queen's solar. And a Lionguard knight posted like a statue. He faced the servant door, his golden armor glowing beneath the light of a hundred candles.

The knight jolted, jumping to attention.

"What is it? What was that sound below?" he blurted out, until his gaze sharpened, his eyes tracing the lines of an unfamiliar face beneath a too-familiar helmet.

He moved for his sword, but far too slowly.

The hesitation was all Dom needed.

He cut once, sword angling through the air. Blood spurted through the space between the knight's helmet and his steel gorget, a red river running from his throat.

Two more Lionguard charged from the far side of the solar, closing the distance down the long room. One of them called out to the fallen and the other roared, his blade drawn.

Dom moved better than they did in heavy armor, weaving between the arcs of two whirling swords. Gallish knights were built for the melee, to overpower any opponent with good steel and the strength of their arm. The Lionguard were most revered of all, handpicked to defend the ruler of Galland from all danger. Many kings were saved by their skill, many battles turned by the swing of their sword.

It would not be so today.

Against Domacridhan, they had no advantage at all. He held more speed, skill, and brute force than both of them put together. Not to mention sheer will.

Steel bit steel, clanging through the solar. The other knight came around to flank Dom but the immortal perceived, dropping to a knee to throw the first off balance. When the Lionguard stumbled, Dom lunged. His sword drove straight through the lion's snarling face, shearing through steel, chain mail, and cloth, into flesh and bone beneath.

The skewered knight screamed in agony, grasping at the sword sticking out of his chest. With a jerk of his arm, Dom drew it loose and let the knight collapse, a hole through his center.

It was the work of only a few quick seconds, stunning to mortal eyes.

The surviving Lionguard rolled back on his heels, almost falling over himself. Dom expected him to surrender. Instead, the knight kept his sword raised, a guard between them. As if it would do anything at all.

"You will not touch the Queen," the knight said, his voice wavering. Beneath his helmet, tears glimmered.

"I don't care about your queen," Dom growled, slashing.

The force of his blow knocked the blade from the knight's hand, his grip on the hilt breaking. Still, he did not relent, raising his gauntleted fists to fight even as he backed across the solar.

Dom did not break stride, following the knight like a hunter tracking prey. As much as it pained him to do so.

The knight loosed a low hiss of frustration. Sweat beaded down his face, rolling off his chin to drip down his armor.

"I am sworn to defend Prince Taristan too," he said. It sounded like a question.

"Defend him then," Dom answered. He angled his shoulders, so that the servant door appeared behind him. It was a clear invitation. "Or run."

The knight held his ground.

Domacridhan was quick and merciful, a Vederan prayer falling from his lips as the knight fell to the floor.

Grim-faced, the immortal stepped over the body. Flames already licked at the knight's feet, looking for more to consume.

The Queen's apartments were richly furnished, even compared to the halls in the rest of the palace. Dom hated it all, the trappings of conquest and greed. Without thought, he dragged an arm over the closest table, knocking over a row of candles. Wax ran thick over polished wood. He kicked over another candle stand, not bothering to watch as the heavy brocade drapes caught fire.

"Do you know the definition of insanity, Domacridhan?"

He recognized the voice too well, the deep ripples of power woven into each word.

Mortal and demon both.

Taristan stood tall at the far end of the solar, planted in a doorway.

The Queen's bedroom opened behind him, all velvet and gold again. Firelight danced at his back, low and controlled, from an unseen hearth. It edged Taristan's silhouette in pulsing red, the hard lines of his face drawn sharply between scarlet and shadow.

As always, Dom saw Cortael first, brought back to life by the very man that killed him. But Taristan was not Cortael, twins though they were. His eyes were sharper, more cruel, filled with hunger instead of pride. Where Cortael was a loyal hound, Taristan was a starving wolf, always scratching for his next meal. Always alone, surviving through any means necessary.

The son of Old Cor leaned against the heavy doorframe, disheveled by sleep or something else. Dom noted his mussed hair and the open collar of his white shirt. He'd dressed hastily, wearing black leather breeches and no shoes, barefoot on the parquet. White veins spidered up his exposed ankles and chest, reaching his neck. They looked like painful scars against pale skin.

Taristan clutched a sword like an afterthought. He looped it lazily between them, the arcing blade his only smile.

"It's doing the same thing over and over again," Taristan offered, still leaning. "And somehow still expecting a different outcome."

The fire spread like plague behind Dom, the heat of it breaking against his back. Its light grew, throwing lashes of gold against Taristan's face, illuminating him fully.

Dom smirked at Corayne's handiwork, a jagged line torn across Taristan's cheek. The wound was healing but slowly, an ugly thing.

It was not alone.

There were burns on his neck, pink and shining as they trailed down to his exposed collarbone. Cuts crisscrossed his knuckles and a half-healed bruise peeked out beneath the sleeve of his shirt, yellow against a muscled forearm.

Dom felt his own eyes widen, shock coursing through his veins. He sucked down a gasp of air through gritted teeth. It tasted like smoke, tinged with the iron of freshly spilled blood. A monstrous hope leapt up inside him.

He can be wounded.

He can be killed.

"Today is not the same, Taristan," he whispered, raising his own blade. The edge glimmered red, still dripping knightsblood.

Something shifted in Taristan. The wolf in him snarled, cornered. *Dangerous as ever. But vulnerable*, Dom thought.

Dom had never seen fear in Taristan's hateful eyes, but he knew it now.

"Gifts easily given are easily taken away, it seems," the immortal said.

He took a sliding step forward. Centuries of training took hold and he sank into the stance of a skilled swordsman.

For once, Taristan held his tongue.

Dom angled his head, letting his senses flare. Another heartbeat sounded in the room behind him, her pulse thrumming. He could hear the Queen breathing, out of rhythm, ragged. She was afraid too, and rightfully so. Her palace burned and her own knights lay slain behind Domacridhan, with only her prince between them.

"You are alone," Dom said, tasting the sharp tang of blood in his mouth. "No wizard. No guards."

A flicker of rage crossed Taristan's face, the only answer Dom needed.

"I'm surprised your queen has no manner of escape from her own bedroom." Dom took another step. "Though no passages out means no passages in, either."

Taristan mirrored his footing. With a jolt, Dom realized the bastard moved to defend, not attack. As he watched, Taristan's eyes flared red, a ring of flame bursting to match the burning room.

What Waits loomed, like a shadow on the wall. Dom could almost feel Him, the air heavy with His cursed presence. But strong as the Demon King was, He could not cross into the realm.

Yet.

Dom bared his teeth, to Taristan and the dark god inside him.

"I did not think you capable of caring for another. Not even your wizard," he taunted. "But the Queen of Galland?"

Taristan kept still, his voice strangled and forced. "Talk all you like, Elder. It will not change the end of this tale."

"A king of ashes is still a king," Dom cut back, throwing out Taristan's own words spoken long ago.

He felt dangerous, lethal. Once Sorasa called the immortals somewhere between man and beast. In this moment, Dom believed it.

"Will Erida be ashes beneath your feet like the rest of us?"

Silence was Taristan's only reply, louder than the crack of flame.

"If you burn the world, she burns with it," Dom hissed.

Behind Taristan, Erida's heartbeat quickened.

It was not meant to convince Taristan of anything, to turn his heart or mind. Dom held few illusions about Taristan's capacity for remorse. Or love.

To his surprise, Taristan's grim face shifted, a smirk twisting his lips.

"Do you think about her?" the Prince of Old Cor asked in a low growl. "The Elder, the one who died in Gidastern. Died right in front of you."

Ridha.

Her name was a wound Dom could never heal. Just the thought of her made his vision haze.

Taristan's smirk widened and Dom's stomach churned.

"No, *died* isn't the proper word," he said, filled with cruel glee. "*Murdered*, more like it. I killed her. Put a dagger right here, letting the immortal ages bleed out of her."

With his free hand, he touched the flesh between his ribs. Dom remembered all too well the sight of a blade shearing through metal armor, skin, and Ridha's still-beating heart.

"And then—"

Rage seized Dom with both hands and the world blurred. He did not feel the floorboards beneath his boots nor the rush of air against his face. The sword swung seemingly of its own accord, following a path worn by long centuries of training.

Smoke and shadow coiled around Taristan as he moved to dodge the blow. To Dom, he was no longer a mortal man, merely the pet of a demon, but the demon himself. His white hands were claws of bone, his black eyes two hollows. There was no mortal heart in him, not even the one Dom heard beating in his chest.

Taristan was a monster and nothing else.

Their blades met with glancing blows, one edge sliding off the other. Vulnerable though he was, Taristan still carried the strength of What Waits in him. He more than held his own against an immortal, the fall of his sword like a bolt of lightning. Dom turned and parried, using his momentum to deflect. The blade caught the edge of Dom's arm anyway, slicing through the gold-plated steel as a knife cuts through butter.

Taristan smiled as the ruined vambrace fell away, the steel plate and shredded buckles clattering to the ground.

Dom ignored it. He disliked fighting in armor, let alone the armor of a dead man.

He set his jaw and whirled, faster than Taristan. Dom still had some advantage and used it well, striking with a flurry of shrieking blows. Taristan barely weathered them all, breathing hard as their steel screamed, but he refused to move from the doorway.

Dom saw the advantage there too.

At the temple and in Gidastern, Taristan fought for himself. Nothing else, not even Ronin. He wove and leaned, outmaneuvering his enemies. The lack of regard made him more dangerous than anyone else.

But he can't do that here, Dom realized. *Not without leaving the Queen*.

Snarling, Dom barreled forward, forgetting the dance of swords to collide with Taristan. The shock of it was shield enough and Taristan wheeled backward, driven by sheer force. They tumbled together into the Queen's bedroom, destroying everything in their wake. Their swords fell to the floor, sliding over the rich carpets.

The flames followed.

Dom pulled back a gauntleted fist and struck. Steel knuckles found the side of Taristan's jaw. He howled, spitting blood, and crashed to the floor.

Dom followed, crushing Taristan beneath him, pinning him with every inch of his strength. Bone smacked against wood as Taristan's skull snapped back against the floor. His eyes rolled.

Dom wasted no time and rocked back on his knees, curling a fist to swing.

Somewhere in the room, Erida screamed; a broken, hollow sound. Born not of fear but frustration, enraged.

Dom whirled just in time to catch a porcelain vase with his face. It shattered, water and thorny roses spilling over him. The Queen of Galland stood in a simple nightdress, her pale skin flushing red, her blue eyes bright as the fire.

It was the only opportunity Taristan needed. He grasped Dom's neck and pulled him back down. Close enough to slam his skull against Dom's brow.

Stars exploded behind the immortal's eyes. His head spun and he rolled sideways in a daze, fighting the urge to vomit. As his vision angled, Erida ran past him, scrambling for her prince's sword.

Taristan leapt up, bleeding from a cut over one eye. It ran dark red, a bloody tear coursing down his face. Erida of Galland rejoined him and raised her chin, staring down her nose at Dom. Wordless, she held out a sword and pressed it back into Taristan's hands.

"Kill him," she said, all venom.

On the floor, Dom fought through the haze. He heard the hiss of steel slicing air and forced himself to roll, narrowly avoiding a slash of Taristan's sword. On his back, Dom kicked a leg aimlessly and connected with his chest. The prince sprawled backward, giving Dom enough time to retrieve his sword. Gasping, Dom gripped the bed and climbed to his feet.

Half his armor was broken, the golden plates dangling off his body. On his chest, the roaring lion split down the middle.

Dom barely noticed the embers swirling between them, spiraling on the curls of smoke. He stared across the opulent bedroom, facing down Taristan and the Queen. Both of them stared back, statues against the roiling flames. Erida stood behind her prince, one hand on his wrist, as if to hold him back. Or keep him close.

Somehow, clad in her nightclothes, surrounded by ashes, Erida still played the part of imperious queen.

"Even I know immortals can burn," she said.

"So long as you burn with me, I die well," Dom answered.

He raised his blade once more, the steel red.

Taristan mirrored him. Streaked with soot and blood, he seemed more the desperate mercenary Dom first met at the temple, when the end of the Ward was but a storm cloud on the horizon. His sword swung and Dom met it, their blades locking. Taristan fought as Dom remembered too: more frantic, his blows unpredictable, born not of a polished castle training yard but muddy battlefields and back alleys. Even as the small cuts on him increased, slices in his white shirt, mortal blood staining his clothes, Taristan wore on.

Erida watched it all, pressed back against the windows, her eyes wavering between her husband and the flames.

Dom was a lion, but a lion in a cave. Cornered, worn down. Slowing. Taristan won cuts of his own, and Dom hissed, every movement bringing a new pain or ache. The floorboards charred beneath them, each step more precarious than the last.

Until Dom's luck ran out, the burned wood beneath him sagging under his weight. Only his immortal grace kept him from crashing through altogether and he leapt sideways, landing on firmer ground.

With a sword at his throat.

Taristan did not smile, nor laugh. Dom expected him to gloat one last time before he made an ending of it. Before he finally broke Domacridhan of Iona to his fate.

Instead, Taristan stared, black eyes edged in scarlet red. Once more, Dom looked on Taristan and saw Cortael. This time, he tried not to let the illusion fade.

His will not be the last face I look upon, not really.

The blade was cold against fevered skin, the edge of it biting a shallow line of red.

Whatever hope Dom carried guttered in his chest, flames reduced to embers. There were no prayers to be said. The gods would not hear Domacridhan in this realm, so far from Glorian. So far from home, and all he cared for.

Idly, he hoped Sorasa and Sigil were safely away, far into the city. If not already on a ship, sailing into the horizon.

"I will not bring you back, Domacridhan. Your corpse will remain where it falls," Taristan murmured, holding his form. The sword did not waver. "This, I can promise, at the very least."

Dom blinked, stunned. The offer was almost merciful.

A muscle flexed in Taristan's cheek. "You've earned the right to die in peace."

"You have a strange definition of peace."

A heartbeat as familiar as Dom's own thundered in his ears, the rhythm a song. His eyes snapped past Taristan to Erida, still pressed back from the fray.

Behind her stood Sorasa Sarn, a shadow in bloody leather, a bronze dagger in one hand. The edge bit against the Queen of Galland's pale, jumping throat.

Despite the flames leaping all around them, consuming the chamber faster and faster, all four figures froze, unable to move. They sucked down smoky gasps of air, chests heaving, their faces streaked with soot and blood. Each glared across the flames, the circumstances catching up. After all they faced, here they stood. The immortal, the queen, the assassin, and the cursed prince.

It seemed impossible, foolish. The work of a dark god, or sheer, dumb luck.

On the floor, a sword against his neck, Dom could only stare. He dared not even blink, lest this all be an illusion. A last wish before the end.

"Where are your armies, Erida?" Dom muttered, his throat moving against the sword. He almost laughed at the absurdity of it all. "Where is your demon god, Taristan?"

But for all your powers vast and terrible, you are still vulnerable, Dom thought, eyes wavering between the Queen and her rogue. *And still mortal.*

Taristan did not relent, holding steady. But he angled his head just so, enough to hold both the women and the immortal in his vision. The blood drained from his face, his skin going bone-white. In that moment, Dom saw all the Queen meant to Taristan. And what it would mean to lose her.

Erida made a low, strangled sound, hesitant to move, unable to scream. She bared her teeth, as angry as she was afraid.

Dom locked eyes with Sorasa, his breath coming in shallow, smoky gasps. For the first time since Byllskos, he looked on a true assassin. Not exiled, not an outcast. A blooded Amhara in all her lethal glory.

She stared back at him, her face blank, her copper eyes empty of all emotion. Not remorse, not fear. Not even her usual disdain. Her ragged black hair fell around her face, barely brushing her shoulders. A single strand moved, betraying her slow, steady breathing.

"Kill her, Sorasa," Dom said, his voice torn by the smoke. "Kill her."

The Queen of Galland twitched but Sorasa reacted smoothly, moving with her. Her free hand held Erida by the arm, the other still at her throat.

"You know what happens if you do," Erida bit out, coughing hard. Her gaze wavered between Taristan and the flames.

Something passed between them, queen and consort, a flicker in their eyes. Both swallowed hard, impossibly cornered.

"You know what happens either way," Sorasa answered coolly. She glanced to Taristan, taunting. "You decide, Taristan of Old Cor. Do I open your wife's throat, or does she burn?"

Taristan's own throat bobbed as he swallowed. He stared, not at Sorasa, but the Queen. The red sheen in his eyes churned, his pupils like two flaming candles. Dom half expected What Waits to leap out into the realm, fueled by all the rage of the abyss.

"Sorasa, kill her," Dom ground out.

If we cannot kill Taristan, we can remove his greatest ally, he thought, mind spinning. *That will be enough. That will be worth the cost. Perhaps this has been our fate all along.*

Sorasa ignored Dom, to his eternal chagrin.

She held on, pressing the dagger a little harder. A drop of blood coursed down Erida's neck.

"Or do you let Domacridhan go?" Sorasa murmured.

On the ground, Dom loosed a low growl. The sword hissed at his throat.

"*Sorasa*," he hissed.

"Queen of Four Kingdoms. Empress Rising. That's what they call you now," Sorasa purred, pushing Erida sideways, so that she faced Taristan head on. They stepped together, both women bound in a murderous dance.

The assassin's gaze flared. "What will they call your queen tomorrow?"

Erida did not relent, standing tall against Sorasa's grip. But even she could not control her tears. Her eyes filled, shimmering to reflect the flames. Again she choked back a cough, gagging on the smoke.

Behind the Queen, Sorasa held her ground. Behind her, the windows gleamed black, opulent panes of glass looking out on the palace gardens.

I should have known I would die arguing with Sorasa Sarn, Dom thought bitterly. His body tightened with frustration, still kneeling beneath Taristan's blade.

"She's worth more dead than we are alive," he shouted. "Kill her!"

Above him, Taristan remained unblinking. His infernal gaze moved to Sorasa. She met his eye without flinching, unbothered by the demon in his mind.

"I will hunt you, Amhara," Taristan murmured. "Both of you."

The blade was still cold against Dom's skin. Part of him knew he could end this himself. One twist of his neck and Sorasa would have no choice. He would be dead and she would have no reason to leave the Queen alive.

I cannot, he knew, broken by the prospect. *Do it for me, Sorasa. Do this for me.*

His own tears stung his eyes, desperation threatening to choke him. "Sorasa, please—"

"I'm counting on it," Sorasa breathed, still glaring at Taristan.

Dom gulped against the steel. He willed himself to do what Sorasa would not.

But then the sword was gone, pulled back an inch. Above Dom, Taristan's heart rammed. He snarled low in his throat, fighting his own nature.

Across the room, Sorasa did the same.

Their blades moved in careful unison. Behind the Queen, Sorasa's lips pulled into a sharp, small smile. She watched, keen-eyed, weighing every inch.

So did Dom. He knew her well enough, and listened for the telltale change in her heart. When the rhythm shifted, so did he.

Immortal and Amhara exploded together, one rolling beyond the reach of Taristan's sword. The other arced with her bronze blade, her grip on the Queen's arm still tight.

Without blinking, Sorasa laid the screaming Queen's palm flat against a side table. The dagger jumped in the air as she switched her grip, giving herself the most leverage. With a downward stroke, Sorasa speared through the Queen's hand, nailing Erida to the spot. The Queen's scream turned into a ragged howl.

Taristan roared through the flames, a monster in mortal skin. But he went for Erida, forcing Sorasa to dodge. She sprinted, careful with her footing over burning floorboards.

Dom matched her easily, both aiming for the wall of windows. He threw a chair at the glass and it shattered, letting a gust of fresh air into the bedchamber. Without breaking stride, he bent to retrieve his sword, sheathing it in a single motion. Behind him, Taristan loosed the Amhara dagger, drawing it free of wood and flesh. Queen Erida yelled again, her screams almost swallowed by the fire.

There was no time to argue, or even think.

Dom could only trust Sorasa, and Sorasa trust Dom.

They leapt out together, his arm around her waist, the other free to scrabble against tumbled stone. A banner ran slick beneath his fingers and he tightened his grip, enough to slow their fall but keep sliding. Sorasa pressed in tightly, small against his chest, her own heartbeat faster than he ever knew it to be.

He felt his heart matched her own.

The gardens rose up below them, a flaming castle above.

The Queen's screams echoed in Dom's head they collapsed to the winter-bare earth. Sorasa jumped away from him, only to keep sprinting, a shadow among the trees.

Without question, Domacridhan followed.

16

TO BE ENOUGH
Charlon

He knew better than to complain. There were worse paths to walk, or ride. Even so, Charlie winced with every new day, their horses galloping over a broken path of roots and stones.

There were no true pathways through the Castlewood, but two hundred Sirandel Elders drove through the knotted woods as if the uneven ground was an old Cor road. The Elders were expert horsemen and set a wicked pace, their horses trained to traverse the precarious terrain as well as any. Charlie could only hold on, his thighs and fingers aching every night when they made camp for the mortals. Elders did not journey with tents or the usual wares, as they did not need to stop or sleep. At least Charlie never feared for their rations. The Elder company provided more than enough for three mortals. Sometimes too much. They clearly had no idea how much any of them ate, or how often.

Charlie's only comfort was Corayne, her teeth gritted against the same exhaustion, her body just as worn. For her, he kept his mouth shut. Corayne had the world on her shoulders. Charlie just had to follow along.

Garion was more infuriating, mortal though he was. His Amhara training made him accustomed to long days of travel, his body broken and remade by years at the citadel. If the blistering pace through the Castlewood bothered him, he gave no indication. Even at night, when they lay down together, Garion never fell asleep first.

The fallen priest breathed a long sigh of relief when they broke through the tree line a week and a half later, leaving the Castlewood. But Valnir and his Elders skirted the eaves of the forest, careful to keep the company out of plain sight. They would not risk the Cor road or open ground, not with Corayne.

Its shadows remained, the eaves of the forest casting a long twilight. Charlie's horse followed the pack as they turned east, riding the line between the forest and the valley sloping away to the south. The Rivealsor wound below them and an old Cor road too, the ancient paving stones a line of silver next to the river.

Beyond it was Madrence.

Charlie swallowed at the sight of his country, distant as it was. In winter, the fields were barren, glittering with frost. The land looked gray and cold, devoid of any of the joy he remembered. Come spring, he knew the hills would burst into green, covered in farmlands and vineyards.

Or so it used to be, he realized, his stomach churning.

As they rode, the landscape came into sharper focus, and Charlie nearly slid from the saddle.

Next to him, on her own horse, Corayne sucked in a searing gasp.

"Erida," she cursed over the sound of hooves.

Miles to the south, along the river, her castles stood guard of the once border. Now that Madrence had fallen to Erida's conquest, their garrisons were quiet. But the mark of her army remained. Erida's legions had beaten a terrible path over the Cor road, tearing up the earth with a thousand hooves, boots, and wheels. Tree stumps littered the way like a pox, the riverbanks bare of vegetation. The border, once invisible, now bore a terrible scar.

"Madrence falls," Charlie hissed to himself, tightening his grip on the reins. It was one thing to know his homeland had been conquered, but another thing entirely to see it.

Garion glared at the borderlands. Charlie saw his own pain mirrored on his lover's face. Garion was a son of Madrence too, even if he hardly remembered it.

As they rode, Charlie tried to focus on anything else. The sound of hooves, the ache in his legs. It was no use. He thought of his own home, far away along the coast. Partepalas.

In his head, he saw the Madrentine capital, resplendent in pinks and golds and polished white. Flowers bloomed and blue-green waves lapped at the city walls, all of it gilded by the sun. His own church stood on the waterside, in the shadow of the city's great lighthouse. In all the world, there was no city like Partepalas. Now she was under Erida's sway, poisoned by Taristan and What Waits. Charlie mourned her as they journeyed on.

Dawn spread slowly through the gray winter sky, the sun never truly breaking through the clouds. A shivering fog bank crept out of the forest, reaching with ghostly fingers.

Charlie bent against it, burrowing deeper into the warmth of his hood.

When something stopped his horse, he almost jolted out of the saddle. He looked up sharply to find Garion pulling his reins, jerking both their horses to a halt.

The rest of the company did the same around him, Corayne reining up on his left side. She closed ranks quickly, maneuvering her own horse so that their legs almost touched.

"What's happening?" Charlie muttered, squinting through the fog. The silhouettes of the other Elders faded through the gray mist.

"I'm not sure," Corayne answered.

She stood in the stirrups, the way Sigil taught her. The Spindleblade gleamed in its sheath, belted to her saddle.

"Must be the scouts," Garion said. He let go of Charlie's reins but his hand lingered, resting lightly on the priest's glove.

Charlie closed his fingers around Garion's, giving him a gentle squeeze. Even after two arduous weeks, Garion still didn't feel real to Charlie. Without hesitation, Garion squeezed back. They didn't need to speak to communicate. Charlie heard Garion's voice ringing in his head clear as a bell.

I'm not going anywhere.

Through the fog, Valnir's tall silhouette lifted a hand, beckoning them forward. Charlie had little desire to speak with the Elder ruler more than he needed to, but Corayne nudged her horse forward without a second thought.

Reluctant, Charlie followed, with Garion bringing up the rear.

They wove through the Elder company to find Valnir dismounted, standing on a spit of rock. He glared down into the valley below. In the distance, the fortress line of castles marched away along the border. Despite the fox insignia on his cloak, the immortal monarch reminded Charlie of an eagle. Peering and distant, a dangerous creature far beyond the bonds of the earth.

As they approached, Valnir turned away from the landscape, rounding on Corayne. His yellow eyes seemed to glow against the gray world.

Flinching, Charlie recognized fear in the Elder lord.

Corayne saw it too.

"What is it?" she ground out. "The castles?"

"The enemy garrisons are small and slow," Valnir answered, cold as the winter air. "We fear little from mortal soldiers."

"Then what do you fear?" Charlie snapped, immediately regretting it.

Valnir's lurid eyes flicked to his own. Charlie thought of an eagle, its talons curled and cruel.

"My scouts found a ruin along the border," he said.

For once, Charlie knew the map better than Corayne. "Castle Vergon?" he offered.

The Elder lifted and dropped one shoulder slowly. "I do not learn the names of mortal castles. They rise and fall so quickly."

"Of course," Charlie scoffed, exchanging withering glances with the others. "Vergon was one of Galland's border fortresses. It was destroyed by an earthquake twenty years ago."

Little more than a blink in the life span of an Elder, Charlie thought. *Especially one so old as Valnir.*

"The entire fortress came down and was never rebuilt," he added. "I've only seen it from a distance. What's wrong with it now?"

Valnir's jaw tightened. "The castle is no longer a ruin, but a dragon roost."

The earth tipped beneath Charlie's feet and he nearly lost his balance. Only Garion's hand at his back and Corayne by his side kept him standing. A hot flush swept over his body from eyebrows to toes.

He remembered the scream of a dragon, high in the burning clouds of Gidastern, its shadow too big to comprehend. The thump of its wings reverberated in his own chest. A thousand red and black jewels glittered over its body, reflecting the inferno raging through the city below.

Charlie ran from the dragon then, leaving Corayne and the Companions to burn.

He wanted to run now.

But he did not move, holding himself rooted to the spot.

"A dragon roost," Corayne repeated next to him, her voice small.

In recent months, she'd seemed older than her age. Stronger, faster, more skilled. Smarter than any of them. Not so anymore. Charlie saw the teenager, the girl barely gone from home, still taking her first steps in the wider world.

"A large garrison was left at the ruin. A dragon feasts on the corpses," Valnir said. "At least one, a juvenile judging by its size."

A child. Charlie bit his lip, mind spinning. The dragon of Gidastern had looked big as a storm cloud, massive, anything but a young creature. Trembling, he wondered how many dragons roamed the Ward now.

"I remember the dragons of younger days, when this realm still bristled with Spindles." The Elder's hawkish face softened a little, his own eyes filled with memory. "I know what it is to face them."

"Do you?" Corayne bit back harshly. Pink spotted high on her cheeks as Valnir recoiled. "I watched a dragon burn a city before my eyes three weeks ago. And I promise you, it was no juvenile."

"Certainly not," Charlie heard himself murmur.

Valnir wisely chose not to press them.

"If we circle back into the forest," he said, "we should be able to pass without alerting the dragon to our presence. It will cost us time, of course."

"Better a few days lost than all our lives," Garion spat, crossing his arms.

Valnir dipped his head once. He even exhaled a sigh of relief. "I am inclined to agree. War comes and I should not spend my warriors yet."

As much as he wanted to do the same, something gnawed at the back of Charlie's mind. He ran a hand through his hair, mussing the braid with errant fingers. Suddenly he could only look at his boots, watching as the fog curled over his feet. He wished he could disappear into it, lost in the forest again. Instead, his mind swirled with the illuminated pages of old scripture, adorned with calligraphy and a dragon's wing painted in vibrant shades.

"Charlie?" Corayne nudged him, her own dark brow furrowed deep. "What is it?"

He swallowed hard, wishing to swallow his own tongue. *For once, Charlie, keep your mouth shut.*

He spoke anyway.

"In another life," he began, "I was a priest of Tiber, dedicated to my god. And his Dazzling Realm."

Garion's eyes bored into his own, rare fear rising in the Amhara. Charlie ignored it, painful as it was.

"Irridas," Valnir said. "From whence the dragons came."

"*Jeweled their skies, jeweled their hides,*" Charlie murmured, remembering the old words and even older prayers. In his church, they laid offerings of gold, silver, and gems, a weak shadow of Tiber's realm.

"You say the young dragon feasts on the remains of a garrison." He let the words sink in. "From what army?"

"My scouts saw remnants of the Gallish flag," Valnir said.

"Erida is at war with the entire Ward," Corayne muttered. Her eyes worried back and forth. "Why would she leave a legion out here to defend a ruin?"

The answer felt like a blow from a hammer. Charlie went cold beneath his gloves, his fingers tingling with numbness. Across the many years, he heard the sound of a choir. Coins clinking on an altar. The smell of candles burning, the scent of ink all over his hands.

"They weren't defending a ruin," he whispered, meeting Corayne's black eyes.

She stared back, her mouth dropping open. "They were defending a Spindle."

"Gods help us," Charlie cursed, gritting his teeth.

"Vergon holds a Spindle torn," Valnir murmured, one white hand flexing at his side.

He still wore his great bow over one shoulder, the curved black yew like a horn growing out of his back. Beneath his finery, Charlie saw his many thousands of years alive, and countless battles won.

But Corayne looked to Charlon Armont, a wayward priest and fugitive. A coward in most things.

"What should we do, Charlie?" she asked in a small, broken voice.

Charlie opened his mouth. He knew what he wanted. Go back into the forest, avoid the dragons, and gallop all the way across the mountains. *We must run and keep running*, he thought, willing his mouth to say the words. *Every second we waste is another second closer to Taristan's victory.*

Even Charlie could admit it was not logic speaking. But his own wretched fear.

"I've seen enough Spindles to last a lifetime," he said thickly, every word heavy on his tongue. He regretted each letter. "But we can't—we can't leave this one. Not if there's a chance we can close it."

Garion made a strangled, frustrated noise low in his throat, but little else, to Charlie's relief.

Corayne only loosed a long, slow breath, then nodded once. Her eyes went to the Spindleblade, finding the red and purple jewels. They were dull in the dim light, unassuming. As if the blade was not the key to saving or ending the realm.

"You're right," she finally murmured. "I'm sorry you're right."

Charlie tried to smile for Corayne, to lift some of the great burden she carried. The best he could do was a twitching grimace.

"So am I," he answered.

It was a little more than a day's ride to the ruins of Vergon, and Valnir took no chances with his kin. They camped for the night several miles from Vergon, the Elders circling to take council together. Valnir sent his scouts out again, ranging to form a safe perimeter around the dragon's roost. If anything went awry, they could ride back to Sirandel for aid.

Not that help would reach us in time, Elder or not, Charlie knew. Even the swiftest horse and finest rider would arrive to find them all burned or eaten.

From his vantage point above the valley, Charlie watched the changing miles. Some clouds lifted by sunset, the last rays of light chasing away the lingering fog in the river valley.

Vergon stood on a hill on the riverbank, half a mile off the old Cor road. The ruins seemed small from such a distance, barely a smudge. Just another pile of tumbled stone and memory. The sunlight could not penetrate the broken towers and collapsed walls. Shadows pooled in the rubble.

Charlie squinted at it, morbid. He looked for the edge of a jeweled wing or a curl of smoke, but the dragon hid well.

"At least the last sunset we ever see is a good one," Garion sighed, perched on a mossy stone beside him. A sword lay across his knees and he cleaned it diligently, working the edge with an oilcloth.

"Where's your rapier?" Charlie said, noting the unfamiliar blade in Garion's lap.

The assassin raised the Elder-made sword, inspecting its slightly curved edge.

"I thought this better for slaying monsters."

The corner of Charlie's mouth twitched, torn between smirk and frown. "I should trade myself out for someone of more use."

He forced a laugh when Garion would not, the Amhara's lovely face going tight.

Sighing, Charlie eased himself down to sit at Garion's side.

"Am I supposed to clean mine too?" he muttered, indicating the blade, a gift from the Elders, now hanging at his waist.

"Don't bother, this is more for me than the blade," Garion said. His hands moved steadily, his focus on the steel.

Their shoulders touched.

"We don't need to be here, Charlie." The wind almost swallowed Garion's low words. "Two hundred Elders and a Cor princess? They don't need us."

He didn't need to say it out loud for Charlie to understand. *We don't need to die.*

Under his cloak, beneath a leather jerkin and quilted tunic, Charlie's heart quickened. Every second on the hill felt against his own nature. He need only turn away, take a horse, and be gone, returning to the fugitive road. He still had his bags of ink and parchment, his beautiful seals. He could make a life for himself in any forgotten corner he chose. With Garion too. But Charlie remained, the stone cold beneath him.

"'I will try.' That's what you said in the forest," Charlie muttered. "That you would try to believe."

A scoff burst from Garion's lips and he put the sword aside. "I'm surrounded by immortals about to assault a dragon's nest. I *certainly* believe you now."

Charlie only shook his head. "I need you to believe *in* me, too," he replied. "Help me believe in myself. And help me stay alive."

Still glaring at the dead grass, Garion gritted his teeth. "That's what I'm trying to do, my darling."

"I'm not going anywhere."

It came out too harsh, too loud. Impossible to ignore.

Finally Garion raised his eyes. He looked torn between frustration and anger. The killer in him was there, small but enough to see. Amharas were trained to survive, to make it home to the citadel even in failure. They were valuable weapons, honed by long years of brutal training. Garion warred with his own instincts, Charlie knew.

Not for the realm, but for me.

"You can run, but I—" Charlie forced out, his voice faltering.

He looked to the horizon again, and the black ruins. Then to the camp, through the Elders, to Corayne lingering at their edges. She stood out like a sore thumb, a mortal girl in the middle of the end of the world.

It was easy for Charlie to draw a little strength from her own.

"If I run, I still die here," he said, feeling his own heart twist. "Part of me. The part you love."

Garion put a hand to his neck. "You think that now but—"

"I tasted the shame of it before." Charlie forced off the Amhara with a swipe. His cheeks flamed. "When I ran from Gidastern. I know what it feels like to think the worst of your own self. To be *consumed* by regret. And I won't do it again. I *won't* leave her."

Charlie willed Garion to see the resolve he felt as much as feared.

"Stop giving me the chance to give up," he finally murmured, looking back to the horizon.

Across the hills, the sunset faded, the blue cold swallowing up the landscape. Charlie felt the chill of it creep into his limbs, starting in his fingers and toes. Without thought, he seized Garion's hand in his own.

After a second, Garion squeezed back.

"You won't leave Corayne, and I won't leave you. Not again," he said. "So be it."

Amhara though he was, Charlie had long learned to see through the cracks in the assassin's mask. He watched now, looking for any hint of a lie. Instead, he saw only doubt.

His thumb brushed the back of Garion's glove.

"Once upon a time, I was a priest of Tiber. Who would I be if I gave up the chance to see his realm?"

Garion rolled his eyes. "A smart man."

"I suppose the Amhara never trained you to fight dragons," Charlie said quietly.

Garion loosed a self-deprecating laugh, shaking his head. "I've killed princes and peasants both. A leopard in Niron. Too many bears to count. Never a dragon."

Shuddering, Charlie pulled his cloak tighter and pressed in against the assassin.

"What is it your guild says about fear?" he asked.

The answer came swiftly, drilled into Garion since childhood.

"Let it guide, but do not let it rule," the Amhara answered.

"Sorasa told me that once," a voice said.

They both turned to find Corayne standing a polite distance away, her hands clasped in front of her body. The Spindleblade peeked over one shoulder, turning her silhouette warlike. Against the deepening blue, she stood apart, the first light of the stars behind her head like jewels in a crown.

Charlie slid from the rock, landing on his feet. "You should get some sleep before tomorrow, Corayne. We all should."

"At least that we can agree on," Garion grumbled. He stood with far more grace.

When Charlie reached for Corayne, she stepped away from his arm, dodging his grasp.

"After I speak with Valnir and his council," she said with another step back.

Exhaustion loomed and Charlie gritted his teeth. "Corayne—"

"I should be there," she shot over her shoulder. "I'm the only one of us who has seen a dragon in three hundred years." Her voice softened. "Up close, I mean."

"Then I'll go too," Charlie said, slipping his arm into her own, matching her gait. "And see you *do* sleep at some point."

"You know, I haven't had a nursemaid in about ten years," she cut back.

"People your age generally don't need them, but here we are."

She offered a grateful smile in reply.

There were no campfires for the Elder company and the cold night air fell sharply as they crossed the hill. Charlie shuddered against it, drawing Corayne close.

"Dragons and haunted woods and bitter cold," he cursed. "I can't believe I'm going to say this, but I think I'll prefer the mountain passes to my own country."

Behind them, Garion scoffed. "I will remind you of that when we're both frozen solid."

Most of the Elder company waited below the hill, tending to their horses or staring at the stars with vacant expressions. Charlie shook his head at them. No matter how much he tried, he would never truly comprehend the immortals. *Nor do I really want to*, he thought.

Valnir and his Elder lieutenants collected around another rocky outcropping, its face smooth and flat like a table. They spoke in low voices, trading words in the Elder tongue. To Charlie's annoyance, he realized they stood in darkness, their immortal eyes keen enough to see without torches.

At their approach, one of them was good enough to pull out a lantern. It sparked to life with a strike of flint and steel.

"Corayne an-Amarat," Valnir said, putting out a hand of welcome.

At his command, two Elders moved apart to allow them room among the council. The immortals looked neither annoyed nor inviting, apathetic to their mortal presence.

Despite all he had seen, Charlie still felt some apprehension around the Elders. Dom was one thing, but two hundred of them was unsettling. Their ethereal, deadly grace put him on edge. He glanced down the rocky table, noting the mixture of faces. Male and female, pale white or darker skinned. Worst of all were Valnir's kin, with their red hair and yellow eyes. Even against the night, they seemed to glow.

"What plans have you made?" Corayne asked bluntly, laying her gloved hands flat on the stone.

Valnir straightened beneath his opulent cloak. In the semidarkness, he was a statue of polished marble, the lantern light reflecting on his smooth face.

"All that are needed," he answered.

Corayne's hand tightened into a fist, her jaw set with frustration. "Valnir."

With a flick of his eyes, Valnir indicated to his captain of the guard, Castrin.

"A dragon is most dangerous in flight. It is the wings we must attack first," Castrin said. "If this is indeed a young dragon, our arrows should be enough to puncture the skin, and tear enough holes to keep the beast from flying."

Elders or not, Charlie could hardly picture it. He saw the same doubt on Corayne's face.

"It is what we did three hundred years ago," Valnir ground out. His sword was suddenly in his hand, the motion too quick for mortal eyes. The steel reflected the weak lantern, every curve of the metal fluid like a river. "I saw the last dragon on the Ward die. It is fitting I kill the next."

The next is already out there, flying around the realm, Charlie wanted to say. Instead he bit his tongue.

Corayne wisely did the same. "So, archers first. Swordsmen next."

"Yes," Valnir clipped. "The dragon is new to this realm, and we must hope it is not yet under Taristan's sway."

"The other dragon wasn't," Corayne said flatly. A rare look of confusion crossed Valnir's face. "It attacked him as much as the rest of us. Dragons must be difficult to enthrall, even for Taristan and his wizard."

Charlie rolled his eyes. "Oh lovely," he said. "Some good news at last."

"And what about me?" Corayne added, raising her chin.

More than a few Elder gazes flew to her, yellow and blue and brown. They eyed the mortal girl as they would a walking fish, or a fire-breathing rabbit. Unnatural and confusing.

Castrin raised an eyebrow, his disbelief apparent. "Are you skilled with a bow, my lady?"

Intimidating as the Elders were, a hundred of them more deadly than a mortal army, Charlie felt his composure break. He glared at Valnir with frustration.

"Your aim *should* be to get Corayne to the Spindle, before anything else can pass through from the next realm," he all but barked, pointing a finger at Corayne. "One young dragon is obstacle enough. Allward cannot afford another full-grown dragon burning its way across the realm."

Down the stone, a few Elders murmured among each other, the rest staring at Charlie. The weight of their focus felt like being hit with an avalanche.

"Or anything else that may come from Irridas," Corayne added. "The black knight was enough."

Charlie's spine turned to ice.

"Black knight?" he sputtered, whirling to her. "What knight?"

She only blinked up at him, confused.

"In Gidastern. There was a knight in black armor. Not steel, but something stronger, like jewels. Or impossibly hard glass," she said. Every word made Charlie feel sicker and sicker. "He rode a black stallion with red eyes. I don't know who he was or who he fought for, but he hunted the dragon—and anyone who got in his way."

Suddenly Charlie was back in his little church, his sure hands running over the dusty pages of an old manuscript. The fine lettering beneath his fingers bled, black and red ink curving to form the figure of a rider on a murderous horse. He was armored all in black, a single sword raised above his head.

"Morvan the Dragonsbane." The name made Charlie's knees tremble. "You saw *him*?"

At the edge of the lantern light, Valnir looked down his long nose at them, his lips pursed. "I do not know this name."

"You wouldn't," Charlie snapped back, still looking at Corayne. All thoughts of courtesy, good manners, or common sense fell away.

At Valnir's side, Castrin bristled. "Mind your tongue, mortal."

Charlie ignored him. "The Dazzling Realm is not your own, but Tiber's."

"Your god," Corayne replied. "What do you know of the black knight?"

"I used to paint dragons all day long. For Tiber's manuscripts, in church records." His words trembled as he sifted through distant memories. "I illustrated the Dragonsbane too. The scriptures differ, depending on which you read. He could be Tiber's son, the child of a god. He could be an immortal of Glorian, lost to wander the cold jewels of Irridas. Either way, he spends the ages hunting dragons, with no regard for anything in his path."

Something glinted in Corayne's eyes. A well of fresh tears, unshed. She sniffed them away before any could fall.

"He was in Gidastern," she managed to say. "Dom turned back to—to stop him."

Out of the corner of his eye, Charlie saw Valnir bow his head. His lips moved, speaking an Elder prayer even Corayne could not translate. In this pain, at least they were united.

Garion broke the silence when no one else would. He shifted, planting his palms on the stone.

"We can only hope the knight is still in the north and does not turn his sights back to his Spindle," he said.

In spite of himself, Charlie banged a closed fist on the rock beneath him. He immediately regretted it, his hand smarting.

"I'm sick to death of hope," he grumbled.

Sick of Spindles and dragons and this wretched cold.

With one last swipe of her eyes, Corayne shrugged. Her shoulders bowed.

"Unfortunately it's all we have," she said.

Then Valnir laid his sword upon the stone, the blade pointed at Corayne. With quick hands, he pulled out his fine yew bow, the curved wood gleaming as he placed it next to the sword.

"Not all," the Elder ruler said.

All down the stone, his warriors did the same, laying down sword and bow and dagger and bare hands. Their deadly weapons and deadlier resolve thrummed with power beneath the winking stars. Garion wasted no time drawing his own weapons, putting them down in a magnificent array of dagger and sword. Charlie felt stupid putting down his single blade next to Garion's many but did it anyway.

He eyed Corayne, small as she was, dark-haired and dark-eyed, a shadow among them. With shaking hands, she drew the Spindleblade from its sheath. The language of Old Cor winked up at them, inscrutable and ancient. It was not Cortael's blade anymore but Taristan's. The dark steel was long clean, but Charlie still saw blood all over the sword.

She did not speak but Charlie heard her voice. He remembered what she said back in Sirandel, in the sanctuary of the Elder enclave. It was difficult to accept then.

And even more difficult now.

He said it back to her anyway.

"We will have to be enough, Corayne."

17

MERCY

Corayne

We will have to be enough.

Castle Vergon was a giant against the dawn, a broken fist of towers and tumbled walls. A maze of thornbushes grew around the hilltop, forming another wall around the ruins, broken by a long-abandoned road. Overhead, the clouds cleared, leaving only a soft pale blue.

What was once a Gallish legion pockmarked the hillside. Corpses lay burned or dismembered, half-eaten or left to rot among the thorns. Corayne was darkly grateful for the winter. The cold kept the worst of the stench at bay, freezing the bodies left in shadow. A single flag remained standing, its banner tattered, flapping weakly in the light breeze. Half the golden lion was gone, torn apart like its soldiers.

Worst of all was the silence. Not even carrion birds dared the dragon's roost, leaving the massacred legion where it lay.

Bones scattered over the road beneath Corayne's boots. She did her best to avoid breaking any, careful in her steps. The Elders had no such trouble. They moved in disarming silence. All were armored and armed, with blade and bow.

The Spindleblade weighed heavy over Corayne's shoulder, her cloak discarded to give her the best range of motion. The frozen air on her cheeks kept her alert, despite a long night of little sleep. She avoided looking left and right, focusing on the Sirandel company instead of the corpses all around. Her memory filled with too many dead faces.

I don't need to carry any more.

She searched among the ruins for any sign of the young dragon. A curl of smoke, the flashing gleam of a jeweled hide, a bat-like wing.

She searched for the Spindle too. A thread of gold, a glimmer of another realm. She could feel it humming somewhere, barely a breath against her skin. But enough to know their assumption was correct. A Spindle was close, though she couldn't see it yet.

Ahead was nothing but the empty castle and the empty sky.

Valnir and the immortals of Sirandel were a formidable force, armed to the teeth. The Monarch led silently, half crouched, his great black bow aimed with an arrow to the string. His hair ran down his back in a single braid of red and silver, one jeweled hand glinting purple in the sunlight. Corayne admired his bravery. Most rulers would hardly lead an army into battle themselves, let alone against a dragon.

She dared not speak, but glanced sidelong. Next to her, Charlie did his best to move quietly too. He lips moved without words, one hand on his brow as he walked.

Save your prayers for us, she wanted to say. *These men are already dead and in the hands of their god.*

He felt Corayne's gaze and tried to smile, his mouth pulling in a weak gesture.

Corayne did not blame him.

His fear was her own, all-consuming, threatening to swallow them up.

Her only comfort was knowing the fear was in them both.

I am not alone.

Garion said nothing, near silent as the Elders, but his face communicated enough. He was deadly as Sorasa, an Amhara blooded, one of the most fearsome assassins on the Ward. And he was terrified, his eyes never wavering from Charlie's back. He followed as closely as he could, near a shadow to the fallen priest. A sword at his side, and a shield at his back.

He reminded Corayne of someone else, another Companion.

Her breath caught as she remembered a gentle-mannered squire, with warm eyes and sure hands.

She looked through the Elder army again, from Valnir's silhouette to every blade and bow. *I would trade all of them for the others. Every single immortal blade.* For Dom, for Sorasa, for Sigil, for Valtik. And for Andry, her own shield to walk beside her, guarding every step of the way.

Ahead of them, the shadow of a tower fell over Valnir. He slowed, and all thoughts of the Companions faded. Corayne's pulse quickened to a steady drumbeat pounding in her ears.

What the Elder monarch sensed, she did not know. Her grip tightened on her sword anyway. Sorasa and Sigil had taught her well, training her to fight, and above all things, how to survive. Corayne could only hope the lessons stuck.

At the vanguard, Valnir raised his bow, training his arrow on something mortal eyes could not see. His archers followed his lead and took aim, arrowheads flashing in the sun.

Corayne gritted her teeth, barely daring to breathe. Next to her, Charlie went white-faced.

They heard no order, but every arrow loosed at once, hissing through the air in gentle arcs. Together, they disappeared over the crest of the hill, among the broken walls of the ruins.

The dragon's cry was like claws on stone, high and keening.

A bolt of terror shot through Corayne and she crouched low, scraping up against a thornbush. Black branches and winter-dead rose vines curled at her back. She could already feel the shadow of wings falling over her, the dragon of Gidastern fresh in her mind. Her breath rattled in her chest and she fought to steady it, counting through every inhale and exhale.

The Elders wasted no time, another volley already arcing over the hill as the first beat of wings sounded. Through the thorns, Corayne caught the first glimpse of the Spindle monster, its wings a deep ruby red.

"To the tomb with this," Garion cursed somewhere. Amhara though he was, even he couldn't keep the fear from his voice. "We can still run."

Corayne swallowed hard, a stone in her stomach. "No we can't," she snapped back.

Her legs moved beneath her, seemingly of their own accord. The old road up to the ruins blurred as she sprinted forward, her boots kicking up dirt and bone dust. The Elders fell in beside her, protectors as much as warriors. She caught sight of Castrin out of the corner of her eye and Charlie too, red-faced, arms pumping with his cloak strewn out behind him.

Valnir was a flag at the head of the company, black bow raised high.

The red dragon leapt into the air with another screech, the joint of each wing needled with arrows. It was indeed small compared to the dragon from Gidastern, but still brutally fearsome. Its body was the size of a carriage, with wings splayed four times as wide, the points hooked into wicked claws. Jewels glittered along its hide, rubies and garnets and carnelian, flashing a firestorm. Roaring, it blew a stream of flame across the sky.

Valnir put an arrow in its eye for the trouble. This time, when the dragon screamed, Corayne had to cover her ears.

They reached the hilltop and the ruins as one, arrows whistling overhead. Many glanced off the red dragon's jeweled skin, but a few found spare inches of soft flesh. Smoking blood rained with every beat of the dragon's wings.

Corayne kept one eye on the beast while sprinting over the uneven ground, careful not to trip on broken stone or body parts. She entered what must have been a great hall once, its columns broken, a single wall remaining, its windows long shattered. The dragon's tail swept overhead like a battering ram and she threw herself to the ground, narrowly avoiding the blow.

Her voice cracked as she yelled, "Charlie!"

"I'm here!" he shouted back from behind a collapsed wall. Garion stood over him, blade drawn, his sharp eyes trained on the dragon wheeling among the towers.

It shrieked and screamed, bellowing another stream of fire down on the Elders. They dodged in graceful unison, moving like a school of fish.

"Another," Valnir shouted, directing the next volley of arrows. His Elders emptied their quivers and the red dragon wailed, its screams of rage devolving into screams of pain.

"Another," Corayne murmured, climbing to her feet. Her breath came in short gasps, some tightness she didn't understand closing around her throat.

She turned in a circle, surveying the ruins and the Elder company. Corpses lay among the stones, barely recognizable, their bones broken and flesh torn. There were animals too, cows from surrounding farms, some horses and deer. Bigger game, all of it devoured, leaving little more than hooves and arcing rib cages.

The Elder ranks devolved, swordsmen and archers splaying out to surround the red dragon. It kept low over them, wings fanning the flames as they caught among the overgrown rocks.

The Elders kept on, a steady, merciless flood to wear down the dragon.

With every passing second, it fought harder, even as its wings weakened, its flames losing their heat.

Victory was near, but Corayne felt only dread. She eyed the massacred animals again, some of them almost the size of the young dragon. Too big for it to carry.

Then a cloud crossed the sun, sending the ruins into shadow.

No, not a cloud, Corayne realized, her body going numb. Once more, she looked to the ruins, the echoes of a castle gone, overgrown with moss and scattered bones.

A single dragon did not roost here.

A mother and child did.

The second dragon's roar shook the stones beneath Corayne, rumbling up through her body. A downdraft of wind hit her like a hammer fall and she landed on her knees as the hot air rushed over her. It smelled of blood and smoke, heavy and rotten.

"NOW WE RUN!" Garion boomed, his hand closing on Corayne's collar.

She didn't fight him, letting the Amhara pull her out of the clearing and into the labyrinthine ruins. He dragged Charlie with his other hand, throwing them both ahead of him as they sprinted.

Behind them, the mother dragon crashed down into the great hall, a tower crumbling with a sweep of her tail. Shouts echoed, Valnir's voice loudest of all, commanding his Elder warriors into formation to fight on two fronts. The mother dragon bellowed back, her jeweled hide glittering purple.

Another dragon wind blew through the ruins, pushing at Corayne's back as she ran. Bones and dismembered limbs rolled underfoot, sticky with old blood. She dodged, leaning on Garion to keep her footing.

"Where is it?" Charlie hunted as they ran, a hand trailing over the broken walls. "Can you feel anything?"

As much as she wanted to keep running and abandon Vergon for good, Corayne forced herself to slow. Panting, she slid up against an archway, putting the stone to her back. She flinched when a blast of fire split the sky, the flames nearly blue with heat.

"It's here," she muttered, trying to feel anything but her thundering heart. At the edge of her mind, a Spindle hissed. And beyond it, something worse. "It's here somewhere."

Charlie eyed the surrounding walls, the passages of the old castle like a maze. Years ago, the earthquake destroyed most of Vergon. The dragons had destroyed the rest, leaving everything in shambles.

He put a hand to Corayne's shoulder and inhaled deeply, in through his nose.

"Take a moment," he said softly. With the other hand, he motioned for her to mirror his breathing. "Valnir can handle the dragons. You focus on the Spindle."

She heard the lie in him, plain as day. Elders or not, two dragons were a death sentence.

But I can make sure it is not in vain.

"This way," she said finally, heaving one more breath.

Without giving herself time to doubt, Corayne sprinted off again, forcing the other two to keep up. She wound among the ruins, through passages without ceilings, over piled bones and black patches of dried blood. A young forest grew within the walls, or at least it had before the dragons. Charred branches and overturned trunks fell across the stones, another obstacle in their path. Ash trees, judging by the crunching dead leaves. In the few places without blood or burn scars, moss carpeted the ground.

The Spindle flickered through it all, stronger with every step, until Corayne could almost feel it between her fingers. She followed the warmth of it like a beckoning hand.

Then the young dragon landed screaming in a heap, colliding with the broken path in front of them. It curled over on itself, kicking up debris with every shudder of pain. One eye was gone, the socket a smoking ruin, skewered by an arrow. It roared again, smoke rasping from its jaws.

In spite of herself, Corayne felt her heart twist.

Its wings flapped uselessly, too weak to take to the sky again. Instead, it snapped and snarled, teeth bared and claws scraping the ground. Hot blood dripped from its many wounds.

Garion stepped neatly between Corayne and the dragon, his Elder sword held to strike. With his free hand, he kept Charlie back, protecting them all as best he could.

"Keep going, leave this to me," he said, hardly convincing in his terror.

Behind him, Charlie all but latched on to his shoulder. "Garion—"

The Amhara shrugged him off gracefully and took a step forward, his focus on the young dragon. It hissed again, a great black tongue lashing the air. Its single remaining eye fixed on Garion, the pupil blown wide, ringed with a thin line of gold.

But the dragon did not strike. Its head bobbed on a serpentine neck, smoke whistling through its teeth as it tracked Garion. The jewels of its body ran slick, their shine dulled by dark blood.

One swing of the assassin's blade might very well end its agony.

"Garion, move slowly," Corayne said, sliding one foot back.

The dragon's eye flickered to her. Strangely, Corayne felt like both predator and prey. She stared back.

It shuddered again, giving a weak cry, its teeth stained scarlet. Corayne saw the monster plainly, a beast that would only grow and destroy. A young dragon taken from its home, forced into a new world, through no fault of its own.

"Garion," Charlie said again, his teeth gritted. He mirrored her steps, angling off the path. "Do as she says."

"It is only a child," Corayne murmured. "Let it be."

The Amhara were no strangers to killing children. But Garion was not Amhara anymore, not with Charlie by his side.

He relented as Sorasa never would.

The young dragon did not follow as they hurried away, deeper into the rubble. But its screams echoed, high and piercing. Corayne tried to block it out, to no avail. It sounded too much like a crying baby now, wailing for its mother.

Her senses flared, trying to feel for any whisper of the Spindle. It was nearly impossible against the chaos, and Corayne let her feet go. They vaulted over moss and blackened bone, turning corners with abandon.

"The chapel," she heard Charlie mutter as she skidded to a halt.

The walls on either side of them curved to a once-vaulted ceiling. Now there was only sky and the single empty window. It stared down the aisle of a small chapel. Stained glass glittered in fragments over the moss, shards of red and blue catching the sun.

In the distance, dragon battle raged, another unearthly shriek shaking the ruins. Corayne barely noticed, her eyes locked on the shivering thread of pure gold.

The Spindle idled before the window, pulsing slightly.

Garion sputtered out a gasp. "Is that it?"

Next to him, Charlie fell to his knees. Not in exhaustion, but reverence. His eyes went wide as he stared. This was the doorway to his god's realm, to Irridas and the land of holy Tiber. Home of the dragons and the black knight.

"This is the fourth Spindle I've seen, and still it manages to surprise me. They look so small," Corayne breathed, taking a shaking step forward.

Her Elder sword fell to the mossy ground and her fingers closed around another hilt. Singing, the Spindleblade loosed from its sheath.

The jewels of the hilt reflected the Spindle's gleaming light, filling them with an unworldly glow. As if the sword knew its own kind, the steel calling to the Spindle's depths.

The golden thread winked back at her, barely a sliver. It trembled as she approached and the air crackled like the sky before a thunderstorm.

Corayne willed herself to move faster, but fear slowed her down. She remembered another Spindle all too well. At the temple, she fell through the Spindle to the weathered, wasted realm of the Ashlands. What Waits loomed within, a shadow and a curse, wandering a broken land of His own making. The Ashlands met a brutal fate beneath His rule, its people reduced to walking corpses, the land choked with ash and dust.

The same fate waits for us now, Corayne knew. *If we fail.*

The Spindleblade felt cold in her grasp, humming with its own magic. She eyed the threadlike Spindle again and searched the gold for some glimpse of the realm beyond. *Does He wait for me there too?* she wondered, shivering with fear.

On the ground, Charlie whispered a prayer and touched his brow. Then he looked over his shoulder, warm brown eyes locking on her own.

"Put an end to it," he said. "Before anything else comes out."

Irridas is not the Ashlands, she told herself, raising the Spindleblade. With a single sharp motion, she ran her bare palm along the edge of the blade, coating it with her own blood. *This realm has not been overtaken. He is not there. Yet.*

The Spindle seemed to stare back at her, the pulse of its light matching the beat of her own heart. Even as she felt its power, Corayne waited, hesitant.

She braced herself for the touch of What Waits. The burning, heavy clasp of a dark hand around her throat.

It never came.

The Spindleblade carried in a smooth arc, the weight of it perfectly balanced. Blood-dipped steel met Spindle and the golden thread severed, the light of it winking and dying.

Somewhere in the ruins, both dragons roared, mother and child screaming up at the sky.

The closing of a Spindle would not kill its own. This Corayne knew too well. Krakens and serpents still swam the oceans. The Ashlander army still walked. And closing the Spindle in Vergon would not destroy the dragons, in the roost or far across the Ward.

They ran from the chapel half bent, pressed up against the stone walls for cover. Garion led with a scowl, his dark brown eyes flickering in every direction. He reminded Corayne of Sorasa, always looking for an escape, plans stacked upon plans.

"If we can get into the thorns, we have a chance," he muttered, waving them through an archway. It crumbled a moment later, spitting dust and debris. "Like Charlie said, we leave the dragons to Valnir."

"Leave Valnir to die, you mean," Corayne bit out, checking around a corner. It was clear but for a few corpses stripped of meat.

"Better Valnir than you," Charlie shot back harshly. He sounded more like the fugitive she first met in Adira, focused on his own survival.

But she couldn't argue his point. The logic was sound, undeniable. With every step forward, Corayne cursed her wretched blood. Her useless birthright. All the things that made her matter more, for no reason other than bad luck. *For nothing.*

They ran with abandon, vaulting over old skeletons and fresh bodies, the armor of Sirandel painted red. Tears stung Corayne's eyes as she recognized fresh immortal corpses scattered throughout the rubble. By the entryway, Castrin stared at the now bright blue sky, his yellow eyes unseeing.

The mother dragon made a feast of the ruins, bringing down the remains of the castle stone by stone. She roared and raged, wings spread wide, Elder arrows glancing off her impenetrable hide. The red dragon cowered beneath her, wings curled over its body, shielding itself from attack. Its shrieking whines threatened to split Corayne's head in two.

Only a dozen Elders remained, all battered, streaked with blood and ash.

Valnir limped among them, his great yew bow snapped in two, abandoned at his feet. But he still held a sword, brandishing it like a king's scepter.

"Another volley!" he roared, the veins in his neck pulsing. The scar around his throat stood out starkly, above his collar of chain mail.

Bows twanged as arrows hissed through the air.

"It's done!" Corayne shouted, to Garion's dismay. He would sooner leave the Elders as a diversion than save a single one. "It's done, get out of here!"

Valnir's yellow eyes met hers through the dust and smoke, his head dipping once in acknowledgment. With a twist of his hand, he directed his warriors to retreat.

They closed ranks around Corayne as she ran, her fear eating up every other emotion. Charlie sprinted alongside, Garion with him, their hands clasped together. The last archway passed overhead and the ground sloped away beneath her feet, angling down the hill. Thorns rose up on either side of the road. It was too early for roses, but corpses bloomed among the vines.

Corayne expected flame at any moment. Cold air smacked her face instead. Only then did she look back, chancing a glimpse at the ruins above. The silhouette was already changed, more towers fallen, smoke and debris rising in the air.

The mother dragon coiled within it, her glowing eyes watching them flee. Through the smoke, Corayne held her serpentine gaze. Until the dragon dropped its head, its scaled nose prodding over the infant beneath her. The red dragon gave a shudder, still alive, but gravely wounded.

In spite of all the death, Corayne felt another well of pity. And relief.

The dragon won't leave its young, she realized, watching the castle grow smaller and smaller.

Another cry echoed over the winter hills, a child's haunting call. Its mother's roar followed, then faded.

For once, victory hung not on who they killed, but who they left alive.

They did not stop until they were well across the border, beyond the Alsor and the Rose, into the great foothills of the mountains. Night fell heavy there, and Valnir stopped the battered company only when the darkness grew so thick even the horses could not see their own hooves. The next dawn was already a soft tinge above the jagged peaks to the east, its light glowing on their snowcaps.

Corayne hardly noticed the mountains, the new stars, or the alpine kingdom of Calidon. Her exhaustion ran bone-deep and heart-through, leaving her only the strength to slide down from the saddle. She was barely to the ground before her eyes slid shut, a void of dreamless sleep already waiting.

She awoke at midday, her face to a weak campfire. It burned low to embers, throwing off a dying heat. Across the ring of stones, Charlie slept on, bundled up alongside Garion.

Even the Amhara are dulled by dragons, she thought, stretching her arms. The Spindleblade lay beside her, close as a lover. Her empty stomach ached and she twisted, searching for her saddlebags.

She nearly jumped out of her skin instead.

Valnir crouched beside her, silent and staring. It felt like coming nose to nose with a hawk, yellow eyes boring into her own.

"By the gods," Corayne cursed, collapsing back on her elbows.

The Elder monarch only blinked, his rich cloak falling across his crouched form. "What?"

She gritted her teeth. "You surprised me is all."

"That was not my intent," he answered coolly.

"I know," she bit back, angry at his Elder manner and terrible social skills. Angrier still at how much he reminded her of Dom.

Valnir stood with a sweeping grace, extending a white hand down to her in open invitation. "Walk with me, Lady Corayne."

"Very well."

With a yawn, she took it, letting the Elder pull her to her feet. It was second nature to slip the Spindleblade over her shoulder.

The remaining Elders stood guard, their silhouettes ringing the camp like statues. For the first time since Vergon, Corayne counted their number. A dozen remained. As they walked over the hilltop, Valnir followed her eyeline. It was not difficult to guess her thoughts.

"I left the Castlewood with two hundred of my people," he murmured. "Two hundred of Sirandel, immortals all. All the ages of this realm within them, all the memory of too many years to count. All lost."

To the west, Allward spread below them like a quilt. A patchwork of farms and forest, kingdoms, peoples. Languages and trade routes. Corayne eyed the land without her usual curiosity. She was tired still, weary of all things. Even the knowledge that used to make her happy once, when the only world she knew was a cliff edge on the Long Sea.

She heaved a great sigh, unable to look Valnir in the face again.

"I am sorry, my lord. I cannot tell you how sorry I am," she said, hugging herself against the cold. "I will mourn them all."

To her surprise, Valnir shook his head. His hair was loose today, falling in a long red curtain. It still smelled of smoke. With a scowl, Corayne realized everything did.

"You mourn for too many already," he said thoughtfully. "Do not take on a burden you do not need to bear."

"They died for me," she answered. "I say that far too often these days."

The Elder faced the west as she did. Overhead, the sun began its slow arc toward nightfall.

"They died for the Ward, for their own, for their families. They died for *me*, Corayne." His voice took on a ragged edge. A strange thing for an Elder. "It is a death they would have chosen. I would do it again if I had to, and give my own life gladly."

Corayne felt a familiar burst of pity for the Elder monarch. As Dom had so many times, Valnir wrestled with all-too-mortal grief. His eyes shone, gleaming with unshed tears as he stared at the sky, the ground, the hills below, the mountains behind. Anywhere but Corayne.

He does not understand it. Sorrow or shame.

"It isn't your fault, Valnir," she said, reaching out to touch his arm. "None of this is."

His cloak was smooth under her hand, the purple fabric finely woven, rich in color. Where it was not torn by dragon claw, burned, or bloodied.

Slowly, he leaned into her palm. It felt like comforting an old tree.

"That is a question of perspective," he forced out, looking down on her. She did not miss the way his eyes traced the Spindleblade over her shoulder, the sword of his making. "Again, I say—I am glad to die for this, if I must."

Corayne had little will to smile, but she tried anyway.

"Get me to Iona, and perhaps the gods will call it even."

He bared his teeth back at her, his own version of a grin. "Perhaps they will, Corayne of Old Cor."

The name felt wrong, like a map without a legend or the sun rising in the west. Again, she thought of her father, Cortael of Old Cor. She was as much of him as she was anyone else, distant though he was. Forever lost to her.

Even so, she stretched out a hand in the darkness of her head. And wished he could somehow reach back.

The dream came two days later. Not of What Waits, the shadow always at the edge of her mind.

But of Erida, Queen of Galland.

Corayne stared at her across a great ridge, a castle she did not know behind the Queen. A strong wind blew, swelling with the scent of blood and smoke. Erida stood firm against it, like a statue against a storm. She wore scarlet silk, her ash-brown hair braided into an opulent crown of rainbow jewels. The young Queen was as beautiful and magnificent as Corayne remembered, more fearsome than any soldier.

Then her eyes narrowed, her lips pulling into a terrible smirk. Steadily, the blue sapphire of her eyes gave over to burning red.

Fear leapt up inside Corayne, so sharp and sudden she felt struck by lightning. Without thinking, she drew the Spindleblade on her back, moving to cut the Queen in two, and destroy whatever monster she had become.

Corayne woke before the sword edge reached the Queen, dawn light spilling over the rest of the Elder camp. Sweat covered her body, her clothes damp against her skin. Her pulse rammed in her ears, every breath a short, shallow gasp.

What the dream meant, she could not say. It hung over her like a cloud, across many days. Every night, she feared to sleep, lest Erida return, closer and more terrible, her burning eyes threatening to devour the world.

18

THE LION'S TEETH
Sorasa

I should have killed her.

Sorasa broke the surface of the canal with a searing breath, trying not to choke down any more of the river water. Her arms worked, carrying her the last few feet to the wall of the canal. Dripping wet, she hauled herself up onto the dark street. She listened for the horns of the palace garrison, or the tromping feet of guards. But nothing came.

After sprinting through the palace gardens and diving into the Queen's private lagoon, it was only a question of riding the current downstream. They emerged in a wealthy merchant quarter, close enough to the palace to warrant roving patrols of city watch. Timber-framed walls and shingle roofs marched away in ordered rows, the streets crisscrossed through the sector. Like the palace, this was another island in the city archipelago, surrounded by water on all sides.

Princesiden, Sorasa knew, spotting the telltale golden crowns stamped on the doors and signposts. Most of the merchants served the royal court of Galland, their shops the finest in the city. The storefronts were dark, shut up for the night. Windows glowed on the upper floors, betraying the people within. But no city watch, to Sorasa's relief. The street was nearly empty, save for a few beggars, come out from their alleys and gutters. Three of them idled at the edge of the canal, paying no mind to an Amhara assassin and an immortal Elder climbing out of the river.

Their eyes were on the New Palace, and the fire consuming all within its walls.

Sorasa felt the heat of it on her back as she stood, a puddle growing under her feet. She dared not look at it, walled across the water. She knew well enough what lay behind, what she herself had done. Even so, she could not ignore the pop of exploding glass or roar of flame. Nor the shouting below it all, as servants and courtiers alike fled across the distant bridge or jumped into the canals.

They run like rats fleeing a sinking ship, Sorasa thought. *I am a rat too, running from the best opportunity the realm will ever get.*

Her eyes stung and she wrung out her hair, examining the streets. Her internal compass moved, adjusting to the grand city of Ascal as it splayed out around them.

A tower crumbled on the palace island, the sound a thunderclap. Sorasa kept on into the shadows, the darkness her only comfort in the world.

Dom followed, the last of his armor at the bottom of the canal. He wore only a leather jerkin and pants again, his old boots sloshing with every swift step. His hair fell wet and golden over one shoulder, his days in the dungeon still bruised beneath his eyes. Bedraggled as he was, Dom was still an Elder, immortal and dangerous, his green eyes bright as the fire behind them.

His voice hissed on her bare neck.

"You should have killed her."

Sorasa gritted her teeth, navigating the fetid alley.

"Keep moving," she snapped, ignoring the chill setting into her bones. Her leathers were soaked through.

Dom kept pace with annoying ease, in step with her. The alley narrowed, walls closing overhead, forcing them shoulder to shoulder. Sorasa used every inch of her will not to trip him against the bricks.

"Sarn," he growled, ferocious.

She rolled her eyes and ducked down a tighter walkway. Dom had to move sidelong, his shoulders too broad to fit where Sorasa could walk freely.

"Snarl all you want, just keep up."

She was careful to keep her face forward, her cheeks hot and red. Not for all the realm would she let Dom see her shame.

"Do you even know where you're going?" he muttered.

Sorasa turned into a small square courtyard beneath narrow windows, a single dead tree at its center. Alleys fanned out in every direction. She knew each little path and where it would lead, growing out to streets and wide avenues, over bridges and canals, to the many gates set along the city walls.

East to Conqueror's Gate, north to the Little Doors, west to Godherda.

She remembered the last gate well, from the last time they escaped Ascal. She could still hear the warning horns blaring through the city. Dom was injured then, half-conscious across the back of a stolen horse. He bled all the way through the night, until Sorasa worried he would not open his eyes at all. Back then she feared she might be left alone with Corayne and Andry, a nursemaid to the end of the world.

I would go back to that moment gladly, she thought. *If only to walk the path again, with both eyes open.*

Dom loomed, silent as she weighed the options of every road. She felt his gaze too keenly.

"Wayfarer's Port," Sorasa finally muttered, choosing the alley going east. Scowling, she glanced back over one shoulder. "I can do it blindfolded if you wish."

He grimaced but followed along without argument. "That will not be necessary."

"At least you finally trust some part of me," Sorasa grumbled back, to her own surprise. Again she felt the slow creep of heat across her face.

You are wrong to trust a coward, she thought bitterly. *Too afraid to do what I should have, and doom us both to whatever hell waits.*

If Dom noticed her discomfort, he did not show it.

"You should have killed her," he said again, for no good reason.

Again Sorasa shivered and cursed her wet clothing. "I already regret leaving you alive."

His blond brow furrowed. "The Queen of Galland is worth more than both of us."

At her side, Sorasa's fingers closed into a tight fist. She could still feel the bronze dagger in her hand, the warm leather of the hilt familiar as her own face. It was lost forever now, stained with the blood of a queen.

"You think I don't know that, Elder?" she snapped, voice echoing off the stone walls. Her body whirled to face him, nearly colliding with his broad form.

He glared down at her, lips parted, eyes wide, all the pain and frustration written plainly. Sorasa felt the same in her own heart, alongside the regret. *I could not do it. I could not let us both die there. Not even with Erida in the balance.* Sorasa's fist trembled and he continued to stare, his eyes unblinking. Green met copper-gold.

Somewhere in the distance, another rumble boomed, followed by a massive slosh of moving water. Another piece of the palace collapsed, this time into the canals. Wall or tower, Sorasa could not say. Behind it all, the roar of fire continued to rage, swallowing up the sounds of any mortal screams. As the destruction spread, so did the panic. Candles flared up in windows and citizens poked out into the streets, voices rising across Ascal.

Sorasa knew chaos would soon follow. They need only stay ahead of it.

"She may yet be dead," Sorasa heard herself murmur.

The tower was on fire, the palace crumbling around us. And I left her nailed to a table.

Dom's low chuckle was more akin to a scoff. "I know better than to hope, Sarn. We are not so lucky, are we?"

"We are still alive," Sorasa said. "I guess that's lucky enough."

Then she heaved a ragged breath, leaving such thoughts behind.

"Keep moving," she said again, softer. "I don't know what kind of time we have, but we must use what we can."

For once, Domacridhan did not argue. He did as commanded, a shadow at her back.

The pair of them passed through the alleys and side streets like a dark wind. Sorasa avoided the grander avenues as much as she could, and the market squares. Even at night, there would be a good amount of traffic, with half the city frequenting the taverns, playhouses, brothels, and gambling halls. Not to mention soldiers of the city garrison and guards of the watch. Both would be rushing toward the palace, to help the evacuation—and to hunt for those responsible.

"What of Sigil?" Dom whispered behind her.

Sorasa winced and pressed up against the wall behind her, narrowly avoiding a pair of washerwomen ambling by.

"Sigil will be at the port with the Temur ambassador," Sorasa replied, firm. She refused to entertain the possibility of anything else. "From there, we can all get out of the city. Stow away with the Temur, sail out under the ambassador's protection. Simple."

Nothing in this life is ever simple. Sorasa knew that lesson too well.

Above her, Dom narrowed his eyes. Elder though he was, foolish to mortal emotion, Sorasa felt studied. It made her skin crawl.

"We have escaped this city once," he said, gesturing for her to walk on. "We can do it again."

Sorasa spun on her heel with some relief, grateful to put Dom behind her. She did not like the way he stared, reading her as he never had before. She had never spent so much unbroken time with another before. Not even in the citadel, where the acolytes were separated for weeks at a time. By now, she'd been six months with Dom, every second like the scratch of nails on glass.

As they walked, Sorasa found herself longing for a few minutes alone. If only to tie her mask a little tighter and don a bit more armor over her heart.

"The Temur ship will have a copper-colored flag with a black wing on it," she said after a few minutes.

Dom's voice darkened. "Why would I need to know that?"

"Because you should know things, Dom," she muttered back, exasperated. "Just in case."

In case we are separated. Or worse.

The Elder drew closer to her, so close she could hear the feral click of his teeth.

"If you do something foolish and get yourself killed," he hissed, "know you could've just ended the Queen instead."

Sorasa thought about pushing him into a gutter. Instead, she scowled at him, lip curled.

"That is a very strange way to tell someone you don't want them to die."

The ambassador did not relent. His brow set into a grim, gray line.

"A trade will do for now," he said.

"I doubt you can carry enough treasure to tempt the Temur Emperor," Erida shot back, shaking her head. *Perhaps Salbhai is not so capable as I assumed.*

He only stared, his eyes boring into the side of Erida's face.

"I don't want anything in your vaults, Your Majesty," Salbhai growled, his good manners cast aside.

Erida whirled at his sharp tone, half shocked. Taristan heard it too and his chair slid back from the table a few inches, giving him room to stand.

"Ambassador—" the Queen said.

But Salbhai held up his hand, silencing her. It felt like a slap across the face. And Erida wasn't the only one to notice. She felt his brazen display of disrespect travel across the room, like ripples across a pond.

Salbhai's black eyes gleamed and Erida saw the warrior in him, buried beneath the decades.

"I want the Temur woman in your dungeons."

The demand was a thunderbolt down Erida's spine. A thousand things ran through her mind all at once, even as she schooled her face to careful disinterest. She hoped Taristan would follow her lead just this once, and keep his seat.

Too many questions weighed in her head, and too few solutions.

She brought a hand to her chin and leaned, elbow against the table-top, putting herself between Salbhai and her husband.

I am subject to nothing and no one, she thought again.

Scowling, Salbhai held her gaze, unblinking.

Erida scowled back.

"She is my prisoner—"

Salbhai's chair crashed to the ground as he stood, both hands clenched into fists. Taristan was already standing, his own chair on its side, with only Erida between them.

"She is a subject of the Temur Emperor," the ambassador spat, unafraid, bolstered by his Born Shield.

"And a wanted fugitive, who attempted to kill the prince consort," Erida said, raising her voice for all the chamber to hear.

Out of the corner of her eye, she saw the Temur delegation jump to their feet, abandoning their cups. Her own Lionguard drew their swords with a ring of singing steel, moving to flank their queen.

Salbhai glared down on her, livid.

Sneering, Erida settled back in her chair, as if it were her throne. She basked in his fury. It tasted like victory.

"And she will face justice," she said. "*Mine*."

Graceful to a fault, she pushed back from her seat. Her knights were already around her, their golden armor flashing.

"Now if you excuse me, Ambassador, I've lost my appetite."

His face twisted, his scars catching the edge of the lantern light.

"If I wanted you dead you would be a skeleton in Byllskos," he hissed back.

Her teeth clenched. "And you would still be chained up in the bowels of Erida's dungeon, if not dead a thousand times over by now."

To her surprise, Dom slowed next to her, hemmed in by the walls of an alley.

"Yes," he said, looking her over. A muscle ticced in his cheek. "Yes, I would be."

The admission felt like an apology and Sorasa nodded once, accepting it with little fuss. She had the energy and inclination for little else.

"Copper flag. Black wing," she said again, turning to move.

His reply was barely a whisper.

"Thank you for saving her."

It takes a great deal to make an Amhara lose their balance. Sorasa whirled too fast, almost slipping on the loose stones of the alleyway. Her eyes widened against the dim light, trying to see a little more of Dom's shadowed face.

He stared back, unmoving. His pulse thrummed in his throat, a vein throbbing with every pound of his stupid, noble heart.

She swallowed hard, her own heartbeat thundering in her ears.

"This isn't the time for that, Dom."

The Elder ignored her.

"Corayne would have died in Gidastern if not for you," he said. "You saved the realm, Sorasa."

Too many emotions laced his words, each one easy to see as it flashed across his face. Gratitude, shame, regret. Pride. Respect.

Above all things, respect.

"You sound like an idiot," she snapped.

Even so, her throat tightened. No one had looked on her in such a way in all her life. In the Guild, there was only success or failure. Success was expected, never rewarded. Never regarded. There were no accolades for the assassins, only the bite of another tattoo, and another contract given. Absently, Sorasa's hand trailed for her only touchstone.

But the Amhara dagger was gone, sacrificed to a burning tower and a devouring queen. She had nothing but her own mind. And Domacridhan.

"You saved the realm," Dom said again, his voice carrying.

Her hand closed into a fist.

"Not yet."

Wayfarer's Port was chaotic in the best of times, the streets crowded with all manner of folk. Priests, thieves, merchants, smugglers, runaways, foreign diplomats. Sails of every color, flags of every kingdom, shouts in every language of the Ward. As they crossed the Moonbridge, arcing over the Fifth Canal, Sorasa breathed a low sigh of relief. Neither she nor Dom would stick out. They were just two more weary travelers in the throng, chewed up and spit out by Ascal.

Or so Sorasa thought.

They were only steps from the port island, caught up in a throng of pilgrims, when the horns sounded.

And not from the palace.

Without thought, Sorasa spun on her heel, facing down the Grand Canal toward the entrance to the harbor. To another port, grander than Wayfarer's in every way.

Fleethaven.

Her eyes widened as she drank in the impossible sight. What was once the heart of Erida's navy, a circular port built to house war galleys like horses in a stable, bloomed into an inferno. Storehouses and docks caught light, barrels and crates bursting open. Masts stood black against red flames, sails billowing in the gushing torrent of hot air. One by one, the masts crumbled, the galleys consumed beneath them, splintering into the water.

Sorasa's gaze jumped to the sky, searching the smoke for any hint of the dragon. A bat-like wing, a jeweled limb, a pair of jaws stretched perilously wide.

But the clouds were empty.

Her mind whirred, the air going hot against her face, the burning fleet like another sun on the horizon. The walls of the city seemed to close around her throat, threatening to choke the life out of her. She elbowed her way across the crowded bridge, through dazed folk staring at the glowing flames.

"Have you somehow lit a match to burn down the entire city?" Dom hissed in her ear, his legs moving alongside her own.

Sorasa gnashed her teeth. "That wasn't me."

His voice dropped. "Sigil?"

"She wouldn't dare risk her kin."

"Then who?"

Sorasa's thoughts tangled again, sifting through too many possibilities. *Accident, sabotage, a single disgruntled captain finally at his wit's end.* She looked back over her shoulder, straining to see through the crowd of the port even as she moved.

The light of the flames undulated against billowing smoke, rising in a black column to join the already low clouds. Other buildings obscured much of Fleethaven, but Sorasa glimpsed enough. Galleys fought their way out of the cothon, fleeing their docks, only to meet a blockade of their own ships, the great hulks burning as they sank into the water. Whatever had set Fleethaven ablaze did so perfectly, trapping war galleys and sailors alike. Only little boats managed to slip through, skiffs and even rowboats manned by whatever sailor was lucky enough to grab an oar. Sorasa could see them splashing through the water, like insects on the surface of a burning pond.

"We need to get on a ship, any ship," she bit out, turning forward again. "It won't be long until the Queen calls the city to arms, and closes the port entirely."

Until we are trapped.

To her relief, Dom did not argue.

Out of the corner of her eye, she watched, not the burning fleet, but the towers at the end of the canal. The Lion's Teeth. They stood like two sentinels, guarding the only way to the sea, the only escape for so many ships still at harbor.

They reached the docks of Wayfarer's Port under the cover of a teeming crowd, half of them slack-jawed at the sight of Fleethaven on fire. Guard patrols roved but they ran for the flaming navy yard.

Sorasa felt herself uncoil a little. Fleethaven was a better distraction than she could have ever asked for.

Opportunity, she thought, the delicious hint of it singing in her blood.

But why? the rest of her wondered. *Who?*

More horns went up over the city, like trumpets in a forest calling out the hunt. A chill went down Sorasa's spine. The horns summoned the city garrison, calling out to the watchtowers and guard posts all over the city. All the soldiers in Ascal would rouse to Erida's command, to flood the city and everything within its walls.

Wayfarer's Port was not the palace grounds or Princesiden. This district was far less organized and upstanding, as befitting the port of a major city. Sorasa glimpsed all manner of dangerous folk as they moved, avoiding brawlers in the alleys and cutthroats in the gutters. Thieves prowled alongside errand runners and swaying sailors.

She feared none of them.

But she feared the towers. Again, she glanced at the Lion's Teeth, dreading what she might see at the mouth of the canal. At any moment, she expected another horn blast, or even the murderous shriek of chain.

"Sorasa."

Dom's breath was cool at her ear. Sorasa froze to keep from jumping in her skin.

Before she could snarl a response, Dom pointed ahead, along the crowded docks jammed with ships of all sizes, and crews of all colors. She squinted, her mortal eyes fighting against the shifting shadows and general chaos. First, she searched the many faces for Sigil, hope leaping in her chest.

But it was not Sigil he found.

"I've seen that ship before," he growled above her.

Her eyes widened, reading the lines of a massive galley as she would a familiar face.

"So have I."

Purple sails, a double deck of oars, two masts. Big enough to rival any trade galley or even a warship. She flew a flag of Siscaria, a golden torch on purple. But Sorasa knew better.

This ship sailed under no flag.

And neither did her captain.

19

THE COST OF EMPIRE
Erida

The palace burned as her hand burned, chewed from the inside out. Red-hot and blinding. Erida could not mourn. She could not even watch as the Amhara and the Elder leapt through the windows, their fate known only to the gods.

She could barely think around the pain, her world narrowed to the blade through her palm, the dagger skewered through her own flesh. Hot flames licked at the walls, demons at the corners of her eyes. Sweat poured over her skin, soaking through her nightgown, as blood poured over the wood of the little table, gushing from the open wound.

"This will hurt," a voice said in her ear, one familiar hand pressing her head to his chest.

His other fist closed around the hilt of the dagger. She flinched, already screaming against him.

Steel seared on bone, nerve, muscle, and skin.

Erida's vision went white.

Her knees buckled and she expected the thud of her body on the floor. It never came. Taristan caught her deftly, one arm around her back, the other looped under her bent knees. She dangled, weightless and help-less in his arms.

"You must stem the bleeding," he rasped above her, his own focus on getting out of their bedchamber alive.

Erida wanted to vomit. Instead, she forced down a breath of smoky air, choking as she gasped. With her good hand, she wrapped the loose fabric of her nightgown around her wounded palm, hissing in agony. Every inch of movement sent a lightning bolt of pain shooting through her hand and up her arm.

Only her anger kept her awake. It coursed through her with the pain, the two entwined like lovers.

She squinted through the smoky room, her once magnificent chamber reduced to embers. Their bed went up in flames, the intricately carved framing crumbling apart. Fire licked along the lacquered wood, consum-ing every beautiful thing. The curtains edged in Madrentine lace, the rare mirrors, the Rhashiran carpets. Crystal candlesticks. Fine clothing. Feather pillows. Cut flowers in jeweled vases. Priceless books, their pages gone to ashes.

On the floor, the bronze dagger lay where Taristan had thrown it. She committed it to memory, her bloodshot, weeping eyes tracing the curve of the edge, the black leather of the hilt.

Amhara, she knew, as she knew the look of the woman who held the blade.

Tattooed, agile, smart. It was she who first saved Corayne so many months ago, when the Corblood girl was in Erida's grasp. The Amhara woman stole victory then, and she stole it again now.

Smoke still spiraled in the wake of her enemies, stirred up by Doma-cridhan and the Amhara's escape. Part of her hoped they were broken at the base of the palace tower, their bodies destroyed by the fall. The rest of her knew the Amhara would not give her life so foolishly.

As Taristan ran from the room, fighting his way past fire and collapsing floorboards, Erida cursed to her god, the taste of blood welling up in her mouth. But even What Waits did not answer, his whispers gone in her hour of need.

She should have killed me, Erida thought, teeth clenched against every agonizing step forward. *That is the blessing from What Waits. I am still alive, to fight and to win.*

She pressed closer into Taristan, her free arm thrown around his neck. His skin burned against hers, blazing like the flames. She was literally in Taristan's hands, at the mercy of his strength and his bravery. Somehow, she found that easy to trust. It felt second nature, like breathing.

The salon was worse than the bedchamber, the tapestries charring off the walls as beams fell overhead, kicking up embers like fireflies. Between slitted eyes, she caught sight of the bodies on the floor. Erida did not grieve the loss of her Lionguard knights. It was their duty to die for her.

Pain and rage drummed back and forth, ruling one heartbeat and then the next. Her hand pulsed, blood welling between her fingers. Try as she might, she could not curl her hand, her fingers barely responding.

It was too much to bear.

Taristan looked pale against the firelight, his own blood running freely from many wounds. Again, Erida cursed the Elder, Corayne, and all their ilk.

When she squeezed her eyes shut again, she reached deeper into herself, grasping for the last drops of her strength.

Taristan murmured something above her, breaking her concentration.

She could barely decipher the words through the weight of the pain, the smoke too heavy in her lungs.

"She burns," she heard Taristan whisper, gasping down a breath. "She burns with it."

The Elder had said as much only moments ago, his voice an echo, still lingering though he was long gone. Erida could not understand, the world spiraling red and black, blood and ash.

She burns with it.

But Erida of Galland refused to burn.

She blinked up the grand column of the Konrada, the vaulted spire rising three hundred feet above her. Lanterns hung in the many stained-glass windows, and a few priests peered down from the spiraling balconies. The faces of every god stared from the twenty-sided chamber, their granite eyes watching the Queen bleed. She glared back at the familiar figures. Lasreen and her dragon Amavar. Tiber with his mouth of coins. Fyriad among his redeeming flames. Syrek, his sword raised like a beacon fire.

What Waits did not have a statue in this place, but she felt His presence all the same. Behind every god, in every candle. And in her own mind, lingering at the edges, come to watch her like all the rest.

Smoke clung to her hair and stained nightgown, ashes and blood crusted under her fingernails. Destruction painted her body, and the bodies around her. Her attendants stood out sharply against the pristine tower, most of them covered in soot. Taristan looked worst of all, the whites of his eyes violent against an ash-streaked face. He watched her with a manic look, half-mad with anger.

As her mind cleared, Erida realized she lay against a divan sofa, dragged to the center of the cathedral. Her physician, Dr. Bahi, perched next to her, his focus on her hand.

Dr. Bahi worked diligently to bandage her wound, moving with excruciatingly slow movements. It still hurt and she hissed a breath, steady hot tears coursing down her cheeks.

She did not weep. The tears would not stop, her eyes burning with the heat of them. But she would not give anything else. Not a sob, not a curse. Her rage boiled beneath the surface, unseen by any of her many attendants.

They buzzed around her like flies on a corpse. Servants, ladies-in-waiting. Lady Harrsing, her nostrils black from breathing smoke. Thornwall and his lieutenants kept a polite distance, with the Queen in her state of undress. Taristan and the physician were the only men permitted to be near the Queen. Even Ronin idled, more bleary-eyed than usual, at the edge of the hall, half-shadowed by the sculptures of the cathedral.

"What do you think, Doctor?" she muttered.

Bahi bit his lip, his voice halting and unsure. Uncertain not in his skill, but in the Queen. She could have his head with a word, and he knew it too well.

"You will not lose the hand," he finally said. "If there is no infection."

The weight of *if* hit the Queen like a kick in the gut. Erida tried to make a fist, the same fingers seemingly detached from the rest of her. She tried not to imagine the whole hand gone, her wrist ending in a bloody stump.

She saw the bob of Bahi's throat over the collar of his nightrobe. Like the rest of them, he'd escaped the palace with little more than the clothes on his back.

"I can say you were lucky, Your Majesty," he continued. "Any lower and the blow would have left the entire hand useless, if not forced amputation."

"An Amhara did this. She knew where to strike, and how. There was no luck to it," Erida bit back, the words sour in her mouth. "Thank you, Dr. Bahi," she added, a little softer for the doctor's sake.

Grateful, Bahi rose and bowed, slipping away to join the rest of the lingering brood.

Harrsing stood over Erida with a grim look, leaning on her cane. Her unbound hair trailed to the small of her back, wispy and gray. She coughed and drew a borrowed cloak tighter around her thin frame. Old as she was, she looked positively murderous.

"So the Amhara have a mark on you. We should march a legion into Mercury's citadel and cut the contract out of him," she said, seething. "We must know who bought your death. Perhaps the Temur? And the Amhara slipped in with the ambassador?"

Slowly, Taristan shook his head.

"This was not the Amhara Guild's doing, but the work of a single assassin pursuing her own ends," he rumbled, still staring at Erida's wound.

The Queen glanced between them, advisor and consort. "The ambassador fled, didn't he?"

Lady Harrsing nodded. "Along with the rest of the palace and half the ships in port."

A chill went down Erida's spine. Ambassador Salbhai had revealed his cards in their last moments together, before everything went to ashes. He had not come to broker peace between their nations, but to bargain for the Temur woman. How he knew about her, Erida could not say. But it concerned her deeply.

What more does the Emperor know of my plans, and Taristan's?

"If he makes it back to Bhur," she murmured, meeting Taristan's gaze, "I fear we might find an army of the Countless at the city gates."

To her chagrin, her husband snarled in frustration. "I care little for the politics of the Ward. It means less every day."

On the divan, Erida clenched her good hand. Her wound throbbed painfully, made worse by the rising beat of her heart. She met Lady Harrsing's eyes, the pair of them exchanging frustrated glances.

"Excuse us, Bella," she said through tight teeth.

Lady Harrsing knew better than to argue, and waved the rest of the fluttering maids away with her. Her cane echoed as she paced across the cathedral floor, leaving Taristan and Erida alone at the center.

It was not privacy, but it was the best Erida could hope for at the moment. Golden armor flashed at the corner of her eye, the remains of her Lionguard posted around the hall.

Erida looked away from them to the grand altar of the Konrada, magnificent in marble and gilding. She remembered what it felt like to stand there, before the faces of the gods, a veil on her head, a sword in her hand, with Taristan beside her. She did not love him then, when she pledged her life to his own. She had no idea what path lay before her, what fate was already made.

Her right hand lay curled in her lap now, half-covered in bandages. A little blood had already begun to seep through, staining everything around it.

"The last time you and I were here, we held the marriage sword between us," she said.

Taristan's face went stone-blank in his usual way. It was his shield and crutch, Erida knew. After a childhood like his own, abandoned to the world, his emotions were always a burden. Always a weakness.

"Good that I am not a man," she continued. "I will never hold a sword again."

One of his fingers twitched at his side, the only indication of Taristan's discomfort.

"Your heart is sword enough," he ground out, his eyes on her face.

She stared back at him, trying to glimpse behind the wall he built so terribly high. Something hid within him, something she could not yet grasp.

"Lord Thornwall commanded the city be locked down," he added, taking on a more serious air. "Every gate, the ports. And they have quelled the fire in Fleethaven. We were lucky, he says."

Erida blew out a pained sigh. She wanted nothing more than for her husband to sit, to feel his closeness and warmth in the cold cathedral. But the eyes of so many were too difficult to ignore. Like him, she put up the usual wall, receding behind her court mask.

She straightened instead, sitting on the divan as she would her throne. Her body screamed in protest, but she did her best to ignore it.

"He raised the port chain," she said. "They will be rats in a trap, then." Her heart dropped. "If they have not escaped already. Those two are slippery as eels."

"Erida."

His low whisper stopped her short, softer than she knew Taristan to be. He looked down on her, frozen to the spot, his expression still veiled. But there was a chink in the armor, a flash of something deeper still.

Not the red sheen of What Waits. Taristan's eyes were still black all the way through. His own.

They welled with pain.

"Taristan" was all she could think to reply, her own whisper weak and measured.

The breath he drew went ragged through clenched teeth, his chest rising and falling rapidly beneath the open collar of his shirt. His white veins stood out against pale skin, made worse by the cut along his collarbone. Erida stared at his wounds as he stared at her own. Realization dawned slowly, and her breath hitched in her chest.

She remembered her fear that morning when he told her of his wounds. Of the Spindle lost, a gift taken away. He was vulnerable, and it terrified her.

She saw the same terror in him now. *For me.* His eyes traced her wounded hand, then the ash clinging to her smooth skin. Erida felt her heart break for him, knowing how great his fear must be if she could see it.

Taristan had only ever known her as a queen, surrounded by guards, impervious on a throne. Her armor was meant for show, not function, her weaponry made of gilt and not steel. She led an army but never in battle, lived in an army camp but never unguarded, never in harm's way. Her wars were waged from the throne, not the battlefield.

Until today.

Slowly, she reached out for him, taking his wrist in her good hand. His pulse thrummed hard against her touch.

"Taristan," she said again, barely a whisper.

He glared above, lips pressed together as his expression wavered between fear and fury.

"This path is mine to walk," he said. "My danger to face."

Erida raised her chin. "And victory? Is that only yours too?"

His answer was swift.

"It is not."

With a will, she raised her bandaged hand, holding it up for him to see. It stung beneath the dressing but she kept a strong face, letting her resolve overtake the injury.

"If this is the cost of empire, I accept the payment," she said firmly. "And I will not allow my own blood to be spilled in vain. Is that understood?"

Without hesitation, Taristan sank to one knee, his wrist still in her grasp. Slowly, he bent his fevered forehead to her knuckles, pressing skin against skin for a long moment.

"Yes, my queen," he murmured.

To her surprise, he did not move. Over his shoulder, the eyes of their many attendants went round, watching the rare display of affection between queen and consort.

Erida bent her head, close enough to press her cheek to his own. "What is it?"

"A king of ashes is still a king," he hissed.

Her grip tightened on his wrist, the bones beneath her fingers.

"Don't dwell on anything that foolish Elder has to say."

"I said it first," he growled. His skin flamed hotter, his cheek flushing against her face.

In spite of the heat of him, Erida went cold. Fear was rare in Taristan of Old Cor. Embarrassment rarer still.

"At the temple, in the foothills. When I was just a mercenary with a wizard and a stolen blade," he pressed on, the whisper spilling from his lips like blood from her hand. "I do not want to rule over ashes, Erida. And I certainly don't want you to burn so I may claim my fate."

Something flared at the edge of her mind, an anger that was not Erida's own. But she understood it. It mirrored her frustration. *We've done too much to turn away now, afraid of our own triumph.*

She released Taristan's wrist and took his chin sharply, raising his eyes to face her.

"Then I won't," she answered, her voice iron, unyielding.

Erida of Galland refused to burn.

The Gallish court was massive, and most courtiers made it out of the palace safely, taking refuge through the city. Erida sent out her advisors to placate her noble lords, while Lord Thornwall and his men went back to inspect the damage by dawn's light. As for the servants, the many hundreds who worked and lived within the palace walls, Erida did not know. She hoped they were good enough to fill a few buckets of water and slow the destruction through the night.

That left the Konrada to serve as Erida's refuge, surrounded by her Lionguard knights and half the city garrison. They lined the cathedral island and the cathedral itself, ensuring no one could access the Queen. Not even an Amhara assassin.

Dawn broke red through the stained-glass windows, spilling shafts of light across the cathedral. Erida paced the floor, too restless to sit any longer. With the guards around the room, she felt like an animal caged, even if it was for her own protection.

Taristan prowled as she did, still in his bloody nightshirt, boots, and breeches.

"I should be hunting with the rest of the garrison," he muttered, casting another glance at the arched doorway.

It was an empty threat. Erida knew he would not leave her side, not with the Amhara still loose.

"Peace, Taristan."

The wizard's hiss stung worse than Erida's hand. She winced as she passed him, now lounging on the divan like a cat on a windowsill. She half expected him to produce a bowl of grapes from his sleeve.

Instead, he watched Taristan's steps with red-rimmed eyes, his white-blond hair dirty with soot. He also worried after the Prince of Old Cor.

In that, at least, we are alike.

"Vexing as the Elder may be, he is not our focus," Ronin said, waving a white hand. "First, we must get the sword back. Without it—"

"Without it, you still have two Spindles, in Gidastern and at Castle Vergon," Erida cut in sharply. She was less than eager to send Taristan against Domacridhan and the Amhara, vulnerable as he was now. "Does that not count for something? Is that not enough for What Waits?"

Ronin eyed her with something between annoyance and amusement.

"In time, it could be," he said. "But Corayne an-Amarat has proven herself too dangerous. Her fate cannot be left to chance while we sit and wait for the realms to wear through."

Erida curled a lip at the thought of Corayne, a little mouse in the middle of a storm.

"Her continued survival makes no sense to me," Erida clipped.

Scowling, Taristan stopped in his tracks, planting himself in Erida's path. She looked up at him, seeing the hunger in his eyes. Not for her, but the Spindleblade.

"If I cannot hunt Domacridhan, I will hunt her instead," he said. "Give me a legion, and I'll drag her back here myself."

The Queen hesitated; certainly a legion would be enough to protect her consort, but she could not shake the new feeling of dread.

"Better to kill her and be done with it, my love," she muttered, dry. "Where will she go?"

On the divan, Ronin loosed a needling laugh.

"Where do little girls go when they are afraid?" He giggled up at the vaulted ceiling. "Home, I suppose. Whatever hovel she rolled out of."

But Taristan's face only darkened, his brow furrowing.

"You underestimate her Ronin, even now." A muscle flexed in his jaw. "Corayne will go where she can stand and fight."

Beneath his anger, Erida sensed a begrudging respect, small as it was. She could not blame him for it. Corayne had survived more than they ever expected, a steel thorn in their side.

"There are many great fortresses across the Ward, and armies fearsome enough to face the Gallish legions," Erida muttered, tapping her lip.

"Ibal, Kasa, the Temurijon."

She pictured the old map of Allward in her council chambers. It encompassed the world from Rhashir to the Jyd, and all the thousands of miles in between.

With a wince, she realized the map was probably ashes by now, like everything else in the old keep.

"No, the Long Sea is thick with pirates. She would never survive the crossing," Erida continued with a shake of her head. She remembered ships of her own fleet falling victim to the sea devils. "Would the Temur take her in?"

Across the floor, Taristan met her eye. He went silent, thinking, then growled low in his throat.

"The Elders would," he spit out, sneering.

Erida narrowed her eyes, unconvinced. "They refused the call to fight before. At the first sign of failure."

"They will not now," Taristan answered bitterly. "With the defeat on their doorstep."

A year ago, a summons arrived in Erida's court. Simple parchment, sealed with the emblem of a stag. It belonged to no kingdom Erida knew. But she knew it now. *Iona*. The immortals asked for aid, to stop a madman before he could break the realm apart.

And I married him instead, she thought, her lips curling with amusement.

"How many enclaves are there across the Ward?" she asked aloud.

"Nine or ten," Ronin answered, speaking up when Taristan did not.

Again she remembered the map, and the endless stretches of Allward. *How many Elders hid within it*, she wondered. *How many might we have to fight?*

The prince busied himself with his sleeve, rolling it up to the elbow to expose a burn across his forearm. The flesh was half-healed, the scar ugly and mottled.

"From the tower?" she asked, indicating his arm.

Taristan shook his head. "The dragon."

A dizziness swept over Erida, too quick to blame on her injury or blood loss. She swallowed hard against the sensation, even as her mind spun with the thought of immortal warriors and monstrous dragons.

Fearsome, ferocious, she thought. *And invaluable.*

Erida spun on her heel, facing the wizard.

"Ronin."

"Your Majesty?" he drawled up at her. Somehow he also managed to make her title sound disrespectful.

She shrugged it off, undeterred.

"If we are to battle half the Ward, and all the immortals in it, we will need more than the legions and the Ashlanders," Erida said, her voice going hard as the marble beneath her feet. "Show us the power we *hope* you possess."

On the divan, Ronin frowned at the insult. He opened his mouth to fire back, but Erida held up her wounded hand, stopping him short.

She held his glare, matching it with her own blue fire.

"Bring us a dragon."

The wizard's white face dropped, his resentment disappearing for once. Fear shimmered in his eyes, unfamiliar and strange. But greed wove through it, stronger than any fear the wizard possessed. He nodded, only once, raising his hands in mock prayer. As with all things related to Red Ronin, Erida suspected there was more at play, a magic she could not understand flowing through his veins.

"The dragons are greater beings. To bind one requires greater sacrifice," Ronin answered. "As do all the gifts of What Waits."

Sneering, Erida raised her wounded hand.

"Is this not sacrifice?" she snarled.

Ronin's rat smile sent a shiver down her spine.

"If it can be done, I will do it," he said. "Your Majesty."

Behind him, the rose window of the cathedral tower glowed red, the sun rising higher across Ascal. It bathed them all in a circle of scarlet warmth, the chinks of light playing over the three. Queen, rogue, and wizard, standing like game pieces on a board. They felt united together, each one with their own part to play. In spite of her still-bleeding hand, Erida almost smiled.

Then Taristan dropped a knee, stricken, his hands scrabbling for purchase against the marble tile. A groan escaped his gritted teeth, a red flush traveling over his pale face. Around the perimeter of the hall, the Lionguard jumped to attention, sprinting forward to attend their prince.

Erida was quicker, all but sliding down next to him, her good hand braced against his shoulder. She searched his face, terror gripping her with icy fingers.

"What is it?" she demanded, pressing her palm to his fevered cheek.

Taristan could only gasp for air, his gaze fixed on the ground.

Ronin's shadow fell over them, his smile long gone. He watched for a silent moment, then cursed in a hissing language Erida did not know.

"Another Spindle has been lost," the wizard said, hollow.

Beneath her hand, Taristan slowed his breathing, his eyes gone all to red. Erida shifted carefully, blocking his face from view of the knights as they closed in.

"He is well," she said coldly, waving them off. "Back to your posts."

They obeyed without question, but Erida barely heard them,

distracted by the harried beating of her own heart. She felt the fury of What Waits on the other side of the door in her mind, his howls of rage echoing across the realms.

Her hand shifted, so that Taristan's jaw rested against her palm. It took only a little push to force him to meet her gaze.

What Waits stared out from her husband's eyes, all the black burned away, eaten by infernal scarlet.

"We must have a dragon," Erida hissed. The air tasted like smoke through her teeth. "And we must have her head."

20

CITY OF STONE
Corayne

By the end of the third week in the mountains, Corayne forgot what warmth felt like. No matter how many cloaks she wore or furs she burrowed under at night, the chill never truly disappeared. She envied Charlie and Garion, who clung to each other by the campfire. She could not even think about the Elders, stoic against the snow and freezing cliffs, lest she dissolve into jealous rage. They seemed only inconvenienced by the weather, not completely incapacitated as she was.

At the last town on the western slopes, Garion was kind enough to go into the market, paying in Elder coin for more suitable clothing. He did not worry about spies among the small towns of the valleys and foothills. Calidon was a frozen country, isolated by the mountains, their cities few and far away on the coast. The people here feared the winter more than any Gallish queen, and knew little of the world beyond their hills.

It was enough to keep Corayne and Charlie alive as they climbed up the mountain pass.

"And so we cross the Monadhrian," Garion said, his face barely visible below his hood. His breath steamed as they began the slow descent down.

"I thought we did that last week," Charlie replied from Corayne's other side, teeth chattering.

"That was the Monadhrion," Corayne said for what felt like the thousandth time.

Not that she could blame Charlie for his confusion. The three mountain ranges in Calidon, drawn down the kingdom like parallel claw marks, were all similarly named. And annoyingly so. They were the Monadhrion, the Monadhrian, and the Monadhstoirm. *We crossed the Monadhrion first,* she knew, remembering her maps. The Mountains of the Star formed the border of Calidon and Madrence, as good as a wall between the kingdoms.

"These are the Monadhrian, the Mountains of the Sun," she added, translating roughly from the Calidonian language.

"Whoever named them has a terrible sense of humor." Charlie snickered.

On a clear day, the sight would be breathtaking, the line of mountain ranges stretching in every direction. But they had not seen the sun in many days, since they began the climb out of the long valley of the River Airdha.

"We should be grateful." Garion raised a gloved hand and blew into it, warming numb fingers. "Even the Queen of Galland cannot send an army over this."

He gestured to the heights of the pass, thousands of feet above the unseen valley floor. Mountains speared higher still on either side, their peaks shrouded by shifting cloud. Snow lay perilously deep, the path ahead painstakingly carved by Valnir's Elders.

They would already be in Iona if not for us, Corayne knew. For all her days of travel, she felt like a child toddling after veteran soldiers.

But terrible as the crossing was, she felt safe through the mountains.

The only danger here was the terrain. An avalanche, a bear, a sudden blizzard. Nothing compared to what already lay behind her.

Or what lies ahead.

The descent into the final valley took another two days, the air growing warmer by the hour. Even so, snow still lay thick and deep as they left the rocky crags of the Monadhrian. They broke through the cloud bank as they reached the tree line. Ancient pines and black yew trees gnarled together, impassable as the Castlewood, obscuring all but a glimpse of the River Avanar winding through the valley.

Shifting fog and mist streaked the landscape, like ink spilled over a page. As it shifted, Corayne caught a rare glimpse of a distant ridge, a long spit of rock thrust out of the valley. The river wound around its base, pooling to form a long lake between the hills.

There was a wall along the ridge, blending into the landscape, gray and white and green. Towers seemed to grow from the ridge itself, straight as granite fingers.

Iona.

Then the mist shifted, the yew trees closed in, and the Elder city disappeared again. Corayne heaved a cold breath, her heart pounding in her ears.

She tried to balance what she remembered from Domacridhan's tales with what she saw now. Iona appeared to be more fortress than city, the entire ridge walled with gray stone, and a high-towered castle at its crown. It filled Corayne with equal parts relief and dread. Their long march was over, but battle loomed, black as a storm on the horizon.

Charlie lowered his furred hood, his breath steaming in the air. Since Gidastern, he always searched the sky first, his gaze sweeping through the clouds. Corayne knew why. She did the same, bracing herself for a flash of jeweled scale or an arc of flame. They could not predict the movements of one dragon, let alone three. The threat hung over them still.

"Dom called it the largest enclave on the Ward," Corayne mumbled to him. She pointed her chin through the trees. "Certainly we will be safe among them."

"I thought the same in Sirandel," Charlie replied. "I only got a single night of peace."

"That's my fault," she said, apologetic. "Like everything, it seems."

Tsking, Charlie grinned at her. "Now, now, let's not make it all about you."

Their laughter echoed off the trees, breaking the muffled silence of a snowy forest. A bird fluttered somewhere and rose with a burst of flapping wings.

Garion wheeled to the sound, his face tight with worry. Charlie only laughed louder, amused.

"Elders or not, a city is a city," Garion snapped. Again, Corayne was reminded of Sorasa and her well-honed skepticism. "We must be on the lookout for spies in their midst. And assassins too."

Before Corayne could open her mouth, Charlie raised a finger and pointed. He jabbed directly at Garion's chest.

"There's one," the priest said, chuckling.

A twitch of a smile betrayed Garion and he looked away to the woods again, hiding his own smirk.

"I pity the Amhara who tries Iona," Corayne said, feeling a little warmth bloom in her chest.

The sun broke weakly through the clouds and treetops, a few shafts of light fighting their way through the branches. Corayne tipped her head, enjoying for a moment the silence and the sun.

* * *

The gates of Iona swung wide, like welcoming arms. Or open jaws.

Elder bowmen stood the ramparts above, silhouetted against the rapidly moving clouds and shifting rays of sunlight. A cold wind roared over the city, stirring the mist through the gray walls and round towers.

It shivered Corayne down to her toes.

She tightened her grip on the reins of her horse, letting it follow along with the rest of the company.

Corayne tried to take in everything she could. Great slabs of granite and sandstone made up Iona, the city worn gray and brown by long centuries of wind and rain. As Sirandel seemed grown from the forest, Iona was born from the ridge, its walls and towers like jagged cliffs. Moss grew over the roofs and ramparts, peeking out beneath the melting snow.

Stags were carved into the iron-banded gates, their heads raised proudly. More were sculpted from granite, set into the ramparts, and gray-green flags snapped in the harsh wind, embroidered with antlers. The Ionian soldiers wore similar. With a pang of sadness, Corayne remembered Domacridhan's old cloak, its edge woven with silver stags. It was lost to Gidastern now, burned with the rest of him.

Only his memory remains.

Her heart twisted again when she raised her eyes to the unfolding city, the stone streets laid out in a straight line climbing up the ridge.

She saw Domacridhan everywhere, in too many faces. Most of the Ionians looked like him, not only in appearance but also manner. They were stiff, scowling, more statue than living flesh, cold as the mountains around their enclave. Clad in gray or green clothing, fine embossed leather or embroidered silk. They stared after the company as they passed, their lips pursed and silent, fair heads turned and pale eyes round. It felt strange to know many of the Elders were older than their own city, their flesh and blood more ancient than the stone.

To Corayne's relief, it was not just her they studied, but Valnir too. The sight of another Elder monarch was clearly out of the ordinary, especially one fresh from battle, with too few soldiers left in his company.

The Monarch of Sirandel stared forward, his high-boned face tipped up, yellow eyes steady. His fine cloak and armor were dirty from the road and the dragon battle, but he wore them as proudly as any court regalia. Many an Ionian Elder stared after him, something strange passing across their white faces.

Corayne remembered how Valnir's court looked when he rallied to war. *I lay down the branch*, he said then. *I take up the bow.*

She saw the same shock in the Elders now. Their illusion of calm shattered as whispers rippled through the growing crowd, following them up to the castle at the crown of the city.

Tiarma.

Her heart leapt in her chest as they approached it, her body going cold beneath her clothes. The castle was a mountain in itself, with moss and snow clinging to every hollow. Corayne counted a dozen towers of varying size, some grand with arched glass windows, others thick-walled, with arrow slits, built for a siege.

All of it gave her a strange feeling, some unsettling doubt deep in her mind. Like a thread out of place in a tapestry, or a word just beyond her grasp. The castle felt oddly familiar, though she could not say why.

Valnir led them to a stone landing before the castle, flat and wide. It offered a dazzling view of the city below and the valley beyond, the mountain peaks still hidden among the clouds. With no shelter from the wind, Corayne slid off her horse before the howling gale could throw her from the saddle.

She was grateful to be on even ground, the many days traversing the mountains still evident in her sore legs. The wind buffeted her again, blowing her black hair loose from her usual braid. She did her best to fight it back into submission, fingers working as she walked.

Charlie followed and batted her hands away, retying her braid with an annoyed hiss.

"Thanks," Corayne mumbled back, dropping her voice as low as she could. *Not that whispers mean much around Elder ears.*

Across the landing, a set of shallow stairs led up to the castle and a set of oaken doors, polished to a high sheen. Like the gates, a pair of stags reared on either side, their antlers impossibly large and complicated. Two guards mimicked the stags, flanking the doorway in overwrought armor, with silver antlers on their helms.

Corayne doubted they could fight in such a monstrosity. But both bore spears, the tips sharp and glinting.

They did not move as Valnir approached, his own horse left behind. No one stood in his way or stopped his company trailing behind.

The oak doors swung inward, revealing only darkness. Corayne could not hesitate, as much as she wanted to.

This was Dom's home, she reminded herself, trying to calm her rising fear. *Dom trusted these Elders, Dom loved them. These are his people.*

A sour taste filled her mouth.

These people left him to fight, and die, alone.

Her heart hardened beneath her leather armor, the Spindleblade heavy along her spine. Grimly, she hoisted the sword higher over her shoulder. As much as she hated Taristan's blade, it brought her some comfort as they entered the castle.

Here is proof of what we have done, and what we must still do.

The castle felt cold as the streets, its vaulted ceilings and arching halls devoid of all warmth. There were no crackling fires in merry hearths, no courtiers peering from corners. Not even servants scurrying to and fro. If there were guards, Corayne could not see them. Though she strongly suspected they could see her.

Like the city, all was gray and white and green. But instead of cloud and snow and moss, it was granite and marble and green velvet worked through with silver thread. She glimpsed a dark feasting hall set with long tables, big enough to hold two hundred at least. Corayne wagered there were real gemstones sewn into the tapestries, while the glass windows sparkled without a hint of stain. A wall of arched windows looked down on a courtyard, a tangle of dead rosebushes at its center. The vines spiraled and climbed, working up the courtyard walls with thorny fingers.

Beautiful as it was, Corayne could not help but feel uneasy. It reminded her too much of Domacridhan. Worse than that, it reminded her of Cortael, the father she would never meet.

This was his home once too, she thought, swallowing around a hard lump in her throat. She tried not to picture him, a man, a teenager, a young boy, mortal among the Elders, given all and nothing at the same time.

She blinked rapidly, refusing to be betrayed by her own tears, and followed Valnir through an intricately carved set of doors. Corayne glimpsed magnificent animals worked into the wood—stags, bears, foxes, and so many others. Representing all the enclaves, and every Elder still clinging to the Ward.

With wide eyes, she drank in the carving. In her heart, she reached out to every sigil, every enclave. The shark, the panther, the stallion, the hawk, the ram, the tiger, the wolf. Hope beyond hope exploded in her heart, almost too much to hold.

Her breath caught when the doors flung open, beckoning into the great hall of Iona.

Green marble stared up at her, while columns marched the length of the hall, limestone statues between them. Monarchs or gods, Corayne did not know.

Gods, she thought suddenly, raising her eyes to the throne at the far end of the hall. *There is only one Monarch here.*

Isibel of Iona stared down from her high throne, the living branch of an ash tree across her knees. Its leaves stood out, sharply green against her muted clothing.

She wore soft gray silk embroidered with jewels, sewn in the pattern of stars or snowflakes. Sunlight flared through one of the high windows, filling the hall as the clouds blew past. Her gems caught the light, winking across her gown and in her long, blond hair. She had no overcoat or furs, despite the chill clinging to the marble hall.

Corayne remembered Erida, resplendent in velvet and emeralds, hair coiled to complex perfection, a heavy golden crown across her brow. She smiled, charming even as she lied, manipulative as she was beautiful. Erida was a burning candle, throwing off a deceptive warmth, her sapphire eyes holding every promise of the world.

Isibel was the opposite. Ancient, distant, cold as the winter.

Her eyes promised nothing.

Only her resemblance to Domacridhan gave Corayne pause. They shared the same carved features and tall frame, evident even as Isibel remained sitting. But her eyes were not Dom's. His were a merry, dancing green. Her own were gray, impossibly pale, with a faraway look.

Corayne saw the same eyes in Valnir.

She is Glorian-born, and carries the light of different stars, she thought, remembering the old phrase. She felt such light in her own blood, in the little pieces of another realm long forgotten. It lay in the steel of the

Spindleblade, forged in the heart of a Spindle crossing. Such a light blazed from Isibel now, too ancient for a mortal to grasp.

The Monarch was not alone on her dais. Two pale advisors flanked her, one with long gray braids and the other with short bronze hair streaked silver. Both watched the company with calculating eyes.

Corayne felt dirty and windblown, a gutter rat before a swan. Ruefully, she wished they'd had time to clean up before meeting the ruler of an immortal city. She halted behind Valnir, and instinctively bowed.

Out of the corner of her eye, she saw Charlie and Garion do the same, along with the rest of the Sirandels. Only Valnir remained upright, barely inclining his chin.

On the throne, Isibel offered the same, dipping her head.

"Valnir."

Her voice was both light and deep, layered with great power. It made Corayne shiver.

"Isibel," Valnir replied. His stern manner softened a little, and he put a hand to his own heart. The other still gripped the yew bow. "I grieve for your daughter, and your nephew."

Corayne's throat tightened, but Isibel's serene expression did not change.

"I have no use for grief," she said, too sharp for Corayne's liking. Then she tipped a finger, dismissing the subject entirely.

Sadness turned to anger, itching beneath Corayne's skin.

"It is not like you to travel with so few, Valnir," the Monarch said, her pale eyes spearing through them. "And certainly not with the Realm's Hope under your protection."

Corayne straightened under Isibel's attention. Her fist curled at her side, nails biting into the palm of her hand. The sting helped ground

Corayne against the scrutiny of an Elder monarch, and the frustration roaring inside her.

The Realm's Hope. The title smarted like salt in a wound and Corayne held back a disdainful scoff.

Slowly, with unnatural grace, Isibel unfolded herself from the throne. She stood monstrously tall and lean, the ash branch still in one hand.

"Corayne of Old Cor," Isibel said. As with Valnir, she dipped her chin in rare deference.

This time, Corayne did not bow, or return the courtesy. Her teeth clenched, the Spindleblade hard against her back. *Corayne of Old Cor.* The name stung again, the pain of it too sharp to ignore this time.

"My name is Corayne an-Amarat," she said, her voice echoing off the endless marble.

Next to her, Charlie pursed his lips and shut his eyes, as if bracing for a blow.

Isibel only took a step forward, not smiling or scowling. Unlike Domacridhan, she kept her emotions well in check, her face unreadable as a stone mask.

"I wish we could have met under different circumstances," she said, descending to the green marble.

Valnir neatly stepped aside, allowing room for Isibel to face Corayne fully. The weight of her stare felt like being struck by lightning. Even so, Corayne would not look away.

"I wish we never had to meet at all," she said, hot anger eating away at her fear.

Charlie visibly winced.

Behind the Monarch, Valnir's yellow eyes flared wide. A muscle clenched in his sculpted cheek.

Corayne wanted to melt into the floor.

To the surprise of everyone, Isibel only tipped her head and extended her free arm, bending it at the elbow. She offered it as if she were a friend, and not a frustration.

"I have something to show you," Isibel said. Up close, her eyes were luminous, like pearls or the full, haunting moon. "Walk with me, Corayne."

21

PRECIOUS CARGO
Domacridhan

Fleethaven burned, its fires licking out along the canals, the wrecks of half-sunken warships like skeletons against the smoke.

Dom felt like a carrion bird, scanning the docks for some opportunity, his immortal eyes noting every soldier of the city watch. Most ran for the flames, their attention elsewhere. If word of the turmoil at the New Palace reached the dockside, it was certainly not a priority now.

Sorasa and Dom used the distraction to their full advantage.

They moved in unison, without discussion, their boots slapping the planks of the dockside. As the way narrowed, hemmed in by bodies, Dom allowed Sorasa to take lead. She slipped through the crowd with ease, heading for the galley with purple sails.

She turned neatly down the dock splits, avoiding the crew of another ship as they hastily loaded whatever cargo they could. There was a gangway, but Sorasa moved past it without thought, making her way to the back of the long galley. Dom glimpsed a flag hanging limp from the stern, emblazoned with a golden torch. He did not know which kingdom it marked, but he knew this ship owed no allegiance to any crown.

His ears prickled, a familiar voice weaving down from the deck above them.

"They knew the risks," she muttered, her voice blunt and cold.

Someone else answered. "We can wait for them another moment. You remember Corranport—"

Her reply was venomous. "In Corranport they burned a granary, not half the Gallish navy. We need to go. Now."

There was a thud as someone banged a fist on the rail of the ship. "The palace is on fire too, it will buy us time, no one's looking at the docks while the Queen's own castle burns. They can't order the port closed—"

"*Now*," the woman snarled.

A long sigh answered, then a rattling breath.

"Yes, Captain."

Boots scuffed on the deck and orders were whispered, oars creaking as the crew adjusted their grips. Overhead, sailors balanced in the rigging, ready to drop sail the second the ship hit open water.

Sorasa jumped quietly from the dock, landing softly in the rope net lashed alongside the hull above the waterline. Dom followed, the pair of them holding tight to the ship, their breath low and even, their figures obscured by the darkness and the smoke settling over the city.

The docks teemed, crowded and noisy, but a shout rang out across the fray. On the deck of the ship, voices answered, one loudest of all.

"Move," the captain bellowed, running to the rail.

Dom shrank back against the ropes, Sorasa right beside him, the two of them clinging to the ship like barnacles on the belly of a whale.

On the docks, the crowd surged, parting in two as if cut down the middle. Two men charged through, aiming for the galley. One was a massive Jydi brawler throwing people aside, his bare arms tattooed in whorls and knots. The other was lean and small, black-skinned, far more agile, with a wide grin on his face. He laughed as they rumbled up the gangway, the plank pulling up a second behind them.

And then the ship was moving, the ropes cast off, the oars rising and falling, the fetid water of the Ascal canals breaking against the hull.

Their ship was not the only one to sense the danger. Quick-minded captains forced their own boats out into the canal, rope lines tangling in their wake. All down the port, the sailors of Wayfarer did their best to flee before more disaster befell the docks.

Dom did not dare to hope, his jaw so tight he thought his teeth might shatter. Sorasa's own heart pounded in his head, her fear all but poisoning the air. Neither seemed to breathe, their arms clawed into the ropes, the spray of the water hissing over them with every pull of the oars.

The air grew hotter as they sailed for freedom, the blaze that was Fleethaven lighting up the black sky. Dom heard the shouts of sailors in the water and guards on the dock, orders barked while cries for help filled the air. In spite of himself, he felt pity for the men of Galland, enemies though they were. It wasn't their fault they served a queen and her demon.

Then the Lion's Teeth loomed, both towers filled with soldiers. Dom could see their silhouettes in the windows and on the ramparts, all of them in disarray. The black chain hung from either side of the canal, disappearing into the water, the thick links menacing as a coiled snake.

Dom strained his ears, waiting for the chain to move, waiting for their doom. He could almost feel it, the shackles around his wrists again, the collar around his neck. The darkness of the prison cells, inescapable and endless.

A rush of air hissed from his mouth as the towers passed over the ship, menacing and monstrous.

And then—the towers fell behind them, already fading behind the wall of smoke.

On the deck, the crew of the *Tempestborn* whooped a cheer, their pace increasing as the purple sails unfurled to catch the wind rolling them into the Long Sea.

Captain Meliz an-Amarat cheered loudest of all, her figure silhouetted against the flames.

Her cry sent a chill down Dom's spine.

She sounds like Corayne, he thought, shivering.

Then the splash of a wave hit the ship hard, the water colder than the river canals. It felt like a slap, washing over Dom and Sorasa. He put out a hand instinctively, pressing her against the ropes. Her scowl burned through the fading light, wet hair plastered to her face. But Sorasa said nothing, letting Dom hold her steady.

Dom gave a shake of his head, his stomach already rolling with the current as it caught the galley. He clenched his teeth against the familiar nausea. Already he dreaded whatever voyage lay ahead.

When the waves abated enough, Sorasa climbed, using the lattice of ropes to haul herself up the side and onto the deck. Dom followed with ease, half-soaked. Both landed with a splatter, looking like drowned creatures of the deep.

They were met with a veteran pirate crew, a dozen blades drawn and waiting. Their faces glowed in the light of a few lanterns, the weak flames washing them all orange. Beneath the aggression and bravado, Dom read the fear in their faces.

He blinked wearily at them all and shook himself off like a wet dog.

Next to him, Sorasa curled a lip with disdain. She wrung out her hair with a sniff, as if she had simply stepped in from a rainstorm, and not the black sea itself.

"Captain an-Amarat," she drawled, her voice carrying over the deck. "Your hospitality has not improved."

At the forecastle, Meliz an-Amarat was already moving, her dark brown eyes wide, reflecting the distant firelight of Ascal. Though she wore plain clothing, there was no mistaking her for anything but the ship's ruthless captain. She glared between Elder and Amhara, a crease appearing between her eyebrows. Her teeth gleamed, set at a hard edge between parted lips.

She reached the deck but gave no order to her ravenous crew. Their blades remained, poised to strike.

Her eyes traveled over them, fast and sharp as a whip crack. "You look worse than the last time I saw you," Meliz said. "And you looked quite terrible then."

Sorasa sneered. "The Queen's dungeons tend to do that to a person."

At that, Meliz's face dropped, her snarling shield cast away. Her gaze hardened and she took another step, waving a hand to her crew. They released behind her, lowering their weapons, but not their eyes.

The captain's voice shook.

"Where is my daughter?"

Dom's heart clenched, his cheeks going hot.

"We do not know," he said with a heavy sigh. Internally, he braced for the storm that was a mother's fury.

Meliz an-Amarat did not disappoint. Her own blade snapped from a sheath at her hip, the short sword rigid in the air, the edge of the blade catching the lantern light. She looked wild, seaborn, chaotic as any wave beneath the ship. Merciless as the Long Sea.

Then she glanced back to the black horizon, and the glimmering embers of Ascal. Dom saw the war inside her, raging between her need to escape and her will to turn back.

"Is Corayne in—?"

Sorasa stepped forward, within an inch of Meliz's sword. She paid little mind to the steel and held out her tattooed palm. As if calming a spooked horse, and not a murderous pirate.

"Corayne is still in the north. Somewhere," she said, forceful and stern. Her copper eyes widened, filled with resolve. "She is alive, I promise you that, Meliz."

Lies came so easily to Sorasa Sarn. Dom saw how difficult it was for her to tell the truth.

Meliz's sword lowered an inch. "You're going after her."

"With all we have," Dom offered, matching step with the assassin. They presented a united front, or at least their own strange version of it. "Whatever that may be."

The captain's eyes narrowed as she scoffed.

"My daughter, alone in the wilderness," Meliz muttered, even as she sheathed her sword. "Alone against all this—I should throw you both overboard."

I do not disagree, Dom thought ruefully, his shame returning tenfold. He looked to the waves, dappled with lantern light before fading into darkness. Even the burning city on the horizon glowed weaker and weaker, as the *Tempestborn* pushed farther out into the Long Sea.

He swallowed hard, fighting back both seasickness and revulsion. Ascal was the largest city in the world. *How many innocents did we leave to burn?*

Meliz's sharp command cut through his thoughts.

"Kireem, clear your cabin," she barked, waving at one of the crew. "These two look ready to drop."

In a flurry of motion, the crewmember leapt down from the forecastle only to disappear into the lower decks. Dom recognized him not only from their previous meeting on the Long Sea, but also from Adira. In the tea shop, when Corayne realized her mother's ship was in port. Kireem and the Jydi bruiser were there, whispering about the ship's narrow escape from a kraken. As before, Kireem still wore an eyepatch, his brown skin like dusk in the lantern light.

Dom eyed the deck again, weighing the brutish crew and the menacing *Tempestborn*. One of the masts was new, the wood a different color than the rest of the ship. *The work of the kraken.*

"Come along," Meliz grumbled under her breath, indicating for the pair to follow.

They did so without question.

"Can we avoid any more swimming in the future?" Dom muttered, stripping off his leather jerkin, then his undershirt. He was glad to be rid of the wet, filthy clothes.

Sorasa gave him a withering glance as they walked down the deck. Her cloak was gone, discarded in an alleyway, leaving only her battered leathers.

"I shall take your comfort into account for our next escape," she said acidly.

Overhead, they were finally out from under the smoky clouds of Ascal, and a few stars winked to life in the night sky. Dom scowled, noting the pink haze to the once-bright constellations. He remembered the sunset in the city, as they fought their way up out of the dungeons. The sky looked red as blood, unnaturally so. It unsettled him deeply, and he longed for the empty blue of Iona, crisp and cold.

Worse still was Sorasa. She squinted up at the sky as he did, concern evident even through her emotionless mask. They exchanged worried glances, but kept their mouths shut.

This is the realm breaking, Dom knew, one hand trembling at his side. *Little by little.*

All the pirates watched as they passed, the oarsmen looking up from their benches and crew looking down from the rigging. They were fearsome as mortals could be, armed even on the deck of their own ship, marked by scars and tattoos and sun-worn skin. Sorasa stared back at them darkly, reading faces as Dom did.

"How quiet is your crew, Captain?" the assassin bit out.

Meliz glared over her shoulder with a look to freeze blood. "There isn't a soul aboard who would sell you to the Lioness, or her Rose Prince."

It sounded like the truth, at least to Domacridhan. He looked to Sorasa, weighing her reply. She understood mortals better than he ever would.

She seemed satisfied, and Dom relaxed a little.

"Good," Sorasa said, as close to a thank-you as someone like her could manage. "And hang a red marker on your flag."

This time, the captain furrowed her brow, confused if not annoyed.

"A spare shirt, a sheet, a rag," Sorasa added, explaining. "Anything, just red."

"Who are you signaling to?" Meliz wondered, her eyes narrowed.

"Perhaps no one," the assassin muttered.

Sigil, Dom thought. *Wherever she may be.*

The single door on deck opened into shadow, a cramped set of stairs falling away below. Meliz led them without breaking stride, well-used to the sway of the sea and the tight quarters. Only Dom's immortal grace kept him from pitching sideways or tumbling down to the deck below.

The Lioness and the Rose Prince. Dom turned the titles over in his mind. They sounded like characters from legend, not flesh-and-blood mortals.

"What do you know of Erida and Taristan?" Dom asked, watching Meliz through the dim light.

The pirate frowned, reaching the bottom of the stair. Over the collar of her jacket, her throat bobbed.

"I know little of queens and conquerors . . . but what I've seen with my own eyes is terrible enough," she said, indicating her own neck, showing the edge of a circular scar.

Dom knew the sight too well. He thought of the kraken's tentacles, puckered with fleshy, sucking circles.

"And the rumors," Meliz pressed on, her voice harsh in the close air of the lower deck. "The red sky. Whispers of the dead walking."

A cold chill went down Dom's bare spine. He was too familiar with the corpse army, men and women slaughtered only to rise again. The Ashlanders and their rotten skeletons, lurching from one realm to poison the next. And What Waits behind it all, a puppeteer with Taristan on His strings.

"Something is wrong in the realm, and it seems to flow from the Queen and her prince," Meliz muttered.

Dom glanced to Sorasa to find her already staring, hard-eyed against the shadows. Her lips pursed to nothing, her gaze shining with the same memories Dom carried.

"You have no idea," the Elder muttered.

Dom had to hunch as they walked, his ear half-pressed up against the ceiling. The floor below made a hollow sound. It was a false bottom, hiding another few feet of storage. What the *Tempestborn* carried beneath the decks, he did not know and could not care.

At last they reached a door at the far end of a collection of hammocks, a few occupied by snoring crew. Kireem left the door to his cabin open, the interior lit by a lantern. He was even good enough to leave a jug of water and a basin.

Meliz eyed the interior with a sniff. "I'll have some food and fresh clothes sent down."

"That isn't necessary," Dom replied without thought, forgetting his own bare chest.

The captain gave him a withering look. "Yes it is."

Flushing, Dom made a low sound like a grumble. "Thank you," he ground out.

"Make yourself worthy of my kindness, Elder," Meliz snapped back, before leaving them both with a sweep of her coat and long, black hair.

Sorasa wasted no time, pushing into the cabin as she unlaced her leathers, fingers skipping neatly down the seams of her ruined jacket.

Dom lingered in the doorway, examining the walls of the narrow cabin with a sour look. There was a single small window, the glass so thick it barely let in any light at all, a little ledge for the basin, and a thin bed against the wall.

"Hardly an Elder palace," Sorasa offered, filling the silence. She threw off her jacket with little regard, then kicked off her old boots. "I think you'll survive."

Her heartbeat did not change, but Dom's thrummed. His bare skin suddenly felt hot against the close, damp air.

Swallowing, he looked to the walls again. A twitchy cabin boy appeared in the doorway, leaving behind a pile of clothes before disappearing again.

"I had more room in my dungeon," Dom muttered, measuring the space in his mind.

Sorasa inspected the clothing, laying out a pair of shirts. Both were worn but clean, thick white cotton with laces at the collar.

"You're welcome to go back," she said, turning her back to the door.

Her ruined undershirt slipped over her head and fell to the floor, her muscled back exposed to the cold air. Dom spun on one heel, avoiding the sight of bare skin and fresh bruises. A few of the scars he knew, courtesy of a sea serpent or an Ashlander. Even just a passing glance had burned her many tattoos into his mind. A line of letters marched along her spine, another set of symbols inked down her skeletal ribs. The last of them stood out painfully, more scar than tattoo. Dom knew it marked her as an exile, cast out of the Amhara Guild.

The sight of it seared something in him, his own ribs itching. He had to restrain himself from holding on to the image, counting the tattoos and scars, each mark another letter in the long tale of Sorasa Sarn.

"You should have more to eat," he said without looking back to her. His keen ears picked up the sound of fabric sliding over skin as she pulled the shirt over her head.

"*You* should take care of yourself for once, Elder," Sorasa bit back at him, all venom. "Here."

He turned in time to catch the other long tunic, snatching it out of the air. She faced him across the doorway, still undressing. The tunic covered most of her, too long, and she shucked off her breeches without a thought.

Dom wanted to turn around again but it felt like admitting defeat. Everything about Sorasa was a challenge, no matter the circumstance. Tightening his jaw, he pulled the stolen clothing over his head. It stretched wide over his chest and shoulders, barely fitting his broad frame. With a burst of satisfaction, he noticed Sorasa's own concentration falter, her eyes flickering over his skin for a brief second.

It didn't last long.

"Stand guard or sleep, but do something useful." Her voice sharpened. "I can take first watch if you need."

He bristled, falling into his usual scowl. "I do not trust a ship of pirates."

"Even Corayne's mother?" Sorasa all but laughed, shaking her head. "Even I know to trust her. Besides, I'll take pirates over a Spindle."

"And what of Sigil? Will your scrap of red signal to her across the endless miles of the realm?"

The beat of Sorasa's heart betrayed her. Dom heard her pulse quicken and saw the feather thrum of the vein in her neck.

"Sigil is either trapped back in the harbor, or free on the waves, her ship escaping with our own," she finally said, her voice cold. "I can only hope for the latter now."

Then her face softened a little.

"We have a long road ahead of us, Dom. Make ready for it."

Much as she tried to hide it, Dom saw the exhaustion creep over her. He felt it too, heavier than anything he'd ever carried. It ran bone-deep now, after so many months. Only moving forward kept it at bay.

Dom did not know what to do now, when he could run no further, and do nothing but wait.

"Where does that road go?" he asked bitterly. Slowly, he unbuckled the belt around his hips, and laid down the greatsword among Sorasa's things.

She sat on the cramped bed, if only to give him room to move around the narrow cabin.

"Your guess is as good as mine," she huffed. "Better, probably."

He quirked a blond brow at her. "How so?"

"You have good hearts, you and Corayne. You think differently than I can."

"Is that a compliment?" he asked, confused.

Her laugh was menacing as she leaned back against a meager pillow, her eyes half-lidded.

"No."

Dom pushed back against the opposite wall, folding his arms. The air stirred as the door eased closed, shutting them both into the cabin together.

"She's had a three-week head start, and then some," he said, watching the pink stars through the window. "If Oscovko survived, she could go back to Vodin."

"Too many spies. Erida would know it soon enough and drag her out of the city." Sorasa yawned into one hand. The other traced lines in mid-air, walking a map only she could see. "The Jydi might take her in. She would not go into the Castlewood."

"Why?"

She shook her head sharply.

"That forest is Spindlerotten, too dangerous, even for her."

Something needled at the back of Dom's mind.

"What of Sirandel?" he asked.

Sorasa's eyes flashed with rare confusion.

"There is an immortal enclave in the Castlewood," he offered with a smug curl of his mouth. Part of him delighted in knowing something Sorasa did not.

Her face darkened with disgust. "We could have used them in Gidastern."

Dom's heart dropped in his chest. He could not help but agree, nodding.

"Ridha failed to sway them before," he said bitterly. "Perhaps they have changed their minds."

His cousin's name was still a knife in his chest, always twisting. It was easier to ignore the pain of her loss in the escape, but now it returned tenfold. As much as he tried to cling to happier memories, of centuries and decades past, he could not shake the sight of her dying. Her green armor awash in blood. Taristan kneeling over her, watching as the light left her eyes. And then, worse than anything Dom had ever seen—the light returned, corrupted and infernal.

Sorasa watched him carefully from the bed, her face still. He expected some sort of reprimand, or unfeeling Amhara advice.

Put the pain away, she told him once.

I cannot, he answered in his mind. *No matter how hard I try.*

"She did not survive," Sorasa said quietly. "Your cousin."

He stared at the floorboards, knotted and uneven, slightly curved beneath his boots. Silence fell over the cabin, but not truly. Dom heard everything above deck, from the scrape of rope through iron rings to the jolly curses of the crew.

"Worse than that," Dom finally spat.

She made a low hum in her throat, almost a purr.

"No wonder you went back to kill him."

Dom raised his eyes with a flick, expecting pity. He saw pride instead.

"You knew I would," he muttered.

It was the closest thing to a thank-you he could muster.

I would be dead in the palace, my body burned to ashes, if not for you.

"You are painfully easy to predict, Elder," Sorasa scoffed, fluffing the pillow behind her head. With a satisfied sigh, her lids fell shut.

Dom did not move from his place against the wall, as much as he wanted to lie down on the floor to sleep.

"Is that a compliment, Amhara?" he muttered, if only to himself.

Without opening her eyes, she grinned.

"No."

22

THE BLOOD OF OLD COR
Corayne

Cold as the throne room was, the vaults below the castle were even colder. Isibel led them down a spiraling passage, into the ridge itself, the smooth walls turning to black volcanic rock. The air was stale, undisturbed this deep underground. Doorways and alcoves opened on either side, holding statues or chests of gods knew what. Corayne imagined rooms piled high with Elder gold, artifacts of Glorian, or even tombs. The last made her shiver again, as much as it intrigued her.

Isibel required no guards and carried no weapons Corayne could see. There was only the ash branch, still in hand.

They walked in bitter silence, Corayne's footsteps echoing like the thump of her heart.

She wondered if this was punishment for her disrespect in the throne room, and hoped Isibel did not mean to abandon her deep beneath the castle. Some part of her knew the Monarch could not. *For I am the Realm's Hope*, she thought, sneering to herself.

"I don't believe you," Corayne said suddenly. Like her footsteps, her voice echoed down the curving passage.

Isibel halted, perplexed, and turned her piercing eyes on Corayne.

"You do grieve for them," Corayne explained. "For Ridha and Dom."

A shadow crossed the Monarch's pale face. She held Corayne's stare for a long, seemingly endless minute. Time passed differently to Elders.

"Of course I do," the Monarch finally said, her voice heavy.

Then she returned to walking, moving faster through the cold stone passages. After so many days of travel and endless worry, Corayne wanted to curl up on the floor. But she trudged along, stubborn. Her resentment was fuel enough.

"I saw what you overcame. How you escaped. What you left behind." Isibel's voice echoed down the passage. "And what I lost."

It was Corayne's turn for confusion. She eyed the Monarch, from her slippered feet to her long, white fingers. All of her glowed, power trembled in the air, as if stirred up by her presence.

"Dom said you had some magic," she muttered, trying to remember. "Rare even for your kind. *Sendings.*"

"Yes, that is what it is called," Isibel said. "I can send a shadow of myself some distances, to see what I wish. And speak if I can."

Corayne saw Domacridhan in his aunt's face, in her inability to understand such terrible pain.

"I was in Gidastern," she explained, her voice catching. Her eyes shone. "With my daughter, in her last moments. As much as I could have been."

It was impossible not to feel for Isibel, as much as Corayne disliked her. Corayne saw her own mother, desperate on the deck of a ship, trying to save her child from the end of the world. Isibel was the same once. And she failed.

"I watched Taristan end her life," Isibel continued. "And I watched him began it anew."

She broke then, a low gasp escaping her lips. Then her teeth flashed, catching her lip, as if to cage all her sorrow.

Corayne could only watch, sick at heart. Corayne had not been there to see Taristan raise the dead of Gidastern. She could barely imagine what horrors befell his victims. No one was safe from him, even in death. Her own eyes stung and she brushed away a hot tear, scrubbing at her face.

She could not think of the others beneath Taristan's sway. Dom, Sorasa. Andry. It would break her heart too deeply.

"I did not know I could wish my own daughter dead, but the alternative—" Isibel cut herself off, her eyes welling again. It felt like watching an old tree battle a storm and refuse to bend. "It is a curse beyond all else."

A curse you could have avoided, Corayne thought bitterly. But for all her frustration, she could not twist the knife.

"I grieve for them too," she said, her own voice echoing to the stone.

The truth of it sobered them both, and they settled into uneasy silence as they walked. Isibel was blank-faced again by the time they reached her destination, a door of polished ebony on iron hinges. When Isibel put a hand to it, it swung open easily.

"I am two thousand years old, and have known few mortals in my later days," Isibel said, stepping into the vault. "I knew your father best of them."

Corayne's mouth fell open, her eyes flying in every direction, trying to hold more than she could ever carry.

The vault was perfectly round, with an arched ceiling. Tables and shelves lined the exterior, each laden with some artifact, relic, or book. Only the stone slab at the center of the room was empty, bare but for a red velvet cloth. An iron hoop of new candles hung overhead, already burning. One of Isibel's attendants had clearly prepared the vault for them, lighting the torches as well as laying out a side table of provisions. Hungry as she was, Corayne ignored the plates of dried fruit and bottles of wine.

In this moment, she cared only for the vault, and its treasures.

It was not gold, silver, or jewels that entranced her, though there were many.

Her fingers trembled as she reached out to the closest shelf, her vision tunneling to a painstakingly piled stack of scrolls. She hesitated, reluctant to touch something so ancient and fragile. Instead, she tipped her head sideways, to read the lettering on the parchment.

"This is the language of Old Cor," she breathed.

Without thought, she slid the Spindleblade from her shoulder and drew the sword a few inches, revealing the steel beneath.

"*A thread of gold against hammer and anvil, and steel between all three. A crossing made, in blood and blade, and both become the key,*" she quoted from memory, remembering Valnir's translation.

The letters etched into the blade matched the ones on the scrolls, the piled parchments, the books, and the many inscriptions scrawled across the relics. They called out to her, with voices she could not understand, singing a song at the edge of memory.

Corayne whirled again, going from table to table, running her hands over gilded cups and silver tablets. Old coins stamped with roses. Ink pots. Arrowheads still sharp and gleaming. Gold, silver, gemstones of every color. A magnificent helmet of bronze and gold stared out from a table all its own, the faceplate inscribed with more words Corayne could not read. Real rubies glittered along the helm, dotted with pear-shaped emeralds. *Roses*, Corayne knew, tracing the symbol of Old Cor.

The same flowers bloomed over the velvet draped across the empty slab, painstakingly picked out in shining thread. Slowly, Corayne drew the rest of the Spindleblade, revealing the rippling steel of another realm. It seemed to hum to her, joining the song haunting her mind.

Her throat tightened when she laid it down on the cloth, a little to the side, careful to leave room for the sword that would never return. It lay shattered in a burning city, the steel of it returned to the Spindles from whence it came.

"You are of these people, Old Cor," Isibel murmured, taking the opposite side of the slab. The steel reflected the candlelight up at her, making her features dance.

Corayne could only stare, every breath harder than the last.

"I knew them once," Isibel said. "I remember when they first crossed into Allward, from another realm that was not their own. We welcomed them, and they welcomed us." A small smile spread across her face. "The kings and queens of Old Cor were the best of mortal blood. Brave, intelligent, noble, curious. Always reaching for the stars. Searching for another Spindle, tracing the lines of the realms as they shifted and moved. Never satisfied with the world beneath their own two feet."

In the old cottage in Lemarta, Corayne had spent most of her time reading maps, charting the next course of her mother's ship, or arranging a trade. She saw little of the world, the boundaries of her life reduced to the Siscarian cliffs. She remembered the longing in her own heart, though she could not name it, or explain how deeply it pulled.

Back then, Corayne spent most of her time looking at the sea, pondering the horizon. Hoping for a little glimpse past the walls she knew.

"Growing up I felt wrong in my skin, unmoored," Corayne bit out. Her vision swam, her eyes stinging. "Never *satisfied*. And I never knew why."

Isibel kindly dropped her gaze.

"It is a trait you share with us, the Veder. We feel closer to your kind, your people. Dwindling as you are," she said. "You are lost too. But we still remember our home. And that is far more painful. Our years are long, our memories longer still. Every day we hope for the road home, another Spindle born, another Spindle shifting back into existence."

Again, Corayne scrubbed at her raw eyes, her cheeks flaming hot. She allowed herself a single undignified sniff.

Another Spindle born. Her ears rang with the implication.

"And so you raised my father to be a king. To claim the empire of our ancestors," she said sharply. "Why?"

To the left, the ruby helmet seemed to stare at her, the empty eyes of its faceplate fixed. She tried not to imagine her father in it, or any other part of the room. It was no use. She felt his ghost everywhere.

Isibel grazed a finger across the Spindleblade, her movements sure and careful. Her cool expression hardened, her lips twisting into a scowl.

"The mortal kingdoms war and squabble like children over toys. Mortals of the Ward break everything they hold." Her voice turned venomous. "They spill blood for no good reason. And they hunger without end."

Corayne knew the evils of the Ward better than most, particularly the sins of its greatest queen. She remembered Ascal, a grand city with horror at its center, like the jeweled eye of a rotting skull. Even in Lemarta, sailors fought over lost bets and assumed insults. Criminals paid off city watch. The crew of the *Tempestborn* were worst of all, pirates who preyed upon any ship of the Long Sea. And there was her mother, a fearsome captain who earned her reputation with gold and blood. Charlie, a criminal fugitive. Sigil, a murderous bounty hunter. Sorasa, a blooded assassin.

Wardborn mortals, all of them.

So was Andry, Corayne thought suddenly. A talented swordsman, noble-hearted, kinder than anyone Corayne had ever met. *He was Wardborn, and better than all the rest of us put together.*

Isibel took her silence for agreement and forged on. She crossed to the jeweled helmet, raising it level with her own face.

"When the throne of Old Cor fell, the Spindles soon followed," she said, letting the rubies catch the light. "So many doors closed. So many lights snuffed out. Including our own."

Glorian Lost. Corayne had heard enough of the Elder realm to last a lifetime. First from Dom, then Valnir. It was too much from Isibel.

She scoffed openly, disgusted.

"So you took my father in to rebuild the throne, and find a way home to Glorian," she spat. "In exchange, you cast another out. You left an orphan child alone in the world."

The helmet dropped with a clang of metal, the ancient artifact discarded like garbage.

"And I was right," Isibel replied coolly. "Look at what Taristan became. Can you imagine who he would be if *we* raised him?"

Sadly, Corayne shook her head. "No, I can't."

For all her self-control, a curl of anger twitched across Isibel's face.

"No man is born to evil," Corayne continued, as much as it pained her. "They are molded to it."

Isibel drew in a sharp breath. "You believe that? After all Taristan has done to this realm, to *you?*"

Again she looked to the Spindleblade and pictured its lost twin alongside. *As Cortael and Taristan should have been.* But instead of two children in the cold halls of Iona, alone together, there was only one. The other left to die, or worse.

Corayne bit her own lip, letting the sting rip her back.

"I must believe it," she said bitterly. "Just as I believe my blood, my Cor ancestry, all this—does not make me a queen."

True confusion crossed Isibel's face. "Then what are you?"

Corayne's answer came easily.

"A pirate's daughter."

Laughter rang from the immortal, echoing off the stone walls.

Corayne winced against it and went for the Spindleblade, grabbing the hilt.

With motions too quick to see, Isibel laid a hand over her own, holding it down.

"Brave, intelligent, noble, curious," she said, blinking at Corayne as if she too were another relic in her collection. "You are Corblood in your bones. The Spindles are in your heart, as they are in this sword."

Then her gaze dropped to the sword itself, worrying over the steel and jewels. Her brow curved.

"This is not the blade I gave Cortael," she said.

"That blade is broken," Corayne muttered, sheathing the sword with a harsh click.

The empty slab lay between them still, the candlelight pooling over the velvet. Corayne forcibly turned herself away, going back to the shelves to look anywhere but the Elder monarch.

Her fingers passed over a folded cloak, red as the velvet behind her. It was dusty but clearly newer than the other artifacts, the collar and hem set with neat gold threading.

"Was this my father's?" she asked softly. Half of her didn't want to know.

"It was," Isibel answered, still frozen to the spot. "I underestimated Taristan and the red wizard once. I will not do so again."

Corayne forced herself to drop the cloak and turned back to face Isibel. It felt like tearing her own skin.

"I'm sorry it took so much bloodshed to convince you," she said harshly. "Put down the branch, Isibel. Fight with us now, or never fight again."

The ash branch trembled in Isibel's hand, the green leaves turned golden by candlelight. Isibel raised it briefly and Corayne's heart leapt.

"I cannot," Isibel said. Her voice sounded like the slamming of a door.

Something snapped in Corayne, her hands shaking with anger, weariness, or frustration. Or perhaps all three.

"You say Corblood makes me different than other mortals," Corayne hissed, near to spitting. "Better."

Isibel did not flinch. "It does."

"Well, Taristan is Corblood too," Corayne shot back, going to the door of the vault.

"Taristan was fated to break this realm." Isibel glared at her, finally revealing a bit of her own frustration. "I saw it decades ago, and I see it now."

Corayne barely heard her, all sense narrowed to the spiraling passage and the halls above. She wanted nothing more than a clean bed, a hot bath, and a pillow to scream into.

"Would you like to know what I see in you?"

In spite of herself, Corayne caught herself by the doorframe, stopping short with a skid of her boots. She would not look back, her jaw clenched tight.

"Hope, Corayne," the ancient immortal said. "I see hope."

Your hope feels like a curse, Corayne thought, throat tight and eyes stinging.

Another Spindle born.

Isibel's words played over and over in Corayne's head as she committed them to memory. Something twisted at the edge of her mind, another hum too deep to name. Like the Spindleblade in its steel, or the relics of Old Cor calling to her. But bigger. Stronger.

And worse.

Her feet knew what her brain could not, carrying Corayne through the long halls of Tíarma. One of the Sirandels kindly directed her to the upper levels, up a tower of spiraling stairs. Half of them were icy, treacherous for mortal feet.

"Are the Elders trying to freeze us to death?"

Garion's voice carried down a hall and Corayne followed it, turning into an open room. Garion sat in the open window, one eye on the landscape, while Charlie bent over a brazier of hot coals. He blew on them, coaxing them to life.

Corayne heaved a sigh of relief, both to see her friends, and experience some warmth.

"They don't feel cold like we do," Charlie grumbled, still wearing his long cloak. He nodded to Corayne as she entered.

There was no hearth in the bedroom, nor even a small fireplace. The brazier had clearly been dragged in. Even against its heat, Corayne shivered. No tapestries covered the walls to keep the heat in and the beautifully framed bed was thin, with no pillows and a single blanket. Corayne made a mental note to ask someone to better outfit their rooms, as befitting mortal bodies.

"They don't feel many things," she said darkly, extending her hands to the brazier. A little feeling returned to her numb fingers.

Garion smirked, one leg dangling out in open air. "Will they even remember to feed us?"

Indeed, Corayne had forgotten her growling belly. It rumbled now, begging for dinner.

Charlie watched her over the brazier, his eyes reflecting the embers. Since the throne room, he'd managed to wash up, his cheeks clean-shaven and eyebrows groomed again. He had not managed to steal new clothes yet, but Corayne wagered he would soon.

"What did she say?" he said, reading her frustration. "Will Isibel fight?"

Corayne pursed her lips. "Remember Dom's pride?"

"I try not to," he replied.

"Isibel is a thousand times worse."

Charlie's shoulders dropped, his face mirroring her own disappointment.

"Will they send out scouts at least?" he said, brow furrowed.

She could only shrug. "They have Elders who patrol the perimeter of the enclave."

Charlie's round cheeks went pink and he pulled at his braid in frustration. "But do they hear anything of the realm? Is anyone even paying attention to the rest of the world?"

At the windowsill, Garion laughed into the open air.

"I knew the Elders were isolated but I didn't think they would be so stupid," he muttered, incredulous.

"I thought if we made it here . . ." Charlie's voice broke with weariness. "I thought—I knew we wouldn't be safe. I knew Taristan would come. But I didn't think the immortals would be so blind as to simply wait for him to knock on the city gates."

He poked at the coals again, sending up a spray of sparks.

To Corayne, they looked like a constellation of red stars, winking out one by one.

"We could be anywhere," she hissed, turning away from the coals. "We could have fled to the ends of the earth, we could have gone to my *mother*—why did my heart lead me here?"

Instead of giving space, Charlie closed the distance, coming around the brazier to take her arm. Corayne expected some judgment from the fugitive priest, but found only compassion in his dark eyes.

"Perhaps your heart knows something the rest of us don't," he said softly.

Corayne's mouth opened to turn him aside with a smart remark, but something caught. Again, she wondered, and listened for a sound no one else could hear. The distant hum, the echoes of power. For a moment, she forgot to breathe.

Something only my heart knows, she thought, turning Charlie's words over in her head.

Like a panther, Garion stepped down from the window. He did not know Corayne well, but he read her as Sorasa would, eyes flitting over her face.

"What is it?" he asked sternly.

Her teeth clenched shut, the words heavy on the tip of her tongue. She eyed the open door, then the window. Then the walls themselves. The castle filled with immortal Elders, with too many eyes and ears to count.

Instead, she went to Charlie's saddlebags piled in the corner. In a few seconds, she plucked out a scrap of paper, a quill, and a stoppered pot of ink.

Garion and Charlie leaned over each of her shoulders, watching with narrowed eyes as she scratched a message.

The quill shook in her hand, her careful lettering crooked. As she wrote, the hum deepened, until she felt it tuning in her bones. It was obvious now, unmistakable.

Both assassin and priest drew in a shocked gasp.

Quickly, Corayne tossed the parchment into the brazier, letting the paper curl and burn. The ink stared up at her, the letters consumed. She watched, wide-eyed, reading them one last time before they fell to ashes.

I think there is a Spindle here.

Her voice quivered, her whisper barely louder than the crackling coals.

"Not open. Not yet," she breathed. "But waiting."

23

SUNLIGHT IN THE RAIN
Andry

The Jydi called him *Safyrsar*. The Blue Star.

At first, Andry thought they meant it as an insult, both to his dirty tunic and his Gallish heritage. He soon learned the Jydi were nothing like the Gallish court. They spoke openly. A smile was a smile, a scowl a scowl. There was no cause for political machinations or intrigue, not with war looming over all else. Halla, the Sornlonda chief, was quick to invite Andry to train with her warriors. Even Kalmo, the hot-tempered, red-bearded chief of Hjorn, gifted Andry an ax, to dispel any hard feelings between them.

The raiders still held no love for the southern kingdoms, let alone Galland and her knights. They spoke often of Erida, spitting whenever someone brought up her name. Andry could not blame them. He'd seen for himself what her greed had done to the realm, and what more she intended to do with Taristan at her side. Once, he admired Erida's bravery and her intelligence, the way she balanced her court and kept the kingdom flourishing. Now he hated her political machinations, and her wretched ambition.

The Jydi mourned as Andry did, building funeral pyres to the Yrla, and all the tribesmen who died in Gidastern. No bodies topped the pyres but the flames jumped up into the heavens anyway, burning for many long nights. The few Yrla survivors took it upon themselves to keep the fires lit.

Like beacons, the pyres drew more tribes into Ghald, until Andry felt the city might burst at the seams.

He spent long weeks watching the people of the Jyd prepare for war. Weapons were forged, leather tanned, mail linked, arrows fletched. Provisions counted, barrels filled. Sails mended, rope woven, oars sanded, hulls sealed with tar. Andry soon lost count of the many tribes, their flags as varied as snowflakes. But every morning, he counted the longships in the harbor, both docked or anchored offshore. Their number grew steadily, until the horizon was a forest of masts.

War councils and endless debate spiraled, more than two dozen chiefs of the Jydi arguing over tactics. At least everyone agreed on one thing. If Erida and Taristan's legions rose to war, the Jydi would slow them down.

In his heart, Andry itched to be gone, away with the wind and the tide. But he could go nowhere without the Elders of Kovalinn, who idled in Ghald despite his best efforts. The days felt endless, sliding by slowly, as if time itself had frozen. Andry found himself praying to the god of time. He begged for less and more in equal measure. More time for the Ward. And less time for Corayne to wander, alone in the wilderness.

Above all things, Andry prayed she was safe. And he prayed Valtik was right.

The old witch said nothing more about Corayne, but told him the same thing every day:

"Beware the halls of graying woe, our doom rises from below. The fates collide on ragged wing, snow melts to blood in coming spring."

That rhyme, at least, was clear enough.

Andry spent his free time training with the Jydi, turning axes with his own sword. The raiders fought more fiercely than knights, but without any organization. Andry knew the intricate steps of dueling and advised the raiders on how to fight a trained Gallish army. Most were farmers outside the raiding season, and it showed. He only hoped it would be enough, to strike Taristan's army from the sea, and retreat to safety before the full might of his legions could strike back.

On one cold, pink dawn, Andry awoke to find the sky streaked red, and the sea a still mirror. He stepped out of his warm tent with a shiver, almost enjoying the slap of cold air. It woke him better than anything else.

He sipped at a hot cup of tea, enjoying the taste of honey and crushed juniper. His scalp still felt tight, his black hair newly wound into neat braids.

In Galland, he would have shorn his hair down to the root every time it grew too long. But that felt wrong now, like putting on a jacket he had grown out of. Instead, one of the Jydi obliged. She was of Kasa originally, his mother's country, and knew how to set his springy black curls.

Finishing his tea, Andry ran a hand down his head. The braids felt right beneath his fingers. They remined him of his mother, and her own intricate braids woven with keen fingers.

As always, his throat bobbed when he thought of Valeri Trelland.

Is she alive? he wondered for the thousandth time. *Is she safe with our kin in Kasa?*

To that, there was no answer, and perhaps never would be.

Andry sighed, looking back to the city.

Ferocious as the winter was, the calm hours were just as beautiful. The cold gave everything a diamond sheen of frost, freezing the muddy streets, with ice crusting on the shoreline. The longships glittered in the harbor, the clouds sharp against a blooming sky. Andry hoped it would not burn, crushed beneath the fist of What Waits.

To Andry's surprise, Eyda and her Elders stood above the city gates, watching the single road along the coast.

He left the tent behind, pulling on his cloak at a run. By now he knew the streets of Ghald well enough to sprint all the way to the gates, taking a few shortcuts along the route.

"What is it?" he gasped, breathless as he bounded up the steps.

The other Elders parted to allow him room next to their lady, who only nodded in greeting. Eyda did not blink, her gaze locked on the tree line obscuring a bend in the rutted old road.

Her silence was answer enough. Andry gave a grim nod of his own before searching the pines with a squint, though his own eyesight could hardly compare to the Elders'.

Something lurched through the trees and his stomach lurched with it, trying to place the lumbering shadow as it picked through the snow. It looked like a boulder at first, shadowed by the endless trees.

It was not alone.

The great bear came through the trees with a dozen Elders marching behind it. Andry's heart leapt up in his throat as he realized a child sat astride the bear's back, swaying like a rider on a pony. At the sight, a cry went up among the Jydi gate wardens. They crowed and pointed, all but hanging off the wall in disbelief.

Andry looked to Eyda sharply, expecting surprise. To his shock, he watched a smile spread across the lady's cold face.

"That is Dyrian," she explained in a soft voice. "Monarch of Kovalinn. My son."

The immortal squared her broad shoulders to face the squire. With a jolt, Andry realized Eyda wore her armor again. It gleamed beneath her torn cloak, wiped clean of the battle of Gidastern. She wore a sword at her hip, as did her company.

The Elders of Kovalinn were outfitted for a long journey, and war.

"Now, Andry Trelland," Eyda said, making for the steps down to the gate. "Now we can go."

Valtik was already aboard one of the longships earmarked for the Elders of Kovalinn, folded up at the prow. The carved image of an eagle rose over her, its beak hooked, its wings flowing out on either side to form the hull. It gave her a godly look, as if the wings were her own. Only her leering cackle ruined the image.

They sailed at noon, or at least what counted as noon this far north. The glassy water, beautiful at dawn, felt foreboding as the two ships slipped out into the Watchful Sea. At the stern, Andry watched Ghald grow smaller and smaller. Much as he wanted to leave, he felt some pang of regret too. As a child in Galland, he'd learned to hate the Jydi raiders. Now he would miss them dearly.

Dyrian and his escorts were the last survivors of Kovalinn, who had not made the crossing to fight in Gidastern. Despite his boyish face, Dyrian was a century old. He was less grave than his mother, keen to walk the deck with his monstrous bear. Andry gave the beast a careful berth, though it seemed tame as a trained hound.

The cold was easier to weather on land, and Andry had nearly forgotten the blistering winds out to sea. He was soon reminded.

But as the days felt too long in Ghald, they passed in a blink on the journey south.

Before Andry knew it, they were gliding toward another shore. The mountains of Calidon rose out of the Watchful Sea, their peaks white with snow. Fog lay heavy through the central valley, obscuring most of the lowlands between the mountain ranges. Andry's breath still rose in clouds but the air was markedly warmer, the winter already less harsh than it was in Ghald.

He was sweating by the time they docked, and threw back his fur cloak, leaving his torso and arms free. But for his blue-starred tunic, Andry looked more raider than knight. A gray wolf pelt lay across his shoulders, its tail clasped in its own jaws. He wore newly made leather armor, belted and buckled across the chest, thick enough to turn the worst of a knife, but not so heavy as to drown him. His head was bare to his braids, his hood lowered, and his eyes fixed into the fog.

The Elders did not need to consult a map or wait for the mists to clear. They knew their path through the hills of Calidon. Andry remembered it too.

He'd landed on these same shores with Sir Grandel and the Norths, too long ago. They left a galleon behind, the lion flag waving in the breeze of early spring. Together, the three knights and their squire had marched south, fumbling through unfamiliar lands. It was only by chance did they find Iona, the mist clearing enough to spot the castle city on a distant ridge.

Nearly a year ago exactly, he thought, his boots crunching on the rocky beach. Valtik walked on beside him, ignoring the sting of stones on bare feet.

Led by Dyrian and his bear, the company walked on and on and on, with Andry fighting to keep his eyes open. Only when he stumbled did they stop to let the mortal rest. So it went through the hill country, over mud and winter grass and snow.

The days seemed a dream. Andry could not tell the fog from ghosts, the shape of Sir Grandel or Dom in every shadow. But another shape kept him moving, walking along beside too many ghosts.

Corayne.

He saw her in the rare beams of sunlight, fighting through the low clouds. She was not a ghost but a beacon, a lantern beckoning him onward. A promise of light when all light seemed gone from the world.

The land was mostly barren in winter, left to the wilderness. A perfect place for Elders to hide these many centuries. Andry trudged on, barely aware of the shifting ground beneath his boots. They seemed a grim funeral march, the survivors of Kovalinn in their earthen cloaks, too graceful to be mortal, too grave to be living.

A river chattered somewhere, rolling over stones Andry could not see. He squinted through the soupy air, the sun low and weak, barely a ball of white above the cloud bank. His Jydi ax clinked at his belt, hanging alongside his sheathed sword.

Then darkness crept across the landscape, a spreading shadow looming out of the fog. The Elders did not break stride and neither did Andry. His breath caught as the darkness solidified. Not into another forest or a rising slope, but a stone wall.

His knees buckled and Andry nearly fell to the ground, his limbs going weak.

The twin stags of Iona stared out from the great gates, their antlers like crowns. The portcullis was already raised, the lattice of iron drawn up into the gatehouse.

Silhouettes crowded the rampart above, the Elder archers standing guard. Their bows stood out in intricate arcs, black against the gray sky. Only their faces were obscured, shadowed by gray-green hoods.

The Ionian guardsmen did not strike. They saw the Elders of Kovalinn, the bear, and their monarch well enough. They knew their own kind, even through the mist.

One of them gave a command in the Elder language, and something creaked. Chains clattered and spun, great wheels turning to open the gates inward.

Iona beckoned, the stone city yawning wide.

Andry exhaled slowly, loosing a long breath. A small part of him had expected Corayne on the other side, whole and real, a blaze of warmth against cold stone. There were only the Elder gate wardens, waiting to escort the company.

Andry flushed down to his toes, a sick warmth replacing the numbness in his fingers. He wanted to sprint all the way up the ridge to the castle at its peak. Instead, he matched the long strides of Elders, falling in among them. His teeth ground together, every step forward painstakingly slow.

Iona was as Andry remembered, his hazy memories solidifying around him. The stag loomed everywhere, the towers crowned in antlers as the guards' cloaks were embroidered with them.

His stomach twisted. The guards around him all looked like Domacridhan, looming at the corners of his vision. Broad shouldered, golden haired, with the same cloak and the same proud manner. Andry was nearly sick with it.

When they reached the flat landing at the top of the ridge, the castle doors were open, a contingent of Elders gathering in the rain. Gray fog shifted over the stone and it felt like climbing up into a cloud.

Raindrops clung to the wolf around Andry's shoulders, his face slick and cold. Ahead of him, Dyrian's bear gave a great shake, sending up a spray of freezing water.

Elder though he was, Dyrian was still a child. He laughed, patting the bear on the nose.

Andry could not help but crook a smile.

Then a flurry of motion caught his eye, and his legs truly gave out, a knee hitting the slick pavement with a bruising jolt. His heartbeat rammed in his ears, the breath stolen from his chest.

One of the Elders waiting in front of the castle—was not an Elder at all.

She lunged forward, forcing herself to the front of the line, her black eyes ringed with ferocious white. She was not so tall as the immortals, her face tinged bronze, still clinging to the Siscarian sun through the depths of winter. A black braid flew out behind her, the loose strands wet and sticking to her skin.

Andry fought to breathe, fought to think. It felt like his body might fall apart. All he could do was stare, eyes fixed, seeing nothing but her. He didn't even feel the rain anymore.

Corayne skidded over the wet tiled stones, fighting to stay upright. She all but toppled into him, bending to seize him around the shoulders as his shaking arms reached out to her in turn.

They ended up kneeling together, her dress soaking through, his leathers and furs drenched. Corayne's head fit over Andry's shoulder, the high point of her cheek against the corner of his jaw. Her body trembled in his grasp, her lips still moving, her voice the last part of her to return to him.

He trembled too. All the pain welled up in him again, every black night of lost hope, every empty dawn.

"Corayne," Andry whispered, tasting raindrops.

She drew a shuddering breath and Andry felt the hitch in her chest as if it were his own. Her arms tightened, pressing them closer together. They held each other through the freezing rain and shifting fog, the gray like a wall around them.

For a moment, the world disappeared, swallowed up by the mist. There was only Corayne, alive and bright.

"Andry," she answered, her voice quivering like her body. Slowly, she pulled back, enough to see his face.

Her wide smile flared in Andry's chest, warm enough to weather any storm. He could only stare at her, eyes roving over features more familiar than his own. The light freckles beneath one eye, her strong, black brow. A long nose. Calculations always spinning behind her gaze, the wheels of her mind forever turning.

They whirled now, faster than Andry had ever seen before. A low current of dread wove through his happiness, like something sour added to sweet.

Whatever it was, Andry knew better than to ask before an audience.

"With me," Corayne said, pulling them both to their feet. Her fingers gripped the edges of his cloak, using it to leverage him up.

Andry matched her grin as best he could. He shivered as her hands lingered. Her palm brushed the edge of the wolf pelt.

The same palm he kissed in a burning city, before sending her on to live, while he turned away to die.

"With me," he echoed.

Nothing seemed real, as much as Andry's surroundings tried to remind him.

Rainwater pooled beneath his cloak, spreading steadily over the fine marble floor. Corayne's dress did the same, leaving a dripping trail behind her. She wore gray and green like the immortals of Iona, her sleeves split to show velvet beneath. It was the finest thing Andry had ever seen her wear.

He preferred her cloak and old boots.

"I don't think they'll miss us," Corayne said, fighting a manic smile. She pulled him gently away from the throne room, leaving the great Elders to speak alone.

Andry heaved a sigh of relief. The thought of another council, especially one filled with grim immortals, made his head spin.

"Thank the gods," he grumbled.

"A Spindle torn for flames, a Spindle torn for flood."

Valtik's haunting voice echoed down the grand passage, her words lilting with a strange melody. She all but skipped toward them, her gnarled hands clasped behind her back.

Corayne beamed and shook her head. "It's good to see you too, Valtik."

Grinning, Valtik chucked Corayne under her chin, as if she were a simple grandmother instead of a bone witch.

"A Spindle lost for bones, a Spindle lost for blood," she added with an airy wave, disappearing into the throne room.

"That's new," Corayne mumbled after her, her brow crinkling in concentration.

Andry shrugged. "It started a few weeks ago, in Ghald."

"No wonder they thought you were a raider," she said, brushing at his wolf pelt again. Then she eyed the ax at his hip, then his braids, taking in the full measure of him. "You certainly look it."

"And I thought you were an Elder at first," he replied, leaning down to her eye level. "Albeit a very short one."

When she snorted out a laugh, the doors to the throne room eased shut. Clearly the Elder wardens had little patience for mortal laughter. They laughed all the more.

"Valtik was the only one I didn't fear for," Corayne added, putting her back to the throne room. She sobered a little. "Somehow, I knew the old witch would find a way to survive."

"She's the reason I lived," Andry said plainly, the memory stark in his mind. *I would have been lost in Gidastern.*

"Then every aggravating second of her has been worth it," Corayne said, her smile grimmer than before.

The vaulted hallways of Tíarma echoed their voices back at them. Again, Andry was reminded of a tomb. *Hopefully not our own.*

They stared at each other again, each sizing the other up. Andry knew Corayne saw the weight of the long weeks on him, just as he saw them in her.

"I look a ruin, don't I?" Corayne muttered, looking down at her dress. "The Elders gave me some better clothing but it's no use. I'm not suited to it."

Fine as her clothes were, Corayne looked threadbare, run through with worry. He felt the same, cold to the bone.

"I don't mind that," Andry said too quickly. He fought back a wince, trying to explain. "It makes you look real. It—" His breath caught, his pulse hammering. "I can't believe you're real. I'm sorry, that doesn't make sense either, of course you're *real*."

To his surprise, Corayne flushed, a lovely shade of pink spotting the tops of her cheeks. Slowly, she took one of his hands, rubbing his raw knuckles. His skin went hot and cold, all at the same time.

"I know what you mean, Andry," she replied. "Trust me, I know."

Andry Trelland recognized what it was to want to kiss someone. He'd felt it a few times in Ascal, at one of the many nameless feasts and galas. Not that the squires were ever permitted to do much more than attend their knights. But he remembered what it was to catch a pretty girl's eye and wonder what her hand would feel like. Wonder how well she knew the steps of a particular dance.

Corayne was not the same. Not because she walked a different path, but because she was simply *more*. Bolder, braver, smarter. Brighter in every way. She was *more* to Andry, more than anyone else had ever been.

Or perhaps ever would be.

His breath caught again, his fingers going numb in her hand.

"Follow me," she said suddenly, turning him aside. Her fingers slipped through his own.

It is all I ever really want to do, he thought to himself ruefully.

He trailed after her, eyes on her back as she navigated the castle halls. Andry knew it had only been a month and a half since Gidastern, but the long days felt like a lifetime. She seemed changed since then, more sure of herself. Her shoulders squared, her back straight as she walked, a little more grace in her step than Andry remembered. She seemed leaner too. *And her hands*, he thought, remembering the old feel of her fingers.

She has more calluses. Worn by the hilt of a sword.

Beneath her sleeves, Corayne still wore her vambraces, gifted months ago in the Ibalet desert. Gold chased through the black leather, outlining the image of dragon scales. The sight gave him pause.

Andry opened his mouth to ask but thought better of it. The halls echoed, seemingly empty, but he knew Elders too well to assume. Immortal guards hid well, and listened even better.

The castle walls and buildings ringed the top of the city ridge like a crown, with a courtyard at its center. Many windows looked onto it, down into a vast garden of winter-dead roses. Corayne climbed higher, up to a long gallery of windows. It looked down to the rose courtyard on one side, and the valley on the other.

Andry slowed to watch, transfixed by the mountain kingdom stretched out like another tapestry. Rain passed in sheets across the golden hills, shimmering with streaks of sun. The light changed with every passing moment, the bands of cloud and rain dueling against cold sunshine.

Corayne stopped with him, looking giddy. Before Andry could think to ask why, she called out down the gallery.

"I'm here!" she said to seemingly no one.

"It's Valtik, isn't it?" a familiar voice answered from the next chamber, sounding weary. "Elders traveling with a raider and a Jydi witch? It has to be, of course that old crone weaseled her way out of—"

"I'm a raider now?" Andry said, a smile splitting his face.

The fugitive priest came around the corner and froze. Like Corayne, Charlie wore Elder-made clothing, done up in soft greens and a sleek fur vest. The finery suited him, his brown hair braided and set with a jeweled clasp. He carried a satchel at his side, no doubt bursting with his usual collection of quills and ink.

"All my squinting at parchment has truly done my eyes in," Charlie sputtered, closing the distance between them. He reached up to take Andry by the face. "By the gods, you lived, Squire."

"So far. Glad you made it, Charlie," Andry replied, embracing him with a firm thump. Then he dropped his voice to a whisper. "I'm glad she wasn't alone."

It dulled Charlie's mood a little. He pushed back to meet Andry's eye.

"I did my best, which isn't saying much of anything." Then he shouldered the satchel, the flap hanging open. To his surprise, Andry glimpsed folded clothes and provisions inside.

Charlie followed his gaze. "I'm trying to make myself useful."

"Are you . . . ?" Andry searched for the correct word. Upon closer inspection, he realized Charlie was dressed for travel.

"I'm not running," the fallen priest said with a half smile. "I'm done with that now. But I am going to see what's going on out there in the world. We're blind here, thanks to the Elders."

Again, Andry took in the sight of Charlon Armont. He was far from the wanted fugitive they first met in Adira, ensconced in his basement of forged papers and spilled ink. Still, Andry felt his throat tighten.

"Certainly you aren't going alone," he muttered, just as another man joined them.

He stood silent as an Elder, but clearly mortal. Unlike the other two, the stranger wore battle-worn leathers beneath his Elder robe.

Andry tensed, ready to grab for his sword or ax. But Corayne's mood stayed his hand. Whoever the man was, she was clearly comfortable in his presence.

"Aren't you going to introduce them?" Corayne said, waggling an eyebrow at the priest.

Charlie went scarlet.

"Oh, ah," he said, scratching his head. Then he waved a hand between the two dismissively. "Garion, this is Andry Trelland. Andry, this is Garion."

Garion who, Andry wanted to ask, before he spotted the telltale dagger belted at his hip. It was only black leather and bronze, unremarkable at a passing glance. But Andry had spent too many days with Sorasa Sarn to forget what an Amhara blade looked like.

An assassin, Andry thought, torn between fear and relief. The Amhara were hunting Corayne, but a friendly assassin was a powerful ally. Then the name snapped across his mind again, joined by a foggy memory. His eyes widened, jumping between Charlie and the Amhara. Though they stood a few feet apart, both were clearly bound together.

A swell of relief washed over Andry.

"*Garion,*" Andry said aloud, feeling his own smirk spread across his lips. He remembered the same name whispered across campfires and saddles, overheard in snatches of conversation.

Somehow, Charlie went even redder.

The squire put out a hand in friendship. "I've heard so much about you."

The assassin's eyes gleamed. "Do tell."

Charlie was quick to step between them, palms raised to stop anyone from pressing further.

"Save it for the dinner table when we return," he grumbled. "After all, we are the only ones who seem to *eat* around here."

Then he grabbed Garion by the wrist and dragged the smiling assassin after him. Garion allowed himself to be led, giving a tiny wave over his shoulder.

Corayne stared after them. "Now where are you off to? I thought you weren't leaving until tomorrow?"

Without breaking stride, Charlie shouted back to her. "I will find more blankets if I have to weave them myself!"

Andry wanted to follow, but Corayne stayed rooted by the arched windows. His heart filled, near to bursting. After so many weeks of misery, the sudden joy was almost too much to bear.

The air was stiller on the courtyard side, the rain reduced to a mist. Corayne leaned out into it, her hands braced to hold her weight lest she fall through the open archway.

"What is it?" Andry muttered, coming alongside her.

The courtyard yawned below, centered on a fountain and a spiraling pathway through the dead vines. Other arches and galleries looked down around them, figures gliding along with immortal grace. Corayne followed them, her eyes tracking the Elders.

"Corayne?" he said, dropping his voice.

His body tensed when she suddenly seized him by the wolf pelt around his shoulders, pulling him down to her height. Her breath was warm on his ear, her whisper barely audible, even an inch away. Andry fought to hear her over the low hum of his own frenzied thoughts.

"There is a Spindle here, somewhere," she breathed, stepping back to show eyes wide with worry.

Andry's heart skipped a beat. "Are you sure?"

Her grim nod was answer enough.

"And what of Isibel?" he murmured.

Andry had barely glimpsed the immortal queen when they arrived, all his focus on Corayne. The Monarch of Iona was but a shadow to her. But Andry remembered Isibel from days past. Stern, silver-eyed, cold as her castle. And he knew she'd turned Domacridhan away, refusing his call to fight after the first Spindle was torn open.

Corayne bit her lip, weighing her answer.

"I don't know," she finally said. "I still don't know if she will fight. And we—I have the last Spindleblade. Taristan will come for it. We must be ready to fight, to make a stand *somewhere*."

She sighed heavily and cast a weary glance over the castle hall.

"I hoped this was the right place to go, but—" she muttered, shaking her head.

Andry bled to watch her darken, her eyes already shadowed with defeat. "We will be ready," he said forcefully, taking her by the hand.

Her face snapped up sharply, eyes finding his own.

Both were grimly aware of their position, and the last time Andry Trelland held the hand of Corayne an-Amarat. For a brief second, flames flickered behind her head, the ruin of Gidastern looming over them both. Andry smelled smoke and blood and death, the wings of a dragon pounding overhead.

Ruefully, Andry dropped her hand.

"Have you kept up with your lessons?"

She blinked, caught off guard.

"Yes," she said, stumbling. "Well, as best I can alone."

That was enough for Andry Trelland. He forced a step back, resting a hand on the hilt of his sword.

"You're not alone anymore," he said, nodding back to the stairs. "Let's find some space and grab your sword."

24

THE ROAD CHOSEN
Sorasa

She awoke to voices up on deck, stirring in the narrow bed as Dom loomed in the doorway. The little cabin window was less dark than she remembered, the first haze of dawn creeping through the little window. With a jolt, Sorasa realized she slept far more hours than she planned. *I am truly exhausted*, she thought, yawning as she stood. She stepped into her leather breeches and worn boots but left on the stolen shirt. Then she threw her ruined jacket over it, the shoulder seams barely holding together.

There was a plate of dried meat and cheese set on the floor next to the bed. The meat was old and tough, but she forced it down with the tasteless cheese. After so many days of hunger, she would happily eat anything in her vicinity.

"What are they saying?" Sorasa asked around a mouthful of cheese.

Dom glowered over her, clad as she was in breeches and a similar white shirt. If he managed to sleep, she could not tell.

"We match," Sorasa muttered, disgusted.

He sneered back at her.

"There's very little I can do about that at the moment," he snapped.

Then he glanced overhead. "The wind and the current are pushing us toward the rest of the ships that escaped the harbor. We're spotting more every hour. Traders, mostly."

Sorasa slowed a little, relieved.

"Good," she said. "We're faster than any trader on the water."

While Sorasa felt dirty and rumpled, Dom looked clean. His blond hair had been combed out, braided over each ear again, with his golden beard trimmed. Quietly, Sorasa seethed, shoving her ragged hair behind her ears. She wished for a comb but saw none in the cabin.

"Maybe we should shave your head," she muttered, eyeing his scalp.

Dom blanched, disgusted and confused. "Excuse me?"

"You're on wanted posters all over the realm. We should do anything we can to make you less recognizable."

"I refuse," he said curtly, green eyes flaring.

Then the ceiling overhead thumped as boots ran across the ship deck. Sorasa counted three pairs of feet at least, heading for the starboard side of the *Tempestborn*.

She brushed by Dom without thought, making for the stairs outside the cabin. Silent as he was, she knew the Elder followed. He was too easy to predict after so many long months. At the top of the cramped staircase, Sorasa even pressed aside, letting Dom go first so he would not pull her back himself.

He shouldered up to the door, pressing it open a few inches to glimpse the main deck of the *Tempestborn*. Sorasa peered under his arm, close as she could be without laying herself against the immortal brute.

They were out of sight of land, far enough into Mirror Bay as to leave the smoke of Ascal behind entirely. But to the east, the dawn broke in a harsh pink line. While Taristan was miles away, they were not beyond the corruption of his demon god.

Her eyes lashed the line where sky met sea, noting the black dots of other ships. One was closer than the rest, its prow pointed directly at the *Tempestborn*. A pit formed in Sorasa's stomach, filled with equal parts dread and wretched hope.

At the stern, a scrap of red wavered in the wind, dancing alongside Meliz's false flag.

Carefully, Sorasa mussed her hair, letting it fall around her ears to brush the tops of her shoulders, hiding her tattoos. She laced up the collar of the shirt tightly to cover any more exposed skin before striding out onto the open deck, indistinguishable from the other members of the crew. Only her Amhara dagger would have marked her as anything else, and it was gone now, melted to nothing.

Meliz and a few other members of the crew stood at the starboard railing, eyeing the Madrentine galley with furrowed brows. In the stronger light, Sorasa took in the sight of the formidable captain again. While Corayne favored her father's looks, she had her mother in her too. In the keen flash of her eyes, the deep black of her hair. In the way she always seemed to face the blowing wind.

The resemblance made Sorasa's heart ache in a way she did not understand, and deeply disliked.

Out on the waves, the other ship kept up its approach, the dawn lifting behind it. Unlike the *Tempestborn*, it was clearly a merchant vessel, well funded with a fresh coat of paint and new sails. Built for coastal trade, with a flatter hull to navigate shallows and rivers. At the top of its mast, a flag hung limp. Sorasa squinted at it.

"What do you see?" she muttered, digging an elbow into Dom's ribs.

Above her, his eyes widened with shock.

"A black wing on bronze."

Her own mouth opened, jaw hanging slack.

As the ship came closer, its flag caught the wind, waving for all to see. Beneath it, a red scrap fluttered to match their own.

Sorasa Sarn did not lend herself much to happiness. It unmoored her, too bright to understand. But it bloomed in her chest, riotous as a field in spring. Even her eyes stung as a true smile split her face, pulling so wide she thought her skin might tear in two.

The sun was up by the time the Temur vessel drew close, shining an odd pink light over the calm waters of Mirror Bay. The Temur were not a seafaring people, better suited to the high steppe and their famed horses. But they showed no fear as they leapt from their ship, swinging across the open space between the *Tempestborn* and their own galley. Even the ambassador, gray-haired as he was, made the daring jump.

Sigil landed right beside him, still pale from the dungeons, her armor streaked in soot. But she grinned wide and white, a sharp contrast to her copper skin.

Before Sorasa could stop her, the bounty hunter lunged, her boots hammering the deck. The assassin braced for impact, two muscled arms wrapping around her to lift her clean off her feet.

The crew of the *Tempestborn*, as well as Meliz, watched with eyes narrowed against the rising sun. They looked on the Temur with curiosity, if not trepidation.

Embarrassing as the display was, Sorasa loosened a little in Sigil's grasp, allowing herself to be held, even if she would not return the gesture.

"He did the stupid thing, didn't he?" Sigil laughed, putting Sorasa back down again. Her black eyes flashed over to Dom, who kept close to the rail lest he lose his breakfast over the side.

Sorasa gave a huff. "Of course he did."

"And?" Sigil said, a dark brow raised.

"The Queen lives," Sorasa answered, "but she may be short a hand."

Sigil gave a raking scoff, low in her throat. "She'd be short a head if I were there."

Beneath her, Sorasa felt her cheeks go hot again, and not from the light of the sun. She blinked, turning her face away from the wind, letting it blow her hair forward to obscure her shame.

She should be dead, she thought, cursing herself once more.

When she turned back, Sigil was still staring, concern in her gaze. Despite her warrior frame and taste for fighting, the bounty hunter had a bigger heart than all the rest of them put together. And it made Sorasa's skin crawl.

"It seems there is no end to strange folk aboard my ship," Meliz called out, stepping into the fray. She wore nothing to mark her as captain of the ship, just an old shirt and breeches, her dark hair in a loose, thick braid.

Even so, the ambassador saw the way she walked the deck, as if it were a kingdom and she its king. He gave her a short bow, and his retinue followed.

"We will be more comfortable below," Meliz added with a winning smile, her grin charming and even seductive. But Sorasa saw the hard edge beneath.

As she saw the pirates on the deck, busy in their duties. But a few inched toward the rail, eager to *explore* the galley alongside their own. Sorasa wagered the Temur would be short some cargo before the morning was out.

Meliz went ahead of them below deck, lighting lanterns and shooing sailors out of their hammocks. She waved their group to a low table, nothing more than stacked crates surrounded by empty barrels for chairs.

Ambassador Salbhai sniffed at the interior of the pirate ship. He was still dressed for a courtly feast, the rose-gold chasings of his black silk reflecting the weak light. Like many politicians, he appeared small among his warriors, but Sorasa knew better than to underestimate a Temur ambassador. Especially one with a Born Shield bodyguard looming behind him.

Sigil slid onto a low stool, her long legs nearly doubled over, while Meliz took a spot against the wall. She folded into the shadows well, content to listen and watch. Dom elected to stand, positioning himself behind Sorasa.

Salbhai glared around the makeshift table, his look shrewd.

"*The Empress Rising,*" he spat, shaking his head. "She makes enemies as easily as she breathes."

Sigil's easy smile lit up the lower deck better than any lantern. "Perhaps Erida has finally made too many. And the scales will tip against her."

"Not so long as the Spindles still burn holes in this realm," Dom growled.

From across the table, Sorasa studied the ambassador, weighing his reaction. His grave, polite manner folded into an annoyed expression, and he swept a hand as if to dismiss the Elder. A brave act indeed.

"More of this Spindle business," he said, glaring again. "Is it you who filled my daughter's head with such nonsense?"

A jolt went down Sorasa's spine. She sat up straighter on her barrel, doing her best to keep her expression blank and unreadable. Even so, she could not help but glance to Sigil out of the corner of her eye.

Sigil went red, her cheeks flaming. For a moment, she seemed more like an embarrassed child than a deadly bounty hunter of great renown.

"How rude of me," she said dryly. "This is my father, Ambassador Salbhai Bhur Bhar."

Across the table, Salbhai did not break his stare. While he was gray-haired, bearded, and smaller than Sigil, with crow's-feet and sunspots,

Sorasa saw the resemblance. Their eyes were the same, brown-black, the kind to flare in sunlight, and darken in shadow.

"Etva," Sigil said, speaking the Temur word for father. "This is Prince Domacridhan of Iona, and Sorasa Sarn of Ibal."

A burst of gratitude exploded in Sorasa's chest, taking her off guard. She pushed it down as she did other emotions, even as she tried to understand it. *Sorasa of Ibal. Not Sorasa of the Amhara,* she thought. *Not anymore.*

Her happiness was short-lived.

"An Amhara assassin and an Elder prince," Salbhai muttered darkly, and Sorasa hardened again. "What strange company you always find, Sigaalbeta. But then, these are strange days."

Sorasa fought around the sour taste in her mouth.

"Indeed the days are strange," she echoed. Then she quirked a dark brow. "Strange enough to draw the Countless across the mountains?"

Again the ambassador waved a hand. "That is not my choice to make."

Sorasa heard her own frustration mirrored in Dom's steady rasp of breath, drawn through clenched teeth. *We heard this before in Ibal,* she cursed to herself. It was frustrating enough in the Heir's tent, when Isadere could offer little more than honeyed words and distant promises of aid.

Now, on the edge of calamity, it stung all the more.

Salbhai was a diplomat, one of the handpicked few ambassadors in direct service to Emperor Bhur. Sorasa knew he was no fool, nor was he compulsive or rash. He eyed them all again, noting their irritation, and weighing his response in heavy silence.

He held Sigil's gaze the longest.

"But I will go to the Emperor with all speed, and bring word of what I've seen here in Ascal," he finally said.

"Bemut," Sigil muttered.

Thank you.

Such gratitude was beyond Sorasa's grasp. Already she pictured the Emperor on his throne, listening to Salbhai's tidings—and doing nothing.

Suddenly, Dom's fist met the top of the crate, thumping a frustrated blow. The wood only cracked, but did not explode.

Someone is learning to control his temper, Sorasa thought, amused.

"It is not only Erida you must fear," he bit out, his eyes like raging green fire. "Taristan of Old Cor *will* destroy this realm. It has already begun."

Across the table, Salbhai gave a shake of his head and a shrug. "I care little for the Queen's dour prince, his supposed bloodline, and whatever foolish magic he claims to have."

Sigil hissed out a breath and stood, bracing herself against the crate. "I explained—"

The ambassador did not flinch, familiar with Sigil's anger. His stare stopped her cold.

Sorasa leaned forward into the light, looking at Salbhai dead on. Her hands splayed on the top of the crate, showing every tattooed finger.

Name me Amhara and Amhara I will be.

"What do you know of the Amhara, my lord ambassador?" she said. Carefully, she flicked her eyes from Salbhai to the Temur warrior at his back, as if to size him up.

The ambassador pursed his lips.

"You are trained from childhood, crafted into the finest assassins in the Ward," he said. "You are unfeeling, intelligent, practical—and deadly."

Sorasa inclined her head. "And what do you know of your daughter? Of the Temur Wolf?"

Salbhai shrank a little on his seat. He raised his gaze to Sigil, still standing, her head scraping the roof of the lower deck. His voice softened in a way Sorasa could not understand.

"She is a fine warrior," he answered. Above him, Sigil's furious expression melted. "Who leads with her heart and sees the world for what it is. Wide, dangerous, and filled with opportunity."

"Are we fools?" Sorasa asked.

Salbhai sighed and shook his head, hopelessly trapped.

"No, you are not," he mumbled. "But I cannot believe—I cannot repeat what you said to the Emperor without proof."

The answer was sharply clear.

Sorasa gave a shrug, as if it was the most obvious thing in the world. "Sigil will go herself."

Black eyes met copper, bounty hunter and Amhara.

"Sorasa," Sigil forced through gritted teeth.

Like her, Sorasa rose from her seat. Between Dom and Sigil, she was of no great height, too small to be of much consequence. Her presence filled the deck anyway, her voice low and stern. She stared up at the bounty hunter, unblinking, challenging the other woman. It felt like running into a brick wall. Sorasa did it anyway.

"The Emperor must be made to understand what you have seen," she said. "What you know to be true, and what you know will happen if the Temurijon does not fight."

Sigil furrowed her brow in confusion, a pained look crossing her face.

"You want me to run away?" she sputtered. "Dom, tell her she's being foolish."

The Elder held his ground. Sorasa felt his stare hit her shoulder but she could not turn around. If she moved, she might break.

"I will not," he murmured.

She loosed a low breath of relief, even as Sigil darkened, her pain turning to anger.

Sorasa felt the same in her own heart, as much as she tried to ignore it. *Put the pain away,* she told herself.

The ambassador stood with a small smile, his brighter mood a sharp contrast.

"Very well," he said. "We will sail for Trisad. Bhur is already on his way from Korbij, with the Countless in tow."

In her head, Sorasa saw the moving city that was the Countless, a vast cavalry to outnumber even the Gallish legions. Where the Countless marched, it left a miles-wide path in its wake, carving roads across the steppe. She could hardly fathom the sight if the Emperor marched with them, the entire realm trembling beneath the hooves of his horse.

"The Emperor is already moving?" Sorasa said, incredulous.

Ambassador Salbhai nodded.

"He received correspondence some weeks ago," he said, his smile turning smug. "One from the now-dead King of Madrence, calling for aid. A desperate measure indeed."

He shook his head, lamenting the fate of King Robart.

Sorasa had heard enough of it in the dungeons, through the gossip of her torturers and jailers. Robart threw himself into the sea during Erida's coronation. Sorasa could not help but commend him for such an insult.

"If war was coming to the realm, he did not want to be a thousand miles away, caught unawares. And there was another letter from Prince Oscovko of Trec. Impossible as *that* sounds," Salbhai added.

Quickly, Sorasa traded glances with Dom and Sigil, all three of them wise enough to hold their tongues. *I venture the seal on that letter is just off, the signature of Prince Oscovko not quite right*, she thought with an invisible smile.

"The priest did something right," Sigil muttered under her breath.

Salbhai paid her no attention, carrying on. "Enemies though we are, Oscovko implored Bhur to fight. The prince spoke of Erida's attempt to conquer the realm, both with her legions and . . . something worse."

A shadow crossed his face, one Sorasa and the others understood all too well.

"You know what that is, Sigil," Sorasa said, willing her to agree. "Make sure the Emperor knows it too."

Be the final nail in Erida's coffin. Bring the Emperor crashing down on her legions.

This time, the bounty hunter did not argue. Instead, she threw up her hands with a huff.

"And what about you?" she snapped. "The entire kingdom still hunts for an Amhara and an Elder."

"We will be fine." It felt like a lie in Sorasa's mouth, but the hope of it was all she had. "When the time comes, you must be ready to go. So will we."

Sigil gestured to the cramped deck of a pirate ship. "Go *where*, Sorasa?"

I don't know.

But it went against everything in Sorasa's nature to admit such a thing out loud.

"We will not leave Corayne to fight alone," she snapped, turning from the rest of them.

On the wall, Meliz shifted at the mention of her daughter.

Undeterred, Sigil moved to block Sorasa's path.

"And where is Corayne?" she demanded. "Neither of you have any idea!"

The once Amhara danced around the Temur woman, too quick and agile.

"That's our problem," she said over her shoulder, the steps of the lower deck passing beneath her boots.

The fresh air seared down her lungs, sharp as a splash of cold water. Sorasa nearly screamed when she heard Sigil's boots behind her, stomping up the stairwell.

"It's a rather large one!" she called, popping up onto the main deck.

Sorasa did not wait, already striding past the mast to reach the prow of the *Tempestborn*. Crew scattered out of her path, eager to be out of her way, but close enough to eavesdrop. She paid them little attention, hoisting herself up onto the edge of the ship, letting her legs dangle over the side.

With a deep breath, Sorasa looked down to her hands, laying both palm up. Her tattoos looked back at her, the sun in her right hand, the crescent moon in her left. The symbols of Lasreen, her goddess. She let the ink still her.

All the world stretched between sun and moon, life and death. Everyone was fated to both. *Everyone, with no exception.*

It was another lesson hard-learned at the Guild. And learned a thousand more times over, in shadows and on battlefields.

She let Sigil join her, the bounty hunter taking the other side of the prow with a dramatic sigh. She leaned back against the rail, elbows braced against the wooden edge.

Voices echoed behind them, from the lower deck.

Wincing, Sorasa braced for the entire Temur retinue to follow. Instead, a low, deep voice rumbled up from below. She could not decipher his words, but she felt the intent.

"When did Dom get so perceptive?" Sorasa grumbled, eyeing the water below. Annoying as Domacridhan's Elder ignorance was, his newfound empathy was just as unsettling. "He seems almost mortal these days."

"He had a long time to think in the dungeons," Sigil offered. Her eyes darkened with memory. "So did I."

"And what was I doing?" Sorasa shot back. A few of her newer scars itched, born of Erida's jailers and Ronin's interrogation.

"Screaming, probably." Sigil rolled her shoulders in a shrug. "You never were one for pain."

Their joined laughter echoed over the water, only to be lost to the waves and wind.

"I don't enjoy this, Sigil," Sorasa muttered, picking at the hem of her shirt. "I'd send Dom to Bhur if I could."

Sigil stared at her across the bow, her lip curling into a sneer.

"No, you wouldn't, Sorasa," she said sharply, and the assassin flushed. "If anyone can find Corayne before the world ends, it's you two."

"If anyone can convince the Emperor to fight, it's you."

Another lie that only luck will make true, Sorasa thought.

"Quite a bit of pressure, that," Sigil huffed.

Sorasa nodded, feeling the same weight across her own shoulders. The sea suddenly felt like open jaws, stretching in every direction. Sorasa hoped it did not snap shut on them all.

"It's the road we chose," she whispered. "When we chose Corayne. And all the rest of them."

Wherever they may be, dead or alive.

Sigil scratched a hand over her scalp, setting her short black hair on end.

"Who knew I'd be glad I never killed the priest," she said, incredulous.

"Good of him to finally pull his weight."

Sorasa nodded, thanking the gods for Charlie's quill and his far-flung letters, their truth written in lying ink. They were enough to give pause, to raise alarm. To turn eyes toward Galland and see the evil growing there. She hoped the letters reached every court upon the Ward, from Rhashir to Kasa to Calidon.

"I will see you again, Sorasa Sarn."

Sigil's whisper trailed, hanging between them.

"The iron bones of the Countless," Sorasa murmured.

In the dim light, Sigil put a closed fist to her chest.

"Will never be broken."

She could not bear to watch the Temur ship disappear into the horizon, and turned herself south, to the warmer wind blowing up from hotter lands. Sorasa inhaled slowly, as if she could taste the heat of Ibal, the sweet pang of juniper and jasmine. There was only salt, and the edge of smoke still clinging to her hair.

"And how do you intend to find my daughter?"

Meliz's voice was not unlike Corayne's, and it made Sorasa's stomach flip. She turned in time to see the captain lean up against the ship's rail, one hand planted on her hip.

Her stare was the same too. Sharp, piercing. And hungry.

Sorasa wanted nothing more than to escape below deck but stood her ground.

"The two most powerful people in the realm hunt your daughter," she said. "They'll find her for us."

The captain tossed back her braid, sneering. "I am a pirate, not a gambler."

"You're a realist, as I am," Sorasa shot back. "You see the world as it is."

Meliz could only nod. Her sword still hung at her hip, and there was another dagger in her boot. She had a scar through one eyebrow, and far worse markings on her hands, from rope burn, sun damage, all manner of injury. Like Sorasa, she was a woman of the Ward, accustomed to danger and harder lives lived.

"That world no longer exists." Sorasa leaned forward, bracing both elbows against the rail of the ship. "Spindles torn, monsters walk. And the worst monster of all controls the throne of Galland."

"I've done what I can to slow them down," Meliz muttered.

"There is more still to do," Sorasa said sharply. "Where are you bound for?"

"Orisi, but we'll take on supplies in Lecorra."

An island city in Tyriot, weeks away. And before it, the capital of Siscaria?

The assassin's brow furrowed, a pounding headache joining the many pains she already ignored.

"Is that not dangerous? Lecorra and the rest of Siscaria are loyal to the Queen."

A grin split Meliz's tanned face and she gave a shrug.

"Cowards though they are, Lecorra still honors good coin and bad paperwork." The captain reached inside her shirt, drawing out a folded leather envelope, papers stuffed within. "That priest of yours is the reason I was able to infiltrate so many harbors with a single ship."

Sorasa's eyes caught on the parchment, studying the snatches of ink and writing. She remembered them too, drawn up hastily on the deck of another ship, the seals and letters of mark created by a master's hand.

A master forger.

"Is he dead too?" Meliz said softly.

Charlie. Andry. Valtik.

Corayne.

Sorasa's heart bled again.

"I don't know."

To her relief, Meliz looked out to sea, shading her eyes against the flashes of sunlight reflecting off the waves. Again, Sorasa turned into her hair, giving herself a moment to recover, even as her throat threatened to close.

The pirate captain did not speak for a long moment, lost in her own thoughts, whatever they were. She leaned forward, out over the water, catching the cold spray. It seemed to soothe her.

"I tried to protect my daughter as best I could," Meliz whispered, so low Sorasa almost missed the words. "Tried to make her happy where she was."

"It is not in Corayne to stay in one place," she replied without thought. Then she winced. It was wrong to tell a mother what her daughter was, what her daughter had become.

But Meliz did not look angry, or even sad. Her eyes were dark mahogany, molten, as if lit from within. They churned like the sea below.

"Thank you," she bit out.

Sorasa remained blank, her face unmoving, even as her mind puzzled.

"You were a mother to her where I could not be," Meliz explained. Her eyes flickered over her shoulder, across the deck to the immortal boulder. "And I suppose he was a father too."

"Keeping Corayne alive keeps me alive," Sorasa shot back, bristling. "Nothing more."

That amused Meliz more than anything, and she smiled again, half laughing. It was a musical sound but laced with something darker. In that moment, Sorasa understood how a woman came to rule the pirates of the Long Sea.

"They taught you many things in your guild, Amhara. But they never taught you how to love," Meliz said, her eyes flickering again. "It's a lesson you're still learning, I see."

Swiftly, Sorasa pushed off the rail, her lips pressed into a thin line.

"To Lecorra," she forced out, turning away.

"To Lecorra," the captain echoed behind her.

The farther they sailed from Ascal, the clearer the sky became, until the heavens opened to a sharp, endless blue and a soft yellow sun. Sorasa basked in it, expelling a heavy breath as she felt some tension loosen from her shoulders. But not all. Taristan's influence was behind them, but not the danger.

As Meliz promised, they met no opposition at the Lecorra harbor, though port officers searched the ship and combed through the captain's passage papers. Sorasa and Dom lay quietly beneath the false boards of the lower deck, counting the seconds until the officers were gone, and the *Tempestborn* safely into port.

Dom remained on the ship. There was no disguising a six-and-a-half-foot Elder, especially one who refused to change anything about his appearance.

Sorasa was less fettered. Her shadowed face was still on the wanted posters, but she knew how to evade a manhunt, having done so too many times to count. And while Lecorra was less than half the size of Ascal, she was still a massive city. Sorasa slipped out easily, leaving Dom to prowl the *Tempestborn*.

She kept to the less desirous sectors of the ancient city, all of them well known to her. Nothing in Lecorra had changed, but for the green flags of Galland waving above the Siscarian banners, to illustrate their new conqueror and queen. Sorasa listened for news, from a dark tavern corner or tucked away in an alley. And she steadily procured wares for their journey, wherever it may lead.

When she returned to the ship, she moved up the rope ladder in a

blink, eager to get over the rail and onto the deck. Dom was already waiting, his hood raised against the setting sun.

"Anything of use?" he asked, relieving her of her pack.

Sorasa handed over her trove of stolen goods. A few waterskins, accu-
rate maps of Allward, thread and a good sewing needle. The rest of her
haul, the result of a very fruitful stroll through an apothecary, she kept
tucked away in the pouches at her belt.

"Too much," she answered, scoffing. "The Queen is dead, the Queen
lives, Prince Taristan has seized the throne, the Queen's usurping cousin
paid the Amhara to kill her."

Sorasa despised that particular rumor. Assassins did not kill for fame,
or to be remembered. Their service was to the Amhara, their names and
memories for the Guild alone. Even so, she hated that Lord Konegin
might take credit for her blade.

Dom followed her doggedly below, into the too-familiar cramped
cabin. It was good of the ship's navigator to let them continue to use it,
but the little room was starting to make her skin itch.

The tight space was made even worse by the growing pile of provisions spilling over the floor. A new cloak for Dom, fresh leathers,
weapons, undershirts, gloves, saddlebags for nonexistent horses, whatever
food would keep, and mixed coin from every corner of the Ward.

"And what of their movements?" he said, settling against the
doorframe.

Sorasa gritted her teeth, wishing for a little quiet. Or for another bout
of nausea to level the Elder.

"Nothing yet," she replied, busying herself with her wares. "But we'll
hear soon enough."

"And if we don't?"

"We will. Whole armies cannot move unnoticed."

"You lie too much, Sorasa Sarn," Dom replied in a low, shuddering voice. "Can you even tell the difference between falsehood and truth anymore?"

Gritting her teeth, Sorasa tore off her new leather jacket. She debated throwing it at him, then sat to inspect the seams and fix a few broken buckles.

"Does it matter?" she scoffed back at him, a needle braced between her fingers.

Quickly, she set to working on the leather, adding a few interior pockets to supplement the pouches on her belt. It was soothing, thread and fabric and soft, old leather. The needle passed through as easily as a knife through flesh. The repetitive motion stilled even Sorasa Sarn, and she thought of younger days doing the exact same thing. Washing away blood, sewing up her torn clothes as she would an open wound.

Dom said nothing, watching her work. As the shadows grew, he even lit a lantern, sparing her eyes from squinting in the dim light.

"Erida did survive," Sorasa finally murmured, breaking the silence. "I spoke to a merchant who saw her, from a distance. She's taken up refuge in one of the cathedrals."

Suddenly Dom stood over her, nearly filling the cabin. His chest rose and fell beneath his leather jerkin, his teeth parted to inhale sharply.

"And Taristan?"

"By her side," she answered, raising her eyes to his. The furious green darkened.

"Let it go, Domacridhan. He's vulnerable, but still beyond your reach."

His lip curled, exposing more of his teeth. "I am still standing here, am I not?"

"There were also rumors that someone left the city, under the Queen's own command," she added, if only to distract him. "A small man, robed in red."

"Ronin," Dom muttered with disgust. He braced a hand against the cabin wall, above the window, and leaned down to peer out. "Would that Valtik had broken his spine and not just a leg."

"You know Valtik." Sorasa turned back to her sewing and bit off a line of thread. "Useless until the second she isn't, and then useless again. You can relate, I'm sure."

Dom gave a low snarl, and the little peace between them broke. "I leave you to your work, Sarn," he grumbled.

"Enjoy pacing the deck a thousand times," she replied, grateful to continue her work in silence.

25

THE SKIN OF A GOD
Erida

.

"We were lucky, Your Majesty."

Wounded hand or not, Erida wanted to rip Lord Thornwall's head from his bowed shoulders.

As Taristan stood at her side, the commander of her armies knelt before her seat. Thornwall still wore his armor, hastily donned the night before, when ratty pirates decided to burn down half of Ascal. He was red-faced, flushed with shame, embarrassment, and fear above all things. Erida could smell it on him.

She ached for her throne, for a crown, for any trapping of the mighty queen she'd made herself into. But Erida was just herself, small in a wrinkled dress, with no gold, no jewels, no furs, seated on an ordinary chair in the cathedral.

She only had her spine. That, at least, was made of steel.

"Four ships of the fleet at the bottom of the canals," she said through clenched teeth. Fire burned through her body as it had burned through her city. "Ten more incapacitated for gods know how long. Fleethaven half in ruins. My palace is in ashes and those rioting fools out in the streets will burn the rest of the city down if given the chance. Pirates infiltrated my own *navy yard*, Lord Thornwall. Sea rats bested *your* soldiers!"

Behind Lord Thornwall, his many attendants and lieutenants shuddered. They were smart enough to keep their eyes on the floor, still kneeling like Thornwall. Her own courtiers, including her ladies and even Lady Harrsing, knew to make themselves scarce. They would spare themselves the Queen's anger.

"And you say we were *lucky*, Lord Thornwall?"

Her voice echoed off the marble, the only sound in the world besides Erida's own ramming heartbeat.

"Most of the fleet is still intact, albeit scattered." Thornwall's leg quivered beneath him. He was not accustomed to kneeling for so long. His old body could not stand it.

Still, Erida did not gesture for him to rise. *He does not deserve to stand.*

"The galleys lost were not our heavy warships," he added hastily, as if it meant something.

Erida curled her lip.

"No, Lord Thornwall," she replied icily. "Our warships are merely trapped in their own docks at Fleethaven, until the city engineers can be bothered to dig out the wreckage."

The commander gave another twitch.

"Precedence should be given to the civilian ships still waiting at anchor," he said, half a whisper.

"Of course it will be," Erida snapped, disgusted. *Would that those ships burned instead of my own, and shut up every yowling sailor in Wayfarer's Port.* "The ships are not trapped here by my hand," she seethed. "Anymore."

After hunting through the locked-down streets of Ascal, Erida had

had no choice but to open the city gates and harbors. Lest the entire city rise in revolt against her and tear down her walls with their own two hands. Crowds had broken through the gates like waves, streaming out in every direction.

Within the walls of the Konrada, she could not see the sky, but enough red light seeped through the stained-glass windows. It unsettled her here as it did in Partepalas, when the strange scarlet haze spread across the horizon. Enough of her knew to blame herself. And Taristan. And What Waits.

His influence was seeping into the world, bit by bit.

She could feel it in her own fingertips, a soft buzz like the hum of bees in a grove.

Thornwall took her silence for fury. He stammered, watery eyes crinkled above his beard.

"I have already sent word through the kingdom, to every castle, fort, outpost, and broken old watchtower," he said, half-pleading. "They will be found, Your Majesty. The Elder and the Amhara."

She twisted on her chair. The very mention of Domacridhan and his Amhara whore made her skin crawl. She saw them both out of the corner of her eye, ghosts lingering just beyond her grasp. The Elder in his stolen armor, the golden steel streaked with blood. The Amhara with her empty expression, dull but for gleaming copper eyes. She was a snake in human skin.

Beside her, Taristan loosed a hissing breath. Like the Queen, he had since procured some more suitable clothing. He looked like his old roguish self, dressed simply, a new sword belted at his waist.

"Just as Corayne an-Amarat was found, Lord Thornwall?" he said, as if scolding a child. "And Konegin too?"

Konegin.

His name ripped down her spine and Erida stood, all but lunging onto her feet. Beneath her, Thornwall flinched.

"I am Queen of Four Kingdoms, the Empress Rising," she said, half snarling. "And I cannot even hunt an old man properly, let alone a teenage girl. What hope do we have for a trained Amhara and an immortal Elder?"

After years of service to both Erida and her own father, Lord Thornwall was not the kind to speak out of turn. Or speak when there was simply nothing to say. Erida knew that much of him. She saw his confusion too, written in the lines of his furrowed brow.

He does not understand, she thought. *But how could he know that Corayne is the key to this realm? He does not see what we see, not truly.*

Lord Thornwall kept his distance from Taristan's corpse army. Terrifying as it was to her nobles, the army had proved its worth more than once. Thornwall's own command was of living soldiers, and he knew nothing of Spindles torn. Only that Erida and Taristan were the glory of Old Cor reborn, their destiny written in blood.

He does not need to understand, Erida knew. *He only needs to follow orders.*

Finally, she gestured for the old man to stand.

Thornwall gave a grateful gasp as he rose, his leg still shaking.

"You Majesty," he muttered.

Her scowl remained.

"Bring me a head, Lord Thornwall," she commanded. "You choose which."

Theirs, or your own.

Thornwall heard the threat clear as a bell, his red face going white. His eyes searched her, looking for any softness, any indication of Erida's own loyalty to her great commander. The Queen remained as stone beneath his scrutiny, daring him to find a chink in her armor.

There was none.

"Yes, Your Majesty," he whispered, bowing away from the simple chair that was her throne.

She watched him go, his lieutenants scurrying after him like hounds behind a hunter. They would not say a word until they were well out of the cathedral, returned to the legion's makeshift camp in the cathedral square.

The doors shut behind them, the slam a dull echo up the cathedral tower. Erida loosened a little. Her shoulders dropped an inch, the hard set of her jaw relaxing. Around the central chamber, her Lionguard remained, golden statues set at intervals. Already Thornwall and Lady Harrsing had replaced her fallen knights, bolstering their ranks.

That nonsense is at least taken care of, Erida thought, grateful to be rid of one more task.

Before Harrsing and the ladies could flock back, Erida took another step from her chair. Taristan moved with her, offering his arm in a courtly gesture.

Erida twisted a smirk at him, rankled as she was by the circumstance.

"Now you decide to have some manners," she muttered, letting him lead her away to their bedchamber.

She spent her rage on his body.

As her enemies had ravaged her city, so did Erida ravage Taristan. He was happy to oblige, his own muscles corded tight with anger, the white veins bursting under his skin. New wounds trailed beneath her fingertips, each one hot as the wick of a candle. She mourned every scratch and scar. They were a terrible, indisputable testament of Taristan's weakness. He hated them too, as much as he pretended not to care. She felt it in the way he held her wrist.

As the minutes stretched, Erida let herself be lost, until her own anger and his frustration fell away. She forgot most things, even the pain in her wounded hand. Their oblivion consumed, until even the warrior prince lay still but for the rise and fall of his bare chest.

For the first time, Erida left marks on him.

She would not trace them, and subject Taristan to yet another reminder.

Their bedchamber in the Konrada once belonged to the high priest of the Godly Pantheon, and his things reflected the life of a mortal approaching death. Fat, waxy candles covered every surface, to provide enough light for aging eyes to read by. His bed was small and too hard, the mattress overstuffed, the pillows little more than two feathers put together. A single glass eye of a window peered out on the plaza, offering a clear view over the smoldering remains of the New Palace.

Erida would not look at it, not yet. She'd heard enough reports of the damage to know the blow struck was astronomical. But she could not force herself to see it, and accept the destruction the Amhara wrought. On Erida, on her authority. And on the palace her forefathers built, king after king.

All lost by a queen.

Erida bit the inside of her cheek, tasting blood. She winced and leapt from the priest's bed, crossing to a washbasin set on the sideboard. After gulping water from a cup, she spit pink into the hammered copper bowl.

A warped shadow of her own face stared back at her, distorted by the metal. Blood and water swirled over it.

"What do we do, Taristan?" she murmured to the shadows. "I've raised bounties, hired assassins. I have the largest army this side of the mountains looking for her."

Erida thought of the realm, the lands of Allward spread wide and vast, filled with so many places to hide.

All of them, somehow, out of her magnificent reach.

"Perhaps we sent Ronin off in haste," Taristan murmured from the bed.

As much as all mentions of the wizard annoyed her, especially in their private quarters, Erida could not help but nod.

"I can't believe I agree," she hissed.

"Have you grown fond of the wizard?" Taristan replied, a smirk in his voice.

"Hardly," she answered, pulling on her nightdress. "But if he returns with a dragon I'll kneel and kiss his feet."

"I will hold you to that." He chuckled darkly.

Erida turned to watch him sit up, a sheen of sweat across his pale skin. His many collected injuries stood out sharply, red against white, haloed by the fall of light from the window.

He tightened beneath her scrutiny, a muscle flexing in his jaw.

"Does it feel—different? The loss of the Spindles?" she breathed.

To be vulnerable, mortal. Her mouth filled with a sour taste. *Like any other man upon the Ward.*

Taristan took a long time in answering, chewing his words as one would a tough cut of meat.

"I spent most of my years as I am now," he finally said. "But it is strange, to wear the skin of a god, and then be stripped of it."

Erida understood. *It would be like losing my crown,* she thought, shuddering. She could hardly picture what it would mean, to feel the throne in her bones, but never sit it again. To be queen. And then *nothing.*

"The temple. Nezri. Vergon." She spit out each word like poison. "All destroyed by that wretched child."

"Gidastern remains," Taristan said coolly.

He shifted to put his bare feet on the floor, the thin blanket across his thighs. One hand flexed in mid-air, white fingers long and callused. He stared at it as if transfixed.

Erida knew what those hands could still do. She remembered the corpse army too well, marching in their huddled ranks. Many were Ashlanders, but others were of Gidastern now, dead farmers and dockworkers and merchants alongside the obliterated remains of her own soldiers.

My soldiers serve Galland still, even in death.

"Gidastern remains," Erida echoed, reaching out to take his hand. "And with the gift of that Spindle, our armies will never waver. No matter how many of our soldiers fall. They will always rise again." Her grip tightened as his fingers wound through her own. "As will we. Together."

Together.

The word lingered in her head. After so many years alone, with only the crown for company, the thought of another still felt unfamiliar. Even Taristan.

The pain began in earnest, a dull needle stabbing at her temples. Erida winced again, shaking her head.

"Erida?" Taristan said, pulling her closer.

"Just a headache," she answered sharply. Whatever brief respite she found from her burdens steadily slipped away, water through her fingers. Her teeth clenched, bone on bone, even as the pressure made the headache worse.

Taristan watched with his endless black eyes.

Erida waited, expecting the flash of red in them. It never came.

"Can't He tell you where she is?" she bit out, dropping his hand. "Isn't He part of you? Is What Waits not a god?"

With the grace of an alley cat, Taristan rose to stand, looming over her. A lock of wavy red hair fell over one eye, the rest brushing the top of his collarbone.

"He does not speak, you know this," he said, matching her exasperated tone. "Not in the way you think, at least. Ronin could hear Him, but
even those whispers were not . . . whole."

She replied without thinking, putting a hand to her temple.

"He speaks to me."

The silence was strangling. The same tightness in her head wound
around her throat, firmer than a lover's hand.

Again, she expected the flare of red. She *hoped* for it, even.

But Taristan remained. A line creased between his brows. Even as
Erida pulled back, he pushed forward, holding the inches between them.

"What does He tell you?"

His voice grated, lower than she ever knew it could be.

"Let me stay," she said. It sounded like an admission or an apology.
"Let me in."

Taristan seized her by the shoulders, his grasp hard and unbreakable.
It was not a lover's embrace, but something more desperate.

"Do not," he whispered. "Do not give Him that."

Erida stared back at him, tracing the veins along his neck and the
shifting presence behind his eyes. It moved even as Taristan held her, as
if simply standing to the side. She wondered if What Waits would do the
same to her. Would her blue eyes burn red and golden, alive with the light
of a dark god?

Would it be worth it?

Taristan's teeth gnashed together, exasperation on his face.

"It is as Ronin says. What Waits requires sacrifice. I have given
enough," he forced out. "You need not do the same."

Gently, she took his hand, turning it over. She examined it as she
would the pages of a book, reading every callus and scratch. There was no
gash across his palm anymore. The Spindle wound disappeared before he

lost the ability to heal. But she remembered his blood welling up between his fingers, dark red against the edge of a Spindleblade. He shed blood to tear every Spindle, giving pieces of himself every time.

Strangely, she thought of Ronin out in the wilderness. *What will he have to give to bind a dragon? What price will he pay?*

"What did you give, Taristan?" Her voice hitched as his hand flinched in her own. "When Ronin first came to you?"

He pulled away from her, his expression going sharp and tight.

"I promised a price," he murmured, his face shadowed. "I promised a price, and before the doors of a forgotten temple, I paid."

With your brother's life, Erida knew, finishing what he could not say.

"What would anyone give to earn their destiny? To rule their fate?" he pushed on, shaking his head. "Imagine you are not queen of all you see, but still feel that power in you, just waiting to be grasped? What would you give to take it?"

Erida did not need to think long. She felt sick and determined, all at the same time.

"Anything."

It was not yet dawn when Erida rose, unable to sleep. Taristan did not stir when she slipped from the bedchamber. He was a heavy sleeper, near dead against the blankets. She looked back once. Only sleeping did his face smooth, his cares worn away, the weight of blood and destiny finally lifted.

In the corridor, the Lionguard waited, all ten lined up outside the antechamber to their bedroom. Erida let them fall in behind her, trailing like her nightgown and heavy robe.

She paced slowly, thinking, her mind a blur of too many thoughts.

Most of the Konrada tower was open to the cathedral floor below.

Sculptures loomed down from the twenty sides of the tower, the gods and goddess of the Ward frozen in stone. Lanterns on massive chains hung from the vaulted ceiling, trailing a hundred feet down. They burned all night, casting a warm glow over everything.

To Erida, half-asleep, the soft light turned the world into a dream. It made her steps easier.

She could pretend this wasn't real.

Lady Harrsing was one of the few courtiers to take up residence in the Konrada with the Queen. Most nobles had their own townhouses and villas throughout Ascal, but Bella chose to stay close. As she always did, since Erida was just a girl.

A maid answered the door, yawning in the Queen's face.

Immediately, her eyes widened in shock, all but dropping to the ground to kneel.

"Your Majesty," she murmured, quivering as she looked at the floor. "I shall wake Lady Harrsing."

"I can do that," Erida said, waving the maid out of the way.

With a glare, she commanded the Lionguard to remain in the corridor. The maid did the same, scurrying out to give the Queen whatever privacy she required.

Bella Harrsing was the wealthiest woman in Galland after Erida herself. With a dead husband behind her and a web of children married across the realm, she could have spent her days in the utmost luxury. Visiting grandchildren, savoring the hospitality of every foreign court across the Ward. Instead, she braided herself to the Queen's service, staying on to mentor Erida when she first took the throne.

In recent days, her uses grew few, as Bella grew old.

She has uses still, Erida thought, entering the narrow antechamber separating the corridor from Bella's bedroom.

The space was little more than a cupboard, the walls paneled wood, bare but for a high window and an icon painting of the goddess Lasreen. Erida sneered at it, despairing of the sun and moon in Lasreen's hands, the dragon Amavar curling behind her.

To her surprise, Bella hobbled to the bedroom door herself, peering out in her nightshift. Her gray hair trailed down her back, set in a loose braid. It was rare to see Lady Harrsing without her jewels, rich as she was. But she did not look small without them. Her shrewd expression was strong enough.

"Your Majesty," she gasped, throwing the door wide. In her haste, she left her cane behind, and leaned heavily on the wall. "Are you well?"

Erida's heart twisted in her chest. People asked her so many questions—what color dress would she like, which crown, what do we say to this lord, how do we placate this noble? Few cared to ask after Erida herself.

"I am well, Bella," she said, moving to join the old woman.

Harrsing's pale green eyes glinted, her gaze narrowing. She was unconvinced.

"Then what are you doing in my bedroom under the cover of darkness?" she said, her voice sharper.

In earlier days, Erida made such visits rarely, always seeking a tiny bottle of maiden's tea. Brewed from an herb all women knew, smelling of mint, looking of lavender. She could still remember the taste, and the desperation that drove her to it.

Quickly, Erida shook her head.

"Nothing like that, Bella," she said warmly. "Come, let me walk you back into bed."

"Very well."

With a small smile, Erida put out both hands to hold Lady Harrsing upright. She did her best not to wince as the old woman put pressure on her wounded hand. Together, they paced into the bedchamber, just as cramped as the receiving room. A single candle burned in the corner, casting a gentle pool of light.

"Well," Harrsing said, settling back under her blankets. "What is it then? What counsel can I give my queen?" Her breath caught. "What counsel can I not give freely in the light of day?"

Erida pulled a small chair to the side of the bed. Her heartbeat quickened, even as she sat calmly. Part of her wanted to get up and run. But not enough.

"There is much I cannot say, Bella," she muttered.

Harrsing touched her gently. "You are afraid."

Blinking, Erida weighed her response. The candle flickered and she sighed. There was no use in lying.

"I am," she admitted.

For so many reasons.

To her surprise, Harrsing only shrugged, her narrow shoulders rising and falling beneath the swoop of her nightgown.

"That is necessary."

Erida could not help but balk. "What?"

The old woman shrugged again.

"Fear is not so terrible as we make it out to be," she said. "Fear means you have a head on your shoulders, a good one. It means you have a heart, as much as you try to hide it from the rest of us."

Like Erida, Lady Harrsing had her own mask, shaped from decades in the royal court. She let it slip to show a smile of her own, warmer and softer than the candle. It made Erida's heart twist.

"A king or queen without fear would be a horrific thing indeed," she added with a scoff.

Erida could not agree. Her own fears seemed endless, looped around her neck in an unbreakable chain. She wondered what it would mean to be free of her misgivings and worst thoughts. To be so strong as to be beyond fear itself. Where only glory and greatness remained.

Lady Harrsing arched an eyebrow, watching the Queen. "To *be* feared is another thing entirely."

"That is necessary too," Erida replied swiftly.

"To an extent," Harrsing said, careful and deliberate. Her gaze wavered, dropping to the blanket beneath her hands. "But—"

"But?" Erida echoed, heart in her teeth.

From the bed, Harrsing leaned forward, whispering without cause. Her little smile returned but her pale eyes went icy.

"Would you permit the ramblings of a feeble-minded old woman?"

Erida knew Lady Harrsing to be the smartest person in her circle, calculating as any courtier and wiser than a priest. Withering as she was, Erida would never describe her as feeble-minded.

Still, she nodded, allowing her to continue.

"You are feared, Erida," she said plainly. "But you are also loved. By me, by Lord Thornwall, by the legions. Even by your pestering nobles. Most of them, anyway. We have all watched you grow into something magnificent, and make your kingdom magnificent too."

Erida blinked fiercely, her eyes suddenly stinging. Again, she wanted to run from the room. Again, her mind outweighed her heart.

"Thank you," she bit out.

Lady Harrsing leaned again, reaching for Erida's wrist. Her grip was surprisingly firm, her touch cold.

"Taristan is not loved," the old woman murmured. Soft as her voice was, every word another razor cut. "And he never will be."

Erida's fingers curled in the old woman's hand, her own body itching against the truth.

"*I love him,*" Erida said stiffly. Instead of fire, she felt ice creep into her heart.

Lady Harrsing pursed her lips. "If only that were enough, my dear."

The ice spread, working its way through Erida's body, numbing her to all feeling. She raised her chin, feeling the crown on her bare head.

"Without Taristan, I would not be the Empress Rising. I would not be Queen of Four Kingdoms. My nobles would not be richer than they ever dreamed, their lands expanded, their treasuries overflowing." The words spilled from her like blood from a wound. "Lord Thornwall would not command an army stretching across the continent. And *you* would not have the ear of the most powerful person in the realm."

She expected an apology at the very least. Harrsing only shrugged and dropped her grasp to throw up her hands in lazy defeat. Her head shook, her pride wiped away. She looked on Erida not with love, but pity.

It was worse than a slap across the face.

And Harrsing knew it.

"As I said," she sighed, raising her only defense. "These are just the ramblings of a feeble old woman."

Erida could only blink. "Taristan of Old Cor will sit the throne long after you are dead."

Harrsing glared back up at her.

"I hope you sit it beside him," she said, truthful. "And not beneath."

Beneath a king of ashes.

The truth burned, hotter than the fire still too close in her memory. More painful even than the scratching at the edges of her mind. Erida of Galland was not a foolish child, not anymore. She knew war, she knew politics. She knew how to balance lords and foreign kings, winter famine and summer bounty.

She knew what Taristan was, as much as she loved him.

He is a sword, not a shovel. He can only destroy, and never create.

Tears stung but would not fall.

Another voice answered her thoughts. Not Bella, but the hissing shadow of What Waits.

My price is named, he said.

The ice in her heart shattered, tearing her with it.

At her side, Erida's good hand clenched, forming a fist. Her nails bit into her palm. She let the sting ground her and forced a false smile.

"There are few people I care for in this world, Bella," she said. "You have been a mother to me, as much as anyone could."

Harrsing loosed a sigh of relief, some tightness dropping in her shoulders.

"It is only what your own mother wished for, before the end," she muttered, lowering her eyes. But not before Erida caught the gleam of unshed tears. "Someone to watch over you, and make sure you are walking the right path."

"Am I?" Erida bit out.

"I think you still can," the old woman answered. When she raised her gaze again, the tears were gone, replaced by steel determination. "And I can help you do it. I can free you of your burdens."

Erida knew Lady Harrsing well enough to hear the words she would not speak aloud. *I will have Taristan removed for you, if only you ask it.*

A low, sucking breath whistled through Erida's teeth. She tasted ash and blood again, as if the palace still burned around her. Whatever doubt she felt, small as it was, evaporated in an instant. Only cruel resolve remained.

"How will you be remembered, I wonder?" Erida said.

Lady Harrsing wasted no time in her response.

"Loyal. Willing to carry any burden you ask of me."

Her pale eyes narrowed as she reached out for Erida's hand again. The Queen did not move, letting Harrsing take her by the wrist and pull her close.

"Yes, I think so," Erida said. The old woman's body felt frail against her, bones poking out beneath paper-thin skin. "Loyal Bella Harrsing."

Erida ignored the throbbing pain in her wounded hand, her arm reaching behind Lady Harrsing's head. Her fingers closed on the pillow, wrenching it out.

The old woman's eyes widened, her mouth dropping open to scream.

Erida was too quick.

"I relieve you of your burdens."

She held the pillow for a long time, for many minutes after Harrsing stopped thrashing. The pressure made her hand sting and when she finally relented, pulling back, there was fresh blood on her bandages. And on the pillow too.

Erida considered the smear of scarlet for a moment before tossing the pillow aside, letting it land stain up on the ground. She cared little for evidence. It was a maid's word against a queen's.

On the bed, Bella lay still, her eyes closed, her mouth agape. As if only asleep.

Erida left her there. She left part of herself too.

After Marguerite, sleep was difficult. Many nights Erida lay awake, remembering the feel of a dagger in her hand, and the warm spray of blood from the girl's abdomen. The young princess falling in front of her, spilling red across a marble hall that was once her home. Her eyes dying last, the light leaving them after her chest stilled, her last gasp of breath already echoed and gone. It was not Erida's plan to kill her, but her death ended the Madrentine line. And removed a valuable pawn from Konegin's grasp.

It served a purpose.

So did this, she thought.

Taristan lay undisturbed next to her, the steady sound of his breathing better than a lullaby.

Tonight, sleep came easily. And Erida dreamed as she never had before. Of great columns of fire, golden and bright. Beacons across the realm, unifying the continent. A dragon's jeweled wings. Her army marching across fields of green and fields of snow. Across rivers and over mountains. The rose of Old Cor and the lion of Galland held high, flags snapping in a harsh wind. No more truce flags, no more opposition. Only surrender ahead, only conquest and victory. Beneath it all, a familiar voice, whispering as He always did.

Then the dream changed. She saw Corayne an-Amarat, a sword on her shoulder, a purple cloak thrown out behind her. She stood on a high ridge, silhouetted against a blue sky torn with white clouds. Another wind blew, sending out her raven hair like a black standard. The girl stared back at her, as if seeing her through the dream.

She has Taristan's eyes, Erida knew. She remembered that from their brief meeting, so long ago.

The whispers rose, hissing, too many to understand, in every language. Erida held Corayne's gaze even as she strained to listen, trying to decipher the message of What Waits.

Across from her, Corayne drew the sword sheathed at her back, slow and deliberate. Red and purple jewels glinted at the hilt, and Erida recognized it immediately.

Corayne raised the Spindleblade, her face grim, her jaw set into a hard line. Her black eyes seemed to swallow the light of the world, dimming the bright flames burning at Erida's side. The air turned cold and the Queen shivered, cursing her own fear.

Then the blade slashed downward in a careful stroke. Erida braced, eyes open, watching as the steel passed through the air like a falling star. It blazed toward her, the air singing with its passage.

In the blade, something reflected, a single flash. Fast, but not fast enough. Erida glimpsed a castle of stone, surrounded by towers, its battlements crowned with stags carved from granite. Flags flung out in the buffeting wind, gray-green, embroidered with silver antlers.

Then the sword fell and Erida could not help but close her eyes, raising her hands to defend against the killing blow.

Air seared from her lungs as she sat up sharply, still in bed, the windows filled with sunrise. Her breath came in heavy gasps, her good hand pressed to her throat. She expected a rush of blood from an open wound. There was only hot skin, fevered to the touch, burning like the candle across the room.

Her mind burned too, branded by a single image, her lips forming a single word.

"Iona," she whispered, the flag still waving in her head.

Beneath her own thoughts, something else moved. Like a shadow, but heavier, a weight behind her own heart. It did not speak.

She knew Him anyway.

26

A BROKEN SHIELD
Corayne

She woke with a gentle sigh, grateful for another night empty of dreams. There had been few nightmares since Gidastern, but enough to make Corayne wary every time she lay down to sleep. Erida's burning eyes or the memory of What Waits, his shadow across the ground, his whispers in her head, were more than enough to give her pause.

It was easier to get out of bed since Andry's arrival. Instead of turning over to sleep another hour, she got to her feet, leaving the warm nest of piled blankets. She still was not used to the chill of the castle. She doubted her body would ever adjust.

As she pulled on her clothes, she wondered if her father did.

Her stomach growled as she stepped into her boots, an easy distraction from spiraling thoughts. She followed the sensation all the way down the tower of guest apartments, making her way to the great feasting hall the Elders never seemed to use.

Charlie and Garion were still gone, near two weeks now. She was not afraid for them, not truly. She imagined they were in Lenava by now, the nearest Calidonian city. Listening for rumors, waiting for any news that might herald the storm to come.

Andry was already in the feasting hall, seated with his back to her, at a table set with an array of food. It was an overwhelming amount, far too much for the few mortals in the castle. But Corayne wagered the Elder cook had no idea how much to feed them, so they made everything possible just in case. There were platters of porridge, freshly baked bread, apples drizzled with honey, a glistening ham, eggs still sizzling in oil, good hard cheese, and creamy butter. Corayne's stomach growled again at the sight.

Smiling, Andry turned over his shoulder. He still wore his Jydi furs. "Hungry?"

"A little," Corayne replied, filling a plate with a bit of everything from the Elder pantries.

"Their cooks are probably exhausted, preparing three meals a day instead of the usual zero," she said, biting into an apple as she sat. "They must be cursing us for making them work so hard. So, what is it today?"

She nodded across the table, to the little teapot next to his plate. One of the matching cups steamed, half filled with hot liquid. The other sat empty, waiting for her.

Andry grinned wider, proud of himself. "I found ginger," he said, pouring her a cup. A spicy-sweet scent wafted up with the steam. "Have you ever had it?"

In her head, Corayne saw the old cottage, a pot boiling slowly over the fireplace. She remembered her mother at the little table, one hand on her head, the other crushing a brown root into fine paste.

"Yes," she said. "My mother would bring it back from her voyages and make me ginger tea when I was sick."

Then her voice faltered. "When she was home, I mean. Usually Kastio would do it if we had any left."

Andry quirked a dark eyebrow. "Kastio?"

Another memory sharpened. An old man, tanned and wrinkled, followed her dutifully into Lemarta port, his vivid blue eyes half-hidden beneath bushy gray eyebrows. He walked strangely, never quite losing his sea legs. In younger days, he even held her hand, his wavering gait making her giggle.

"An old sailor my mother press-ganged into being my nursemaid," Corayne said fondly.

Andry's dark brown eyes crinkled. "I wonder what he found more difficult. Minding you or being a pirate?"

"Most days he would say me," she replied, the memory turning bitter. Her voice dropped and she forced a gulp of tea. "I left without saying goodbye."

On the tabletop, Andry's fingers twitched an inch. Corayne half expected him to reach over the food and take her by the hand. But he only stared, his gaze softening. His brown face, warm and kind, looked out of place against Jydi furs. But the new braids suited him.

"You'll see him again *because* you left," he said, his voice so firm she couldn't help but believe it.

"I hope so," she sighed, apple in hand.

While she returned to her food, steadily working through everything on her plate, he leaned back in his seat. Slowly, he nudged his breakfast away.

"I tell myself the same thing," he muttered, looking to the tall windows. They opened out onto the ridge, the valley stretching beyond.

Corayne noted his stare. *He looks south, toward Kasa.*

"I'm sure the letter will reach her in good time."

Andry shrugged beneath his furs. "I know, I trust Charlie to send it off the first chance he gets."

"Part of me hopes he doesn't come back," Corayne mumbled.

Across the table, Andry raised an eyebrow in question. "Because when he returns, it will be with grave news?"

Her heart bled. "Because he probably won't survive if he comes back."

And neither will I, she thought, careful to keep such words to herself.

Andry stared through her anyway, as if she spoke her thoughts aloud.

"Well, you certainly won't be making any speeches before the final battle," he said sharply. Then he stood up from the table, somehow taller than she remembered him to be. Broad-shouldered, lean, halfway between a knight and a raider.

No longer a boy, but a man grown.

"My mother is safe in Kasa," he added, half for himself. "That's the best I can ask for."

The table ran between them, a dividing wall of wasted food. Corayne eyed him over it, weighing what she knew to be true—and what she hoped to be possible.

"You will see her again. I promise you that, Andry Trelland," she finally forced out. The look on his face made her blush, her cheeks heating against the cold air.

"For whatever my promise is worth," she added, looking away.

His footsteps echoed on the stone tile of the hall, one boot after the other. Not around the table toward her, but back into the adjoining hall. She looked up, startled, only to find him staring from the connecting archway.

"Come on," he said, beckoning her with a flick of his hand. "I'm going to teach you how to use a shield today."

Cold and strange as Tíarma seemed, the Elder fortress was still a castle, and Iona still a city. Daily life unfolded, but more slowly, the passage of time odd among the Elders. At first, as in Sirandel, Corayne assumed such lives were boring. The immortals spent most of their time contemplating the sky, staring out at the ever-changing mists. Some read or wrote or painted, bent over stacks of parchment or empty canvas. Isibel herself spent most of her time shut up in the throne room with Valnir, Eyda, and their collected advisors. Corayne didn't have the stomach to suffer their long-winded, useless droning.

Only the guards seemed to have anything to do, and most of that was pacing. A few scouts ranged out every day, guarding a close perimeter around the enclave. All of them cycled through the training yards within the castle walls. Every day a new contingent of Elder guards went through their exercises, their motions too fast for mortal eyes. Every sweep of a sword or loosed arrow moved elegantly, honed to perfection by centuries of practice.

The mist hung low, pressing down on the Iona ridge in a heavy, gray ceiling. It obscured most of the castle, turning the towers to looming shadows.

Corayne shuddered under them as she followed Andry down the familiar path to the training yard of slabbed stone. He slowed as they descended the steps to the yard, lingering to watch the soldiers in their training. He carried a tall shield under one arm, a sword belted at his hip alongside his Jydi ax.

Corayne halted next to him, the Spindleblade belted in place over her shoulder. She was loath to leave it behind, even here.

Below, a squadron of Elder guards dueled. Twelve of them in all, half with spears, half with swords. The blades sang and the spears danced, sparks flying with every clash of steel. They moved together in strange tandem, perfectly balanced. The endless wind of the mountain valley continued to blow, stirring the mist and their golden hair.

"They aren't trying to win," Corayne muttered. "They're just going through the motions to stay sharp."

Andry eyed her with a sweep of dark lashes.

"And stay connected to each other. A soldier is only as good as the person next to him," he said, giving her a nudge with his elbow. Beneath his furs, he wore chain mail. "Trust is as much a weapon as anything else."

She nearly rolled her eyes. "I'll keep that in mind when Taristan brings the full weight of his empire crashing down on this place."

The joke landed poorly and Andry's face darkened.

"You think he will?"

What do you expect, Andry? she wanted to shout. *To stay here, cocooned from the world forever, while the realm ends in fire?*

Her reply was far more diplomatic.

"It's only a matter of time before he figures out where I am," she said, moving again.

This time, Andry followed her.

"Well then, let's use the time we have," he said behind her. Not even the mist, or the circumstances, could truly dampen his sunny disposition.

It annoyed and calmed Corayne in equal measure. If not for Andry, she might spend most of her days studying the horizon, watching for a legion to crest the mountain pass. Still as the Elders, waiting for the world to end.

By now, the Ionian guards knew both Andry and Corayne. They greeted them with stern glances as Andry led her to a place at the edge of the stone landing. Two blunted training swords were already waiting.

Andry loosened the clasp holding his furs in place, shrugging them off onto a nearby bench. A hand ax dangled at his waist, but without the Jydi wolf pelt around his shoulders, he looked more like himself. Out of place among the immortals, but still Andry Trelland. Noble to a fault, somehow warm without a ray of sun.

He was only missing his tunic, the old white fabric emblazoned with the blue star. Corayne had not seen it since he arrived in Iona. She could only hope it was safely tucked away in his room, and not lost like all the other pieces of his home.

Corayne made herself ready, unbuckling the Spindleblade to lay it next to his furs. She unsheathed her Sirandel blade too, replacing it with the dull-edged sword.

"If you don't know how to use a shield, it's not going to help you," Andry said, watching her carefully.

He clasped the tall shield between his hands. It was half her height, flat across the top and tapered at the bottom, made of reinforced wood and worn red leather.

"This is your shortest lesson yet," she replied, forcing a laugh.

"Perhaps," Andry countered. "The great advantage of a shield, of course, is to defend yourself. You can strike and still keep most of your body covered."

He slipped an arm into the strap on the back of the shield, the other motioning the swing of a sword. Beneath him, his feet slid into a fighting stance, his body weight shifting. Corayne watched keenly, half taking notes for herself. The rest watched the tall young man with the kind eyes, tracking every flex of his long-fingered hand or the clench of his jaw.

It was his focus, more than anything, that drew her in.

"You can also use a shield to push your opponent back," he added, stepping forward with his body braced behind the shield. Corayne stepped neatly out of his way. "You can even smash him in the face. But rely on your sword first."

Corayne blanched as he passed it over to her, surprised by the weight.

Andry raised an eyebrow. "Too heavy?"

She shook her head, slipping her arm into the strap at the back of the shield. The old leather was soft but strong, freshly oiled.

"The opposite," she said. "I thought an Elder shield would be impossible for me to lift."

"It's not Elder," Andry replied casually. "Some of the Ionian guards offered me a few things from the armory."

Not Elder. Her grip tightened on the shield strap, fingers feeling for the old hand that once held it. It was like trying to hold hands with a ghost.

"Not an Elder's shield," Corayne murmured. "*His.*"

Across from her, Andry's eyes went round, his own realization dawning. "Oh," he said, stumbling over his words. "Corayne, I didn't realize—"

She sucked in a painful breath, her chest tight beneath her leather jerkin. The air smelled of rain and nothing else. *As if a shield could smell like my father*, she thought, cursing her own stupidity.

"What else was there?" Corayne asked sharply. Half of her wanted to fight the Elder soldiers for disturbing her father's belongings. The rest wanted to see what else they still had.

Andry frowned, shaking his head. "They only gave me the shield. The rest is not my business," he answered. His throat bobbed as he swallowed. "My father had a shield too."

Corayne remembered it, a ruin nearly cracked in half, fixed against the wall of the Trelland apartments. Like his tunic, it bore the blue star.

"It was the only part of him to come back," Andry murmured, his own grief rising up to meet hers. "We can take a moment, if you like."

Corayne showed her teeth. Her grip tightened on the shield strap, her other hand going for the training blade at her hip.

"We don't have a moment," she hissed, loosing the sword.

Immediately, she caught the edge of the shield, the dull blade sliding against the wood. Corayne winced, her cheeks flaming red.

"Sorasa and Sigil never taught me any of this."

There was no judgment in Andry Trelland. He merely dropped into the proper stance again, modeling for her.

"Sorasa and Sigil never trained to be a knight," he said. As she mirrored his form, he nodded. "If war comes to this castle, you won't be striking from dark alleys and slitting throats behind corners. You're going to face an army head on."

His army once. His knights and companions. His fellow squires. His friends. She saw the same heavy thoughts on his face, shadowing his eyes.

The wind blew again, sending a chill through Corayne. But she knew better than to throw her cloak back on. They would work up a sweat quickly enough.

"Let's see how you move with it first, so I can tell you what to fix," Andry offered. He drew his own training sword, holding it between them.

The flush still burned on Corayne's face. "That will do wonders for my self-confidence."

He only shrugged. The blade twirled in his hand, betraying the deadly swordsman beneath Andry's gentle facade. Sometimes it was easy to forget he was trained to be a knight, and had survived many battles since.

"It's all right to get things wrong," he said. "It's how we learn to do things properly."

Over the next few minutes, Corayne was wrong many times.

Andry danced within her guard or tripped her up, using the weight of the shield to send her off balance. He moved too quickly, more agile than Corayne still struggling to strike and hold the shield in place. He corrected her gently, adjusting her stance or her grip, giving advice in a low voice.

Corayne expected to feel stupid and embarrassed. Instead, she felt only encouraged, prodded on by the promise of Andry's delighted cheer or proud smile.

"You're a good teacher," she finally said, panting a little. Across from her, Andry halted in his steps. "You must have been the envy of the other squires."

His soft expression changed, going sour. Immediately Corayne regretted her words, though she couldn't say why.

"I did my best," Andry said. His smile returned, horribly forced. "Sometimes it was enough. Again."

Back and forth they went, with Corayne learning little by little. Until she realized exactly how well Andry fought, and how much he allowed her to win.

His left hand went to his hip too quickly, loosing the Jydi ax. She nearly missed the motion, distracted by his still-moving sword. Then the ax hooked around the edge of the shield. With a snap of his arm, he struck open her guard as one might open a book.

Leaving Corayne completely exposed, his training sword at her throat. All instinct, she fell backward, landing hard against the stone beneath her.

Before Andry could apologize, she laughed up at him.

"You're more raider than squire now, Trelland," she chuckled, indicating the gleaming ax.

He shook his head back at her, extending a hand to help her up. Grinning, Corayne took it, leaving her training sword where it fell.

Then her eyes narrowed, her gaze fixed not on Andry, but the castle behind him. Tíarma, towers gray against the retreating clouds, half shrouded in mist, half ribboned with sunlight. Elders patrolled the ramparts, moving slowly along the battlements crowned in antlers and sculpted stags.

"Corayne?"

Andry's voice sounded far away, rippling as if through deep water. It did nothing to stop the nausea rising in Corayne's body, her own teeth clenched against a sudden gasp.

"I've seen this before," she breathed, pulling herself up on shaky feet.

Her eyes never left the castle, her mind whirling as she tried to place the image. The exact spread of light, the exact shadows. The exact position from this spot in the training yard.

Andry frowned over her, rightfully confused. "Yes, we've been here for weeks now."

She barely heard him.

"I dreamed of this place." Her breath hitched and she nearly fell to the ground again. Only Andry kept her standing, his hand still firm in her own. "I dreamed of it before I ever set foot here."

If Andry said something, she did not know.

A roaring in her ears drowned him out.

"I stood here with the Spindleblade, and Erida stood with me," she forced out, her body shaking. "Her eyes were burning."

A flush crept up on Andry's face, his own eyes widening. "Like . . . ?"

"Like Taristan."

Again, the wind howled.

"It was not a dream, not really." She tightened her grip on Andry's hand, nails digging. He didn't flinch. "I saw her—I felt her here as closely as I feel you now. And she—"

Corayne's voice broke.

"She saw me. She saw me here," she bit out. Nausea roiled up inside her, until Corayne feared she might be sick all over the training yard.

Andry held firm, never letting her go. He stared down on her with concerned eyes, brow furrowed in a grim line. "Erida saw you—in your dream?" he asked, hesitant. "Corayne—"

A chill ran through her. "She is not the only one who does."

Even awake, Corayne felt the blistering touch of a demon, his shadow creeping at the corners of her eyes. They were only memories, but sharp as the castle above her. As real as the stone beneath her body.

"What Waits showed me to her," she whispered, curling into Andry. Her eyes squeezed shut, and the shadow of What Waits loomed, somehow darker than the darkness.

Her mouth filled with a vile taste.

"They know where I am, Andry."

Reluctantly, Corayne opened her eyes and looked back up at the castle. Now a figure stood the ramparts, small in her gray shift, her braids fluttering in the wind.

Valtik looked down on her with a grave expression, her blue eyes lighting across the distance between them. For once, she looked stern, her playful manner gone entirely.

Corayne's head spun, her breath catching even as she forced out the words.

"Our time has run out."

27

THE WORST POSSIBLE
Charlon

The wet cold persisted after they left Iona. Winter ran harsh in the long glen between the mountains, occupying a cruel balance. It did not snow, but freezing rain persisted every day, punctuated by sudden bursts of sunlight through the streaking clouds. After a week traveling south, Charlie felt worn as an old rock, eroded by wind and rain. Even Garion could not hide his discomfort, his alabaster cheeks tinged pink over the collar of his cloak.

It was noon when they rode into Lenava, though Charlie could hardly tell. The gray sky frowned over them, the sun stubborn and hidden.

Lenava seemed quaint compared to metropolitan Ascal or beautiful, pink-hued Partepalas. Even the criminal haven of Adira had more of a heartbeat. The Calidonian capital was a sleepy backwater, to Charlie's eye. A dark blue flag flapped above the city gates, the image of a white boar waving in the howling wind. The city appeared to be little more than a large town ringed with a stone wall, a castle perched on the hill above the River Avanar. The port sat where the river met the icy waters of the Auroran Ocean, with only a few ships in harbor.

People walked the streets, heading into market or out to the farmlands outside the walls. A herd of sheep shuffled by, driven on by a brusque shepherd and a pair of dogs. Carts wheeled, piled high with peat. But the steady rain muffled most noise, pressing down like a gray blanket.

The quiet should have been a comfort. Charlie only felt more unease, his horse squelching through muddy streets.

Garion remained alert, his collar laced high and tight to hide his Amhara tattoos. With his pale face and dark hair, he fit in smoothly with the other cityfolk, all of them milk-skinned beneath their heavy coats and fur hoods.

This seemed like a good idea in Iona, Charlie thought, swallowing hard. The Elder enclave had felt so cut off from the world, but Lenava looked just as isolated.

He eyed the street again, seemingly the main road through the city. Workshops and houses lined the sides, most of them wattle-and-daub, with thatched roofs and timber framing. In Lenava, the market teemed despite the rain, the square of stalls safe beneath a timber roof with open sides.

"Where to first?" Charlie muttered under his breath, leaning toward Garion.

The Amhara gave a devastating smirk. With a tip of a finger, he indicated a nearby building, its wooden sign swaying in the wind. Charlie glimpsed the painted image of a cup. Beneath it, windows glowed with warmth, the stone walls streaked with age.

Garion slid from his horse, grasping at the reins. "Where else?"

The inn and tavern had a small courtyard, and Charlie expected the least. Instead, two grooms jumped to attention, eager to stable their horses. And eager for payment.

Charlie did not miss the way they squinted at the Elder coin, rubbing fingers over the stamped image of a stag. Both grooms, young men with easy smiles, turned sour. But they did not return the coin and led the horses away with curt nods.

"The first time I don't use counterfeit coin, they turn up their noses at it," Charlie grumbled under his breath.

The common room of the tavern had a low ceiling and smoky air born of the hearth fire, with a few patrons seated or standing at the bar. It was a suitable establishment, and Charlie was pleasantly surprised with the service. In a few moments, he and Garion had a room for the next few days, their bags and provisions stowed, and a fine lunch laid out. The wine was half-sour but Charlie drank it down anyway, allowing himself to lean back in the little chair.

Exiled or not, Garion did not discard his Amhara ways. He sat with his back in the corner, one eye on the room at all times. Charlie hardly minded. It felt good to shirk off his worries, if only a little.

"Well," Garion finally said, raising an eyebrow across the table.

"Well," Charlie answered with a huff.

Outside, the rain turned from heavy mist to a steady downpour, leaving fat drops coursing down the pitted windows.

Beneath the table, Charlie's knee bounced, despite all his attempts to relax.

Garion tipped his head, his glossy dark eyes narrowed. "What worries you, darling?"

"What doesn't?" Charlie cut back.

He winced at his own tone, sharper than it needed to be. A low ache throbbed in his temple and he loosed his hair from its tight braid, working out the damp chestnut waves. Then he shrugged off his cloak, too hot for the close, warm air of the tavern. While the rest of their things had been brought upstairs, he'd kept his satchel. His forged seals and inks were worth more than anything in their saddlebags. Not to mention Andry's letter to his mother, tucked away safely between pages of parchment.

"There are worse places in the realm to be," Garion said gently.

"I've been in most of them," Charlie replied, remembering too much.

The wings of a dragon, a kraken's salty brine stench, ash on his tongue, the corpse army of hundreds churning in the mud. It washed over him, impossible to ignore.

"I'm sorry, I don't know," he muttered. "It's difficult to—"

Garion's hand crept over the tabletop to land on Charlie's own. "Stay still?"

"It's difficult to see my place in all this." Charlie kept his eyes on their joined fingers, his ink-stained skin against Garion's. "I thought this was the right idea. I thought this was how I could help."

"It *is* a good idea, but we've been here all of an hour, Charlie. Breathe a bit," the assassin said. "Besides, Queen Erida isn't going to jump out of a closet and punch you in the face. And if she does—"

Beneath the table, something glimmered, bronze and deadly. Garion's other hand spun the dagger with lethal intent, the blade blurring with his skilled motions.

"That's all our worries ended," he said, slipping the dagger away again.

"Killing her is only part of it." Reluctantly, Charlie pulled his hand back. "There's Taristan to consider, and worse things behind him."

The mask of the Amhara slid down over Garion's face, his expression going blank. "What Waits."

Charlie gritted his teeth. "I know. It still sounds foolish, even to me."

"I saw the dragons with my own two eyes. I'll believe anything now," Garion bit out, frustrated. "And I'll follow you wherever it is you wish to go."

Again, Charlie's head throbbed. He sensed the implication laced through his paramour's words, and it set his hair on end.

"I won't abandon her, Garion," he said through clenched teeth. "I told you before."

He expected Garion to argue. To lay out every good and logical reason to run. Instead, the assassin shoved back from the table, a winning smile plastered across his face. Even his eyes sparkled, matching the easy grin. But Charlie saw through it, to the tightness in his shoulders, the twitching of his hands.

"Garion—"

"I know," the assassin said, before crossing the common room.

To Charlie's horror, he did the worst thing possible.

With a smile and a word of greeting, Garion talked to the other patrons. His Amhara-trained charisma crackled through the room, enticing the barkeep and the innkeeper, and pulling the other Calidonian regulars under his sway.

Charlie wanted to sink into the floor.

Instead, he forced down the rest of his wine, and stood to join.

To the folk of Lenava, Charlie was a priest on a pilgrimage to Tiber's holy temple at Turadir, set among the famed silver mines of the eastern mountains. Garion was his hired bodyguard, a mercenary from one of the lesser guilds in Partepalas. It was an easy arrangement, and an easy lie to tell.

Charlie even blessed a few merchants in the market, trading prayers for less conspicuous coin. They spent most days tramping between market and harbor, under the guise of preparing for the journey north along the coast. Truly, they collected what little they could: news, rumors, stories from old sailors and young farmers alike.

Garion was the more charming of the pair, his easy manner trained into him by the Amhara Guild. He charmed all manner of folk, filling the tavern with patrons every night, only to listen rapturously to their tales of the greater realm.

Most stories conflicted, and Charlie's head spun trying to piece together the truth of it all.

If nothing else, I have done this, Charlie thought one morning, Andry's letter in hand.

He passed it over to a ship bound for Kasa, its crew sailing for warmer waters beyond the gray horizon.

Charlie hoped the letter would find Andry's mother safe and cared for, among her own family, far away from the grim fate of the world. If anyone in the realm deserved something, Andry Trelland deserved that.

Every day, Charlie felt a little less useless, even as they sat and contemplated the rain. Now, when he woke, it took a moment to remember the world was ending, and the warm body next to him was real. Not a dream, not a wish. But Garion, right beside him, already awake and staring. Lenava was as far from a golden summer in Partepalas as one could be, but the slow moments felt the same. Unburdened, good.

And slipping away, sand through his fingers.

He dreaded the second they would end.

It was the shouts of the innkeeper one morning that sent them both rolling from their bed, scrambling for boots and clothes. Garion slipped out first, his rapier belted into place, his fingers lazy on the Amhara dagger. He moved like water, dancing out into the hall before Charlie had a shirt over his head.

Cursing, he followed, grabbing for his own sword as an afterthought. Charlie doubted he would be much use against bandits or pirates or whatever else caused such a commotion, but knew better than to walk into a fight empty-handed.

He barreled down the narrow stairs to the common room, only to find Garion already with the innkeeper. The old man was white-faced, stumbling over his words, one finger shaking as he pointed out toward the street.

After more than a week at the inn, Charlie had never seen the man so fearful, let alone at such a loss for words.

"It's all right, it's all right," Garion said, soothing the old innkeeper as he would a spooked animal.

It seemed to work a little. The old man pointed again, his long white beard waggling.

"Invasion," he forced out, barely a hiss. "Invasion."

Charlie's insides turned to ice.

Garion's soft manner dropped away, his mask of encouraging calm shattered. His dark brow furrowed, his eyes black and sharp. Without a word, he went to the door to the street and yanked it open, stepping out into the rare sunlight.

Charlie followed, trembling. His mind whirled, a tangle of thoughts. *Grab our things, get the horses, make for the hills.* But he did none of them, following Garion instead.

Outside the tavern, the street turned and angled up a slight hill, offering a clear view across the harbor and out into the Auroran Ocean. Charlie had to shade his eyes, squinting as he looked westward into the coastal hills, toward the border with Madrence.

He expected the flash of sun on steel. The gleam of armor and swords, the thunder of a marching legion. His throat tightened as he braced for the sight of a green flag and a golden lion. Or worse, a prince all in red, a bloody wizard at his side.

To his surprise, there was nothing but the mountains, the forested slopes fading to stone and snow.

Then Garion touched him, slipping a hand under his chin. Gently, he directed Charlie's gaze away from the west, and out to frigid ocean.

But for Garion's hand, Charlie feared his jaw might drop clean off.

The horizon filled with sails, their flags caught in the still blustering wind, one unfurling after the other.

Tears stung Charlie's eyes as he studied them one by one, their flags unmistakable.

28

THE RIVER
Erida

She was half-dressed by the time Taristan rolled over, blinking forcefully, his hair a red mess across one side of his face. He sat up slowly, the remnants of sleep still clinging to him as he surveyed the commandeered bedchamber. Erida watched him from the adjoining room, her arms spread wide as her servants clothed her.

In the Konrada, they had smaller apartments, forcing Taristan into closer proximity with the Queen's dizzying array of attendants. His disdain for them was well known, and impossible to overlook. As he rose for the day, the maids quickened their pace.

Jeweled rings slid onto Erida's fingers, a ruby bracelet over one wrist. She chose a gray gown from the few available, an artwork of pale silver brocade over dove silk. The maids braided her hair last, weaving together a great many strands to form a long plait down her back. It felt like a rope swinging between her shoulder blades.

"A little early for full battledress."

Taristan leaned against the doorframe, naked to the waist, his breeches belted low over bare skin. If he meant to frighten the maids, he succeeded. Their eyes shot to the floor. Erida smirked over their heads and pulled out of their grasp.

She raised an eyebrow at Taristan's appearance, from his white-veined chest to his bare feet. "Shall I call for your manservants?"

"Is that a threat?" he answered roughly.

"That will be enough," she said, dismissing her maids with a curt wave.

A half second later, the door to the hall clicked shut behind them, leaving Erida to glitter in the cramped salon. Outside the window, the red sky glowed, the sun well above the horizon.

My mind is my own.

She repeated the old refrain, the one she used to tell herself to remain steady when she felt alone. Now she held on to it tightly, as she would a shield. A gentle divider between herself, and what crawled through her thoughts.

To her surprise, she felt something like a tug, gentle but firm. Half of her wanted to walk out too, eager to face what had only begun. She need only convene her council and speak the command that would set all in motion.

The other half of her smiled, all but vibrating in her skin. She checked the door again, then swept forward so quickly Taristan flinched. Her skirts swirled across the floor as she took him by the shoulders, her teeth bared into a too-wide smile.

"Iona," she said, barely daring to speak the word aloud.

His own hands closed over her arms, his fingers blazing even through her sleeves. The line of his brow tightened with concern. Red stirred in the black of his eyes. Only a glimmer, sparks beneath steel. Enough to betray the thin veil that existed between Taristan's mind, and something else. For now, the black abyss of his own soul won out, devouring.

"Iona?" he echoed.

"Corayne flees to the Elder enclave," she said, ignoring the sharp pressure of his grasp. "She has the Spindleblade, she's alive, and she thinks she can outlast us within the walls of a crumbling castle."

Taristan was many things. A prince of an ancient bloodline. A queen's consort. A demon's tool. A mercenary, a murderer, a jealous orphan grasping at some semblance of a future. They all flashed across his face, pulled to the surface.

"How do you know this?" His voice shook.

It was both a question and an accusation.

"How do you know this?" he asked again, shaking her shoulders harshly.

This time, Erida did not flinch. She held his gaze, resolute and proud. The phantom pull remained, like a river current flowing past her legs, gently nudging her toward the hall. She held her ground, even as the pressure mounted.

Slowly, without blinking, Taristan undid the laces at her neck. With one hand, he pulled aside the silk fabric, laying bare the top of her collarbone. His breath turned shallow as he laid his palm to her skin.

She flamed beneath him, burning as he burned.

"Erida," he whispered, a broken edge to his voice.

She could only blink, trembling beneath his hand. Too many words stuck in her mouth, rattling the cage of teeth. She searched his face, his eyes, his inches, trying to read the emotions as they welled up in him.

The Queen expected him to be impressed, proud, intrigued.

I am joined to you in every way now, she thought. *You should kneel at my feet and be grateful for my choice.*

Instead, her heart twisted.

Taristan was furious.

"I am following the path you already walk," she hissed, her rage rising to match his own. "So that we might walk it forever. *Together.*"

Still he held her, bruises blooming beneath his fingers. The pain was dull in comparison to the pain in her own chest. They braided together, fury and sorrow, until she could not distinguish one from the other.

Finally, Taristan loosened his grip but did not step back, holding his ground. He towered over her, dangerous as the day she first saw him. All his scars stood out, white against flushing skin, laying bare the truth of Taristan's life. He was a survivor first, above all things.

"I did not want this for you," he hissed. "You do not know what you have done."

"You paid your price to What Waits. And I have paid mine," Erida snapped. She refused to think of the old woman tucked away in her bed, her eyes open and glassy, unseeing in death.

"Does that bother you?" she pressed on, half-mad. She felt like a galloping horse with no rider to rein her in. "That I am your equal in His eyes?"

"Erida," he warned. The low timbre of his voice rattled the air.

She did not care, her blood turned to venom, stinging in her veins. Her own skin blazed, and she feared her silk gown might turn to embers.

"You are the same as all the rest, no matter what I let myself believe," she spat out, jabbing a finger at the hollow beneath his throat. Her eyes stung, tears hot against her lashes. "You see me as they do. A broodmare. An object."

That is not true, some little part of her whispered. She remembered how he knelt, so easily, without shame. How he waited for her order to kill. Every time he hung back, shifting to stand just a little bit behind her, holding her flank like a soldier on the front line of battle. How he froze, a sword to Domacridhan's neck, the Elder's death in his hands. But for

Erida's own life hanging in the balance.

Even so, she could not stop.

"I have been alone all my life. And I thought you—" Her breath caught, choking. She blinked fiercely, trying to force back the hot, stinging sensation. "I suppose now I'll never be alone again."

The river still flowed against her legs, pressing, begging to be followed. She wanted to lean into it and be swept away. To follow and not lead, if only for a single moment.

Taristan only stared, the hard edge of his jaw clenched tight. He watched her, eyes ticking up her frame, *judging* her. She could feel it, his gaze. It burned like her skin, threatening to consume everything.

"You must learn to balance," he finally said, his shoulders dropping.

Her eyes flared wide.

"How dare you lecture me?" she sneered.

But he only shook his head. Again, he closed the distance between them, reaching out to touch her exposed throat. Erida shrugged away, nearly tripping over her own skirts.

"Balance what He is, and who you are. Both exist now, in here." His voice shifted, oddly kind for the circumstances. Erida did not trust it.

"*Both,*" he said again.

This time, when his hand closed over the space where neck met shoulder, Erida held herself steady. She swallowed hard, throat bobbing against his thumb. As much as the feel of him burned, it grounded her too.

Balance, the small voice, her own voice, said. She reached for it, past the rage and wild abandon.

Her eyes went round and she looked up to Taristan of Old Cor. It felt like seeing him for the first time. But now, she saw beneath. To the battle under his skin, behind his eyes, the weight always tipping back and forth.

The river current.

With a shudder, she realized it was not a gentle pull tugging at her body, cool and sweet as freshwater. It was a fountain of magma, red and endless, angry. It was the slow, inexorable motion of stars in the black sky, who could not stop their dance even if they tried.

"Taristan," she whispered.

My mind is my own.

Again, her eyes stung. She could not see them herself, but some part of her knew. The sapphire blue was no more.

Her eyes burned red.

"I know," he answered, laying his fevered forehead to her fevered neck. "I know."

She smelled smoke again. From her dress or the demon in her head, Erida did not know. And, she knew, it did not matter.

Then the door burst open, a white-faced lady behind it. She stood half in the hall, the other ladies-in-waiting behind her, all of them pale and trembling. It was no small thing to disturb the Queen and her consort. At the back of Erida's mind, something snarled for their heads. It overwhelmed her at first, her vision shining white, and she had to turn away.

Taristan let her, bracing her against his still-bare chest. *Hiding me,* she realized. *Hiding what I've done.*

"My lady, the council has convened in the cathedral. But—"

Erida went stiff against Taristan, her back too straight, both hands fisting at the folds of her dress. Her good hand curled, nails biting into her palm.

Still she would not turn. Not while her eyes stung, her sight edged with a black-and-red haze.

Even so, she knew what came next.

"Lady Harrsing is gone, Your Majesty."

It was easy to slump against her husband, letting her limbs turn to water. To the ladies, it would seem their queen was overtaken by grief. They all knew Harrsing was as a mother to her, not to mention a valued advisor.

"Oh," she mumbled against Taristan's shoulder, her face pressed against him. She felt his arm go around her back, keeping her steady.

"She went in her sleep, it seems. It was peaceful," the foolish woman kept on. "I cannot tell you how sorry—"

"Leave us," Taristan snarled.

Confronted with the full weight of the prince's fury, the lady gave a sound like a mouse being stepped on. Then slammed the door, leaving them both in silence.

Safely alone, Erida swallowed around a lump in her throat. Sighing, she stepped back from Taristan and looked up at him with dry, unyielding eyes. Once more, he studied her, and she let him stare. If he searched for grief, he would not find it.

"At least I am already wearing the colors of mourning," she said, gesturing down to the gray and silver.

It was admission enough.

"You knew," he muttered.

"I knew," she answered, re-lacing her collar over her exposed throat. "What's done is done."

Taristan curled his lip. "What's done is done."

It was easier than Erida thought, in the end.

She unfurled one of Thornwall's maps, the one marked with every fortress, every garrison, the legions mapped out in red ink. Her advisors looked on in silence as she traced a line from Ascal across the continent.

Calidon.

There had been opposition. Calidon was a poor kingdom. She would be a small jewel in an already blazing crown. The Gallish legions had just returned. It was still winter, and provisions would be expensive, if not impossible to find. Feeding the armies might empty the royal treasury, let alone seed revolt among the minor lords and their men-at-arms. She heard none of it. Not the state of the mountain passes. Not the danger of traveling by sea.

Nothing was impossible, not for her. Not for Taristan.

Not for the demon god in their veins.

She felt him as she could feel the crown on her head, the jewels on her hands.

Taristan was right.

It was like being a god in human skin, pure power sliding through her veins.

What Waits did not speak as she imagined He would, now that the door was opened, the table set. The feast prepared and waiting to be devoured. *Let me in, let me stay* still echoed, but only in memory. His whispers were no longer in a language she knew, but something hissing and tangled, punctuated by the click of teeth. She felt His breath on the back of her neck, sometimes hot and humid, sometimes shivering cold. The darkness never changed, though, black and empty as the space between stars. Deeper even than Taristan's eyes.

To her relief, she understood Him still. His wishes moved in her, prodding, sometimes the lava flow, sometimes the river. She could fight them whenever she liked, letting the water break against her. Digging her feet into the mud, steeling her body against the never-ending pressure.

Sometimes it was easier to be swept along.

The touch of Him was terrible and glorious. And as Taristan said, the only answer was balance.

Erida practiced it every day, safe behind her intricate veils. It was better to wear them, sheer silk studded with gemstones or embroidered with delicate lace. The last thing she needed was a noble to run screaming, telling everyone their queen was possessed, her eyes made of flame.

Let them think I mourn Bella Harrsing, she thought as she donned the veils. *Let them think me softhearted, if only for a little while.*

The death of Lady Harrsing came and went, old news by the next morning. Her advisors and nobles forgot the loss of a single old woman. There was the business of war to think about.

But Erida did not forget, not in the last untouched corners of her heart. *Bella wanted to help me,* she told herself. *And she has.*

The city cheered as they rode out again, Erida and Taristan in all their splendor. They left behind a palace half destroyed, the harbor still in shambles, the smoldering wreck of the pirate attack still shifting on the wind. And somehow, none of it mattered to the commoners, not in the face of another victory. Another kingdom to win, another crown to bring home.

She was the Lioness, the Empress Rising. Her place was on the battlefield, not the throne.

Lord Thornwall chose the rally point at Rouleine. He sent word to the legions and forts across Galland, as well as their emissaries in Siscaria, Madrence, and Tyriot. Armies were called from every corner of Erida's vastly growing empire, their spears pointed toward Rouleine.

In the first campaign, Erida had despised the long march and the military camp. She hated the dust, hated the smell, hated the heavy ache that came with bouncing in a carriage or swaying in the saddle. Most of all, she hated the council tent, the posturing up and down the long table of every lord and half-stupid heir. All that changed now. Thornwall handled most of her council, with few advisors daring to disturb the Queen and her consort. So long as the army moved, the eastern horizon fixed in front of them, Erida was satisfied.

Every mile on felt like a good meal sucked through her teeth. Her blood surged, heart thumping, the cold winter wind a mild breeze against her fevered face. She felt the river current always. Today it wound around her like a happy puppy, bouncing along. It was a firm reminder of her place, her purpose, and what promise lay ahead.

As much as What Waits frightened her, Erida delighted in Him too.

She felt meant for this, as she was meant for the throne.

Mile by mile, her army grew, its length a shadow across the sprawling countryside. The supply train alone doubled their number. There was cavalry, infantry, men-at-arms, archers, pikemen, and knights. Professional soldiers of the legions or peasant farmers clutching shovels. Noble lords with their infinite sons, done up in ridiculous armor and brocade. And the corpse army too, following at a distance so as not to terrify the living.

Taristan was careful to keep them downwind.

By now, her lords knew their worth. What's more, they knew better than to argue against an army of the undead.

There were reports of villages picked clean, barren farmland stripped to the roots, forests burned for fuel or chopped down for firewood. Rivers ran with refuse from the grand camps. Open fields turned to muddy wastes. Erida waved off every concern. Such was the price of empire.

All will give. As I have given.

The days blurred. She practiced balance, awash in the hissing love of What Waits, but never slipping under the surface. Even so, she had to be reminded to eat, to sleep, to acknowledge the existence of her ladies as they dressed her or tended to her body.

She understood Taristan's mask now. His placid, unconcerned

manner. The still surface hid a churning whirlpool beneath. Erida felt it too, her mind balanced between her own thoughts and the creeping wishes of What Waits.

For many weeks, her army navigated the stretch of land between the waters of the Old Lion and the dark shadows of the Castlewood, hemmed in between river and forest. The army line moved like an inchworm, stretching and contracting. Supplies traveled upriver with them, making it easier to outfit the grand legions and keep their bellies full. That was enough for soldiers, as well as raised wages, promised by the Queen herself. Their loyalty was easy to buy, with promises of glory and good coin.

The land was familiar. It was the same road the first campaign took, the wake of their passing still evident across the ground. Erida watched as the hooves of her horse navigated the ruts of cart wheels and churned earth, the eaves of the forest glittering with frost.

There were no borders here anymore. Not with Madrence or Siscaria. The horizon belonged to Erida and the army did not fear enemies as it did before. They moved like the victory was already won.

Her retinue traveled at the head of the line, with the cavalry, moving faster than the slow carts and foot soldiers. Their aim was Rouleine, where the rest of the legions would rally, and Erida's company made for it with all speed.

Taristan rode beside her through it all, ramrod straight in the saddle of his horse, a red cape billowing behind him. The light shimmered oddly on him now, as if she glimpsed him through a chink of thick glass.

"Vergon is near," he said one morning, his shoulders still squared to the road. But his head turned, his eyes raised to the hills above the river valley.

Her teeth clenched. Erida could not see Castle Vergon from their place on the road, but she knew the ruins lay only a few miles off. She remembered the hill of thorns rising up to the castle walls, the chapel, where stained glass still sparkled among the moss, the face of a goddess broken in two. A Spindle burned there, a single thread of gold, a seam in the making of the realm.

It burned no more, and never would again.

Taristan had no Spindleblade, no blessed steel. He could not tear the Spindle open again even if he marched up to Vergon and clawed the air himself.

Erida reached across the space between their two horses, grasping for Taristan's gloved hand. He gripped her back, almost too tightly, and his face flushed, lips pulled into a scowl.

"I'm sorry" was all she could think to say.

He gave no reply, but his thoughts were easy to read.

Near a month ago, he'd crumbled to the floor of the Konrada, clutching at his own chest. He felt the loss of the Spindle as Corayne tore it apart, with his Spindleblade in her hand. Erida knew he felt the agony of it again, so close as to touch the Spindle lost.

But without a Spindleblade, there was nothing to be done. By either of them.

Anger curled in Erida's mind, weaving with the same anger of What Waits. Both seethed. Neither knew what it was to be helpless, without power.

We have that in common, Erida thought, still holding Taristan's hand.

She felt another presence nudging at their joined fingers. What Waits wove between them, a coursing river of hunger.

Erida hissed with annoyance when Thornwall stopped the march for the evening, the whistles of his lieutenants carrying up and down the line. The sun had barely begun to set, red behind the low clouds. They had hours yet until darkness, and Erida wanted nothing more than to press on.

Instead, she allowed Taristan to help her dismount. Both stalked off while grooms attended to their horses, to the grand tent already waiting at the crest of a nearby hill.

To her surprise, Lord Thornwall followed them, his face pulled in trepidation. As before, the campaign suited him. He was a soldier above all things. But something shadowed his eyes.

"My lord?" Erida asked.

Thornwall gave a shallow bow. "You should join the council tonight, Your Majesty."

Erida only blinked. "Is there something I don't know?"

Quickly, Thornwall shook his head. "No, of course not. My reports to you have been complete."

Indeed, every morning he delivered painstakingly written reports of the campaign, from army movements to the bickering of her lords over their campfires.

She narrowed her eyes, searching her commander. "Then is there something you cannot handle, Lord Thornwall?"

Again, he shook his head violently. "No."

The wound on her palm itched, still throbbing from a day of riding. Erida fought the urge to clench a fist and worsen the pain.

"Then?" she bit out.

Thornwall looked between Erida and Taristan, his teeth on edge. He drew a long breath.

"It would do your lords well to see you," he said. "Both of you."

The Queen could not help but loose a long peal of laughter, even as the shadow inside her sneered.

"Do they not see enough of me on the campaign?" she balked. "I ride among them, at the head of my own cavalry. Not even my father did that, did he?"

Not even my father. Nor any king before him. Only I am brave enough to ride with the vanguard, to travel as a soldier would. Her thoughts spiraled, each one sharper than the last. Darker and darker, threatening to tip her over. *Balance,* she told herself, clenching her teeth. Her fist curled, and pain lanced up her arm. It steadied her.

My mind is my own.

"That is true, Your Majesty," Thornwall allowed, lowering his eyes.

Erida only straightened, her voice firmer. "I am finished doting on the whims of petty lords. It is beneath me," she said plainly. "Coddle them yourself. I will not."

To her shock, Thornwall's head snapped back up, his eyes meeting hers with resolve usually saved for the battlefield.

"Those petty lords command thousands of soldiers," he replied, harsher than she knew he could be.

Her knuckles turned white, her curled fist tightening until the pain turned the edge of her vision red. It was all she could do to keep level.

"No, my lord Thornwall," she hissed back. "You do."

And you answer to me.

Despite the vast war camp organizing around them, many thousands of horse and soldiers settling in for the night, Erida heard only silence. It pooled between queen and commander, but Lord Thornwall held his ground. He said nothing, only staring, and Erida saw a little of the soldier beneath the facade of an old man. Determined, intelligent, and deadly.

Any response died in her throat, as Erida searched for something to say.

"You promised my queen a head, Lord Thornwall."

Taristan's voice shattered the silent wall. He glared down at the military commander, his simmering fury on full display.

Bring me a head. You choose which. Erida commanded as much back in Ascal. *Corayne. Domacridhan. The Amhara. Konegin. Bring me my enemies.*

Lord Thornwall had failed to find a single one.

It was enough to make Thornwall remember himself, and he dropped his eyes, demure again. A deep flush washed over his cheeks, giving him an even ruddier look. His shame was palpable, all but perfuming the air. Despite the gray beard, Thornwall looked like a scolded squire.

In it, Erida saw opportunity.

Thornwall blanched when he felt the Queen's hand take his arm, her touch gentle despite her fierce disposition.

"You are not a hunter, Otto," she murmured. She did her best to soothe, though she did not know how. Erida of Galland had never soothed anything in her life. "You are not a betrayer either."

The commander flagged beneath her touch, heaving another sigh.

"It is not in you to think like usurpers and snakes," Erida continued. With her free hand, she raised her veil, a look of compassion on her face. "I cannot fault you for this failure."

Swiftly, Thornwall bowed, this time as low as he could. His knees creaked as he moved, his face aimed at the ground.

"Thank you, Your Majesty," he murmured, rising to meet her gaze again.

She stared back. "I am the head of this army, but you are its heart. Keep beating for me."

"I will, Your Majesty," he answered, putting a hand to his heart in salute.

Erida smiled in return, the pull of her lips so painful she thought her mouth might split at the corners.

"What a war," she murmured, echoing his own words from so long ago in the council chamber. When they talked of the Temurijon, and their legions meeting the Countless on the open field.

Even now, beneath the exhaustion and the dirt of the road, Thornwall perked up.

"What a war," he echoed, the memory warm in his eyes.

It was enough. Erida turned into the tent on her heel, retreating into the cool darkness.

The flap swished closed behind Taristan, plunging them both into half shadow. He set to lighting the candles laid out on the table, until the small space glowed.

"You are too soft with him," he grumbled, glancing at her as she sat to remove her boots.

Erida gave a huff and a wave of her good hand.

"I am exactly what I must be," she replied wearily. "He sees me as a daughter, no matter how many crowns I wear. If that is the role I must play to keep him loyal and obedient, so be it."

In the candlelight, Taristan's black eyes gleamed.

"You are a fearsome thing indeed," he said, looking proud. "Even without Him."

"I am exactly what I must be," Erida said again, too gentle. Then she winced. *I sound like a little girl.*

The low bed sagged as Taristan sat next to her, his weight nearly bowing the mattress to the floor. Erida leaned into him, letting his arm prop her up.

He took her hand. "And who are you with me?"

"Myself," she replied. "Whoever that is."

Again, What Waits wove between them, tight as their clasped fingers. This time, Erida could not say if He meant to bind them closer or slide them apart.

Her brow furrowed, her eyelids drooping. She was too tired to contemplate which.

My mind is my own.

Taristan stiffened next to her, his shoulders going tense with some worry. Erida angled her head to look up at him, reading the stern line of his brow.

"I am sorry about Vergon," she said again. In her heart, Erida knew she could not fathom what it felt like to lose a Spindle. And the gift with it.

"It is not Vergon that concerns me," he growled low in his throat. It shivered her. "But what came from it."

Erida shivered again, this time with fear. *The dragon.* It was still loose in the Ward, somewhere. Beholden to nothing but its own will. She bit her lip sharply, and tried not to think about what a dragon could do to her cavalry. To Taristan. And to her.

But I refuse to burn, she thought, squeezing her eyes shut. *I refuse to burn.*

At her core, the river turned hot, as if it could wash away her fear. Her skin flamed, her eyes stinging. She blinked rapidly, wishing for a splash of cold water.

"We must trust in Ronin," she finally said, moving to stand.

On the bed, Taristan scoffed in disbelief. She could not blame him. She hardly believed herself, or her own sudden faith in the red wizard.

"And above all things," she added, the words tumbling, "we must trust in Him."

On the table, the candles jumped and danced, each tongue of flame a little golden star. Erida watched them for a moment, before turning to face their own shadows on the wall of the tent. Like the candles, they wavered, shifting, never holding steady. Taristan's hunched, mirroring his position as he sat.

Her own shadow grew tall, distorted. For a moment, she glimpsed the silhouette of a crown she did not wear.

No, not a crown, she thought, narrowing her eyes.

The shadow changed again, sharpening.

Horns.

Come spring, Erida knew the hills would flourish green and bountiful. She imagined shimmering fields of golden wheat and woodlands filled with game, the Alsor flush with snowmelt, overflowing its banks. Merchants and caravans would rut the roads, not armies. But the land still clung to winter, the first bursts of spring some weeks away. The trees hung bare, the fields pitted and gray, the river low over smooth stones.

She recognized the landscape anyway. The first march to Rouleine was still fresh in her mind, and growing sharper by the mile. The same road unfurled now, eaten up by the Queen's cavalry as they charged along the river. Overhead, the green flags of Galland streamed out, the lion roaring above the great army. Roses of Old Cor wound around the lion's neck, a thorny necklace of flowers and vines. Beneath the lion's paws ran the silver stallion, the mermaid, and the blazing torch.

Madrence, Tyriot, Siscaria, Erida knew. *United beneath the lion, beneath me.*

No flags flew over Rouleine.

Erida looked down on the scarred ground where the city once lay, wedged into the joining of the Alsor and the Rose. It would be their rally point for the legions, until the full army could assemble and march into Calidon. She could hardly picture it, the entire might of Galland gathered to win the realm. The low thrum of power sang beneath her skin, enveloping her like a warm embrace.

The city walls remained below, blackened by fire. They formed a rough outline of the city that once was. The rest lay in ruins, burned or flooded. Buried in ashes or mud.

Let it burn.

She could still taste the command on her tongue, still see Lord Thornwall nod. It was his own suggestion, to destroy Rouleine so that no enemy might use the border city against Galland. But the border it marked no longer existed, swept from the map like pieces from a game board.

More than anything, she remembered the girl she was before the siege of Rouleine. Nineteen, but a girl still. Unknowing of the world, simple. She did not truly know what it meant to fight a war, let alone win it.

It was not Erida's army that beat down the gates and drew surrender from the city. It was something else entirely, crawling up out of the river. Corpses with dangling flesh, half skeletons, born of another realm and another Spindle. They frightened her then, as she watched across the river, under the shroud of night. Taristan held her back, forcing her to see what their conquest actually looked like.

Erida looked on with open eyes.

And she was never a girl again.

29

ROOTS AND WINGS
Domacridhan

The Elder ventured he would never get used to sea travel. He cursed the waves as the ship rocked beneath him. He wished for a horse and the open wilderness. He would rather gallop the Ward twice over than suffer another minute at sea.

They were long free from Ascal, but his torture wore on.

He was seasick no less than an hour into the next leg of the voyage. Domacridhan avoided the incredulous looks and backhanded smirks from the crew, going down to the little cabin to sleep off the worst of his illness. He felt Sorasa on his heels, silent as a mortal could be.

"If you need the cabin—" he began.

Sorasa cut him off with a whipcrack glare, her face pulled with disgust.

"I have little desire to share a sickbed with you," she snapped.

Instead, she put a bucket at the door in a rare display of kindness, along with a tiny sachet of powder. The latter, he assumed, would kill a mortal man. Elder though he was, Dom carefully avoided it.

Dom knew better than to press. Even exiled, Sorasa was a blooded

Amhara. She had little to fear sleeping on a ship filled with pirates who could barely look her in the eye. Let alone make trouble.

By now, he knew her manner well enough to understand when she meant to attack. Or simply deflect. As she stared back at Corranport, the harbor destroyed with a half-burned city slouching over it, he guessed it was the latter. She studied the coastline, her gaze flicking between smoke and sea. Her thoughts remained a mystery, shrouded behind the mask she wore so well.

His own churned in his mind, sickening as the waves beneath them.

"Every mile forward could be another mile closer to Corayne. Or not," he said, voice full of meaning.

The prospect weighed heavy in his mind, filling his waking thoughts. *If we don't know where she is, we don't know where we're going. Or how best to help her.*

Sorasa remained silent, but she did not argue, setting her mouth in a grim line. From the Amhara, that was agreement enough.

She looked better than she had in weeks. Lighter somehow. It was an unseasonably mild day outside and she wore only a light shirt and breeches, her short hair gathered at the nape of her neck. Her tattoos were on full display, oil-black against bronze skin. She had no cause to hide her identity here. The crew of the *Tempestborn* knew her measure. As always, she wore her belt of tricks—poison, powders, and a new dagger.

The little window looked out on the bobbing sea, pitching up and down. One glance sent Dom hurtling for the bed, to lie flat and hopefully weather the worst of his sickness.

Sorasa chuckled to herself, still amused by his inability to stomach the sea.

She crossed the narrow cabin, bending to peer out the thick glass.

"Three more today," she said idly, counting the number of ships following alongside the *Tempestborn*. "That makes ten in the last week."

Dom watched her through slitted eyes, trying to read her expression. "More pirates?"

She gave a hum of agreement. "And Tyri ships. I can see the flags. Meliz has been busy these last few months, burning ports and building alliances."

Then her copper eyes glittered.

"It seems they are united in their hatred of Queen Erida."

Dom knew little of the mortal kingdoms, but even he understood what a feat that was. The Tyri princes and the pirates had a long history of mutual disdain.

"We all have that in common these days," he muttered. "Hopefully that hatred is enough to raise the realm to war and stand against Erida before Taristan makes her too strong to fight."

"Hopefully." Sorasa cursed, shaking her head.

On the bed, Dom let himself be rocked by the ship, trying to lean into the sensation even as it shook his body. He stared at the low ceiling above him, studying the whorls in the planks of wood, each one of them familiar by now.

"We will be in Orisi soon enough and gather more news there. When Erida marches to war, we need only follow," he muttered, repeating the plan like a prayer.

"Well, not follow. Hopefully," Sorasa added, wincing. "I hate that word."

Dom looked down on her, watching her mouth curve with distaste.

"Follow?" he offered.

Her frown deepened.

"Hope."

* * *

After another week of maritime torture, Dom glimpsed the island city of Orisi. Most of him wanted to leap from the deck and swim the last mile into the harbor, leaving the *Tempestborn* behind. Only a stern look from Sorasa kept him standing.

To his surprise, a row of hunter ships guarded the mouth of the city port. They reminded him of the embargo wall across the Strait of the Ward. Half flew the turquoise flags of Tyriot, embroidered with the golden mermaid. The rest flew no flags at all.

Pirates, Dom knew.

While the rest of Tyriot was under Erida's control, the rebelling princes and the pirate alliance held the city island.

At the prow of the ship, Meliz stood proudly, one hand on a rope, her body like another sail as her hair caught the wind. She grinned at the island, the blockade, and the ships in harbor. Pride radiated off her, evident even to the immortal.

Orisi was not like the criminal haven of Adira. This was a true city, sprouting across most of the wedge-shaped island. The western side rose to jagged cliffs, the east flat into the blue-green shallows. White-walled temples and red-tiled villas looked out over the water, with market quarters and the docks across the flat below. Even from the port, Dom caught the scent of wild herbs and cypress groves.

While winter fog hung low to the north, the sun shone on Orisi, gilding the sea and the streets.

"It is as if the gods smile on this place, a city in open rebellion," Sorasa mused as they navigated into the port.

Once docked, the disembarkment was swift, to Dom's great pleasure. He followed Meliz and Sorasa down the gangway, all but sprinting onto dry land.

Immediately, he swayed on stable ground, kept upright only by his immortal grace. Thankfully, Sorasa swayed too. And Meliz swayed worst of all of them, her sea legs permanent as she wove her way down the gangplank. Her navigator, Kireem, followed, along with the Jydi bruiser Ehjer. Both took up flanking position, as if their captain needed protecting in the shadow of an immortal prince.

"If there's news of Erida's movements, it will reach the Sea Prince first," Meliz said, pointing up the hill. "I'll take you to him."

The docks of Orisi bustled, the streets bristling. Sailors of every stripe milled about, in all shades of skin. Pirates were easy to pick out, though the Tyri sailors were just as sun-worn and seaworthy. But far more grim, gray despite the sunshine. Trapped beneath the cloud of open war.

The Amhara followed Meliz closely, crouched low in her cloak to hide her tattoos again, her hair hanging loose.

"Should we be on the lookout for bounty hunters or assassins?" Dom asked, bending down to her ear.

He remembered the wanted posters in Almasad and Ascal, emblazoned with their faces and his name. Quickly, he scanned the walls of the buildings edging the dockyard and braced for the familiar sight of his own face.

Sorasa shook her head but pulled up her hood. "You have nothing to fear, Elder. Orisi stands against the Queen. Few here would try to turn you over to her. And I pity any who might try."

You have nothing to fear.

He eyed her as they walked the jostling streets, hearing what she would not say.

You.

Sorasa Sarn had many enemies, not just the Queen of Galland. She was not only wanted by the crown, but by her own guild. After the slaying of her Amhara kin, Dom suspected another assassin would kill her on sight. If they were not already hunting her across the Ward.

His chest burned with the thought. Suddenly, he felt the urge to open his cloak, to pull her closer. To put himself between Sorasa Sarn and anyone who wished her harm. *Not that she needs me for such things*, he thought sharply, dismissing the foolish idea with a shake of his head.

She watched him as they walked, a look of disdain on her face. As if she could read his mind.

"Worry about yourself, Dom," Sorasa spat, walking on. "And hope you don't make a fool of yourself in front of the Sea Prince. Better not to talk at all, really."

They wound up the wedge of the rocky island, leaving the docks and the ships behind. But not the sailors. Orisi seemed filled to bursting with Tyri crews, their families in tow. Many had fled the mainland after Erida claimed Tyriot for her own, and left her lords behind to govern. It gave the city the feel of a military fort or a refugee camp. Every door and window hung wide, the people of Orisi welcoming their countrymen.

Dom stuck out as usual, too pale and fair to be of the islands. He stood taller than most, his shoulders jutting out above the rest. Under her hood, Sorasa could be any Tyri woman, bronze-skinned and sharp-eyed.

But they were lost in the chaotic crowd of sailors, pirates, and refugees fleeing their conquered lands. The plaza near the docks looked like an encampment, with canopies stretching from the white walls. Men stood in winding lines, approaching makeshift desks and squinting navy officers. Names were signed and coins passed, along with uniforms.

Someone shouted at Dom in Tyri, pointing from beneath one of the canopies.

He tensed, his body going rigid beneath his cloak. While one hand went for his sword, the other flew to Sorasa's shoulder, pulling her into his shadow.

"He's asking if you sail, Elder," she said, her body tense beneath his hand. But she lingered, if only a moment, before shrugging him off.

He glanced down to catch a flash of teeth as she smirked.

"Erida is in for a terrible surprise," Sorasa muttered.

"Didn't Tyriot surrender to her?" he asked, puzzled.

Beneath her hood, Sorasa's copper eyes gleamed. "She may think so. But this isn't surrender. This is war, and she is too proud to see it coming. All that remains now is choosing where they might strike."

Dom wanted to trust in her excitement, as he reluctantly trusted her in most things. Instead, he felt a heavy sense of foreboding.

"Erida and Taristan's true strength is on land," he said in a low voice. "You mortals can fill the Long Sea with warships but that won't stop Erida's legions or Taristan's corpse army from rolling over every city upon the Ward."

And it brings us no closer to Corayne. No closer to even a hint of where she might be.

Meliz did not idle, despite a great many sailors calling to her on the streets. A few even applauded, all of them pirates. The Tyri were less effusive. The pirates were their old enemies, and only a common foe made allies of them. For now.

The pirate captain led them up to a blue-and-white-painted doorway. Guards flanked the door, their helmets patterned in fish scales, with golden spears in hand, and short, aquamarine capes draped over their armor.

Neither bothered to stop Meliz an-Amarat, who strode through with ease, the rest tromping along behind her. The captain was clearly well known in the Sea Prince's company.

Inside, the villa was cool and shaded, the building centered on courtyards of tiled stone and fresh greenery. A good many officers and aides cluttered the halls but were careful to let Meliz pass. In her salt-worn clothes with her unbound, curling hair, Meliz looked like a rag doll against statues. She led the rest through the passages, to a central courtyard with a fountain at its center.

Guards lined the whitewashed walls, watching over a trio of men. All three jerked their heads toward Meliz as she stepped out into the light, her golden smile crooked on her face.

She gave an exaggerated bow, sweeping back an arm like a dancer.

"Your Highness," she chuckled, as if the title was some wonderful joke.

The Sea Prince did not return the gesture, but his lips twitched, amused by the captain's posturing. Like his sailors, he was bronze-skinned with curly black hair, close in color to Meliz herself. But his eyes were honey and he wore a simple circlet of hammered gold, a single aquamarine jewel set at his brow.

"Captain an-Amarat," he said, striding toward them. "We were just discussing you."

Meliz gave a wave of a scarred hand. "When are you not?"

Then her eyes flicked over the other two, both seated at a little table.

"Admiral Kyros, Lord Malek," she said, inclining her head to each.

Dom guessed Kyros to be the one in uniform. The other, Lord Malek, wore iridescent purple robes. He had pale eyes and the warm, dark skin of the southern kingdoms.

"It seems first reports are not what we hoped," Kyros said, his stare burning at Meliz. He wore the telltale blue of a Tyri sailor, and a jeweled sash to denote high rank. "Fleethaven burned but it is not destroyed, and most of the Gallish navy were not yet in port."

Meliz laughed outright. "Would you like to keep reading your reports, or would you like to hear directly from those who were actually there?"

While Sorasa tucked her face, hiding a smirk, Lord Malek answered with a look of disgust.

"You struck too quickly," he grumbled. "You did not have the patience to wait for the rest of Erida's fleet. Nor the courage for it."

"Courage?" Meliz's smile dropped, her eyes flashing in a dangerous way.

"Peace, Lord Malek," the Sea Prince said, pacing again.

"My prince." Kyros blanched at his lord. "I cannot believe I would live to see the day you defend pirate scum like Meliz an-Amarat."

"Let us cage the Lioness, and then we can return to hunting sharks," the Sea Prince replied, smiling directly at Meliz. She only grinned back.

It was like watching two bolts of lightning meet in mid-air.

"Impatience did not force my hand," Meliz said, swaying as she walked. "But these two."

All eyes snapped to the Elder and the assassin, spearing through both. Dom shook off their scrutiny, well used to the gaping looks of mortals by now. But he rankled when he saw how they watched Sorasa, each man studying the tattoos peeking out from her clothes.

She did not move under their attention, though he could hear her heartbeat quicken.

The Sea Prince gave an incredulous shake of his head.

"You try my manners every time you walk my halls, Meliz," he said. "First you bring squabbling pirate rabble onto my streets, and now an Amhara into my courtyard."

Sorasa's voice was acid. "I promise you, I am not the first Amhara to walk the halls of a Sea Prince."

"That's precisely what concerns me," he shot back. "Does the other one speak?"

Dom straightened instinctively, facing the Sea Prince as he would any other dignitary. It made for an imposing sight, even as his stomach rolled with the last waves of seasickness.

"I am Prince Domacridhan of Iona, a son of Glorian Lost," he rumbled.

He did not miss the way Sorasa scoffed low in her throat.

The Prince whistled a low note. "You do have strange friends, Meliz."

"No stranger than the Sea Prince himself," she replied.

That seemed to amuse the Prince most of all. With one last look to Sorasa, and her many daggers, he gave a shrug. "Well? What did they do exactly, to ruin weeks of careful planning?"

A chair scraped along the fine tile of the courtyard, screeching as Meliz dragged it into place between Kyros and Lord Malek. Sighing, she collapsed into it, putting one boot on the table, to the disgust of the two men.

"They set the palace on fire," she said, satisfied. "And almost killed the Queen, yes?"

"*Almost*," Sorasa replied coldly.

The three men exchanged glances, both horrified and impressed.

"After that, I knew our time had run out," Meliz kept on. "Patrols would triple once the city was set to rights, and Erida would close the harbor. I did what I could to salvage our mission, with my ship and my crew intact."

"Very well," Kyros grumbled. It clearly pained him to give any credit to a pirate. "I suppose that is the best we can hope for at the moment."

"And what is this moment precisely?" Sorasa's voice echoed through the courtyard, low as it was. "Where does your alliance stand?"

While the other two men fell silent, cowed in the face of a live Amhara, the Sea Prince took a daring step toward her.

"On uneven ground," he answered.

"Have you word from Lord Konegin?" Malek said. "Or has he disappeared after his failure?"

Konegin. Dom turned the name over in his mind, trying to place it. Judging by the way Sorasa's eyes widened, she understood far more than he did. The Amhara pressed her lips together, content to keep silent and listen. Dom resolved to do the same.

The Sea Prince chuckled at Meliz. "Which failure? When he tried to kill Prince Taristan in the middle of a court feast? Or when he tried to supplant Erida with a Madrentine princess, and got the girl killed for her trouble?"

Malek shrugged broad shoulders. "Idiot or not, Konegin is the only chance to usurp Erida. Before she becomes too powerful to overthrow."

"Our spies in Lecorra intercepted orders bound for Duke Reccio, from Erida herself," Kyros said. He drew out a piece of parchment and smoothed it out over the table. "Sent by military scout, at all speed from Ascal."

The Sea Prince rounded the fountain to bend over the scroll. He leaned, one finger on the page, the other clasped behind his back. Sorasa and Meliz leaned right alongside him, to the dismay of his guards.

Dom hung back, eyeing the page. It was written in a mortal language he did not know.

"It is a hasty copy," Kyros explained. "But word for word."

"She calls her legions to mass at Rouleine." The Sea Prince straightened, his handsome face going stern. "Is Rouleine not a shattered waste? Destroyed by her own hand?"

"Her campaign in the north is far from finished. She isn't even waiting for the snows to melt, the bloodthirsty fool," Lord Malek said roughly. He examined the paper for himself. "She means to march on Calidon."

"Through the mountain passes." Still seated, Kyros puffed out his chest proudly. "She knows she cannot land an army by sea."

Meliz gave a shake of her head. "Calidon is a small kingdom. All but useless to her. She'll march across half the realm to claim little more than rock and snow."

Calidon.

The word was a bell in Domacridhan's mind, tolling endlessly, over and over. It echoed with five hundred years of memory. Black yew trees veining through the mist. A brutal wind striping a mountain valley between golden sun and bitter shadow. Deathless snow on the highest peaks. And a high ridge of gray stone, crowned by a fortress city most would never see.

Calidon is what the mortals call it.

He knew it as Iona.

Home.

Sweat broke across his brow and he staggered only one step, but that was enough. His stomach lurched, as if he were still on the deck of a ship.

Sorasa whirled from the table, her copper eyes meeting his own with rare concern. Her brow twitched, her lips parted in confusion. He willed her to see, to read him as she so easily could.

"Corayne," Dom managed to hiss, barely more than a breath.

At the table, Meliz went cold, her charming manner forgotten.

She is in Iona. She is with my kin, safe, whole. Still alive. He swallowed against the wave of revulsion. *And Erida knows it. Her armies are already moving to her.*

His heart nearly stopped, the world tilting beneath him.

Taristan knows it.

But for Sorasa, he would have toppled sideways. Instead, she held Dom steady, both arms around him.

"Steady," she muttered. "Steady."

He heaved a breath, gasping against the suddenly close air of the courtyard. *In through the nose, out through the mouth.* Sorasa told him that once, after they first encountered shades of the Spindle army. She did it now, eyes fierce, her chest rising and falling with exaggerated motion as she mimicked the technique for him again. He matched her rhythm as best he could, using her body to set his own breathing.

"We know where she is now," Sorasa murmured, so close he could feel her voice vibrating in her throat. "We can do something now."

"You know where my daughter is."

Meliz's harsh tone brought him crashing back. She pushed away from the table, jumping up to glare across the courtyard.

"I do," he ground out.

Dom nodded and Sorasa stepped away, leaving him to stand on his own two feet. He still leaned against the wall, half-slumped, but under his own power.

Thank you, he wanted to stay.

Even unspoken, Sorasa heard the words anyway. She gave him a curt nod.

He felt the sudden attention of the room, every eye following his face. All but Sorasa, who looked back to the fountain, her eyes out of focus. She knew as he did. She understood the burden he suddenly carried, his body threatening to collapse under the weight of it.

"Queen Erida and Taristan are marching to Iona, the Elder enclave in Calidon," Dom said, willing his voice to remain steady. Even as he spoke, his mind was consumed by horrifying images of his home burned and broken, his people slaughtered. "My enclave."

With blistering speed, Meliz closed the distance between them. She took Dom by the arm, her grip hard and desperate.

"What can we do?" she demanded.

Dom heard the meaning beneath her words as plain as daylight.

How can I help her?

Hissing to herself, Sorasa began to pace as the Prince had. "The full force of the legions will march with them," she muttered. "Their entire army crashing down in one place."

The Sea Prince winced.

"Our power is on the sea," he said, sounding apologetic.

At that, Sorasa stopped short. Her head snapped up, her hair tossing back to show a curve of a tattoo at her neck. Dom knew it at a glance. *The scorpion.*

"*Your* power," she said, breathless. Then her eyes went to Dom, boring into his own, until he felt like he could see the inside of her mind.

His heartbeat quickened, his own breath going shallow. Realization ripped down his spine.

Dom's voice shook. "The Temurijon marches too."

Something pinched his forearm, and Dom realized Meliz still gripped him, her fingers digging in. Her face lit from within, fiery resolve settling over the pirate captain.

"The Emperor and his Countless will need swift passage," she barked, releasing Dom. "As many ships as we can muster."

Meliz an-Amarat was small compared to the Sea Prince and his lords, clad in rough clothing, her body swaying as if still at sea. But she faced them like a giant, unyielding and unafraid.

The Sea Prince bent at the waist, a wink in his eye, a smirk playing on his lips. When he smiled, a single gold tooth gleamed.

"It will be done," he said, to the chagrin of his companions.

Both Malek and Kyros crowed in shock, kicking up a fuss of noise.

Sorasa's own voice was nearly lost in the din, but Dom heard her over all others.

"We will require a ship too."

"I'm ashamed I can't go with you."

The blue-green waters of the Orisi port shimmered, the sun hazing golden as it dipped toward the western horizon. Meliz stood beside Dom at the railing above the docks, the pair of them like statues watching the sea. She did not look at him, nor the small ship being provisioned for his journey northeast. Her gaze was somewhere else, her eyes shadowed, her heart thumping a ragged beat in Dom's ears.

Dom let her words linger, choosing his own carefully.

"You will be more useful with the armada." It was the truth. "Both to your allies, and to Corayne."

The captain drew a short breath, stilling herself. On the docks, Sorasa watched over another boat, directing provisions and stores onto the deck. Their new ship was tiny in comparison to the *Tempestborn*, crewed by half a dozen men, but seaworthy enough for the voyage to Calidon.

"And if we do not reach you in time?" Meliz muttered, shaking her head. Something caught in her voice. "If a storm blows in, or the Emperor is delayed—"

"It does no good to think of such things," Dom said bluntly. "We can only trust in each other."

The words sounded hollow, even in his own head. But Dom believed them all the same. He had to, for there was nothing else.

"And we must trust in the gods, wherever they may be." Meliz went sour, her lip curling. She bent a finger, making some gesture at the sea. "If they exist at all."

"My own gods are silent, but I've seen enough to know gods still speak in this realm," he muttered. The Spindles burned in his mind, golden and brutal, each one another merciless doorway.

Meliz raised her gaze to glare at the sky. "What kind of god allows such times as these?"

Shuddering, Dom went cold, despite the sunlight and the warm southern breeze.

"It is not only a god who brings about this doom," he said. "But the heart of a mortal man."

The wind stirred in Meliz's hair, blowing a black curl across her face. It glinted dark red with the light, a streak of color within the abyss black. If Dom squinted, her face blurring, she could be Corayne. It was an illusion, but he relaxed into it.

"Corayne's uncle," Meliz said slowly. Her cheeks flushed. "A twin, you say."

The illusion shattered into a thousand pieces.

Dom's hand clenched into a fist, knuckles white beneath pale skin. He refused to think of Taristan and Cortael in the same breath, their images intertwined. Lest the memory of Cortael rot, corrupted by his brother's face.

"He did speak of you. I remember that much." Meliz's voice took on a dreamy edge, her eyes faraway again, in a memory Dom did not share. "Cortael called you his brother, in heart if not blood."

Elders healed quicker than mortals; Dom himself was a testament to that. *The trade, it seems, is that our hearts, once broken, never heal at all.* He felt the pain of it sharply in his chest, beneath quilted wool, skin, and bone.

Part of him wanted to turn away and leave Meliz to her memories. But he could not move, frozen to the spot.

The reason was obvious, even to him.

She held a little piece of Cortael, one he had never seen. As she spoke, it was like he lived again, even for an instant.

"He was seventeen when we met," she said.

Dom remembered. Cortael was gangly, his limbs too long, still growing into his frame. His dark red hair hung loose, brushing his shoulders, his black eyes always piercing, always fixed on the horizon. And he was diligent, talented, honed like good steel. He already had the makings of a king.

"Cortael was barely more than a boy, but already different." Meliz wavered, her brow furrowing. "Graver. Older in some way. And restless. Haunted."

"So are all his kind," Dom mumbled. He remembered the same, the way Cortael always took one last glance at the stars before they forced him to sleep. Always searching.

"I thought I could save Corayne from it." Her voice thickened, catching in her throat. "I thought I could give her roots. But what do I know of such things?"

The pirate captain waved dismissively at herself, salt-worn and sun-damaged, swaying idly as her ship swayed on the tide.

Dom felt the odd urge to embrace the woman but elected not to. He wagered Meliz an-Amarat did not enjoy being coddled, least of all by him.

"She will never have roots, Meliz," he said slowly, as much for himself as for her. "But perhaps we can give her wings."

Her eyes gleamed, unshed tears reflecting the dipping sun. As in the villa, she took him by the arm. This time, her touch was gentle, her hand feather-light.

"Protect her for me," she breathed. "And for Cortael."

"I will."

With my dying breath. With every fiber of my being.

"I loved him too, in my own way." Her hand pulled back, dropping to her side. Meliz did not weep, her tears held at bay. "Before I let him go."

Dom's own eyes stung, the image of the port swimming out of focus, until even Sorasa was a blur before his eyes.

"I am still learning to do that," he bit out.

"The memories can stay," she said gravely. Her aura of command returned, falling around her like a cloak. "But the rest is an anchor. The grief. Even you can drown, Domacridhan."

Stricken as he was, Dom could not help but twist a bitter smile.

"A strange thing to say before a voyage."

To his surprise, Meliz smiled too, shaking her head at him. With the sun in her hair and the smile on her face, Dom understood what Cortael saw in her, so many years ago.

"You are odder than I expected," she chuckled.

He quirked a brow at her. "And what did you expect?"

The pirate captain paused, licking her lips.

"Someone colder," she finally said, looking him up and down. "Made of stone instead of flesh. Less mortal. Like all the things Cortael tried to be."

The wind blew over the harbor again, smelling of salt. He turned into it, facing the docks and the little ship. A familiar figure ran its deck, checking the rigging, though she was no sailor. It was not like Sorasa Sarn to remain still.

Dom heaved a breath. "I was that way once."

The shadow of a smile crossed Meliz's face as she followed his gaze. "Love does that."

His throat tightened and his jaw clenched, teeth gritted so tightly Dom could not speak if he tried.

Meliz only gave a wave of her hand. "I'm referring to my daughter, and the love you bear her." Her grin widened mischievously. "Of course."

"Of course," Dom managed, wrenching his eyes from the port. His entire body felt hot with embarrassment, if not indignance.

Satisfied, Meliz folded her arms across her chest, taking in the sight of so many ships as a general would survey his troops. The *Tempestborn* loomed among them, purple-sailed and magnificent, as fearsome a ship as to ever roam the seas. Her eyes narrowed, studying the galley.

"I wonder how many horses my ship can hold," she mused.

Once more, Dom wished his gods could hear him in this realm. If they could, he would have prayed, asking for Meliz's safety, and swift winds.

"I hope I live to find out," he answered before setting off to board yet another wretched ship.

30

THE TORTURE OF HOPE

Sorasa

Pain lanced through her head. It felt like an ax splitting her skull over and over again, thumping in time with the beat of her heart. Sorasa hissed against the agony, trying to think. Her Amhara instincts flared and she forced herself to breathe evenly despite the tightness of her chest. It helped a little, grounding her. She blinked, nearly blinded by the white light around her. Hissing again, she wriggled her toes in her boots. To her relief, they responded. And they *squelched*, her boots filled with water. Her hands curled, something soft and cool sifting between her fingers. *Sand*, she knew instantly. No matter what, Sorasa Sarn would always recognize the feel of sand.

The world came into focus slowly, the brightness fading little by little. Gingerly, she rolled off her front and onto her back, to stare up at a vivid blue sky. She tasted salt and smelled ocean. It did not take a scholar to piece such a puzzle.

The beach ran along in either direction, turning rocky above the shore, riddled with white stones that rose into murderous cliffs.

Fear threatened to swallow her up. It clawed at her inside, a beast with too many teeth. *Do not let it rule*, she told herself, repeating the old Amhara teaching. *Do not let it rule. Do not let it rule.*

She refused to think beyond the world in front of her. Refused to let her mind spiral with hideous possibility. It was a hole she would never dig out of.

With a snarl of pain, she forced herself to sit up, her head spinning with the sudden movement. One hand touched her temple, sticky with dried blood. She winced, feeling a gash along her eyebrow. It was long but shallow, and already scabbing over.

She clenched her jaw, teeth grinding, as she surveyed the beach with squinting eyes. The ocean stared back at her, empty and endless, a wall of iron blue. Then she noticed shapes along the beach, some half-buried in the sand, others caught in the rhythmic pull of the tide. She narrowed her eyes and the shapes solidified.

A torn length of sail floated, tangled up with rope. A shattered piece of the mast angled out of the sand like a pike. Smashed crates littered the beach, along with other debris from the ship. Bits of hull. Rigging. Oars snapped in half.

The bodies moved with the waves.

Her steady breathing lost its rhythm, coming in shorter and shorter gasps until she feared her throat might close.

Her thoughts scattered, impossible to grasp.

All thoughts but one.

"DOMACRIDHAN!"

Her shout echoed, desperate and ragged.

"DOMACRIDHAN!"

Only the waves answered, crashing endless against the shore.

She forgot her training and forced herself to stand, nearly falling over with dizziness. Her limbs ached but she ignored it, lunging toward the waterline. Her lips moved, her voice shouting his name again, though she couldn't hear it above the pummel of her own heart.

Sorasa Sarn was no stranger to corpses. She splashed into the waves with abandon, even as her head spun.

Sailor, sailor, sailor, she noted, her desperation rising with every Tyri uniform and head of black hair. One of them looked ripped in half, missing everything from the waist down. His entrails floated with the rest of him, like a length of bleached rope.

She suspected a shark got the best of him.

Then her memories returned with a crash like the waves.

The Tyri ship. Nightfall. The sea serpent slithering up out of the deep. The breaking of a lantern. Fire across the deck, slick scales running over my hands. The swing of a greatsword, Elder-made. Dom silhouetted against a sky awash with lightning. And then the cold, drowning darkness of the ocean.

A wave splashed up against her and Sorasa stumbled back to shore, shivering. She had not waded more than waist deep, but her face felt wet, water she could not understand streaking her cheeks.

Her knees buckled and she fell, exhausted. She heaved a breath, then two.

And screamed.

Somehow, the pain in her head paled in comparison to the pain in her heart. It dismayed and destroyed her in equal measure. The wind blew, stirring salt-crusted hair across her face, sending a chill down to her soul. It was like the wilderness all over again, the bodies of her Amhara kin splayed around her.

No, she realized, her throat raw. *This is worse. There is not even a body to mourn.*

She contemplated the emptiness for a while, the beach and the waves, and the bodies gently pressing into shore. If she squinted, they could only be debris from the ship, bits of wood instead of bloated flesh and bone.

The sun glimmered on the water. Sorasa hated it.

Nothing but clouds since Orisi, and now you choose to shine.

It was not like her to lose her senses. The ability to drift was beaten from her long ago. But Sorasa drifted now, pacing the beach.

She did not hear the shift of sand, or the heavy scuff of boots over the loose stones. There was only the wind.

Until a strand of gold blew across her vision, joined by a warm, unyielding palm against her shoulder. Her body jolted as she turned, nose to nose with Domacridhan of Iona. His green eyes glittered, his mouth open as he shouted something again, his voice swallowed up by the droning in her own head.

"Sorasa."

It came to her slowly, as if through deep water. Her own name, over and over again. She could only stare back into the verdant green, lost in the fields of his eyes. In her chest, her heart stumbled. She expected her body to follow.

Instead, her fist closed and her knuckles met cheekbone.

Dom was good enough to turn his head, letting the blow glance off. Begrudgingly, Sorasa knew he had spared her a broken hand on top of everything else.

"How dare you," she forced out, trembling.

Whatever concern he wore burned away in an instant.

"How dare I what? Save your *life?*" he snarled, letting her go.

Sorasa swayed without his support. She clenched her own jaw, fighting to maintain her balance lest she fall to pieces entirely.

"Is that another Amhara lesson?" he raged on, throwing up both arms. "When given the choice between death or indignity, choose *death*?!"

Hissing, Sorasa looked back to the spot where she woke up. Heat crept up her face as she realized her body left a trail through the sand when he dragged her up from the tide line. A blind man would have noticed it. But not Sorasa in her fury and grief.

"Oh" was all she could manage. Her mouth flapped open, her mind spinning. Only the truth came, and that was far too embarrassing. "I did not see. I—"

Her head throbbed again and she pressed a hand to her temple, wincing away from his stern glare.

"I will feel better if you sit," Dom said stiffly.

Despite the pain, Sorasa loosed a low growl. She wanted to stand just to spite him, but thought better of it. With a huff, she sank, cross-legged on the cool sand.

Dom was quick to follow, almost blurring. It made her head spin again.

"So you saved me from the shipwreck just to abandon me here?" Sorasa muttered as Dom opened his mouth to protest. "I don't blame you. Time is of the essence now. A wounded mortal will only slow you down."

She expected him to bluster and lie. Instead, his brow furrowed, lines creasing between his still vivid eyes. The light off the ocean suited him.

"Are you? Wounded?" he asked gently, his gaze raking over her. His focus snagged on her temple, and the gash there. "Anywhere else, I mean?"

For the first time since she woke, Sorasa tried to still herself. Her breath slowed as she assessed herself, feeling her own body from toes to scalp. As her awareness traveled, she noted every blooming bruise and cut, every dull ache and shooting pain.

Bruised ribs. A sprained wrist.

Her tongue flicked in her mouth. Scowling, she spit out a broken tooth.

"No, I'm not wounded," she said aloud.

Dom's desperate smile broke wide. He went slack against the sand for an instant, falling back on his elbows to tip his face to the sky. His eyes fluttered shut only for a moment.

Sorasa knew his gods were too far. He said so himself. The gods of Glorian could not hear their children in this realm.

Even so, Sorasa saw it on his face. Dom prayed anyway. In gratitude or anger, she did not know.

"Good," he finally said, sitting back up.

The wind stirred in his loose hair and Sorasa assessed him for the first time since her memory failed. Since the deck of the Tyri ship caught fire, and someone seized her around the middle, plunging them both into the dark waves.

She did not need to guess to know who.

Dom's clothing was torn but long dry. He still wore the leather jerkin with the undershirt, but his borrowed cloak had been left to feed sea serpents. The rest of him looked intact. He had only a few fresh cuts across the backs of his hands, like terrible rope burn. *Scales*, Sorasa knew. The sea serpent coiled in her head, bigger than the mast, its scales flashing a dark rainbow.

Her breath caught when she realized he wore no sword belt, nor sheath. Nor sword.

"Dom," she bit out, reaching out between them. Only her instincts caught her, her hand freezing inches above his hip.

His brow furrowed again, carving a line of concern.

"Your sword."

The line deepened, and Sorasa understood. She mourned her own dagger, earned so many decades ago, now lost to a burning palace. She could not imagine what Dom felt for a blade centuries old.

"It is done," he finally said, fishing into his shirt.

The collar pulled, showing a line of white flesh, the planes of hard muscle rippling beneath. Sorasa dropped her eyes, letting him fuss.

Only when something soft touched her temple did she look up again.

Her heart thumped.

Dom did not meet her gaze, focused on his work, cleaning her wound with a length of cloth.

It was the fabric that made her breath catch.

Little more than a scrap of gray green. Thin but finely made by master hands. Embroidered with silver antlers.

It was a piece of Dom's old cloak, the last remnant of Iona. It survived a kraken, an undead army, a dragon, and the dungeons of a mad queen.

But it would not survive Sorasa Sarn.

She let him work, her skin aflame beneath his fingers. Until the last bits of blood were gone, and the last piece of his home tossed away.

"Thank you," she finally said to no reply.

The pain in her head lessened with every passing moment, just as the sun dipped toward the west. She glared into it, squinting, trying to read the silhouette of mountains marching into the distance. Snow clung to the heights, frowning over the bitter coast.

Despite the sun, Sorasa shivered beneath her own tattered clothes.

"We are in Calidon," she muttered, eyeing the mountains again. It was not yet spring, but purple flowers clung between shore and rising cliff. "Your country."

Dom shook his head. "Hardly mine. Most Calidonians do not believe my people exist anymore, and the ones who do wish they could forget us entirely."

"I share the sentiment," Sorasa answered dryly.

Next to her, Dom grinned. "Mortal humor. I know it too well by now."

Sorasa tried to smile but failed, squinting at the landscape.

His face wiped clean. "What?"

"I know little of this place," she answered, grinding her teeth. It made her temple throb again.

Dom's smirk felt worse. He eyed her with a rare look, mischievous, like a child with a secret.

"Are you asking for help, Sorasa Sarn?" the Elder teased.

Sorasa wanted to stand up, but doubted she could with any grace. Instead, she stayed rooted, her fists curling in the sand until tiny stones pressed between her fingers.

"I will deny it if you tell anyone," she hissed, regretting the words as soon as they left her mouth.

To her horror, Dom's smirk only widened and Sorasa realized she had made a terrible error. A grave miscalculation. Dom understood more than she realized. And knew the Amhara better than she ever thought possible.

Then his hand found her wrist. She jumped in her skin, almost yelping as he helped her to her feet.

Thankfully, she did not falter.

"I thought you hated it," he said, the smirk still curling. It made her want to hit him again.

"What?" Sorasa snapped.

Dom let her wrist drop.

"Hope."

* * *

Sorasa cursed the feel of it with every step over the rocky shore. Hope hung heavy, a weight across her shoulders, a stone in her heart, a chain around each ankle. She felt dragged by it, as if tied to a mad horse charging in the opposite direction. Every instinct in her screamed for sense. Reason. Cold logic and careful calculations.

Hope burned through them all, try as she might to snuff it out.

Lord Mercury would weep to see me now. Or laugh.

Her stomach turned at the thought of her old master. She hoped he was still ensconced across the Long Sea, shut up in his citadel, content to watch the world consume itself.

Hoped.

She gritted her teeth, biting back a snarl of frustration. Lest she reveal her vexation to Domacridhan. It would only put him in a better mood, and his mood was already trying enough.

"Stop whistling," she snapped, tossing a stick at his back.

She doubted he felt it. The Elder did not break stride as he navigated between waves and cliff wall. They hugged the Calidonian coastline for a week now, marching east at Dom's direction. Sorasa knew the way ahead only vaguely. They crossed the River Airdha yesterday, leaving its valley behind to climb again. To the north, jagged above them, were the mountains of Monadhrian. *The mountains of the sun.*

Shivering, Sorasa glanced at the so-called namesake, well hidden behind stormy clouds.

"I have been told I whistle quite well," Dom finally said, glancing over his shoulder. His hair was still wet from a passing rainstorm, braided back in strands of dark gold.

Sorasa pursed her lips. "Do Elders go deaf?"

In reply, he whistled again. It was a low, haunting sound to echo against the rocks, and perhaps carry into the mountain heights. More birdcall than melody, carrying no tune she recognized. Like the hoot of an owl, but deeper.

"It's how we Vedera find each other in mortal lands," he explained, whistling again. Then he paused, head angled toward the snows. The hoot echoed without any response and Dom shuffled on.

As they walked, he brushed his hands here and there, touching boulders carpeted with moss or tide pools swirling with brine. Sorasa was careful not to slip over the wet stones, but Dom paid them no mind, leaping with his usual Elder grace. And something more.

This land was familiar to him like nothing else. Sorasa had never seen him so at ease, like a captured hawk finally returned to the sky.

"I patrolled the southern coast in my youth," he said, as if sensing her thoughts. His fingers brushed a copse of purple heather, stubbornly clinging to life between the rocks.

Sorasa tried to picture him, younger, smaller, more enamored of the world. It felt impossible.

"And what do you consider youth?" she wondered, settling in to walk next to him.

He shrugged his broad shoulders. "I suppose I was more than a century and a half old then."

One hundred and fifty years old, and still young, Sorasa thought, balking. She could not wrap her mind around the years of Elders, and the sprawl of time they occupied upon the realm. Not to mention their relative indifference to the world as it spun around them, shifting and changing and breaking apart.

And Dom is the best of them, the first to fight, the last to lose faith.

"It's difficult to believe you are the least annoying of your kin," she muttered.

The wind blew again and she wished for something better than the salt-stiff blanket around her shoulders, salvaged from the wreckage on shore.

Dom surveyed her with a strange look, his eyes losing a bit of their glimmer. Whatever warmth he carried went cold, the embers snuffed out.

"I suppose that's true now, with Ridha gone," he said tightly.

Sorasa swallowed around a sudden lump in her throat. She cursed her poor attempt at a compliment.

"I did not mean to speak of Ridha," she said, only for Dom to quicken his pace.

After a few strides, he turned to sneer at her, walking backward over the rocky ground.

"What is it you mortals say when you are in grave pain but don't want to admit it?" His voice echoed harshly off the cliffs, loud enough to overtake the crash of waves. "Oh yes. *I'm fine.*"

A dozen sharp retorts rose up but she bit them back, clenching her teeth. Dom still mourned the loss of his cousin, and Sorasa could not blame him. She remembered her last glimpse of the Elder princess, tall in her green armor, black hair like a standard, a greatsword in hand. The immortal woman turned back to guard Corayne's escape, and Dom went with her, to hold off the horrors of a Spindle as best they could. The dragon roared overhead, the Infyrna hounds yelped and burned. The undead marched in their unending rows. And a black knight rode through them all, his blade a merciless shadow.

It was a miracle Dom survived at all.

"Very well," she muttered. "I am useless at that sort of talk anyway."

Dom did not relent.

"I know," he answered. "The last time you experienced any feeling at all, you stopped speaking for two months."

His pain was suddenly her own. It lanced down her spine, the edge of her vision going white. Though the shipwreck beach was far behind them, she saw bodies again. Not in Tyri uniforms, but Amhara leathers, their faces familiar, their wounds still bleeding.

Sorasa wanted to retch.

"*I'm fine*," she forced out.

Dom's lips twisted, forming his usual scowl. With that, he turned around, and they fell back into their rhythm.

Slowly, the tide washed in, forcing them higher up the slopes, until the way became too perilous for even Sorasa to traverse. They would have to wait for the water to roll out again, clearing the path forward. Part of her wondered if she might be dashed against the cliffs, the waves breaking only a few yards away. But Dom showed no such worry, and it put her at ease.

He stood at the edge of the slope, on an outcropping over the churning ocean. To the west, the sun descended, glimpsed through gaps in the clouds. It streaked red and bloody, giving the air a strange scarlet haze.

Like Ascal, Sorasa thought, remembering the strange sky over Erida's city. Her stomach turned. As Erida's empire spread, so did Taristan's evil. Like wildfire. Like fever.

Dom glared at the red sun, eyes slitted.

"Do you think Sigil will convince her emperor to fight?" he murmured, so low Sorasa almost missed it. "Do you think Meliz will reach them in time?"

She joined him at the cliff-edge, the ragged blanket wrapped around her shoulders. Her own face tipped westward, not to the sunset, or the raging coastline. But the lands beyond, farther than either of them could see. She traced the way back to Ascal, and then deeper into the continent. Through field and forest, foothills, winding rivers, swamps and cities. Across the sentinel Mountains of the Ward, a wall cutting the continent in two.

Her thoughts raced over the peaks and into the golden steppe, through endless lengths of grass and sky. To the Temurijon. To Sigil's home.

"I am only glad Sigil is safe from all this," Sorasa said. Truly, she did not know what the Emperor would do, or if the Countless would ever march. "As much as she can be."

Dom gave a gruff nod. "We will see her afterward."

Afterward. Again, her stomach turned. Again, she cursed the weight of hope and all its heartbreaks.

"Fine," she clipped.

He eyed her sidelong, trying to read her expression.

"Do you mean that in the good way or the bad way?"

Sorasa drew a cold breath through her teeth.

"I'm not sure," she answered.

It was the truth, whether she liked it or not.

"Afterward. I would like to go home," she blurted out, the words coming too quickly to stop. Despite the cold, heat crept into her face.

Dom turned to her fully, blinking in confusion. He looked almost angry. "To the Amhara?"

She almost laughed aloud at his idiocy.

"No," she said sharply. It was frustrating to spell out, both to Dom and herself. Her voice flagged, going small. Her eyes swept over the ocean. "To whatever home really is for me."

He only continued to stare, reading her still.

"What about you?" she challenged. "What is your afterward?"

His usually crinkled brow went smooth, his stern expression melting away. Like Sorasa, he searched the ocean, eyes flicking back and forth as he weighed an answer.

"I suppose I must look for a home too," he finally said, a look of surprise taking hold.

As much as she wanted to, Sorasa knew better than to push. Dom had a home, an entire enclave, with family and friends of many centuries. She could not understand such a thing, but she understood betrayal. The pain of it dogged him every day, in clear view. While Dom stood to fight, they hung back. It was as good as exile to him.

She knew what that felt like too.

"And I will go to Kasa," he added.

Sorasa bit her lip. "To Andry's mother."

The Elder bowed his head. The setting sun cast him in silhouette, his shadow streaking out beside them, his golden hair edged in glowing red. Sorasa had never seen a god, but she ventured Domacridhan came close enough.

"She deserves to know her son was a hero," he said. "And better than any knight."

Sorasa cared little for noble deeds or chivalry. But even she could not argue. If there was a single man alive who deserved to be a knight, it was Andry Trelland.

Would that he were alive still to know it.

"I will join you in that," she murmured, knowing it could never be.

Shivering, she lay down against the rocks, eager to sleep, even as the cold seeped up through her clothes. In spite of herself, her teeth chattered. Eyes shut, she heard Dom attempt a fire, only for the constant wind to blow it out half a dozen times.

When he at last lay down beside her, his warmth like the sun, she did not move, her eyes still closed, the mask of sleep drawn tight over her face.

Even so, she knew her heart betrayed her. The slow, methodic beat jumped with every shift of his body, and her own.

31

THE FIRST ARMY
Andry

Despite his best efforts, the Ionian guards would not let him pass. The doors to the throne room remained barred to him, so Andry was forced to pace. He could not hear beyond the doors but strained to listen anyway. Murmurs echoed, Corayne's higher voice easy to pick out. She spoke quickly, with desperation.

Our time has run out, she said just moments ago, outside the castle. He could only hope Isibel believed her. The Monarch's own voice was lower, more grave. Like the distant tolling of a heavy bell.

He could not hear other Elder leaders, but Andry knew they were never far from Isibel's side. Lord Valnir and Lady Eyda spent many days trying to sway Isibel to war, the immortal siblings openly frustrated by her lack of action.

Andry wished for Garion, who might have better luck sneaking into the throne room. But he was still with Charlie, in Lenava to await news.

Corayne is alone in there, he thought with a wince. *Not that I would be much use.*

The murmurs echoed, harsher than before. Arguing.

His heart twisted and he halted, facing the guards.

I cannot make her fight alone.

"Let me pass," he said. It was not a request, but a command rising up from somewhere deep, spoken in a voice Andry did not know he possessed.

The guards only blinked, unmoving and silent.

Andry deflated, all but huffing. "Very well," he grumbled. "I shall just wear a hole in my boots then."

He began pacing again, only to halt at the echoing sound of approaching feet. Behind him, the Elder guards straightened even taller, at attention, their chins raised.

The Monarch of Kovalinn came around a corner at speed, the young immortal flanked by a contingent of his own guards. His pet bear was not with him, relegated to the stables of Tíarma.

"Your Highness," Andry said, dropping into a well-practiced bow.

Dyrian fixed him with a gray-eyed stare, his stern manner at odds with such a young face.

"Andry Trelland," Dyrian replied, giving him a curt nod. Then he glanced past, gaze shifting to the guards and the throne room beyond. "It seems we have something in common, sir."

Sir. Andry all but jumped at the title, even if the young lord did not understand its weight.

"Certainly the guards will let you pass, my lord," he offered, glancing to the throne room.

Dyrian fidgeted with the silver chain holding his sable cloak in place. "They would. But I know better than to go where I will only be in the way."

Andry could not help but be amused by the child Elder. He heaved a sigh in agreement. "If only I learned that lesson months ago."

"From what I hear, the world would be ended already," Dyrian said, peering up at him. "If not for the brave work of Andry Trelland."

Heat crept up Andry's face.

"I do not think that is true, my lord."

"Oh?" Dyrian raised a fair eyebrow against freckled skin. "Am I mistaken? Did you not save a Spindleblade from Taristan of Old Cor's grasp?"

"Yes, but—" Andry faltered. He curled a fist to stave off a fresh wave of painful memories. "I suppose that feels like a long time ago now."

"For you," Dyrian said thoughtfully, holding his gaze.

Andry's flush deepened.

"True," he muttered, finding little else to say. *A year must seem like a few days to him, if that.*

He eyed the doors again, and the guards pretending to ignore them both. "Can you hear what they're saying in there?"

"Yes," Dyrian answered, as if it were the most obvious thing in the world. Then it was his turn to blush, a rare pink creeping over his face. "Oh, can you not?"

Andry stifled a laugh and shook his head. "No, my lord."

Dyrian's eyes went round with fascination. Elder though he was, dozens of years old, his wonderment betrayed his true age.

"How strange," he said, clapping his hands together. "Shall I tell you?"

It felt wrong to manipulate a child, but Andry brushed it off as best he could.

"I'd like that immensely."

The young lord grinned, showing a gap in otherwise perfect teeth.

"Isibel is angry with my uncle Valnir," he said, his focus shifting to the throne room beyond. "She says he is driven by guilt, not sense."

Corayne had explained as much to Andry when he first arrived. Valnir was not only the brother of Lady Eyda, but forcibly exiled to Allward, cast out of Glorian before the Elders lost their realm. Because he feared the Spindles and made weapons to destroy them.

He forged the Spindleblades, and now we all pay the price.

"Isibel says . . ." Dyrian's voice faltered, his conspiratorial smile fading. A shadow crossed his face. "She says that Valnir and my mother proved war is too dangerous. They spilled too much Elder blood. She will not make the same mistake."

The Monarch of Kovalinn was too young to hide his emotions well. Tears shimmered in his eyes, a red flush creeping up his neck as he did his best not to cry. Andry's hand twitched and he nearly embraced him, forgetting for a moment that Dyrian was an Elder lord, and not a homesick boy crying in the barracks.

"I'm sorry about your people," Andry murmured, crouching so they were eye level. "And your home."

Dyrian wrinkled his nose, as if scrunching his face might keep the tears from falling. He scrubbed at his eyes with the back of his hand, embarrassed.

"Kovalinn was never our home. Not truly. We are children of Glorian," he said stiffly, as if reciting a prayer. It did not help his mood. "But Kovalinn was the only home I ever knew," he added, half whispering.

Elders and lords be damned.

Andry could not help himself. He reached out to take the young immortal by the shoulder. Behind him, the Kovalinn guards went tense, but Dyrian relaxed into his grip. He even sniffled.

"My home is gone too," Andry said, his own voice breaking. He thought of Ascal, the palace, the knights and squires he'd lived all his life beside. The queen he served, who betrayed them all. Andry mourned for it all, as he mourned for himself, and a fate long dead.

"Burn the life behind you," he murmured, remembering Valtik's words from a lifetime ago.

Dyrian peered up at him. "What?"

"Just something a friend said once," Andry answered. "That I needed to burn the life behind me, to save the realm. And that life is certainly ashes now."

"My life burned too." Dyrian sniffled.

Then the Ionians jumped to attention, a flurry of motion as they reached for the doors. Andry turned in time to see them swing open, revealing the Elder nobles in all their splendor.

Isibel led the other two, still in her white robes, her silver-gold hair unbound and streaming. Her moon-gray eyes pierced through Andry as if he were only mist. The ash branch shivered in her hand, its leaves gleaming as she strode forward, forceful in her steps. Valnir and Lady Eyda followed inches behind, alike in their pale skin and red hair.

Corayne followed like an afterthought, her face pulled with confusion. She struggled to keep up with their long strides, looking between the three fearsome Elders.

"Dyrian, come," Eyda said brusquely.

The young lord gave Andry a soft look, then did as commanded, falling in next to his mother. Andry was quick to do the same, flanking Corayne.

"Well?" he muttered, trying to match her pace without losing the pack entirely.

Corayne scowled, a fire in her black eyes. "I was hardly given room to speak, let alone explain," she hissed. "All they do is talk back and forth. Time means nothing to these folk."

Andry knew the Elders heard them as they walked. He wagered Corayne was counting on it.

"Taristan and Erida are coming. They won't leave me alive, let alone with a Spindleblade," she pressed on as they navigated the hall. "The only question now is how long do we have? And what can we do before the full weight of Erida's throne crashes down on us?"

More than any in Iona, Andry knew what that looked like. The legions were vast, many thousands strong, consisting of career soldiers trained for war and conquest. Cavalry, infantry, siege engines. He shook his head, trying to dispel the image of catapults firing on the walls of the Elder city.

"At least Charlie had some sense," Corayne bit out.

Andry nodded. Lenava was a small city, but better than the cocoon that was Iona, completely cut off from the mortal world.

Ahead of them, Isibel reached the entryway. Light spilled over the marble floor, the doors to the castle ridge thrown wide open. Outside, the clouds streaked in ribbons, torn by the blustering wind.

Isibel stepped out into the sunlight first, her hair flashing like a blade. She needed no armor to look fearsome, or a sword to seem dangerous. She was both with a single cut of her eyes.

They followed her out onto the flat landing before the gate of the castle, the city laid out below, with the valley beyond. The mist remained across the hills, obscuring anything more than a few miles away.

As a pair of Ionian guards fought through the gate, too fast for mortal eyes to comprehend, a horn sounded over the city. Andry and Corayne jumped in their skin, reaching for each other without thought.

Their hands brushed and Andry jumped again, all nerves.

"My lady, the scouts," one of the new guards said, all but collapsing to a knee before his monarch.

Isibel silenced him with a wave of her branch. She looked down the ridge, past the gray walls and towers of Iona. Then she turned her eyes south, to the long, mirror-glass lake fading into the mist. Lochlara, the Lake of the Dawn.

Her pale eyes narrowed, her fair brow drawing tight.

Neither Andry nor Corayne could see what she scrutinized, their mortal eyes useless against the mist. Instead, Andry looked to Valnir and Eyda, and even Dyrian. Stoic as they were, they were easier to read than Isibel, who remained distant and unfeeling as a star.

Eyda drew herself to her full, menacing height, one hand gripping her son's shoulder. Below her, Dyrian's eyes went round again, this time with fear.

It sent a shiver down Andry's spine.

Hawklike, Valnir glared across the miles, his thin lips pressed into a grim line, and one hand went to the bow at his shoulder, touching it briefly. As a priest would an icon, or a relic.

"Is anyone going to tell us what's going on?" Corayne snapped. "Or must we guess?"

A shadow of annoyance flickered across Isibel's face. She glanced to Corayne as if spotting her for the first time.

"There is a mortal army marching north," she said softly. There was no fear in her, but no courage either. She went blank as a stone. "Toward Iona."

Whatever terror Andry felt disappeared, easily eclipsed by his anger. A fist clenched at his side, the sword and ax at his hip suddenly heavy. He was glad to have both close enough, especially now. *The Elders have wasted what little time we had to prepare, and now we pay the price for it*, he thought, seething.

Next to him, Corayne flushed with fury, a lip quivering.

He turned his back to Isibel and took Corayne by the arm, leaning to speak into her ear. "We will outrun them," he said forcefully. "I'll get you out of here, I promise."

To his surprise, Corayne didn't move. She held Isibel's gaze instead. Silence strung between them, tight as coiled rope.

"How many?" Corayne finally said, sounding hoarse.

"We need to run," Andry hissed, his breath stirring her black hair.

She shrugged him off.

"How many, Isibel of Iona?" Corayne snarled. "How many mortals are you Elders too afraid to fight?"

The Monarch's eyes flared wide but she did not answer.

"I venture ten thousand." Valnir's deep voice rang over the gateyard.

Ten thousand, Andry thought. He puzzled over the number, trying to make sense of it. *Barely two legions. Too small to be Erida's great army, unless this is the vanguard. Or the first wave.*

"Most on foot, but there are perhaps a thousand on horseback." Valnir squinted into the mist again, his teeth on edge. "And there are twenty or so elephants."

"Elephants?!" Corayne sputtered, whirling to Andry. She looked torn between disbelief—and joy.

Andry felt the same, even as his mind spun. He looked down on her, his heart leaping in his chest, loud as a beating drum.

"There are no elephants in the Gallish army," he said, all but breathless.

Beneath him, Corayne's face split into an uncontrollable grin. Laughter followed, spilling forth until it overtook Andry too. The pair of them went slack against each other, trembling with relief.

Still tucked next to his mother, Dyrian gasped to himself. "Elephants," he murmured, as if enchanted.

"What army marches on my enclave?" Isibel said forcefully over the din of their joy.

Corayne threw back her own piercing glare. "You'll have to leave it to find out."

The rain held off, confined to the higher slopes of the mountains in a wall of hazing gray. But the valley floor seemed to glow, bathed in the sun of waning winter. Andry's horse charged alongside Corayne's, the pair of them neck and neck as they thundered across the golden fields. Behind them, the ridge of Iona knifed into the sky, casting a long black shadow.

They were not the only riders. Isibel refused to leave the enclave but her advisors journeyed in her stead, alongside Valnir, Eyda, and enough Elder soldiers to overthrow a fortress. Many hooves beat against the ground, kicking up mud as they followed the River Avanar. The cold, dark water flowed into Lochlara, flattening out to fill the valley floor like it was a shallow bowl.

The army marched toward them, spears flashing in the sun, flags streaming in the bitter wind.

Blue with a golden dragon.

Purple with a white eagle.

Ibal.

Kasa.

He felt wings of his own, strong enough to rival the eagle on the flag. When the army came into sharper focus, he feared he might fly right off his horse.

Valnir's eye was true. Thousands of soldiers marched along the lake, many of them cavalry riders, all of them armed to the teeth. And there were indeed elephants. Each great beast was a wonderous thing. They lurched along, hulking gray boulders, their footfalls like low thunder.

Then riders broke apart from the great host, barreling forward to meet the retinue from Iona. Standard-bearers rode with them, holding the flags high even as their horses charged ahead.

It felt like being on top of a cresting wave, with another wave crashing right into it.

Both companies slowed before they could slam together, drawing to a halt.

Andry barely felt the ground beneath his boots as he dismounted. Corayne moved with him, keeping stride, her smile brighter than any sun.

He glimpsed familiar faces beneath the Ibalet flags, their golden robes overlaid with gilded armor blazing with sapphires. The Heir of Ibal raised their head in greeting. Next to them, their brother Sibrez gave a sharp look. Commander lin-Lira sat on the horse next to them, the sigil of the Crown's Falcons flapping over his head. Andry nearly wept to see them all, shivering as they were, out of place against the cold and wet of Calidon, better suited to the blazing deserts of Ibal.

A trio of knights in white armor rode next to them, their own standard held high. *Eagle knights*, Andry knew. His joy ebbed a little, remembering Lord Okran, who gave his life at the temple Spindle. The knights stared back at him, all of them brown-skinned or black beneath their white helmets, their armor set with amethysts. The trio clutched magnificent spears.

As much as Andry wanted to ask for news from Kasa, there was one thing he wanted more.

"Good to see you two are still attached at the hip," Charlie crowed from the line of riders. He bumbled off his horse but did not fall, thanks to Garion at his back.

With a grin, the fugitive priest squelched toward them through the mud. Andry had never seen the man so happy, or so wonderfully proud.

Charlie plucked at his clothing, brushing away imaginary dust. Then he sighed back at the army, looking them over, and planted his hands on his hips.

"I will be collecting a finder's fee."

32

A GIFT FIT FOR A QUEEN
Erida

The war camp grew, joined by new companies and fresh legions. Annoying as it was, Erida knew she could no longer avoid her more tedious duties as queen. To Thornwall's relief and her own irritation, she returned to the council tent, feasting with a ragged collection of nobles and officers.

Erida wore her veils still, though she was vastly improving in her ability to balance the beast within. *My mind is my own,* she thought over and over again, the words like a prayer. It worked mostly, and the veils became a precaution.

But sometimes, the nobles were too frustrating to bear, and the veils gave her a place to hide.

She rolled her eyes behind them now, listening to her bickering lords as they ate. In the war camp or the throne room, the conversation never truly changed. They spoke always of petty rivalries and wealth. They argued over who would control which silver mine or administrate which port city. Back and forth, they carved up the empire, as if they had any true say in what the realm would become.

Erida allowed them their delusions.

None of it interested her in the slightest.

Taristan did not have the benefit of veils to hide behind. He sat white-faced in his chair, his eyes glaring into the tabletop, until Erida thought it might crack beneath the lightning force of his gaze.

"To the Queen," one of the nobles said, his voice breaking through the low buzz of conversation.

Erida snapped to attention and raised her glass without thought. Red wine rippled behind facets of cut crystal, catching the candlelight. It looked like blood.

She bowed her head as another glass rose, another lord toasting her.

"To the Empress Rising!" he said, louder than the first, as if that proved anything.

Fists banged against wood and wine sloshed as the toasts carried. It was the same every night, near the end of dinner, when her lords swayed in their chairs, and the tent went hazy with the smoke from too many candles.

As always, Taristan drank little, sipping politely at his cup. She understood that now too. He remained clearheaded at all times, and therefore, in better control. In better *balance*.

Erida did the same. The wine sloshed against her closed lips, never touching her tongue.

"To Lady Harrsing," one of her lords, Morly, muttered, and the cheers fell silent.

Heads turned, looking between the drunken Morly and the Queen. In the corners of the tent, even the servants watched with trepidation.

On her left, Lord Thornwall's mouth twitched beneath his beard, betraying a frown. He shot a warning look at Morly across the table. The lord only shrugged, slurping at his glass. His face was near purple as his wine.

He is well past drunk, Erida knew, her smile fixed in place, visible behind the lace of her veil. She kept her glass high, careful to mask the anger rippling beneath her skin. *He means nothing by it.*

But her own voice in her head faded, losing strength. She gritted her teeth, trying to hold on to it, even as the edge of her vision flared hot. Beneath the table, her free hand gripped Taristan's, her knuckles bone-white, her nails digging into his fingers.

His hand clenched back, offering her an anchor against the swirling rage.

"To Lady Harrsing," Erida forced out, her voice hoarser than she meant it to be.

The table of lords gave a collective sigh of relief. Lord Thornwall shot her a grateful look and Erida took it in stride. Queen though she was, it would not do to start cutting off her lords' heads. Not now, before a battle for the realm entire.

Even if they deserve it, she thought darkly. *Even if they are useless, little jackals feasting on the scraps of my victory.*

Night fell black outside the council tent, loosing Erida's chains. Her hour of freedom came and she stood from the table eagerly, Taristan alongside. Along the table, the nobles shot to their own feet, even Morly, who could barely stand.

"My lords," she said, dipping her brow.

They bowed back at her.

Safe behind her veil, she glanced down their line one last time, scrutinizing every pink face, ruddy with food and too much drink. She was reminded of peacocks in the palace garden, spoiled and dull. Or turkeys, slowly fattened, picking their way toward slaughter.

Most of them looked to her with respect, if not fear. None dared move until she swept from the tent, Taristan carried along in her wake, the Lionguard behind them both.

The Queen's apartments were a collection of tents, the canvas painted like brocade, the rooms within as well appointed as they could be on the campaign. Grand though they were, her knights took no chances. Half of them ringed the Queen, while the other half searched her tents, passing through the flaps with neat efficiency.

After the attack in Ascal, Erida could not argue. She still felt the Amhara's blade against her throat, almost as well as she remembered the same dagger spearing through her itching hand.

Satisfied with their inspection, the Lionguard emerged again, and took up their posts around the exterior.

Erida glanced at her palm as they entered the tent, walking into the salon set with chairs, the hard ground covered in fine rugs. Candles burned around the tent, too bright for her eyes. She squinted and blew out a few, her hand stinging. Her wound was healing slowly, thanks to weeks of travel, gripping the reins of a cantering horse.

"Shall I call for Dr. Bahi?" Taristan muttered, watching her as she examined the bandage around her palm. He idled by the wooden screen dividing the salon from their bedchamber. "If there's sign of infection—"

Erida shook her head and threw off the mantle around her shoulders, letting it land in a heap on the carpeted floor. Her maids would attend to it in the morning.

"It's nothing," she replied. "I'm lucky to still have the hand at all."

Then a shadow stepped out from behind the screen, the weak light setting him in silhouette.

"Sorasa Sarn is losing her touch," the man murmured, mouth curled in a half grin.

Taristan reacted first, going for the sword at his waist, while Erida shuddered, stumbling backward against one of the cushioned chairs. Her mind roared, the edge of her vision streaking red, rage and fear leaping up inside her.

The hooded shadow sidestepped the first swipe of Taristan's blade, then the second, swift as the wind.

Even as What Waits twisted inside, all but yanking her away from the shadow, toward the flap of the tent, Erida stayed flat against the chair. Her stinging eyes narrowed, head pounding. She would not leave Taristan behind, not even while every instinct screamed at her to do so.

Again Taristan struck and again the hooded shadow dodged, as if the Prince of Old Cor were only a child playing at swords. His motions were quick and fluid, like water.

Like a *snake*.

"Lord Mercury," Erida breathed, the pieces slotting together in her mind.

Taristan's sword caught the edge of a chair, embedding in the wood. Before he could wrench it free, the shadow kicked it from his hand. Then he turned, sweeping out an arm to bow, his dark cloak billowing.

"At your service," the shadow said.

His hood fell, swept back from a skeletal face, tanned skin drawn tight against murderously high cheekbones. His hair was silver, near translucent, and his eyes were a pale green, the same color as jade.

The same color as the circular seal she'd received, in exchange for a mountain of gold and a contract with the Amhara. It was back in Ascal, but Erida remembered it keenly, the image of a snake carved into the jade.

Her throat tightened, even as What Waits calmed within her. She swallowed against the sensation, trying to make sense of the man before her.

The lord of the Amhara, commander of the deadliest assassins upon the Ward. Here in my tent.

She gritted her teeth, her eyes flicking to Taristan. He stared back at her, panting, a question in his eyes. Slowly, she shook her head, and he relented, backing away from the assassin king.

What will it cost me?

"I did not know the leader of the Amhara Guild could leave his citadel," she said, straightening up in her seat as gracefully as she could. "To what do we owe this great honor?"

Lord Mercury stalked toward her. She thought of the snake again, slithering and poisonous. But he was charming too, still handsome despite his age.

"A common misconception," Mercury said, laughing. "I leave whenever I wish. I am just rarely seen."

Erida forced a cold laugh of her own, all performance. "I can imagine."

To her surprise, the Amhara sank to a knee, his back to Taristan. As if her husband posed no threat at all. It incensed him, his nostrils flaring. Mercury dipped his head.

"I come to offer my apologies. My guild has failed to fulfill your contract, which you so generously gave." He shifted, his cloak opening enough to show the brace of daggers at each hip. They glowed bronze, filled with candlelight. "We Amhara are not accustomed to such shame."

Erida could not help but think about the mountain of gold she'd sent into the desert, paid for the life of one stupid girl. Her cheeks burned.

"Corayne an-Amarat is harder to kill than any of us suspected," she muttered.

"Indeed." Mercury stood again. "I lost a dozen of my own in the attempt."

Good, Erida snapped in her mind. It was only fitting his failure cost him something too.

"Sorasa Sarn." She turned the words over as she would an intriguing book. Again, the tiger-eyed assassin flashed in her mind, little more than a shadow, her smile a sharpened knife. "So that is her name. Gone rogue, has she?"

"Exiled," Mercury offered. "Once I thought it the worst punishment for her. Death would have been a reprieve to abandonment."

His almost cheerful manner did not disappear, but his gaze sharpened, his eyes dangerous and angry, mismatched from the rest of his face. Though Erida carried a demon inside her, she could not help but shudder.

"I promise to remedy that error, Your Majesty," he said, in a low voice to quake the room.

Behind him, Taristan retrieved his sword and sheathed it home. Mercury ignored him. Old man though he was, Erida saw the hard lines of muscle in his wrists and neck, and the calluses on his fingers. She wagered he was one of the most dangerous mortals in the realm.

"Have you come to return my payment, my lord?" she asked, angling her head.

His smile returned in full force, showing a mouth of too many teeth. "I think you'll find my gift far more valuable than gold."

With a wave, he gestured back out into the night.

Side by side, Erida and Taristan followed, letting Mercury lead them outside into the square. Only for Erida's jaw to drop, a gasp escaping her lips as Taristan drew her close. He pulled her in, shielding her with the bulk of his body.

In the center of the camp square, firelight played against golden armor. Every single knight of the Lionguard kneeled in the dirt, Amharas at their backs, and knives at their throats. Two more assassins stood to the side, something huddled between them.

"Do not fear for your knights, Your Majesty," Mercury said, waving a hand. As if that could dismiss Erida's shock or Taristan's concern.

"Lord Mercury—" Erida began, until a shout cut her off.

At the edge of the circle of tents, torches flickered and swords rang, drawn from sheaths. Boots thumped against the ground, guards yelling to each other. Lord Thornwall was loudest of all, sprinting in his nightshirt, skinny legs bared to the firelight. His red face appeared at the edge of the torch ring, a sword in hand, a contingent of soldiers on his heels.

"Wait!" Erida shouted, raising a hand to stop Thornwall before he could plunge into a viper's nest of assassins.

Red-faced, her commander stopped short, his men with him.

"Your Majesty," he panted, eyes wide with fear.

"Wait," Erida said again, softer, but filled with command. "Very well, Lord Mercury. Show me your gift, then."

The Amhara lord did not hesitate.

"Bring him forth," Mercury said, flicking a hand.

Two of his assassins moved, shoving the huddled shape between them. *Him.*

Erida's stomach turned as the shape stumbled forward. He fell over himself, hands bound, a sack over his head, his clothing torn and crusted with mud.

But for the surcoat, she would not have recognized him. It was gold, emblazoned with a green lion. The reverse crest of Galland.

The crest of Lord Konegin.

She felt that same lion leap up inside of her, roaring, triumphant. It was like another conquest, another jewel in her crown. *No,* she realized, laughing to herself. *This is better.*

One of the assassins pushed him again, and Konegin fell to his knees. He gave a muffled yelp beneath the sack.

Erida stared down at him, mouth parted, the air tingling on her tongue. It tasted like victory.

"My lord, this is a mighty gift indeed." Her hands shook, her skin burning. "What will it cost me?"

To her delight, Mercury gave another bow. As he moved, a chain around his neck fell forward, catching the torchlight. The jade snake dangled from it.

"The price is already paid," he said.

She felt Thornwall's eyes on her face, and the attention of his soldiers behind him. They looked, not just at her, but at the Lionguard held at knifepoint.

The Queen raised her chin, remembering herself. "My knights."

With another flick of Mercury's fingers, the Amhara drew back in unison, moving like a school of deadly fish.

The Lionguard knights sprang away as fast as they could, scrambling out of reach of the assassins.

"What of Corayne?" Erida said, turning her attention back to Mercury.

He shot her a dark look.

"The Amhara Guild does not tolerate failure," he hissed. "Nor betrayal."

Satisfaction welled up in Erida, and What Waits purred at the back of her mind. *He wants Corayne and Sarn*, she thought, delighted. *He'll kill them both.*

"Lord Thornwall, prepare a tent for Lord Mercury and his company," she said, her eyes shooting back to Konegin.

Her cousin seemed larger in her memories, clad in fur and velvet, always looking down on her, even when she sat the throne above him.

Now he would never look down on her again.

Erida's hand closed on the sack over his head, the fabric rough in her grasp. Slowly, she pulled it off, revealing the broken man beneath. And Konegin was indeed broken.

A gag rubbed the sides of his mouth raw, his teeth fanged around it. Gone was his luxurious blond beard and mustache, his face red and cheeks shorn. His golden hair was no more, all turned to gray. He was thinner, older than she remembered. His eyes welled, red-rimmed and bloodshot, wavering over her face. The last time she saw him, he'd put poison in her husband's cup, and ran when that poison failed.

Once, he was the spitting image of Erida's father. It haunted her, to look into his face. To know grasping Lord Konegin lived while her father was long dead. Now he was no better than a corpse in Taristan's army, white-faced and hollow, wrung out. Gone was the man who tried to seize her throne and murder her husband. Gone was the last hope of her traitorous lords, simpering men who could not stomach a woman's reign.

Barely a spark remained in his blue eyes, the last bit of fight left in Lord Konegin.

"Hello, cousin," she whispered.

Below her, he trembled, and the spark guttered out.

The knights carried him into her tent. She heard the thud of him hitting the floor, along with a yelp of pain. Taristan went in first, a greedy look on his face. Erida felt the same, her mouth twisted into a devilish smirk. She made to follow, Konegin's heart already in her teeth.

Erida nearly snarled when Thornwall stopped her at the door. Immediately, she dropped her eyes, feeling the telltale burn of flames.

"And what will this accomplish, Your Majesty?" he asked hastily, wringing his hands. He still wore only a long nightshirt, an odd sight under the circumstances.

"Are you joking, my lord?" She hissed back at him, her eyes squeezed shut to hide her rage. "If there are traitors in my court, I will know of them. And deal with them as I see fit."

At the back of her mind, something stung. Painfully, she wondered why Thornwall did not want her to interrogate the treasonous lord.

"Normally, I would agree," he mumbled, glancing back to the tents and the torches.

"But?" Erida blinked rapidly, feeling her vision clear. Just in time to study his face, watching for any tell of a lie. "Is there something you would like to confess, Lord Thornwall?"

Her old commander turned to stone before her eyes, his jaw set beneath his gray beard. His eyes flashed, and she saw the Lion of Galland in him too.

"I am the commander of the armies of Galland," Thornwall said shortly. She imagined this was the man his soldiers saw, intense and unyielding. "If I were guilty of treason, you would know it by now."

Erida nearly choked, words dying in her throat.

Thornwall took it as indication to continue, to her chagrin.

"Lord Konegin will be executed. He knows it, and he knows there is nothing in the realm that can save him from your just punishment," he said. "So he will tear out your heart. He will name every noble who ever smiled at him, who ever entertained a whisper of his plans for the throne. Up to his dying breath, Konegin will *poison* you."

As he tried to poison Taristan. As he tried to poison the realm against me. Her fist curled, the wound singing. It kept her level, even as her anger simmered, rising to a boil.

"Kill him, and be done with it," Thornwall begged. His stern face melted, eyes wide with desperation. "Let the treason die with him."

Erida hated his reason, his logic, his good sense. He was right about Konegin, she knew that plainly. But the temptation loomed, too great to ignore.

"It is good advice, Lord Thornwall," she said, moving past him, leaving her commander alone with the torches, the knights, and the blinking stars.

Inside the tent, Taristan sat waiting, a knife on the table next to him. He eyed her as she crossed the carpets, stopping a yard away from Konegin's crumpled form.

She gave a nod and Taristan cut the gag away. Her cousin gasped and spit, sputtering against the floor. His hands were still bound, tied behind his back. Without them, he could not sit up, and remained slumped, cheek pressed to the carpet, eyes rolling in his head.

Another might pity the old man. Erida would not.

You bring this upon yourself, my lord.

"You will tell me everything," she said, gesturing for the knife.

For a moment, Taristan did not move. He returned her stare, his expression unreadable and distant. Erida tightened her jaw, holding out her good hand.

The hilt of the knife felt right in her palm, well balanced. It was a small blade, the edge gleaming, meant for delicate work.

Konegin stared, eyes flickering between Erida's face and the knife in her grasp.

"You have grown, Erida," he said, his voice hoarse and dry. "Grown into something terrible."

"I am what you made me," she said, taking a step toward him. "I am the punishment you have earned. A woman in the place you sought to fill, a woman who holds all you tried to take. Better than you in every single way, greater than you could ever dream to become. You tried to put me on the pyre, my lord. But it is you who will burn."

With a smile, she bent low, stooping so they were eye-to-eye. Her blood sang, the river coursing in her. What Waits did not push, so much as make His presence known. She leaned into Him, bracing against Him as if He were a wall behind her.

Her eyes flamed, her vision going red. She could not help but smile, knowing what Konegin saw in her.

His mouth dropped, the blood draining from his face.

"I am what you made me," she said again.

In the morning, twelve lords swung from twelve ropes. The rains of early spring dripped down their bodies, washing them clean of their treasons. Konegin's body hung highest, above the rest of his conspirators. She would not let him wear the lion to the gallows, and he was dressed as a lowly prisoner, in little more than an undershirt and breeches. Gone were his velvets and jeweled chains. Gone was the circlet of gold.

Erida watched the corpses for a long while, the crowd of nobles dissipating around her. They whispered and stared, dark-eyed and pale-faced. Thornwall walked among them, silent but dutiful.

Erida cared little for the opinion of noble sheep. She was a lion, and she would not answer to them any longer.

Only Taristan remained at her side, bareheaded beneath the rain. His hair ran dark against his face, the red locks near to black.

It was still cold, but not so cold as it once was.

"Winter is ending," Erida said to the open air. It tasted of rain and mud, and growing things beneath. *Spring.*

His eyes met her own, the scarlet sparking beneath the black.

Erida felt the same in her own eyes, the twisted roots of the same infernal tree.

"I will wait no longer," she breathed. What Waits coiled, wrapping around her wrists, her ankles, her throat. "Let the rest of the armies follow. We march today."

Taristan's hand met her fevered cheek, his skin burning as she burned. His thumb ran the length of her cheekbone, tracing the lines of her face.

His kiss burned too.

"And I will follow," he muttered against her. "Anywhere you go."

Her heart hammered. "Once, we promised each other the world entire."

His eyes bored into her own. Once she feared the black abyss of his gaze. Now it was a familiar comfort. But something stirred, his focus wavering.

"Yes, we did," Taristan finally answered, his voice thick.

He did not blink, holding her stare, and she let his words echo in her head, turning each letter over. As before, Erida felt him waiting, letting her take the first step so he might follow.

"The world entire," she said again.

"The world entire," he echoed.

This time, it sounded like a surrender, like an ending.

She devoured it whole.

33

THE DREAM WAKING
Corayne

"I am Isadere, the Heir to Ibal."

Their voice echoed up to the vaulted ceiling of the throne room, singing off the marble. Though Isadere was mortal, they seemed to suit the proud halls of the Elder castle. As sunlight filled the windows, so did it gleam off Isadere's armor, gilded and jeweled, their long black hair a smooth curtain over one shoulder. The Heir's illegitimate brother, Sibrez, held their left while Commander lin-Lira stood the right. All three made for an imposing sight, grand as the kingdom they hailed from.

Corayne could not help but feel excited, fidgeting a little in her seat. She adjusted her grip on the hilt of the Spindleblade, holding it as she would a staff, one hand on the hilt. Andry and Charlie sat on either side of her, both watching Isadere with wide eyes.

They were not the only ones.

Chairs lined both sides of Isibel's raised dais, so that the lady of Iona could receive her guests properly. Valnir and Dyrian sat to her right and left. Lady Eyda stood behind her son, his bear alongside her, half-asleep.

"You are welcome here, Isadere," Isibel replied, though she sounded anything but welcoming.

On the floor, Isadere gave a bow of their head and a sweep of an arm. It was half a curtsy, more fluid, their spine never bending.

"The legends of your people speak of your bravery, your strength, but not your kindness," Isadere answered with their shark smile.

Corayne winced into her hand. Eager as she was to see the Heir match wits with the Elder monarch, Corayne hoped they might do so without the world hanging in the balance. Next to her, Charlie tsked under his breath. He held little fondness for Isadere, but even less for Isibel.

Together with Commander lin-Lira and Sibrez, Isadere stepped back from the center of the hall. The three knights of Kasa quickly replaced them, each one kneeling with a clank of white armor. They leaned on their spears, the steel tips glinting at the ceiling.

Isibel eyed them coolly.

The first stood, short but broad, and removed his helmet to better face the assembled company. The knight was black-skinned, darker than Andry and his mother, with velvety brown eyes beneath thick brows.

"I am Sir Gamon of Kin Debes," the knight said, putting a gauntleted fist to his breastplate. The eagle screamed across his chest, worked in white steel. "These are my cousins, Sir Enais and Lady Farra."

Still kneeling, both Kasans raised their helmets. Enais was lighter-skinned and tall, all limbs, while Farra could have been Gamon's twin.

"We come at the behest of our queen, who extends a hand in friend-ship and alliance," he said, bowing again. Then he turned on a booted heel, his warm eyes roving. "To you, and to Corayne an-Amarat. The Realm's Hope."

While her fingers tightened on the hilt of the Spindleblade, Corayne flushed, her cheeks going warm.

"Thank you," she forced out, her voice embarrassingly small. It barely echoed in the cavernous chamber.

"I must also acknowledge you, Andry Trelland," Sir Gamon added, his gaze shifting to the seat beside her.

A low gasp escaped Andry's lips and he sat a bit straighter, blinking fiercely.

Sir Gamon quirked a half smile. "Your mother is well."

Without thinking, Corayne reached out to take Andry by the hand, squeezing hard. He fell slack against his seat, unable to speak. He could only nod his thanks across the hall, which Sir Gamon accepted dutifully.

On the throne, Isibel curled her lip.

"Perhaps I am mistaken in my understanding of the mortal kingdoms." Her voice took on a sharp edge, demanding attention. "But I was under the impression that the lands of Kasa and Ibal were vast, with sprawling cities. And grand armies."

The accusation shot through the chamber like an arrow. It made the hairs on Corayne's neck stand on end. Scowling, she dropped Andry's hand.

"More will come," she blurted out, before anyone could think to say something more damning. "These are simply the first."

Across the hall, Isadere gave a curt nod, their eyes tight with frustration.

"More will come," they said in agreement. "But there are many miles from our shores to your city. And the Long Sea is rife with dangers, thanks to our enemy."

Beside Isadere, Sibrez's face darkened. He was quicker to anger than his sibling, and Corayne prayed he kept in line.

"We lost a good many ships on the crossing," the Heir added bitterly.

On the dais, Valnir's eyes gleamed. "You will lose more than that in the days ahead. Steel yourself to it."

Corayne wanted to scream and sink into the floor. Judging by the sudden clench of Andry's fist, his knuckles bony beneath brown skin, he shared the sentiment.

Helmet still tucked under his arm, Gamon gave a weary, withering shake of his head. He glanced through the Elders again.

"Perhaps *I* am mistaken in my understanding of immortals," he said neatly. "But is one of your warriors not worth a hundred of our own? A hundred of Erida's soldiers? If not more?"

Silence echoed, and Isadere took it as an invitation. Gold cloak sweeping, they marched to Gamon's side, presenting a united front. Anger spotted on the Heir's golden cheeks.

"You three are the monarchs of your enclaves," Isadere growled, eyeing each in turn. Dyrian drew back in his seat, the young lord going pale. "Three rulers. Where are *your* armies, my lords and lady?"

The Heir's teeth snapped together.

"And where were *you* when all this began?"

Doing nothing, their heads buried, Corayne thought, feeling the same rage she saw on Isadere's face.

Isibel only turned her head away, to look anywhere but at the gathered faces watching her.

"I will not be questioned by a mortal," she said stiffly.

Murmurs rippled through the hall, whispered in languages the Elders did not know. But Corayne did. She gritted her teeth, hoping Isibel would not drive away their only allies against the oncoming storm.

Isadere's voice shook with fury. "We will spill our blood to save the realm, but you could have spilled your own first. And saved thousands for it. This I have seen."

Valnir eyed Isibel with distaste. Then he leaned forward in his seat, to address the assembled with a softer manner.

"I have sent word back to my enclave, calling my folk here," he said.

"They are to leave behind a skeleton force, enough to make trouble for Erida's legions should they march through our territory."

Across the hall, Corayne shot him a grateful look.

"The Elders of Kovalinn fought bravely against the dragon of Irridas," she offered.

Lady Eyda gave a grim nod while Dyrian perked up on his chair.

"Twice," the young lord added, holding up two fingers.

Next to her, Andry stood, his wolf pelt fastened around his shoulders, its jaws wide as if frozen mid-bite. He puffed out his chest a little, drawing himself up to face the chamber. To everyone else, he seemed stoic and calm.

Corayne saw the worry beneath, written in the trembling of his hand. She wanted to grab it and squeeze, to give him some support. Instead, she gripped the Spindleblade tighter.

"The Jydi will guard the Watchful Sea, and Trec holds the north," Andry reported. "They will attack what legions they can, and hopefully slow Erida's progress." A muscle flexed in his cheek. "Her armies are many, but it will take time to rally the full might of Galland. They will have to travel overland, across the mountains. That is our advantage."

Corayne rose to stand next to him, if only so he did not have to stand alone. The backs of their arms brushed, sending jolts of lightning under her skin.

"But when she does come," Corayne said, "her fist will be powerful indeed."

The legions, the Ashlanders, and whatever else Taristan rains down on us. Her heart skipped a beat. As always, she felt the shadow over her, heavy and cold. *Or What Waits Himself, waiting no longer.*

"Erida and Taristan *will* strike here." Isadere's voice rang hollow. "I have seen it."

"You see what lies in front of you, mortal. Little else," Isibel bit back at them. One white hand waved dismissively through the air, her white sleeve shimmering like snow.

The Heir of Ibal fumed, their face burning.

"I see what the gods of the Ward show me," Isadere growled, forgetting all manners or etiquette. "I see by the light and dark of Blessed Lasreen."

"The gods of the Ward." Isibel surveyed the chamber, letting her voice echo. Then she shook her head, the branch of the ash tree trembling across her knees. "The gods of the Ward are silent. They will let this realm shatter. Perhaps that is your fate?"

"*Our* fate," Corayne snapped, boiling over. With a clang, she let the tip of the Spindleblade smack the marble floor. "If you do nothing."

Next to her, Andry shifted just an inch, so that his arm pressed into her own, steady as a wall. It was both support, and a warning.

With blurring motion, Isibel suddenly stood from her throne, her eyes downcast. She contemplated the branch in her hand, and for a moment, Corayne could not breathe. She remembered how Valnir threw down the silver branch of golden leaves, the aspen replaced by his yew bow. It roused his enclave to war.

Isibel did not do the same. Her grip only tightened on the branch of the ash tree.

"If your armies have need, give word," she said, waving to one of her advisors. "We will host whoever we can inside the city walls, but I fear Iona cannot shelter all your soldiers. Nor the . . . elephants," she added, sounding almost apologetic.

On the floor, Sir Gamon and his knights bowed again.

"We are grateful for your hospitality," he said.

Isadere stiffly ducked their head, the only thanks they would show.

At her seat, Corayne let go a long, slow breath. She watched as Isibel all but fled the throne room, her advisors in tow.

"That went well," Charlie grumbled, standing from his chair.

After long weeks of cold silence stalking the halls of Tíarma, the presence of other mortals was almost jarring to Corayne. The Elder castle, once a tomb, bustled like a city market. Much to the chagrin of the Elders themselves, who seemed perturbed by the mortal chaos. Despite Isibel's promises, her advisors were little help in administrating the new lay of the castle. Thankfully, Andry delighted in the organization, arranging for sleeping pallets and linens until the passages became a parade of laundry. When everyone had a place to sleep, he turned his attentions on the stables and the armory.

Even Charlie made himself useful, quickly dashing off requests for provisions to the King of Calidon in Lenava, and the nobles in Turadir. He included grand promises of payment. For once, the signatures on his letters were not forged. Both Isadere and Sir Gamon signed their names without issue, eager to secure enough food for their army.

Like the castle, the city of Iona threatened to burst at the seams. They fit as many soldiers as they could within the walls, but most made camp at the bottom of the ridge, digging in with their backs against the gates and the rising cliffs.

The next morning, Corayne watched the palisade walls go up around the war camp, along with a ditch and field of sharpened pikes. It would not hold off Erida's legions for long, but it would be something.

It was not yet spring, but the air felt warmer on her face. Corayne flinched against it, the sun streaking through the clouds. Spring was coming, and with it, melting snows. Easier passage through the mountains. A safer road for all that sought to destroy the realm.

Her chest tightened beneath her cloak, until she felt her ribs might collapse inward.

She was not alone on the landing, but most gave her a wide berth, leaving Corayne an-Amarat to her thoughts.

Isadere an-Amdiras was not most.

Corayne felt their stare like a knife at the neck, and turned to find the Heir of Ibal watching from a distance.

"Your Highness," Corayne muttered, dipping into a quick bow. "Do you have everything you need?"

"Everything within possibility, yes," Isadere answered, walking to Corayne's side at the edge of the terrace. "The squire will be made a seneschal if he keeps up his good work."

Corayne smiled and tipped her face into the sun's warmth. Foreboding as it was, she reveled in it for a moment. *Andry deserves a warm castle filled with laughter, not a war bearing down on him.*

"I admit, my mirror did not warn me of the cold," Isadere grumbled, burrowing into a cloak of tawny furs.

"Your goddess showed you Iona," Corayne said.

Isadere barely nodded. "I mustered what army I could, with my father's blessing."

Corayne was the daughter of a pirate, well versed in the matters of the Long Sea. She knew how dangerous the Ibalet navy could be, if truly roused to war. *There will be no chance Erida moves by sea.*

"What of the Kasans?" she said, thinking of the elephants penned up outside the city wall.

"Queen Berin has been wary for some time. She received summons and warnings from across the Ward," Isadere replied. "We sailed to Nkonabo first, to prepare for the crossing. She was more than willing to send soldiers north with us, despite the danger."

Corayne tried to call up the feeling of relief and joy when she first spotted the unified army. It was difficult to grasp now, with the realities of their circumstance on full display.

"It feels like a cruel joke of the gods," Corayne cursed. "Drawing us all here, making us think we have a chance."

Isadere only blinked.

"Do we not have a chance, Corayne?" they asked plainly. "It does not matter what Isibel of Iona commands or believes. Taristan and Erida are coming whether she chooses to fight or not."

Fire licked up Corayne's spine, hot and angry. "What then? We kill ourselves out there while she watches and weeps over a realm she will never see again?"

"The Monarch can do as she wishes. But the others around her can not stand by, not while the realm crumbles beneath them," Isadere said, too serene. "They will fight with us, when it comes to it. Even Elders fear to die."

"Comforting," Corayne snapped, letting them both lapse into uneasy silence.

As in the desert, Isadere's blind faith in the goddess set Corayne on edge. She could not understand it, no matter all she had seen. Sorasa was not so zealous, though she served the same god. The memory of her made Corayne heartsick.

"You cannot break it, can you?" Isadere asked in a low voice. Their black eyes flashed to the Spindleblade, still close at Corayne's shoulder.

The steel pressed against her back, the jewels of the hilt winking in the corner of her eye. Taunting her.

"If only we could," she replied. "But a Spindle still burns in Gidastern. If we break the last blade, then hope is truly lost. And the realm too."

She could still smell the city in flames, the golden thread of a Spindle glowing through the inferno. Corayne despaired of ever truly reaching it again, but knew they were doomed if she did not. Even if Taristan fell, the Spindle he left behind would one day tear the realm in two.

"Even Elders fear to die," Isadere said again, their eyes boring into Corayne's own. Their voice deepened, filled with meaning.

Corayne's tongue felt heavy. She wanted to tell Isadere about her misgivings, to ask for advice. To unload her worries about the echo of a Spindle humming somewhere in the castle. It grew stronger every day, until Corayne feared she might walk through a portal on her way to breakfast.

But her voice died in her throat, the words turning to ash in her mouth. Instead, Corayne forced a bow, and turned to leave.

"I did not see the Amhara. Nor your Elder bodyguard," Isadere called after her. "I am sorry for your loss."

Corayne faltered but did not stop. She would not let the Heir see her frustration, or the weariness threatening to split her apart.

She wanted to retreat to her bedchamber, which she now shared with Lady Farra. Instead, her feet carried her through the receiving hall, past the long feasting tables crowded with soldiers, and up the dais of the empty throne room. Isibel's carved seat stood out against the other assembled chairs. Like its lady, the throne stood cold and distant, apart from the rest.

Corayne glared at it as she walked, continuing into the hall behind the dais. It led to the Monarch's private wing of the castle, the only part of Tíarma that did not teem with life.

The passage was frigid, lined with archways on one side, all open to the valley and the elements. Corayne shivered to think what it would be in winter.

She expected a guard to stop her, but no one came.

She crossed into a gallery hung with tapestries, its windows facing the misty north. There were maps on the walls like none she had ever seen, and a pair of tables drawn together to form a massive desk. Parchment covered the top, covered in scribbled notes and drawn lines. It reminded Corayne of her sea maps and charts, used to track the paths of the stars. But these used no stars that she understood, the constellations unfamiliar, the writing indecipherable.

She glanced at the map on the wall again, narrowing her eyes.

Glorian, she realized, tracing the strange coastlines of the Elder realm. As she did in the vaults, she felt a low pressure ripple against her skin. It seemed to tremble through her flesh, down to her bones.

She felt it in the Spindleblade too, the steel straight against her back.

Her spine turned to ice. Again, she thought of the Spindle, burning somewhere, leading to only the gods knew what. Her stomach twisted.

Does Isibel know? she thought, trembling. Her fingers shook on the parchment and she shoved it away, turning from the table with a sick feeling.

Only to find the Monarch of Iona staring at her, silent as a ghost. Corayne's heart leapt up in her chest, her body buzzing as if struck by lightning.

"Curse you Elders," Corayne bit out, trying to calm herself down.

Isibel only quirked her head, a curtain of silver-gold hair falling over one shoulder. As always, she carried a glow in her, alive in her pearl eyes and pale skin. The Monarch was cruelly beautiful, like frost on a flower.

"Corayne of Old Cor," she said, enunciating the letters sharply.

Her skin crawled. *That is not my name*, she wanted to snap.

"Are you lost," Isibel pushed on, "or did you intend to intrude upon my private chambers?"

Swallowing hard, Corayne set her feet. In another life she would have felt shame upon being caught, but not anymore. Too much hung in the balance for such things. There were too many obstacles in their way, one of them being Isibel herself.

"You said you saw hope in me," Corayne said, her eyes on Isibel's face. She watched every small tic and pull, trying to read her expression. "Hope for what?"

The Monarch looked past her, to the books on the shelves and the windows filled with golden light. The sun set early in the valley, slipping behind the high peaks of the Monadhrian. Shadows pooled across the floor.

"I am afraid I do not know," Isibel muttered, shaking her head. "I wish I could tell you. I wish— I wish I could give you what you ask for."

Corayne set her jaw. "Why can't you?"

She did not miss the minute flicker of Isibel's gaze, almost too quick to see. They wavered from Corayne, only for a moment, spearing a spot on the wall behind her.

The map, Corayne knew, her insides twisting.

"The price is too great," the Elder lamented. Her white hands clasped together, fingers wringing. "And now I have no heirs to my enclave. There is no future for my people in this realm."

Isibel's voice broke, but Corayne could not pity her. Even if they mourned the same dead.

Her stomach twisted again, this time with terrible realization. The truth buzzed in her skin like the sensation of magic, like the touch of a Spindle somewhere close.

A Spindle only Taristan would dare open.

"The Ward's fate is not yet written," Corayne said harshly.

Isibel answered with a melancholy look. "It is already etched in stone."

With a will, Corayne turned from the gallery, leaving the Elder ruler in her wake.

"Then I will break it."

* * *

Corayne did not know who convinced Isibel to assemble their gathered council again, but she suspected Valnir and Eyda had some part in it.

They were fewer in number than before, with only Isadere and Sir Gamon joining, their chairs arranged in a semicircle before the throne and dais. It was not lost on Corayne how the Elders sat elevated above the rest, with the mortals forced to look up. She ground her teeth together as she sat, hoping Isadere or Sir Gamon did not take offense.

"I feel put on trial again," Charlie muttered as he took the seat beside her. He at least dressed the part, clad in soft robes of gray, his brown hair freshly washed and curling over his shoulders.

Annoyed as she was, Corayne relaxed a little. "What number would this be?"

The fugitive priest gave a glancing wave, shrugging. "Oh, I've lost count by now."

"Seven," Garion muttered next to him. The Amhara still wore his leathers, but favored a long black sable fur to keep warm within the shivering halls.

It suited him as the wolf pelt suited Andry, who remained standing. His fingers drummed on the back of his chair, betraying his unease.

"What is it?" Corayne said, laying a careful hand on his wrist.

He stilled immediately.

"Let Isibel say whatever she wants," he said, sharper than usual. "It does not matter. We're here, we're digging in. We'll fight what comes, and her Ionians can fight alongside us if they so choose. In fact, they'll have to. I doubt Taristan will differentiate one body from another."

"Isadere said as much," Corayne mumbled back, seeing the truth of it, depressing as it may be.

On the dais, the Elders stiffened, all of them in clear earshot. Only

Isibel did not react, peering down on them with her cold, silver eyes.

"I've had word from my enclave in the Castlewood," Valnir boomed, silencing all conversation. "They confirmed the legions are massing at Rouleine, drawn from every corner of the Gallish empire."

Grave looks rippled through the council, and Corayne felt sick to her core. This was truly the end, if Erida was willing to leave her kingdom undefended.

All for me.

Andry cursed under his breath, then began to count on his fingers. He shook his head, despair darkening his eyes.

"How many men can the Queen of Galland muster?" she heard herself ask, her voice tight.

Next to her, Andry continued to count. Her heart sank with every finger he curled and uncurled.

"Whatever it is, it does not take into account what Taristan can do," Lady Eyda said from the dais, her lips twitching. "And what kind of army he can command."

The implication shattered Isibel's indifference. Her eyes dropped, her throat working above the collar of her dress. In her hand, her knuckles went white, fingers gripping the ash branch.

"I will not watch my daughter's corpse march upon these walls," she hissed out, her eyes shimmering.

It felt like a knife in Corayne's gut. She tried not to picture it, Ridha in her green armor. Or Dom with his cloak. Sorasa. Sigil. Their silhouettes familiar, their eyes strange. Their bodies rotting beneath them.

"When they come, we will target Taristan first. And destroy him. I promise you this, Isibel," Valnir said, fervent as a prayer. His hand closed over her free one, still clawed to her throne.

To his dismay, she only pulled back. "None but Corayne can harm him now. None but a mortal girl."

Corayne flinched, though it was the truth. She remembered how even Dom could do nothing against Taristan, only blessed weapons in her own hand able to leave scratches on her demon uncle's skin. The Dragon-claw gauntlets. The Jydi charms. And the Spindleblade too.

"None but Corayne," Valnir echoed, setting his jaw. His yellow eyes found her own. "So be it."

Then the Elder lord cocked his head, eyes narrowing as he scrutinized some sound Corayne could not hear.

"Is that a horse?"

The bang of the doors behind them cut him off, followed by the thunderous clatter of hooves on marble. While the Elders jumped to stand, slack-jawed, Corayne turned in her chair. Next to her, Andry went for the ax at his hip.

Two horses reined to a halt at the center of the throne room, the first of them rearing up with a pawing of hooves. It obscured the rider on his back, only for a moment. Behind them, the statues of the Elder gods looked on, fearsome in white marble.

Then a ghost slid from the saddle. Muddy, roadworn, his broad shoulders wrapped in old, stained wool, his blond hair dark with rain.

Corayne's chair fell backward as she lurched from it.

This is a dream. This is a dream, she told herself, tears already stinging her eyes. She could not bear the thought of waking up.

This is a dream.

Then the second rider jumped to the ground, landing with her lethal grace. She looked worse than ever, her leathers torn and re-sewn, her tell-tale dagger missing from her belt. There were bruise-like circles beneath her eyes and her cheekbones cut more sharply in her face.

But there was no mistaking the tattoos.

Dull pain radiated up from Corayne's knees as they hit the marble beneath her. She did not feel it, as she could hardly feel anything at all.

"This is a dream," Corayne said aloud. She expected her eyes to open. She expected the now familiar rush of grief.

Instead, she found only warm, strong arms and the smell of horse. She forgot the council, forgot the war, forgot Erida and Taristan and all their horrors.

Someone lifted her clean off the floor, his grip carefully gentle. She felt herself spin, her head already whirling, her heart torn in every single direction.

"This is a dream," she said again, trembling as her boots touched the ground.

Above her, Domacridhan of Iona grinned with the full force of the blazing sun.

"It is not," he said. "I promise you, it is not."

34

WHAT YOU CHOOSE
Domacridhan

"This is a dream."

Corayne's voice brought him spiraling back to the world. Gently, he lowered her down to the marble. She stared up at him, eyes too wide, as if she feared to blink. Fine clothing flowed around her, embroidered velvet, silk, and fur. Her hair gleamed, freshly washed, woven into a black braid over one shoulder. She looked healthy, despite the shadows beneath her eyes.

"It is not," he said, his voice trembling. "I promise you it is not."

She stared up at him, her eyes shining. Dom's breath caught and he realized she had the same look her father did as a young boy. Cortael wore the same wonderment when he learned a new twist of the sword, or felled his first deer.

Even as his heart swelled with happiness, it bled a little too.

Reluctantly, he looked up from Corayne to survey the rest of the great hall. What he found stole his breath away. He looked, not to the dais of Elder monarchs, all of them stoic and cold. But to the assembled council below.

Charlie stared back at him, eyes round as dinner plates. He gripped the back of his chair for support, his mouth open in shock.

There was Andry, unmistakable, and somehow taller than Dom remembered. He had a wolf pelt around his shoulders, looking more raider than squire. He stood with an ax in one hand, ready to defend Corayne at a second's notice. Dom expected nothing less.

The squire lowered his weapon with a sheepish grin, almost laughing.

Dom felt as if his legs might give out, but he kept his footing. Sorasa would certainly torture him if he made it all this way only to faint.

The assassin hung back, her usual mask donned to hide her own emotions. She stiffened as Corayne pulled her into a tight embrace, her head laid against the assassin's shoulder. Dom could not help but smirk, meeting her eye over Corayne's head. Sorasa simply glared back, exhaustion written all over her face. Gingerly, she extricated herself from Corayne's grip.

"That would be my broken rib," she said tightly, pressing a hand to her side. It was only half a joke.

Corayne's face fell. "Oh gods, Sorasa."

The Amhara waved her off before she could make a fuss.

"It's nothing," she muttered. "We have weathered worse."

Charlie approached them all with a smile, his arms crossed over his stomach. His eyes flicked over them both, examining Dom and Sorasa with his artist's eye.

"It certainly looks like it," he chuckled.

Sorasa staved him off with a piercing glare, before looking to Andry beside him. "Please do not hug me, either of you."

While Charlie only chuckled again, Andry gave a stilted sort of bow. Then he turned to Dom, his eyes the soft color of swirling tea. It felt like standing before a blazing hearth, safe and delightfully warm.

Grinning, Dom reached out an arm to the young man. Andry clasped it eagerly in return.

"We thought you were dead, my lord," he murmured.

"Squire Trelland," Dom said, giving his arm a shake. Then he dropped his voice. "Thank you for keeping her safe."

Andry's lips curved, halfway between a smile and something more forlorn.

"She kept herself safe," he answered. To that, Dom could only nod.

Then Andry's voice dropped again, near a whisper. "Where is Sigil?"

Corayne went grave, her face falling. Pain pulled at Andry, while even Charlie gave a little look of regret, his eyebrows knitting together.

Again, Sorasa waved a hand, the tattooed sun blazing on her palm.

"She's fine," the Amhara said to their relief. "Or she's safer than us, at least." Her copper eyes swept the room again, scanning the collected faces, mortal and immortal. "I assume the witch is well enough?"

"Somewhere in the castle," Andry offered, shrugging beneath an odd wolf pelt. "You know Valtik."

"Indeed," Sorasa spat back. "She's the only one I did not fear for."

Next to her, Corayne gave a sly grin. "Careful. You're showing that heart you try so hard to hide."

Sorasa's expression did not change, but pink spotted high on her bronze cheeks. Dom heard her teeth grind together, bone on bone.

"Good of you to join us, Amhara," one of the assembled council said, calling from their chair. After a moment, Dom realized it was Isadere, the Heir of Ibal.

Sneering, Sorasa inclined her head to both the Heir and their brother, the tempestuous Sibrez. Both huddled in thick furs, their noses red with cold.

"Good of you to finally listen," Sorasa snapped back at them. "Try not to freeze."

With a roll of her eyes, Corayne stepped in front of Sorasa, her jaw set.

"Tell us everything," she demanded.

Dom only loosed a weary sigh, the long road to Iona unfurling in his mind. He knew Sorasa shared the sentiment, her teeth bared as she forced a painful breath.

"In due time," he said. Tired as he was, there was still work to be done.

He faced the dais, the anger of many months eclipsing whatever joy he felt. From her throne, Isibel held his furious gaze, matching it with her own icy stare. It felt like a challenge, but Dom had faced far worse since the last time he challenged the throne of Iona.

"There is barely a guard on the city gates. I saw no archers on the walls, no trebuchets, no ballistas. No proper defense on Iona, or the castle. Not even *scouts* at the border, to watch the shores. Do you even have anyone guarding the mountain passes?" he ground out, spearing his aunt with accusation. *Treachery*, he wanted to scream. "Have you surrendered already, Isibel? Will you doom the realm with your own cowardice?"

Next to the throne, the noble Vedera stared on in shocked silence. He remembered Valnir from centuries past, the Sirandel lord red in the face. Lady Eyda remained stoic, with only a glint of satisfaction in her eye. Even Dyrian's bear woke to the sound of his booming voice, blinking sleepily at his master's side.

"It is good to see you alive, my beloved nephew," Isibel said slowly, as if commenting on the weather.

It only incensed Dom further.

"You did not even send for me, not once," he hissed, his face flushing with heat. "What I would have given for a spark of your light in that dungeon."

He expected her usual coldness. Instead, his aunt seemed to waver, her chest rising and falling beneath the folds of her gown. Rare emotion shimmered in her eyes.

Dom clenched his teeth, bracing himself for the icy touch of Isibel's magic. He knew the power of her sendings; she would weave through his head, whispering what she could not say aloud.

Instead, she spoke, her voice breaking. "I could not bear it, Domacridhan. I could not bear to send my magic forth, and find you a walking corpse."

Like Ridha, he knew, hearing the words she would not speak. He felt the pain of it in his own chest.

"Put down the branch, Isibel," he urged, gesturing to the ash branch across her knees. "You are at war whether you will it or not. There is nothing upon this realm that will save you from it."

"The Prince of Iona returns," she said, her voice thick with emotion. "And he speaks the truth. There is nothing in this realm that will save us from Taristan of Old Cor. Not now."

It felt like standing on the edge of a cliff. Dom took another step toward the dais, willing his aunt to see reason.

"Put down the branch," he said again, pleading. "Put down the branch and send word to every enclave. Ask for help. Give us a *chance*, my lady."

Her silence boiled his blood. Dom gnashed his teeth, biting back every harsh word he wanted to throw. Every horror he wanted to lay at Isibel's feet. Ridha. Cortael. Countless innocents across the Ward.

"You have an heir again, Isibel." Corayne's voice rang out behind him, high and clear and confident. It sounded like the voice of a queen. "You and your people have a future still."

It was as if something broke in Isibel of Iona. Her pearl-gray eyes turned stormy, her gaze lowered to her lap. And the branch of the ash tree.

Dom's heart thudded against his rib cage. His eyes never wavered from the branch, watching her white fingers among the leaves. They were silver with winter, but within bloomed the first green of spring.

With a great crack to shake the foundations of the castle, she snapped the branch in two. Dom felt the rush of old magic wash over him, rippling out from the throne to cover the room. It felt like lightning over his skin. Without thought, he fell to a knee, bowing his head.

Above them all, Isibel stood. She cast aside the pieces of the ash branch, letting them scatter across the steps up the dais.

"I lay down the branch," she said, the ancient words filled with meaning.

Dom shuddered. He had only heard such words once in his lifetime, an age ago, when the last dragon haunted the Ward.

At the corner of the room, an Ionian guard appeared from a doorway. His armor was ceremonial, gilding over steel, the antlers on his helm banded in gold and silver. He bore a sword across his open palms, the steel of it unsheathed, thick as Dom's own hand.

It was not a beautiful blade. There were no jewels in the hilt, no lovely script etched down the steel. The greatsword looked better suited to a butcher's shop. Dom went cold at the sight of the blade. This was a sword of Glorian, a veteran of battles older than the Ward itself.

Isibel took it with ease, holding the greatsword in one hand. With a twist of her wrist, she tested it in the air, the edge still singing.

"I take up the sword," she murmured. "I take up the sword."

Her eyes danced, some light moving in them, white behind the gray.

Dom swallowed hard, willing her voice to travel. Willing her magic to carry through every corner of the Ward.

Dom tried to picture it, her voice rousing the Monarchs to war.

In Tirakrion, Karias put down the vibrant hyacinth flower, and took up the spear.

In Salahae, Ramia let the palm fall, calling for her dagger.

In Barasa, Shan broke the ebony branch, and drew out the war hammer.

In Hizir, Asaro cast aside a clutch of juniper for the lance.

In Syrene, Empir dropped the gnarled cypress to uncurl his whip.

In Tarima, Gida scattered stalks of wheat to raise the scythe.

And in Ghishan, Anarim burned her jasmine to bring forth a swinging mace.

Though no battle had been won, it felt like a victory. Across the throne room, eyes lit with fresh determination. Andry and Corayne shone brightest of all, clasping arms like champions in a competition. Dom wanted to share in their celebration. Gods knew they deserved it. Instead, his gaze slid past them, to Sorasa hanging back, her face half in shadow. She was already staring, copper eyes fixed to his.

Her heart thumped, steady and slow. Constant.

In that instant, Dom understood why Sorasa hated hope so much. It looped around his throat, tight as a noose.

After so many days and weeks in dungeons and wilderness, a blade at his neck or free beneath the stars, it felt odd to sit surrounded, at a table laden with food, chairs filled, familiar voices chattering back and forth. Dom looked around at them, the Companions, gathered in the salon. Andry and Corayne sharing a spiced cake, both bent over a map of the mountains. Charlie kicked his feet up alongside them, savoring a glass of wine. Even Valtik sat in the corner, humming to herself. They were whole but for Sigil, and she was far from danger at least.

A sun shower pattered at the window, sending sparkling dots of light across the floor. It passed slowly, lingering over the castle. As Dom wished to linger in this moment, content to sit and listen, his fingers laced together as he leaned back in his cushioned chair. He spent many centuries in Tíarma, raised within the castle walls. Not once could he remember so much laughter in one room, not even with Ridha and Cortael.

It felt bittersweet, to remember. And, for a moment, to forget.

The others wove their tales together, Andry, Corayne, and Charlie. Through the Castlewood, to the frozen shores of the Jyd. All ending here in Iona. In return, Dom and Sorasa detailed their journey, piecing together all that befell them since Gidastern. The shortest version, at least. He did not mention how he panicked in the Sea Prince's villa, anchored only by Sorasa's sure hands. And Sorasa did not tell them how she screamed on the Calidonian beach, weeping when she thought herself finally alone.

She stood in the corner, somehow finding the shadows even in the brightly lit room. Garion perched next to her, muttering in a low voice. He was another Amhara, the one Charlie spoke of so many times. Dom quickly gathered he was not Amhara anymore either. They whispered of Lord Mercury, the Amhara Guild, of problems long behind them both.

"So every Spindle we closed, we took something back from him." Corayne grinned down at her map and brushed away a few crumbs, bolstered by their news. "He can be wounded by any one of us. He is mortal again, vulnerable?"

"But still dangerous," Sorasa interjected, looking up from her conversation. "As is Erida. You are to go nowhere without me or Dom, and never let the Spindleblade out of your sight."

A low current of anger rippled over Dom. Grimly, he nodded. "Taristan stole the sword from this castle once. He may try to do so again."

"I can understand how. I saw the vaults for myself," Corayne huffed. "You Elders don't believe in locks."

We Vedera have never had to, Dom thought bitterly. Then he raised an eyebrow.

"You went into the vaults?"

"Isibel took me," she replied, her eyes filled with meaning. And longing.

He knew the feeling well. Dom did not need to ask to know which vault she visited, or what relics she saw within. The remnants of Old Cor—and the remnants of her father, now left to gather dust.

The conversation ebbed away from more dire things, all of them loath to destroy their reunion with dark tidings. Dom fell silent, content to watch his friends as they smiled and talked, the candles gleaming brightly in their eyes. The fire crackled in the hearth and even Charlie threw off his furs, basking in the warmth. It thrummed against Dom's skin, holding him, until his eyes grew heavy, the voices around him distant, the patter of rain fading.

Sure fingers gripped his shoulder, sending a jolt down his arm. He started in his seat, looking up to see Sorasa standing over him. She surveyed him sharply, her brow furrowed with concern.

"You fell asleep," she said, half in disbelief.

Dom blinked and straightened, only to find the others staring at him.

"You must be exhausted, both of you," Corayne said, glancing between them. "You should rest, we have time to talk."

Time.

He saw the word break against Sorasa, as he felt it break against himself. She eyed him again, speaking without words. Dom heard her as easily as he heard her heartbeat. Her face was not so difficult to read anymore. Her tells were there. The pull at the corner of her mouth, the thrum of a vein in her neck, fluttering beneath the tattooed image of a snake.

Corayne studied them both, her scrutiny sharp as ever. Slowly, she stood, all cheer draining from her face.

"We have time, don't we?" she asked gently.

Next to her, Andry wore a grave look. "It will take weeks for Erida to rally her full strength at Rouleine. And weeks more to march them across the mountains here." He spoke firmly, but with desperation. Not confidence.

"That is all true," Sorasa said, matter-of-fact. "We have three weeks from the moment the army leaves Rouleine. Three weeks. *Maybe.*"

The warm air seemed sucked from the room, the sun fading behind a cloud, leaving only gray rain to spatter the windows.

In the back of his mind, Dom wished Sorasa had let him sleep, and enjoy his peace a little bit longer. Instead, he stood from his chair, too awake now to bother. He wished for a bath, for a cold walk in the rain, for a spar in the training yard. For something to distract him.

He caught Corayne's eye instead.

"Come with me," he said, gesturing to the door.

She was eager to follow.

Corayne walked with the Spindleblade sheathed across her back. It looked uncomfortable but Dom knew she was well accustomed to the sword by now. He glared at it as they navigated the castle, noting the small imperfections and differences from the blade broken in Gidastern.

"I hate it too," Corayne muttered, returning his gaze. "The hilt is wrong. The grip." She reached up to touch the hilt. "It wore to his hand first."

"We will take it to the armorer in the morning, and see what she can do to change that," he rumbled, wrenching his eyes away. He could not help but remember all the lives the sword claimed, Cortael's among them.

He could still hear the sound of steel shearing through armor, and then flesh.

Domacridhan did not enjoy the vaults below the castle. The spiraling passages, drilled down into the rock, had frightened him as a youth. They unsettled him now, the air too close and stale, as if the full weight of Tíarma pressed down on top of them. Even he did not know how deep they ran. Perhaps to the roots of the world itself.

He eyed the doors of each vault, some of them cracked ajar, some of them undisturbed for centuries. Treasure and useless cast-offs in each. Then he stopped short before a familiar door, blowing out a pained breath. He stared at the wood as if he could see through it, to the small room on the other side.

Corayne halted beside him, puzzled.

"The Cor vaults are deeper," she said, pointing down into the bowels of the rock. "My father's things—"

"Your father's memory is not in jeweled armor," Dom bit out.

His palm lay flat against the wood, pale skin sharp in contrast to the black ebony. It swung open below his hand, yawning onto darkness, the only light spilling inward from the passage.

He did not hesitate, stepping into the shadows. His Vederan eyes did not need much light to see by, but he lit a few candles for Corayne's benefit, illuminating the chamber.

She lingered in the doorway, staring at the stone floor. As if she could not bear it.

Dom shared the feeling. He forced himself to look anyway.

He knew what it felt like to be stabbed, burned, chained in darkness, drowned, and smothered. He knew what it was to look death in the eye.

Life was worse.

Cortael's entire life sprawled around them, written in the objects left behind. Training swords, blunted, short as Dom's forearm, too small for a man but perfectly sized for a mortal boy. Stacks of parchment, letters painstakingly written, Paramount translated into High Vederan and back again.

Cortael once practiced their language more than anything, even his swordsmanship, so dedicated was he to learning the tongue of the immortals he lived beside. He spoke it better than Dom ever thought he could, his pronunciation near perfect by the end.

The memory made his throat tighten, and he tore his gaze away, to the other shelves laden with clothes. Breeches, tunics, cloaks, and jerkins. Some sized for a child, others for a man full grown. All of it lay folded neatly in shelves and in trunks, never to see the light of day again.

"There is no dust," Corayne said in a hushed voice. Slowly, her eyes shining, she stepped into the vault.

"These chambers are well tended," Dom replied hoarsely. He ran a hand over a wooden horse, whittled to smooth perfection. It was missing a leg, snapped clean off.

"I remember when he broke this," he muttered, picking up the toy. His finger traced the rough edge of broken wood. "Not two days after I finished making it for him."

Corayne drew closer, her breath ragged. She stared at the horse but would not touch it.

"What was he like?" she breathed. "As a boy?"

"Wild," Dom said, without hesitation. "Wild and curious."

"And as a man?"

"Noble. Grave. Proud." His voice broke. "And haunted too. By what he could never be."

Her face collapsed, the corners of her mouth dragging down as her eyes squeezed shut, a single sob escaping her lips.

This time, when Dom embraced her, he squeezed a little tighter. Just enough to let her stifle her tears and draw a little strength from whatever he could give.

"He would have been so proud of you," Dom said, pulling back to look at her fully.

Corayne looked back up in disbelief, her eyes swimming. The candlelight wavered on her face, sharpening the lines of her cheeks and nose. What little she carried of her mother faded in the soft light, until Cortael stared out from her black eyes.

Then she shook her head and went back to the clothes. "Who knows what he would have thought of me," she said roughly.

Her hands roved over the folded clothes, until they pulled out an old cape from years long past. The fabric was red and dusty, but well made. When she held it up to herself, the hem barely reached the floor, just her size.

"This was his," she said, smoothing the soft scarlet. Roses bloomed along the edges, the thread still gleaming. "When he was young."

I wish he could have met you, Dom thought, his heart bleeding. *I wish he could have known you as I do.*

"I am proud of you too," he added, though he thought it too obvious to have to say.

This time, Corayne beamed, smiling through still rolling tears. Hastily, she wiped at her face and draped the cape over her arm.

"I have come far indeed from that girl on the steps of a cottage," she said, laughing at herself.

Dom gave her a stern look.

"I am not proud of what you've done already, Corayne," he said quickly. "But what you choose to do. You are braver than any one of us. Without you—" He faltered, weighing his words carefully. "If you turned and ran, so would we. All of us."

Her face fell again, and Dom winced. *I have said the wrong thing. Curse my Vederan manner,* he thought angrily.

But she did not cry again. Instead, her expression tightened, her thin lips pressing to nothing. She looked up at him through dark lashes, her tears disappearing.

"I think your monarch still plans to," she hissed, so low even Dom could barely hear her.

He staggered back, head tipped in confusion.

"Isibel would not flee from Iona," he whispered fiercely. "She is a coward, but she has nowhere to turn. She will fight because she must, and that will be enough."

But Corayne was unconvinced.

"She does have somewhere to flee, Dom," she shot back at him, teeth bared in frustration. "She may not know it yet, but—"

Her voice rose too high and she stopped herself, glancing back to the open doorway. Dom read the worry on her face plain as daylight.

"There is no one anywhere near us," he said softly, listening for a heartbeat. There was only his own and Corayne's, both pulsing quicker and quicker.

Her throat bobbed as she swallowed. Then nodded.

"I can feel a Spindle, here in Iona. Not fully, but there is *something*."

Dom felt his jaw drop, his confusion giving way to pure shock. And then disbelief, as much as he wanted to trust in Corayne.

She grabbed for his hand, holding it in her own, all but begging. "I know it in my bones, Dom."

He could only blink, feeling the vault spin around him. "Cortael would have felt one, certainly."

Corayne shook her head. "Spindles move, don't they? Over years and years." She did not let go of his hand, squeezing his fingers so tightly Dom feared for her bones. "Perhaps one is shifting here, returning to the place where your kind first came."

The possibility was too grave to consider. It made him sick at heart.

"Isibel would not dare," he murmured, shaking his head. "Another Spindle torn might break the realm in two."

We are already on the edge of a cliff, and Gidastern still burns open, inching us closer to ruin with every passing second. His heart thudded, louder and faster.

Corayne gave him a sad look, her eyes welling up with . . .

Pity, he realized.

"She only cares for one realm, Dom," she whispered. "And it isn't this one."

Glorian.

The vault spun again, and the world with it.

He gripped her hand back, careful not to break anything.

"Who else have you told this?" he hissed, dipping his head closer.

Corayne stared up at him, brow drawn and black eyes wide. "Just us. Our own."

His relief was short-lived. Again, he felt the weight of the castle bearing down, along with the rest of the realm.

"Let us keep it that way."

35

BLINDED
Erida

Her breath spiraled in the cold, like smoke against the breaking dawn.

Frost clung to the tents, the carts and wagons, the horses, and even the sentries at their posts, waiting for the change in the guard. They stood against snowbanks piled higher than their spears, hastily cleared by the engineers and laborers. The workmen slowed the passage of the cavalry, but they widened the pass, cutting through the snow, until even the packed trebuchets might lumber through.

Erida did not feel the cold as she used to. Fire burned in her flesh, warming her better than any fur. While the others shivered, she kept still, frozen as the mountains around them. She felt like a mountain herself, her head raised above all others.

While her soldiers began the work of breaking down the camp, Erida remained still, alone but for the demon inside. She stood at the pinnacle of the mountain pass, the slope falling away on either side of her.

The west lay behind, back to the foothills and her own kingdoms, where spring already bloomed. Erida faced east, into the long valley on the far side of the Monadhrion. Gray fog carpeted the land below, obscuring the valley floor. The Queen thought little of it. They would cross the valley without issue, cutting through the heart of Calidon to the next mountain range.

It was the Monadhrian she stared at, the ragged peaks many miles away, silhouetted against the pink dawn. They stood on the far side of the valley, like islands poking up out of the gray-cloud sea. The last obstacle between her army and Iona. Between Taristan and Corayne.

Between Erida and empire.

What Waits glowered beneath it all, tugging at her skirts. She shared the sentiment. But some things were beyond even the Queen of Galland. Erida could not force the army to move any faster than it did already. She could not melt the snows or level the mountains, no matter how hard she tried.

Shouts echoed through the pass, and boots crunched through the snow. Horses and oxen lumbered awake, snorting against their rope paddocks. Erida gave a sigh of her own, and turned away, following her own footsteps back through the snow.

She wore fur-lined boots and a thick cloak over quilted wool, dressed more like a maid than a queen. But there was no call for finery in the mountains, not even among her lords who still clung to their overwrought armor and patterned silk. Erida's manner was crown enough.

His red cloak over one shoulder, Taristan waited at the tent flap, his eyes glassy with sleep. But he already had a sword belted at his hip, his traveling clothes donned. Like Erida, he was eager to be gone and back on the march.

"You should not wander," he said gruffly.

Erida gave a shrug. She eyed the clear sky overhead, fading from soft purple to more vibrant pink. There was not even a cloud to threaten snow.

"We have been lucky. A blizzard would have closed the pass to us or stranded us up here." Her lips curled. "A blessing."

"You should not wander," Taristan said again, his voice sharper.

"I am surrounded by knights at all times, not to mention an army of thousands who would die for me if given the chance," she answered, shaking her head.

Some already have, she thought, thinking of the men who froze in their tents or slipped on the climb, falling to the rocks below. It had been weeks since they left Rouleine, and Erida demanded a grueling pace from her army. No matter the cost.

"And I have you," she added, taking her consort by the arm.

Taristan shifted. "The closer we get to Iona, the more careful we must be. All it takes is one arrow from an Elder bow," he said, pointing a finger to her chest, directly over her heart.

With a soft smile, Erida wrapped her hand around his own. "Now you choose to fear for me," she said, amused. "We've come too far for that."

"I fear for you always," he muttered, as if admitting a crime. "Always, Erida."

Her grin widened, her grip on his hand going tight.

Then a wind buffeted the tent, strong and sudden, like a howling gale. Erida tucked against Taristan, his cloak billowing around them in a scarlet curtain. Across the camp, her soldiers braced, tents and flags flapping against the gust.

The high mountains were no stranger to rough winds. But Erida furrowed her brow, tensing against the wall of Taristan's body.

The wind was oddly warmed. And it smelled of . . .

"Smoke?" Erida said aloud, her face drawn in confusion.

Above her, the blood drained from Taristan's face, leaving him pale as a ghost. His arms tightened around her, all but crushing her into his embrace.

"What is it?" she snapped, pushing against him, her heartbeat quickening.

Something like a drum boomed in the sky, deep and shuddering. The air quivered with the sound, and another gust of wind blew. This time, the soldiers of Erida's army threw themselves to the ground, some of them screaming. Some of them going for their weapons. Some of them sprinting down the pass in either direction, scattering like mice fleeing a cat.

Taristan cursed above her, low in his throat, the sound reverberating in her core. She glanced up through the cage of his arms, watching as a shadow crossed the camp.

A shadow cast by a cloudless sky.

She wanted to be afraid. All reason told her to be afraid. Instead she felt only grim satisfaction, welling up from a mind that was not her own.

The dragon was too big for her mind to comprehend, a storm cloud over the mountain peaks. It shot through the cold air like a bird of prey, steam rising from its scales. It had bat-like wings and four legs folded against its massive body, claws as big as wagon wheels. The rising sun flashed ruby and jet against its back, its bejeweled hide reflecting the light.

It landed against the mountain peak above the pass, dislodging rocks and snow to rain down on the camp. The beast seemed as large as the mountain itself, its tail curling around jagged stone. Her men continued to run, yelping and shouting, crying out to the gods in their desperation.

Erida knew only one god, and He laughed within her, delighted by their fear.

The dragon gave a roar into the heavens, arching its serpentine neck, jaws gaping wide. The sound threatened to split the mountains in two.

Embers glowed at the back of its throat, waves of heat rippling from its mouth.

Something dragged at her legs, begging her to move. Without thought, Erida obeyed, extricating herself from Taristan's arms. He shouted after her, but she ignored him, sweeping across the camp to face the dragon head on.

He is not afraid, so I have nothing to fear, she thought, her heart singing.

The dragon's wings splayed wide, the points hooked with smaller claws, the membrane thin between the joints. At close range, Erida could see scars and arrow holes, the edge of its wings ripped and torn.

As her husband wore the battle of Gidastern on his skin, so did the dragon.

It fixed on her with a single eye, the pupil swirling with red and gold, like the heart of a flame. Erida could not help but smile.

She recognized those eyes.

She saw them in her husband.

She felt them in herself.

Painfully slow, the dragon took a step down the slope, and then another, climbing down into the pass. The rocks shuddered beneath it, threatening to shake apart the mountainside.

Erida held her ground, even as every instinct told her to run. Not that she trusted her own instincts much anymore.

Her soldiers kept up their retreat, the Lionguard shouting for her to run. Only Taristan dared follow, charging across the snow.

She felt him at her side, blazing with heat, his own eyes awash with consuming flame.

Then the dragon lowered its head to them both, jaws closed, its belly scraping along the ground. The snow hissed beneath it, melting on contact, filling the pass with a boiling heat and a curtain of steam.

Grinning, a figure all in red slid from its back, his white face like a ghastly moon.

And his eyes, his horrible eyes.

Erida stopped short, almost slipping in the snow. A wave of revulsion passed over her, the image of the wizard wavering before her as her head spun.

She'd hated his eyes before, so watery and pale, always rimmed with red, as if he'd spent the last hours crying. Bloodshot like no eyes she had ever seen in her life.

To her horror, Erida found herself missing such eyes.

Two sunken holes were all that remained now, the lids bruised and crusted with blood, the sockets sunken. White veins and black webbed over his face, mottling his skin in a terrible mask. The wizard wavered, shaky over the snow, one hand cast out to catch himself lest he fall. The other still clutched his cane, using it to feel his way forward.

"Ronin," Erida whispered, falling to her knees.

Behind her, she heard Taristan suck in a hissing breath.

"The price," he murmured, his boots crunching in the snow.

Somehow, Ronin managed to sneer despite his injury. His pride remained.

"It is done," he said, laughing to himself, following the sound of their voices "It is—"

The red wizard faltered, craning his neck. Erida felt sick again as his head turned, his sightless eyes somehow finding her on the ground. His lips moved, soundless.

Ronin went paler, white as the snow. Slowly, he sank to a knee, reverent as she had never seen him. He bowed his head, red cloak spilling around him like fresh blood.

"It is done," he said again, and Erida knew he did not mean the dragon.

She could not help but feel a grim sense of satisfaction. She understood what he sensed in her, what he saw without seeing.

"My queen," he murmured, raising his palms to them both. "My king."

"First an army of corpses, then a dragon."

Behind her veil, Erida rolled her stinging eyes at one of her lords.

The gaps in the council table were still painfully apparent, the seats of executed lords left empty. Erida wished the other nobles would fill them in, for her own sake. It felt like an attempt at punishment, to make her stare at what she did.

What I did justly, she reminded herself from the head of the table. Taristan glowered beside her, near to smoldering. *Every lord who died with Konegin deserved it. They were traitors, all of them.*

One of the surviving lords stared at her from halfway down the table, his fleshy face folded up with worry. He was a weak man, with no chin.

"A *dragon*," he exclaimed, repeating himself.

"Thank you for the astute observation, Lord Bullen," Erida bit out, her voice acid. "What is your point?"

To her left, Lord Thornwall pursed his lips, but said nothing. Lord Bullen did the same, lowering his eyes.

Ronin tittered into his hand, laughing openly at the noble coward. Once, Erida might have stopped him. Instead, she let him laugh; his mutilated appearance set the entire council on edge, most of them refusing to even look at the twisted little wizard.

"We are the glory of Old Cor reborn. There is no denying our victory, our conquest, is the will of the gods," Erida said to the table, pointing down the long line of chairs to the open tent flap. "Tell me that is not proof of it. A lethal army. A *dragon*."

She kept her hand raised, careful to use her wounded hand. It was still bandaged, the gash beneath never quite healing. Her lords did not miss it, a symbol of their queen's own sacrifice.

"There is no kingdom that can stand against us now," Erida said, rising from her seat. Every eye followed her movements, even Ronin's unseeing stare. "Not even the Temurijon. Not even the Emperor and his Countless."

Silence spread down the council table, punctuated only by the whistle of wind sweeping through the foothills. The camp echoed like an empty graveyard, her soldiers exhausted by the climb down the pass, and the fear of a dragon overhead.

Thornwall leaned back in his chair.

"I've had reports, Your Majesty," he said, his lips twisting.

"Reports?" she spat back at him, mocking his grave tone.

Down the table, a few nobles flinched, but her commander did not.

"Reports," Thornwall said again, sharpening each letter. "The Temurijon on the move. The Countless crossed the mountains, perhaps months ago."

In her head, Erida loosed a string of curses, and What Waits cursed with her. She warred against the urge to run from the tent, holding herself steady as her own lords sputtered and complained.

"Crossing the mountains?" "This is war!" "Ascal is undefended!"

"If they march across Galland, they will cut a line of destruction across our entire kingdom," one of her lords said. "They could raze Ascal before we even make it back to our own borders."

Thornwall looked grim and worn, his face going gray. "We do not know their aim. There's word of an armada with them, to ferry the Countless by sea."

Too many voices wound together, almost drowning out Erida's thoughts in her own head. She leaned heavily, a hand to her brow, willing them to be silent and *obey*.

If the Temur take Ascal, I will simply take it back, she thought, laughing at the prospect. *The Emperor does not know my wrath, nor my power.*

"Send word to Lenava," Thornwall urged. "Demand the King of Calidon kneel or be destroyed."

Erida stared at him, his face softened by her veils and a haze of candlelight. Quickly, she weighed her options in her mind.

"Fine, send what letters you must," she finally muttered, twisting her hand.

One of the lords made a scoffing sound, his eyes wide. "Then we—turn around. March back to Ascal and ram through the Countless ourselves."

Whispers rippled down the table, rare smiles loosed on pale faces. Erida scowled at them.

"Hardly," she snapped. "Our battle is with Iona."

Thornwall squinted at her side, his own confusion palpable. "The Elder enclave?"

Erida's head thumped, a dull ache beginning in her temples. Dimly, she wished she had left her lords in the mountains and let them freeze to death.

"Dragons and Elders, what madness is this?" One of them mumbled, hissing under his breath.

Taristan speared him with a glare.

"Madness, my lord?" he snarled, and the whispers dropped. "Are you accusing the Queen of something?"

"Never," the lord stammered back, terrified. "It is only—yours is a mortal empire. We have no cause to bother with immortals, hidden in their ancient holes. Few as they are. Inconsequential to the rest of us. Especially not while our grand city hangs in the balance. The jewel in *your* crown."

With a smack, Erida slammed her bandaged hand down on the flat of the table. The sound rang through the tent, the pain of it shooting up her arm like a spike. A low groan escaped her lips. Around the table, her lords winced, cowed into silence again.

"Yes. *My* crown."

Shaking, Erida raised her fist again, her meaning clear.

"The Elders of Iona sent assassins against me," she said, holding up her bandages for all to see. Her teeth bared behind her veil, gleaming. "They destroyed my palace, they set fire to Ascal. Make no mistake, they are behind every opposition to my reign. And to *our* victory. We must destroy them at the root, lest they continue to destroy what we seek to build."

She looked at each of her lords in turn, weighing their measure. They stared back at her, grim or fearful, determined or resigned to her rule. None would dare speak, nor stand.

And that was enough.

"We march on, my lords," she said, rolling her shoulders back. "To glory."

36

ON THE MATTER OF SMALL THINGS
Charlon

A storm broke after midnight, drenching Iona in a downpour. Charlie woke fitfully from an already fading dream. He tried to grasp it as the rain hammered the window, and the wind howled. But the dream slipped away, leaving only hazy echoes. The shadow of a dragon on snow. The smell of death through the cavernous castle halls. He shivered and turned to look at Garion asleep next to him.

The assassin's eyes flew open, alert in an instant.

But Charlie waved him back down.

"It's fine," he said, swinging out of their bed. "Just a nightmare."

After donning a thick robe and rabbit-fur slippers, he padded out into the hall. Charlie did not fear the Elder castle, nor the guards placed around its passages. He was a mortal, and one of the useless ones at that. Even their enemies hardly paid him any mind.

Hearths burned in the grander chambers, while candles lit the halls, creating islands of light in the darkness. The rain continued its onslaught, louder in the public corridors, where the windows remained open, without shutters or glass to keep out the elements.

Pulling his robe tighter, Charlie cursed the Elders and their too-high tolerance for discomfort.

"Good evening."

A voice echoed down the passage, from one of the open galleries. Despite his shivering, Charlie walked toward it, careful to avoid the puddles of rainwater pooling on the stone floor.

He stepped out onto the long balcony, looking out over the Elder enclave. Even in the rain, he could see the dark silhouettes of catapults in the streets, and slings fixed to the city walls.

Isadere of Ibal stared from one of the arches, wrapped in a coat of golden fur. They eyed him over their collar, their curling black hair pulled back into a neat tail.

"Looking for an altar, Priest?" they said, smirking behind the furs.

Charlie sneered in reply. "Looking for a mirror?"

They gave a soft flick of their hand. "It is in my chambers."

Of course, Charlie thought bitterly.

"See anything interesting lately?" he needled.

"Only shadows and darkness. Lasreen shows me less and less every day." A muscle ticced in Isadere's cheek, their eyes narrowing. "The closer I came to this place, the more distant she has been."

Charlie scoffed. "Convenient."

"Much as you try to hide it, you are a believer, Charlon Armont," Isadere bit back, fixing him with a black glare.

"In some things," he answered with a shrug. "In some people, too."

Their expression loosened, if only a little. "I must admit, I was surprised to find *you* waiting for my army in Lenava."

In spite of himself, Charlie gave a half smile. "I was surprised you showed up at all."

Isadere did not return the favor. "For a man of faith, you have very little of it."

"Me? Oh, I have buckets of faith." His smile widened, pleased to incense the Heir. "I just put it where it should be."

Beyond the city ridge, lightning veined through the storm clouds, purple white. It illuminated them both for a moment, their shadows flashing against the castle walls.

"In Corayne?" Isadere murmured after the crack of thunder subsided.

"She is the only hope the realm has," he said plainly. "So I'd be foolish not to."

The simple logic took Isadere off guard, then they frowned. "I see your point," they said. "I suppose I feel the same."

They lapsed into silence, watching the storm roll down the valley, the lightning shifting farther and farther away. It crackled and roared, a force like no other.

"Do you think the gods are watching?" he breathed. Charlie watched the sky with wide eyes, not daring to blink lest he miss another flash in the clouds.

He expected some blustering speech about the goddess Lasreen, her infallibility, her presence in all things. And perhaps an accusation of blasphemy to round things out.

Instead, Isadere whispered, "I don't know."

Charlie tore his eyes from the storm, incredulous.

"How could they look away?" he asked, his voice rising with his frustration. "If this is to be the end of Allward?"

Isadere only stared back at him, their confusion all the more irritating. Charlie bit hard, teeth grinding, even as he cursed the gods in every language he knew.

"How can they remain silent?" he hissed, balling a fist at his side.

How can they let this happen? If they are real—how can they let us fall?

"I don't know," Isadere said again. To his surprise, they took him by the shoulder. Their touch was surprisingly gentle, and kind. "Perhaps you should take a little of your faith and give it to the gods."

Charlie scowled, thinking of churches and altars, stained glass, coins in the offering plates. Ink on parchment, chanted prayers. Scripture. And silence. Never an answer. Not even a whisper or the lightest touch.

"I will when they earn it," he muttered, angrier than he knew himself to be.

Isadere's fingers tightened.

"Then it is not faith anymore," they said.

A warm flush washed over his cheeks. Charlie chewed his lip, reluctant to give the Heir an inch. As politely as he could, Charlie extricated himself from the Heir's grasp.

"I see your point," he finally ground out, echoing their words a moment before. "We are not warriors, you and I," he added, eyeing the Heir's fine furs and their smooth, soft hands.

The Heir made a low sound, barely cousin to a laugh. "And yet we find ourselves in the middle of the greatest war this realm has ever seen. It must be for something, shouldn't it?"

"I must think so," Charlie answered. "I must think there is some reason for me to still be here. That there is something yet I can do, small as it may be."

"Or perhaps it is done already, our parts played," the Heir said serenely, their eyes going back to the landscape and the distant lightning.

Charlie followed their gaze. The sky took on a purple tinge as night wore slowly toward dawn. The first rays of sun would not appear for hours, if they broke through the clouds at all.

"The mirror truly showed you nothing?" he murmured, incredulous.

Isadere sighed low, showing a rare glimpse of their frustration.

"I did not say it showed me nothing," they replied. "I said it showed me shadows and darkness." Something flickered in their gaze, their dark brows knitting together with concern. "And deep places, spiraling downward through blackness. And at the bottom, a dim red light."

The image made Charlie shiver.

"What else?" he breathed.

Next to him, Isadere's breath caught.

"I could not— I did not want to look," they said, ashamed. "Something in me knew not to press further, lest I fall into something I could not escape."

Charlie swallowed hard around a lump in his throat, his chest suddenly tight.

"What Waits hangs heavy over us all, it seems," the Heir added, shaking their head.

"And heaviest on Corayne." Charlie shrugged beneath his furs, cursing the realm. "It isn't fair."

Isadere of Ibal, born royal and holy, gave him a withering, almost pitying look.

"When have you ever known the world to be fair, Priest?"

"True" was all he could muster, watching the last rolls of thunder, and the wretched lightning.

In the following days, the first roses in the grand courtyard began to bloom, bloodred buds peeking out from green vines.

Charlie sat among them, breathing in the sweet scent of fresh flowers and air after rain. He relished the rare sunlight, beaming directly down into the garden. The walls of Tíarma would cast shadows soon enough, but Charlie lingered, enjoying what seconds of warmth he could. As the rest of the castle and city buzzed in preparation, silence ruled here. They could not hear the hammers on wood, nor the roll of endless wagons traveling up and down the ridge of Iona. There were only the roses, and the sky.

Next to him, Garion sprawled out on one of their jealously hoarded blankets, his eyes heavy-lidded. He clutched a half-eaten apple in one hand, the last of the fall harvest. He watched the clouds race overhead.

"I'm surprised you aren't down in the training yard with the rest of them," Charlie said, quirking a pleased smile at the assassin.

Indeed, Sorasa spent most of her days near the castle barracks, drilling Corayne for hours on end, with Dom and Andry watching over them both. They fell back into their rhythm so quickly, it was as if the months apart never existed. Corayne and her loyal bodyguard, the squire of Galland. Domacridhan and the surly assassin snapping at his heels.

Though she doesn't snap at him quite so often these days, Charlie thought with a smirk.

Garion angled his head, meeting Charlie's gaze. His dark mahogany curls splayed out against the blanket.

"Corayne has enough nannies," he said with a sigh. Wordlessly, he passed the apple to Charlie, who finished it off. "I have my own charge to mind."

"I assure you, I can manage," Charlie replied, tossing the apple core away.

"I disagree." Garion straightened up to face him fully, his eyes narrowed in concentration. "Besides, I have wasted our time enough. I won't waste any more."

Guilt twisted in Charlie's stomach.

"Garion—" he began, but the other man cut him off with a sharp look.

"I regret it, Charlie," he said fervently, an admission as much as a prayer. "I regret the choice I made. Let me at least apologize for it."

For many long days, Charlie imagined hearing the same words from the same mouth. He dreamed of them night and day, at his desk in his basement workshop, or curled up in his musty bed. In his imagination, he would feel triumph, if not vindication. Instead, he felt hollow, almost ashamed.

The words were not worth the pain on Garion's face, nor the regret they both carried.

"Amhara are not supposed to form attachment to anyone or anything but the Guild. It creates weakness, confusion—" Garion's voice broke, his head shaking. "Our loyalty belongs to one person, only. Ever."

Lord Mercury, Charlie thought, imagining the shadow of the Amhara leader. He did not know what he looked like, but Garion and Sorasa's fear painted the picture well enough.

"I suppose that is still true," Garion muttered, his frown fading. "My loyalty lies in one place still."

Warmth burst in Charlie's chest, a balm to the stinging agony. Charlie reached across the inches between them, putting a hand to Garion's neck.

"I was a coward too," the priest said. "Hiding behind the walls of a backwater, too afraid to step out into the world."

Garion gave him a look. "For good reason."

A dozen bounties on my head, Charlie thought, counting off his charges. *And one very large, very capable Temur woman who intended to collect.*

"I imprisoned myself in Adira to save my own skin," he said aloud, his face going hot. "I could have left for yours. I could have followed—"

"Enough," Garion snapped, all but rolling his eyes. Swiftly, he gripped Charlie's neck, mirroring his stance. "I am sorry, my love. Accept it, please."

Grinning, Charlie leaned forward to kiss him soundly on the lips. "Oh, very well," he said, grinning. "Besides, Mercury would have killed you if you abandoned the Guild."

Shrugging, Garion rolled his neck. "I suppose I could've gotten myself exiled like Sorasa."

"True."

"Though she always was his favorite," he added ruefully. Envy flickered in his eyes, even now. "He would have killed the rest of us for disobedience. But not her."

For many years, Charlie had hated Lord Mercury. That hatred only deepened, seeing how perfectly he laid his hooks in people like Garion and Sorasa. Alone, but for the Guild. Easily manipulated, weapons made to be controlled. And cast off.

"Whatever path we walked before, we're here now," Charlie sighed, pushing a curl out of Garion's eyes.

"We're here now," Garion echoed. "Here being the end of the world."

The fugitive priest tsked, clicking his tongue. "The *potential* end of the world."

"Fine." He lay back again, splayed out against the blanket. But for the Amhara dagger at his belt, he looked like a poet, contemplating the heavens. "Not that I understand the Spindle talk anyways. Other realms and demon lords. Corblood princes. Magical swords. Quite the mess you've put us in."

With another tsk, Charlie settled down next to him, tucking himself tight against the assassin.

"If you recall, I was dragged into this against my will," he muttered.

Garion glanced at him sidelong, eyes sharp. "And you chose to stay in it."

"I did," Charlie replied, thoughtful. As much for himself as for Garion. His voice softened. "I chose to do something with myself, if only something small."

He expected Garion to laugh at him. Instead, the man held his gaze, his dark eyes melting. Their fingers brushed, then wove together.

"Small things matter too," Garion muttered, looking back to the sky.

Charlie did not, memorizing instead the lines of Garion's face and the feel of the sun on their joined hands. The smell of roses, and more rain, not yet fallen, but soon to come.

"Yes, indeed."

37

WITH ME
Andry

Squires did not only tend to their knights, but learned how to be knights themselves. How to act, how to speak, swing a sword, tend armor, groom horses, set up camp. The geography of the land they were bound to protect, as they would be oathed to serve its ruler. Their education came not only in the training yard or by the campfire, but in the classroom as well. Before Andry set out into the realm, he learned the land from books and scholars.

And he learned its history too.

Old Cor and the empire. Galland's humble beginnings and its bloody rise, the borders expanding with every new conquest. He studied battle in all its forms, from minor skirmishes to thunderous wars. Ambushes, false retreats, pincer movements, cavalry charges. Sieges.

It is a siege we will face, he knew, terrified of the prospect already. *No matter what happens on the field, they will encircle us eventually. And grind us down, day after day.*

Andry Trelland walked the walls of Iona every morning, studying the city as he would a map. He learned where the wall was thickest—*at the bottom of the ridge, around the gates*—and how far the top of that ridge jutted out above the valley floor—*more than four hundred feet down over the cliffs, higher still from the top of the walls.* He thought of how much grain the castle vaults could hold, and how deep the wells beneath the city ran. Which bits of stone would best suit the catapults. What provisions a mortal army would need—and how much longer an immortal army could hold out, after the mortals starved to death.

He looked at Iona from all angles, as a defender and an attacker. As a son of Galland, raised to fight for the lion. And as a traitor, set to defeat the legions at all cost.

It made him sick at heart, but still he walked the walls.

And he was not the only one. Corayne often joined him after her training, along with the two Amhara. Isadere and their lieutenants frowned at the landscape. The eagle knights of Kasa were friendly, but despaired of the ridge city. Andry understood. It felt like standing on a rock in the ocean, watching a tidal wave on the horizon. The Elders were more distant, silently carrying out the orders of their monarchs. The Sirandels in their purple armor, the Elders of Kovalinn in chain mail. The Ionians favored their green cloaks and steel plate.

Andry thought of Ghald, chaotic in its preparation for war. Iona was the same, like a tick swelled up with blood. Ready to burst.

Worst of all things was the sky.

The rain passed, leaving white clouds across the empty blue. But every morning, the sun rose a bit redder, a bit weaker. A haze settled over the valley, threatening to choke them all. It felt like looking at the sun through smoke, or the shimmering air of high summer in a sweltering city.

Andry watched as dawn crept over the eastern mountains, the Monadhstoirm like a wall.

"It looked like this in Ascal."

Dom towered beside him, frowning at the sky.

Despite his Elder nature, Dom looked terrible. Even washed, his hair freshly combed and braided, his blond beard trimmed, a new cloak over his shoulder, and fine leather armor beneath, he wore exhaustion plainly, his face drawn, his complexion gray, the green spark gone from his eyes.

While the Monarch of Iona remained deep in her halls, unseen by the rest of the city, Dom took up the mantle of leadership she cast aside. He was as Andry first remembered him to be. Duty-bound, stoic, and distant.

Like Andry, he walked the walls, both a guardian and a ghost.

"They are close," Dom murmured.

"Good that the Sirandels arrived yesterday," Andry said, thinking of the grand procession of Elders. Another hundred of them entered the city gates, together with wagons loaded with food and weaponry. "Will other enclaves send help?"

The Sirandels were not the only immortals joining Iona. A small force had arrived from Tirakrion a week prior, tiny in number, but better than nothing. They were golden-skinned, bronzed by centuries on their island, hidden among the warm waters of the Long Sea. Though they were more suited to sailing, they were warriors all.

"I cannot say. Many of my people are half the realm away. And even immortals cannot fly," Dom answered. Then he cursed under his breath.

Andry well knew the object of Dom's frustration. "It is not your fault."

The Elder ignored him. "If I had come sooner—if I was here, I could have swayed Isibel. There would have been more time. We could have rallied the realm, all the enclaves—"

"You escaped the dungeons of Ascal," Andry said forcefully, cutting him off. He put a hand to the Elder's broad shoulder. "You survived to be here, now. That is enough, Dom."

"It must be enough," Dom murmured, his green eyes still murky with frustration.

Much as he shared the sentiment, Andry knew they could not dwell on what they could not change. He turned back to the landscape, his jaw tightening.

"Is the ditch finished?" he asked, changing the subject. "And the stakes?"

"As much as will be," Dom replied.

Andry clenched his jaw. The Elders had made quick work of digging out a long ditch on either side of the city ridge, with sharpened tree trunks jutting out. It would force Erida's army to funnel, reducing their advantage in the assault on the city gates. But it was too late to dig around the entire city, leaving the higher cliffs vulnerable.

"Ten thousand soldiers of Ibal and Kasa. Cavalry, infantry, archers, *elephants*," Dom muttered, rattling off their forces. "And a city of Elders behind them."

A formidable army, to be sure. But nothing compared to the onslaught marching toward them. Andry winced to himself. *We will have to eat the horses before long.*

Though it was only morning, Andry's eyes burned with exhaustion. While he spent his days studying the battlefield or training in the yard, meetings consumed his evenings. Between the Elders and the mortal commanders, along with Sorasa and Garion's input, they had some semblance of a strategy. Much of it Andry's own suggestion.

"With any luck," Andry said, "we can turn back the first wave. Then the real trouble begins."

Siege.

He shuddered to think of it, locked up like a rat in a trap. Doomed to spend his final days starving, watching Erida and Taristan from afar.

Dom looked just as uneasy. "It is not the city we hope to save, but Corayne."

"Corayne," Andry echoed. Their plans for her were far more detailed. "Half of me wishes we had more time."

The Elder gave him a stern look. "And the rest?"

"I wish it was over," Andry blurted out. He leaned into the air, hands braced against the ramparts of the city wall. "Whatever our fates may be. I just want to know what comes after, and finally be done with all this."

Despite the cold breeze, his cheeks flushed hot, going red with shame. Andry tucked his chin, looking down the walls to the sheer granite cliffs, and then the valley below. The great height made his head spin.

A warm hand closed on his shoulder, heavy through Andry's cloak and furs. He turned to see Dom watching him, a thoughtful look on his face. Without judgment. It anchored Andry a little.

"Think of after," Dom said. "Think of *your* after. Where you will go, what you will do. All the things you're fighting for, big and small."

Andry wanted to lose himself in such an endeavor. It was one thing to dream, and wish. It was another entirely to hide himself in a delusion, especially now, as the red sun rose and time wore out.

"What about you?" Andry muttered, turning the question back on the Elder.

Dom replied too quickly, without thought or care. "Sorasa wants to return to Ibal. If she can," he said with a shrug, as if it were the most obvious answer.

Andry felt his eyebrows nearly disappear into his hairline. He blinked at Dom, shocked, waiting for the Elder to understand what his words meant.

"And you would . . . go with her?" Andry said in a halting voice.

Suddenly, he found himself replaying Dom and Sorasa's journey over in his head. Trying to read between the lines of what they'd told the Companions. And what they hadn't.

The realization swept over Dom, his expression changing inch by inch. His usual scowl loosened, his eyes going wide, blinking rapidly. He turned to Andry.

"I don't know why I said that," he muttered.

Despite the circumstances, Andry grinned.

I do.

Dom did not smile back. He glowered out at the valley, darker than a storm cloud.

And then Andry was laughing, doubled over the ramparts, clutching at his sides. He felt overwhelmed, every emotion overflowing.

Other soldiers on the wall looked at him as if he were a madman. Dom only seethed, his teeth bared.

"I am tired, Trelland," he bit out, his face going scarlet as the sky. "I misspoke."

"Indeed," Andry teased.

Domacridhan was an immortal Elder, five hundred years old, a fearsome warrior, a true hero. Andry had seen him stabbed, burned, and left for dead. But never so fragile as he was now, red-faced and blinking, contemplating the valley as a scholar would a book.

Andry laughed again. Dom was a fighter above all things, and he fought like a tiger against his own heart.

But Andry's amusement was short-lived.

A horn blast echoed over the city, a long, deep sound carrying out of the east. Andry and Dom turned toward it in unison, color draining from both their faces. All down the walls and on the streets, it was the same. Terror washed over Iona, from the mortal soldiers outside the gates to Isibel enshrined on her throne, the greatsword laid across her knees.

It was Dom who ordered Elder scouts into the mountains, but the horn relay was Andry's idea.

The horn sounded again, then another blew, louder and closer. And then another, the horn blasts traveling rapidly across the valley, from the mountain pass all the way to Iona. At the city gates, an Elder raised a spiraling horn, blowing a call to shake the city.

The message was clear.

"They are coming down the Godhead Pass," Dom breathed, running a careful hand over his weary face. He glared into the mountain range, as if he could see all the way up into the jagged slopes.

Perhaps he can, Andry thought darkly.

Somewhere deeper in the city, the sound of hoofbeats clattered through the stone streets. Andry's heart rammed in time with the galloping horses, a pair of them, carrying two Elder riders. They flew down from the stables, fast as birds of prey, tearing through the city gates.

One will ride north, and one south, Andry knew. It was another one of his own suggestions. *To make sure someone lives to tell of what happened here. What we fought, and what we fell to.*

Beneath his beard, Dom grimaced. "We have until nightfall."

Andry slowly shook his head. In his mind, he saw the great cavalry charging across the valley, spurred on by Taristan's fury and Erida's hunger.

His voice broke.

"Before nightfall."

Quiet, cold Tíarma was no more. The marble halls of the Elders rang with noise, filled with boots trailing mud and mortal soldiers alongside Elder lords. It felt more like a military fortress than a grand castle, given over to the messy business of war.

Andry knew the many precautions taken to fortify the castle against attack. Hammers still sounded as the last wood planks were nailed into place, covering up the delicate glass windows or open archways. Provisions filled the vaults below the castle, tucked away for long weeks of siege. And the feasting tables barricaded all but one way into the castle, forming another funnel point. Andry even had caches of weapons stowed throughout the city, strategically placed to aid a slow retreat up the ridge. Bows and quivers of arrows, spears, sharpened swords, daggers, shields. Alongside food and water, bandages, herbs, whatever medicines the Elders had.

The last defense, Andry thought darkly as he entered the great castle, close on Dom's heels. Shadows rose up to meet them, the sun filtering through the boarded windows in weak shafts of light.

The Ibalets argued with Elder commanders, bickering over formations. Isadere looked on in golden chain mail, while the eagle knights waited, their armor donned, gleaming in white steel with their spears in hand.

Andry's heart rose up in his throat as he passed by. He wondered if it would be the last time he saw any of them alive.

None dared stand in Dom's way. The hall cleared before him as he walked, allowing the Prince of Iona to sweep through without issue. Andry stalked along in his wake, eyes downcast. Too many faces swirled around them, faces he might never see again after sunset.

Despite the disarray of the halls, the castle armory was far more organized, thanks to days of Andry's careful preparation. The Companions were already there, waiting as instructed in days past.

In the center of the chamber, Sorasa inspected an array of swords, her nose wrinkled despite the good quality of the Elder steel. She sneered at everything, but even her mask of disdain could not hide the fear beneath.

"Are the riders away?" she called out, meeting Dom's eye.

The Elder gave a silent nod and threw off his gray-green cloak. His suit of armor lay waiting in the corner, polished to a mirror shine. It had a pale green hue. *Like his cousin's armor*, Andry realized, remembering the Elder princess who died in Gidastern.

Corayne already wore armor of her own, a combination of steel plate and chain mail so as not to weigh her down too much. Her spiked vambraces were laced tightly over her forearms, patterned in scales. Like Dom, she wore no cloak, the Spindleblade strapped to her back instead. She gave Andry a shrug, indicating the helmet tucked under her arm.

"I look ridiculous," Corayne muttered, testing her range of motion. She clanked horribly as she reached for the sword belted at her hip.

"Well, I look marvelous," Charlie said from across the armory. Like Corayne, he did not suit the armor. The man was already red in the face, sweating above the gorget around his throat.

Sorasa gave them both a withering glance, before going back to the weapons, running her hands over a selection of spears.

"I don't see you stuffing yourself into a steel coffin," Charlie shot at her.

Over his shoulder, Garion snickered into his hand. He too wore a light suit of armor, good steel buckled over his leathers.

Shaking her head, the Amhara woman went to another table, this one laid out with daggers. Andry did not miss the way she pointedly put her back to Dom, her gaze anywhere but him.

"I move better without armor," she said over her shoulder. Her fingers danced among the blades, testing the edges, spinning a few of them for good measure.

In the corner, Dom scoffed so low it could have been a growl. "Your leathers can't turn an arrow, Sarn."

"You know I won't be anywhere near the archers, Elder," she answered back hotly.

As they bickered back and forth, Andry maneuvered to Corayne's side. She gave him a little smile, barely more than a curl of her lips. But enough.

"Where's Valtik?" he asked, eyeing the chamber again. Red sunlight bled through the shuttered windows, giving the armory a bloody glow.

The old witch was nowhere to be found.

"She actually slept with us last night," Corayne said, incredulous. "Right next to Sorasa on the floor."

Andry raised an eyebrow. "Brave."

"She giggles in her sleep. We almost murdered her," she added. Then her eyes darkened, so black as to swallow the light. "Though I suppose we'll have enough bloodshed tonight."

"Corayne," Andry muttered, wincing.

Her cheeks went pink. "Sorry."

They both fell into uneasy silence, broken only by Dom and Sorasa's errant sniping. Back and forth they went, Elder and Amhara, needling each other over everything and nothing. All the while, Dom stripped off his princely clothes, until he stood in only his thin breeches. Then, piece by piece, he donned his battle gear, slow enough to drive Sorasa into a rage.

Andry shuffled through his own things, neatly tucked away in the corner. It was a ramshackle collection. Elder-made armor, his own sword, the Jydi ax and wolf pelt. Along with his old tunic, washed clean, the blue star brighter than he remembered it could be. He laid it out flat on the table, smoothing over the fabric. The stitches ran beneath his fingers, the thread older than he was.

Corayne's hand joined his own, just inches away. She ran a finger along the edge of the star, careful not to snag anything.

"We will make them proud tonight," she said in a low voice. "Your father and mine."

"We will," Andry replied.

I hope.

After donning his own gear in the privacy of the corner, all was ready. But no one moved, hesitant to leave the armory. To face the coming storm.

Dom stood, massive in his green steel, his greatsword slung across his back like the Spindleblade slung behind Corayne. Across from him, Sorasa glared at her arm, picking at the chain mail beneath her leathers. It was not armor, but a good compromise, and she hated it. Charlie continued to twist at the waist, looking like a lord in a military parade, his brown hair freshly oiled and braided. Like Corayne, he would be far from the fighting, for however long he could be.

And Corayne stood alone, framed against one of the windows, the boards behind her bleeding red light. Her silhouette burned.

Andry eyed the Companions one by one, balancing the strangers he first met, and the friends he faced now. His throat tightened as he looked them over, memorizing every face.

The armory echoed with the distant sounds of the castle and the city. The Companions remained, frozen, unwilling to break the spell holding them all in place.

But we must move, Andry knew.

For a moment, his eyes slipped shut. When they opened again, he set his jaw, hardened his heart, and took the first step.

"With me," Andry growled, making for the doorway.

The others did not hesitate.

"With me," they echoed, one by one.

The castle blurred, the walls of stone and marble floors running like a river. More joined their throng, until Elder guards and mortal soldiers hemmed in the Companions. Andry saw nothing, heard no one, his blood surging in his veins. There was only Corayne at the corner of his eye, her armor etched with roses, the jewels of the Spindleblade glowing over her shoulder. Red and purple they winked, like a terrible sunrise.

Andry followed the others out onto the terrace in front of the castle. There was no mist today, only a bloody sky, turning redder by the second. Nothing hid the mountains from view. Nor the dark line of the legions picking their way steadily down the mountainside, the flash of their steel evident even to mortal eyes.

"Dom asked what I will do afterward," he said softly, barely audible over the clank of armor. "After all this."

Corayne stilled next to him, stopping to let the rest flow around her. Even Sorasa gave them space, if only a few yards.

"You believe there will be an afterward," she murmured.

The wind blew cold and clean. One last gasp of freedom. Andry pushed against it, breathing in.

"I have to," he said, eyes stinging. He knew he sounded foolish, but he spoke the words anyway. As if it would make them real. "I'll go to my mother, to Nkonabo. The house with the fountains and the purple fish. She used to tell me stories of her kin, their lives. Our family."

He expected Corayne to pity him. Instead, she took him by the hand, her gloves meeting his gauntlet.

"It will be wonderful," she said, her grip tight. Her face tipped up to his, so close he could see the freckles spattered across the bridge of her long nose. "I always wanted to see Kasa too."

Come with me, he wanted to say, so badly his heart ached. *Come with me. Even if it is only a dream.*

The wind blew harder, catching her long braid of black hair. Without letting go, she turned into the wind, a wistful look on her face. She stared, not to the army in the mountains, but south across the valley.

To the waters of the Long Sea.

"How fare the winds?" Corayne murmured to herself, so low he barely heard her. Her throat bobbed over the collar of her mail, the only bit of exposed skin below her face.

Slowly, she turned back to face him. "I wonder if I'll ever see my mother again."

"You will, Corayne." His grip tightened. "I promise you will."

As in Gidastern, something came over Andry Trelland. Before he knew it, her gloved hand was at his mouth, his lips brushing over her knuckles.

She did not pull away, only staring, holding his gaze. For a moment, only her eyes existed, a black sky. He wanted to fill it with blazing stars.

"Hold on to afterward," he said to her hand. "Whatever your afterward is, hold on to it."

With a twist, she broke his grip, only to raise both palms to his face, her gloves flat against his cheeks. Andry felt himself burn beneath her grasp and thought his heart might pound right out of his chest.

"I'll try," she said. "I promise I'll try."

Her breath ghosted over his face and he felt his helmet slip from under his arm. Andry did not care, letting it drop. Tentatively, his hands went to her waist, though he could not feel her through the armor. It did not matter. The shape of her was enough. Her eyes were enough.

And he was enough too.

The dragon's distant roar split them apart, the pair of them flinching at the all-too-familiar sound. Andry threw out an arm, shoving Corayne behind his body. The crowd around them reacted in kind, turning toward the source of the noise.

Below them on the landing, Sorasa loosed a string of curses, each one worse than the last.

The black line of Erida's army wove on. And above it, the dragon circled, terrible and enormous.

Andry squinted, hoping to see a burst of flame. In Gidastern, the dragon attacked with abandon, loyal to no side. It did not serve Taristan, or any other master, then.

The dragon roared again and his heart sank to his toes.

It did not attack, content to wheel over the army in lazy circles. Instead, the dragon followed the Gallish legions as a dog would its master.

Below him, Corayne raised her chin, pale with fear. But still defiant.

"With me," she murmured.

"With me," he answered.

38

THE GODS WILL ANSWER
Corayne

This was not like Nezri, or the forest temple, or even Gidastern. Break-neck battles all, with no time to think. They could only charge forward into whatever lay ahead, monsters and Spindles both.

Corayne wished for only monsters and Spindles now. Instead, she faced a long, tormenting tide riding out of the mountains, like a snake writhing down onto the valley floor. She did not know how many legions Erida commanded, and could not bear to ask, even now. Like the rest, she could only suffer and watch, the seconds sliding by, the great black serpent drawing closer and closer. Until the light shifted and she realized the snake was not black, but horrid steel and glistening green.

The dragon hovered over the great army, as if kept on a leash.

Her hands trembled, still burning from the feel of Andry's face. He stood in front of her, shielding her as if one squire could defend her from all the armies of the Ward. In her heart, she knew he would certainly try.

On the steps below, Dom and Sorasa lingered. They waited like islands in the churning sea of bodies. Neither moved, watching the army and the dragon as soldiers broke around them, hurrying to their posts.

Then Dom shuddered, his great shoulders rising. The steel on his back flashed, catching the red sun. The time had come. Corayne knew it as well as he did, as well as any of them. Dom would not remain in the castle, but march down with his own people. To face the first wave of attack, and perhaps his very last.

He barely took a step before Corayne lunged toward him, grabbing for his arm.

He did not move, letting her hold him back.

"The Elders can fight without you," Corayne said, tears blurring her vision. She had not won this battle in the council room. Judging by the look on his face, she would not win it now.

But she tried anyway.

His golden brow bent, and for a moment, she thought he might cry too.

"I am the Prince of Iona," Domacridhan said tightly. "It is my duty."

"Your duty is to *me*," Corayne shot back, her teeth bared. It was the only card she could think to play. "To my father."

Gently, he broke her grip, shrugging away from her.

"Sorasa will keep you safe until I return."

Next to him, the Amhara looked at the ground, refusing to raise her black-lined eyes. The makeup was war paint now, sharpening her copper glare until it glowed like molten glass. Her full lips pressed to nothing, teeth clenched to hold something at bay.

"Dom." Corayne grabbed for him again.

This time, he dodged her, as if she were only a shaky toddler.

"It is my duty," he said again, a well of regret bubbling up in his green eyes.

"And mine," another voice answered, cool and distant.

Corayne turned and was nearly blinded by the glint of sunlight on bright silver. Isibel's armor gleamed red beneath the strange sky. Like

Dom, the antlers splayed across her chest, each point set with a jewel. The Monarch of Iona was a vision, as close to a god as Corayne had ever seen.

In one hand, she grasped the greatsword of Iona, a brutal piece of metal, heavy and ancient. Isibel spun it once, as if it were made of feathers and not steel.

Corayne could only stare, even as her mind raged, torn between gratitude and anger.

Isibel did not smile, nor apologize. The Elder only stepped down to join Dom, her own guards flowing behind them. It was the last push Dom needed, and he finally turned aside, shoulder to shoulder with his aunt. They marched in step, a drumbeat of steel.

Sorasa walked the first few yards with him, as if she too might go down to the gates. But Corayne knew she would not. Such was the plan. Sorasa Sarn had no place on the battlefield. Still, she walked alongside Dom, seeking one last goodbye, a farewell for no one else to hear.

Corayne's heart twisted as the assassin and immortal traded words, their eyes speaking as much as their lips. Then a haunted look crossed Sorasa's face and she halted, letting Dom move forward without her.

Like Isibel, Dom wore his golden hair braided back from his face. Corayne stared at it, tracking the back of his head as he walked. Usually Dom stood well above a crowd, but among the Ionians, he was one of many. Fair, tall, lethal. Her eyes burned and Corayne had to blink. When she opened her eyes, she could not find him again. Domacridhan was lost to the sea of soldiers, swept down the ridge in a wave to meet the oncoming tide.

Her breath rattled in her body, her ribs tight, straining against the buckles of her armor. Suddenly it felt impossible to breathe, as if something pressed the air from her lungs.

She knew the battle plans. She had listened to them every evening, whispered around the feasting table or shouted across the throne room. A ditch here, a catapult there. This many in reserve, this much time to retreat. Near a thousand Ionian soldiers stood in the field with Isadere's army and the Kasans, with the Elders of Sirandel and Tirakrion manning the walls. Eyda and the Elders of Kovalinn remained in the castle, as Corayne's personal guard. And Dom would lead his people below, as long as he could. Until the endless wave of Gallish legions forced them back.

All this, Corayne knew. And it broke her heart.

Sorasa stared too, long after the Ionians passed through the castle gates, until only the echoes of them remained. Her shoulders bowed once, the only indication of her own pain.

Corayne knew better than to expect tears. When Sorasa finally turned around, her eyes were dry, her face arranged into her usual mask of pride and disdain. She took a step up to join Sorasa and Andry, before spinning again to face the battlefield.

Overhead, the sun threw off a heavy, scarlet light, bathing the world in an eclipsing haze.

Corayne's stomach twisted, the buzz of a Spindle ever-present on her skin. She could not help but remember the Ashlands, the wasted realm of dust and corpses. *That sky was red too*, she thought, trembling.

"It will be a long night," Sorasa said to no one.

There was no good way to pass the time. Conversation sputtered, all of them too fearful to talk much. Even Charlie had nothing to say, standing pale and silent next to Garion. Sorasa did her best, listing off all the ways to kill a man. She demonstrated a few, pointing to a spot on Corayne's neck, then a place between specific ribs. All of it Corayne knew already. Sorasa's lessons were drilled into her by now. Still, she listened, but not for her own sake. There was desperation in Sorasa's eyes, and fear too. She needed this more than Corayne did.

In the distance, the army continued to march, the thunder of many thousands of feet undercut by the beat of battle drums and the thump of the dragon's wings. It felt like being struck in the chest with a hammer, over and over again.

"This is torture," Corayne murmured.

Sorasa gritted her teeth against the relentless echoes. "No, this is worse."

Minute by minute, the worry grew, until Corayne thought she might be sick all over herself. Then the black snake closed the last mile. The sound of charging horses joined the din, along with the shouts of too many soldiers to fathom. When the horns went up on the battlefield, signaling the Gallish charge toward Iona, she swayed on the spot. But Andry would not let her fall. He shifted, as good as a wall beside her, allowing Corayne to lean.

"A Spindle born for flame, a Spindle born for flood."

Corayne whirled to find Valtik standing much too close, clad only in her usual shift. She looked weak and small against the armored ranks. But Valtik stared straight ahead, at the dragon circling over the army.

Sorasa eyed the old witch, then the dragon again.

"You should go inside, Valtik," she warned, only for the witch to hold up a white hand, cutting her off.

"A Spindle born for riches, a Spindle born for blood."

Flame. Flood. Gold. Blood. Corayne saw each Spindle in her mind, and the realms they led to. Infyrna. Meer. Irridas. The Ashlands. She winced, wondering which Spindle lay here.

Next to her, Valtik's eyes tracked the dragon. It circled over the battlefield, snarling. Corayne wagered Taristan rode directly beneath it, with

Ronin at his side. Though her uncle had lost his ability to heal his body, and his great strength, he had gained a formidable bodyguard.

"The gods of Irridas have spoken, the beasts of their treasures awoken," Valtik murmured. Her gnarled fingers worried at her pouch of bones, still belted at her waist.

Corayne's heart rose in her throat. She remembered the rhyme. It was almost exactly the same as the spell she used to force the kraken back into the Spindle. In spite of herself, she dared to hope, watching the old witch sway. Gently, she touched Valtik on the arm, encouraging her to continue.

The witch turned to her, eyes going wide. Even against the red light, they remained an impossible, vibrant blue. Even so, she looked like any other old woman, her skin thin as paper, veins webbing beneath the lines of age. Spots dusted over her cheeks, and the scent of lavender clung to the air. For a moment, it overpowered all else.

"The enemy is at the gates," the Jydi witch said, her mad laughter gone.

Corayne stooped to meet her eyeline. "I know, Valtik. Help us defeat them. Tell us what to do."

But Valtik only laid a palm to Corayne's face, her hand icy cold against her cheek. "Be well, Breaker of Fates."

Out on the battlefield, the dragon gave a scream like nothing Corayne had ever heard. She flinched, ducking down as it suddenly shot up into the sky, wings beating furiously to send a hot, ashen wind tearing over the castle.

"Inside!" she heard Sorasa scream. The Amhara caught one of the straps on her armor, using it to drag her back up the landing.

Corayne's legs scrabbled over the stone, trying to run. It only sent her tumbling sideways, knocking herself off balance, and taking Andry with her. They sprawled together, hitting the ground with a painful smack. Corayne's head rung like a bell and she wished she had her helmet, foolish as it looked. Her vision spun but she looked up in time to see Valtik still rooted to the spot, the dragon's wings blowing her hair back in a silver curtain.

Again, Corayne smelled lavender. And snow.

"Valtik!" she shouted, crawling to her feet. "Valtik, run!"

The dragon wheeled around the city in a terrible arc, flame spouting from its jaws. A ribbon of fire danced along the walls, breaking against stone and Elder alike. Screams pierced the air even as arrows twanged, a hundred bows raised to fend off the circling monster. Most glanced off the dragon's jeweled hide. Hardly enough to deter a dragon, enraged and ensnared to the will of What Waits.

Then it turned on Tíarma.

The old woman did not move, somehow tall against the tormenting wind. She only squinted, her mythic blue eyes narrowing to slits. But they did not dull or diminish.

If anything, her eyes seemed to glow, stronger and more fearsome.

"Valtik," Corayne said again, her voice weak, lost to the chaos.

Lavender. Snow.

Her mind spun, her focus still fixed on the witch, small as she was. A single old tree before a ruinous storm.

I know those eyes, she thought suddenly, images crashing through her head. Every memory of Valtik, cackling and rhyming, her bones spilling over her bare feet. And then another pair of the same eyes, the same shade, the same luminous, impossible blue.

They looked out from an old man's face, swaying in his step, kind in his manner. Old, insignificant, a weary sailor doomed to chase after a pirate's daughter.

"Kastio," she whispered, too soft for anyone to hear her.

But somehow, Valtik did.

She glanced at Corayne once, her hair streaming. And winked.

With a single beat of massive wings, the dragon sprang a hundred feet into the sky, its shadow covering the castle gateyard. Its wings pounded and another gust bore down on them all. Corayne fell back again, landing like a turtle on its shell, the weight of her armor holding her down. She choked on the smoky air, fighting to keep her eyes open.

There was only the dragon above her, the red sky behind it.

Corayne did not need to pass through another Spindle to see the hell of What Waits.

I am already there.

Then she was sliding across the stone, dragged like a sack of washing.

Valtik remained, silhouetted against the sudden blast of smoke.

"The gods of Asunder have spoken," the old woman chanted, raising a hand to the dragon.

It roared down at her in an ear-splitting screech, so powerful Corayne expected the stone to crack beneath them. Weakly, she reached for the old woman, as if she could still catch Valtik. Kastio. Whoever the bone witch might truly be.

Her fingers met only smoky air, embers raining down from the dragon's jeweled hide.

In the sky, its jaws opened wide, lines of relentless heat spilling from its mouth. Corayne knew what came next.

Valtik held her ground.

"And the gods of the Ward will answer."

The world slowed and flames bloomed, pouring out of the dragon's jaws. Its wings splayed wide, its jeweled body dropping to land. Below, the old witch waited, her face upturned, hands bowled at her sides, as if she might simply catch the dragon flame.

Corayne wanted to shut her eyes but could not, squinting through the smoke.

The first curl of fire licked at Valtik's face. The rest consumed and Corayne screamed.

The dragon screamed with her, changing directions rapidly, flapping its wings like a spooked bird. Its eyes widened, its flames glowing hotter and bigger, red giving over to burning yellow, then searing white.

Then icy blue.

A second dragon burst upward and out of the flames, its hide like ice and turquoise, like glacial water. It wore no jewels, but scales like a fish. Its wings unfurled in graceful arcs, the skin of it like cold winter sky. Beautiful somehow. And lethal. Its low neck bowed, its own fangs bared. It was smaller but agile, fast as a winter wind.

Then the second dragon's eyes flared open, pupils surrounded by a bright, familiar blue.

The demon dragon screeched, curling in the air to dodge the blue dragon's snapping jaws. When the second beast roared, it breathed an arrow of cobalt flame. But instead of heat, it threw off a blistering cold.

On the ground, Corayne could only watch, slack-jawed, as the blue dragon drove the other higher and higher into the sky. Their wings pumping, their bodies twisting, all snapping teeth and ripping claws. Red flame and blue ice battled into the hellish sky, until both looked small as birds.

Corayne's head spun. Then the doors of the castle passed over her, and marble slid beneath as she was dragged inside.

39

GHOSTS
Domacridhan

As his own people assembled in front of the castle, Dom expected to feel some kind of fellowship. He knew the soldiers around him, the Vedera of Iona, his own immortal kin. He thought of Ridha, and what he would give to have her standing there with them, ready to fight for the survival of their people, and the realm itself. It only made him feel more hollow, disconnected. He did not want to die on the battlefield below the city, alone but for the thousand other soldiers slaughtered with them.

His breath caught. He wanted to die right here on the castle steps, with the Companions beside him.

If we cannot live, we can at least go together.

But Dom knew it was not to be. He was a Prince of Iona, and his duty lay below, with his people. With the army. To hold off Taristan for as long as they could, however they could.

Gently, he shrugged off Corayne's hand, and took a step down with the other Ionians, his aunt among them.

To his surprise, Sorasa moved with him. She looked straight ahead, refusing to meet his eye. Instead, she fussed with the chain mail beneath her jacket, trying to adjust the metal rings. Clearly she despised it, her usually fluid motions slower and more stilted.

He opened his mouth to taunt her, to say anything, to grasp one more second at her side.

"Thank you for wearing armor," he growled. It was the only thing left to say.

He expected a quick, poisonous retort. Instead, Sorasa looked up at him. Her copper eyes wavered, filled with all the emotion she no longer cared to hide.

"Iron and steel won't save us from dragon fire," she said, all regret, her mouth barely moving.

Again, Dom wanted to stay, lingering one last moment, his eyes locked on her own.

"I know you don't believe in ghosts," Sorasa murmured, holding her ground. She did not move closer, or move at all, letting the crowd of Elders break around her.

A Vedera who falls in this realm falls forever, Dom thought, the old belief a sudden curse.

Sorasa's eyes shimmered, swimming with tears she would never allow herself to shed. She looked like she did on the beach after the shipwreck, torn apart by grief.

"But I do," she said.

His chest filled with unfamiliar feeling, an ache he could not name.

"Sorasa," he began, but the crowd surged around them, his Vederan soldiers too many to ignore. Every part of him wanted to stay rooted, though he knew he could not.

She would not reach for him, her hands pressed to her sides, her chin raised and jaw set. Whatever tears she carried faded, pushed down into the unfeeling well of an Amhara heart.

"Haunt me, Domacridhan."

The tide of the army swelled before he could muster an answer. While Sorasa stood against it, Dom let himself be carried. While his body marched, his heart stayed behind, broken as it was, already burning.

Her last words followed him all the way down to the city gates. They echoed in his head, lingering like Sorasa's tiger eyes, like Corayne's face. He tried to push it all away as Sorasa could. But there was no forgetting. Not Sorasa's voice, nor Andry's concern. Charlie small against the steps, sweating in his armor. And nothing in the realm could wipe away Corayne's heartbreak as he turned to go, every instinct screaming to stay behind.

She will be safe, he told himself, repeating it over and over, as if that might make it true. Indeed, she had Sorasa and Andry both, not to mention her Kovalinn guards. *She will be safe.*

Then he glimpsed the black snake of the legions curled down the mountains, the dragon moving with it. His belief shattered, his hope scattering like leaves in the cruel wind.

Safe until the moment she isn't. Until the second all this comes crashing down, and we die scattered, separated from each other one last time.

An arrow in the heart would be less painful.

One thousand Vedera of Iona marched around him, the sound of their armor like the ringing of a thousand bells. All were outfitted with swords, arrows, as many daggers as they could carry. Wagons brought up the rear, carrying stacks of long pikes. Male and female alike fought, leaving most of the city empty but the few Vedera too young to fight, and the rest guarding the city walls. The Vedera of Sirandel and Tirakrion saluted them as they passed. They stood, silhouetted against the red sky, watching as their immortal kin marched to their doom.

It felt like a funeral procession, and Domacridhan one of the dead.

Beneath a cloud of dread, the Vederan company reached the city gates at the base of the ridge. Stone jaws opened wide, and they marched onto what would become the battlefield. Ditches ran out along either side of the gates, forming a bottleneck. Sharpened stakes lined the bottom of each, tipped red by the odd light. They looked like too-long mouths of crooked jaws, ready to consume anyone who came too close.

Dom tried not to see what he knew the future held, what the field before him would become. Bodies and ragged earth, burn scars and a swamp of blood.

Instead he focused on Isibel, a gleaming star as she marched in silence. His anger toward her did not dissipate, but he did understand the anger at least. Like Isibel, he wore the mantle of command across his shoulders. It grew heavier with every passing second.

His stomach turned. A thousand immortals of Iona marched together. *How many of them will be dead by morning? Is it even possible to mourn so many lost?*

He despised Isibel's cowardice, but he could not blame her for it.

"To the head of the field," Dom called in High Vedera, raising his sword to rally the army.

His kin gave a resounding shout, moving into their tight lines. In seconds, Dom found himself at the head of the immortal column, with Isibel on his right. They fell into step together, the ground shuddering as they marched between the fanged ditches, to the great plain beyond it.

Dom remembered the war council, and Andry's quill scratching over parchment, drawing out the battle plans. Marking the different armies, the different flags. Archers, shield walls, infantry, pikemen. Spears, swords. The range of their catapults. And the elephants too. It was all there on the page, in black ink and golden paper.

Now it lay before Dom's own eyes, a terrible nightmare brought to life.

To the left was the Kasan army, organized in neat rows. At their head, the three eagle knights blazed in their white armor. The Ibalets held the right, Sibrez and Commander lin-Lira at the front of the battle lines. Their elephants waited at the back of their company, ready to charge when called for. Flags caught the wind, the white eagle and the golden dragon wavering against the red sky.

The immortals of Iona would hold the center, where the attack would fall hardest.

As they marched into formation, Dom swelled with gratitude toward the mortal kingdoms. Not just Kasa and Ibal, but the others fighting throughout the Ward. Without the Jydi and the pirates defending the seas, Iona would face an even larger force, with even less time to prepare. Now at least, their joint effort forced Erida's legions through the mountains, wearing them out with bitter cold and lethal climbs.

Dom stared across the valley, to the foothills sloping up into the mountainous heights. His heartbeat quickened as the Gallish legions appeared, weaving swiftly through the foothills. Above them, the dragon wheeled in circles, the beat of its wings shuddering the air.

Even from this distance, Dom saw the horses trotting at the head of the line.

It was as Andry suspected.

"Pike wall," he shouted, and the Vedera snapped to his command.

They moved like water, one thousand immortals falling into position across the battlefield, swooping out to defend the entire length of their unified army. The pikes rolled out with them, distributed swiftly, until every hand held a long, murderous spear, the iron tips glinting. The formation took shape, three rows deep, with each line of pikes set at a different angle. Their front line was no longer a collection of soldiers, but a wall of spikes. Archers fell into step behind, arrows at the ready, with the rest of the combined army beyond them.

Pikes, archers, infantry.

Dom kneeled in the first row, dead center. He planted his pike against the ground, his immortal strength driving the first foot of it deep into the earth, the tip set at the correct angle.

Isibel did not hang back from the front line. She glowed in her pearly armor, standing just behind Dom, her own pike clutched between her hands, held level with the ground.

"You look like your father," she said suddenly, breaking Dom's focus.

He blinked beneath his helmet, hesitating to look at her and change his stance.

She took it as an invitation to continue. "He led our kin against the Old Dragon, as you lead today."

And he died, Dom thought, heart twisting.

Isibel's voice dropped as the sound of hoofbeats grew. "He would be proud of you. As would your mother."

Try as he might, Dom could not picture them. The memory was too old, the moment too dire. He glimpsed wisps of golden hair, green eyes, and nothing more.

Isibel held the pike steady but one hand dropped, touching him on the shoulder for only a moment. "I am proud of you too. No matter what happens today."

Something wet dripped down Dom's cheek and onto his chin, tickling its way down his face. He held his position, steeled against the sensation.

Part of him could not forgive Isibel. Her inaction cost them Ridha's life, and countless others. Her hesitance left them vulnerable. Her cowardice may have doomed the Ward. But while his anger burned, fuel to a fire he so desperately needed, it consumed too.

"For Ridha," he murmured, the only acceptance he could give.

He could not see Isibel's face, but he heard her breath catch with pain.

And then there was no more time to mourn, or regret. There was only the battlefield, the legions, and the red sky.

Across the field, the Gallish line grew and grew and grew, fanning out as the column reached the valley floor. The legions were a proper army, not a rabble of the undead or a lazy company of the city watch. They were trained soldiers, hard drilled, molded to the battlefield, the greatest weapon Galland could ever wield. Dom saw it written in the way they moved, even the cavalry horses in lockstep.

They marched on, until Dom could pick out individual stallions, still trotting, saving their strength for the last charge. He searched the line of green flags and iron armor, hunting for a bloody burst of red. But there were only heavy knights on the front line, spears tucked beneath their arms.

Dom cursed to himself and eyed the dragon again, set back from the front line.

Of course they will not risk themselves in the vanguard, he thought bitterly, picturing Taristan and Ronin. *They will hang back beneath the protection of a dragon and leave the worst to Erida's mortal soldiers.*

Though the legions were his enemy, a wall of steel pressing forward with every second, Dom found it in his heart to pity them too. They did not know what they marched for. They did not know they fought for their own doom.

Or, Dom thought darkly, *they have no choice in the matter at all.*

"Hold firm, together," Dom called out along the line. "They will break before we do."

He remembered what Andry had said about battle tactics. *Galland relies on their knights to charge first, using the cavalry to sweep away the front line of an opposing army.* Andry's fingers illustrated across a table in the library. *We can stop them with a pike wall, an Elder pike wall, no less. It will be like charging into the side of a castle.*

Dom tightened against his own pike now, setting his shoulder to reinforce the wood. He hoped Andry was right.

The Gallish horns blew, bellowing over their own army. The knights reacted to the command, spurring the horses beneath them. They couched their lances, one hand on the reins, the red light flashing through the endless column.

Closer and closer they came, until the ground shook beneath Dom's boots, trembling under the weight of many hundreds of heavy horse. He could hear the knights shouting, voices raised in a battle cry, as he could hear the snorting breath of their horses, the jingle of tack, the bray of horns, the clang of armor. And the constant, cloying sweep of the dragon's wings.

The air turned hot, smelling of smoke.

To the east, the sun began its descent behind the mountains, sending the first shadows streaking over the valley like another army.

"They will break before we do," he growled again.

The Vedera responded with a cry of victory, speaking the old words from a realm lost. Even Isibel joined the call, the air trembling with her power.

Behind their line, he heard a thousand bowstrings pull taut, a thousand arrows aimed. He prayed to every god, in the Ward and Glorian, for those arrows to fly true.

Somehow, he forgot the dragon, the red sky, the city behind him. Even Taristan. Even Corayne. There was only the pike against his shoulder, the line of cavalry, and the breath in his body. This was the only place in the world, the only moment in all of existence. His senses flared, overwhelmed by the sound, the smell, the feel of the tidal wave crashing toward him.

They will break before we do.

The arrows arced, suspended for an instant before curving down into the charge.

Earth and dirt kicked up beneath the many hooves, a cloud rising with the oncoming cavalry. Flags still waved over them, the men of Galland roaring beneath their helmets, teeth bared, as fearsome as their galloping horses. The Vederan arrows found home among them, downing knights and their steeds in equal measure, each one collapsing in a heap of twitching limbs.

But there were more soldiers than arrows, and the cavalry charged on.

Dom braced, his jaw set, every muscle in his body tensed for the crushing blow. All down the line, his people did the same.

They will break before we do, he prayed.

And the legions broke.

The first knights careened into the wall, their eyes going wide in the last seconds, the horses screaming beneath them. The Vedera held their line as lances splintered and pikes sheared through flesh, man and horse both. Blood ran hot, legs flailing, hooves pawing as the ground turned to red mud. It was a crush of bodies and broken bones, the lines charging into each other, until the cavalry was forced to wheel, lest they be crushed too. Flags fell streaming, drums faltered, and mortal commanders screamed out above the fray, trying to re-form their destroyed line.

Dom saw the chance.

"FORWARD," he bellowed.

As one, the Vedera moved, pushing against the piled corpses, their bloody pikes creeping ahead. The archers went with them, firing again, raining death.

Part of the Gallish cavalry tried to wheel around the pike line, to attack the army from the flank, only to meet the ditches instead. Horses flailed in the muck, their knights impaled, blood filling their armor. The bottleneck held, forcing the cavalry right into their jaws.

But the charge did not end, the long column of Erida's calvary forming up again. They were a river and Domacridhan the dam.

"Forward," Dom shouted again, the line moving carefully.

Out of the corner of his eye, he noted the edge of the ditch wall, making sure to keep level with the funnel, lest they leave their sides undefended. The last thing they needed was the cavalry to worm around them, and attack from behind.

Then the dragon gave a ragged scream from behind the cavalry, spooking the horses. Dom went cold. Taristan would not hesitate to scorch a thousand of his own men, not if it meant conquering the city. His heart stopped in his chest and he braced himself, preparing to be burned alive.

Instead, the dragon leapt up into the air like another arrow from the bow, arcing high into the red sky. Dom watched it, puzzled.

Only to wish it would simply burn them all.

The dragon soared high over the Ionian army, ignoring them as it would too-small prey. A few arrows glanced uselessly off its jeweled hide, but the dragon did not seem to notice. Jaws open, it made for Iona—and the castle.

"Hold the line." Isibel's voice in his ear shuddered him.

Dom blinked, looking down to find he was already turning from the battle, ready to charge through his own ranks and up the city ridge. He swallowed, wishing he could, wishing he was back at the castle with the rest of them.

Instead, he turned into the fray.

It was all he could do. There was nowhere to go, no way to turn around, even if he wanted to.

Dom could only hope the castle held, that fire would not overcome stone. He willed it to be so, giving over any hope of his own survival. It was Corayne he thought of, and Sorasa beside her, keeping them both alive.

Then another screech joined the sounds of the roaring dragon. It was higher, like the keen of an eagle. Flinching, Dom looked up through the pikes to see the dragon of Gidastern twisting in the air, streams of flame sprouting from its jaws.

Dom narrowed his gaze, unwilling to believe his own eyes. Beneath his helmet, his jaw dropped. He was not the only one. Both armies slowed in their battle, looking up to watch not one, but *two* dragons spiral furiously through the scarlet heavens.

The other dragon was blue-scaled, its wings impossibly wide, fading to lavender gray. As he watched, the new monster loosed a blast of icy blue flame. Its wings stirred up a blast of bitter cold, even as the black dragon filled the air with cloying heat.

But there was no time to puzzle over the new dragon, impossible as it seemed. The battle raged on below, as the dragons raged above.

So it went. The cavalry. The pike wall. Dom's shoulder ached, his own pike splintering down the wood, until he feared it might finally snap in two. Behind him, the archers kept up their onslaught, but their quivers were not endless. They could not keep up their volleys forever.

The battlefield became a dizzying display of fallen bodies. They piled in little walls, the horses fallen in heaps. The knights died slowly, calling weakly for aid. Dom ignored the sounds of dying. He would not bear it.

Another horn blast went up from the Gallish lines, from a hill over the rise of the battlefield. Dom glimpsed a wall of commanders, old men on steady horses, a forest of flags over them. Dom assumed Taristan was there, cowering away from the worst of the battle. Whoever commanded the Gallish army had finally given up the hope of a cavalry charge, calling back the knights with another blast of the horn. They left a wasteland in their wake, the ground torn up and pocked with pools of blood.

"Back to the original line," Dom ordered.

As they marched backward to the first line of formation, the Gallish line dismounted, the knights joined by infantry. Lances lay discarded and swords were drawn, lines of archers forming behind them. Dom gritted his teeth and looked down at his own steel. The once-green armor ran scarlet, awash in enemy blood.

If the charge fails, they will rely on their numbers to overwhelm us. Andry's advice echoed in Dom's head, grim as the tidings were. Over the heads of the opposing line, he glimpsed the mountains again, and the serpentine march of the legions still coming out of the pass. *Galland can throw a thousand men to every one of us, and never blink.*

Dom and his Vedera slammed their pikes into the ground, hammering them into the mud to stand at the same angle. It would hold, but only for a few moments. Then they retreated behind the defenses, their own swords drawn, to join the Ibalets and Kasans.

Again, Dom searched through the Gallish soldiers, reading each face. He raised his gaze to the little hill, where the commanders still watched beyond arrow range. Again, he saw no spot of scarlet. No red wizard. No son of Old Cor. A flag shifted, falling limp, and he spotted the Queen, resplendent in armor. But Taristan was not there.

A whoosh rippled overhead and Dom ducked, expecting another dragon to swoop out of the sky. Instead, a great stone fell, exploding through the Gallish infantry. *Catapults,* Dom thought, remembering the siege engines within the walls of Iona. More followed, made of rocks and mortar, crashing down as the Gallish advanced.

Dom barely noticed, horror creeping up through his body. He hardly felt the sword gripped in his hand, nor smelled the blood drying all over his body. But his mind whirled.

He remembered Taristan in the palace of Ascal. Silhouetted in the doorway of a burning tower, still dangerous but fighting with more restraint than Dom knew he possessed. He did not attack Domacridhan so much as defend the Queen, trying to hold him off. And when the chance came to kill Dom outright, with only Erida in the balance, Taristan chose her. Above all things, Taristan chose Erida.

Dom felt sick.

Taristan would not abandon her to the battlefield alone, he thought, almost retching. *Unless he is not on the battlefield at all.*

The Gallish charged through the downfall of stones, ringing their armor and waving their swords. The pike wall only slowed them down, forcing the soldiers to maneuver through a forest of bloody stumps. But Dom barely saw it.

Taristan is not here.

The army met the breaking wave of the Gallish legions, their singing arrows landing in every direction. Swords crossed and shields clanged, spears dancing through the ordered line of veteran soldiers. Dom glimpsed Isibel out of the corner of his eye, her greatsword a red mirror, awash in blood.

He is not here.

Dom reacted on instinct, his own sword rising up to parry, letting a knight slide by him. And then his feet slowed, boots sticking in the mud.

He is not here.

The battle spun, and Dom spun with it. Moving, breathing, still alive, his heart pounding louder than the screams of the dying, and the roars of the dragons.

In another life, Dom lived quietly in Iona. He hunted, he trained, he spent most days with his cousin and Cortael. The trio wandered as they willed, climbing the mountains, walking the coasts. Until Isibel called them back with a sending, her voice as grave as her face.

A Spindleblade has been stolen.

They returned to find the Cor vault undisturbed, but for a missing sword. A blade that could rip the world apart.

There was no way for Taristan and Ronin to enter the city unnoticed. Even they could not slip past Vederan guards, in Iona or in the castle.

They did not come through the city, Dom realized, raising his eyes to the ridge behind them. Iona crawled up its length, a hulk of granite beneath the darkening scarlet sky. At its peak, Tíarma sat, watching over all, her towers tall against the clouds.

And her vaults deep. Endless. Spiraling down into the rock, so deep not even Dom knew where they ended. If they ended at all.

Or if they led out to open air, a terrible weakness overlooked for centuries.

Despite the battle, Dom felt himself turn.

But someone grabbed at his shoulder, her grip too strong to break.

"Let me go," Dom growled, fighting against the Monarch of Iona herself.

Isibel stood next to him, holding him back, her helmet gone, her curtain of silver hair hanging free.

"Are you running, Domacridhan?" she hissed, something like shock in her gray eyes. "Have you lost sight already?"

"No," he answered, shoving against her. "I see clearly. Taristan isn't here, neither is the wizard. This is a diversion—this is *all* a diversion."

Her shock bled to horror, her grip on Dom's shoulder releasing as she took in his words.

In a flash, he jumped to his feet. Isibel rose with him, her own gaze looking back to the castle frowning over all.

"Diversion," she murmured, as if dazed. The ancient sword still hung in her grasp, its edge painted scarlet. "We must go."

It was all the opening Dom needed. With a word to a lieutenant, he turned from the front lines, letting the Vederan move to plug the hole he left behind. There was no time to wonder if his absence would strike fear into the army. If Corayne died, they were all doomed anyway.

His body exploded beneath him, running at full speed despite his suit of armor.

Overhead, the dragons continued to battle, blue flame and red pouring back and forth. No side seemed to be winning, until the pair hurtled to the ground together, limbs and claws locked, their wings tangled and torn.

Dom threw himself sideways in time to dodge the hurtling dragons, their bodies giving off waves of hot and cold. They hit the ground like falling stars, sending up a plume of destroyed earth. They writhed through the haze, both unharmed, still tearing at each other, even as Dom struggled to his feet. Soldiers of either side gave the dragons a wide berth, mortal and immortal alike.

He barely ducked in time when a hiss of steel passed through the air, moving through the space where his head was a moment ago.

Dom blinked up incredulously to see a rider blaze past, menacing and tall in the saddle, his familiar form like a shadow turned to steel.

The black knight, Dom thought, remembering Gidastern, remembering the way the cursed warrior destroyed everything in his path. Charlie gave him a name. *Morvan the Dragonsbane. Another monster of Irridas, bound to hunt dragons until the ending of the realms.*

One way or another, his time will soon be at an end, Dom thought, even as his vision spun.

Morvan. The name sounded wrong, twisted, even in his own head.

He remembered Ridha, her green armor, her sword swinging, her black hair undone. She was fierce and beautiful, and broken beneath the black knight's hand. Left to die.

No, Dom thought, flinching. *Worse.*

The knight wheeled on his horse, his own sword raised. Though his face was obscured by the panes of his helmet, Dom still felt his stare like a spear. Morvan looked straight through him, to the dragons scrabbling at each other. Heat broke against Dom's back, then icy cold, as the monsters bellowed back and forth.

Even Morvan's horse did not seem to care about the landscape, trampling soldiers beneath its hooves. He moved with his master, careening in a circle to charge.

Dom wanted to hold his ground, to raise his own sword to meet Morvan's. Perhaps then Ridha would be avenged, in some small way. And one of his many wounds would finally begin to heal.

He tightened his grip on his greatsword, squaring his shoulders to Morvan. Some feral part of him roared in pleasure, begging to be loosed upon the black knight.

Another voice answered, echoing from the quieter corners of his mind.

Corayne.

Her name was a bell in his head, tolling still.

Morvan lowered his sword as the stallion beneath him reared.

It took everything in Dom to turn, to leave the black knight in his silence. And leave Ridha unavenged, her death unanswered.

But turn Domacridhan did.

40

BETWEEN HAMMER AND ANVIL
Sorasa

She felt torn between awe and annoyance. The dragon that was Valtik shot through the sky, her claws ripping at the other monstrous beast, the pair of them locked together in aerial combat.

Sorasa could not believe her own eyes.

Nor could she believe Valtik had possessed such earth-shattering magic *all this time.*

The realization came quickly. *No, it is not only magic,* she thought, all her anger melting away. *This is not the work of a witch, but a god.*

She turned to run, following Andry as he dragged Corayne backward over the threshold of the castle. Charlie was already inside, Garion with him, both white-faced with shock. The Elders of Kovalinn thronged around Corayne, pulling her to her feet. Isadere was there too, flanked by a pair of Falcons. The Heir was no warrior and pressed into the castle with the rest of them.

Sorasa lingered in the doorway, her body braced against the arch, peering out to watch the dragons race each other across a bloody sky. Her lip curled, watching the blue dragon as its lavender wings unfurled.

Then Sorasa raised a palm, the one tattooed with the crescent moon. A mark of Lasreen, the goddess of death.

"Thank you," she murmured to the wind before turning back inside.

The receiving hall looked more like a military barracks, piled with provisions and weapons, not to mention mountainous stores of bandages. *Optimistic*, Sorasa thought, eyeing the medical supplies. *That would require someone left alive to tend the wounded.*

Corayne steadied herself in the open doorway, eyes impossibly wide.

"Valtik is—" she breathed, overcome.

Sorasa put a steadying hand to her shoulder, gently guiding the Realm's Hope away from the outside. "She is beyond all of us, now."

In the shadows, Charlie worried at his lip, looking foolish in his over-padded armor.

"Is it time to barricade the castle?" he asked. His eyes flickered to the doorway, the sky red beyond it, the sounds of battle rising up from the field. "I think it is, just to be safe."

Sorasa shook her head. Again she pulled at the chain mail beneath her jacket, trying to adjust the fit. It felt like being slowly compressed.

"Not yet," she huffed. The plan was well known, gone over a thousand times. "We wait until the signal. If the city is breached, we seal the castle gates, and move backward through the keep." She thought of the vaults beneath the castle, so deep as to escape even dragonfire. "We will outlast them."

She tasted the lie, bitter on her tongue. Judging by the darkness in Corayne's eyes, the girl felt the same.

"We will outlast them," Corayne echoed, her voice hollow.

So they lingered, waiting for news. The Sirandel Elders were quick with their reports, dashing back and forth from their posts on the walls.

Sorasa's heart leapt up into her throat whenever one of the immortals appeared at the door, breathless with fresh news. Each time, she made her peace with surrender, failure, death. Each time, she said a small goodbye to Domacridhan, and whatever hope remained in her withered heart.

It was a torturous experience, and after an hour, she felt wrung out by it.

At the doorway, another Sirandel gave his report, detailing the last charge of the Gallish line. It sounded like a massacre. Sorasa listened too intently, bent toward him, tight as coiled rope.

"Any word from the Prince of Iona?" she muttered. Again she braced for the worst.

"No word," the Sirandel answered. "But he fights alongside the Monarch. I saw them both on the pike line before I left the walls."

Sorasa blew out a long sigh, her eyes fluttering shut for a moment. "Very well."

Her body itched. It was not the Amhara way to charge recklessly into a battle. They struck from the shadows. But every part of her felt wrong in the castle, hiding while Dom fought below. *He is safe among an Elder army*, she told herself. Irritating as he was, Sorasa knew no greater warrior than Domacridhan. And there were hundreds more just like him.

With any luck, they might cut through enough of Erida's army, and the legions would scatter, their commanders broken by immortal endurance.

She turned away, letting Lady Eyda speak to the Sirandel scout. The warrior maiden was done up in a dress of chain mail, her great cloak discarded, an ax on her back. Her own people numbered less than twenty now, set at intervals down the receiving hall.

The shaggy bear lumbered among them, yawning. Sorasa made a point to keep her distance from the animal, no matter how well trained they assured her it was.

Corayne scratched it behind the ears, as if it were only a puppy, and not a massive beast. It shuddered, tongue lolling as it leaned heavily into her hand.

"You miss your boy, don't you?" Corayne said to the bear. Indeed, Dyrian was down in the vaults with the other younger immortals, hidden away from the bloodshed. "You'll see him soon enough."

Andry hung back a few paces, uneasy.

Though a grim air hung over the hall, Isadere could not help but smile. The weak candles and thin shafts of light illuminated their bronze face and a flash of white teeth.

"We should give thanks to the goddess Lasreen," Isadere said excitedly, gesturing to the dragons. "She has answered our prayers."

Across the hall, Charlie gave an echoing scoff. "You think the goddess of death sent Valtik to us?"

Sorasa ignored them and peered out the door, tracking the blue dragon. In the sky, Valtik dueled bitterly, jaws snapping as icy flame shot through the sky. But the other dragon never gave an inch.

Amavar? she wondered, naming Lasreen's faithful servant. *Or the goddess herself?*

The gods of the Ward have answered, Valtik had said before transforming.

Sorasa only hoped it was enough. Her body went cold as she watched the battle, gaze wavering between the field and the dragons in the sky. She winced as Taristan's dragon tore through Valtik's defenses, raking a claw down the length of her neck. Rivulets of iridescent blood shimmered in the air before raining down on the city.

Next to her, Isadere flinched, their bronze face going pale.

"She cannot win this battle alone," the Heir muttered. "I must try my mirror. Certainly the goddess will speak to me now, her eye is upon us."

The gods are not ours to call upon, Sorasa wanted to say, but held her tongue. Instead, she gave a grim nod.

With a swish of their robes, Isadere marched off, the bodyguards in tow. All three headed for the vaults of Iona, where the valuables were stored.

"Maybe they'll get lost." Charlie chuckled darkly, drawing a rare laugh from Sorasa.

It was short-lived.

A piercing scream split the halls of Tíarma, the sound of it like lightning down Sorasa's spine. She turned toward the noise in time to watch Isadere stagger back into the receiving hall, the Falcon bodyguards half carrying them.

Isadere looked to Charlie first, their black eyes filled with terror.

"This is what the goddess showed me," they moaned, their voice breaking.

Without thought, Charlie ran to Isadere's side. "What is it?"

"The path I saw, down and down into darkness . . ."

Isadere's eyes widened with terror, one hand pointing back toward the vaults.

"Shadows, and a red light beneath it all," the Heir whispered. "A path my feet would not follow."

"What are they talking about, Charlie?" Sorasa demanded hotly, coming to stand beside the two. Fear licked at her insides, but she ignored it.

The fallen priest gave a strange look as he searched Isadere's face. No matter the enmity between Charlie and Isadere, he certainly believed their words, whatever they meant. Sorasa cursed under her breath. The last thing they needed was a bout of religious hysteria.

The Elders looked on in confusion, their faces blank. Until Lady Eyda raised her head, her eyes lifting from Isadere, back toward the passage.

"Do you hear that?" the Elder breathed. Her white hand trailed, reaching for the battle-ax across her shoulders.

The fear in Sorasa's heart grew, burning like the dragon flames.

"Hear what?" she said softly, only to see the Elders around the room go wide-eyed.

Their focus shifted to something beyond Sorasa's mortal perception. As they strained to listen, all others fell quiet, until the castle went silent as a tomb. The only sound was the battle far away, and their own heavy breathing.

It was not the quiet that bothered Sorasa, but the looks of terror rippling through the immortal Elders. Even Eyda, a warrior of great renown.

Without thought, Sorasa pulled Corayne close, her grip harsh on the collar of her armor. Andry followed, a wall behind them both.

"Hear what?" Sorasa said again, sharper. Her free hand went to a dagger, while Andry's sword sang from its sheath.

Across the room, Garion caught her eye, his own rapier dancing free.

But Eyda did not answer. The ax swung in her hand, her face white as milk.

"Dyrian," she whispered, charging from the room.

Dyrian. Sorasa's stomach churned. *Down in the vaults with the other young ones.*

"Wait!" Sorasa screamed, trying to stop the other Elders. They hesitated, torn between following Eyda and protecting Corayne.

Whirling, Sorasa pointed to the scout still waiting at the door. "Send word to the walls," she barked. "Get help. Something is wrong in this castle."

The Elder runner disappeared in a swirl of purple leathers, sprinting out into the dying light. Sorasa wanted to follow, to get Corayne out into the open. Suddenly the castle felt like a trap. Already she could feel the walls closing over her, threatening to collapse and bury them all.

Another scream shattered through the halls of Tíarma, reverberating off the marble and stone. The last of the Kovalinn guard charged away, following the sound of Eyda's wailing.

Sorasa gnashed her teeth, at war with her own instincts. Again she wanted to run. Instead, she dragged them all along, chasing after the Elders who were meant to guard Corayne, and not run off at the first sign of trouble. Charlie and Garion moved too, close at her heels. All they could do was follow, to stay behind the Elders, and stay within their circle of protection.

The Elders only made it a few feet into the next hall before they stopped short. Some yards down the long passage, Eyda stood alone, staring down the steps into the deeper bowels of the castle. Into the spiraling tunnel that was the vaults.

The Lady of Kovalinn remained in silhouette, a shuttered window above her. The last, dark rays of sunshine broke weakly through the gaps in the boards, flashing red against her chain mail. The Elder woman turned to ice, near frozen to the spot.

Sorasa clung to Corayne, holding the girl behind her. Every instinct she ever had, the ones she was born with and the ones the Amhara drilled into her, exploded in Sorasa's body. They tore at her, screaming, until she could barely hear anything beyond her own body.

It was the smell that hit her first.

Sorasa knew it instantly.

There is nothing like rotting flesh. Nothing like the bodies of the undead.

The first of them lurched, their movements jerky and strange, their limbs dangling on rotting tendons and crumbling bones. Red light illuminated the corpses as they moved, edging them all in scarlet, drenched in old blood.

"Run," Sorasa hissed, pushing Corayne.

In her heart, Sorasa was already out of the castle, to the stables, shoving Corayne onto a horse, and galloping out of Iona as fast as four hooves would carry them.

They only made it a few steps backward.

Sorasa turned toward the entrance hall and freedom, Corayne safe in her grip.

Again the lightning crackled up the assassin's spine.

Thirteen figures stood across the entrance hall, their forms sharp against the dying light spilling over the marble. As the undead writhed up from the vaults, so did the Amhara slither into the castle.

We are surrounded.

"Run," Sorasa said again, softer now. Her arm unwound from Corayne's body, one hand pushing her to the side, to the other corridors branching away. "Run."

Corayne stared, sputtering. Her lips moved, shouting something Sorasa would not hear. She did not have the focus for it. There was only the Amhara ahead, the undead behind.

Garion was the same. Like Sorasa, he shoved Charlie away without warning. The priest fell hard but scrambled back to his feet.

"Run, church mouse," Garion echoed, all his charm forgotten.

Andry gathered them up, Corayne and Charlie, pirate's daughter and priest. He was their protector now. Not a squire, but a true knight, his armor donned and sword raised. Sorasa spared a single glance for him, meeting Andry's stare. His warm eyes were black with fear, but he nodded to her. Slowly, he backed all three of them down the other corridor, away from the crossing of assassins and undead.

"Keep them safe, Andry," Sorasa whispered.

"Follow me," a voice said, grave and cold.

Sorasa gasped, the tiniest flicker of relief jumping up in her. "Isibel."

How the Monarch found her way past the assassins, Sorasa did not know, but this was not the time to ask. And this was Isibel's own fortress, her own castle. Certainly she knew it better than anyone alive.

Isibel beckoned from farther down the corridor, her armor shimmering like a mirror. Blood splattered every inch of her, but her silver hair hung free, making her seem paler in the fading light. Her ancient sword, brutal and cruel, looked worse than her armor.

"Come," Isibel said, raising a hand to Corayne and her Companions. "I know the way."

There was no time to argue, nor hesitate.

Corayne spared one last look for Sorasa, before Andry dragged her off. Charlie fought Andry's grip, too, but he was no match for the squire. They disappeared after Isibel, fleeing both the crossing of the passages, and the two-pronged attack on the castle.

In a heartbeat, they faded from Sorasa's thoughts, her mind clearing, until she felt only her dagger, and the pulse of her own heart.

A rapier swished through the air, dancing lazily in Garion's hand. His body relaxed, fluid as a dancer as he dropped into his fighting stance. Beneath his mahogany curls, his face was bone white. He knew the danger as Sorasa did.

The clang of weapons sounded behind them, the Elders of Kovalinn standing their ground against the undead army welling up from the vaults. Their grunts of exertion echoed off the stone walls and up to the ceilings, ringing the entire castle like some horrendous bell. As their swords and axes swung, chopping limbs and severing heads, the corpses rasped. They dragged themselves inexorably up from the vaults in a grim tide, flooding Tiarma from below.

Sorasa swallowed hard.

There would be no Elder rescue from the Amhara. The Ashlanders were challenge enough.

She could only pray for the immortals behind her, and hope they held the passage. Hope someone arrived in time to save them.

Hope Isibel has the sense to get Corayne out of here, even if it means carrying her down the cliffs herself.

They were pinned, Sorasa and Garion, nailed down between the vaults and the entrance hall. Their only advantage was the high ground, small as it was, with the entryway sunken below.

The last rays of sunlight bled over the floor, and battle still raged in the field. Sorasa could hear the distant thud of catapults, the twang of arrows. Her heart rose up in her throat. Again she prayed, this time for a familiar silhouette to charge up the street. Broad shoulders and golden hair. A furious disposition.

She shook away the useless hope, squaring to the Amhara.

The Amhara only stared back, waiting for their exiled kin to strike.

Sorasa took whatever they would give. She hunted for opportunity, reading every face, noting every name, every weakness, every strength. Cataloguing all she knew of them in a heartbeat. Anything to give herself the upper hand.

And anything to last one second longer.

One of the Amhara stood out from the others. Not in height or weight, but in age. He was the oldest of them by decades, his skin bronzed and sun-worn by half a century in the deserts of Ibal. His pale green eyes crinkled, as close to a smile as Sorasa had ever seen on his face.

"I am flattered, Lord Mercury," Sorasa said, taking a step back into the hall. Behind her, corpses roared and screamed.

Garion moved to match, his lips pursed into a thin line.

Lord Mercury looked between them both, taking his time. Sorasa knew he was sizing them up as she had done, reading their bodies and their histories. While the assassins on either side of him clutched their weapons, swords and daggers and axes and whips, Mercury held nothing. He did not move, hands clasped in front of his long black robes.

Sorasa knew better. She remembered the knives he carried, all tucked carefully beneath the folds of his clothes. It was jarring to see him standing here, in front of her, a nightmare made flesh.

After so many years, I convinced myself he was just a ghost.

"What a mess you have made, Sorasa Sarn," he sighed, shrugging.

His voice tore something inside. Too many memories streaked across her mind, from childhood on. Every lesson, every torture. Every kind word, few as they were. In another life, she considered Mercury her father. But that life was gone.

No, Sorasa knew. She was only a tool to him, even then. *It never existed at all.*

Mercury stared through her, as if she were still that little girl, weeping beneath a desert moon.

"A pity I must clean it up."

Sorasa bared her teeth. She took another step into the entrance hall, closing the distance between them.

"A pity you did not do so years ago," she snapped.

"Yes, I agree," Mercury said evenly. "I know that now. Such is my weakness, to leave a failure like you alive." He angled his head, spearing Garion with his pale stare. "I see you've poisoned Garion too."

Sorasa gave a dark laugh. "I'm afraid I can't claim responsibility for that."

"If you kill Corayne an-Amarat, the realm ends," Garion said lightly, as if discussing the weather. "That is what Erida truly wants, you old fool."

Mercury only grinned, deepening the lines of his face. His teeth gleamed red in the odd light, sharp as Sorasa remembered.

"I will give you a chance to stand aside, Garion," he said, waving toward the door. "But not you. Your fate is sealed, Sarn. As it has been sealed since the day you were born."

Her heart hammered and she cursed the chain mail. It would turn an arrow on the battlefield, but it would only weigh her down against the Amhara. *Fucking Domacridhan, a gargantuan nuisance until the very end.*

Sorasa gave a shake of her head, slowly, letting her frustration rise to the surface. Her brow furrowed, a single gasping sob escaping her mouth. She could feel Mercury watching, his eyes devouring her pain.

She gave it to him gladly, letting the seconds slide by. Each one well earned.

When she raised her eyes again, Mercury sneered. And Sorasa's face wiped blank. Over his shoulder, outside in the castle gateyard, figures moved soundlessly over the stone. Swift as the wind, their purple leathers like shadows.

"Bring me my fate then," Sorasa said, leaping.

As her feet left the ground, the Sirandel scouts crashed through the door, immortals all of them. Deadly and silent, even to the Amhara.

The assassins whirled, only to face a new company of Elder warriors. Red-haired, yellow-eyed, fearsome and sly as the foxes embroidered on their cloaks. Lord Valnir led them, his bow twanging, a contingent of guards flowing in his wake. The first arrow skewered an Amhara, sending her falling to her knees.

Sorasa landed hard, her dagger dragging a ragged line through an Amhara throat. Next to her, Garion spun, deflecting the first blow of a hammering sword.

In the Guild, the acolytes sparred as often as they ate. In the training yards, but also in the halls and dormitories. Rivalries and alliances bloomed through the years together, their histories interwoven. Sorasa knew each face in front of her. Some older, some younger, but all acolytes once. As close as siblings, beloved or reviled. She used such knowledge to her advantage, and her opponents did the same.

Mercury leered through it all, hanging back to watch his pets devour each other.

As on the hill on the Wolf's Way, Sorasa closed her heart to emotion, refusing to acknowledge the blood she spilled until the task was done.

Battle raged inside the castle, like two tides crashing on a beach. The Sirandels, the Amhara, the Kovalinn, the undead steadily gaining ground. All warred back and forth, with Sorasa and Garion smashed in the middle, stuck between hammer and anvil. Her survival instincts took over, her body moving without thought. She could only step, dodge, parry, stab. Again and again and again. A corpse grabbed at her ankles, an Amhara whip curled around her arm. *Strike, slice.* It all blurred, sweeping her away in the current.

She lost Garion in the fray but glimpsed Dyrian's bear, an Amhara's head in its jaws. It shook the assassin's body back and forth like a toy.

On the floor, Eyda wept over the broken figure of her son. The young lord lay still, white-faced in death. A small sword lay broken beside them. He died fighting, at the very least.

Sorasa's stomach churned as she realized Dyrian met a better fate than the other Elder children.

The young immortals clambered through the fray, lurching and sluggish as they surmounted the stairs. All were dead-eyed, jaws slack. The dead walking.

The vaults had not saved them. Instead, they were their doom.

Her mind spun with the implication. New dead walked, raised from corpses.

Raised by—

"Taristan is here," she breathed to no one, head pounding.

Then a boot caught her jaw and she sailed sideways. Instinctively, her body went limp as she flew through the air. Tension would only hurt her more, a lesson she learned a hundred times. She landed and rolled, body curling against the wretched chain mail.

But Mercury was there, faster than she thought a mortal could move. He took her by the throat, one hand closing, the other holding one of his precious daggers to her ribs.

"I meant what I said, Sarn," Mercury snarled, his breath washing over her face. "You were my greatest failure. But the flaw was in your making, in me. Take heart in that."

Then he drove the dagger home.

Or at least he tried to.

The chain mail held, saving her lung, though her side throbbed as if struck by a hammer.

"Armor?" Mercury laughed, his breath on her face. He held on, squeezing her throat. "You have changed."

Sorasa clawed at his face, drawing ragged, bloody lines. He didn't seem to notice. This time, he raised the dagger, putting it to her face. The blade felt cold against her cheek, the tip a hair's breadth from her eye.

Then a blur struck the lord of the Amhara, a larger body slamming into him, knocking the old man to the ground. A demon stood over him, his armor streaked in blood, his helmet torn away. He loomed, monstrous, chest rising and falling with ragged gasps of breath. But for the golden hair and green steel, Sorasa would have suspected Dyrian's bear.

Dom certainly fought like one.

On the ground, Mercury flipped to his feet but Dom caught him, gripping him by the neck and the leg. He lifted Mercury clean over his head, as if he were no more than a bundle of twigs, and tossed him bodily across the hall. The assassin landed with a sickening crack, his body smacking against the marble.

Sorasa wanted to fall, exhausted. She wanted to embrace Dom, grateful.

Instead, she spun to face the next enemy.

"Thank you," Sorasa bit out over her shoulder, letting her sword dance. She would not bother asking what happened on the battlefield, or why he'd returned.

"You are welcome," Dom answered, putting his back to her.

For a moment, she leaned against his steel, feeling Domacridhan behind her. His presence bought her seconds only, but enough time to gather her wits.

She assessed the hall, reading the blood on the floor, the tide of bodies whirling back and forth. The undead were still coming, foaming up from the vaults in endless rows, flooding through the castle. The Elders did their best to mop them up. Some fell apart on the steps, reduced to rolling heads and clawing torsos. But most surged forward, scattering and snarling in all directions.

Six Amhara remained, but they ran to Mercury's body, leaving Garion panting in their wake. One of them scooped their lord up, slinging him over his shoulder.

Sorasa wanted to chase after them, to slit Mercury's throat and watch the light leave his eyes for good. Her fingers twitched, still tight on her dagger, her heartbeat ragged in her chest. Memories welled, each more painful than the last. Being abandoned in the desert as a small child. Her body broken by training. Her first kill and how terrible it made her feel. Mercury's smile and favor, bestowed like a gift, but so easily taken away. And then her face pressed to the cold stone of the citadel, her body bare, a horrible tattoo inked across her ribs. Mercury did not smile then, as he took away everything she ever tried to build.

Mercury's voice loomed out of the back of her mind. *My greatest failure.*

But Sorasa could not move.

The Amhara—and Mercury—grew smaller, fleeing out into the city. They ran, but she could not, watching as they disappeared out into the gateyard. Her lip quivered. In the back of her mind, she sent up a prayer to Lasreen.

Let him be dead.

Their figures faded, just like the memories. Like the Amhara she once was.

"Where is Taristan?" Dom snarled, his head craning back and forth.

"I don't know," Sorasa replied, desperate. She prayed he had not slipped by her in the melee.

Dom whirled to her, taking her by the neck as Mercury did. But the immortal's touch was far more gentle, his thumb light across her throat. In spite of herself, Sorasa pushed into his grasp, his skin cool against her flaming body.

His green eyes danced, explosive, his face streaked in blood.

"Then where is Corayne?"

"With Isibel," Sorasa cut back. "She returned before you did. Andry and Charlie are with them."

Some tension released and Dom gave a great sigh, heaving his shoulders. It was enough for Sorasa, relief ebbing through her. She tipped her head, bracing her brow against the flat of Dom's chest, the steel cold beneath her hot skin.

In through the nose, out through the mouth, she told herself, schooling her breathing. Slowing her heart. Letting the fear shrink into something she could control.

Dom is here now.

"*Fuck*," he said above her, a rare mortal curse sliding through his teeth.

Sorasa raised her head, turning as he turned, looking where he looked. Again the world narrowed. Again sound fell away.

She glimpsed Ronin first, his robes scarlet against the tide of rotting corpses. But it was his face that stood out, his head bobbing back and forth. He threw out a hand, clutching someone next to him, letting them lead.

Because the wizard no longer had eyes.

Only two bruised sockets remained, weeping blood between the eyelids, as if the wound was still fresh. Red rivers wound down his pale cheeks.

Sorasa felt her knees buckle even as Dom held her, time slowing for them both.

Another head appeared above the corpse tide, coming into view with every step upward. The face, the neck, the shoulders. Red hair, black eyes, white veins like lightning in his skin. Like Ronin, he wore scarlet over one shoulder, a cloak billowing out behind him. But his leathers were old, stained and worn, a testament to a life of bitter hardship.

Taristan of Old Cor.

Though the Elders stood in the way, still fighting, Taristan looked right through them. Sorasa expected his leering smile, horrendous and cruel. Instead he glared across the yards, unfurling more of himself with every step up into Tíarma. His pace was languid, lazy even. Like he had already won.

Without thought, she threw out an arm, meaning to bar Dom's way. She remembered how he charged into a burning palace for even the chance to kill Taristan. But the Elder did not move. To her shock, he even took a step back, pulling her with him.

"Where did Isibel go?" Dom breathed in her ear, his grasp on her tightening.

Sorasa gripped him back, her eyes still on Taristan as he advanced.

"Let's find out."

41

THE CLASH OF EMPIRES
Erida

It seemed a simple endeavor.

The mist cleared beneath the rising sun, revealing Iona to them as they descended the last miles of the pass. The Elder city sat upon a wedge of granite, thrust up from the valley floor. Little more than a large town to Erida's eyes, paltry in comparison to the great cities of her empire. And dwarfed by the massive army around her.

The legions will swallow this place whole, she thought, staring down at Iona.

Her eyes stung, her gaze fixed so intently Erida forgot to blink.

Behind her veils and beneath her armor, her skin prickled. She felt as if a thousand hooks had embedded themselves in her flesh. Each one stung only a little, dragging her down and down over the rocky terrain. The more ground she covered, the more insistently they pulled. Erida twitched her heels, urging her horse to quicken her pace.

The mare was skittish beneath her, oddly on edge. Erida wondered if the horse could sense the demon in her, or if she simply smelled the dragon wheeling higher up in the mountains.

Taristan had left her alone among her commanders. He set out with

Ronin and the Ashlanders under the cover of darkness, his own plans keenly drawn. Once, she might have feared for him or mistrusted his path. But What Waits did not fear, His presence calming and sure. And so Erida would not either.

Besides, they would be reunited in victory soon enough.

Lord Thornwall did not speak to her, to Erida's delight. Her lords gave her a wide berth, letting the Lionguard surround their queen, leaving her in a pleasant cocoon of silence. She preferred it to coddling her weak nobles, some of them already pissing themselves with fear.

Erida despaired of them. *We command the largest army upon the Ward. We should never fear anything, ever again.*

They whispered of Ascal but she did not listen. Her mind was forward, not behind.

Earlier that morning, the scouts had reported on the Ionian defenses. As they reached the lower foothills, the distance closing, Erida could see them with her own two eyes. She almost laughed at the meager ditches around the city gates. They would barely slow her legions, let alone turn the course of the future.

Despite the war with Madrence and her conquest of the southern kingdoms, Erida had never seen a battlefield quite like this. Two armies laid out, facing each other across the barren plain. While the legions marched onward, following their captains and field officers, a guard led Erida's horse to a rise above the chosen ground.

The flags of Galland tossed high overhead. Beneath them, her commanders assembled, Lord Thornwall chief among them. He looked small compared to his burly lieutenants or noble lords in overwrought armor. But Erida knew better than to underestimate her general.

All remained in the saddle and so did Erida, easing her horse in alongside Thornwall. Her own cloak trailed down her back and over her horse's haunches, the green velvet trimmed with roses. Her armor was not so ornate, thicker than Erida was used to. It weighed heavy across her body, the steel gleaming. Such was the cost of being so close to battle. There was no cause for useless gilding or crowns.

"Assemble," Lord Thornwall called from horseback.

At his command, the army formed up into endless lines, the infantry falling back to allow the knights of her heavy cavalry to take the vanguard.

It was a beautiful sight, enough to make the breath catch in Erida's chest.

"Magnificent," she breathed.

Next to her, Thornwall could not help but agree, his eyes alight with the flame of war.

Then the dragon swung low overhead, its jeweled body throwing off heat like a furnace. It shrieked like a raptor bird, a foul wind following in its wake. The flags tugged against their poles, while her commanders ducked low in the saddle. Even the Lionguard flinched, but Erida alone sat tall, unbothered by the Spindle monster.

The dragon answered to her husband now.

And Taristan answers to me.

In spite of her faith in him, and What Waits, Erida felt a pang of longing. Again, she squinted across the valley, looking for some dark smudge against the landscape. From the lake, not the mountains. But there was nothing. Either Taristan and Ronin were well hidden, or they were already inside the tunnels, winding up the city from the inside, like worms eating a corpse.

She sighed beneath her veils, willing her husband to succeed.

Iona looked even smaller than it had a few hours ago. Let alone any kind of prize for the Empress Rising.

It is not the city, she knew. *But the girl inside it. Corayne and the Spindleblade.*

The defending force seemed bigger than the enclave itself, spilling out of the city gates to take formation. Erida thought she might pity them, but felt only disgust for the soldiers marching against her. They would fight in vain and die useless deaths.

"At least ten thousand," Thornwall muttered to one of his lieutenants, answering a question Erida did not hear. She peered at him, studying his frown.

A little of the light guttered from his eyes, his eager manner fading. Erida puzzled at it. The battlefield was the only place Thornwall truly belonged, and he attacked it with dogged determination. But his look turned grim, his lips pressed into a hard line.

"Ten thousand," Erida laughed, smirking beneath her veil. *Barely two legions.* "We will run through them."

Most of the nobles mirrored her sentiment, false as they were.

Thornwall did not.

"Ten thousand, beneath the flag of Ibal and the flag of Kasa," he said sharply, pointing to the armies assembled on the field.

"Ibal and Kasa do not frighten me, my lord," Erida replied coolly.

He was undeterred, his ruddy face going red as the sky. "Not to mention however many Elders there are among them. They form the center."

The Queen of Galland reined her horse to look Thornwall head on. He stared back at her, stone-faced. Though he was small in frame, Erida had never thought of him as a small man.

Until now.

"Elders do not frighten me either," she hissed. "Do they frighten you, Lord Thornwall?"

The insult was clear, thrown like a javelin. Her nobles looked on, speechless, their gazes wavering between queen and commander. Erida may as well have stabbed Thornwall through the heart.

He curled his lip and Erida braced for treason. Instead, he bowed as much as he could from the saddle of a horse.

"No, Your Majesty," he murmured.

"Good," she spat back at him. "Then proceed. Sound the charge."

It took all her will to remain silent in the saddle, her hands still on the reins. She was glad for her gloves to hide her knuckles, bone white as they gripped the reins tighter and tighter. Her armor felt stifling, the chain mail and good steel like an anchor holding her in place. It felt strange to wear true battle armor instead of skirts, dressed as a warrior instead of a queen. Again, the hooks in her skin tugged, and the river of influence flowed around her limbs. They pulled at her, What Waits nudging always.

But Erida held to the saddle. She watched the dragons dancing in the sky, locked together in a conflict not seen since the age of Spindles. If What Waits knew where the second dragon came from, she could not tell. But she could feel His hatred. It dripped from her own pores, seething with every beat of the blue dragon's wings.

It was difficult to know where to look. The dragons above, trading bouts of flame, or the battlefield below. Her own army was a wave, the tide of knights crashing against a merciless shore.

With every pass of the cavalry, every re-formed line, her throat tightened, until Erida feared she might gasp another breath. Each time, she prayed for the Elder line to collapse inward. For just one of them to falter.

They never did.

Erida snarled to herself. What Waits worked through her body, like poison in her veins, his rage fueling her own.

Balance, she told herself, clutching the reins. *Balance*.

"Their line won't break," Thornwall muttered. Then he leaned to a lieutenant, "Pull back the calvary, bring forth the archers. Defend the retreat."

Erida felt her anger flare.

"Retreat?" she snapped. "The lion does not retreat."

"Recover, I mean," Thornwall said quickly. "So we can send in the infantry."

Below, the Gallish army shifted, responding to Thornwall's orders, the Ionian army responding in kind. The Elders drew back, carrying their pikes with them. They were certainly stronger than mortal men, the pike line like a moving forest until they re-formed some yards back.

Erida felt the hooks in her skin, pulling and pulling, weak but incessant.

Soon, she told herself, and the thing inside her.

Again, her eyes burned. Again, she forgot to blink.

This time, she was not the only one. All down the rise, her lords and commanders held their breath, not daring to look away.

The infantry marched across the wasteland of blood, meeting the wall of Elders and mortals in a clash of shrieking metal, steel on steel, iron and bronze and copper ringing. Strong as the Elders were, they were hopelessly outnumbered. Erida's army ate at their edges, where the mortal soldiers were weaker. Flags of Ibal fell, the golden dragon trampled beneath the lion's feet. Eagle knights of Kasa stood out among the soldiers, their white armor gleaming up against the red sky. One by one they disappeared, overcome by the waves of battle.

Slowly but surely, the line drew back, the defense losing ground minute by minute, inch by bloody inch.

"What a war," Erida murmured, turning to Thornwall to smile at him, a peace flag between queen and commander.

She expected to see pride, or at least a flicker of triumph. Instead, Thornwall stared blankly at the field, stone-faced. All along the line of commanders, she saw the same, even in her Lionguard.

"This is not war," Thornwall murmured, glancing between the field and the castle above it. "This is slaughter. Death for no reason."

"Galland prevails. That is reason enough," Erida sneered. Again, the hooks pulled, again the river pushed at her legs, begging to sweep her forward into the city. At any cost.

Even her horse seemed to feel it, pawing the ground impatiently.

"Bring the cavalry around again, my lord," she said.

Thornwall blanched. "The knights need time to recover, Your Majesty. Let the infantry and archers do what they were trained for. I will not give that order."

Her eyes stung, her anger leaping.

"Will not?" Erida replied, wheeling on him. Her voice went dangerously low. "Their line is breaking. Sound another charge, and we will sweep them away."

There was some truth in it. The pike wall had collapsed, leaving the Ionians vulnerable.

"I will not," Thornwall said again. "The cavalry must recover. We will only lose—"

"Do you deny me? That is treason, my lord," she purred, leaning close. Her veils stirred in the dragon wind, the edge of her face exposed for a second.

And her burning, glowing eyes.

Thornwall's face went slack.

His mouth opened, only to be cut off by a blowing horn.

Not from their own line, but the Ionian army, echoing out over their massed companies. It was a high keening sound, not like the deep bellows of the Gallish horns. Erida rankled, squinting into the chaos, watching as the armies shifted.

Her breath caught.

"The elephants," Thornwall said flatly.

Before their eyes, a marching wall of war elephants tramped across the field, their armored legs crashing through Erida's infantry. Ibalet archers swayed on their backs, raining arrows on any Gallish soldier who managed to dodge their living siege engines.

Erida fought down a frustrated scream, her body buzzing, overcome with the urge to move. It was almost too much to bear.

"They will be worn down in time," Thornwall said distantly, his voice weak and already fading in her mind. "We can outlast any army in this valley."

Another horn blast stopped him cold.

This was not the trilling sound of the Ibalets calling another charge, nor the Gallish troops communicating through the battlefield. Not Kasa. Not the Elders. Not even the dragons could make such a sound, the long, shuddering call deep and metallic.

Erida whirled in the saddle, looking toward the southern horizon, to the long lake below the ridge of the castle. It shimmered red, turned to blood by the hellish sky.

"I have not heard that horn in decades," Thornwall murmured. His face went white, his hands shaking on the reins.

His officers whispered, exchanging confused glances. Erida's lords were less tactful. One of them choked out a sob. Another wheeled his horse and fled entirely, spurring his mount to a gallop.

The hooks in her skin threatened to tear her apart, so strong was their pull. Erida grimaced against them, trying to read the horizon and her commander.

"Thornwall?" she hissed through gritted teeth.

His throat bobbed, his eyes glassy.

"The Temurijon comes," he whispered.

Again the horn sounded, again her commander trembled. And the Countless wavered into being, a shadow crawling along the shores of the lake. The southern horizon turned black with their number, their flags streaming over the great army like a flock of birds. All were on horseback, armed with bow and blade.

Even as a girl, Erida learned the tales of the Temurijon. People of the steppes, a great warrior empire, Galland's only true rival in all the realm. Her advisors used to whisper they were lucky the Temur Emperor lost his taste for war.

It has certainly returned, Erida thought through the painful haze clouding her mind.

To his credit, Thornwall recovered before anyone else.

"Call up the rest of the cavalry, send word to the legions still marching to make haste," he said quickly. "Have them gallop out of the mountains if they must, pull back the infantry, we must re-form and brace for a Temur charge."

"Or tell them to turn and run," another lord spat, his face pale with fear.

The Temur will tear through us, devouring legion after legion as they come out of the mountains, Erida thought, reading the battle like a book.

Her head felt split in two, a lightning bolt forking down her body. Thornwall's voice echoed in one ear, a hissing language she did not know in the other. She understood it anyway, what it wanted, what He told her.

What she had to do, lest she lose everything she bled, fought, and killed for.

Erida barely thought the word before it left her mouth, her lips and tongue moving of their own accord.

"CHARGE," the Queen of Galland roared, her horse rearing beneath her.

For a moment, she rose up, like a hero in a tapestry, horse and rider framed against the red sky, her armor shining, her piercing gaze on the castle high above. Then the charger exploded into a gallop, hooves pounding over the darkening earth.

Dimly, she heard her Lionguard follow, spurring their horses to keep up with the Queen. Some tried to stop her, reaching for her reins, only for her horse to pull out of range. At a glance, Erida realized her mare's eyes burned, ringed red like her own.

Behind them, the cries of her commanders sounded loud and long, Thornwall's sharpest of all.

"Charge!" he echoed, directing the shattered cavalry after his queen. Even from a distance, Erida heard the regret in his voice. But there was no other choice her commander could make, not with the Queen herself on the battlefield.

Erida did not know where What Waits led, but she followed, letting Him direct their path down into the melee. The knights formed up with her, weary as they were, their horses foaming with sweat.

Through the scarlet haze, Erida realized her own soldiers cheered her on, bolstered by the presence of their lioness queen. They joined the charge too, sprinting as fast as they could, hammering swords and shields in a roar of sound.

One elephant reared, then another, spooked by the howling noise, and the oncoming horses. Their eyes rolled white, trunks raised to trumpet their fear as archers fell from their backs.

When one of the war elephants turned tail, its massive body

thundering back through the defensive lines, Erida pulled at the reins, directing her horse to follow, letting the elephant cut through the enemy army for her.

Somewhere, the Temur horn sounded again, a roar of thousands going up with it. Erida did not care and dared not look back. A defeated army did not bother her, even if the doomed soldiers were her own.

We can still use corpses, she thought, grinning.

The great elephant ran all the way to the city gates, soldiers of all kingdoms jumping from its path. To Erida's delight, the gates were still open, her enemy retreating with their wounded, streaming into the walled city. Erida and her charge followed, eating at the retreat.

What Waits dragged at her body, directing her up the ridge of the city. There were other Elders within, archers and spearmen, but few. They whittled at her Lionguard, felling one knight after another, until only the Queen remained, galloping alone. Protected by luck, or her demon god, she could not say.

The streets felt oddly deserted, but Erida did not have time to wonder about an enemy garrison. All she knew was the horse beneath her, and the fire burning beneath her skin.

Whoever remained to defend Iona was gone, drawn into the battle raging at the gates.

Or something worse ahead.

42

THE IMMORTAL TOMB
Domacridhan

Five hundred years he walked the castle of Tíarma, but tonight it was a stranger to him. Dom had never seen the castle like this, torn apart by battle, awash in blood. He knew her in crushing silence, in almost maddening peace. Now the smell of death permeated the passages no matter how far he ran, leaving the vaults behind. And the echoes were somehow worse. He mourned for Garion and the Vedera fighting, holding back the dauntless tide of undead.

He only hoped they slowed Taristan and Ronin, buying enough time.

The sun finally slipped behind the mountains, plunging the valley into shadow. Somehow the darkness was not so terrible as the cursed red light.

Sorasa kept stride next to him, her jacket torn open, the chain mail still glinting beneath. Bruises already bloomed on her neck, angry as a brand. They followed the pattern of Mercury's fingers. Dom could still see the Amhara lord's hands wrapped around her throat, her face turning blue, her eyes rolling as he squeezed the life from her.

Her heart still beats, he told himself as they ran, letting the sound of her pulse fill his head. The rhythm thumped until his heart matched her own, the pair of them in perfect tandem.

He listened beyond Sorasa's heart, searching the castle with his senses. Waiting for a familiar voice or scent to cross his path.

A horn blast sounded instead, echoing through the castle.

From the opposite direction of the battlefield, Dom realized, slowing his pace.

Sorasa paused, her bloody face tightening with concern. "I heard it too."

"Gallish reinforcements?" He winced at the thought, impossible as it felt. There were already so many legions bearing down on them. He hardly believed there could be more.

The horns rang out again and Sorasa grinned, showing equally bloody teeth.

"Who are they?" Dom asked, though he feared the answer.

"A chance," she breathed. As much as the Amhara despised hope, Dom saw it written all over her face. "The Temur have come."

He knew little of the Temurijon, but trusted Sorasa Sarn above almost all others. If she dared to believe in the Temur army, Dom would too.

His feet followed the familiar path through the endless corridors, until they reached the garden at the center of Tíarma. He let out a gasp of relief, stepping into the weak torchlight of the courtyard. Rose vines curled beneath his feet, still bare, the first buds still fighting to be born.

His eyes went to Corayne first, safe in Isibel's shadow, with Andry and Charlie on either side of her. All three gave a shout, calling to them across the courtyard.

"Domacridhan," the Monarch said, a tremor in her voice. She still had her sword and her armor, her silver hair loose across one shoulder.

There was little time for reunion, as much as Dom wanted to sweep the younger Companions into his arms. Instead, he crossed the garden, his brow furrowed into a hard line.

"Taristan is in the castle, along with the wizard," he barked, beckoning for Corayne with one hand.

Her eyes went round, eating up the weak light of the rose garden. "Shit," she murmured.

Shit indeed, Dom thought.

Sorasa spat blood on the ground. "We're going to get you out of here. The Temur have arrived. If we can make it to their army—"

At that, Isibel made a low noise in her throat, her pearlescent eyes flashing. With a weary sigh, she lowered her ancient sword, resting the blade against the dirt.

"The dead walk in my castle," she said bitterly, shaking her head. The Monarch gave a mournful look at the walls of the courtyard. Battle echoed through the open air. "I suppose this place has always been a tomb."

Even as time ran against them, Dom felt a pang of true sorrow for his aunt. Already he saw her staying behind, to die defending her throne.

"Come with us," he said, taking a step toward her. Again he beckoned, one hand outstretched to her.

Isibel squared her shoulders to her nephew. Her words took on a hard edge. "A graveyard for all of us, our souls trapped here, doomed to waste so far from home."

"The Ward is our home," he answered sharply.

"We need to go," Sorasa muttered next to him. "Leave her if we must."

The Monarch offered the assassin the lightest curve of a smile before her eyes returned to Dom.

"You do not know, Domacridhan, *Wardborn*. And you never will," she said, showing too many teeth. Her voice deepened. "I have seen the light of different stars. And I *will* see them again."

A sound like roaring wind filled Dom's ears.

Even among the Vedera, there were legends and old stories. Histories of Glorian. Tales of heroes and mighty kings. Isibel stood among them once, alive in another realm. She was mighty too, one of the most ancient beings left to walk the Ward.

"Isibel," he began.

Her sword moved so quickly even Dom could not see the steel, nor feel the blade as it plunged through his body. There was only the hole it left behind, through steel, cloth, and immortal flesh.

The roaring in his head intensified, as if a hurricane tore through the castle. He blinked slowly, his knees going weak.

Andry grabbed for Corayne, restraining her before she could lunge at his traitorous aunt.

"My daughter is dead because of you," Isibel screamed, her gray eyes gone to white fire. Dom heard her as if through water, distant and muffled. "It is only fair I return the favor."

As her voice worked through his mind, so did the pain work through his shock. It was dull at first, then so sharp his vision spun. Dom expected the smack of his body hitting the ground, but it never came.

Small, wiry arms caught him instead, lowering him to the ground with her, until his back rested against her chest. Bronze fingers worked at the buckles of his armor, tearing off the plates of steel and tossing them away to expose the wound beneath. The same hands ripped his shirt apart and pressed the scraps against the hole in his torso. Despite her quick thinking, blood bubbled through Sorasa's fingers. Her face crumpled at the sight of it, and Dom knew.

This would not be like the dagger in his ribs. Sorasa Sarn could not sew up this wound.

"It's fine," she hissed, lying, one hand still holding pressure. The other went around his chest, drawing him into her, letting him lean back into her body. "It's fine."

"That is what mortals say when they are in grave pain," he sputtered, choking on his own blood.

A tear hit his cheek, the only one Sorasa would spare.

"TRAITOR," Corayne shouted somewhere, bucking against Andry's grasp.

Her legs kicked out into open air, arms swinging, fighting like a cat in an alley. Only Andry's long arms kept her from attacking the Monarch with her bare hands.

Charlie was not so lucky.

The fallen priest was not a warrior. He held no skill with a sword, nor fist. Nor was he tremendously brave. Or so Dom thought.

The Prince of Iona blinked laboriously, watching as Charlon Armont launched himself at Isibel. A mortal criminal against an ancient queen.

She batted him aside as she would an insect. He landed hard, rolling into the vines, his eyes closed and jaw slack.

Corayne's shouts turned to sobs as the world began to dim around him.

"Taristan never stole the Spindleblade," Dom forced out. "You gave it to him."

Isibel did not meet his gaze.

"Cortael would never risk the realm for Spindlepower. You raised too noble a son," she replied with a huff. "Lucky that I did not kill Taristan in the cradle. Lucky that another remained, with the spine to do what must be done."

The pieces slotted together in Dom's mind. He shuddered against Sorasa.

So that is why you sent such a small force against him. Why you did nothing after we failed. He cursed Isibel to every god he knew, in this realm and any other. *Why you waited and wasted what little hope we had.*

"He did not find a secret way into the city," Dom whispered. "You showed him."

Isibel gave no answer, and that was answer enough.

Another arm went around his shoulders, more gentle than Sorasa's, her touch light as a feather. But her tears landed hard, cold against his bare shoulder. Corayne embraced him even as he bled, red staining over her own armor.

He wanted to hug her one last time, but found his strength failing, too weak to move.

Instead, Dom glared over Corayne's head, spearing Isibel with all the fury he had left.

"What Waits will destroy everything, even your Glorian," he spat.

To his dismay, Isibel only shrugged. "That is a chance I am willing to take."

43

ROSES GROWN IN BLOOD
Andry

It was the temple all over again. The Companions defeated, caught in the jaws of a trap none of them saw coming.

Sorasa cradled Dom where he lay, doing what she could to stem the flow of blood. It was a fool's errand, hopeless. Even Andry could admit it, a sob rising up in his throat. But he forced it down, telling himself to focus. There was no time to mourn, not with the Monarch of Iona looming over them.

Gently, Andry tugged Corayne away from Dom, putting some distance between her and Isibel. It would not matter much. But it mattered enough to Andry.

The torchlight flickered over Isibel's silver armor, turning her to liquid flame. She tossed her proud head and raised her nose, assessing Corayne as if she were an object, and not a person. Andry supposed that was how Isibel felt all along. Mortals were so far beneath her, she did not have the ability to see them as anything more than tools.

"You can feel it, can't you?" the Monarch said imperiously.

Corayne tightened in his arms, her armor against his own.

"I feel nothing," she snarled, lunging.

Andry held firm, his grip unyielding. He gritted his teeth, doing all he could to keep Corayne from ending up like Charlie, unconscious among the roses. Andry wished he could split himself in two, so he could stay with Corayne and go to Charlie in the same second.

Isibel continued at her languid pace. Her boots scuffed over paved stone and packed dirt, crushing vines beneath her feet. She glanced at the buds and thorns, her stare broken.

"Roses grow where Spindles cross, in their wake, their absence, and in their coming," she said, bending down to inspect the tangle of vines. "It's why the people of Old Cor took the rose as their sigil. To symbolize their own heritage as children of crossing."

Andry's breath caught as the rosebuds around Isibel began to bloom, growing before his very eyes. All over the courtyard, the roses unfurled, their scarlet petals like bursts of fresh blood.

"No," Corayne whispered, her voice thick with emotion. "Not now."

The Spindle, Andry thought, barely daring to say it even in his own head. *The Spindle is right here among the roses, waiting for us. Waiting for this moment.*

This has always been our fate, he thought bitterly. *Since the beginning.*

Distantly, he thought of his mother. Painful as it was, Andry let go of her, and any belief he might see her again. He could only hope she died of her sickness, and not slaughter. That she would never live to look upon a realm broken, the Ward in ashes around her.

The smell of roses perfumed the air, sickly sweet over the scent of blood, until Andry thought he might retch. He tipped his head, hoping for a fresh gust of wind. The red stars stared back, the open sky taunting him above the walls of the courtyard.

A dragon roared somewhere, and Andry prayed it was Valtik. *Come back, we need you. We are all going to die here if help does not come.*

"I know what it is to feel trapped between two worlds," he blurted out suddenly, stopping Isibel in her tracks.

She glared at him from a yard away and tipped her head, a look of disgust curdling her beautiful face.

"You know nothing of this pain, Mortal. *Wardborn*," she replied, the title a curse.

Slowly, Andry inched backward, pulling Corayne with him. *Valtik, Valtik, Valtik*, he screamed in his head, willing the dragon witch to hear him.

"I saw it in my mother. Born of Kasa, though she came to serve a northern queen." He swallowed hard. "She was forever torn between two kingdoms, between where she came from and where she ended up."

The Monarch shook her head. Sneering, she took another step forward, closing the distance again, until they were only a sword's length apart. Andry debated his own sword, and how quickly he could draw it while pushing Corayne to safety.

"I saw enough of your quick thinking in the council meetings, Andry Trelland," Isibel said. "I will not be drawn into your attempt to stall for time."

Beneath his armor, Andry trembled.

"Damn," he heard himself mutter.

The ancient blade of Iona rose, still edged in Domacridhan's blood. It leveled at Andry's head, the point narrowed to a lethal gleam.

"Kneel, Mortal," she commanded.

Andry only stood straighter, pulling Corayne away from the danger.

"Never," he said, backing away, crushing roses under his feet. He moved surely, his steps carrying him over to where Charlie lay.

To his relief, Andry spotted the slow rise and fall of the priest's chest.

For all her disdain, Isibel made a very mortal gesture, and rolled her gray eyes.

"Very well," she sighed.

Lightning fast, the immortal moved, throwing Corayne to the ground and taking Andry by the neck in the same motion, turning his body, forcing him to kneel beneath her. Her hand dug into his throat, her grip bruising. Then her blade raised against his skin. It happened so quickly, Andry barely knew it, realizing his doom long after he felt the cold bite of steel at his throat.

He braced himself for the slash of Isibel's sword through his neck.

But Isibel held him there, suspended between life and death, the blade perilously close.

"Kneel," she said again, her voice ragged in his ear.

On the ground, Corayne turned onto her back, pushing up on her elbows. Tears tracked down her dirty face. Andry wanted so badly to wipe them away, to feel her cheek against the palm of his hand. To hold her a little bit longer, until they were parted forever.

"Andry," Corayne bit out, not daring to move another inch. "Andry, I'm sorry."

He held her stare. *If she is the last thing I see, then so be it.*

"There is nothing to be sorry for," he whispered back, meaning every word.

"Yet," Isibel said behind him, the sword still against his throat. "Corayne an-Amarat, do what you were meant for."

One side of the Elder's mouth lifted in a cruel excuse for a smile. "Or watch him die."

On the ground, Corayne choked back another sob. Around her, the roses continued to open, taunting in their scarlet bloom. Shakily, she moved to stand. The Spindleblade remained against her back, the jewels of it winking.

"I will not," she said, though her voice quivered.

"Run, Corayne," Domacridhan sputtered, still slumped against Sorasa. Her hands still pressed against his wound. "You must run."

"Foolish counsel from a foolish soul," Isibel said, her hold on Andry tightening. He swallowed carefully, his skin bobbing just below the deadly steel. "Blood the sword, Corayne. And succumb to your fate."

"Don't," Andry said carefully, keenly aware of the cliff he stood upon. And what lay below.

So they stood, in terrible balance, one side against the other. But any semblance of a chance was just an illusion. Isibel could force Corayne to open the Spindle. She could kill them all where they stood to give the sword to Taristan, and everyone knew it. This was only torture, plain and simple.

Corayne shifted her gaze, her black eyes downcast. Another tear worked its way down her face. To his horror, her arm rose, a hand angling for the sheath at her back.

"Don't," he said again, softer this time.

The ring of a drawn sword drowned him out, the Spindleblade loosing with a flash of torchlight and roses. At the hilt, the amethysts and rubies glowed.

In the center of the courtyard, at the heart of the blooming flowers, something else glowed too. Thin, near invisible, little more than a thread of impossible gold.

Behind him, Isibel sighed out a low breath of satisfaction.

Corayne curled with pain, heartbreak written all over her face.

Andry gave a curse through gritted teeth, pushing back against the Monarch. It was like slamming himself against a wall. She did not give.

"Corayne," he said, his voice breaking.

She did not stop, nor look at him. Her eyes were on the sword, and her palm. She winced as her hand ran the blade's edge, drawing a line of red blood. *Cor blood.*

Shaking, she held out the sword, as if offering it to Isibel.

The Elder ruler stared back at her, eyes narrowed in confusion.

"There is your key," Corayne spat. "You want the Spindle, you do it yourself."

On his knees, Andry braced for the end, waiting for Isibel to claim her terrible prize. But she did not move, her sword still pressed against his neck. She didn't even blink.

Her hesitation was damnation enough.

Corayne gave a withering laugh to pierce the courtyard.

"You walk us all to the edge of doom, but cannot move the final inch," Corayne said, her voice dripping with cold judgment. "Coward."

Isibel answered with silence, her jaw clenched.

Then footsteps echoed from the halls, through the open archways of the courtyard, and Corayne froze. Slumped against Sorasa, Dom gave a low growl, hearing what Andry could not.

"So this is how it ends."

The sneering, hateful voice burned. If Andry was not already kneeling, he would have fallen to the ground.

Taristan of Old Cor stood silhouetted, looking down into the rose garden. He was as Andry remembered in Gidastern. Bloodstained, ragged, his eyes a deep well of bottomless hunger. When his gaze raked over the courtyard, Andry could not help but shiver. *No, he is worse than my memories*, he thought. Taristan seemed weary, his fingers bruised and bleeding even as they held an unremarkable sword. And the white veins splayed beneath his skin, creeping up his neck. He seemed to rot from within. Andry supposed that might be true.

The red wizard hunched next to him and Andry's stomach churned. Ronin's eyes, or what remained of them, wept blood over his face. His head turned, sightless; his nostrils flared as if he could smell the Spindle. *Perhaps he can.* Somehow, the wizard grinned, showing his rat teeth.

Behind them, shadows guttered along the passageways, outlining lurching shapes of twisted figures. Andry almost laughed at the circumstances. *What's a few more corpses now?*

Isibel turned her head, grimacing to Taristan and Ronin.

"I give you everything you need for victory, and still you mortals are so slow," she grumbled. "Well then, come. Claim what is yours, and I will do the same."

Ronin descended the stairs first, giggling, his steps haltingly slow as he limped into the garden. He swayed, one hand cast out lest he fall.

Corayne remained frozen, the Spindleblade in hand. Her own blood splattered the ground beneath the sword, falling in ruby drops. She sucked in a steadying breath.

Her uncle held her gaze as he approached, sparing only a glance for Domacridhan and Sorasa on the ground. Andry half expected the assassin to leap up and attack.

"You fought bravely," Taristan murmured as he passed.

Sorasa hissed back up at him like a snake. "You will regret this moment for the rest of your days."

In her arms, Dom gave a wet, halting laugh more akin to a death rattle.

"A king of ashes," the Elder said, blood flecking the air. "And ashes only."

A king of ashes is still a king. Andry remembered how Taristan snarled the same words so long ago, when Cortael was still alive, when all this had only begun. Then, he was a wolf, dangerous and desperate.

With a jolt, Andry realized that desperate, ravenous edge was gone. Taristan was a wolf still, but less reckless, less emotional. The man who laughed at his brother's dying body was stoic now, without smirk or reply.

His aim was the Spindle and nothing else.

"You may do the honors," he said flatly, gesturing to Corayne.

"Cowards, both of you," she cursed. "So eager for the ending of the world, but not by your own hands."

Her eyes flickered between her uncle and the wizard, then Andry again.

Andry watched the wheels turn in her head, her brilliant mind searching for some chance.

Then the dead appeared in the archways, the horror of them worse than Andry remembered. Some were skeletal, little more than animated remains, held together by rotting tendon and loose skin. Others were fresh, in Gallish uniforms, rough-spun clothes, even silks. Andry tried not to look at their faces, and glimpse who the corpses used to be before they fell under Taristan's sway.

But one face caught his eye.

From the roses, Dom gave a terrible moan, his face lined with sorrow.

An Elder princess stumbled among the undead as they surrounded the courtyard, still in the green armor she wore in Gidastern. Some plates were missing, others cracked, spattered with old, dark blood. What hair she had left hung loose across her face, a black curtain to hide a gruesome, rotting face.

"Ridha."

Isibel inhaled sharply, her body going taut behind Andry. He could not help but pity her, hateful as she was. Hers was a fate no parent deserved.

Gingerly, Andry turned his head an inch, peering out of the corner of his eye. Isibel wept silent tears, her eyes following her daughter's halting corpse. In her grief, her hands shook.

And her sword lowered an inch.

A storm broke inside the courtyard then, as Charlie leapt up from the ground, his long knife flashing in his hand.

Isibel screamed like a demon, woken from her stupor as Charlie's blade stabbed through the back of her thigh, between the plates of armor. Andry leapt away as she collapsed to the ground, clutching at her leg.

Time ceased to exist, everything happening through a dreamlike haze.

Andry's boot crunched down on Isibel's wrist, breaking her grip on her sword. With a kick, he sent the ancient blade spiraling into the roses, shearing petals and thorns as it skittered through the dirt.

Across the garden, Corayne's Spindleblade whistled through the air, slicing inches from Ronin's head. The blind wizard managed to dodge under the blow just in time, ducking Corayne's sword as she advanced, a furious battle cry on her lips. He curled his fingers, lunging out of her way, as Corayne rounded on Taristan.

Her sword met his own in a spray of sparks.

As they dueled, Sorasa clambered over the ground like a spider, leaving Dom to fall backward as she leapt onto Isibel's back. The Elder woman hissed, still on the ground, her wounded leg bent beneath her. Sorasa's own legs clenched, thighs wrapped around the Monarch's throat, threatening to choke the life out of her.

Blades crashed, hammering again as Corayne danced around Taristan.

Out of the corner of his eye, Andry saw Charlie take Sorasa's place, pressing the torn clothing back over Dom's wound.

For his part, the squire turned on the wizard, his sword in one hand, the ax in the other.

The scale balanced.

If only for a moment.

44

NAMELESS
Corayne

The Spindle shimmered, even as Corayne turned to put the golden thread behind her. She felt it always, as keenly as a needle in her skin. It called out to her with a voice like the wind, rising to a steady howl. And beneath, What Waits called too, His hissing whispers lacing through her mind.

The infinite realms wait for you, Corayne an-Amarat. The crossing of all roads, the center of every map. All of it is yours, you need only claim it.

Taristan's sword crashed against her own, the force of his blow making her arms shake. But he was not the Spindlerotten monster she remembered, gifted by a demon king, over-strong and invincible. He was as close to mortal as Corayne had ever known him, the testament of his new weakness written in every blooming bruise and new scar.

Her uncle wheeled in front of her, and her own life hung in the balance of every sword thrust.

Claim your fate, Corayne, the demon in her mind whispered.

"My fate is my own," she shouted, turning her shoulder to let a glancing blow slide off her armor. All her training came rushing back, every bit of footwork and swordplay.

Taristan puzzled over her as he sparred, his brow tightening even as he kicked at her legs. She barely dodged, almost losing her balance.

As she spun, Corayne caught a glimpse of Sorasa scuffling with Isibel. Her legs still squeezed her throat, using the strongest part of her body to subdue the Elder. It lasted only seconds, before Isibel recovered enough to throw Sorasa off, letting the assassin roll into the roses. Sorasa was up again in a second, a dagger in hand.

Andry was luckier, facing down a blind wizard. It seemed an even match, despite Ronin's magic. His curled fingers, powerful as they were, aimed and missed. The force of his magic blasted mere inches from Andry's face, blowing a hole through the roses.

"You are beaten, Corayne."

Taristan's voice made her whirl and she reacted, dropping under another sweep of his sword. He glared at her over the blade, his grand cloak torn away to show the old leathers beneath.

Corayne saw him as he was once, before the Queen of Galland joined her fate to his own. A rogue alone in the world, a mortal man born to nothing—and somehow everything.

"This realm will fall," he continued, grim. She expected him to gloat, but his pale face remained as stone, unfeeling.

"And you will fall with it," Corayne snapped back at him, adjusting her grip. Her vambraces lashed tight against her forearms, the clawed edges gleaming like the edge of the Spindleblade. "Don't you understand that by now?"

His next strike was lazy, tauntingly so. No matter her training of the last few months, Corayne was still no match for her uncle's long life in the gutters of the world. He danced within her guard and slammed his shoulder against her chest, sending her sprawling backward to land in a heap of armor.

He looked down on her with a grimace. "Better to stand victorious at the right hand of a god than to die nameless and forgotten."

His sword fell like a bolt of lightning.

Corayne raised her forearms, the steel edge of her vambraces catching the blow. The force of it shook her entire body and her muscles screamed in protest.

"There is no victory, Taristan!" she growled as he recoiled from the strike. In an instant, she scrambled to her feet again. "I have seen the Ashlands. I have seen what he will do to this realm and every other."

Dust. Death, she thought, even as the same tempting whisper braided through her mind. What Waits hissed, inches away, yearning to cross through. She remembered His shadow in the Ashlands, the outline of a monstrous king. It wavered beneath a dying sun, surrounded by a land of echoes and corpses. *The destruction of everything anyone ever held dear.*

Corayne set her feet, wrapping another hand around the Spindle-blade to grasp it with all her strength. Taristan glared, the pair locked together as the rest of the world boiled around them.

"You will be forgotten either way, another mind broken beneath the temptation of What Waits," Corayne said, desperation in every word. "You are just a tool, Taristan. Mortal as the rest of us. *Nameless.*"

She did not expect Taristan to care, if he even listened to her at all.

Her voice shook. "Useful until the second you aren't, until the moment he casts you away to find another fool."

To her shock, Taristan did not move forward, though his sword remained between them. Locks of dark red hair stuck to his sweaty face, a few strands moving with gasps of breath. Despite the white veins crawling under his skin, and the edge of red flaring around his eyes, he looked more mortal than Corayne knew he could be.

Rare emotion darkened his gaze, the black eating up the hellish red.

Confusion, Corayne saw. *Regret.*

"I know what he promised you," she bit out. "A purpose. A fate."

Again the whispers curled. *The infinite realms wait for you.* Cursed as Corayne knew the offer to be, some part of her heart sang for it anyway.

"I know what that feels like, to someone like us. Torn as we are, abandoned and lost." Her eyes stung again, her gaze swimming. "But it isn't real. All He brings is death."

It erupted around them now, the evidence of it in every inch. Blood poisoned the air. The corpse army still surrounded the courtyard. They hung back, as if watching some horrific play.

"Be done with this, Taristan," the wizard sneered, his empty eyes trailing red tears. He sent a blast of magic over Andry's head. The squire dropped, narrowly avoiding the spell. It caught Isibel instead and she snarled, stumbling back.

"The Spindle is here," Ronin continued, oblivious. "We need only open the door and walk through."

"To *what?*" Corayne roared back. "Where do you think this ends for you?"

Taristan's gaze shifted, his eyes sliding out of focus as something crossed his mind.

Someone, Corayne realized with a burst of energy.

"Where do you think this ends for *her?*" she shouted, taking a daring step forward.

Whatever mask her uncle wore cracked, his face going whiter than she thought possible. A war broke in his mind, his eyes suddenly spiraling between red flame and black abyss.

"What Waits will consume Erida, as He consumes all things," Corayne pleaded, another step closer. The whispers, the howling wind, the chaos of battle. It all raged, overwhelming her senses. "If you will not save the realm, you can at least save *her*."

A low grunt of pain turned her aside, the voice too familiar. Corayne spun, unguarded, to watch Andry's sword fall from his grasp and land at his feet. He bowed backward, his arms splayed wide, his mouth opening and sputtering, gasping for breath.

Among the roses, Ronin stood, his fist clenched. He could not see, but his ruined eyes pointed at Andry, his arm thrust out in the squire's direction. With a horrible smile, he raised a fist. And Andry's body rose with it.

"NO!" Corayne screamed, forgetting all things as she lunged across the distance.

Ronin did not flinch, throwing out his free hand. A blast of air followed, striking Corayne dead on. She fell backward over herself, the Spindleblade landing inches away.

"Take the sword, Taristan," Ronin said, his teeth bared, spittle spraying from his mouth. "The Spindleblade is yours."

In front of him, Andry dangled, toes scraping at the ground as he rose higher and higher.

Ronin's fist curled tighter, and Andry screamed.

The wizard grinned again, the blood coursing down his face. "Do what you were made for."

On the ground, Corayne watched helplessly, tears streaming, the sight too horrible to bear. Andry writhed in pain. Dom's face drained of color, his breath weakening with every second. Behind him, Charlie kneeled, praying to every god. And Sorasa held off Isibel with every trick she knew, dwindling as they were.

Taristan was worst of all. His boots crunched through the roses, trampling red petals underfoot. He reached the Spindleblade, fingers wrapping around the hilt of the sword.

Over his shoulder, the Spindle still danced. It looked like the crack in a door, separating one dark room from another filled with light.

"What I was made for," Taristan of Old Cor said, raising the Spindleblade.

In front of him, Ronin tipped his head back, his mouth opened wide, his teeth too sharp, the blood still trailing down his face and over his neck, spattered all down his robes.

"It is done, my lord," the wizard hissed, a rat in all things. Smiling, he tipped his head back, as if basking in the light of a terrible sun.

"It is done," Taristan echoed, slicing the Spindleblade through open air, the edge of it still red with Corayne's blood.

And then Ronin's.

Two men fell to the ground in the same instant. Andry dropped first, released from the wizard's dark magic. He collapsed to the dirt, groaning.

Ronin made no noise at all. The two halves of his body fell with a dull, final thud.

45

A QUEEN OF ASHES
Erida

Erida hated Iona, every part. The immortal city was an ugly, gray thing to her, little more than another smudge to be wiped from the map.

She expected to meet some opposition in the gateyard of the Elder castle. But most of the guards were wounded if not dead, and she rode through unaccosted. Cobblestone and pavings turned to marble as she galloped into what was once a grand hall. She smelled death in all its forms, fresh and rotting. The marble floor ran slick with blood, a war raging within the walls. The remaining Elders battled at the overwhelming number of undead as they flooded the passages of the castle. Bodies lay everywhere, Elder and mortal and Ashlander corpses. Erida glanced at them, looking for familiar faces. She saw none.

The horse skidded on the slick floor and she leapt from its back, landing in the carnage. Her feet moved without thought, following a path she did not know through the castle. The hooks dragged, the river pulled, the wind howled—Erida felt unmoored in her own skin. It terrified and thrilled her in the same measure.

We are so close.

She turned a corner, her armor heavy on her limbs. But What Waits pushed, until the cloying smell of roses hit her in a wave.

Death stank beneath the flowers, until she could not distinguish one from the other.

Her eyes burned, every step more difficult. And yet Erida knew she could not stop running, even if she wanted to. She found a courtyard at the center of the castle, the undead leering around its perimeter. Despite the still early days of spring, impossibly large roses bloomed all over the garden. Red as blood, big as her fist. The vines curled before her eyes, spiked and menacing, the leaves an acid green. She sucked in a shallow breath, her chest tight with anticipation.

Nothing could have prepared her for what she saw in the courtyard below.

There was Domacridhan, gasping for air, his bare chest white and heaving. A round little man in ill-fitting armor tended to him, pressing blood-soaked rags to the Elder's abdomen. Across the garden, the assassin battled like a tiger against a wounded immortal woman.

They meant little to Erida of Galland, in the scheme of things. They were already dead in her eyes, already defeated.

For a Spindle burned, right there in the courtyard of the Elder castle. The golden thread gleamed, almost disarming in its smallness. But Erida knew better by now. Small things changed the course of history.

We were all small things once. And for some, small is all they will ever be, she thought, her eyes landing on Corayne.

The young woman lay crumpled on the ground, her black hair undone. Corayne cut a tragic figure, like some doomed hero in a fairy tale. She wept too, reduced to what she always was.

A little girl at the end of the world, Erida thought. *Nothing, and no one.*

The Prince of Old Cor stood tall over his niece, his body washed black by the shadows. His hair clung to his face, damp with sweat. It was a long climb up the vaults of the castle, in darkness and dread.

Erida's breath hitched. The sight of him was like a cool cloth on a fevered brow, and she felt some heaviness lift from her body.

When he raised his arm, the Spindleblade clutched in his hand, Erida wanted to fly. Taristan was not just alive, but victorious. A conqueror as she always knew he would be.

What Waits hissed inside Erida, His voice joining with her own, until her ears rang with the same three words.

We have won.

Taristan turned the sword over slowly, inspecting the scarlet edge. Blood dripped from its length. Judging by the cut on Corayne's palm, Erida knew who the blood belonged to. And what it meant for the realm.

"It is done, my lord," Ronin hissed, his voice somewhere between man and monster. He stood tall for once in his rotten life, one hand clawed into the air, holding a body aloft.

Andry Trelland.

In spite of herself, the smallest pang of regret worked through Erida of Galland. She swallowed hard, trying to push back a rush of unwanted memories. Andry Trelland had grown up a page boy in her palace, and then a squire. Always kind, always noble, everything a true knight could ever be. The other boys despaired of his softness, and even a few knights did too. Erida never could, not then.

And even now, after his betrayal, after all the ruin he brought, Erida still could not find it in herself to hate him.

But she could not find the words to spare his life either.

I am only glad I do not have to give the order myself, she thought, watching as Ronin's magic tightened around the squire. Andry gave a yelp of pain, his eyes too wide, a red flush working beneath the warm brown of his skin.

Beneath him, Ronin leered without eyes, his bloody tears still flowing.

"It is done," Taristan echoed.

With a low grunt of exertion, Taristan swung the Spindleblade. It arced in a flash of steel, reflecting the torchlight and the red stars. For a moment, Erida glimpsed something else in the mirror edge. The shadow of a figure, its outline black, two burning flames where eyes should be.

Erida braced for the feel of a shattering Spindle, waiting for the telltale crackle of power as it hummed through the air. But it never came.

The Spindleblade sliced through Ronin's body instead, severing him at the waist.

Erida let out a guttural scream as the wizard fell apart, and Andry tumbled back to the ground. She howled out her rage and confusion, even as the steps down into the courtyard tripped away beneath her feet. It was not her body that moved, but something within, pulling at her limbs, guiding her as it guided her wretched horse.

The undead moaned with her, stumbling through the archways around the rose garden. Their wizard was dead, their leashes dropped. Some fell to pieces entirely, whatever magic held them together disappearing.

"Erida," Taristan said, his voice rasping and low.

She heard him as if he spoke directly in her ear. Her eyes burned, so hot as to be icy cold. The edge of her vision hazed white, pulsing with the beat of her own heart.

Around the garden, Corayne and her allies scrambled, drawing together.

Erida cared little for them, her focus on Taristan—and his eyes. She willed his eyes to be like her own. Gone the fathomless black, replaced by swirling lines of red and gold.

Andry Trelland watched her from a distance, his jaw falling open.

"What have you done to yourself, Erida?" Andry murmured.

"What I must," she answered, before grabbing for Taristan with both hands.

It was the truth. This was the cost of freedom. From commanders, councilors, from usurpers and jailer husbands. From every man who would betray her, trick her, trap her, until she was just another old woman leaning on a cane, whispering in corners, all her life behind her, and only regret ahead.

Taristan caught her by the wrist, holding her up as much as he held her back.

"Look what your god did to her," Corayne called out across the roses. "Look at what he demands."

Erida felt the demon scream up inside her, so fierce her body lurched. She snarled against it, lunging for Corayne, only for Taristan to reel her in.

"It is done," he said again, echoing the words of his dead wizard.

To her horror, Erida watched as Taristan cast the sword aside, letting it drop at their feet. The Spindle pulsed again, calling out to the sword. *Calling out to me.*

His palm was cold against her cheek, sickly so. No longer a balm but a block of ice, too painful to stand. Erida tried to turn out of his grip, only to meet his abyss-black eyes. Her own eyes seared, her tears like acid.

"I will not let you burn, Erida," Taristan growled, forcing her to hold his gaze.

Her body bucked in his grasp, a puppet jumping on someone else's string. "You promised me," she rasped. "You promised me the realm entire."

"You are realm enough for me," he answered.

Part of her wanted to relent. To fall into Taristan's arms, to let go.

But the map of the world swam before her eyes, the edges of it carved into her. She knew Galland's borders like the lines of her own face, like the feel of the throne, like the weight of the crown. They were born into her, born *to* her. Just like her fate.

His hands still pressed against fevered skin, at her cheeks and her wrist.

"Balance," he hissed to her, his own eyes a battlefield for control. "Balance."

Erida swam in her own head, through hot and cold, light and dark. Her voice sounded weak, distant, her thoughts struggling to form. As before, something wove around Taristan's grip on her, working its way along their bodies. This time, it did not pull them closer. But it wormed between, pushing them apart.

Her breath rattled, the voices in her head blurring and blending.

Until only one remained. And the world went shockingly clear.

This is the cost.

Something changed in her voice, a lacing of power she did not possess before.

"There is no balance between mortal and god," she said coldly. "If you will not be a king of ashes, then I will be its queen."

She did not know where the strength came from, but her wrist twisted, breaking his grasp as she lunged to the ground. Her wounded hand closed around the hilt of the Spindleblade, the leather still warm, the jewels flashing red and purple. Pain lanced up her arm, but she held on as tightly as she could, the ground moving beneath her, the Spindle like a beacon.

And then the blade moved too, the edge of it still wet with Corayne's blood.

The blood of Old Cor.

46

CLAIM YOUR FATE
Corayne

Whatever you decide, possible death or certain death, be quick about it.

Sorasa said that once, in the shadows of Ascal, on a night so far from where they were now it made Corayne's head spin. She remembered the lesson too well.

Certain death, she thought as Erida seized the Spindleblade, and cut the golden thread in two.

A light flashed and Corayne ducked, squeezing her eyes shut against the terrible brightness. Someone pressed in against her, his touch gentle but firm. *Andry*, she knew, his embrace familiar as he tried to shield her with his own body.

Power and magic crackled over their skin, the sensation impossible to comprehend.

Then the smell of death and roses disappeared, wiped away. Replaced by something impossible.

Corayne expected the Ashlands. A red world of dust and ruin. Another realm broken. *Or worse*, she thought. *His realm. Asunder, the abyss.*

Instead, her eyes snapped open to see lush green grass under her hands, rich and dark. A warm breeze rustled her hair, as it rustled the branches in the countless trees. Verdant leaves shimmered all around them, dancing beneath the light of a gentle, unseen sun.

Slowly, Corayne straightened, her mouth agape. She wheeled, drinking in the impossible place.

Next to her, Andry did the same, his dark eyes wide.

"What is this realm?" he murmured over her.

Gone was Tíarma and the courtyard. Gone were Sorasa, Dom, Charlie, and even Isibel. Gone were the undead corpses, their withering bodies already a memory. Instead, Andry and Corayne stood in the middle of an endless forest, surrounded by impossibly perfect trees, each one the same, silver-barked with lush green branches. Even the temperature was perfect, like a lovely spring day. The land ran flat in every direction, without undergrowth, bare but for a level carpet of cool, soft grass.

The trees arced together, like the buttresses of a vaulted cathedral, forming a maze of perfect corridors in every direction, each one as far as the eye could see. Except one. A single passage through the trees ended a few yards away, blocked by a set of carved marble stairs. They rose sharply into the treetops, with no indication as to where they ended. If they ended at all.

Their own Spindle thread sparkled a few feet away, glowing with inner light.

It was not alone.

Other threads glimmered through the trees, just waiting to be opened. Countless Spindles leading to countless realms.

"The Crossroads," Corayne finally answered, her heart in her throat. "The door to all doorways."

Andry stared at the trees, the light of endless Spindles turning his brown eyes to molten gold. "By the gods," he breathed. "Every realm."

By the gods indeed, Corayne thought, trying to fathom the sheer weight of the world around her. What each Spindle contained. What lay just behind the flickering threads, what lands and new realms. Her mind spun with possibility.

And temptation.

Anywhere I wished, I could go. Farther than any mortal thought possible, beyond every horizon that ever existed. Her Corblood heart sang and ached, beating so hard Corayne feared her ribs might shatter.

Anywhere. Perhaps even home.

Corayne did not know where her ancestors came from, but it haunted her just the same. Since childhood, or even longer, she realized. Since she first looked up at the sky and wondered what lay behind the stars, what called to her across the endless blue.

A wretched snarl brought her back to her body.

Across the clearing, Taristan gathered Erida in his arms. She lurched against him, her once beautiful face drawn and pale, her eyes too terrible to comprehend. White veins wriggled beneath her skin, like worms on a corpse.

"Erida, remember yourself, remember who you are, what we have built," Taristan growled, his wife struggling against him. He took her with both hands, and the Spindleblade fell from her grip.

As much as Corayne hated him, she paused at the sight of Taristan's face. He looked stricken, heartbroken even, his unfeeling air replaced by sorrow. Fire danced in his eyes, but the black was there too, warring for control. Not like the Queen. Whatever sapphire blue there was in Erida had long disappeared, eaten up by the demon in her head.

"I am what you made me," Erida screamed back at her consort, trying to claw out of his grasp. "I could not sit by and watch you falter. Not after all we have given."

With Taristan distracted by the Queen, their opening was clear.

Corayne and Andry ran together, the grass soft beneath their boots. His sword was left behind in Allward, so Andry drew his dagger and his ax. Corayne had nothing but her own two hands and her clawed vambraces, their edges glinting.

She made for the Spindleblade, all her focus bent on the sword.

Then a clap like thunder went through the trees and all the Crossroads rumbled, the ground shaking under their feet. Corayne almost lost her footing and dropped to her knees to steady herself, Andry crouching beside her as the earth shook.

Taristan froze, what little color he had left draining from his face. In his arms, Erida continued to squirm, her expression desperate and devastating, like a starved woman seeing food for the first time. Like a priest before her waking god.

She pulled in Taristan's grasp, her livid, burning eyes on the marble steps. A hideous smile split her face as she sensed something Corayne could not.

Another ferocious crack split the air and the marble split with it. A long fissure spiderwebbed down the otherwise flawless white stone, the line like a jagged bolt of lightning.

Corayne shivered, her body jumping with the noise.

Something is coming.

"Get back to the Spindle," Corayne hissed, shoving Andry away. "Run."

But Andry Trelland did not move. Instead, his fingers wove through her own, his touch warm and familiar.

For once in her life, Corayne understood what home must feel like.

"With me," Andry said, dragging them both to their feet.

The ground shook again but they kept their footing, staggering only a little as they ran for the sword.

Across the clearing Erida threw herself out of Taristan's arms, laughing wildly when another crack ran through the marble.

Taristan moved to follow her, only to whirl back. He looked between Erida and the Spindleblade still lying in the grass. Anguish and anger warred across his face, as he warred within himself. His eyes darkened, going blacker by the second, until his brow furrowed. He looked like someone waking up from a nightmare.

Corayne slowed and met his eyes across the steel of the Spindleblade. The sword reflected both their faces, similar as they were, chained together by blood and destiny.

She expected him to lunge for the blade, but Taristan did not move, his breath coming in short, ragged gasps.

"Claim your fate, Taristan of Old Cor," she said softly.

Claim yours, Corayne an-Amarat.

The voice was a needle between her eyes. She screamed against it, almost collapsing, only for Andry to hold her steady. What Waits scratched at the edges of her mind, begging to be let in. Begging to hold Corayne as he held Taristan. As he consumed Erida.

"My fate is my own," Corayne snarled aloud, to Taristan and the demon god hammering his way through the realms. "To claim or break."

Another rumble shook the earth as another crack ran down the stairs. This time the noise was unmistakable.

A footstep.

The air shuddered, and a flash of light swept through the green forest, blinding them all for an instant. When it cleared, Corayne opened her eyes to embers, the trees burned black, the branches crumbling, the beautiful leaves blown to ashes in a merciless wind.

The destruction raged, the flames voracious and churning around them. It felt like being at the eye of a storm. Corayne gritted her teeth against the sudden heat, her eyes slitted through the smoke. Even as the fires burned and What Waits screamed, she pushed through, holding on to her mind and her goal.

She grabbed for the Spindleblade, its jewels leering red and purple. Her fingers brushed the gems, but another hand was faster, the fingers white, bones all but showing through tight skin. Veins wriggled like pearly worms.

Erida.

Corayne leapt backward just as the Queen swung, arcing the blade with all the strength in her body. She was no swordsman, her movement jerky and unpracticed.

Andry swept his knife to meet her blade, eager to block her next harried blow.

He met Taristan's own dagger instead.

"Run while you can, Squire," Taristan bit out, twisting his wrist to disarm Andry and throw him back in the same motion. "Run as you did so long ago."

In reply, Andry reached for the hand ax still belted at his waist. He spun it deftly. "I will not."

"Dutiful squire," Erida sneered, hateful with every breath. Rage rotted through her. "What an ending for you. To die trying to kill the queen you swore to protect. Your father would be ashamed."

Andry gave a roar and spun, the ax circling with him only to meet Taristan's dagger again. They both parried, exploding into a furious duel. The squire was not Taristan's better, but he was close to his equal. Enough to hold him off.

Torn as she was between Andry and the sword, Corayne could not hesitate. She lunged after Erida, dodging every clumsy swipe of the Spindleblade.

Livid, burning eyes looked back at her, fiery as the inferno around them. Erida pulled her lips into something like a smile, but worse, her mouth too wide, showing too many teeth. Little by little, she backed toward the steps, even as Corayne bore down.

"I did not think I would get to kill you myself," Erida said, her voice raspy.

Corayne's training came back to her in flashes, her lessons hard-learned. She struck with her free hand, swiping her spiked vambraces at Erida's face. The Queen dodged, but barely, sparing herself the worst of the blow. Still she stumbled, a trail of blood across her cheek.

Somewhere, Taristan shouted, his concentration split between Andry and the Queen.

"I did not think you were stupid enough to listen to What Waits," Corayne spat back. "And give Him everything you ever could be."

Another crack ran through the marble, another step resounded through the Crossroads. The wind shifted, the air shuddering with embers.

Corayne struck again, forcing Erida to her knees, the Spindleblade shakily held between them. But Erida was still ferocious, her teeth bared, even as her face bled.

Corayne almost laughed at the sight. The Queen of Galland kneeling to a pirate's daughter. Then pity washed over her. Erida was a girl once too, surrounded by enemies, grasping for any way to survive the pit of vipers she called a home.

But Corayne's compassion soon ebbed. She had not forgotten every-one dead for Erida's hunger. For her own will, long before What Waits crept into her heart.

When Erida struck again, Corayne caught her by the arm. She broke the Queen's hold on the Spindleblade with a well-practiced twist, compliments of Sorasa Sarn. This time Corayne was faster, snatching the sword off the ground to raise the gruesome steel painted in too much blood.

Shaking, Corayne laid the sword to Erida's exposed neck, the edge of it against skin.

Beneath her, Erida choked back a gasp of frustration. There was no remorse in her, only bitter acceptance.

"This is the cost," she said, breathless, torn between a scream and a sob. "This is the price I must pay."

Corayne wanted to slap Erida, to scream in her face. *This was your own doing, your own choice*, she wanted to yell. *Your greed brought us here long before What Waits wormed into your head. You destroyed half the world for nothing more than another crown.* Around the hilt of the Spindleblade, her fingers curled, itching to wrap around Erida's throat.

But Corayne held her ground. Her eyes flicked up, to the steps now inches away. They splintered, ashes sweeping across crumbling marble. She still could not see the top, the upper levels engulfed in shadow.

A red light pulsed among the branches, thumping like the beat of a ragged heart.

"We can only walk the path in front of us," Corayne said, repeating Erida's own words from so long ago. From another life, when they first met, queen and pirate's daughter.

On the ground, the Queen's ruined face crumbled, tears gathering in her eyes. Corayne half expected them to turn to steam.

"I leave you to the path you've chosen, Erida," Corayne murmured, taking a step backward. The sword still angled between them, keeping the Queen at bay. "The fate you deserve."

The steps rumbled, the earth shaking. Erida swayed with it, her ash-brown hair singed at the edges as embers landed. For a moment, they flared up, beautiful as a crown.

You do not have the spine for it, my dearest love.

Corayne flinched as if stabbed, almost losing her grip on the sword.

Insider her head, What Waits spoke with another voice, the only one that could break Corayne's heart.

Mother.

Something shifted in the smoke, a shadow at the top of the marble stairs. It took form slowly, solidifying into the silhouette of a figure too horrifying to comprehend. He was too tall, His limbs too long, His head dipped beneath the weight of impossible horns. As Corayne looked, frozen to the spot, the red light flared and pulsed faster, until two slitted eyes opened in the shadows, bright as the heart of a lightning bolt, burning hotter than any fire ever could.

As the terrible pulse pounded, so did Corayne's.

How I despise that flame inside you, that restless heart of yours, What Waits said with her mother's voice. *And how I envy it too.*

Though she could not see them, Corayne could feel His too-long fingers reaching across the Crossroads, His claws dragging lightly over her skin. She shivered and tried to turn away, tried to run, tried to scream.

Let me in, and I will make you queen of any kingdom you wish. The voice wavered, her mother's playful tone fading into something darker, heavier. *I will save the life of your Elder. I will spare your friends in the castle. I will keep the Ward as it is now, green and alive, its people free and safe. I will make your realm the jewel in my crown, and you its keeper.*

What Waits purred and snarled.

Let me in.

"I will not," Corayne hissed through gritted teeth, the battle raging inside her own head. "I will not."

Her legs shook, but slowly, one foot moved, sliding inch by awful inch. And then an arm hooked across her chest, throwing her backward with reckless abandon.

It was enough to break the spell, and What Waits howled, His rage so absolute it shook the trees, echoing through the ashen Crossroads.

Corayne landed in Andry's arms, the Spindleblade still in hand. She could only watch, slack-jawed, as Taristan pushed them both away, back toward the Spindle. He threw one last glance at his niece, his eyes black all the way through.

They were her father's eyes, and her own too.

Her body shook as Taristan turned around, never to look at them again.

If he feared the steps, and the shadow at the top, he did not show it. Instead, he sank to his knees, facing Queen Erida. Slowly, he took her head in his hands, brushing away the ashes clinging to her torn and bloody cheeks. Erida shuddered in his grasp, her body twitching, trying to get away even as she pulled him closer.

For a moment, Corayne thought she glimpsed a flash of blue in Erida's eyes.

Then the steps rumbled, the earth shaking.

This is not over, Corayne of Old Cor.

The voice hissed and whispered, speaking in all languages. Corayne turned from it as she turned from her uncle and the Queen, leaving them with the embers.

The Spindle slid over Andry and Corayne, the Spindleblade with them.

When her boots hit stone, Corayne whirled, gripping the sword with both hands, all her strength poured into a single motion. The Spindleblade cut through the air, severing the portal, leaving Taristan and Erida behind forever.

However long forever was.

* * *

They returned to a crater of corpses, the Ashlander army withering where they stood. Whatever had kept them alive seeped out of them, like blood into the ground. One was fallen already, her green armor dull; the Princess of Iona finally returned home. Isibel lay next to her, her eyes closed, as if only sleeping. In a glance, Corayne knew she would never wake up.

The living flooded through the courtyard, Elder soldiers dispatching the few corpses still clinging to cursed life. Their figures blurred, unimportant to Corayne. She searched the ground instead, eyes roving over paved stone and roses.

Domacridhan lay in the same place, with Sorasa kneeling over him again. His blood dried on her hands, turning them a horrific black color. His eyes were still open, wavering, but always fixed on her face. She did not blink, holding his gaze.

Charlie was there too, slumped against a battered but breathing Garion. The assassin held a bloody rag to one side of his face.

When Charlie's eyes met hers, his mouth dropped, his feet already moving to meet her.

Corayne did not know how to feel. Triumph sounded wrong. There was no victory, only survival.

One hand still clutched Andry's, the other the Spindleblade. It felt strange in her grasp now, the hum of it dimmed. It was the same with the Spindle, the light of the golden thread sputtering, and then fading away. Closing the door to the Crossroads forever.

It was the last thing Corayne saw before her vision slanted, dark spots dancing in front of her eyes. Until the blackness ate up the world, and there was nothing at all.

* * *

Dawn broke cold and yellow over Iona, the relentless clouds of Calidon blown away by a cleansing wind. The red light was gone from the sky, as if it never existed at all. Small fires still burned within the city, and out on the field. Most flickered around the jeweled corpse of a fallen dragon, its gemstone hide gone dull, its wings like black sails against the ground.

On the battlefield, a company of Temur riders made another pass, rounding up survivors of every army. Kasa, Ibal, the immortals. And Galland too, whoever remained, too injured to run with the rest of the legions. The lucky ones scattered into the mountains, fleeing before the full might of the Temur Emperor, and his magnificent Countless.

Corayne leaned against the ramparts of the city wall, facing into the cold wind, letting it shiver her to the bone. She still could not believe her eyes. The massive Temur army was a brown and black sea across the valley floor, their numbers too numerous to comprehend. She could hardly fathom how many ships were needed to ferry them across the Long Sea. Or how her own mother could lead such an armada.

Many flags streamed in the air. A black wing on bronze danced for the Temur. The flags of Iona still held, the flags of Kasa and Ibal too. Green and silver. Purple. Blue and gold. Bronze. Flags from every corner of the map. From far-flung kingdoms. Mortal and immortal both.

They answered the call. They saw what faced us, what threatened the realm entire. And they came.

For all the death, all the loss, Corayne could hold on to that.

We are, at the end of all things, a realm united, and not apart.

EPILOGUE
Afterward

It was not Charlie's first time at the gallows, nor even his second. Still, he did not enjoy the feeling of rough rope on his soft neck. It chafed and itched.

He eyed the small crowd gathered around the platform, most of them slack-jawed peasants who were only just hearing of the war, months after it ended. Only two guards bothered to watch. Charlie was hardly a threat, a round little fugitive finally caught for his otherwise boring crimes. At least the air was warm. Spring had come bursting, all the world in bloom, as if to make up for a long, bloody winter. And now summer reigned, the realm edged in hazy gold.

There was no executioner in a black hood. Just a toothless man who worked odd jobs in the town. Charlie supposed anyone could kick a bucket out from under a man's feet.

When he approached, Charlie braced for the worst. No matter how many times he stood the gallows, he always wondered which would be his last.

Then the rope broke over him, sliced clean by a perfectly aimed arrow. The crowd gave a cry of shock as Charlie leapt off the barrel, leaving the toothless man behind. He scrambled to the edge of the platform, just as the horse and rider burst through the fray. The guards had only just roused from their stupor by the time Charlie was safe in the saddle, holding on to Garion in front of him.

The pair laughed all the way out of town and into the Madrentine hills.

It was not long before they found Sigil's camp, the Temur woman cutting a broad silhouette against the trees.

"I was beginning to think something went wrong," she said, smiling. "It's not every day a one-eyed man can hit a target."

Garion gave her a wink with his good eye. The other was scarred shut, still healing even months after the battle of Iona.

"I did my best," he said, sliding off the horse.

Charlie jumped down behind him, proud of his own performance. *I'm getting better at this.*

"What's the take?" he asked, eager.

"Less than I'd hoped," Sigil answered. She bent to her things and pulled out a clinking pouch, upending it to show a spray of gold coins. "Your bounty has gone down. Something about worse problems than you in the Ward?"

Frowning, Charlie counted the coins in a glance.

"Well, I suppose I should get back to work, then."

Sorasa Sarn stood at the edge of the city, the desert stretching wide and golden, shimmering with the last rays of sunset. It was already cooling, the heat of the day driven off by lengthening shadows. She patted at the horse beneath her, a sand mare. The pride of Ibal, faster than any other horses in the Ward. And a gift from the Heir.

It was still strange, to have friends in the highest of places. And enemies in the lowest of them.

She eyed the desert again. Almasad was the closest city to the citadel, though the seat of the Amhara Guild was still many days off. It was a grueling journey through the sands, the path unmarked, known only to those who already knew the way.

Her heart trembled at the prospect, both in fear and anticipation. She did not know what waited for her among the Amhara. Was Mercury alive, as the rumors said? Or did he die in Iona like so many others? There was only one way to find out.

The wind curled, blowing a strand of black hair across her eyes. And then a strand of gold.

Domacridhan sat placidly at her side, his own horse still beneath him, his emerald gaze fixed on the horizon. His hair was longer, his scars fading, but he still leaned to one side, accommodating the wound beneath his arm. It was healing too, thanks to his Elder nature. Not to mention a good deal of luck, prayer, and Amhara skill.

A mortal would have died months ago, bleeding into the roses, his body going cold beneath her.

"Thank you for coming with me."

She knew it was no small thing. Dom was Monarch of Iona now, the leader of an enclave shattered by war and betrayal. He should have been at home with his people, helping them restore what was nearly lost forever.

Instead, he looked grimly down a sand dune, his clothes poorly suited to the climate, his appearance sticking out of the desert like the sorest of thumbs. While so many things had changed, Dom's ability to look out of place never did. He even wore his usual cloak, a twin to the one he lost months ago. The gray green had become a comfort like nothing else, just like the silhouette of his familiar form. He loomed always, never far from her side.

It was enough to make Sorasa's eyes sting, and turn her face to hide in her hood for a long moment.

Dom paid it no notice, letting her recover. Instead, he fished an apple from his saddlebags and took a noisy bite.

"I saved the realm," he said, shrugging. "The least I can do is try to see some of it."

Sorasa was used to Elder manners by now. Their distant ways, their inability to understand subtle hints. The side of her mouth raised against her hood, and she turned back to face him, smirking.

"Thank you for coming *with me*," she said again.

"Oh," he answered, shifting to look at her. The green of his eyes danced, bright against the desert. "Where else would I go?"

Then he passed the apple over to her. She finished the rest without a thought.

His hand lingered, though, scarred knuckles on a tattooed arm.

She did not push him away. Instead, Sorasa leaned, so that her shoulder brushed his own, putting some of her weight on him.

"Am I still a waste of arsenic?" he said, his eyes never moving from her face.

Sorasa stopped short, blinking in confusion. "What?"

"When we first met." His own smirk unfurled. "You called me a waste of arsenic."

In a tavern in Byllskos, after I dumped poison in his cup, and watched him drink it all. Sorasa laughed at the memory, her voice echoing over the empty dunes. In that moment, she thought Domacridhan was her death, another assassin sent to kill her. Now she knew he was the opposite entirely.

Slowly, she raised her arm and he did not flinch. It felt strange still, terrifying and thrilling in equal measure.

His cheek was cool under her hand, his scars now familiar against her palm. Elders were less affected by the desert heat, a fact Sorasa used to her full advantage.

"No," she answered, pulling his face down to her own. "I would waste all the arsenic in the world on you."

"Is that a compliment, Amhara?" Dom muttered against her lips.

No, she tried to reply.

On the golden sand, their shadows met, grain by grain, until there was no space left at all.

The deck of the ship rolled beneath her, the warm breeze of the Long Sea tangled in her black hair. Corayne gulped down the taste of salt greedily, as if she could drink the seas themselves. Her face turned toward the sun, still rising in the east, yellow and bright.

In younger days, Corayne would have killed to work the deck of the *Tempest*. It was freedom, it was the whole world. Now the ship seemed small, little more than a piece of driftwood bobbing in the endless sea.

Her heart still yearned, but what heart did not?

"How fare the winds?" a voice asked.

She turned to see her mother standing at the rail, Meliz an-Amarat in all her terrible glory. The sun glinted red in her black hair and softened the already gentle curves of her golden face. Even after everything, Corayne still envied her mother's beauty. But she treasured it too.

"Fine," Corayne answered, "for they bring me home."

Home. The *Tempestborn* was not home, but it felt close. A place she could belong one day, if she wished it. Perhaps that is what home really was. Not a place or a single person, but a moment in time.

"We're making good time," Corayne said idly, studying the arc of the sun. Judging by the angle and the sea charts, they would make landfall in a few days.

Next to her, Meliz gave an incredulous scoff. She shook her head, grinning. "How would you know?"

Heat spread across Corayne's cheeks and she fought the urge to duck her head. Indeed, she did not know anything of this route. Not firsthand, at least. She knew only what her maps and charts told her, what other sailors discovered. What her mother experienced too many times to count.

Instead of shrinking away, Corayne straightened her spine.

"I suppose I am learning," she admitted. "Finally."

Meliz grinned. "Good. I don't tolerate stupidity on my ship."

Instead of smiling with her, Corayne looked back to the sea. Not in anger but peace.

"Thank you for this," she muttered.

Next to her, Meliz shifted, leaning forward on her elbows to inspect the waves. Even the ending of the world had not changed her aversion to emotion, good or bad. She gave a shrug and another grin.

"There are worse places in the world for you to be."

Corayne fought the all-too-familiar urge to roll her eyes. Turning, she faced her mother, refusing to blink, holding her gaze. Forcing Meliz to see exactly what she meant.

"Thank you," she said again, too many meanings rushing up, her voice thick with emotion.

For your love, for your bravery, for standing back when I needed to move forward.

For everything you ever made me, and everything you would not let me become.

Corayne expected the days after the war to be difficult, for pain and regret and anguish. To hate herself, to see blood everywhere. Death, destruction. What Waits in every shadow. To feel tormented by all she survived and all she did to survive it.

Instead, she remembered the young dragon. Crying for its mother. Wounded but stubbornly alive. Protected by Corayne's mercy.

And then Erida. Defenseless beneath her. An easy ending, a deserved death. But Corayne would not give it. Though the Spindleblade ran with blood and all the world seemed to burn, Corayne's soul was clean.

"You said once I did not have the spine for it. This life," she said, looking at the endless horizon. It held so much possibility her head spun. "You're right."

Something gleamed in Meliz's eye. A tear or a trick of the light, Corayne could not say.

"Of course I'm right, I'm your mother," she answered, moving closer.

Meliz was warm as she rested her head on Corayne's shoulder, one arm wrapped around her back. They leaned together, each holding the other up, mother and daughter. Their paths would part again, as all are destined to do. But for the moment, they ran together, side by side.

The port of Nkonabo was a riot of color, sound, and smell. Andry tried to take it all in from the deck of the ship. The white eagle on purple flags, voices calling in every language, the tang of saltwater and the spice market. The alabaster monuments, famed throughout the Ward, rose all over the city, carved in the likenesses of the many gods. Their eyes gleamed, studded with flawless amethysts.

From his elevated position on the ship, Andry soon found the statue of Lasreen. At her feet wound her loyal dragon, Amavar. Despite the purple gems, its jeweled eyes seemed to wink blue.

Then something down on the dock caught his attention, and all thoughts of the dragon disappeared.

Andry nearly leapt from the ship, tripping over himself to disembark. Like the city, the docks were chaotic, teeming with sailors and merchants. He stared through all of them, gaze fixed on a single point.

A single person.

Valeri Trelland did not need her wheeled chair anymore. She leaned heavily on a cane but walked under her own power. Even from a distance, her spring-green eyes sparked, her polished ebony skin gleaming beneath the Kasan sun. Members of her family, Kin Kiane, walked with her, matching her slow pace.

Andry wanted to run for her but held his ground. His mother was a lady, and she despised poor manners. Instead, he waited like a polite, dutiful son, even as his throat threatened to close, unshed tears stinging.

"*Madero*," she said, putting out a hand to him. *My dear.*

He fitted his cheek into her palm, her skin softer than he remembered.

"It is so good to see you," he said, almost choking on the words.

Valeri smiled, brushing away his tears. "When I left you were still a boy."

He could not help but laugh. "Are you going to say I'm a man now?"

"No," she replied, and smoothed his collar. "You are a hero."

But for the onlookers, Andry would have wept in the middle of the dock. Instead, he forced back his tears, taking his mother by the free hand.

"There's someone I want you to meet," he said, gesturing back to the ship.

The purple sails of the *Tempestborn* were already stowed, its crew beginning the careful business of docking down the galley. Corayne appeared at the rail, her hair tied back in her braid, a fresh tan across her face.

"We have met already," Valeri said, half-scolding her son. Then she looked at him sidelong. "Unless I am meeting her in some other capacity."

"I would hope so," Andry answered, grinning as Corayne joined them.

She stood straight, a blue cloak over one arm, a satchel strung from one shoulder. These days she carried only a long knife, stowed in her boot.

And nothing else.

Valeri Trelland greeted her fondly, kissing Corayne on both cheeks. Andry could only watch, a little shocked by the moment as it unfolded. He dreamed of this so many times he could hardly believe it was real. *Corayne. My mother. The land of my ancestors.* His eyes prickled and his heart swelled in his chest until it was almost too much to bear.

Then Corayne's shoulder brushed his own and he shivered. Still unsure of their closeness, of where each side stood. But she grinned up at him in an encouraging way, gesturing for him to join them. Her smile was like the sun, bathing him in a warm glow.

"With me," Corayne said under her breath, so only he could hear.

Slowly, the young man loosed a breath. And with it, the last weight hanging from his shoulders. Whatever darkness remained disappeared, chased away by golden light.

"With me," Andry whispered back.

The realm entire.

Erida thought of her crowns, varied as they were. Gold, silver, every kind of jewel. Some for celebration, some for war. All meant to mark her as what she was—the Queen of Galland, the most powerful person to walk the Ward.

Her crown was ashes now, her jewels embers.

Her realm was barely what she held in her body, and even that was no longer hers.

My mind is my own. She repeated it over and over again, until some feeling came back to her limbs, some control to her mind. Her hands still twitched, the scratch of What Waits ever-present in her head. But it was a little bit easier to bear.

"You should have gone with them," she said, lifting her chin to look at Taristan. The smoke grew so thick she could hardly see him through the shadows, the strange realm burning around them.

But she could still feel his arms, wrapped around her as they were, holding them both together until some kind of ending came.

"To what?" he answered, his voice raspy with smoke.

Erida heaved another choking breath, the heat of the flames buffeting her back. Tears slipped from her eyes and Erida curled into him, as if she might disappear into Taristan entirely.

"To anything but this," she cried out, looking back to where the Spindle used to be. "There is nothing for you here."

Taristan only stared. "Yes, there is."

The fires spread, so close now Erida feared her armor might melt off her body. But there was nowhere to go, nothing to do. They had no blade. They had no doorways. There was only Taristan in front of her, the long years of his life welling up in his eyes.

She knew them as much as anyone could. An orphan, a mercenary, a prince. A discarded child ripe for the picking, set on this terrible path for so terribly long.

Did it always lead here? she wondered. *Has this always been our fate?*

The steps shuddered behind her, one of them crumbling entirely. What Waits hissed with the cracking stone, closer by the second. The demon within called to the demon without, the two of them connected like a piece of rope pulling taut.

Erida swallowed against the sensation, feeling her control slip.

She gripped Taristan tighter, blinking fiercely.

My mind is my own. My mind is my own.

But her own voice began to fade, even in her head. She saw the same in Taristan, the same war raging behind his eyes. Before it could seize them both, Erida seized her prince by the neck, pulling his face to her own. He tasted like blood and smoke, but she reveled in it.

"Does this make you mine?" Taristan whispered, his hand against her jaw.

It was the same question he once asked so long ago, when Erida could give no answer. It felt foolish now, a stupid thing to hesitate over. Especially as another took over her head, conquering her mind as she tried to conquer the world.

"Yes," she answered, kissing him again. Kissing him until the flames pressed in, until she couldn't breathe. Until her vision went black.

Until the first footstep landed on the grass, the dirt going to ashes beneath Him, and all the realms shook with the weight of it.

ACKNOWLEDGMENTS

I am truly stunned to be writing these words, because writing them means that *Fate Breaker* is done, and the Realm Breaker series has finished. You would think I'd get used to this after publishing eight books, but you never get used to it. Or at least I never will. How does someone get used to living their dreams? Because this has truly been a dream for me. Every second of my publishing career has been a gift, and I am so grateful for it all.

This series was written as much for me as it was for my readers, because Realm Breaker is everything I wanted as a dorky teenager combing through fan fiction. To get to even attempt to write what my teenage self needed is such a privilege. And I am continuously shocked to find readers just like me, looking for stories just like this. To all of you who love Realm Breaker as I do, who see what I see in these pages, thank you. We belong to each other.

Of course, I would never be in this position without the immense support of my family. Both my parents are educators, who gave me my love of stories, and perhaps more important, my curiosity and drive. Thank you to Mom, Dad, and Andy, for everything always.

I am also blessed to have an incredible circle of support here in California, my new home (by new I mean I've lived here fifteen years). Thank you to my chosen family—Morgan, Jen, Tori, and all our dear friends who have somehow tolerated me for ten-plus years.

Since publishing my last book, I married my husband, who continues to be my grounding center. And somehow, a Realm Breaker superfan. Along with the best pal to our darling girl, Indy, the furry light of my life. I love you both more than words can say, and I'm pretty okay with words. Oh, and thanks for giving me the best in-laws a girl could ever ask for. Somehow I find myself gaining another pair of fantastic parents, wonderful sisters- and brothers-in-law, and a bonus grandmother, our dearest Shirley.

I would list all my literary colleagues who have become dear friends, but it feels like bragging. You are a murderers' row of phenomenal artists and even better people. Thank you for your advice, your encouragement, and most of all, for understanding this weird space we occupy together.

The small-town kid I was could never have dreamed the woman I am today, with the career I've enjoyed. None of it would be possible without my literary agent, Suzie Townsend. Here's to another five years, and as many books as the world will let me write. Thank you for being my true north. I would be remiss if I didn't mention the rest of the smash team at New Leaf Literary—Pouya, Sophia, Olivia, Jo, Tracy, Keifer, Katherine, Hilary, and Eileen. Thank you for your genius, in getting my words around the world, on the screen, and everywhere in between. And thank you forever to Steve, my legal warrior and true friend.

At HarperCollins, I have been so lucky to work with an incredible team to get my stories onto shelves. First and foremost is Alice, my editor for four books now, who has successfully ferried me from one series through another. Thank you for your genius, your kindness, and your endless support. Thank you to Erica for your guidance and steadfast leadership. And many endless thanks to Clare, who wrangles all of us with tremendous grace. I am so lucky to have the team I have, and my books are so lucky too. Thank you to Alexandra, Jenna, Alison, Vanessa, Shannon, Audrey, Sammy, and Christina—I would be a mess without you! And special shout-out to Sasha Vinogradova, your covers have been a dream come true.

Somehow my books have managed to find their way across the globe, to countries I've never set foot in, printed in too many languages to learn. Thank you to every foreign agent, every editor, every translator, every publicist. You perform miracles and magic. I hope I am lucky enough to meet you all one day.

I would say the same of my readers, but there are honestly too many of you for me to imagine. I still cannot believe you exist, let alone care about anything I've written. Thank you forever to every bookseller, librarian, teacher, blogger, reader—for every post or video, every word of encouragement, every recommendation you pass along. I would not exist without you, and neither would my stories. I promise I will do everything to protect your faith in me, and keep creating worlds for you to live in, and characters for you to love. Or hate. ☺

Of course, at last, I must thank J. R. R. Tolkien. His influence is all over this series, both in what stories he gave me, and what stories he didn't. I would not be myself without Middle-earth, and for that I will always be grateful. Now, back to my hobbit hole. And the next adventure.

All my love, forever,
Victoria